LOST TREASURE OF THE
CHINA BAR

LOST TREASURE OF THE CHINA BAR

Douglas Withrow

THANK YOU:

To my wife and daughters for putting up with my counterculture ways

To my editor… Laura Belanger

To the IBEW L.U. 191 and L.U. 77

To Kris, Jim, Tom, and Gina

To Charlie Dool… Ollala Canyon

To Noble and Vicki Horn, Odell (Haulk) Texas… for tending my grandparents' grave

To Willis Allen Ramsey and Leon Russell… for defining who I am

To the Colville Confederated Tribes… Wendell George, Cindy Miller, Bub Moon, Joe Lazard, Sonny Moses, Andy Joseph… and Chief Bertram (Corn Chief) Hopi tribe, Oraibi

To the People of Leyte

To President Duterte… for demanding the bells be returned… and succeeding

To my Mother and Father

To J.J. Kerr

Dorothy Cordova… Filipino National Historical Society

And most of all to Jesus Christ, my Savior… forgive me LORD for the cursing language….

LOST TREASURE OF THE CHINA BAR - TABLE OF CONTENTS

Matalom

The tropical sunrise was beginning to blink out the last of the morning stars. Like clockwork, a distant red rooster in the coconut jungle crowed the first call of the morning. Another distant rooster answered on the mountain, and within moments, a dozen could be heard echoing from all across the river valley.

It was a new day in the Philippines in the year 1849. Juana Melendres' rooster was announcing the day also, the rascal being right under her this morning. Juana's nipa hut was on six-foot stilts. The ground level was an open kitchen and jungle workshop. Above was the sleeping quarters, a split bamboo floor with woven mats for walls. The roof was laced palm leaves of thatch, gabled in the middle with bamboo beams.

Juana, now twelve years old, arose early to start her chores before the long trek to school. She was a middle child in a family of eight brothers and sisters. Her younger siblings were five, seven and nine years old, while her four older brothers were fourteen, fifteen, sixteen, and seventeen years of age.

"Pinto," she whispered to her older brother, "help me light the mosquito husks." Pinto, her favorite brother, rubbed his eyes with a heavy sigh and stood up. Climbing down the bamboo ladder, she shooed the rooster from his perch. She fetched a dozen dried, split coconut husks and built four little pyramids on the ground around the nipa hut.

"Mornin' sis," was offered by Pinto as he climbed down the ladder. Juana nodded, and handed him four candle stubs. Last night's kitchen fire still smoldered in the hearth. A few puffs of air and a little tinder brought the flames back to life. Lighting one candle, Pinto placed it under one pyramid and moved to the next, until all four were smoking nicely and pushing the mosquitoes away.

Maxima, their mother, came down the ladder and cheerfully greeted them. Her hair was now turning white, as the rigors of raising and feeding a large family had taken its toll. "Pinto, collect some eggs while I start the rice and fish," she said as she patted him on the head. He then took her hand and pressed it to his forehead as a sign of respect.

Maxima, or Nanay, as she was called by her family, was light-skinned and recognized as one of the barangay's prettiest women.

Juana's father was from a large family dating back to Captain Francisco Melendres, a Castilian who was commissioned in 1588 by the King of Spain to deliver galleons, newly built, from the shipyard of Biliran, to the docks of Manila.

Known far and wide as a ladies' man, Francisco had fathered two dozen children with the local sweethearts of Biliran. The large family spread all through the Visaya's over the following two centuries.

Nanay was impatient with Pinto. "Where are those eggs?" she called into the jungle. Juana had by now pitched water from the spring and settled down on her mat to weave a fresh mat. Her split bamboo mat was five feet by seven feet in size and could be woven to completion in two hours if she was diligent. It was her meal ticket for the day, as she would roll it up and carry it to the market on her walk to school.

Here, life had been much easier than two years earlier when calamity struck the family. Her father, a fisherman by trade, had kept a corn patch to help feed the family. With his daily fish catch, the corn patch, and help from her two oldest brothers, there was a surplus to trade with and prosper.

A bully of a man lived within the barangay and would let his carabao roam untethered. One day, the cow got in the corn patch, resulting in a confrontation between Juana's father and the bully. Both men drew their bolos and the bully swung wildly at her father's arm, slicing it off at the bicep. Screaming in pain and rage, he attacked the bully until he ran off. He was able to pull his thong off and tie a noose around the stub to stop the bleeding.

Crawling to the nipa hut, the brothers found him and borrowed a cart and donkey. They took him to the Chinese doctor in Matalom. The old Chinaman was able to save his life by convalescing at the Chinaman's house for a month. Juana had been ten years old at the time. She had stayed at her father's bedside and worked long hours for the Chinaman, cleaning the wound and making teas and powders.

When her father had finally enough strength to go home after a month, the Chinaman had grown fond of Juana's help, and he requested her servitude as payment for saving her father's life.

Shortly after her father had been stabilized at the Chinaman's, the brothers went after the bully on a mission to kill him, which they did. They set an ambush on a jungle trail as the bully was carrying a bundle stock of bananas on his shoulder and walking by. So swift and deadly was the bolo attack, that there were no blood curdling cries. The boys fled for refuge and hid in the mountains. Three days later when the body was discovered, the Spanish authorities quickly assessed who the suspects were through local interrogation, and so Juana's two older brothers became desperados. Her brothers had not been seen since, and her father, who was once a prosperous fisherman, now wandered for days up river, setting shrimp traps in the shallows.

The corn and fish days of plenty were gone. Now she must weave mats five days a week and deliver them to the doctor's wife who gave her breakfast. She then attended school in the Matalom nunnery and after school, worked for the old Chinaman's wife in payment for her servitude.

The old woman traded the mats for food and cooked for the girl as she did laundry, pitched water, and did household chores. At sundown she would walk the path back home and arrive at the nipa hut at dark, then repeat the routine the next day.

The sun was up and heating up the morning as she finished her mat and rolled it up. She grabbed a banana and put the mat on her shoulder, told her mother she loved her and started her one hour trek to the town. The trail through the jungle was the fastest way to get to Matalom. She wound her way down the muddy path through banana and coconut groves, always watching the ground for snakes and poisonous insects. If it was raining, she would pick a giant banana leaf and use it as an umbrella.

Matalom was an old Spanish settlement consisting of the church, nunnery school and an array of nipa huts, that were the homes of fishermen, as the town sat on the beach of the Canigao Sea.

An old Spanish stone watchtower had been constructed on the beach one hundred years earlier, to guard and warn the town against marauding pirates that plundered up and down the coast. The danger was still very real and the tower was manned around the clock. A large gong was banged if the Pirates were spotted approaching. Large conch shells were blown, to warn the town to flee toward the jungle and mountains if an attack was occurring. The Pirates were "Moros"... Islamic raiders from the southern islands that plundered for food, booty and most of all slaves.

Her walk to town was uneventful this morning and she hurried to deliver her mat to the old China woman. "Juana, you're late this morning," she scolded in Mandarin Chinese. "Eat your fish soup. It's getting cold." The old woman only spoke Chinese, and after several months of working for her, the girl had learned to understand and communicate with the woman in her tongue.

She gulped down her soup, thanked her in Chinese and bolted out the kitchen, as the school bell was beginning to ring. The nuns did not like tardiness and punishment was staying after school to do the task of cleaning the church and nunnery. She slipped through the door just as the last bell was chiming. This was a much anticipated week in Matalom. It was their feast week to celebrate her town's patron saint. A king and queen had been selected amongst the students of the school, with a grand parade through town, culminating at the school ground with dancing contests, food and celebration. She had been selected as a princess of the king and queen's court and would dance in a contest before the assembled town, celebrating with a number of prizes to be awarded. The bamboo dance and the water glass dance were her favorite, and she had practiced many days with her schoolmates to get the intricacies of the dance correct.

Today was the last day of practice, as the celebration was to start the next day. The Chinese granny had helped her with her costume and her confidence of winning the contest was assured. And so the day was spent rehearsing the program. The competition was keen, as the winners of the contest were celebrities for the following year within the town. The school day passed quickly and she hurried to complete her chores for the old woman. They needed to put the final touches on her costume.

Arriving back at home at dark, she was happy to find her father. He had returned after a three-day trek up the river and was back now from checking his rock cairn shrimp traps. His bamboo bag was full of freshwater shrimp, and there was plenty for feasts and some to sell as well. He hugged her with his one arm and she blessed his hand. That evening, camotes yams, fruits, shrimp and cornbread with tuba coconut wine were consumed. Many friends stopped to gossip and celebrate life. She wanted to stay up and listen to her Tatay's stories, but she knew she must sleep if she was to have a chance in the dance contest.

She awoke and the roosters were crowing again across the morning river valley. Juana shivered with excitement in her veins, knowing the coming day would be one to remember. Quickly she woke Pinto and went about her usual tasks. She set coconut husk pyres burning and then a frenzied fast weaving job, loose and a second grade weave today. She didn't care, her mind was elsewhere. Her father had departed earlier back to the river traps. There were leftover camotes from the night before, and she grabbed two. She rolled up her mat, blessed her mother's hand, and jogged down the trail to town. She needed time at the China woman's house to finalize preparation of her costume. Arriving early, the old woman cackled with joy, as she was excited for the girl. She had sewn a purple cotton tunic, decorated in hand made sewn flowers, with a crown of fresh flowers for her head and a skirt of palm fronds, with anklets of cocoa beans. The old woman carefully placed the trappings in a woven basket with a shoulder strap for Juana to carry to school. The bell was ringing. "Quickly, go child," she urged in Chinese. This was a big event, a "fiesta," and everyone in the school was somehow involved in presenting the festivities.

The students assembled on the parade ground in front of the school. They formed little groups and each helped the other with his or her costume. The king and queen had their court and entourage. Then came the princes and princesses, then the warriors and dancing maidens, and finally the musicians. At the head of the parade was the Patron Saint, carried on a litter by twelve of the

4

strongest athletes. The royalty was to remember the days of old before the Spanish Inquisition and how they were subjugated to their Saint now.

Blowing conch horns ahead of the patron saint litter, the whole procession left the parade ground, marched down the length of the waterfront fishing village, passed the pirate guard tower, then on to the beach, where offerings were made to the sea for good fishing. Having completed the offering and prayer, the parade marched back to the parade grounds, where the whole town celebrated with games, dancing and sharing of food. The dancing took place in front of the king and queen and their court. Five judges sat to the side to declare best dancer in the competition. There were ten princesses, each doing her techniques to the bamboo dance. Two long bamboos, twelve feet long, were held at both ends by two people, who are on their knees, opening and closing the bamboos while the princess' stepped in and out, without being touched, doing a graceful dance to drums, bells and flutes. It was Juana's day. She never missed a beat and got clapping and cheering when she was done. The water glass dance, not so. She spilled a small amount, which was seen by the judges. Afterwards, the king announced the winners, and to her amazement, "Juana Melendres, step forward for outstanding achievement and grace, costume choice and beauty. I award you the princess necklace." He placed a beautiful mother of pearl round medallion that shown with brilliant colors around her neck. The necklace beads were drilled Puka shell, a stunning piece of native craftsmanship.

An afternoon of basking in her new celebrity and eating fruits came to a conclusion, and it was back to the China woman's house with the exciting news. Of course the Chinese granny was just as excited to learn about her winning. She admired her necklace award and sat and had tea, listening to all the details that Juana could translate in broken Mandarin. And so the kind old woman let her leave early, as it was Friday, knowing that her family would be excited and would want to hear the details. Juana hurried as fast as she could on the jungle trail. One had to carefully watch the trail ahead for jumping black snakes and cobras. But this was like a sixth sense, which had been taught to her by her brothers. Carlito and Pinto had become the family's source of support, as they had taken up the family banca boat that her father and oldest brothers had abandoned. Her father, with one arm, could no longer pull the net or manage the banca. He had become a recluse hermit of the river jungle, and disappeared sometimes for many days. With the two older brothers on the run for the revenge killing, the two younger boys were now the men of the house.

Arriving at the nipa hut, bursting with the good news, Juana immediately sensed something wrong. She called up to the nipa hut, "Nanay, what is wrong?"

5

"Juana, fetch some cool spring water quickly!" The tone of her voice sounded of urgency, so she quickly fetched gourds of spring water. "Nanay, what is wrong?" she called out again, as she climbed the ladder. "Bring it here!" ordered Nanay. Juana held the gourd out to her mother who was sitting by Carlito, who was lying on the mat, sweating profusely. His eyes were half rolled back in his head. "Pinto and Carlito came back early today from fishing, Carlito has the fever," Nanay explained. "Fan the banana leaf while I bathe him in cool water."

"Where is Pinto? asked Juana.

"He's back down river with the banca, repairing a leak and mending the nets."

"Is he going to be okay, Nanay?" she asked.

"He needs medicine. Your Kuya has the cure. You need to take some food and go to him quickly."

Juana hesitated. "But Nanay, I've only been there twice. I'm not sure of the trail." The truth was Juana was terrified of her old uncle. He was recognized far and wide as the "black ghost," or the "ghost in the tree"; a powerful shaman who lived deep in the jungle, in a massive banyan tree.

Juana's father was the shaman's youngest brother. Her father, or "Tatay," had given up the old ways and been baptized a Catholic. The "Black Ghost" on the other hand, had been taught the old ways and practiced his black magic in solitude. He could cure many ailments, as the ancient medicines of the jungle had been conveyed to him by another older hermit of the jungle. He was tattooed from the neck down with bazaar designs done with black ash of the tugas tree. He would smear more black grease on his face, giving the appearance of the devil in the flesh.

The Spanish had named his people "Visayan," or "The Painted Ones." The old tradition of tattooing had disappeared after the "Inquisition," being tattooed a sign to the Spanish that you had not converted.

"But there's only three hours of daylight left," Juana said in a soft voice.

"You'll be okay Juana. Climb the ridge and you can see his tree across the valley. You'll know it by the birds that constantly fly in a circle around it. Now go, take some of the cooked shrimp to him, you'll have to hurry to make it back by nightfall. Hurry, your brother's life depends on it."

"I won the bamboo dance contest today. I won this necklace" the girl blurted out.

"Yes that's nice, we'll talk about it later, now hurry and go!"

Juana summoned her younger siblings, all unaware of their brother's serious condition. She gave each instructions, to help Nanay, and quickly packed some shrimp in a banana leaf. She grabbed a bolo and scabbard hanging on the post, and hurried to the trail climbing the ridge.

A thick canopy of jungle vegetation had consumed the trail, as it was not often used. She pulled her bolo and began to cut away at the muddy trail. Swarms of insects would rise up in clouds, as she pushed up along the mountain trail. She had been to the Banyan tree only twice before, both times with her father.

Upon arriving at the tree, her father made her stay back at a distance. As he approached, he called out to the tree. Hearing him, the "Black Ghost" would answer. After a heated exchange of curses between the two, he would lower a bucket with the prescribed cure, and her father would send back up ears of corn. Her father would retrieve her from her hiding place each time, and rant and curse his brother down the trail as they returned home. In both cases, a snake bite cure and fever cure had worked miraculously, and the afflicted person had recovered quickly. And so she knew the fever cure worked, but the dread of approaching the tree and calling out for the "Ghost" terrified her.

Finally, she reached the top of the ridge, but the canopy was so dense, she could not see across the valley. The trail divided on top of the ridge, and she wasn't sure which way to go. She hung her shrimp basket on a branch and her bolo on another. Spotting the tallest coconut tree in the grove, she pulled herself up the trunk the way Pinto had taught her. Finally, another fifty feet in the air, she was staring at a huge jungle valley, in a sweeping vista as far as she could see. And there it was, the "tree," no doubt about it, just as her Nanay had said. A wisp of smoke across the valley on top of the ridge could be seen trailing out of its canopy. Large birds could be seen flying in circular, gliding patterns around its height. It looked ominous and at least another hour away.

It would be dark in two hours and fear began to run through her thoughts. She hung on to the coconut trunk and shielded her eyes from the sun, trying to see into the canopy of the huge tree. She noticed the golden reflection from her medallion on the back of her hand. A faint trail could be seen below leading down and across the valley floor. If she hurried, she could get medicine and make it home by dark. Climbing down and gathering her bolo and shrimp, she hastily moved down the trail, all the time scanning ahead for danger.

Reaching the valley floor, she came to a small jungle stream rushing under the canopy. Using stepping stones to cross the stream, she continued through the dense growth. Suddenly, she stopped dead in her tracks. Three steps ahead lay the skin of a giant, eight-foot black cobra. The snake had molted on the trail, leaving a paper thin mold and shadow of his body behind. As she stood there in startled fear, not wanting to move, her left foot began to burn like

7

fire. Pulling her gaze away from the snakeskin, she looked down to see her left barefoot standing on the mound of a fire ant colony. Too late! Two dozen ants had swarmed her foot and bitten her mercilessly. She yelped out in a low cry and brushed the venomous ants from her foot. She knew what was coming, having been bitten before, but never in this quantity. Within sixty seconds the burning pain stabbed her foot. She hobbled along, tears of pain and fear falling on her cheeks. She put a green stick in her teeth, grimaced, and found a stick to hobble on as a crutch.

What was that up ahead? Gathering her composure, she recognized the large rock she would sit on and wait for her father on the previous two visits. Languishing in pain, she stumbled on, remembering her father talking about the snakes in the area.

All of a sudden, there it was! She stepped into the clearing and the fortress tree loomed before her. High up in the midsection of the tree, several platforms at different elevations spread out across the massive branches. A great commotion of bird caws and monkey chatter all of a sudden exploded, announcing her presence. She took two steps forward, and instantly a black jungle cobra that was lurking in the grass stood up and billowed his hood, hissing savagely. A loud screeching command came from the tree. "Matar, Matar, Matar!"

Now, two large macaque monkeys came leaping out of the tree, brandishing large sticks and screaming at the top of their lungs. By the time the snake realized he was being attacked from the rear, it was too late. Engaging the snake, one masterfully got the serpent to strike at his stick, and at that moment, the other macaque swung and broke the snakes back. With screams of delight, showing their dagger teeth and blood rage in their eyes, they beat the snake to a pulp… all of this happening in the period of a few moments.

The cawing and macaque screams were at a multitude now, and the girl stood and trembled with her eyes closed. "God dammit, that's enough! Get your wretched asses back in the tree!" Suddenly, a large green coconut came flying out of the tree and landed close to the murdering macaques. "You sons of bitches, don't make me throw another one! Be gone, you filthy butt pickers!" Both macaques snarled at Juana and then lumbered away, jumping up into the lower branches of the colossal tree.

"Who the hell are you and what do you want?" She tipped her head back, and looking down at her was a large black feathered face with a beak protruding from it. She stood terrified, not being able to answer for fear. "God dammit answer me! Are you lost?"

Her foot was burning in pain, but she managed to choke out, "I came for fever medicine."

"God dammit, the sun's going down and you want medicine? Who are you? Who the hell sends their child into this jungle at this time of day? God dammit!"

She lowered her head and began to sob, crying softly and rubbing her burning foot. "What's wrong with your damn foot? Stop crying! Did a snake bite you on the foot?"

"No, I stepped on a fire ant mound." And with that, she collapsed and fainted from the pain.

Now came a barrage of expletive cursing in a long continuous ramble. A long ladder all of a sudden came swinging down from a lower platform. Hurling curses at the crowd of macaques watching, he came down the ladder and stood over the girl. Tilting her head back, he put a gourd of cool water to her lips, reviving her conscious. Was she dreaming, or was this happening? The "ghost" was covered in black tattoos, and a hideous bird mask covered his face. A gourd and thong were all that covered his loins. He could have been the reincarnation of the devil himself.

She felt him lift her up, and the fear caused her to pass out again. Slowly the shaman carried her lifeless body up the ladder, where he promptly pulled the stair backup into the canopy, with an attached vine. Realizing he was dealing with a child, the old man removed his mask, sensing that it was contributing to her fear.

The *caw, caws* were now building in crescendo and realizing it, he bellowed, "Enough! Shut the hell up!" and immediately, a quiet calm encompassed the tree. Putting damp, cool rags on her forehead, arms and chest, he quickly mixed a solution of herbs in a large shell bowl, and bathed the swollen foot repeatedly, chanting a discernible prayer. Fanning her with a large banana leaf, she regained her wits and quietly stared around her.

Her fear and pain had diminished, as she assessed her surroundings and situation. Where was she? A large bamboo floor spread out to other little staircases, that climbed to the platforms above her. Giant tortoise shells for collecting water were strategically situated all about, with a series of split bamboo running through the branches to collect water. Off to the side a large stone hearth with clay pots and cooking apparatus was emitting a smoldering flame. Hung everywhere were bundles of herbs, snake skins, clay hanging pots and various jungle bird plumages.

"Ah, you're awake now, good. Drink this tea and your foot will stop aching." The old man's demeanor had totally changed now. He smiled and patted her on the head, handing her the gourd of tea. With the bird mask gone, she was able to look at him now. "Drink the tea, all of it," he demanded. A euphoric calm suddenly overwhelmed her. She stared down at her swollen foot, realizing the burning had been neutralized.

"All right, so who might you be and who needs fever medicine?" the shaman asked.

"I am Juana Melendres, the daughter of your brother."

"What? You are Dionisio's daughter?"

"Yes" she answered, and immediately a rage of expletive curses spewed from the old man.

"God dammit, what's wrong with that one armed idiot? Does he not value his own child's life? This god damn jungle will eat you up and make you disappear. Why didn't he come himself?" the "ghost" cursed under his breath.

"He's shrimping up river and has been gone. My older brothers have run off, and my other two brothers fish for our food. One brother caught the fever yesterday and I'm the only one that Nanay could send."

The shaman scratched his chin, "Oh that father of yours. I told him to come see me before he lost his arm. I have a potion that will make the carabao go blind. That would've solved his problem. But instead he chose combat and he lost.... Serves him right!"

Seeing her on the verge of tears again after saying this, he quickly soothed her and said, "Don't worry, I'll make a medicine to save your brother. But it will take a couple of hours and it's starting to get dark. You can stay here tonight."

"No, I must return immediately, to save his life."

"When did this fever first appear. Yesterday?"

"Yes."

"He still has time. I'll walk you back to the trail in the morning. Calm down, he'll be alright."

"But I must go."

"Well then, your brother will never see the medicine, as you will disappear in the jungle by morning. What's in your bamboo bag?"

"Nanay sent you shrimp to pay for the medicine."

"I see, well I'm hungry. I'll cook it up here for us, while you rest that foot." Soon the smell of boiling shrimp permeated the air, and he dumped the steaming mass on a banana leaf, mixing a lime and pepper dip in a scallop shell.

Again, realizing his wild demeanor and cursing was scaring the girl, he quietly spoke, "You look just like my mother… your nose and your eyes are hers. Why have I never met you?"

"Tatay thinks you're evil because you are of the old ways and reject

10

Jesus. He said that he does not want your sorcerer ways taught to his children."

"Is that so!? And yet they all come running to me for fever cure, snake bite and voodoo hexes. And you, what do you think? Has the pain in your foot disappeared?"

Reminding her of her affliction, she realized that the pain had totally disappeared and her foot had returned to its normal size. "But why do you live in the middle of nowhere? Why not share your gifts of curing in town?"

"Bah! Why? So I can get my arm cut off, catch the fever, or killed by a pirate? I belong here, I've been in this tree fifty years, my little friends and protectors watch out for me, I am a creature of the jungle."

"What do you mean, your little friends and protectors?"

"We all depend on each other here. The macaques are my little friends, they keep the snakes away. The ravens are my protectors. They see danger and the enemy from the top of the tree and warn me. They told me you were coming today."

"What?" Juana questioned.

"Fifty ravens live in this tree. One of them, Duto, saw your medallion flash in the sun across the valley and told me of your presence."

"What, this 'Duto' talks to you?"

"Yes, he talks to me."

"What, like we're talking now?"

"Yes, like we're talking now. The ravens bring fruit from all over the jungle and drop lots of it here on the ground. The macaques get the leftovers. The jungle rats eat what's left. That's why the snakes are here. The snakes on the ground, the macaques in the lower branches and the ravens up above, as sentinels. No one can get to me. I live between the macaques and the ravens to keep the peace. The macaques would rob the raven's nests if I weren't here and so we all help each other."

"Why do you wear that scary bird mask?"

"Ahh that. I raise the raven chicks from the hatchlings. I wear the mask when they are young, and they bond to me as one of their own."

"But why?"

"You have a lot of questions for someone who doesn't believe in the old ways! I'll tell you a story Juana, as I like you. Your heart is good and innocent. A long list of shamans have lived in this tree for over two hundred years. As a young boy, I became curious of the old ways, witnessing some of its magic. The old shaman that lived here took me in as an apprentice, whereas I left your father's family and became a hermit here in the jungle with the shaman.

"The secrets of the black birds and their wisdom was divulged to me by the shaman. By living here in the tree with them, many secrets eventually became evident. The Raven is a highly intelligent bird, able to remember things and places, and use them to their advantage. They have a structured society and communicate amongst themselves, using intonation, different caws, clicking sounds and body language. One of their most remarkable traits is their ability to mimic sound. And if you're around one long enough, he will begin to mimic the sounds you make, and eventually an understandable conversation can happen. They have keen eyesight and can see long distances, one reason why you were spotted today. And they have one big weakness. Anything that is bright, smooth, shiny and can be transported in their beaks back to their nests becomes their treasure. They will fight and die for their treasure and will follow it wherever it goes.

"That's the secret. Steal a piece of treasure from their nest, and when they realize it's gone, make sure they see you drop it into a leather bag, and tie it around your neck. Now, you own this bird and he will never let you out of his sight."

Juana looked big eyed and her jaw dropped. Around the old man's neck were no less than ten little leather bags of different qualities to each. "But where are these magic birds Lolung?" She realized she had called him uncle. He beamed a big smile.

"They're all around you, don't you see them? Look up," and he raised his eyes. Juana stared out into the dark canopy of the massive tree, and then suddenly realized they were everywhere, holding motionless, staring at her from fifty different angles from above.

"Lolung, I see them now," she softly whispered.

He chuckled. "Yes, you are the first human to be in the tree in a very long time. They are fascinated."

"Lolung, your house is so magical, I like it!"

"How do you feed yourself, Lolung?"

"Well, just like you Juana. People of the jungle bring me food for my services. I lower a basket with the prescribed cure and get corn, rice, and fish sent back up the bucket. In the lower branch on the far side, I have a wild pig snare I use once a month. And the chickens, they bring them live and there's a free-for-all for the bones. It's easy living in the tree Juana. I have all the protection I need. You're the one that needs protection Juana, I'll work on that one, it can be applied in many forms." She now felt at ease in his presence. He had saved her from the snake, cured her ant bites, fed her, and she was calling him Lolung now.

"So Lolung, you say you talk to your birds, can you show me?"

12

Lolung leaned and smiled and stared at Juana for a long minute. Suddenly, he took both palms and made a *po, po, po* sound, followed by two tongue clicks and another *po, po, po*. And from a far outer branch burst a huge black crow, lighting on the back of the chair. The bird uttered a tremendous amount of *caw, caw, caw*ing and paced back and forth. Lolung now made a shrill *ta, ta, ta* and the raven sat motionless.

"Wow! Uncle he is beautiful," cried Juana.

"Oh yes, he's just getting warmed up. He's being Mr. Asshole right now."

"Lolung, what is his name?" whispered Juana.

"That one's called 'Duto.' I've had him for forty-five years, and I have his treasure. We don't like each other too much. I have other protectors and he is jealous. He's the one that spotted you today and sounded the alarm. So this is his reward, to meet you face to face. Come here Juana, let me see your medallion."

Juana sat up on her palette and rubbed her foot. "Can I walk on it now, Lolung?"

"Yes, you can walk now. Come to the table." Rising up, she took several slow steps, arriving between the bird and the old man. The old man now lit a candle from the hearth and placed it on the table.

"Juana, tell me about your medallion. May I look at it?" *At last*, she thought, *someone has admired my medallion*, as she quickly lifted it from her neck and held it out to the old man. Just as she was about to transfer it to his hand, Duto exploded from his roost and had the thong in his beak, just as the old shaman's hand closed around it. A tussle of feathers and squawks and curses and tugging resulted. Finally, Lolung had the necklace. Lolung screamed in Visayan, "You son-of-a-bitch devil bird piece of macaque shit!"

Duto screamed in Visayan. "You dirty fucking bastard!"

And Lolung screamed back in Visayan, "Get back in your shit hole nest you rotten wormy puke!"

Duto replied "Blow it out your ass old man!"

The old man now held the medallion up at arms-length and taunted the furious raven. "Is this what you wanted?" waving it back and forth. Perched on the chair, refusing to obey, Duto became transfixed by the medallion. With his free hand, Lolung quickly grabbed Duto by the legs, and another tussle proceeded. And just like that, Lolung had a leash on the birds leg, and he instantly quieted down. Lolung swore a slurry of unholy Visayan cuss words under his breath. He handed Juana back the necklace, and she quickly put it back on. Now on his tether, Duto paced back and forth on the table, eyeing the medallion.

13

"Well, we just solved part of your problem Juana, you now have a protector. That was the last straw between me and this bird." Lolung stood up, and picking up a long cane pole, reached into the rafters and unhung a bamboo cage, bringing it down to the table. Duto paced back and forth on his tether, sensing what was coming. The tether had a slipknot tied to the chair with a long tail dangling. Lolung proceeded to string the tail into the cage and out the back. Undoing the slipknot, he pulled the bird slowly into the cage. Closing the hatch, he smiled and said to Juana, "Stay here, I'll be right back."

From the gloom of the candle light and into the darkness, Lolung disappeared among the trees branches. She could hear twigs snapping and popping all the time, Duto going crazy in his cage. Soon the old man stepped back in to the candlelight, and opened his hand onto the table in front of the cage. Out fell a mother-of-pearl button, a silver peso, a shiny red stag coral, a white shell and a brass ring.

The bird was throwing himself at the cage and cursing in Visayan again. "You bastard of buttholes, those are mine!" the bird cried.

Scooping them up, the old man tied them in a leather pouch and placed them with a thong around Juana's neck.

Duto now calmed down. "He knows what is happening," the shaman told Juana.

Lolung looked down at his chest and pulled off a green bag with the star symbol on it and shouted at Duto, "See, you and I must travel another path." He sneered at the bird, "She needs a protector. She has your treasure." And with that, the old man placed the second bag around Juana's neck.

"Lolung, wait. I can't have a pet. I go to school."

"Juana, he is not a pet. He will never let you out of his sight. He will protect you because you have his treasure. You don't have to feed him, he takes care of himself. He knows his place as your protector and will stay out of your daily activities, always waiting for you on the fringe. It is done child, he belongs to you. You will come to appreciate what he can do for you in life. Go ahead, take him out of the cage, he knows you have the treasure."

Opening the cage, the bird did not hesitate to hop onto the table. He flapped his wings and jumped out to an outer dark branch. Moments later, a voice came in Visayan from the branch. "Bastard." Whereas, Lolung answered, "Piece of shit."

"All right Juana, rest on the pallet... a blanket is rolled up and hanging up there." He pointed. "I will wake you in the morning and get you safely on your way."

"But what about the medicine for my brother? You said it takes two hours to make."

"Ah yes, the medicine, it's in a jar right here. It takes two hours of thought to remember which jar it was in--so many jars and so many cures. Lights out. I only have a little candle."

She didn't hesitate to lie back down. She was in a state of tranquility, and to close her eyes and rest was an easy option. She stared at a bundle of twigs above her head, spinning in the candlelight, and she slept.

She awoke to a chorus of crows cawing, a thunderous upheaval from the branches and sky. Below on the lower branches beneath her, came a howling and screeching of the devil himself. Startled, Juana sat up and stared in every direction, trying to put yesterday's events in focus. Lolung sat by his hearth stone, boiling a tea. He cocked his head when she sat up and gave her a gleaming smile.

"What is it Lolung? Why are they all raising such a racket?"

"They know that one is leaving, they're all gossiping about it!"

Juana smiled, "They're talking about me leaving?"

"Sort of," said Lolung. "They all are protectors, and Duto is one of the old ones. They're both upset and happy that he is leaving." She glanced down at the branch that Duto had been roosting on yesterday, and there he sat sulking and staring at her. As soon as she made eye contact with him, he hopped into the air and flew away.

Immediately the cawing and macaque howling stopped. Juana looked bewildered. Lolung scratched his jaw. "You see Juana your Duto will check in with you usually in the morning and evening. He likes to make eye contact with his treasure. He's off now, to wherever, but be assured he has you in sight, for he can see a mile away."

"But Lolung, I don't know how to take care of him," Juana pleaded with the old man.

"The deed has been done Juana," the old man sighed. "He does need one thing. Long ago, the old ones learned how to prolong the lives of these medicine birds. A secret pellet, and only one, given once a year, when the bird starts molting. He will shed old feathers and grow new ones. The secret pellet is given, and his heart becomes that of a three-year-old bird all over again. I have two birds that are one hundred and twenty-five years old, passed on to me. One pellet a year. Duto is forty-five years old." He reached into a jar, pulled out a handful, and placed them in a snakeskin bag. With a thong, he tied it around her neck.

"But I'm here for my brother," she protested.

From a clay jar with blue stripes on it, he dumped a dried green mass

15

onto a banana leaf and folded it up.

"What is it Lolung?" she asked.

"It's *tawa-tawa*, *kalamansi*, and my secret snake liver ingredient. Make a soup with this, and his fever will break in an hour. Hold on child, the day is young, how is your foot?" She had forgotten all about the ant bites--they no longer bothered her. "Wait, there is a fee for the medicine."

"I have no money Lolung."

"Money! I don't want your money, what good is money to me? The fact is, to complete your protection, I need some of your hair."

"Alright, I don't care. Take what you want, but hurry, my brother needs me."

The old man stepped behind her and gathered her elbow length hair into a tail behind her back. He cut the mane with a black obsidian knife. Three quick hacks, and he dropped the long black tail into a woven bamboo basket. "Drink this tea and we'll go," said Lolung. "I'll take you past the snakes, and then you're on your own."

He lowered the magnificent trees' staircase to the ground and slowly climbed down. He reached the ground and beckoned her to follow. Clutching her purse of fever medicine, she one stepped it down. The shaman pulled a counter weighted vine, and the steps rose back into the tree. Instantly, a troop of macaques surrounded them. Giving a command, the old man began to walk through the clearing, all the while the macaques thrashing their perimeter with sticks. "Where are the snakes Lolung?" she asked nervously.

"They don't like the macaques. They know the macaques will kill them." Soon the large rock came into view, and here the monkey troop stopped. The old man smiled and put his hand on her head. "You are the image of my mother little one. You have protection now. Hurry to your brother, the soup will cure him."

"Thank you Lolung, I must go." And at a brisk walk, she hurried down the trail, looking back one final time. She saw him waving his arms and cursing at the macaques.

A full, pale moon was waning through the morning sky. Arriving at the stone crossing of the stream in the valley floor, she was astonished to see a white hen bathing on one of the stones. The hen, sensing her presence, squawked and flew downstream to a tree, shrouded in mist. Startled, she stared at the tree for a long moment, and suddenly from the sky, came a black crow flying into the hidden mist. A loud cawing and screeching commenced within the vapor cloud. Terrified, she bolted and began to run as fast as she could, swinging her bolo in one hand and grasping the bamboo purse of medicine in

16

the other. Finally arriving at the top of the ridge, she arrived gasping at the tree she had climbed the day before. Adrenaline had turned into exhaustion. She sat, breathing silently, trying to hear for signs of danger. Remembering her sick brother, she composed herself and stood up to embark down the hill. Duto landed in the tree she had climbed, and cawed for her attention. Juana smiled to herself, as she looked up and admired his ebony black brilliance. She made eye contact and rattled her pouches and medallion at him. The bird then took flight into the canopy. No time to lose, she began a slow steady trot down the trail.

Coming around a corner, she came to an old man tapping a donkey with a bamboo cane. The old man and the burro came to a stop. "Young man, you startled me." the old man cried.

"I'm sorry sir, I'm in a hurry. I have medicine for a sick brother."

"I see." The man lowered his tone. "You, boy! You went up to that Ghost tree by yourself?" he quipped.

"Yes, fever medicine," she answered. She realized he was calling her a boy, and now lowering her voice, "Is that your white hen I saw in the stream?"

"Huh? White hen in the stream? Where?" he asked.

She pointed back at the trail. "She was bathing in the stream, and I came upon her suddenly. She squawked and flew into a tree surrounded by a mist of clouds."

The old man's eyes grew large, and quickly he turned his burro around and tapped him fiercely. "The white lady, the she devil of the woods, you saw her? Run quickly! She may be coming!"

Rattled and now scared again, Juana burst into her fastest run now. Legs aching and lungs burning, finally she could see a line of trees that led to her home. At last, some smoke in the trees and the roof of her nipa hut were in sight. She called out, exhausted, and began to sob. Her Nanay heard her, rushing to her voice and crying. She wrapped her arms around her, calming her daughter.

"Is he still alive, Nanay?"

"Yes, he's very sick though."

"Here, Nanay, this pouch has the medicine… make a soup and he will live."

"What happened to your hair, Juana?" her mother asked, bewildered.

"Lolung cut my hair as payment for the medicine."

"Oh, that old devil. God knows what he'll do with it--some kind of voodoo practice. Thank God you're all right. Now hurry and boil the water. We'll make his soup."

Soon, Nanay had a simmering broth bubbling and climbed the ladder to

17

attend the sick boy. Juana's younger siblings stared at her and pointed. A small Chinese trade mirror hung on a post, and she looked startled when she stared into it. Her face was smeared with black dust and her hair cut at the ears. Around her neck hung the medicine pouches and the medallion. She now had the look of a young warrior native of the deep mountain forest. She had transformed from the schoolgirl of yesterday. She fell into a hammock, and just before she closed her eyes, a blackbird silhouetted in the canopy above. She was asleep instantly.

Laughter came louder and louder. She opened her eyes to see Pinto standing over her, pointing and laughing. "The dancing princess of the royal court is now the warrior princess of the forest!"

"It's not funny, where were you, we needed you?" Juana asked, annoyed.

Finally composing himself, he took defense and answered. "I had to go back and get the net. When Carlito got sick, he collapsed in the boat. I had to leave the net and get him to shore."

Ahh, the net! The most valuable thing the family owned. "Were you able to get it back?" she now asked, sympathetically.

"Yes, I was lucky. I got it back before the tide took it away. We need to fish today. We earned nothing yesterday."

"And how is Carlito?" she suddenly asked.

"His fever broke last night. He is resting. Mother is resting," Pinto said. "Juana, if you help me with the boat today, we will have fish. I need help. You can do it, just paddle the banca for me."

"But it's Sunday. I must go to Mass and check on the old China woman."

"They won't miss you one day, Juana, we have to feed our family, it's up to you and me." Hearing the reasoning of Pinto, she realized he was right. Her brother would recover in a couple of days. She must take his place and help on the fishing banca.

Caw, caw, caw, came a call from the coconut tree in the grove, and Pinto picked up a rock to chuck it at him.

"No, no! Don't throw that," Juana loudly protested.

"Huh? He's been jumping around in that tree since sun up. He's being annoying."

"Don't hurt him. He's my friend," she quipped at him. "Lolung gave him to me, or he gave me to him, I'm not sure."

Pinto rolled his eyes. "Yes, I want to hear all about your adventure to the "Ghost Tree." But eat something, if we leave now, we can catch the tide change and catch fish. The bambinos have food and water. Carlito and mother are resting. I told mother I was taking you fishing. She agreed. Now get up, let's go! Nanay bundled some rice and dried mango. It's laced on a string. You carry it. I'll bring the fish buckets."

Shouldering a long pole with both buckets hanging at each end, he headed down the trail. Grabbing her straw coulee hat, she followed along the trail, still trying to wake up. The path was well used, winding down to the river bank. The path ended at a small beach of sand on the shore. The banca was beached, with a long tether to a tree on the bank. Untying the tether, he launched the boat by gently dragging it the short distance in the sand to the water. The net was rolled into a bundle, hanging from a tree to keep it dry. Placing the net bundle and the two fish buckets aboard the center of the craft, he ordered her to get into the boat. With a gentle push and a hop aboard the stern, they were now moving in the current downstream. "Pick up a paddle and help me Juana," said Pinto.

Soon, they were in rhythm together, gliding along past nipa huts on the shoreline. Morning smoke from cooking fires lay motionless in the air over the river bank. The mosquitoes were getting thicker in the air as they approached a mangrove forest on either side. The water was turning brackish as they paddled past several gulls sitting on a dead mangrove tree. All of a sudden, the flock of gulls arose in a loud commotion, as a large raven landed and flapped his wings authoritatively. *Caw, caw, caw!*

"Juana, I think that's your friend the raven, what did you call him?"

Juana giggled, "Yes, that's Duto!"

"Is he going to follow us into the ocean?" Pinto asked.

"I'm not sure, let's see what he does." As they continued to paddle, Duto would relocate downriver a little farther to another convenient mangrove tree, all the time protesting and cawing. At last the river broadened out into a flat, calm sea. As they passed the last mangrove tree, the black bird landed and silently stared, as they paddled by. Their destination could be seen in the distance, a lone bamboo mast, bobbing on the water. Their father had years before constructed a large bamboo raft, anchoring it a mile offshore with a heavy manila rope. It was anchored to the bottom with stones. It was maintained and used almost daily, since they could remember. The shade under the raft was a natural beacon to the fish in the hot tropical sun. By attaching the net on the corner of the raft and peeling or laying the net from the banca in a large circle, one could return to the raft, and pull the giant purse of the net in and onto the floating platform.

To set the net, it took two people, one to release the net or set the net, the other person constantly paddling ahead in a circle, and then back to the raft.

The vista of the Camotes Sea that morning was a vision of tropical paradise. The Camotes Islands, distant to the north, and the island of Cebu to the west, with Bohol to the south and Leyte to the east, was a panorama of unmatched beauty. The clear, warm tropical waters were teeming with fish species of every dimension. Dolphins, schools of Mahi Mahi and whale shark, all feasted on the bounty of the sea. Sprinkled throughout were numerous coral reefs, atolls and islets, harboring sugar white sand beaches, covered with exotic shells.

The sea was the provider for everyone who lived on its shores. Fishermen dotted the waters in every direction on small bancas, as if to claim their territory. Other rafts to the north and south were anchored as well, by now being worked by their owners. Pinto's raft was anchored in the current of the Canigao Channel. The islet of Canigao was another half-mile beyond in the distance.

Leaving the mouth of the river, they now paddled into the current of the sea. Pinto raised a small bamboo mast with a woven bamboo mat, a square sail. Quickly he had the boat crisply splashing through the water toward the raft. Finally, Juana was able to stop and relax. She had been through a whirlwind of events in the last three days, and she was exhausted. She laid her shoulders into the bow and covered her head with her coulee hat. "Wake me up when we get there, Pinto."

The sun was at ten o'clock now, and the tropical heat was heavy. She slipped into a deep slumber, when all of a sudden, she was awakened by a *caw, caw caw*. There sat Duto on top of the mast, glaring down at her and his treasure.

"What's the matter with this bird?" Pinto cried. "He belongs in the jungle, not out here on the sea. What kind of devil bird did the old ghost give you?" Juana lifted her hat and stared with one eye at him, and he back at her with one eye. "No matter, we're almost there, grab the paddle." Quickly, Pinto popped the mast from its bracket and the bird rose up in protest. Circling a couple of times, Duto landed on the mast of the raft, which was a stone's throw away.

Smoothly, they paddled and glided up to the raft. Pinto now gave direction, as she had never been on the raft before. "Grab that line and tie the bow of the banca off," Pinto ordered. Stepping onto the raft, Pinto quickly tied the stern up. "All right Juana, rest while I get the net rigged to the raft." Pulling the end of the net from the banca, he dove in with a weighted rock to drop the net, with the other end attached to the raft. Surfacing for air, he cried out to Juana. "A turtle!" And with that, dove again. For the longest time she waited, almost jumping in to look for him. At last, there he was, thirty feet away, holding a huge flapping sea turtle to his chest. "Juana, throw me a line, quick!"

Brooke Meets Weynton

That same morning, twenty miles to the south and anchored in a Macrohan cove, lay a sleek topsail schooner, bristling with armaments.

Like a sleeping hornet, she lay in a back water coral channel that was lined with coconut trees. The trees disguised her two masts from the Camotes Sea. She flew the Union Jack, and the sight of her left no doubt she was a ship of the Queen's Navy. She carried eighteen, two pound brass swivel cannons on either rail, with six six-pound cannons, three portals on either side, and an array of cutlass rifles. Shotgun cabinets and lockers were across her deck. Her rails had been refitted and shielded in tugas wood, which was hard as iron, and a defensive shield. State-of-the-art and modified, there was no mistake she was built for battle.

Her name was the HMS "Royalist." Her captain, who commissioned her and spent his inheritance to buy her, was a genius at maritime warfare. He was known as the "White Rajah of Sarawak," or Captain James Brooke, as he preferred to be called. He was already a legend in the Spice Islands.

Born in Calcutta, India to wealthy British aristocrats, he was schooled in England at an early age. Brooke enlisted in the Bengal army, as an ensign, and an escort to the British East India Company. He had been wounded twice in two different wars under the Crown Navy. At this point in his life, he had inherited the family estate, whereby he resigned his commission from the British Navy, and purchased the HMS "Royalist." He had rigged her for privateering, with a nod of approval from the crown.

The "Royalist" had been refitted in the shipyards of Singapore, with two inches of tugas wood shielding her sides and gun ports. Her secret weapons were ten British naval brass blunderbusses, mounted on swivels, staggered down the rail between two pound cannons. At one hundred feet, the blunderbusses were deadly.

The crew were soldiers of fortune, who had been trained in survival and hand-to-hand combat. They wore long barong swords on leather belts, that were loaded with smaller knives for throwing. Each carried a double barrel pistol, on either leg, opposite the sword.

Capt. James Brooke had contracted his warship out to the Sultan of Brunei, and quickly destroyed a siege and uprising, thus saving the Sultan's kingdom. In gratitude, the Sultan gave him his own island kingdom and granted him the title "Rajah of Sarawak."

Because he was Rajah in his own kingdom, he chose to cede the valuable island to the British Crown to serve as a trading port. In doing so, the British made him Governor and Commander in Chief of its naval base on the island.

His kingdom had prospered under his rule. The trading of spices and pepper flourished under the protection of his schooner, the "Royalist."

But as years went by, the sea pirates, the Iranum, or more generally known as the Moro's, figured out that the schooner could not be everywhere at once, and began terrorizing his trade routes from all directions.

The Moro had been there since ancient times, and had become expert seafarers. They realized that if several "proa," as their craft were called, were organized into a flotilla, the raiding would be easy pickings in all parts of the archipelago's thousands of islands.

A culture of Islam, the Moro's had no remorse using the krill, or sword in battle, and reveled in the thrill of the raid for booty and slaves.

So vast were the islands of the archipelago, raiding had become a way of life. There was no predictability of where and when they would strike, and very difficult to defend against their numbers. For two centuries, the Spanish had rimmed the Camotes Sea with stone watchtowers at various strategic spots of geography. These watchmen gazed into the sea, searching for signs of sail, indicating a Moro pirate flotilla on the horizon. Seeing danger, the watchmen banged a gong and blew a conch horn shell, warning the village of the onslaught. The warning would allow for quick evacuation into the interior, avoiding capture and slavery. Valuables could be cached in time also.

Gangs of these flotillas (fleets) of pirates had been getting much bolder as of late, and so Brooke had decided to take to the sea again, trading his palace for his love of privateering. Using intelligence of a network of scouts, he now waited in ambush for a flotilla, which had been seen sailing north, a month earlier. He had chosen this hideout, and now waited for their return.

They had been anchored for three days, and his crew were getting bored and lazy. If the pirates were spotted, he needed to get underway quickly, in order to intercept them in the channel. Vigilance was imperative, and Brooke knew it. "Morning Sir," the first mate saluted as the captain stepped out of his salon.

"Morning Colin, have my tea brought to the wheel deck," Brooke replied. He looked up at the rigging. On the mainmast sat two lookouts, gazing down at him. "Any luck lads?" asked Brooke.

"No sir, nothing but fishing boats, sir," the one with the glass replied.

"Dammit, where are those rascals?" Brooke muttered. "This sitting and waiting is so monotonous."

The men were playing dice and dominoes on deck, and others sat whittling. "Patience lads, we know they're coming," Brooke assured them as a whole. "Powder and shot inspected this morning Colin?" Brooke asked.

22

"Yes sir, powder packs dry and shot loads inventoried for attack sir," Colin proudly responded.

Brooke had built on his years of experience at sea warfare, and his twenty men were taught to work as a team under attack. All knew their job and what was expected of them, and they were extremely loyal to Brooke. It was his ship, his kingdom, and their leader.

"Damn, I've never seen anything like this!" came a cry from the mast watch.

"What is it Higgs?" Brooke called out to him.

Higgs was staring into the glass and leaning out over the cross-arm. "Not sure sir, a black swirling cloud is coming down the beach.

"Sir!" he exclaimed. "They're birds sir, thousands of them, coming this way!"

Back at the fishing raft, Juana pulled the rope, and hauled in Pinto with his turtle.

"Juana, take the knife and punch a hole on the edge of his shell," Pinto struggled and yelled. "Now tie him to the raft."

Understanding, she quickly had the turtle tethered with a strong cord, and the creature stopped struggling. Jumping up on the raft, Pinto was exuberant, "Wow, your good luck Juana! "We'll have turtle soup for a week!" Juana let out a yell of joy and the raven, "Duto," celebrated with a *caw, caw, caw!*

As Pinto sat and caught his breath, Juana scanned the horizon. She realized she had never witnessed the marvelous view, as she had never been on the sea, and now she drank in the vista. She was surrounded by a dozen islands, ringed by white sands, and waving coconut trees. The jagged mountains of Leyte, running down the backbone of the big island, were shrouded on the tops by white, wispy clouds. Towards Bohol, blue sky and small white clouds were to the south, and she could see the Hilongos Holy Cross bell tower rising above the coconut forest. She looked back towards Matalom and the river inlet, and could see the Moro watchtower, with a whiff of smoke coming from the top. The watchmen were cooking food. The smoke was a sign that it was occupied, from out at sea. Looking north towards the Camotes, it looked dark and ominous. A giant thunderhead, with a squall riding under it, was coming across the Camotes Sea.

"Pinto that looks like a bad storm," said Juana.

"I see that sister, let's hurry. We can get one net set, maybe it will disappear. Let's keep our eyes on it. C'mon start paddling. I'll play the net," said Pinto. "Just paddle us in a giant circle so we end up back at the raft."

Catching on quickly to his method, the paddling became easier as the net was tossed over. With his guidance and paddling also, they closed the purse, and tied back up at the raft. Very pleased, Pinto gave some praise to her. "Gosh, I want to call you Juan, you act like an old timer fishing the boat and net!"

"Don't call me Juan--I can't help it. Lolung cut my hair for payment."

"Ah yes, tell me about your adventure and this damn crow that's shitting on my raft," he laughed.

"Well, I had to walk through this field of snakes and...."

"Stop, stop," he held his hand up and pointed at the net. The surface was twinkling with hundreds of little fins.

"Tell me later! Pull now!" Both of them began retrieving the net, and pulled a ball of jumping fingerlings onto the raft. Juana and Pinto both laughed excitedly as they filled the two buckets. In their excitement, the squall had crept up on them, with both of them spotting the menace at the same time.

"Juana--let's make for Canigao! Until this storm passes, leave the net. I'll tie it down. Quick, get the fish in the boat."

Feeling urgency now, Pinto pushed off the raft, and got the sail up, with the swift wind that was building. They could be on Canigao in ten minutes and ride the storm out safely with their fish.

"What about the turtle?" asked Juana.

"Oh, he'll be fine. We'll go back in a couple of hours, get the net, pick him up, and head home."

In her whole life of twelve years, she had always stared at Canigao Island in the distance, looking magical and beautiful with its turquoise water, and white sand beach. This would be the first time that she had ever stepped onto it's shore. It was without drinking water, a grove of 1,000 coconut trees and surrounded by endless white sand.

The first raindrops hit them just as they beached. A lucky break, as the sea was now turning white with a squall upon them. *Caw, caw, caw* came the cry from the canopy of coconut trees. Looking up, Juana giggled to herself. This old crow was quite the fellow.

"C'mon, get the buckets in the trees, I'll tie the boat up. There's an old fisherman's hut in the clearing." The wall of rain was upon them now. The wind began breaking coconuts loose, falling everywhere with a *thump, thump, thump* in the sand.

"There! A small hut in the clearing, get out of the wind and rain," pointed Pinto. Soon, he was in the shelter also, laughing at their luck, and the close call

24

at almost getting caught in the stormy sea. "Well, let's make the best of this. I have a flint and a steel fire starter. Let's cook some fish for lunch!" smiled Pinto. "C'mon Juan, pull some of that dry grass tender out of the corner there," said Pinto.

"Stop calling me Juan, or make your own fire," she snapped angrily.

"Okay, okay" laughed Pinto.

He scrounged several burnables in the hut, and sparking the dry grass, had a crackling little fire going. Spearing several fish on a bamboo stick, he built a pyramid of roasting fish around the little flame.

Outside the rain continued to pour. The crow had disappeared apparently, finding a safe place to ride out the bluster. The aroma of roasting fish and warmth of the fire brought a sense of calm again. Pinto stood up and stared out at the storm.

"I think it's passing, I can see blue sky over there. Yes, good its blowing off to the east now." Sitting back down, he rubbed his hands together. "Oh, let's feast on fish!"

Both of them ate all the sticks up. Licking his fingers, he sat back and patted his stomach. "It was a good catch Juana. Sometimes it takes a week to catch that many. I knew we were lucky today when we caught the turtle." Juana pulled her knees up under her cotton smock shirt, and closed her eyes with contentment.

Caw, caw, caw, caw, caw.

"Listen to him, said Pinto. Doesn't he ever rest?"

Juana laughed.

Caw, caw, caw, caw, caw, caw, caw!!!

Bong, bong, bong, bong, bong. Caw, caw.

"What the hell? It's the warning gong! Get up, get to the boat!" Running from the hut to the banca on the beach, they both were horrified at what they were looking at. A dozen proa were scattered between the island of Canigao and the mainland, and were approaching. Plying the water under sail, two of them were almost to the beach where they stood.

The gong and conch horns continued to sound from the watchtower on the mainland. The Pirates had used the cover of the storm, and hid behind its front, as they sailed down the straight, heading south from the northern reaches of the sea. The smoke from Pinto's cooking fire had betrayed their presence on the island. Fortunately for Matalom, the tide was out, making a beach assault too risky. One proa tried to beach on the mainland, and was met by a hail of arrows, spears, and sporadic musket gunfire. The proa quickly backed away out of range of the defensive onslaught.

25

Pinto froze. He could hear their commands coming now, as the two boats landed on the beach a short distance away. They wore turbans on their heads, and had scarlet, striped velvet trousers on. They wore green and red silk jackets, with silk sarongs that were tied around the waist. The Pirates raced forward, running and shouting, and holding up their swords.

"Say nothing Juana!" he muttered. "Let me do the talking." Soon they were surrounded by the fierce looking group of cutthroats. One of them demanded, in their dialect, who they were and who else was on the island.

"We are poor fisherman, we have nothing. Take our fish, take our net on the raft." he pointed at the distant float.

"Ha, you are offering gifts!?" said the big ugly one. "You and your brother, the net and fish and banca belong to Ren Tap now! What are your names?!" he barked.

"My name is Pinto. My brother's name is Juan, but he is deaf and dumb. He cannot speak."

The big, ugly one's companions spread out and searched the island, finding only the bucket of fish. Tying the brother and sisters hands together, they were marched to the boat and pushed onto the deck. Pinto could see another proa tying up to the raft, and could see them loading his prize net. A yell of success came from another one, as he held up the turtle for his companions to admire.

The pounding gong and horns had stopped echoing from the watchtower on the beach in Matalom. The hail of projectiles had discouraged any further attempts to beach and attack. Now came a shout of commands between the dozen boats, and they all turned and headed out to sea. The channel was blocked from Pinto's vision, as they were on the backside of Canigao Island.

Pushing off from the beach, one pirate proa followed, towing Pinto's banca. As they rounded the point of the island, Pinto stared in disbelief. A flotilla of proa's, fifty or more, surrounded a large battleship, the mothership, a long boat known as a "Caracoa." The bow was an alligator head, carved in wood, and the stern carved like the creature's tale. It had massive outriggers, with an upper and lower deck. The lower deck was for oarsmen and galley slaves. It's massive square sales were covered with streamers and silk flags.

As they approached the large mothership, laughing and jeering pirates looked over the rail and down at them, tied and sitting on the proa deck. They continued their mockery as the proa pulled up to the massive outrigger, her oarsmen tying the small boat alongside. The one who spoke Visayan yelled at Pinto and Juana "Get up!" "Move." tapping a sword on Pinto's back. They both ascended the outriggers cross arm to the main deck, via the steps that were built

26

into its design. A large column of smoke arose from the main deck. Two large tents, or canopies, could be seen at either end. All around the Caracoa, smaller boats passed, jeering and laughing at the captives, offering compliments to the success of the slave capture. At the prodding of swords and hostile commands, they both climbed the ladder, and stepped over the rail, and onto the deck of the floating fortress.

Trembling with fright, Juana kept her head lowered, and covered her face with her coulee hat. Pinto stared at the sight. There was a galley in the center of the massive deck, where a whole pig was turning on a spit, along with another of roasting chickens.

A colorful canopy forward of the galley could be seen, with a large robust fellow propped up on silk pillows, and two totally naked women lying on either side of him, stroking his loins and running their fingers through his hair. Another tent was at the stern, at which a rather fat, naked native girl was tied at the hands, kneeling on her knees and elbows, looking over her shoulder at the new arrivals.

The deck and rigging were covered with armed, menacing looking pirates. The lieutenants and underlings were enjoying a feast of food, wine, opium and sex from the infidel slaves, the women having been captured and drugged into euphoria. The two captives were pushed toward the forward tent, and stood before Ren Tap. He bellowed, "What have we here?"

One of his lieutenants quickly answered, "Captured fisherman your highness, the smoke we spotted on the island."

"I see, well their fishing days are over. They will work the Sultan's rice paddies the rest of their days now. Take them below and chain them in the forward bow!" "Bring me more wine and a fresh pipe," he bellowed.

Caw, caw, caw came a cry from the mast top. A sudden hush came over the entire crew. A pirate began yelling, "A curse, a curse, bad luck black bird land on mast at sea."

Looking down at the scene, Duto quickly realized he was a target, and flew off the mast, just as three muskets went off, all of the balls missing him. The last Juana saw was him flying toward the mainland, and thinking to herself *Not much of a protector!* as she was pushed down the deck ladder, into the lower compartment.

The smell was ghastly, of sweat and urine and opium smoke hanging in the air. She was prodded with the kris blade down the center of naked oarsmen, all shackled with blocks and rotten rope at the ankles. Reaching the forward hold in the bow, she and Pinto were shackled with iron rings to the bulkhead. A huge tattooed blacksmith pounded red hot rivets into their wrists shackles, and flattening them with a hammer. Next to them, three live pigs were in a pen. Completing his task, he closed the bowsprit door, leaving them in darkness and oppressive heat.

Juana began to sob and weep softly.

"Shss, quiet, be brave--they must not discover you are a girl!" Pinto begged. The heat and stench from the pigs was unbearable. They could now hear shouts and commands, and a drum began a steady beat. They could hear water splashing on the bow. indicating they were underway. "What will we do Pinto?" she cried.

"I'm not sure, save your strength." he whispered. "Try and rest. There's nothing we can do, I can't even see my feet," said Pinto.

Duto gained altitude as he flew away from the Caracoa. He then found some thermal air, and fell into a glide for the coast. Reaching the shoreline of Leyte finally, he spotted an old, tall nara tree on the beach. He recognized it as one of his old roosting haunts. Duto had roosted here before on his excursions, and had witnessed pirates and ship battles. Looking to the east, Duto spotted the masts and the outline of the "Royalist," hidden behind a spot on a little peninsula. Springing into action, he flew to the very top of the tree above the canopy, and began a chorus of cawing and cackling, without stopping. He continued the cawing for several minutes.

Resting, he stared across the canopy into the interior. He was able to see for miles, all the way up the slope of the jungle covered Cordilla. And there they were! Hundreds of ravens coming from every direction, towards his calling. He began again *caw, caw, caw, caw, caw, caw*. Within fifteen minutes, the tree was black with hundreds of crows, and they were still coming from the distance.

Looking around at his handiwork and sounding the alarm, he flapped his wings, and announced to the multitude to follow him. Leaping from the top branch, he spiraled up for altitude, and headed for the mast of the ship hidden behind the coconut trees. He flew along the beach with the swarm following him.

Arriving at the line of coconut trees on the little spit of land, approximately 2,000 crows landed in their canopy, all of them cawing at once. The sound was so tumultuous, that the deckhands below stared in awe and disbelief at the spectacle. Satisfied with his backup, Duto flew and landed on the top of the forward mast. With that, the cawing mass relocated to the schooner itself, roosting on every conceivable square inch.

Brooke and his men stood in fear and silence. This many ravens could easily peck their eyes out. They were witnessing a phenomena, or a black

28

voodoo curse.

"Steady boys," Brooke hollered above the roar of cawing.

"Maybe we should jump in and swim for it" Colin suggested. Suddenly, the one on the top of the mast flew down to the stern deck, opening his wings and flaring them. He landed a short distance from Brooke. The bird began to pace around in circles. As he did, the flock began to quiet down. After circling for about a minute, silence was on the deck.

Standing sideways and eyeing Brooke, the crow began to speak in the Visayan dialect "Follow me! Moro Oro! Moro Oro! Follow me."

Brooke looked at Colin. "By the devil himself, is that bird talking?"

Again the bird paced in a three foot circle and stopped. Opening his beak again, he spoke, "Moro Oro. Follow me. Moro Oro. Follow me!"

"Sir, he's speaking Visayan. He's saying pirate gold, follow me!"

And once more, Duto spoke, "Moro Oro, follow me," and he then flew to the top of the masthead. Looking down at Brooke, he made eye contact, and flew off toward the west and the southern point. The mass of black crows arose up, and followed him.

"Mr. Colin, weigh anchor!! Look alive mates, a sign from heaven! Fortune has come our way. Man the main! Open the canvass!"

Quickly the sailors jumped into the long tender boat, and pulling at eight oars, pulled the Royalist out of the slack water bite, and into the wind and current. Clearing the coral shoal, with her hands rowing and trimming her sails, she soon was on a course towards the point to the west, in the direction of the cloud of crows. The Royalist came to life like a well-oiled machine.

"Come about, due northwest Mr. Irons!" Brooke commanded. "Full topsail sheets ready?" Brooke barked.

"Ready sir!" Mr. Colin's answered.

"Cinch her down hard lads." "Maintain your bearing, Mr. Irons," Brooke commanded. The schooner was clipping along now at eight knots, with activity on deck in every dimension.

"Mr. Higgs!" Brooke looked up." Do you see the cloud of birds, sir?"

"Aye Captain, they've landed on the beach, at the point, sir."

Brooke rubbed his chin. Was there a treasure chest on the beach, a cache of pirate gold? "Maintain your course, Mr. Irons," he commanded, and then advised the entire crew, "We'll circle off the point lads, and observe these birds. On my command, we'll come about and…"

"Sir, sir!" came the cry from Higgs roost. "A Moro pirate fleet sir. Sails as far as I can see, it's the flotilla sir!"

Quickly realizing that his course and bearing would put them upon the fleet before they could react, Brooke gave the cry. "Battle stations! Battle stations!"

Twelve of his men had been trained as a group, specifically for shooting the Royalist's guns, with each having a specific duty. The other eight were the ship's eyes, course, and direction, maintaining her sail power. Over the years, learning from previous actions and skirmishes, using techniques and experience, combined with the latest British naval firepower, the crew had melded into a deadly, killing machine.

"Close all gun ports Mr. Colin," came the command. Quickly, the hull gun ports were closed, sliding two inch thick tugas wood into the windows. Brooke was now on the high point of the bow, scanning the fleet for the swarm's prize.

There she was! An immense Caracoa came into view in the glass, streamers flying from her two masts, and square sails running with the wind. Behind her were two more large Proa, oars plying the water and under sail. Totally surprised, the Moros now tried to change course downwind, and run from the unknown threat. At the same time, dozens of smaller proa began heading towards the Royalist. These crafts were much smaller, two or three man crews, with a one-shot homemade bamboo lantana cannon protruding from the bow. Black powder and beach pebbles were usually the charge. Getting in close and shooting the one time gun, with several of them at once, was the strategy. They would then board with sword and shield, and glory to the finish.

"Mr. Irons, change course to intercept that Dragon boat!" Brooke bellowed. "Mr. Colin break out the Johnny guns!" Looking at his telltales, and the oncoming attack, he then shouted, "Muster and mount on starboard all Johnny guns."

"Aye aye, Captain!" And then came a scrambling at the salon locker on deck, as the brass blunderbusses were handed out. Each team of two manned two guns. They quickly dropped the swivels into the molded rail slots. The team worked, one as a fuse man, the other as a target aimer, shouldering the beast. Now they were being sprayed with the pebble flack from the firing lantanas, cracking hard on the schooner's bow.

"All hands take cover. Wait for my signal. Mr. Irons, come over hard 90° on my command," Brooke yelled.

"Hard on the port reach! At your command! Aye, Captain!"

Hearing the gongs and bells and war cries of the Moro, they were headed right at the swarm of proa, on a collision course, when came the command. Now arrows were landing on the deck. "Steady lads, steady." Brooke was the only one with his head above the rail. "Now Mr. Irons, hard over on the port reach, fire at will on the starboard lads!" Brooke bellowed.

30

Instantly the rail windows flew open, and proa that were within twenty feet of the schooner were decimated, as each blunderbuss picked one out. The cannoneer's ordered the fuse men to strike, and the huge explosion of lead grapeshot, with a twenty foot circumference pattern, ripped into the sail rigging, hull, and the unlucky pirates on board the sitting duck proa.

Moving to their second gun station, and sliding the shield open, they raked the boats coming up from behind, with a direct hit from the blunderbuss. Now, twelve shattered, sinking burning proa lay in a mass of debris, with dying men trying to stay afloat and swim. The thirty other Moro proa fell off the attack, after seeing the devastation of their bravest and lead commanders. All this time, the battery crew quickly swabbed their blunderbuss, and reloaded with new charges.

"Stay on that Dragon ship Mr. Irons, ignore the attack--we'll pound them again!" Now another attack came, this time on the port.

"Mr. Colin, Johnny guns on the portside. Muster! Engage in two minutes!"

Like clockwork, the guns were removed from their rail brackets, and shifted to the port, dropping each gun's swivel into its prescribed station.

"Maintain course. On my command, gun number six, engage!" The fuseman opened the window, and there was a proa, attempting to come alongside.

BOOM!!!

The craft folded into a heap, with arms flailing, under the collapsed rigging.

"Number three, engage!" came the command. The window slid open, and instantly a thunderous BOOM! Then the window slammed shut.

"Steady lads, those were the brave ones. They're almost upon us. Steady, all guns. Engage! Fire at will!"

The Royalist cook and Brooke's cabin boy were sniping with muskets on the stern now, shooting at trailing attackers. Again the deadly technique sluiced the pirate fleet with lead grapeshot, and another twelve Proa were flattened, drifting off in the channel current. This was too much for the pirates. Half of their attack fleet wiped out in ten minutes. The remaining proa now stayed on a parallel course with the Royalist at a safe distance, out of range of her fire breathing broadsides.

The Royalist was now gaining on the giant Caracoa, with time to reload the blunderbuss for another attack. The cabin boy began spreading sand on the deck, as the blood from hand-to-hand combat was more than likely to be spilled on the deck. The sand would prevent slipping on the blood, in mortal deck fighting with swords.

The Caracoa was armed with two Chinese iron cannon, one on the bow and one on the stern. She had an array of light cannons on her rails, but was no match for the Royalist. Her biggest defense was her fleet of surrounding proa, half of which lay shattered on the horizon. She fired her antique stern cannon, the charge of black powder not enough to push the grapeshot the distance to the Royalist. A spew of spray fell way short, and now the Royalist was coming up alongside the Dragon boat for a broadside. Her slaving oarsmen pulled for their lives on the outriggers, and her lower deck oarsmen were in perfect unison. They had no choice, as they all were tied to their stations. Giving up was no option. It meant death by the justice of the White Rajah.

"Mr. Colin! Muster Johnny guns to the starboard, on my command Mr. Colin. Make your targets the oarsmen on the outriggers lads! I want a full broadside! Gentleman, do your job for God and country. Steady… ready… NOW!"

A fusillade of grapeshot was now unleashed, as missiles and arrows came flying through the air. The blunderbuss raked the poor defenseless oarsmen. A great panic of shouts and cries of pain now came from the wounded vessel. Scores of proa were now rescuing the fleeing hierarchy.

Now Brooke gave the command, "Mr. Irons. Come About! Engage starboard cannonade on my command Mr. Colin. Fire! Fire! Fire!"

The two pound brass cannonade released their grapeshot of fury, aiming at the oar ports on the vessel's hull, knowing the shot would penetrate the interior.

With splintering explosions and screams, the volley was devastating. The coup de grace was the firing of the three six-pounders. Each was loaded with ball and chain, designed to bring down rigging, sail and mast. Boom! Boom! Boom! They exploded, and the forward mast and rigging of the Caracoa all fell into the rear mast, now catching fire. Pirates were jumping and swimming for their lives. Sharks could be seen, having smelled the blood in the water.

"Report damage Mr. Colin. Any wounded sir?" Brooke maintained his composure.

"Mr. Higgs wounded sir, with an arrow. He'll live. And Carlton, a finger shot off. The ship, she's a fighter sir!" came Colin's report.

"Alright. Come about. Pistols and sabers for boarding, be alert lads! They might have booby traps on her!"

Only three of Allah's soldiers of the sea remained, hiding amongst the fallen rigging. Quickly, they were dispatched with pistol shots, as they exposed themselves, and rushed the lads with swords, crying "God is Great!" The slaughter on the deck and below was appalling. A naked woman lay crushed in the stern from the fallen rigging. Scattered on the outriggers and below were corpses, a bloody heap of scalded flesh that had been sluiced by lead shot and wood splinters.

"Let's get this fire out lads! We might be able to save the beast!"

The crew quickly formed a bucket brigade up the outrigger to the deck and managed to extinguish the flames.

"Mr. Colin, search the lower deck for contraband and survivors," Brooke commanded.

The carnage was hard to look at, men shackled in place, all dead with agony etched on their faces. The lower stern cabin contained a dozen barrels of corn and dried fish, the rations for the slaves.

"Check that bow cabin Mr. Johns," came Colin's command. Opening the door, he jumped back at the sight of two sets of eyes staring back at him. He raised his pistol to shoot, and both Pinto and Juana covered their faces. Seeing them both shackled, the sailor, Mr. Johns, lowered his pistol and hollered, "Here sir, over here, some survivors chained to the bulwark!"

Colin came stumbling forward through the blood and fallen corpses.

"My God sir, how did they survive?"

The three pigs lay dead, having sustained a direct hit through the hull. Their bodies had absorbed the lead grapeshot, and had saved Pinto and Juana.

Colin disappeared to report, when Mr. Johns noticed a shattered corpse of a pirate that was wearing gold earrings, and a gilded kris in his belt. He distracted himself to obtain the souvenirs. Good timing, because at that moment, a fluttering of wings landed at the hole blown open in the bow. Seeing Juana, Duto exalted a loud *caw, caw, caw.* He'd come back! Her protector! And her eyes grew wide. A big smile was now on her face. She held the shiny medallion up in the sunlight. "Dirty bastards," said the bird, and flew away.

"Come out with your hands up!" Colin had returned and commanded, pointing his pistol at them.

"Sir, they're chained up, they can't move" reported Mr. Johns.

"Are they wounded, Johns?" Mr. Colin asked.

"No sir, they must be captured slaves," Johns guessed.

"Alright, leave the door open so they can breathe. Poor creatures. We'll deal with them later. Standby, Mr. Johns. I'll tell the captain about these two survivors." Colin returned to the main deck and found Brooke.

"Well Mr. Colin, what is our reward for today's labors?" asked Brooke. Of course he was hoping to hear him say the hold was laden with silk, gunpowder, opium and gold. But Colin was shaking his head as no.

33

"Sir some barrels of corn and fish, and two slaves that appeared to not be wounded."

"Damn, damn, damn. A burned up floating pig sty, some barrels of corn and two slaves. We risked our lives for this." Brooke stared out at the fleeing flotilla, now a mile away. The wise, old Ren Tap had escaped, with his slave boats and treasure.

"Well Mr. Colin, we'll make for Malitbog and collect our bounty for the heads we have. The head bounty and the corn are worth something! Can we get that stern sail up and working Mr. Irons?"

"I believe so sir, we'll give it our best shot."

Soon they had the stern clear of debris, hacking it loose, and throwing the rigging overboard. They managed to haul up what was left of the tattered stern square sail, and now had her underway. Rejoining the Royalist, Brooke hooked a towline to the wallowing Caracoa. Heading east, he soon had the prize underway, leaving the sea, and plowing ahead for the Spanish town of Malitbog. Brooke had hoped for valuable booty to help finance his excursion, but the bounty and reward on the burned up Caracoa would probably only pay for his grog and rations. Powder and lead were costly. The big reward was breaking up Ren Tap's pirate navy, and restoring safe passage for his kingdom in Sarawak.

Malitbog was an old Spanish port, that had been established for over two hundred years. The province had become an important supplier of "abaca hemp," used for braiding quality rope, prized for rigging ships. Two tribes of earlier times realized the wealth of the abaca trade and fought each other for control. To settle the dispute, a church was built on the boundary of the two tribes, and peace was attained through the prosperity of the abaca trade.

The Spanish had beached an old galleon, the 'Dona Marta,' and built a bamboo catwalk out to her, creating a control point for taxation and loading. The old Spanish church was at the center of town. Malitbog lay in a protected bay on the south of the island, with good anchorage, that protected the ships from ocean storms.

A cobbled street led from the church to a large stone quay on the shore. Into the bay protruded a long dock on bamboo stilts, a catwalk reaching out from the shore to deep water. At the end of the catwalk, the old rotten, Spanish galleon Dona Marta rested, her hull grounded on the sand bottom, with her decks and lower cabins well above the waterline. The old galleon provided a loading dock and quarters for a fat old Spanish captain named Garcia. He controlled the export and import through the use of this facility. Captain Garcia was the Spanish authority, in cooperation with the local priest of the church, who held extreme power over the people. Brooke had traded here often, enjoying shore leave with the native population, and replenishing water supplies. The Royalist was paid by the Spanish captain, through the wealth of the church, for protection, and bounty on the heads of pirates. The fat, lazy old Capt. Garcia was corrupt in every dealing, and Brooke always felt the man should be strung up on the yardarm. Yet, it was the only thing close to civilization in this part of the world. So it was on this day, as they rounded the point into the bay, towing his prize, that Brooke could see in his glass, a large three masted barque. She was tied up at the side of the Dona Marta, a Union Jack flying from her stern.

The barque's captain was Alexander Weynton, born in the early part of the nineteenth century, in Kingston Jamaica, which had previously been known as Santiago. A Spanish holding, it had been a colony of Columbus. One hundred years earlier, Britain had conquered and taken the prize island, now a major producer of sugar and rum. Rum, watered down, was known as grog, and was a common ration within the British Navy.

Renaming Santiago to Jamaica, they now imported African slaves, and tripled sugar production, supplying rum for the thirst of the British Navy. Weynton's father was a rum merchant, and so the boy learned Spanish and English growing up on the docks of Kingston. He had listened and learned tales of treachery, and was schooled in the ways of the sea.

Early on, his father purchased two merchant sloops, shipping the barrels of rum to New Orleans, a very lucrative venture. Apprenticing as a cabin boy and deckhand, he quickly became first mate, and at the age of twenty, was made Captain of his father's schooner, after learning to navigate with the sextant. After years of plying the Carribean Sea and working the rum trade, he had become a seasoned and respected Captain.

As fate would have it though, the slave population rebelled, and his father's plantation and enterprise were burned to the ground. Having to satisfy creditors, the sloops and schooner were sold, leaving Weynton stuck in Kingston broke. For years, the Hudson Bay Company had maintained their own wharf in Kingston and were purchasing agents of Jamaican rum. Knowing the disaster that had befallen the Weynton enterprise, and in sympathy, Weynton was offered a job as first mate on a barque, the Cowlitz. She was loaded with lumber, having returned from the Oregon country, by way of the horn.

Trading some of her lumber for barrels of rum, she was on her way back to London. On her crossing the Atlantic, her captain suffered a heart attack, and was found dead in his quarters. Weynton, being the only one who could navigate, took charge of the large vessel, and safely commanded her to the docks of the Thames River. The Hudson Bay Company was so impressed with his ability, that they immediately named him Captain of the Cowlitz.

The Hudson Bay Company had invested heavily at Fort Vancouver, at the mouth of the Columbia River, on the Pacific coast. To the north of the fort, a place they call Cowlitz Farm, they had planted immense fields of wheat, grain and vegetables, including large potato fields. So successful with an immense crop, the company commissioned a large three masted barque, The Cowlitz, to ship the surplus food and carry lumber to the Caribbean.

Having realized the value of the rum and sugar trade, the Hudson Bay Company had also established a trading post in the Sandwich Islands, specifically, Honolulu. Sugar from the plantations, and whale oil from the whaling fleet that home ported in Honolulu were gotten cheap for English gunpowder, cotton cloth and salt going to Victoria. At Victoria, salmon could be traded for the oil and rum.

And so Captain Weynton had set sail for the Sandwich Islands from London, via the Cape of Africa. Upon arriving in Honolulu, he was to proceed to a new colony the Hudson Bay Company had chartered. The Crown had established a place called Fort Victoria, and the Cowlitz was to deliver oil and rum to the colonies warehouse. The cargo from London was several bales of cheap cotton cloth, and fifty kegs of gunpowder, to be traded in Honolulu. It was a very light shipment, so the ship had been ballasted heavily, in preparation for sailing around the Cape of Africa. With Capt. Weynton's navigation abilities and experience, the passage had been uneventful. Safely arriving at the East Indies port of Singapore, at a Hudson Bay trading wharf, the ship was loaded with barrels of rock salt, a major trading commodity, used for preserving fish and meat. The company was exploring a new market source, being Honolulu's salt was twice the Singapore price. The salt was destined to Fort Victoria for barrels of salmon. The Captain had charted his course up the South China Sea, and then would steer east for the open Pacific, and the Sandwich Islands. The Malay Archipelago was known to be rife with pirates, so by staying at sea and avoiding the surrounding islands, odds were better for safe passage.

Now having left Singapore and only two days underway, he noticed how sluggish the ship was handling, not pointing as high as it should on tack. Thinking something not right, he retired to his chart room, and began scrutinizing the ship's log. He compared the weight tonnage aboard of cargo, the salt, gunpowder and cloth. Looking at the ballast tonnage, he found a glaring error.

In London, she had been loaded with extra ballast, 10,000 pounds to be exact. He had ordered the extra ballast removed in Singapore. The work crew of the company, on the dock, were charged with this task, as his crew had been given shore leave. Captain Weynton now realized the wharf crew chief had noted on the manifest, that 1,000 pounds of ballast had been removed. That was it! They were 9,000 pounds overweight, and sluggishly plowing along. Immediately he called for an officer's meeting in the chart room, and showed them the discrepancy, of the weights and measures. The Captain asked for opinions.

"Well, what do you think of it, Mr. Heinz?" the captain asked.

"Sir, we'll have to put in at some cove, find slack water, and weigh the ballast."

"That's exactly right Heinz," replied the captain. "The trouble is, it will take two days, and sitting for two days in these pirate waters is suicide."

"We could remove ballast while we're underway sir. I know it's risky. We could easily wallow and broach." Heinz offered.

"Mr. Patron, what is your opinion?" asked the captain. Dr. Patron was an old Mexican who spoke perfect English and had been schooled in medicine in the Spanish Navy. He had been commissioned as the ship's doctor, having served in the Spanish Navy at an early age. He was captured in a naval battle, and now pressed into the Queens service.

"Well sir, why not make the best of our predicament," said the whiskered old man.

"Go on," said the captain.

"Why not trade the ballast for contraband. By fault of the company, they have put the entire ship at risk. I once made port in the Philippines at a place where we procured the finest abaca waxed ropes, and transported the cargo load to a Biliran shipbuilding yard. It was a long time ago, but the abaca was cheap and easy to be had. Waxed abaca rolled brings a large amount of money, and is scarce in the Sandwich Islands. The whalers would pay huge amounts for it."

"And what are you suggesting Mr. Patron?" looking at him.

"I can find this place on the chart. We put in at the harbor, weigh our ballast, and take on a load of waxed rope."

"You want me to run contraband on the Cowlitz?" angrily the captain bellowed.

"Sir, he is right. Think about it, we need to put in and weigh up. Why not use it to our advantage, and capitalize for our success?" said Mr. Heinz. "The rope is worth far more than the gunpowder. We'll trade ten kegs for three tons of rope--a huge profit," reasoned Heinz.

"Very well. Mr. Heinz, log this meeting, honestly. We're all present and will sign the affidavit, that in light of the circumstances, we will put in at Mr.

Patron's refuge, whereby a load of valuable cargo can be realized for the company. We've been lucky so far, we haven't had heavy seas since leaving Singapore. In our current situation, we could founder and sink. To hell with the affidavit, do I have your word gentleman to back and support me to proceed with this gamble?"

All heartily agreed.

"Show me this place on the charts, Mr. Patron," Weynton commanded.

For a long, five minutes, Dr. Patron studied the different rolls of the charts.

"It's here sir," pointing at the map. Weynton leaned over, putting his eye down close and reading, Malitbog Church.

"My God Patron! That's through the heart of the Moro Empire. Do you gentlemen realize the risk?" the captain looked around. "We have one signal cannon and ten old muskets! We're no match for them!"

"As long as we have full sail, we can hold off an attack sir," Mr. Heinz advised.

The Captain scratched his chin.

"Alright then, Mr. Heinz, at the point of Sabah, we'll change course, and head east into the Sulu Sea. God help us--to the island of Leyte."

The new orders were quickly relayed to the crew, as they were now fully aware of their situation, and anxious to learn what the solution might be. All that day, they carried a full, steady sail, and at sunset, spotted the Sabah point off the starboard bow.

"Come over 90° and hold your course, due east! Keep a sharp watch on the shoreline for trouble," the captain commanded.

The wind began building, and by dark, they were surrounded by a wall of waves and raging wind. Their worst fears were upon them now, as the Cowlitz was taking on water. Waves washed her bow, one taking the cabin boy and another deck hand over the rail, vanishing in the dark howling wind and spray. Below, four men took turns manning the bilge pump. It was too risky to dump ballast, as she needed the balance and stability, but was now taking on water for it.

Finally, it was the first light of the morning. The sea and wind had died down, and they were able to calm their senses from the ordeal, and the loss of two seamen. They continued to pump the water from the bilge. Biscuits and grog were passed around to all hands. On deck, they watched for trouble. Capt. Weynton took his sight on the sextant, and plotted their course on the chart. They were in the center of the Sulu Sea, making way for a channel, that emptied into the Bohol Sea.

Fair wind was with them now, and after two days of heading east, with no sign of trouble, they entered the Bohol Sea, recognized as Spanish territory.

The islands were all around them now, and as they plied onward, several fishing banca finally intercepted them. The old Dr. Patron engaged a lively, friendly conversation, as they came alongside, and conversed under sail. The immediate question was, "Are there pirates in this area?" and Dr. Patron was given the answer, "No, but pirates had been seen going north a month ago. There was no threat right now in this area," came the answer.

After another day of steady wind, they now approached the southern point of Leyte, rounded it, and came to a large open bay. In the distance, smoke was seen rising from the shore. And as they approached, they could make out the old stone church in the trees, and a bamboo catwalk out to a dilapidated galleon, a Spanish pendant flying from her mast.

"It's still here! This is it!" Dr. Patron gleamed, as he lit his pipe.

"By the salvation of our Lord, we have survived, Mr. Patron," said Weynton as he was checking the horizon. His men began sounding the bottom, and he ordered the anchor dropped. "We'll go ashore unarmed, you and I, Dr. Patron. We'll parlay and explain our predicament, test the water for danger," he said.

Already the Cowlitz was surrounded with bancas, offering up fruits, fish, seashells and sex. A couple of brave ones began to scale the side of the ship, and seeing this, Weynton fired a pistol into the air and ordered them off. Now a skiff of four men could be seen leaving the galleon, rowing their way, to instill their authority.

Upon reaching the Cowlitz, their leader stood up, and questioned her purpose. Dr. Patron begin to answer, but Weynton stopped him. The Captain knew perfect Spanish, growing up in Jamaica, and he answered the fat, old rascal.

"Good day sir, we've experienced a shift in cargo due to foul seas. Would you afford us the courtesy of correcting our situation?"

"But of course sir, I am El Capitan Diego Rovales Garcia. Let me be of service to you. And your name, Captain?"

"Alexander Weynton, sir."

"Excellent, excellent, come ashore at your leisure sir, you are welcome here," and with that commanded his oarsmen to return to his sunken bastion.

"We'll put ashore and check the situation out," said Weynton. "I want a four man armed watch, we don't want to let our guard down."

"Aye Captain," came a chorus from the crew.

Rolling out her davits, they lowered the long boat, and soon were rowing toward the galleon. A climbing net was hanging from her side. They tied up alongside, and climbed up to the deck. The galleon was old, maybe one hundred years, full of ship worms. Her sails had long ago rotted, and had been stripped away. She was in disrepair and neglect in every way.

"Welcome aboard Capt. Weynton. Here, come to my cabin for wine," the Capt. Garcia beckoned.

His ragged group of a crew looked remorseful and poorly, and not seem to be any kind of a threat. They entered the grand old salon on the stern, her windows open to the sea. "Sit down gentleman, a cigar and a glass of sherry?" he inquired.

"Of course, thank you captain."

"And how is it that a British merchantman can fail to stow her cargo properly, sir?" Garcia inquired.

"That was a ruse sir. I had to bluff until I felt we were in no danger," Weynton replied. "It's simple," he said, "as a Captain, you will understand. We are grossly overweight with ballast and need to correct the problem."

"There is a scale on my deck for weighing cargo," answered Garcia. "For a small fee, you may pull alongside and weigh out your ballast. I can even assist in labor."

"And what is your fee, sir?" asked Weynton.

"Twenty silver pesos would be the price, sir."

"Captain Garcia, we are merchant men. We carry no silver. We only have cargo." *(Which wasn't the truth.)*

"Ah, you want to trade? What is it you carry?" Capt. Garcia inquired.

"Bolts of cloth and gunpowder," Weynton replied.

Garcia now looked intrigued. "I have no use for cloth, but powder, who does not need powder? Your powder is in kegs, I'm guessing, how many do you carry?"

Not wanting to tip his hand, Weynton replied, "We have only five kegs, the standard issue for ships armament."

"Well then, Captain Weynton, four kegs is the fee, leaving you with enough to get you on your way."

"Too much, Garcia--two kegs to come alongside and correct our misfortune."

"You are a shrewd one Weynton. All right, two kegs. You have two days to complete your weighing."

"Alright your Excellency--agreed, but I wish to commence immediately, as time is of the essence."

"A salute and a toast!" They clinked glasses, with Weynton gulping it down and departing for the Cowlitz.

Back aboard, he parlayed a meeting with the entire crew.

"Lads, we've got two days to come alongside and weigh the ballast. We'll do the job ourselves. I want an armed guard, twenty-four hours a day, on the watch, let's get this done and get out of here."

"Sir, will we be taking on a cargo of rope?" inquired Mr. Heinz.

"There's been no discussion on that. Let's focus on our problem, and if we can shed the weight and take on cargo, we'll negotiate then."

"Aye Captain."

"Alright, heave away and tow us in Mr. Heinz," came the command.

Within an hour the Cowlitz was tied up to the galleon, the old ship being half the size of the huge barque. A large cross arm of weights and measures was set up on the deck. The crew began the laborious task of hauling out the large stones, and weighing them, recording, and then piling them on the galleon's deck. All day and into the next, they worked and finally 9,000 pounds of stones lay on the deck. The Cowlitz was now floating at the correct water line mark, on her hull.

The men began to shoulder the stones and carry them down the bamboo catwalk to the stone quay on shore, tossing them in on the rip-rap. Pleased with their labor, Weynton now approached Garcia and thanked him. Two of his men shouldered the kegs of powder, and set them at Captain Garcia's feet. Weynton proclaimed, "Here is your payment sir, my gratitude is boundless."

"You're welcome, sir. Come, another cigar and cognac, I enjoy your conversation," answered Capt. Garcia. "And where are you bound, Capt. Weynton?" he asked.

"The Sandwich Islands, sir."

"Ah, the Sandwiches. We have sent many a cargo of abaca that way. The whalers seem to like our quality."

"I have heard that rumor sir, that rope can be acquired here. Is there any of this product available for sale?" He curiously asked.

"Of course, we loaded a vessel last month, for shipment to Manila. I could round up a quantity, but it would take four or five days. What are you trading, your last three kegs of powder?" He smiled.

"You read my mind, and how much rope would three kegs of Queen's powder get me?"

"I will give you 2,000 pounds of abaca rope, waxed, for the three kegs."

"But I must wait five days, I can't afford your dock fees. Will you accommodate us?" Weynton asked.

"Nothing is free my friend, you will give me a musket for my hospitality, no?" he bargained.

"All right, done," said Weynton. "We'll remove another 2,000 pounds of ballast and replace it with the rope, do we have a deal?"

"Deal sir." and they clinked glasses, and finished the bottle of cognac.

The next day the crew was informed of the venture, and continued weighing and removing the stone. Another 2,000 pounds of ballast stones were carried to the shore, and tossed in. The ship now had risen two inches above her engineered waterline, ready for the contraband cargo. Garcia now had his workers piling the coils of waxed manila rope up on the deck. The magistrate and crew watched and weighed each one and placed the mass in a separate pile. On the fourth day, 2,000 pounds of rope lay weighed out on the deck.

Bringing Captain Garcia three kegs of powder, and the oldest musket they had, the trade was made complete, and the men began to wrestle and lift the heavy coils, stowing them on the Cowlitz, deep in her hold. It was late afternoon when they finally completed loading their cargo, when a cry from the mast watch rang out.

"Sir! A schooner spotted, rounding the point to the south!" came the cry from the mast watch. Hearing the commotion, Capt. Garcia appeared and stared at the approaching vessel. He let out a loud laugh.

"No alarm gentleman, they're not pirates. It's Capt. James Brooke and the Royalist, and it looks like they've captured a pirate vessel."

"Give me the glass!" barked Weynton, and staring for a long minute, he revealed his observance, still looking. "She's Queen's Navy alright, looks like she's towing a vessel in distress. I think he's flying a pennant of Bath, by God!" cried Weynton. "She's a captured pirate ship, a floating Dragon in distress, burned and shot to pieces, and she's covered with bodies!"

Now seeing the Cowlitz through his glass, James Brooke ordered Mr. Irons to run the Jack up the mainstay.

"Signal we are friendly, Mr. Colin!" bellowed James Brooke.

And a crisp reply, "Sir?"

"Skip one ball starboard side," Brooke rattled off.

"Aye sir, skip one ball, starboard side." Quickly a window popped open with the report.

"Ready sir, one for the Queen's Navy, she's a Queen's merchantman!"

"Fire, Mr. Colin." And the fuse man and cannoneer torched a two pounder, skipping the ball across the ocean as a salute, 90° to the Cowlitz.

Now challenged by the outgoing tide, Brooke put his tow in shallow water, ordering the wreck to drop anchor… a huge, square stone in a rattan cage. Casting off her towline, the smoldering wreck now lay anchored, a hundred yards offshore. Brooke continued with caution, and now each ship hailed the other. Confirming who the Earl of Bath was for proof of identity, both crews let their guard down, and a rousing cheer went up. Suddenly, fiddle music could be heard, as the Royalist tied up to the side of the Cowlitz. Dancing with glee broke out on both decks. One sailor played an old Irish sea tune on a squeezebox.

It was remarkable that they had crossed paths. They all realized the miracle of it, so vast was this island archipelago. The quick formalities were exchanged to dignify the situation, introducing Captains, and then both crews enjoyed the chance to be and speak with their own culture, as Englishmen telling old stories of their homeland.

Western Pacific

Now the celebration was on. Out came the rum and tobacco, and the singing and dancing on deck was raucous. Having called several times at Malitbog in the past, Brooke's crew was very knowledgeable of the local female entertainment, and soon, a dozen were on deck, bare breasted and dancing to the drum and fife. Conversing with Weynton and Garcia on the deck of the Cowlitz and enjoying the celebration, Brooke noticed one of his men missing. "Mr. Colin--I don't see Mr. Johns?" Brooke inquired.

"Uh, yes sir, he's still standing watch on the Pirate boat. Those two slaves are still chained, sir."

"I see. Send Mick to relieve his watch, and take some food and water to those poor wretches chained up. Tell them I'll have them unchained in the morning. The blacksmith is far too drunk now to attempt the task," said Brooke.

"Aye aye Captain," and at once Colin jumped and searched out Mick, finding him rolling with a native girl in a forward deck locker. "Mick, Captain's Order, you need to relieve John's on the wreck's watch. That's an order Mick. Pull yourself out of her!" yelled Colin.

"All right, right away sir," pulling up his breeches and buckle.

Telling his dusky pleasure to stay and wait, he climbed down to the shore skiff. Colin caught him before he pushed off, tossing him a biscuit cake and a canteen of water saying, "And Captain says give them food and water. That's an order Mick. Don't you eat and drink it."

"Aye, aye Mr. Colin," and pulling on the oars, he headed towards the anchored hulk. Coming alongside of the outrigger, he tied up, and stepping his way over the corpses that were still harnessed to their stations, he called out "Johns! God damnit! Johns! Hurry up! Where are you, John's!?" Mick called. Making his way to the bow, he found John's sitting, manning his sentry post over the two chained beings.

"Did you bring me dinner, Mick?" asked Johns.

"No, this is for your heathens. Come along now. I have orders to bring you back--a celebration and feast, you're missing it." Looking down, he saw the body of the Moro pirate, and seeing his ears cut off, shook his head and said nothing else.

"I got his sword, and she is a beauty. Look," holding up the kris for Mick to see.

"That is a fine sword, but you'll have to give it to Captain Brooke. The booty is his. Alright, let's go. Here, give this food and water to them. Tell them Captain will free them in the morning."

"I can't speak their dialect, Mick!" Johns cried.

"Let's go, we're missing the party," said Mick, and quickly they both rowed back to the ships, leaving Pinto and Juana with the meager biscuit and water.

Now, Garcia invited the captains to his quarters, enticing them with more cigars and rare cognac. Removed from the celebration on deck, they loosened up and began casual talk. Brooke began lamenting about his costs of fighting pirates with little return. At that point, he told them of the strange apparition of crows and the raven that spoke and danced on deck. He described in detail Duto's "Moro Oro" dance. He then discussed the headcount of the pirates chained to the Caracoa and made arrangements for payment. "And a head count in the morning," as Garcia offered a toast.

Weynton began to grieve the loss of his cabin boy and deck hand, and being short handed for the steerage to cross the Pacific. Hearing this, Brooke volunteered a solution. "Captain Weynton. I have two poor seaworthy souls that came into my possession today. I'd make a trade for a month's ration of grog. We're down to the last keg on the Royalist, having run almost out. I can't risk mutiny," said Brooke.

"That's a fair offer Mr. Brooke, but I would need to inspect their health before agreeing."

"Fair enough," Brooke responded. "They're on the pirate boat. You can have them in the morning. They're chained at the moment. My blacksmith will free them tomorrow." Then came a knocking at the cabin door. "Come in! Enter!"

It was Colin, and excusing himself, presented the kris sword to Brooke. "Sir, this fine kris was found on the dragon boat. The crew would like to present it to you as your reward."

"Very nice, thank you Mr. Colin. Tell the crew it pleases me," and Mr. Colin spun around and departed.

Pulling the prize from its scabbard, Brooke held it up and examined its crooked blade. "Got a nice balance and pommel," he admired.

"Let me see it, if I may," asked Garcia. Handing it over, Garcia examined it closely. "Mr. Brooke, I've come into possession of some fine British gunpowder. I would trade a keg of powder for this fine weapon sir," Garcia offered.

Instantly, Weynton kicked Brooke in the calf under the table, and looking his way, saw Weynton holding up two fingers on the side of his head. Catching on, Brooke fell right in, not missing the moment, and replied, "Captain Garcia-- this fine sword is worth far more! I should think its value at three kegs of powder." Brooke offered.

45

"All right, two kegs, but no more, is it a deal?"

"Done" said Brooke, handing Garcia the scabbard.

"A fine evening gentlemen" Brooke stood up. "I've got powder and grog, Garcia has his souvenir, and Weynton has solved his manpower dilemma. Gentlemen, I'll take tea with you in the morning. Good evening," he bowed.

And now Weynton arose, toasting his glass to the queen, and swallowed the dram of cognac. "And for me also," bowing to Brooke and then Garcia.

"Salute," Garcia raised his goblet, drained it, and passed out, face down on the salon table.

"He's a harmless old rat. Just don't believe everything he says," Brooke scoffed. He then picked up his traded sword and scabbard. "We'll see if he remembers his trade in the morning."

Walking out now, Weynton asked Brooke how this Captain Garcia had acquired his position, on a stranded galleon.

"The Dona Marta was beached over ten years ago, and since then its quarters have become a brothel and saloon and tax collector. Realizing a surplus of local women, Garcia opened his brothel and saloon, becoming the most important person in town. He had put the Dona Marta on a coral head not far from here at Padre Burgos. Knowing she was drawing water and split open, he sailed her another fifteen miles and was able to dock her here, whereupon she sank, becoming a wharf, dock, and a means for the locals to tax and load abaca. He has become a fixture to the trade, as it was all part of doing business for the Church and the Crown of Spain--on the backs and labors of the native people. It's just how they do business in this culture, Mr. Weynton. You have to accept their method of commerce. Mr. Weynton, I'm going to break up the party. My men need clear heads for tomorrow," Brooke explained.

The orgy of laughter, flesh, and rum and smoke was going to be tough to break up.

"Mr. Colin," hollered Brooke.

"Yes sir, Captain Brooke," Colin saluted.

"All hands on deck. Roll call! And start the watch," Brooke ordered. The Royalist ship's bell was now signaling deck call for all hands, and reluctantly, her crew stopped the festivity, abandoning the Dona Marta, and crossing the Cowlitz to get to the Royalist. Captain Weynton, impressed with the demonstration of Brooke's authority over his men, and not to be outdone, gave the same command, but with not the same punctual effect. The pleasures of the native women were too powerful to just instantly release. By midnight, the scene was quiet. Both ships posted their regular watch. A sleeping, drunk guard was hunched over on the galleon, and dogs barked in the distance on the quay.

It was now first light, the morning after. Down the catwalk from the town's old Spanish barracks, the Constable came with the Magistrate and his record book, asking permission to come aboard. Brooke was shaving in his salon, when notified of the Magistrate calling. The Magistrate would verify and document the pirate headcount, paying the government bounty. Brooke had his crew up and moving, and pushed away from the Cowlitz. The Royalist hoisted a small storm jib, and with perfect trim, sailed the short distance, and brought her alongside the pirate ship. The smell had become putrid. The ripped, exposed human flesh in the tropical sun, chained to their coffin, was a disturbing sight. The flies were beginning to swarm. Brooke wanted the two Chinese cannons and anything that could be stripped and salvaged. The few barrels of corn and dried fish were valuable commodities as well. Soon, they had a yardarm swung over, and the old Chinese cannons were hoisted away.

"Mr. Shepard! Below and forward in the bow are two native slaves, chained to the beam. Please remove their chains and bring them to me," commanded Brooke. "Mr. Colin, show him the way sir." Taking his tool bag, Colin and the ship's blacksmith disappeared below deck.

A pile of eight bodies were laid out on deck, all with tattoos and markings as Iranun pirates. The magistrate made notes in his journal, and pulling out a hidden pouch, dropped forty pesos into Brooke's hand, paying the Spanish bounty. The other twenty corpses were worthless, casualties of war, locals who were in the wrong place at the wrong time--chained and whipped, no choice in the battle, victims of the Royalist's supreme fire power. Up in the forward bow compartment, the dead pigs were beginning to smell horribly. Juana felt nauseated. She and Pinto had a restless, sleepless night, not understanding their situation. Fear and prayer had exhausted her, and now, not knowing the Anglo's language, she was convinced that they would be executed that morning.

As first light shone through the hole blown in the side of the bow compartment, a flapping of wings came and "*Caw! Caw! Caw!*" She cried tears of joy, seeing the crow and pleading, "Help us, Duto!"

Standing in the blown hole in the bow with the sun at his back, he blurted out, "Show treasure! Show treasure!" With a large smile on her face, she pulled the three thongs out from her smock, revealing the medallion in the sun and the two pouches. "Dirty bastards," he cried and flew away.

She called out to him, "Duto! Duto, come back!" and then she heard the voices and clamoring on deck. Fearing their doom, she was weak, and trembled violently.

"Stop shaking, Juana," whispered Pinto. "Don't let them know you're afraid. I'm afraid, too. Try and be brave," he tried to assure her.

"Up here, Mr. Shepard, in that forward cabin! Damn... here's another one! I'll drag him up top for bounty. In there--the slaves are chained in there," pointed Colin.

"Sir, the stench is awful, I can't."

"Shut up Shepard. Do your job. Captain Brooke wants them on deck," barked Colin.

Shepard took a deep breath, and pulling a long file from his bag, he began laboriously to file the pin down on Pinto's wrist shackle, and soon had him free. Now, through gesture and hand sign, he had Pinto assist him to remove Juana's wrist pin. All three came tumbling out of the stifling compartment, gasping for air. Colin now had his pistol out, and waving it at them, commanded Shepard to lead the way, pushing the two behind him at gunpoint. Emerging on the deck and seeing Brooke giving instructions for the salvage, Colin marched the two up behind Brooke.

"Sir, here are your prisoners," called Mr. Colin.

Brooke turned, and seeing Colin with the drawn side arm, cursed him, "God damn it Colin! Put that away! They're not prisoners. They think we're going to shoot them. Put that away!" Brooke ordered.

Now Brooke brought up a translator and began to calmly talk to them in their broken dialect, and soon Pinto and Juana were smiling, given food and water, and taken aboard the Royalist. Brooke commanded to pull up the Caracoa's anchor, and set sail on the Royalist, towing the wreck out to deep water in the bay. He then had it put to the torch and released it. The tide began to pull the flaming hulk to the south.

The Royalist then sailed back to Malitbog, and tied back up to the Cowlitz. By now, it was afternoon, and the Cowlitz crew were preparing to disembark the following day. Her crew were busy on deck as the Royalist came alongside. "Permission to come aboard, Captain Weynton," Brooke hailed the other a short distance away.

"Of course, by all means" came Weynton's reply. Pinto and Juana were assured not to be afraid, as the massive barque was the greatest wonder they had ever beheld. Climbing up onto the deck and following Brooke, he turned and presented the two.

"*Caw! Caw! Caw!*" Came a call from a distant coconut tree.

"I believe we made a bargain last night--a cabin boy and deck hand for a crews' month's ration of grog. Do you recall that conversation, Mr. Weynton?"

"My heavens, you weren't joking! Wretched looking lads. They could use a good scrubbing," exclaimed Captain Weynton.

48

"Mr. Patron, examine these creatures. Are they fit to bring aboard?" ordered Captain Weynton.

"Right away, Captain Weynton." The Doctor nodded.

"Bring them this way to the ship's dispensary." Doctor Patron now ushered the two across the deck to a side door, and into the main salon.

"Sir, Captain Garcia wants permission to come aboard!" came the watch call to Weynton.

"All right, please assist," ordered Weynton. Soon the old Spaniard was waving his arms and pleading a case in front of the two captains, complaining of damages the night before to his establishment and unpaid gratuities that were to be paid to his soiled doves.

"And how much would the damages be?" asked Brooke.

Captain Garcia counted on his fingers and looked skyward. "Around one hundred and twenty pesos should cover it señor," he replied.

There was utter surprise when Brooke answered, "Alright, I'll give you one hundred twenty pesos, but on one condition--that you fulfill our bargain made last night of four kegs of powder for the sword and one barrel of corn and one of fish."

"Yes, I remember the sword. Where is it?" the bewildered Garcia looked.

"Colin, bring me the kris," ordered Brooke. Moments later, he was handing it to the Spaniard, who then looked at Brooke.

"Uh--the corn, fish, and four kegs of powder--for the kris--our gentlemen's agreement last night. That is what we agreed on señor?" Captain Garcia could not remember.

Brooke replied, "Yes, I trust you are a gentleman and will honor our agreement."

"Very well, Brooke. Bring the captain the four kegs of powder," Garcia ordered his men. "I trust you have one hundred and twenty pesos, Captain Brooke?" came the question from Garcia. Brooke pulled a pouch from under his tunic, laughed, and counted out the coins, handing them to Garcia. Four kegs of powder and a barrel of corn and fish. *I'm back in business*, thought Brooke.

Dr. Patron now appeared to Captain Weynton and Brooke, and gave his report. "Sir, the two native fishermen are of good health. Some rest, soap and water, and a couple of meals, and they'll be fit for the task." Looking back and forth at Brooke and Weynton, he further replied, "And sir, at your leisure, may I see you privately in your cabin?"

"Of course, Dr. Patron. Thank you for your examination. I'll be with you shortly. Brooke and I have some business to discuss," said Weynton.

"Very well sir. I'll have the cook feed them, sir," nodding and leaving.

"Well, Captain Brooke, I'm not a man that condones slavery. We're both in a situation, here-- you running low on grog, me shorthanded for the ocean crossing. I can justify the trade on behalf of the company to insure the delivery of our cargo. My men will bring the keg of grog aboard, for the trade, but, for the record, as you are my witness, again, I do not condone slavery, and so next year on my return to these waters, I shall make the effort to deposit them at their fishing village."

"Very well, the best of luck on your crossing. I'll look for your return, and a pleasure doing business with you." They both shook hands and saluted each other.

"Mr. Colin, swing the yardarm and hoist the keg of grog. Be quick! Get ready to make way lads!" Within the hour, the Royalist cast off from the Cowlitz and was heading south, passing a smoldering plume that could be seen in the distance--the pirate wreck.

"What is it, Dr. Patron?" asked Captain Weynton, entering the doctor's dispensary. Laying on a bunk were Juana and Pinto, passed out, sleeping hard.

"I gave them both laudanum in their tea. They'll sleep for several hours."

"Sir, sit down," said Dr. Patron.

"Sir, on examining the two, I was shocked to discover the one with the cotton smock on is a girl!"

"What! You're sure?" Weynton looked stunned.

"Take a look for yourself, Captain," was the answer.

"My God, man, I'm a Captain--not a physician. What should we do, Doctor?"

"Well, sir, a young damsel on a sailing vessel at sea among a bunch of bilge rats can present a problem," said Patron.

"Indeed, Doctor. I can't have this crew distracted from the task at hand."

"Well, sir, no one knows this but you and I. Perhaps in the interest of the ship's welfare, we won't disclose our secret."

"Very well. We'll keep this under wraps. I'll be in the chart room. It's a full moon tonight. We'll set sail after dinner. Keep your eye on them. They may try to jump overboard if they awake."

No one had noticed the black crow alighting in the stern mizzen mast nest, making no sound. He discreetly landed in the stern mast cross arms of the Cowlitz, where he perched, obscuring himself from being seen from the deck below.

The crew was given a quick meal of gruel and hardtack, and finally, the Cowlitz cast off of the old galleon dock. The long skiff boat pulled her into the bay, and soon, they were running with the wind. They were following the same course Brooke had taken, heading south, but upon clearing the bay, they headed for the channel between East Limasawa and the open Pacific Ocean.

"Mr. Heinz, the island off the port bow is Limasawa, the very first place the cross of our Lord was planted in Asia they say. Pray to the cross for a safe voyage!"

Continuing with the landmark in sight, Weynton further commanded, "Alright, bring her over. Set a heading of due east."

"Very well, sir," replied Heinz, barking commands to trim the sail and rudder to the easterly course.

"There she is lads, the mighty Pacific. Maintain this bearing. We'll put in at Agana in the Marianas for food and water." Leaving the protected seas of the Philippines, the barque lumbered along in large, rolling swells in the open ocean.

Juana found her head bobbing back and forth with the movement of the ship, bumping her head on the wall of her bunk, until it woke her up. "Pinto! Wake up!" she said, shaking him. Groggily, Pinto awoke, not knowing his whereabouts.

"Where are we, Juana?" He looked around. The cabin walls were covered with cabinets with glass fronts, behind which were medicines, bandages, and tools of the doctor's trade. A large table sat in the middle of the cabin with two empty chairs. A cabin window was open, letting in fresh air.

"Go look out the window, Pinto," Juana whispered. Peering out the portal, Pinto could only see a deck and the ships sail, with the sea appearing and disappearing with each swell.

"I don't know. We're under sail, though, going somewhere. Hopefully they are taking us back to Matalom." Pinto then whispered, "Someone's coming. Pretend we're asleep!"

Dr. Patron entered his cabin. Checking on his patients and satisfied with their condition, he sat down and lit a cigar after pouring a drink. Draining his glass, he approached Juana and Pinto again, this time pinching Pinto very hard on the ear, forcing him to cry out.

"Alright, wake up you two," the doctor spoke loudly in Spanish, now pinching Juana's toe.

Juana opened her eyes, and understanding him replied, "We are fishermen from Matalom. Don't harm us. We have nothing!" said Juana, also in Spanish.

"Relax. No one will harm you here. You are safe, but tell me the truth, señorita. Why were you on the pirate vessel?" asked Dr. Patron.

"You know that I am a girl, sir?" she asked, giving away her gender.

"Yes, yes. My name is Dr. Patron, the ship's medical officer, and after examining you, I'm honoring your dignity as a woman. Now I see you speak Spanish. Tell me who you are and how you ended up in my care."

Pinto, not understanding, as he only spoke his dialect, asked Juana what was being said.

In their dialect, she explained that he was a doctor, and conferring with each other, Pinto warned her to pretend she was a boy. She now explained to him the ruse was discovered. Feeling a sense of trust, she divulged to the doctor the happenings of the previous hours, the capture, the battle, and the night of misery chained to the floating raft of corpses. "Please, Mr. Patron, are you taking us back home?" asked Juana.

"Let me explain something to you, Juana. Yes, we are taking you home, after you've paid your servitude to the crown. Captain Weynton is the law. He has impressed you and your brother into the Queen's service, yours being in gratitude for being saved from certain slavery or death at the hands of the pirates. We're sailing for the Sandwich Islands, and as luck would have it, you two are needed aboard, as two seamen were lost at sea ten days ago. We're in the ocean now, so don't be foolish and try and swim for it. Stay here. I'll fetch the captain." Soon, he returned with Weynton. Having informed him of his interrogation and conversation, they both sat down at the table, and poured another shot of rum.

Captain Weynton, born and raised in Jamaica, now asked Juana in Spanish, "Señorita, how old are you?"

"I'm twelve years old, sir," she replied meekly.

"The doctor tells me, after questioning you, that you do not have your monthly bleeds--you are still too young--is that correct?" asked Weynton.

Blushing, she meekly replied, "*Si.*"

"Well, Juana, I can't have a young girl in a cotton nightshirt running around on the ship. It won't work. Mr. Patron will supply you with dungarees and a button-down shirt. You will be addressed from this point on as 'Juanito,' and will take charge as my cabin boy. Mr. Heinz will school you in your duties."

"You, Mr. Pinto, for the time being, will help the cook--and refer to your sister as your brother."

"Translate that to him," he directed Juana.

"...do you both understand?" asked Weynton.

They both nodded yes.

"Because of the situation, you'll be employed by the company now, as payment for our services of saving your lives. On our return voyage next year, you'll be returned to your homeland," he advised Juana in spanish. "Dr. Patron, fetch these boys some decent clothing, and see to it they get a good scrubbing!"

"Captain, do you want them bathing on deck? I don't see how..." Mr. Patron stopped Weynton.

"Get Pinto to fetch a bucket of freshwater. Better yet, I'll take him with me. We'll be right back." Pointing at the door, he told "Juanito" to translate to Pinto to follow him for a bucket of water.

Weynton signaled for Pinto to follow him. Once on deck, a chorus of chatter came from the crew, and Weynton boomed out a command. "That will be enough! This man's name is Pinto. He'll be assisting the cook for the time being. His brother, Juanito, will be my cabin boy. I expect fair treatment and behaviour on the crew's part, realizing we are short of manpower."

As Weynton was giving his oratory to his crew, Pinto looked up and momentarily saw a pair of wings open and close upon the yardarm. For a brief moment he saw Duto, his beady eye staring back silently.

A large group of barrels were lashed to the cabin deck, and Weynton picked up a bucket, handing it to Pinto, and pointed at the one to open. Filling the bucket, Pinto looked at the captain for direction, and Weynton signaled for him to follow. He opened the dispensary door, holding it open for Pinto and the bucket of water. "Alright, Doctor. Clean them up, and I'll put them to work. I'll be back in a couple hours to check on you. Till then, don't leave this cabin."

"Yes, sir. No problem, sir. I'll take care of it." And out the door went Weynton.

"Take those necklaces and charms off," the doctor ordered Juana. "Alright, here's a bar of soap. Stand in the bucket--you first, 'Juanito.' I'll just sit over here and read my journal."

The fresh water and soap invigorated Juana. She sighed with relief, as the clean water and soap made her skin glisten.

"On the table, over there, some dungarees and a shirt," Dr. Patron pointed, commanding in spanish.

She stepped into the trousers, a first time, not sure how to pull them on. Sitting down and pulling them on, she stood up and buttoned them. A good fit, being the previous cabin boy's wardrobe. She buttoned the shirt up the front, and stared at herself in the mirror. She didn't recognize herself, the person looking back at her.

Pinto took his bath in the same bucket, anxious to try his new clothes on, having never owned such luxuries.

"Juana--uh, I mean Juanito--I saw Duto up in the mast rigging." Pointing up and looking big-eyed, Pinto whispered excitedly, "He's still with us. I saw him."

Dr. Patron sat them both down at the table now, schooling them in spanish about what and what not to do on board, with Juana always translating to Pinto. They talked for a good hour this way, asking questions, translating, getting clarification on duties, and preparing them for the voyage. Agana was two weeks away. They would not see land until then, and were instructed to say very little. She now remembered her necklaces hanging on a hook, retrieved them, and was putting them on when Weynton knocked.

"Captain Weynton here."

"Come in, Captain," Dr. Patron replied.

"Well, good. I see they look a sight better cleaned up. Good job, Dr. Patron.

"What's that around your neck there, Juanito?" the captain asked.

"This one is an award for dancing," she said, holding up the medallion. "And these other two are medicine for my pet raven."

"What? Bird medicine? What kind of voodoo is that?" asked Weynton.

"Well, sir, he's my pet raven, and follows me everywhere. He's on board now, sir. He's..."

"What! Who's on board? A black raven? We're two hundred miles out on the Pacific. That's nonsense! Talk some sense, Juanito."

"Sir, if I may go on deck--Pinto has seen him--he's... "

"By thunder, this is a knee slapper. Very well, show me where your raven is!" shouted Weynton. The captain led the way, and out the door the four went on to the deck.

Standing on the deck, Pinto pointed up at the aft castle on the stern mast. "Up there," he said to Juana.

"I don't see him. Where?" said Juana.

Still pointing, he was interrupted by Weynton's protest. "Enough of this nonsense!"

Juana stared up at the rigging, searching for him. "Wait!" Pulling out her medallion, it caught the sun, and she shone it up at the mast, whereupon a loud "Caw! Caw! Caw!" was heard, and Duto appeared from his hideout, flying down to the deck and strutting around in circles before Juana.

There was a brief moment of stunned, disbelieving silence as Weynton, the doctor, and the crew could only stare in wonder. "It's the magic crow! The one that landed on the Royalist!" someone called out.

"Yes, I heard that story, too!" came another report.

The magic crow! The story that Brooke had told! It now landed on the deck and was dancing and talking. Weynton thought it was a drunken sea yarn when told the story, but now, here was this raven, strutting on his deck, far out in the ocean.

"Son of bitch, I'm hungry!" said Duto in Visayan.

Juana and Pinto began laughing, hearing his cursing tirade.

"Son of bitch!" again Duto repeated.

"What's he saying?" asked Weynton to the girl.

"He's saying he's hungry, sir," Juana continued to laugh.

"I see. What does he eat?" asked Weynton, now smiling.

"Just about anything, sir. He likes fresh fish guts," said Juana.

"Heinz, fetch some fish guts from the cook. Don't just stand there, he's hungry!"

Heinz quickly returned with the kitchen garbage bucket, setting it down in front of Duto. Not hesitating, he jumped up on the lip of the bucket, and pulled an entrail out, gulping it down. And just like that, the crew, captain and doctor took a keen interest in the bird. In the days ahead, they would treat him like a mascot. Each would come up and touch him kindly, talking nonsense. They admired his plumage, and placed rags in the aft castle for a nest. This first encounter with the captain and crew had gone well, with Duto realizing he was not in danger. Thereafter, he would hop around on the deck and then flutter up onto Juana's shoulder. Cocking his head, he could just see his treasure hanging on her chest.

The novelty of the ship's new pet had now worn off, and it was business as usual. "Trim that Mainsail!" bellowed Weynton. "Mr. Heinz, take Pinto below. He's needed in the galley. Juanito, you and your bird come with me," Weynton ordered.

Following the captain with the bird on her shoulder, they entered his cabin, and closed the door. "So this bird talks to you?" asked Weynton in spanish.

"Yes, sometimes, when he wants to," replied Juana.

"And what do you discuss?" asked Weynton.

"We usually don't discuss anything. He just curses a lot and is always angry about something."

"I see. Well, you see them yonder hooks on the rib timber? Thar's a hammock in that locker and a blanket. You'll have to clean up after your bird. There's a basket of socks. They need to be washed. Take it with your bird. I need to shoot my sextant and take bearings. Run along," he said, laughing at the sight.

Days passed with a good, steady, favoring wind. The monotony and boring hours that can pass at sea, day after day, year after year, are common to the sailor. The curiosity of the cabin boy's talking bird had become a huge entertainment for the sailors. The well-being of the bird became everyone's game, having heard the story of the dance of Moro Oro. He was now a celebrity, each man offering Duto a tidbit daily, and providing him a small pan of fresh water to drink.

"Juanito" had learned her daily tasks and remained undiscovered by the crew as being a girl. Relieving herself in the captain's chamber pot, and being the one to empty it daily over the rail, no one had seemed to notice that she never stood on the fantail to urinate. Pinto was doing well in the galley. His experience of cleaning and filleting fish, and his luck at catching them, had provided the crew with daily fish steaks. He quickly was appreciated and accepted into their world.

On the fourteenth day after leaving Leyte, at morning muster bell, land was sighted. "On the lee--land ho!" came the call. Everyone started to jump for the lee rail to look, but Captain Weynton bellowed.

"Steady! Back in line! Resume roll call, Mr. Heinz."

"All present, sir," reported Heinz.

"Dismissed, sir," Weynton said. "Good morning…. 'Land ho' is it? My glass Juanito, quickly!" he ordered.

Returning with the brass telescope, the captain took a long look at the island. He then checked his watch and compass bearings, recording the information in a little black book. Closing the book and stuffing it into his pocket, he smiled and announced, "That's Guam, lads. We'll pull in to Port Agana for water, chickens, and fruit. Mr. Heinz, bring her up fifteen degrees and mark on that bearing," commanded Weynton.

Shortly thereafter came the call from the yard arms, "Coral heads, one hundred feet ahead, sir!"

"Drop anchor, now!" ordered the captain. "Luft away!"

The crew scrambled, knowing the danger and urgency.

"Drop anchor, Mr. Heinz!" he bellowed again.

And none too soon, as the Cowlitz came to a jolting stop, ten feet from a coral head, which would have ripped her in two.

Calmly assessing the situation, he ordered her to come about and retrim, retrieving her anchor. Retracing her path to safer water, the anchor was dropped again. The captain now reassessed the situation. The coral heads were not on the British charts. A scouting boat, known as a skiff, would be sent to investigate the way through.

As the crew on the skiff were pulling away, a cry came from the mast watch. "Three proa boats are approaching from the island, sir."

Spotting them with his glass, Weynton commanded the search boat to intercept them and parlay. Meeting each other halfway between the Cowlitz and the island, Weynton observed in his glass a conversation between Heinz and a native, wearing a large straw hat. Soon, the skiff was back alongside the Cowlitz, being followed by the three proa, who smiled and waved, encouraging hospitality.

"Well, what's the situation Mr. Heinz?" Weynton leaned over the rail and called down.

"Sir, these are the Chimorro people. Their leader is a Spaniard--in the straw hat, sir. The entrance to the anchorage and dock are further east, a narrow channel through the coral heads. These natives will guide us through."

"Very well. Heave to lads." Quickly, the crew was pulling up anchor. The skiff now pulled the Cowlitz bow into the wind, and soon the massive barque was headed southeast, following the three proa, and towing her skiff. "Keep a sharp eye up there, Rogers," Weynton commanded to his mast watch.

"Aye Captain. I can see the breach in the coral heads, sir. Maintain your course, sir," came the reply.

Now, two dozen canoes were seen paddling furious for them, one hundred natives calling out with excitement. Coming alongside, several natives attempting to scale the side of the Cowlitz and board. Not knowing their intention, Weynton fired a pistol shot into the air, and the frenzied attempt to board was abandoned by the milling crowd of canoes. A call came in spanish from the proa to drop anchor. Seeing the stone quay of the village one hundred yards from shore, Weynton gave the order to drop anchor. Bare-breasted women in bancas surrounded the Cowlitz, trying to entice the crewmen, holding up fruits and drink.

A clamor of bells, whistles, and gongs were accompanying the spectacle, and soon the proa approached the Cowlitz. The one in the straw hat signaled he wanted to come aboard. The boarding ladder was dropped on either side, with a guard posted with a musket. The bronzed, straw-hatted man jumped onto the deck, saluted Captain Weynton, and announced his name in perfect spanish.

"Sir, I am El Capitan Señor Carlos Rodriguez at your service--the mayor of Agana. We welcome you to our island," and he gave a long bow.

Weynton returned the bow then stated, "A pleasure, Señor Rodriguez. We come in peace--a queen's ship of the Hudson Bay Company. We offer silver for water and food. Can you be of help to us?" asked Weynton.

"Yes, yes. But pleasure first. We'll talk business later. Come ashore and let us refresh you from your journey."

Weynton was suspicious now of the mayor, trying to entice his crew ashore, having heard tales of treachery, and being overwhelmed. He politely declined, stating that his crew would not be going ashore, and asked if the good mayor could deliver the water provision, live chickens, and any fruit or produce.

Señor Rodriguez looked disappointed, and continued to plead his case of hospitality. Finally realizing it wasn't going to happen, he began to wrangle about the shortage of chickens, and that the cost was going to be a rather inflated fee. Weynton had a bag of spanish silver pesos provided by the Company for just these kind of situations. He kept them in his cabin in a strong box. The captain then handed over a list of items he hoped to acquire from Sr. Rodriguez. The mayor began haggling the price. He settled on a figure for the items, but then tried to secure advanced payment. Again, Weynton detected deceit, and agreed to pay for the items as they were delivered alongside. Seeing that Weynton was much shrewder than he anticipated, Rodriguez bowed and stated the goods would be delivered tomorrow. Returning to his proa, the whole entourage made their way back to shore silently now, the excitement over with.

"*Caw! Caw! Caw!*" came the cry from his mast nest, and Duto was now flying to the shore, searching for a snack!

"Juanito, I see your friend Duto did not get my order of "No shore leave" said Weynton, smiling and making a joke.

"He'll be back, sir--probably looking for some fresh mangoes," Juanito replied.

"Good job, Mr. Heinz. Set up a double-armed watch. I'll be in my cabin," commanded Weynton. "Dr. Patron, may I see you in my cabin?"

Patron nodded yes.

"Juanito, bring the Dr. and I some lunch."

Now sitting at his table in his cabin, he offered a cigar to the doctor, and congratulated him and the crew's success of the passage so far.

"If I may, Captain, inquire as to the restriction of shore leave--the men would really like to kick up their heels ashore and celebrate," suggested Patron.

"Well, Doctor, I realize that they want shore leave, but let me remind you of our briefing in Singapore. There is the fever and the pox that is circulating the Pacific now, and the less contact we make, the safer we are," answered Weynton.

"Ah yes--perhaps a good decision. We all got caught up in the excitement and forgot the warning. But yes, we have another six weeks to reach the Sandwiches. An epidemic on board would be deadly--I commend your thinking of the consequences," replied the doctor.

"I've heard stories in old Jamaica of ships crews putting in at lone tropical islands, and a week later at sea, they're all dead, bringing some form of pestilence on board. Ghost ships, sir. By the way, have you quinine for fever? Have you any of the pox serum in your cabin, Doctor?" asked Weynton.

"Yes, I have a small vial, perhaps enough for five or six innoculations. Why? The crew was inoculated in England," answered the doctor.

"And the crew was all given a measure of quinine?" asked the captain.

"Yes, as prescribed by the London Board, sir," said the doctor.

"Pinto and Juanito--I've become attached to them, and as their Captain, their well being is my concern. They both have proven worthy, and I see it only fitting that you give them the protective medicine," replied Captain Weynton.

"I'll take care of it, Captain," replied Patron, just as Juanito entered the cabin with a platter of steaming fish steaks and rice.

Finishing their hearty meal, Dr. Patron suggested to the captain that he should advise "Juanito" of the procedure, and she could translate it to Pinto, assuring them both that it was safe, and not to fear. Captain Weynton agreed, and asked the doctor to summon Pinto to his quarters. The doctor excused himself, and shortly thereafter, a knock came at the door. Weynton answered, "Enter," whereupon Pinto and the doctor appeared. The captain motioned for them to sit down. Now, explaining to "Juanito" in spanish, he told her of the ravages of the pox disease. The captain could see fear in her eyes, and told her to translate to Pinto. Hearing the description of the devil disease, his eyes became large and worried. Then the captain went on to explain that a procedure would prevent them from catching it--a scratching of the skin with a sharp needle several times, and then applying the serum. He explained a large scab would appear, but after two weeks, it would fall off and be gone. They would then be protected from the "pox." Pinto and "Juanito" looked at each other, afraid of the unknown. They had come to trust the old captain, and now both accepted to be treated by Dr. Patron, with Weynton's assurances it was safe. Escorting the two to his cabin, the doctor had them both look away as he did his work. He scratched the skin bloody on the outer arm, smearing the cut with the serum, and then applied a cotton bandage.

Pinto now returned to his work in the galley, and Juanito knocked on the captain's door.

"Come in!" said Weynton. "Ah, I see you've taken the cure. You'll thank me someday. Come, sit down," the captain calmly persuaded her. "I have a wife and two daughters in London at home, who I miss dreadfully. You remind me of the oldest one. You and your bird have been good for the ship's morale, and I've observed you daily, noticing a quick ability to learn things. Growing up in Jamaica, I was schooled in English, but learned Spanish on the docks and warehouses. This is an English ship, and I have accommodated you and your spanish tongue, but you must learn English to survive in the Queen's realm. So, after dinner, from now on, I will school you in the English language. Do you agree to that?" asked Weynton.

"Yes sir. *Si...* I, I..."

"Can you read and write in spanish?" asked the captain. He placed a copy of the Spanish Bible on the table. "Read to me! Here," randomly pointing out a scripture.

Juanito began to articulate the words, and realizing her ability, he told her to stop. "Excellent, we'll begin after we leave this port. Now, hang your hammock and to bed with ye."

Swinging in her hammock, she rubbed her sore arm, scratching at the bandage. The sun was dipping into the ocean through the open window, as a flapping of wings and "*Caw! Caw! Caw!*" came from the window sill. Smiling, she waved her medallion at him, and he disappeared from the ledge.

The Chamoro had tried approaching the Cowlitz that night. Her whale oil lamps illuminated the bay too well, defeating any chance of sneaking on board to steal whatever. The attempt was dismissed when a warning shot was fired by the watch. Captain Weynton had anticipated this, staying up late studying charts, and upon hearing the musket shot, he was on deck instantly with his cutlass drawn. "What is it Rogers?" barked Weynton.

"Just a warning shot sir. A shot in the air..."

"By thunder, don't kill one of them. We'll never get out of here alive. Maintain your composure, mister."

"Over there sir--see them" he pointed.

"Yes, I see them. I think your shot had effect--looks like they're beaching. Good eye, Jeffries, stay alert!"

Of course the musket shot had awoken the whole crew, and now several were relieving themselves, and cursing the Chamoros at the same time. It was a long night, but uneventful, with no further drama.

Weynton and Heinz were on deck at first light, watching the shoreline for activity. Morning breakfast smoke could be seen filtering through the coconut trees, and finally, El Capitan Rodriguez's proa could be seen approaching the Cowlitz.

"Good morning, Señor Rodriguez" Weynton called down to the captain.

"I have the provisions you requested, Captain. My people will deliver at your request, sir. May I come aboard?" asked Rodriguez.

Pleased at the answer, Weynton quickly acknowledged, and gave the command to assist the spanish gentleman aboard. Now, standing on the deck and bowing, he asked to be excused for a moment, and pulled a polished mirror from his tunic, signaled a reflective sun shot at the beach. Out of the trees came a mass of Chamoro natives, carrying the cargo down to the beach to the quay, and began loading it onto their banca's.

"And what are you selling me today, Señor Rodriguez?" asked Weynton.

"We have fresh water in buckets from the village well, twenty-five live chickens in cages, and baskets of jackfruit and guava."

"Excellent, Señor Rodriguez. And my fee is...?" asked Weynton.

"A bargain at sixty-five pesos--normally would charge more, but you're Hudson Bay, and we want you to return," said Señor Rodriguez.

"Fair enough, sir. If you will, this way, please," leading him to his cabin.

"Sit down--a drink of rum?" asked Weynton.

"Very well. And where are you headed, Captain?" asked Rodriguez.

"The Sandwiches, sir, delivering a cargo to the company store--whaling provisions," answered Weynton. "Your people acted crazy and surprised to see our ship--is there a reason for that?" he asked.

"We get a spanish galleon once a month, but they are small compared to your fine vessel. The people are struck by the size of your ship. They all wanted to get close and see it."

"I see. Well, let me count out your payment," and opening the box so as not to show its contents, Weynton counted out the 65 pesos, stacking them on the table. "And of course, you'll be staying and oversee the loading, Señor Rodriguez?" the captain with raised eyebrow asked.

"But of course, Captain. In that case, could I beg a cigar and another drink?" he inquired, twisting his moustache.

Weynton poured them both another shot, and saluting, tipped the glasses back. Offering a cigar and light, the captain stood up and headed for the door. "Shall we?"

Back on deck, the banca's were getting close, and Weynton told Rodriguez to line them up under the boom that had been hoisted over the rail. The work took a couple of hours. The water buckets were heavy--hauled to the tank, dumped in, and returned. Having only six buckets, the process had to repeat itself back to the well and then hauled back to the quay. Between water trips, the chickens and baskets of fruit came aboard. By ten o'clock, the operation was completed. The captains exchanged pleasantries, saluted, and El

Capitan was assisted to his proa. No sooner had the proa pushed off of the Cowlitz, when Weynton bellowed, "Mr. Heinz, prepare to make way. Let's take advantage of this wind, sir. Rig her for slow passage, sir."

Just as the anchor cleared water, a familiar *Caw! Caw! Caw!* was heard, and sure enough, Duto was back from shore leave, landing on his roost in the masthead.

"Sharp eye, Rodgers. Be ready on that anchor drop," Weynton reminded the crew. "Bring her about, Mr. Heinz."

They picked their way through the coral channel, found open water, and the immense ocean. Soon the island was a flat spot on the horizon, as they headed due east to the Sandwiches.

The Pacific was living up to Magellan's name for this ocean, as fair weather and a steady, smooth wind stayed with the Cowlitz. Duto had become a great entertainment and pastime for the crew, with the bird enjoying his notoriety also. He would curse filthily in Visayan and do his gold dance, bringing great laughter to his audience. It wasn't long before the sailors had him cussing in English, "You son of a bitch," bringing a roar of laughter from those present.

Pinto always had a couple of baited lures trailing the ship, and upon hooking a fish, a gathering of support and advice was given, as Pinto got the fish over the rail.

By now, Captain Weynton had bonded with Juana, looking at her more as a daughter than his cabin servant, and he wanted to protect her from being discovered as a young girl. The crew was better off with not having that knowledge. The captain kept her busy in his cabin with daily chores, and in the evening began reciting nouns in English. He used a Western dictionary containing drawings and etchings, enabling her to reference and understand. He would pick five nouns each night, have her memorize them, and five more the next night, and so on. After two weeks of this, he taught her a few common verbs, and suddenly, she was talking to Weynton in basic English, picking up the sailors' conversations when on deck, and now understanding what they were referring to. Captain Weynton was proud of his success, but kept the lessons unknown to the crew. "Juanito" said very little on deck at all, only motioning in sign for basic needs to any other crewman.

Dr. Patron, of course, would take dinner with Weynton on a regular basis. The three conversed in spanish in order to include Juana in the conversation, and when it was revealed to the old doctor that she could now speak English, a large smile broke across his face. "So, you are a pupil of our distinguished Captain?" asked the doctor.

Not understanding "distinguished," she asked if it was a good or bad word to the doctor.

"Forgive me. You are Weynton's student! Very good!" The doctor now simplified his sentences.

"Yes. He good man!" replied Juana.

Now, the doctor took up the challenge of teaching her also at dinnertime, and the young girl was soon asking questions in English and answered in English. She looked forward to the daily dinner, the conversation fascinating her. Quite often, she would not understand, and either the captain or the doctor would draw a pencil diagram on the table, explaining the word and meaning.

Duto was always watching from above, landing on her shoulder and following her around on deck. He would circle the ship and *caw caw caw* a couple of times a day, flying around the mast and sail tops. He sometimes landed on the ledge of the captain's open window. Shrieking obscenities in Visayan, Juana would pull her medallion out, and satisfied of its safety, he would fly back to the deck, visiting different deck hands. The crew discovered his fondness for shiny trinkets of no value, and would tease him until he would curse violently. Upon giving him the shiny stone or shell, he would fly up to his hideout in the mizzen cross trees, stashing away his new treasure.

A month had passed since their layover in Agana. The chickens had been consumed, and a strong wind had been with them the last ten days. Their speed had made it too fast for Pinto's fishing lines. Weynton was pleased. They had made up for lost time at the emergency stop in Malitbog. His cargo was timed for delivery in the Sandwiches, just as whalers were arriving, following the annual migration of the creatures in the North Pacific. The HBC had a warehouse and dock in the village called Honolulu. The salt, powder, cloth, and hemp rope would be deposited in the company store. He would recommend a bonus for the crew in securing a profitable cargo, while correcting the ballast problem, as it had been a company mistake in Singapore. The crew was very much aware of this. They were anxious to make payroll, and go ashore, as they well deserved. Clerks would weigh and record the cargo, according to the ship's manifest. The company bought large amounts of fresh fish from the local natives, and after salting these stocks for preservation, they were traded as food provision to the whalers. The whalers also traded their barrels of whale oil for rope, rum, powder, and trade goods. The whale oil would be transported to the Oregon territory and sold to the increasing population at a 100% profit. The product could be sold for twice what they had invested.

63

The climate was pleasant and balmy. The afternoons were enjoyable, spent playing dice, carving, playing the flute, and teasing Duto, who always was cursing his tormentors. He'd play their game until he got his treasure rewards.

Pinto was pulling in a luckless line, checking the bait, when he looked down and saw two coconuts floating past--a sure sign that land was not far. He called for "Juanito" in Visayan, and pointed them out to her, floating in the water. Reporting the sighting to Captain Weynton in his chart room, she explained in English, "Pinto see coconut."

"Ah, yes. Good observation. Let me plot the sighting."

Using his chart compass, he walked it twice across the chart. Scratching his whiskered chin, he looked at her and said, "Tomorrow, Juana! We should make Honolulu tomorrow! The company has quarters for us while we layover for two weeks. I've read books about it and heard stories--a nice place--a paradise, they say. Juana, when we make port, the company will resupply the crew with manpower and provisions. You and your brother can stay and go to school. I'll pick you up on my return and take you back to your island. It's the only gentlemanly thing to do. I'll assure you that you'll be looked after till I return."

"Home? You'll take me home?" She hugged him and wept.

"Yes. We've kept your secret undiscovered. I almost feel like a father to you now, and your safety is important to me. Perhaps your learning ability, and your crazy bird has made my affection grow for you. Whatever it is, we've had good luck and smooth sailing, and I'm grateful for you and your brother's help. Hang your hammock and rest. The day will be long tomorrow."

The next morning, a sun beam shone into the captain's cabin, through the open window. "*Caw! Caw! Caw!*" woke up Juana in her hammock. Knowing the routine, she waved the medallion and pouches at him, to make him stop his cawing. But not this morning. "*Caw! Caw! Caw! ...Caw! Caw! Caw!*" Strutting back and forth on the ledge, he began to recite over and over, "Son of a Bitch today! Son of a Bitch today! *Caw! Caw! Caw!*" but this time, it was in English. Juana swung her legs out of the hammock. The captain was absent from the quarters, and the bird flew off from the open stern window. Washing her face and relieving herself, she carried the thunder pot out to the deck to dump overboard. Walking to the stern, she emptied its contents into the sea, tying its handle to a rope, washing it out, and now pulling it back aboard.

A cry came from the forward yardarm. "Land ho! Land ho! On the leeward!" A loud cheer went up, with everyone shading their eyes in the morning sun, and spotting the mist over a distant mountain. The island began to grow out of the sea, and by noon, sea birds were following the Cowlitz. They were within five miles of Honolulu. Weynton and Patron stood in the forecastle, handing the

64

brass telescope back and forth. They talked about their observations, then traded the looking glass, asking the other about what they were seeing.

"What do you make of that Doctor?" Weynton asked.

"Looks like business is good, Captain," answered Dr. Patron. "I count thirty, maybe more ships at anchor, and no activity on them," he announced.

"There shouldn't be that many ships there, and you're right--I see no one on the decks."

"Could it be an invasion, sir? A foreign navy?" Patron guessed.

"No, Doctor. There's no battle formation and no war banners. It's just odd," Weynton wondered.

"Could it be the 'pox,' sir?" the doctor now questioned.

"Mr. Heinz, prepare a shore party. We'll lay up and await your return and report. Mind you, make your inquiry at a distance, as to why all these ships are anchored here."

The Cowlitz found anchorage to the south of the empty ships, and Heinz, with five armed men, lowered the skiff. Soon, the investigating party of men were under sail towards the mass of ships. The town wharf could be seen, jutting out from the shoreline. A church chapel stood above several adobe and grass homes, with government and trading warehouses in mortared lava stone at the wharf. There seemed to be little activity in the town. As they sailed past one of the empty ships, Heinz spotted a lone figure on the deck. Rather then go ashore, he came about to approach and questioned the human.

Now close to the anchored schooner, Heinz called out to him. "Ahoy! We are men of the Queen's Navy. Who be you?"

"Aloha. I be Ben Scrapper," came the reply from the bewhiskered old man.

"And why are you the only one on this vessel, sir?" hollered Heinz.

"I can't swim," came Ben's reply.

Now confused, Heinz asked directly, "Sir, are there any diseases or fevers on board?"

"Oh no, ha! Nothing like that. Come aboard. I'll throw you the ladder," Ben hollered down. The toothless, grinning and whiskered old sea rat giggled, looking over the rail. "C'mon up. No need for the muskets lads, ha! C'mon up," waving his arm to motion them up.

"Alright, Ben Scrapper, we'll come up, but any trickery, and my men are authorized to shoot."

"Alright, I'll go first." Heinz climbed the rope ladder, landing on the deck of the deserted schooner.

"C'mon up, boys," the old man beckoned. "Look at ye lads, lashed by the sea, hard as biscuits. Ha! Well, quit lookin' goon-eyed! Aloha! Welcome to Owyhee!"

Now, standing on the deck with two of his men, Heinz could see that this vessel had been stripped and cannibalized.

"What happened here, Ben? This vessel is seaworthy, but not a lanyard or hulyard pin remains." asked Heinz.

"Orders of the King----Kamehameha wants all these abandoned ships stripped of valuables," answered Ben.

"Abandoned?" questioned Heinz.

"The gold! The gold! They've all left for the gold fields!" cackled Ben.

"What gold fields, Ben?" asked Heinz.

"Ahh--been at sea awhile. Well, sir, eight or nine months ago, a merchant landed from the Oregon country, and talked of a huge gold strike in California. Must be some truth to it, because in the last six months, half the town has left, and the whalers are abandoning their company ships to catch the next schooner to San Francisco."

"They're just abandoning their ships?" astonished Heinz asked.

"Yup. It's crazy. The crews never go back after coming ashore. Yesterday, two Opium Clippers from the Orient departed, full of passengers-- whalers, Kanaka--the town's almost half empty. With no crew, the captains walk away also. The gold fever makes them crazy."

"And so these are whaling ships... abandoned?" again asked Heinz.

"Yup. You're in Kamehameha country. He ordered his people to strip the ships of valuables, as one by one, they drag anchor and disappear out to sea," replied Ben.

"And so you work for the King?" asked Heinz.

"Oh no, no. I just scrounge whatever is left, after the King's people leave. My boat's mooring line broke yesterday and floated away--been waiting to be rescued--ha!" he laughed.

"Alright, consider yourself rescued. Will you come with us and tell your story to the captain?"

"Ye gots tobacco and rum?" asked Ben.

"We'll see what we can do, Ben Scrapper. You come with us!" answered Heinz. At that point, Heinz realized his two guards were now very excited, having heard this tale of gold fields in the far away place called California. "You two are under strict orders to say nothing!" he told them.

Now, climbing back aboard the skiff, Heinz introduced Ben, and then gave the command to urgently make way back to the Cowlitz. Captain Weynton had been watching Heinz through the glass as he had boarded the whaling vessel, and could see him conversing with the ragged old salt on deck. Now, seeing them returning with the man, he waited alongside, until Heinz climbed up and reported to him. Asking for a conference in private, the two armed seamen, Heinz, Ben, and the captain withdrew to the captain's quarters and closed the door behind them. "What is it Heinz? Who is this man--what's going on?"

Owyhee

"Captain, this is Ben Scrapper. He has a story to tell you."

"Aye, alright, Mr. Scrapper. Can you explain all these empty ships out here?" answered Weynton.

"Whalers--all went to the gold fields in Californy," came Ben's reply, shrugging.

"Wait--who are you? Please explain," came Weynton's questioning.

"I was a warehouseman on the dock here for several years for the Hankel Whaling Company, supplying the ships with provisions--food, water-- and loading their cargoes of oil bound for England. The arctic fleet became very successful, and business was booming, the company having a charter with the King here, paying taxes, everyone enjoying the good life. Last year, a merchantman arrived from San Francisco with newspapers of fabulous gold fields in California. Within weeks, the whalers abandoned their ships, on hearing the news after arriving here. Every packet, merchantman, and opium cutter that left for California was filled with gold seekers. As the captains lost all their crews, they were helpless to sail away, so they too joined the exodus of gold fever. If they had sailed their ships to San Francisco, they would have been charged with piracy and larceny, so by walking away, they all avoid jail. That's why all the ships are here," explained Ben.

Weynton sat quietly and pondered what the old man had said. "What else do you know about this gold rush, Ben?" asked Weynton.

"Well, sir, a dram of grog and a cigar would help me recollect my thoughts," answered Ben. Weynton opened his cigar box and offered the old salt one, and Ben took two. Weynton poured him a glass of bonded rum. Ben proceeded to tell all the rumor, hearsay, and reports coming weekly from arriving ships, reporting the tales of men getting rich quick.

Weynton finally stopped the tales that Ben was talking endlessly about, realizing his two crewmen were hearing all this, but it was too late. The two armed guards were looking wild-eyed and excited. Now, Weynton realized he was in the same situation as the whaling captains. His crew was granted shore leave and bonus pay as written per contract upon arriving in Honolulu, and they all expected to go ashore as soon as the Cowlitz docked.

"Alright, Ben, we'll be going ashore soon. Mr. Heinz, take this man to the galley and feed him," commanded Weynton. "You, men--come with me," commanded the captain. Ringing the ship's bell for muster, the captain soon had his crew on deck.

"Alright, alright, quiet down," came his order. "Gentlemen, I've been given some information that I will pass on to you now. First, let me remind you that all of you are under contract with the company, and that if you willfully abandoned your acknowledged duty, you will be looked upon as a deserter of the Queen's charter, and be hung by the neck if captured. Gold has been discovered in California--that's why all these abandoned whalers are here. *(lots of whispering, excited)* Our orders are to offload our cloth and load oil, bound for the new colony of Victoria, as you all were informed of in London. Shore leave and bonus pay will be granted as the company has contracted with you, so I expect all of you to fulfill your duty and continue this voyage as agreed. I need six volunteers for a shore party. I'll go ashore and check in at the company office and find out more information. Dr. Patron, I'll leave you in charge until we return." Summoning Heinz and Ben Scrapper, the group boarded the long boat and pushed away, pulling for the wharf a half mile away.

Honolulu was a large town in 1850, with platted streets, the King's Palace, several churches, some stone warehouses, and buildings in the wharf area. There were hundreds of grass shacks spread out around the harbor. The surrounding hills were all barren from overgrazing sheep and cattle over the last twenty years. At the wharf, two Kanaka boys were fishing, otherwise very little activity was seen. Ben hollered at the boys to assist, throwing them the mooring line. Climbing the ladder of the wharf, they were all soon standing on the dock.

"This way, boys," guided Ben, walking down Queen Street towards a two-story stone building. "Here's the Hudson Bay office. Good luck, boys. Thanks for rescuing me." Smiling, away he went.

"Heinz, you and the men sit in the shade here. I'll report our arrival," commanded Weynton.

Entering the door of the building, he was confronted with a host of exotic smells. Everywhere were shelves, bins, barrels of food, tools, and assortments of bolts of cloth. A clerk looked up from his desk in the corner asking, "Good day, sir. May I help you?"

"Yes, I am Captain Alexander Weynton of the company ship Cowlitz. Our arrival was this morning. Are you Georgy Pelly?" asked Weynton.

"Ahh, excellent. We've been expecting you, sir. I'm William Bowden, company clerk. Mr. Pelly is upstairs in the accounting office. I'll summon him," and he hurriedly climbed a creaky stair to the above floor.

Soon, down the stairs came the company chief, Georgy Pelly. "Welcome, welcome, Captain. I trust you had a safe passage." George offered his hand. "I was expecting Captain Hornwick--and you are?" asking Pelly.

"Captain Alexander Weynton--Captain Hornwick passed away last year. Sorry to inform you," answered Weynton.

"Come upstairs, Captain. We have a lot to discuss," answered Pelly.

"Indeed we do, sir," answered Weynton.

The office was well-lit and accommodating. Taking a chair, Weynton sat and rubbed his whiskers. "Captain, before you brief me on your voyage and news from London, I need to inform you that the situation here in Honolulu has changed immensely for the company in the last six months. You must know by now that gold has been discovered in California, and with that, the population here has shrunk to half of what it was a year ago. Our labor situation is critical--no one working in the fields, the whalers all abandoning their ships, everyone, school teachers, preachers, merchants, all gone crazy with the lure of gold. The business here has collapsed. Because the company has no facilities in California, our supplies sit here and rot. I've got thousands of yards of Manila rope and barrels of oil to be shipped, but no labor to load it or transport it. There's already talk coming from the mainland of closing this facility," explained Pelly.

"Wait--what talk--whose talk?" asked Weynton.

"Captain, the Chief Factor, James Douglas, sent me a letter last month from Fort Victoria. The company is totally abandoning its fort at Vancouver in the Oregon country. England and the U.S. have settled on the forty-ninth parallel as the official border. The treaty established that we could remain in the business at Fort Vancouver, but we soon realized that asking the U.S. Army for protection of a British business was not going to work. The Crown has given the Hudson Bay Company total control of the "British Columbia," the region above the fort-ninth parallel. The agreement with the Crown is based upon the HBC colonizing the area within a five year period, after which the Crown will assess the company's success, and will then extend the agreement. The whole focus of the company is now all of a sudden charged with this endeavor to colonize--to gain and keep control of

70

this province. The letter states that upon your arrival, you are to offload immediately your bolts of cloth and powder, and take on a herd of sheep-- along with your salt shipment.

"What!? By thunder, the company can't turn my ship into a livestock farm!" shouted Weynton in disbelief.

"You're forgetting, Captain, the ship belongs to them. They decide the cargo," Pelly muttered.

"What about the barrels of oil?" asked Weynton.

"All I can tell you, Captain, is that Chief Factor James Douglas, our man in charge, has designated in this letter what you are to deliver. Here-- read it," handing the document over to Weynton. He took five minutes to read it, looking up at Pelly periodically, and shaking his head.

"Sheep! My men aren't herders. They're sailors!" fumed Weynton.

"We'll send Kanaka sheep men to care for them during the voyage. The arrangements have been made, Captain," answered Pelly.

"The company wants a large supply of wool to manufacture blankets... blankets being our most important trading product with the natives," answered Pelly.

Weynton was in disbelief. "Sheep?" he repeated, shaking his head. "Alright, Mr. Pelly. I assume you have all the manpower to pull us into the wharf," asked Weynton.

"I assume you have Kamehameha's gun powder shipment?," asked Pelly.

"Yes, it's on the manifest," answered Weynton.

"Good. I'll inform the King of his powder arriving. He'll send out two canoes tomorrow to pull your ship in. Your men are welcome to board in the company barracks during your layover, and I trust you'll keep them from disappearing," answered Pelly.

"I'll see you tomorrow, Mr. Pelly. Good day." The captain hurried back down the stairs and nodded at Bowden, the clerk.

"Alright, men, thank you for your patience. Our business is done here today. We'll return to the ship, where I will inform all of you of the situation. No grumbling. Move along now, lads. You'll have your shore leave in due time," revealing some of the unknown to them.

Back on board the skiff, the mood was silent on the row back. Upon tying up again alongside the Cowlitz, a *Caw! Caw! Caw!* came from the stern deck rail, as to announce their return.

71

"Mr. Heinz, lock her down and shape her up for a tow to the wharf tomorrow," was the command, as soon as the crew were all on deck.

"Aye, Captain."

"Dr. Patron, may I see you in my cabin?" asked Weynton.

"Of course, sir. At your service," answered Patron.

"Juanito, bring us some food from the galley," commanded Weynton.

Back in the captain's cabin, Weynton poured two large glasses of rum. Offering a cigar, both men lit them off the candle on the table. "Doctor...." and Weynton proceeded to tell him the information he had been given that day.

Finally, Dr. Patron stopped him. "Wait. You're telling me that there's a river of gold in California, and we're delivering "sheep" to some new outpost that's a year old in the wilderness," muttered the astonished Dr. Patron.

Knock Knock "Come in."

Juana entered with a steaming tray of fish, rice, and gravy with fresh bread. Both men thanked her for serving and resumed their conversations, as if she wasn't there.

"If I may give my opinion, sir," asked Patron.

"Of course, but I know what you're going to say," answered Weynton.

"Sir, our men are no different from anyone else. We can only hope they will honor their contracts and not desert. You must give them leave and pay them. You have no choice as a man of honor," replied the doctor.

"Alright. Assemble the crew on deck, Doctor. I'll be up shortly," came Weynton's reply.

As soon as the doctor had left, Weynton sat and pondered over his unfinished dinner.

"Excuse me sir. Me take plate?" asked Juana.

"Ahh, Juana, my little shining pearl. Uh, no, let me finish here. I see your English has improved," he winked at her.

"Yes, sir. Me listen to Captain," came her smile.

"Good. Juana, tomorrow we will dock, and I'm sure you want to go ashore like everyone else. The school has closed here. Things are not right. I want you and Pinto to not go ashore. Do you understand?" Weynton looked at her.

"Yes. Captain say me and Pinto not go land," she answered.

"Yes, good. Alright, let's go on deck. Come along," Weynton patted her head.

Now, as Weynton came out of his cabin, the ship's bell signaled his presence, and the assembled crew of sixteen men and the cook stood before him. No one spoke, as they all wanted to hear the news.

"Alright, men. Tomorrow the King's tow boats will take us to the wharf. You're all granted three days' leave from the moment the bow line is cleated. Bonus pay will be doled out on deck after dinner." "We will not be rewarded for our efforts in the Philippines, according to the company. The rope is stacked neck deep in the warehouse with no buyers. I will put in a good word in London for your efforts, as it will merit well with your future employments of the company. Of course, you're under the law of Kamehameha, and if you end up in jail, there are no guarantees of the outcome, so I expect good behaviour." "As I said, Mr. Heinz will mark on his clock watch when we tie up, and you have seventy-two hours to return, otherwise, you'll be classified as a 'deserter.' Are we clear, gentlemen?" barked Weynton.

"Aye, Captain," came the simultaneous reply.

"Good day, gentlemen," and a whoop and holler went up, with laughter and merriment. As was promised, they all hastily finished dinner and lined up on deck to receive their bonus, being allotted and recorded by Mr. Heinz. The bonus was company coupon, redeemable at the trading post. They then went back to their deck games, now already gambling away their new wealth.

Duto was a delight on this evening, flitting around on the deck, receiving his treats and rewards, the men feeding him till he could eat no more. The bird was now cursing quite well in English. "Gimme that som' bitch! Gimme that som' bitch!" was Duto's new line, enjoying the raucous laughter every time he said it over and over again. The men turned in early, anticipating being awake for the next three days.

The next morning, the harbor was as smooth as glass. The sun had not been up an hour when a long horn call of a conch shell could be heard in the distance. Out of the coconut groves and down the beach came two outrigger canoes, being skidded into the water by a mass of natives. The horn continued to blow as the craft finally were floating, and now, pulling towards them in unison, the craft came alongside the Cowlitz in ten minutes. Casting off a tow line on either side, the Cowlitz weighed anchor. The Kanaka oarsmen were now singing in cadence a laborious song of the helmsman, calling out verses, and the oarsmen answered with a pull and yelp. Smaller canoes came alongside now, offering fruits up to the sailors, the bare-breasted women enticing the men, holding up pineapples. The tug boats arrived at the wharf, casting up the bow lines to the Kanaka wharf hands. Within minutes, the Cowlitz was tied up on the dock.

"C'mon Yancy, swing that gangplank," pleaded the anxious crew.

Scrambling down the plank, the group was now clamoring up the street, and disappeared into the side street haunts.

"Well, Doctor, again, I ask that you stay with the ship, as my need to discuss our orders are urgent. Heinz is assigned to inventory with the dock crew. The cook, Pinto, and Juana will stay with you."

"No problem, sir. Your ship is my mistress. See if we can get out of this sheep situation," said the doctor.

"Aye, Doctor. I'll try," said Weynton. A parade of Kanaka now came boisterously down the street, pounding drums to a rhythm of horns. They wore the accoutrements of royalty, bearing shields and spears and splendored with exotic feathers. These were the King's Royal Guard to pick up his gunpowder. Seeing this, Weynton quickly walked down the plank to address them at the dock, saluting and bowing to the sergeant of arms. Holding out the King's purchase order, the sergeant requested the powder to be put in his charge. Reading the document, he handed it back and turned to Mr. Heinz saying, "Assist these gentlemen in procuring their powder. I'll be back." Saluting and bowing again, the captain walked on past the contingent, and up the street to George Pelly's office.

Boldly entering, he stormed past the clerk who had his hands full of company men, redeeming coupons for company store goods. Climbing the stairs, he urgently knocked on the door. "Come in, Captain Weynton. I've been expecting you," called out George Pelly. "Sit down. I trust that you've calmed down from yesterday, sir. Have a drink of scotch," offered Pelly.

Accepting the glass, Captain Weynton took a gulp and said, "Mr. Pelly. We have a discrepancy in the powder delivery for the King," and proceeded to tell the truthful whole story, overloaded with ballast in the South China Sea, and putting in at a pirate's nest to correct the problem. "Our only bargaining tool was the powder kegs with the Spanish, having to trade two to tie up. Exploiting the opportunity of the moment, I traded three more kegs for 2,000 pounds of waxed Manila rope, worth five times what the powder is valued."

Pelly raised his eyebrows. "Yes, six months ago your waxed rope was valuable, but now there's so much, it lays out in the rain and rots. Ahh, now I understand your urgency. The King and I are on good terms, Captain. I can get you off the hook, but I need your pledge and allegiance that you will be at sea by the end of this week, on your way to British Columbia with the cargo we have discussed. Otherwise, the King might arrest you for embezzling, Captain," snided Pelly.

"I'm a man of my word, Pelly. Your ship will be under way by the end of the week," hissed Captain Weynton.

"Very well, I'll send a dock crew to offload the cloth and rope. We'll be loading the hay and sheep the day after tomorrow."

"Alright, Mr. Pelly. One other thing. Captain James Brooke of the British Navy requisitioned a month's supply of grog. It was given as a regulation, made note of in ship's log. My stores will need the extra replenished ration."

Pelly looked astonished. "You, sir, met the White Rajah?" asked Pelly in disbelief.

"Yes, we crossed paths in the Philippines. He had been attacking pirates, and his supplies were low," said the captain.

"Well, I'll take you for your word as a gentleman. You'll get your extra grog ration," snapped Pelly.

"Good day, Mr. Pelly." The captain departed, returning to the wharf.

By now, the forty-five kegs were on the dock. The sergeant of arms was making a big scene about the missing five kegs, with Heinz pretending not to understand. At this point, Weynton intervened, explaining it was an accounting error, and that the King needed to talk to Mr. Pelly. Satisfied that he had pleaded his case in public, the sergeant ordered his porters to shoulder the forty-five kegs, and began marching back up the street, banging their drums and blowing their conch horns. Weynton marched back up the gangplank, and strutting past Dr. Patron standing on deck, he slammed his cabin door.

Pinto, Juana, and the doctor all looked at each other and shrugged. The doctor now looked bewildered. "Juana, do your job. Go tend his needs," the doctor nudged his nose towards the cabin. Recognizing the tapping on the door, Weynton knew who it was. "Come in, Juanito," he called.

"Can me get you food?" asked Juana.

75

"Uh, no. Fetch me Dr. Patron," he stated, staring out the window to the sea.

"Yes, sir."

Soon, Dr. Patron was knocking on the door. "Come in, Doctor. Please sit down. Doctor, do you have any business to take care of here in Honolulu? If so, I suggest you take care of it tomorrow, and yes, the company has changed the cargo from whale oil to sheep and hay, to be loaded day after tomorrow. We set sail on this coming Thursday morning."

"I see, sir. When this crew finds out you're shipping sheep, they will desert as sure as there's fire in hell. It's the only excuse they need, with this gold fever running through their drunken minds now," said the doctor.

"Well, Doctor, as both of us are British gentlemen, I'm sure I can count on you, whatever the outcome. We'll have to wait and see. The clock is ticking," said Weynton.

"I'm too old to chase gold down in the wilderness. No, sir, I like my job within the company," said Patron.

"Very well, Doctor. If I may indulge your patience once more, I'm going back to town, have a bath, shave, and a steak, and I'll replenish our whiskey and cigar supply. Tomorrow will be your day ashore, sir," said Weynton.

"Very good, sir, and I might recommend the Honduran El Presidente cigar--better quality," Patron joked and smiled.

"Alright, I'll be back at sundown. That will be all, Doctor," said Weynton.

"Juana, you take care of the doctor. I'll be back."

Stepping out on deck, the dock crew was now unloading the bales of cloth under the watchful eye of Heinz. "All is in order, Heinz?" asked Weynton.

"Ah yes, these Kanaka are hard workers. We should be done by evening, sir," answered Heinz.

"Very well. Carry on." Weynton walked back up to Queen Street, disappearing around the corner.

The afternoon was uneventful, the dock crew being urged on by their superiors, with Heinz stopping and checking the tagging and manifest. The cook was taking a nap, and so Pinto and Juana bided their time fishing over the rail with hand lines. The fish were small but quite plentiful--enough for a fine fish stew. Duto strutted back and forth on the rail, cursing every time a flopping fish came over the rail.

"SOM' BITCH. GOOD BOY.

SOM' BITCH. GOOD BOY."

Duto now began a tirade of foul curse words in their Visayan tongue. Pinto would quickly gut the fish, throwing the treat to Duto who gobbled it, and he'd start again and say

"SOM' BITCH. GOOD BOY.

SOM' BITCH. GOOD BOY."

The harbor was tranquil that afternoon, with the tide going out. Pinto pointed out a reef becoming exposed with the receding tide, and a large flock of gulls feeding on the exposed coral and rock. "That would be a good place to fish, at high tide." Pinto pointed towards the feeding gulls.

"Maybe," said Juana," but our bucket is almost full. Why go over there?" she laughed at Pinto.

"Bigger fish," replied Pinto. The sun was now sinking into the Pacific. The dock crew finished offloading their donkey carts, and the goods were taken up the cobble street to the company warehouse.

Heinz, the doctor, Pinto, and Juana were all feasting on the cook's fresh fish stew, when the galley door popped open. Captain Weynton, smiling, held up two cotton sacks, the contents of clinking glass bottles. "Bought the last two boxes of Hondurans, Doctor--your lucky day!" he announced with a gleam in his eye.

"Ha! I was making a joke. Excellent choice, Captain," the doctor slapped his knee.

"And for you two--some fish hooks for Pinto and some sugar cane candy for Juana--uh--Juanito," he corrected himself, realizing his error in front of the cook and Heinz. "And Doctor, on your visit to town, I do recommend Charlotte's Bath House. The steak across the street was tough as boot leather though, and the whiskey watered, but the hot bath well-appreciated." The captain went on and shared his adventures in town, and looking at his pocket watch, finally yawned and announced he was retiring.

The company had posted a guard on the dock, and Weynton acknowledged his presence as he walked the deck back to his cabin. Juana followed and slipped in before he closed the door. As he turned to address her, she threw her arms around his waist and softly thanked him. Patting her on the head, he laughed and said, "Enough. Into your hammock. The day is done," and blew out the candle.

Juana awoke late the next morning to the sound of hammering and loud banging noises on the Cowlitz. Company workers had come aboard that morning and were constructing a "corral" in the hold of the ship to transport the sheep. Large bundles of hay were being loaded, with the wharf a scene of activity. Lumber and hay sat on the dock, waiting to be carried onto the ship. The worthless abaca rope they had acquired now lay heaped on several carts, being hauled away to be forgotten. Weynton and Patron watched the activity from the stern deck, drinking tea and smoking cigars. "Well, Captain, the word will be out today about shipping these sheep. If we don't have a crew by tomorrow, we won't be going anywhere," said Patron.

"Aye, Doctor. There are handbills and posters all over town about the Gold Strike in California. It's very tempting for any man," said Weynton. "You, sir, need to go to town and tend your business. I'll keep an eye on the ship today."

The doctor, flicking his cigar stub overboard, smiled and said, "I'll see you at dinner," and down the gangplank he went.

The day was long and monotonous. Pinto and Juana again spent the day fishing over the rail of the ship, playing games with Duto. He would fly off periodically, flying down the beach and returning with a shiny stone or shell to add to his collection, up in his stern mast hideout. Weynton spent the afternoon gazing at his charts, checking information and making notes, bringing his log up to date. It was dinnertime when Patron returned with his purchases, a porter lugging his packages back aboard for him. "Well, how was that bath, Doctor?" asked Weynton.

"Superb, sir, and as you said, the steak across the street was boot leather," replied the doctor. "I'm afraid I have some not good news, Captain," the doctor went on. "Seems three of the crew got caught up in a bar room brawl and smashed up the place, and were arrested and placed in jail," the doctor said with raised eyebrows.

"I see. Not good," said Weynton. "I'll talk to Pelly and have the company pay for the damages, and take it out of their pay," said Weynton.

"I don't think it's that simple sir. They beat up some of the King's arresting guards. It's a serious offense," said the doctor.

"How about the rest of the crew? Did you see any of them?" asked Weynton.

"I saw Yancy with two native girls holding him up, he was so drunk," said the doctor. "He was so drunk, I don't think he knew who I was."

"Damn. I was afraid of this happening. Well, it's getting dark. I'll talk to Pelly tomorrow. Perhaps his influence with the King will help," said Weynton.

Another uneventful evening passed, and the next morning, Weynton was off early to seek the help of Pelly. Climbing the stairs to the company office, he knocked and was told to enter. "Good morning, Captain. I've been informed that your ship is made ready. We're on schedule?" asked Pelly.

"Yes, Mr. Pelly. The Cowlitz is in good order," said Weynton. "I've received a report that three of my men are in the King's stockade," replied Weynton.

"And for what reason?" asked Pelly.

"Apparently, drunk and disorderly--and beating up the King's guard," replied Weynton.

"That's not good," said Pelly. "The last time that happened, the men were all given a five year sentence of manual labor in the pineapple fields," said Pelly.

"Can you approach the King and ask for leniency?" asked Weynton.

"Mr. Weynton, there is a huge shortage of manpower on this island, and the King is fully aware of it. A chance to add more laborers to his pineapple fields is not an easy thing to undo. It is your responsibility to maintain discipline with your crew, so I hold you responsible for the situation," said Pelly.

"Hold on here, Pelly. Company contract allows these men for rest and shore time after the Pacific crossing. I can't follow them around town and watch over them," Weynton angrily replied.

"Regardless of your feelings, Weynton, the company holds you responsible for the actions of your crew," replied Pelly.

"I guess you'll be sailing tomorrow minus three crew members," said Pelly. "Your provisions will be delivered this afternoon, and I trust you and your ship will be underway by this time tomorrow. Good day, Captain Weynton." Now Pelly looked back down at his ledger.

Weynton stormed out of the office, slamming the door. Hastily walking briskly back to the ship, he now paced back and forth on the deck, muttering and cursing under his breath. Seeing him and his agitated mood, Patron summoned the captain to his cabin, where scotch and smoke calmed him down. Revealing his information to the doctor, the two sat discussing their options, continually refilling their tankers.

Down the cobble street came a loud commotion--a herd of sheep surrounded by herders, dogs, and helpers. Once on the wharf, the dogs kept them in a tight circle, and catching them one by one, were walked up the gangplank one at a time, two men hold their legs and carrying them upside down.

Weynton and Patron were now on deck again, observing the spectacle, as the sheep did not want anything to do with the ship. A circus soon developed, sheep getting loose and running around on deck, with Weynton cursing and waving his arms, disgusted with the whole scene.

Juana and Pinto again were fishing off the rail. With all the commotion on deck, they climbed over the side and down to a skiff that was floating and tied to her stern. Now trying their luck with the hand lines in the skiff, Pinto noticed the tide was up, and the reef he had spotted days earlier was underwater.

"Let's row over there and try our luck," said Pinto.

"Captain said we can't go ashore," said Juana.

"We're not going ashore. We're still in a boat," said Pinto. "He won't mind. I'll catch a big Mahi Mahi for his dinner," said Pinto. "He's busy with loading these sheep. C'mon, it's not far."

"Alright. For a little while, but if we get in trouble, I told you so," said Juana.

An old canvas sail bag and two oars were in the boat. Dropping the oars into the rail locks, Pinto was pulling away now for the underwater reef. Soon, they were upon the reef, the water only waist deep. The water was crystal clear, and soon, fish were congregating in the shade of the skiff. They began to catch several, but none of them having the size that Pinto had hoped for. Peering over the side and watching her baited hook, she began to stare at the bottom and suddenly realized she was staring at a huge bank of oysters. "Pinto, look at the bottom--you see that?" asked Juana.

Now refocusing, he realized what she was seeing. Hundreds of oysters covered the coral reef. Pinto looked at her with big eyes, and pulled his line in. He dove over the side, careful to keep his feet from touching bottom. Soon, he was surfacing and throwing large clumps of oysters into the boat. Juana pulled the oars and slowly moved down the reef. Within an hour, Pinto had two bushels of oysters piled into the bottom of the skiff. In their exuberance and excitement, they had drifted and rowed quite a distance from the ship, and now, the crack of a pistol and a puff of smoke came from the ship. Weynton had observed their absence, and seeing the skiff gone, quickly scanned the harbor and spotted them with his glass. They could see him waving them back, and now they hurriedly rowed back to the ship, all the time fabricating their excuse to be told to him.

Covering the oysters with the sea bag, they came back alongside the Cowlitz now, with Weynton looking over the rail and barking down at them. "Damn it, you two. I've got enough problems today without having to watch over and worry about you two! Tie that thing up and get back up here," his red face barked and then disappeared.

"Leave the oysters. I'll get them later," said Pinto. "We better get up there." Climbing back aboard, the ship was emitting a strong, farmlike odor of wet wool and manure, now attracting black flies. Seeing both of them, Weynton glared in anger, looking for someone to take his anger out on. Sensing his wrath, both hustled themselves down to the galley and began peeling potatoes.

"Well, Doctor, it's 4 o' clock. These scalawags have until tomorrow morning at 9:00 to return," said Weynton. "If not, we'll run her aground on the beach and make a livestock farm out of her," cursed Weynton.

As the evening rolled along, the odor became more and more overbearing, the sheep relieving themselves in the hold. A sleepless, annoying night seemed to go on forever, and finally, it was 6 o'clock and sunrise. Weynton, Patron, and Heinz were up early, all three pacing the deck, looking at their watches and watching the street, waiting for the crew to return.

It was Yancy and three other crew members that first appeared, staggering down the street with their entourage of harlots, all trying to get whatever last payment they could. Once on the wharf, the company guards shooed the soiled doves away, and the four drunken sots wobbled up the plank and onto the deck. Saluting their captain and slurring their words, Heinz threw a bucket of sea water on the wretches, which had little effect. "Alright, you boys have had your fun. Time to get to work. Where's the rest of them?" asked Weynton.

"Well, sir, Randolph, Butler, and Cooper are in jail, and the rest have run off on an outrigger to Lahaina. They're looking to catch a schooner to the gold fields. They all left yesterday," answered Yancy with his head down.

"My God," said Weynton, "the company will throw us all in jail now," shaking his head.

"They heard we were shipping livestock two days ago, and they all said we didn't sign on to be sheep herders, so away they went, all talking like they were going to be rich," whined Yancy.

"Well, that's that." Patron turned and looked at Weynton. "Now what?"

"Hmm, this ship isn't going anywhere with a crew of four," Weynton now looked perplexed. "I'm gonna have to report this situation to Pelly." "We'll all probably be in irons by the end of the day," fumed Weynton.

So now back up Queen St. the captain trudged, having to report the Cowlitz was now without manpower. Back up the stairs, knocking, and the familiar "Enter," Weynton now stood before Pelly at his desk.

"Well, I see you've come to say goodbye," said Pelly to Weynton.

"I wish that were the case, Mr. Pelly, but gold fever and the vices of your island have reduced my crew to four men," answered Weynton.

Dropping his quill and looking up from his ledger, he swirled his tongue on the inside, his anger beginning to boil.

"God damnit Weynton, you better not be serious," Pelly's steely stare was now unflinching.

"Mr. Pelly, I am a seaman. Your wicked little island here is yours, and yours has taken my crew and scattered it to the wind. I suggest you calm yourself, as this dilemma will not look good for either one of us in London. I need seamen, Mr. Pelly, or the Cowlitz's fate is the same as the rest of these ghosts anchored in the bay."

Pelly's head sunk, and he took his spectacles off and rubbed his face. Looking back up, he acknowledged that cooler heads needed to prevail by shaking his head yes. "Alright, Captain Weynton, you are correct. The company has some Kanaka dock hands under contract, and I have two Makah Indian whalers that were left behind. I've been feeding them for doing errands and work for me. It's the best I can do, Captain, but you are right--if we fail here, the colony in Victoria could fail, and I don't want that on my record."

"How many hands can you give me, Mr. Pelly?" Weynton was now listening.

"I have six Kanaka under contract. I must keep two. Four Kanaka and the two Makahs," answered Pelly.

Weynton now was shaking his head--a totally green crew, no communication possible with these six, and the wild Pacific Ocean to consume them all if one blunder is made.

"Your sheep will start dying if we don't get them fresh air, Captain," reminded Pelly.

"When can you have these men report to the ship?" asked Weynton.

"I'll personally bring them at 11 o'clock, Captain," answered Pelly.

"Very well. Tell your tug canoes we will be debarking at noon." Tipping his hat, he turned to leave.

"Captain Weynton..." the captain turned back around as Pelly stood and held out his hand, "...best of luck--God save the Queen." They shook hands, and Weynton turned and left.

Weynton found himself briskly walking back to the ship, his mind whirling in thought along the way, planning the rest of the day and sizing up his situation. Arriving back on deck, his hungover deckhands were pretending to work. Calling Heinz to the deck, he commanded for the skiff to come aboard, and get ready to get underway. Knocking on the doctor's door, he entered and disappeared.

Pinto was in the galley, helping the cook, and Juana was washing the captain's clothes, in a tub on the stern deck. Duto walked back and forth on a nearby spar, trying to catch a glimpse of his medallion on her neck. Both of them had tried to stay low and not be seen since the incident of the day before, with the captain firing a pistol to call them back to the ship. The oysters were still in the skiff, under the sail bag. The skiff had ringlets at either end for lowering and raising, and so two seamen were ordered to swing the davit arms over the side, and raise the boat to the deck. At this point, Heinz told Yancy to fetch Pinto from the galley. When he appeared, Heinz hand signaled him to dive in off the stern, undo the mooring line and fasten the davit ropes to the ringlets on the skiff. In no time, Pinto was in the water, untying the skiff and attaching the hooks to the eyelets. He rode the boat up to the rail. The davits were then swung inward, landing the skiff on the deck.

"Alright, Yancy, we'll flip her and lash her later. We've got more important things to do. Pinto, block that skiff up and stow those davit lines," commanded Heinz.

Soon, the five seamen had moved forward on the bow deck, greasing block and tackle on the rigging. Taking the opportunity of the moment, Pinto got the oysters into the sail bag, hardly being able to lift the heavy bag out of the boat. Finally succeeding, he was dragging it across the deck, making for the galley, when Heinz called out, "PINTO, COME HERE. I NEED YOU." An ax locker was handy, so he opened the door and pulled the sack in, closed the door, and went trotting forward. Showing Pinto a bucket of grease lard, he handed it to him, and told him to fetch more from the galley.

The morning passed quickly with all of the activity on the ship, and at ten minutes to eleven, Pelly appeared on the wharf with his six conscripts, calling up for Weynton to appear. The four Kanakas had their belongings bundled in sacks, being coerced and ordered to assist the ship on its voyage, with the promise of their return in two months. The Makahs had only the shirts on their backs, but upon learning of a chance to return to their homeland, quickly volunteered for the passage to the mainland.

Weynton appeared and ordered Heinz to assist the newcomers aboard, and show them their quarters. Once aboard, Juana stared at the newcomers, and was intrigued with their skin color and facial looks, being very similar to her own people in the Philippines. Of course, Heinz was instructing them in English, which they did not understand, and so hand signals and patience was needed to get them settled into their new environment.

Within the hour, the Kanaka tug canoes came alongside, and taking advantage of the high tide, Weynton ordered the dock mooring lines to be cast off. The canoe men began their chanting in cadence, slowly pulling the ship out through the coral reef channel. As this was going on, Heinz assigned a Kanaka to each of his four remaining English deckhands, using their brawn to hoist the main sails, and soon the Cowlitz was underway. The fresh air relieved the ship of her pungent barnyard odor.

Weynton and Patron were constantly patrolling the deck now, making observations and corrections, bringing up the morale of all aboard, coaxing the Kanaka to watch and pay attention. Weynton and Patron were now satisfied. They returned to the captain's quarters, studying the charts and began making decisions on navigation.

"Juana, fetch us some hot tea," Weynton addressed the young girl. Soon, she returned with a pot of steaming tea, setting it on the captain's table.

"Juana, did you cut yourself?" asked Patron, noticing blood trickling down her leg. Surprised and confused, Juana looked down and saw the blood trail on the inside of her leg.

"Excuse us, Captain." After a moment of silence, Dr. Patron said, "Juana, come with me," holding out his arm and gesturing towards the door.

Confused now, she followed the doctor to his salon, and after a brief embarrassing look at the source of blood, he spoke. "Well, today you have become a young woman--no longer a girl." Terrified, Juana began to cry, as she feared she might bleed to death. Calming her, Patron explained in spanish that she should be happy, and schooled her how to take care of her monthly situation in a sanitary way, providing her with cotton and gauze bandaging. Patting her on the head, he told her to lie down and rest, and returned to Weynton's quarters.

"Well, Captain, there's no point in hiding the fact from the crew that she's a woman. Our four remaining crew members are all fairly trustworthy. I think you should advise them all of her gender," said Patron.

"Yes, I agree, Doctor. I'll assemble the crew this afternoon and disclose the fact," answered Weynton.

The trade winds were warm and gentle, and the Cowlitz clipped along at a steady pace. The Makah had become transfixed with Duto, the raven in their culture being a supernatural deity. Upon hearing him curse and perform his little dance for bits of food, they became enchanted with him, and visually followed his constant movement and location on the ship. Seeing him roosted up on a spar, they would point and exclaim, "*Kah-kah ta-mah-no-us*," and get a big smile on their face.

Weynton entered the doctor's salon, smiling warmly and assuring Juana. He told her to come with him. Once out on deck, Duto spotted her and flew down and landed on her shoulder. She pulled her medallion and medicine bags out from under her shirt, calming him and assuring him.

"Alright, listen up Heinz, assemble the crew," commanded Weynton. Within minutes, the rag tag sailors were standing before their captain, waiting for his announcement. "Alright, all of you are aware of our situation. We're totally undermanned and need complete cooperation and discipline, if we are to survive this passage to the mainland. All of us are depending on one another, right down to this young lady standing here."

A gasp followed from Heinz and the four original sailors. Weynton continued, "As your captain, I felt it was in the best interest of our ship's crew

85

to not divulge that Juanito here is actually Juana, but as the situation has drastically changed, she may be called upon to do a man's work--and so I demand that she be treated with respect, and if I hear of any provocation towards her being a woman, I will have that man thoroughly flogged and put in irons until we arrive at Victoria. Are we understood, gentlemen?" Now came Weynton's questioning look. "Well!?" bellowed Weynton.

"Aye, aye, Captain," came the weak response.

"I expect you men to somehow translate her gender to these newcomers and make sure they understand the consequences, if they violate this young woman. That is all. Trim that foresail on the secondary, Mr. Heinz!" Weynton spun on his heel and left the deck, returning to his cabin.

The assembled crew now disbanded, wandering off to continue their duties. The Makah stood and stared at the girl and Duto, pointing at her and saying, "*Kah-kah-ta-mah-no-us*." She held out her arm, and he jumped from her shoulder to her extended hand. She beckoned the two Indians to approach and allowed them both to stroke his beak and back, both of them grinning from ear to ear.

Heinz now observed the three and the bird and spoke up, "Juana, go help in the galley. These men have chores to do," gently nudging her in that direction.

Duto flew off to his hideout in the stern mast, and Juana climbed down the stairs into the galley. Seeing Pinto gutting fish on a chop block, she volunteered her help. Acknowledging her with a big, toothy smile, he jokingly asked, "So, Juanito, I mean Juana..." and they both burst into laughter at the same time. "I need help with these oysters. We'll surprise the captain with a big oyster dinner," Pinto told her in their dialect.

"Where are they--the oysters?" asked Juana.

"C'mon." Grabbing a bucket, stool, and a shiv, he climbed up the galley steps. Arriving at the ax locker, Pinto now pulled the sack out onto the deck. Setting up his stool, he gave Juana a quick lesson in the art of shucking, wearing a glove and finding the split on the shell. Shucking three oysters, he asked her, "You got it? Don't cut yourself. Go slow." Handing her the glove, she sat down and handily broke two shells open, scraping the morsel into the bucket. Pinto nodded his head, satisfied she could handle it, and announced, "I need to get back in the galley to keep the fire going. This will help keep you busy," and walked off.

As soon as he left, Duto, who had been observing and catching flashes of the bright opened oyster shells, landed and quickly strutted back and forth on the deck, as if shopping for the proper shell. The bird began cursing, "Dirty bastard, gimme that! Dirty bastard, gimme that!" Annoyed, Juana shooed him away, but he would have none of it. He crow-hopped over to a barrel, flared his wings, and lit upon the barrel lid, now pacing in a circle. She had successfully opened a dozen or so, and upon popping the next one open, she found a shimmering bead puddled in the creature's grasp. Seeing it, she set the shiv down and picked it out, the size of a small marble, and held it up towards the sky.

Caw! Caw! Caw! Duto saw it too and jumped down and hopped to her side. His eyes big and glassy, he craved to have it in his beak. Recognizing this, she pulled the pearl away, and shooed him off again. Using one of the larger opened shells as a container for the pearl, Juana set her prize under the stool, and continued working. Within minutes, she had another and added it to the one under the stool. Now, she had quite a few opened shells piled up, and was relishing her task, hoping for more rewards.

A Kanaka was trimming up a lanyard forward of her, and spotted the activity she was engaged in. Slowly, he cleated off his rope and approached the girl with eyes wide and mouth open. When he got within five feet of her, he let out a shrill whistle and a panicked, "*Ki eee! Ki eee!*" Running back up deck, he pointed and cried out to his fellow Kanaka. They began to wail and cry and rub their hands and shake all over. Heinz came hurriedly from the helm, totally perplexed as to what was wrong, shouting, "What is it? What is it?" as the Kanaka continued to wail and point at Juana shucking oysters.

"Damn it Yancy! What are they saying? What's wrong with them? stammered Heinz.

"*KAMEHAMEHA MAKAMAE MOMI!!*"

"What is it, Yancy?" cried Heinz, desperate for order.

"They're saying, "Those are the King's precious pearls,'" Yancy explained.

"*KAMEHAMEHA CHOP CHOP THE WAHINE!*" the Kanaka cried.

"They say the King will kill the girl and all the Kanaka who take oysters from his harbor. It's part of their culture, sir. Some foods are for the King, only. Taking them is a death sentence," replied Yancy.

"Dammit! Lie to them, Yancy. Tell them the King gave them as a gift to the captain" quick-thinking Heinz tried to control the situation. And so Yancy, in broken jargon, explained them as a gift, and that it was okay.

Now they all huddled, and assuring each other that they were in no danger, they began to congregate around Juana, having never even been allowed to see the process. Soon, they were all laughing, as she held up another pearl, and they began clapping and chattering loudly, hoping that more would be found. She pried a larger one open, and a black, glistening orb lay in the flesh. There was a cry of excitement and laughter, the Kanaka now pointing at her, saying "*You Wahine Momi,*" and howling their pleasure with the rare find.

Hearing all of the excitement on deck, Weynton approached the huddle of men, and seeing Juana surrounded by them now, sounded his displeasure. "Here, here. What is this? You men were told to leave...." Now, seeing her looking up at him and smiling, he suppressed his sentence when he saw the pile of shells.

"We surprise Captain--oyster dinner," Juana smiled.

"Where in tarnation did you get those? I love oysters." He began to boisterously laugh, fully aware of Kamehameha's law regarding Pearl Harbor. "Well, I suppose the King won't miss a couple hundred oysters. We're not turning around to take them back!" he exclaimed and let out another huge belly laugh. "Alright, break it up. Back to work." Weynton struck a match and lit his pipe. "Alright, good job, Juana. Toss those shells over the side when you're done," he said and walked off, breaking into laughter again.

An hour later he returned, just as she was finishing up. She had found twelve pearls, some of them the rare blacks. One of the blacks was huge--the size of a marble. She held her prize shell full of pearls up to him to show him her find. Weynton let out a long whistle, examining the gleamers, and he handed back the shell, carefully. Pulling his tobacco pouch from his pocket, he packed the last bowl in the bag, and handed the empty bag to her saying, "Put your pearls in here. Put them with your belongings in the cabin, and when you get back, clean up this mess," with a gleam and smile in his eye.

That night, the crew all bonded with a feast of fried oysters and oyster stew. The Makah ate them raw, as preferred, and the celebration carried into the night.

The Makah turned out to be able sailors, and Heinz quickly became aware of their natural ability to sense a shift in the wind and trim the sail accordingly. Everyone on the ship was now calling Juana, "Pearl." The Kanaka initially called her "*Momi*," but Weynton was now calling her Pearl as well, and *Momi* was forgotten, its meaning, of course, being "pearl." The trade winds had continued to be fair with following seas, and their progress was good. Weynton had continued teaching Juana English, and he was pleased, seeing her progress.

Duto had befriended the sailor named Yancy, known for his foul, un-Christian language. The bird seemed to love it. Yancy would tease Duto with repetitive vulgar language until the bird became enraged and began screaming the obscenities back at him, one trying to outdo the other. Having heard enough of the tainted obscenities, Weynton would give a sharp command, "That'll be enough, you two!" Whereas Duto repeated the command, "That'll be enough, you two! *Caw! Caw!*"

Pearl had become friends with the two Makah. Their fascination of Duto and her control over him was magic to them. He would land on the deck in her presence and create a fuss of *Caw! Caw! Caw!* until she would flash the medallion. Then satisfied, he would hop off to find some mischief to get into. Wanting to learn her power, the Makah began to teach Pearl Chinook Jargon, the trade language of the Oregon country. Her ability to pick up the conversation was remarkable, and within two weeks, she was having an understandable conversation with the two.

They explained they were Makah whalers, from a tribe off the point of the mainland. Their village could be seen upon entering the channel that approached Fort Victoria, they explained. They had paddled north to hunt whales, but while at sea had been caught in a bad storm. A Yankee whaler had spotted them, and as payment for saving their lives, they were impressed as laborers on the whaling ship. They had not been home in five years, and had been abandoned in Honolulu, their crew mutinying for the gold fields. They were excited to see home again, and they regarded Duto as a spirit of good luck.

The ship had been at sea twenty-three days now, and the smell of the sheep was becoming nauseating to some of the crew. Several of the sheep had died, their carcasses tossed over to the sharks. One day, forward on the bow deck to escape the odor, the Makah and Pearl sat, the bird hopping around them, cursing and pacing. One Makah was teaching her words in

Chinook--feet, hands, nose, teeth--pointing at them and giving the corresponding word. The other Makah slapped him on the shoulder, and told him to stop, pointing at his nose and smelling the wind. The other breathed the rushing air, and then got very excited. "Yes! Yes! I smell it!" They both looked at each other and grinned, and now Pearl wanted to know what it was. They instructed her to smell the air, but she could not comprehend their excitement.

"What is it?" she pleaded. "What?"

"Land, Pearl. We smell land," came their reply. She looked off the bow at their heading but could only see endless rolling sea. And now Duto sensed it, and flying up to the tallest yardarm, *Caw Caw*ed from his new position on the ship. Any new gossip on a ship is craved, and so with this new prediction from the Makah, she found Weynton smoking a cigar in his chart room, compassing over the map. He made notes and calculations in his vest pad notebook.

"Captain Weynton?" asked Pearl.

"What is it, Pearl--I'm busy," not looking up from his calculation.

"The Makah say they smell land, sir," came her reply, and now Weynton looked up and slapped the chart and nodded his head.

"Well, I suppose your Makah boys are right," smiled the captain. "I've got us exactly one hundred miles off the mainland coast," came his answer, as he stared at the chart and rubbed his whiskers. "We'll be at the mouth of the strait by morning, I'm guessing."

That evening, excitement was in the air on the deck, the crew in full awareness that they were approaching land. The watch was doubled that night, and the ship slowed down to half sail in preparation for hidden danger. The entrance to the strait was twelve miles wide, and to be too far north or south would put them on the rocks.

As first light broke on the deck, the ship entered an eerie, dense fog. All but the foresail was up now, keeping the bow into the waves, a monotonous up and down in rolling seas, but totally blind by the fog in the surroundings. A group of seagulls from out of nowhere landed in the rigging, and Duto confronted them, making them take flight. Everyone was on deck listening, for nothing could be seen. The fog was cold and thick, with the Kanaka now shivering from the exposure. When someone would talk, Weynton would bellow, "Silence. Listen." If there was any perception of waves lapping on a close beach without knowing it was there, the anchor

90

was ready to be dropped, to hopefully keep them from running aground. Everyone strained their eyes and searched the fog blanket, listening for sound.

Suddenly, as if the curtain was raised on a large theatre stage, they emerged from the fog bank and into the sunlight. A large, monumental rock to the south could be seen, the waves of the ocean splashing on its walls. The Makah began screaming, "*Tatoosh! Tatoosh!*" pointing at the large rock.

Weynton looked at Patron, winked, and uttered, "We'll be drinking the Queen's whiskey tonight!"

Fort Victoria

Emerging from the fog bank, Weynton now quickly assessed his surroundings, realizing he was riding an incoming tide. Ordering the Cowlitz to proceed under ¾ sail, he guided the ship to the center of the Strait of Juan de Fuca. The sun shone only briefly, and soon gray clouds and a steady drizzle of rain was soaking the ship. The Makah pointed out a distant group of Orca whales, their geysers of spray from their blowholes revealing their presence. To the south, a range of snow capped mountains could be seen, the tops of which were shrouded in cloud cover. Pinto and Pearl stared at the new landscape along the shorelines--massive green forests covered in mist--with no sign of civilization. A cry came from the mast watch, "Canoe dead ahead--off the port bow." Training his glass on the sighting, Weynton could see a native canoe with a dozen men paddling, heading in the same direction as the Colwitz. The Cowlitz was slowly gaining on the craft, and within the hour was alongside the vessel.

The canoe was a large cedar, with carvings of strange eyes and painted spirits in distinct colors. Pearl stared at the oarsmen and marveled at their hats, much like the coulee hats in the rice paddies at home, only squared off on top, and in this case, functioning as umbrellas. As the Cowlitz came alongside, the Makah began conversing with the natives, pointing and gesturing. Not understanding what was being said, Weynton called for Pearl, to see if she could translate what was being communicated.

Now questioning the Makah as to the subject of the conversation, she soon understood, and translated to Weynton. "They are the Songhee people. Fishermen. They are going to Fort Victoria," Pearl explained to the captain.

"Ask them if one can come aboard to pilot us to this Fort Victoria," asked Weynton.

Pearl translated the request to the Makah, and they relayed the message down to the canoe. A reply came, which Pearl understood. "They want tobacco to show you the way, Captain," replied Pearl.

"Very well. Heinz, fetch some plug tobacco out of ship's stores," commanded Weynton. Returning with the rolled plugs, a dozen in his hand, Heinz held the tobacco up for the natives to see. The natives acknowledged their pleasure, and the gift was lowered in a bucket over the side. The natives now grabbed the bucket and rope and used the rope as a means to stay alongside the Cowlitz. Excitedly claiming their reward, a tall one now pulled himself up the rope, and the canoe pushed away, unable to keep up with the ship. The Songhee jumped onto the deck, and immediately a foul odor was overpowering the smell of the sheep. He was covered in rancid fish oil to insulate his skin from cold and ward off insects. The odor was nauseating. The Makah entered into a lively conversation with him, the others on deck staying well away from the offensive odor. Again, Weynton asked Pearl to translate.

"I'm not sure, sir. Something about magic and spirits," replied Pearl.

"Ask them how far is Fort Victoria," prompted Weynton.

Translating the question to the Makah, it was revealed that the Fort was twenty miles ahead, on the North shore in a hidden harbor.

"Heinz, escort this Songhee to the stern, downwind, if you will," urged Weynton. "Pearl, you and the Makah will have to translate. Follow me to the wheel." At the helm wheel, the captain grabbed some deep breaths of air, now upwind of the rotten smell. The Makah seemed to not notice or care about the smell, and talked and hand signed in close proximity to the fishermen. Every few minutes, the Makah would call out some information, and Pearl would tell Weynton the new heading or something that seemed significant along the coastline.

They now changed course to a northeast heading, making for a distant point of land, and finally rounding the point. Smoke trails from distant fires in the evergreen shroud could be seen, wisping and rolling up under the gray cloud cover. Canoes were now visible in the distance, heading straight at the Cowlitz. Concerned, Weynton questioned the girl if they were friendly or a war party. The fishermen assured the Makah that the canoes were friendly Songhee, excited because they had spotted the Union Jack, and at the chance of acquiring new trade goods, all wanted to be first in line.

"Mr. Heinz, fire the signal cannon. A Queen's ship shall not be intimidated," commanded Weynton. The two pound cannon had been primed earlier in the morning, to be used just for this purpose--signaling the Fort and keeping the natives at a distance. The crack of the gun sent a thundering concussion across the water towards an empty bluff, raising a multitude of seagulls on a distant beach.

Within one minute, a distant *KABOOM* came the report of an unseen cannon. Weynton called for lowering sail and began sounding the depth with a drop line, realizing they were out of the channel now. The native canoes--a dozen or more--now lingered all around the Cowlitz, her cannon fire warning them to keep their distance.

Now in fifty feet of calm water, Weynton dropped anchor. The Fort could not be seen from their anchorage, a finger of land between them. Approaching the Cowlitz from around the point was a skiff, pulling with oarsmen and a helmsman. An Englishman, wearing a tunic of the Royal Navy cried up, "Ahoy!

Cowlitz. Welcome. Lieutenant John Baylor, at your service. Is your captain present?" he greeted, searching the faces peering over the rail of the ship.

Captain Weynton acknowledged the man, answering, "I be the captain, Lieutenant Baylor--Alexander Weynton. Lieutenant, are we anchored out of harm's way?" he questioned their situation.

"Yes, yes. Permission to come aboard, Captain?" came Lt. Baylor's call up.

"Of course. Heinz, drop the boarding ladder." Soon, the lieutenant was on deck, saluting Weynton and vigorously shaking hands.

"Sir, the entrance to the harbor is around that small point. Wisely, you have anchored, as the tide is going out, and your ship can only pass at high tide. You'll have to wait until morning. Sir James Douglas welcomes you and will send a detail of tow boats to escort you into the harbor tomorrow. Congratulations on your successful voyage, sir!" More pleasantries were exchanged, and questions answered and asked.

Now, with his new information, he begged to be excused, explaining, "Sir James was and is very anxious to know if you brought the livestock sheep. He will be very pleased to have this new information. I must return with my report. Your crew will be well received tomorrow, Captain. I'll see you in the morning." Saluting, he turned and climbed over the rail and was away in his boat.

Barking commands at the natives in their surrounding canoes, the lieutenant pointed and waved them away, and the whole flotilla disappeared around the point.

Now, joy and laughter spread across the Cowlitz, the stress of navigating the ship in coastal water relieved, and the long voyage over. The safety of land and the food, drink, and debauchery it offered was close by. Weynton and Patron could feel the new excitement, and nodding at each other, Patron invited the captain to his salon for a drink from a bottle that had been saved for such an occasion.

Sitting in the doctor's cabin, Weynton put his boots up on the table, as Patron pulled a bottle out from a chest locker and set it on the table. Weynton picked it up, not understanding the label or the contents. "What kinda medicine is this, Doctor?" laughed Weynton.

"It's called Pisco, a Spanish Brandy from Peru--my only bottle," explained Patron. Setting two crystal glasses on the table, he produced a corkscrew and "popped" the bottle's cork. Pouring two fingers in each glass, he wasted no time and clinked the captain's glass, and in one gulp, inhaled his shot of liquor. He quickly poured himself another, and explained, "I've had that bottle for twenty years--been saving it for something special--my compliments on your seamanship, Captain. Clinking glasses again, they both drank the fine brandy and commented on its smoothness and taste. Weynton pulled out two cigars, offering the doctor one, as another round was poured. The Pisco had a wonderful taste, and soon the bottle was half gone. Now, Patron got out his cigars, as the conversation got louder and looser, as both men began feeling the effects of the brandy.

"Tell me, Doctor, where can we get some more of this Pisco?" The captain now picked up the bottle and admired its contents.

"There is quite a story behind that bottle, Captain," said Patron. "I've never told it, but since you ask, I'll indulge you with the tale," said Patron. "I was born in Vera Cruz, Mexico in the Carribean, not far from your island, Jamaica. As a young boy, I hung around the docks of the Spanish port town, trading fruits and doing odd jobs for the sailors. I was poor, my mother and father peasants. I had become a common recognized beggar on the docks, and no one paid much attention to me. One day, hunger driving me, I sneaked aboard a galleon that was docked, most of the crew in town. Finding the ship galley, I stole a cheese and a bottle of wine. Hiding in the hold of the ship, I devoured the cheese, washing it down with the wine--which, as a young boy, within minutes left me passed out. My stomach content and my brain medicated, I fell into a deep sleep, awakening the next day in a dark compartment, not knowing where I was. Coming to my senses and realizing where I was, I panicked and jumped up. Peering out a portal, I was shocked to see we were at sea. Soon, I was discovered, a stowaway, but because of my youth and the sailors recognizing me, harsh treatment was not given, and within a short time, I was a working crew member."

"As fate would have it, by luck, I had fallen into a group of selective loyal Spaniards, a secret detail and galleon being sent to Lima, Peru to ship silver reales to Panama under heavy guard, to then be transported over the isthmus to Nombre de Dios. There was so much coinage being minted in Lima, several galleons were needed to transport the huge amounts of silver coming out of the Andes. Our galleon, the "Santa Luanna" had been commissioned in Spain for this task. Sailing around the Horn and up to Lima, the ship's doctor took me on as an errand boy and apprentice. Arriving in Callao, the port city of Lima, we were quickly put to work hauling the hoards of silver up the coast, always returning to be loaded again, provisioned, and sent back to sea with another load of silver. The Castillians discipline was harsh--the threat of having one's tongue cut out and thrown to the sharks was the hidden code, and no thought was given to stealing the weighed and manifested hoard. "

"This routine went on for several years, and I had become a valuable medical assistant, and a very knowledgeable part of the crew. We would have layovers in Callao, the men enjoying the vices of the port city. As a teenager, I had little money, so I would wander this certain beach from time to time, enjoying the walking. One day, on one of these walks, I came upon a beautiful young Inca maiden, sitting on a rock, looking out to sea and chanting a beautiful song. Upon seeing me, she stopped her chant, and began talking to me, as if we were old friends. I learned she was from the interior, high in the mountains of the Andes. She was visiting a relative, a grandmother, who lived nearby. We quickly fell in love, and during that short layover, became quite intimate."

"At one point, she confided a deep secret, one that would have her killed if it were known, yet she divulged it. Apparently, back in Inca times, the Gods rewarded the Inca with a great rainbow machine, which, if the Inca activated it, would summon the Gods from the heavens. The Gods showed the Inca this sacred place high in the mountains--a place called Picchu. The Inca were given a giant golden litter on which a giant, clear crystal, the size of a giant pineapple, was mounted on a chassis on the litter, and could be calibrated to certain angles. The entire machine was encrusted in precious gems. The golden litter was so heavy, it took eight men to carry it. At a sacred spot at Picchu, it was brought out of the temple and placed on a pedestal peg, the litter being set down on this stone peg for alignment--a pedestal base. It was known as the Hitching Post to the Sun. Then, the priest would calibrate the crystal, catching the sun and shooting a rainbow beam across the plaza, where a monstrous solid gold shield on a huge flat stone was reflected upward, turning the beam into an enormous rainbow shooting into the heavens, thus making contact with the Gods. Every time the Inca would conquer another kingdom or people, they would bring them to this Picchu. Having displayed the spectacle of the rainbow catcher, they would fall on their knees and weep and pledge their allegiance to the awesome power witnessed."

"When the conquistadors overtook Peru and conquered the Inca, the Spanish demanded a huge ransom in solid gold to release their imprisoned king. The Inca knew that they could replace the giant golden shield, the rainbow reflector, and delivered it as part of the ransom, but the golden litter with the crystal and adjustment chassis was given by the Gods, and could not be replaced. It was too precious to them, and so an elaborate plan was hatched to hide it from the Spanish. According to what had been handed down to her verbally, the golden chassis and magic crystal was secretly carried to an old Inca fishing village, where her grandmother lived. The priceless artifact was then put on a large rattan and reed barge, and sailed straight west to an island called

Eiao. There, a secret Inca sect called the Mametaki hid the treasure in a cave--a place they call Hatutu."

"After she told me the story, she became very fearful that she had done so. So sincere was her fear, that I felt that there might be some truth in the story. That day, I had bought this bottle of Pisco, as we were in the marketplace. Returning to her grandmother's, I asked her to write the names down of the island and people she spoke of. Again, after long persuasion, she finally picked up a quill and drew a map and the names on a guinea pig skin. That afternoon, I was summoned back to the ship, and by that evening was back at sea."

"When I returned six weeks later, the girl was gone, the grandmother had died, and the house was empty. When inquiring about the girl, people would only point at the distant mountains."

"On our next shipment, we were captured and boarded by English privateers. The silver and galleon were brought back to England, and because of my medical skills, the Crown realized I had potential as a naval doctor, whereupon I received my extended education in London, and was impressed into Her Majesty's service."

Weynton stared in silence, wanting to hear more, but that was the end of the tale. "Do you still have the map on the guinea pig skin?" asked Weynton.

Patron, smiling, stood up, and rummaging through the chest locker, he pulled out the animal skin. Stretching it out on the table, he began to point out its secrets, having studied and memorizing it for years. The map showed "sugar loaf peaks" in the mountains, and had "Picchu" written next to it. A dotted trail led to the ocean village, showing a reed barge and sail. The dots continued across the skin to a crescent shaped island called Eiao. Next to this island was an X indicating Tuametaki Hatutu.

Weynton stared for a long time at the map. Sitting back in his chair, he rubbed his temple and pondered. "I've seen this place on the charts, Patron," answered Weynton. "C'mon, let's go to my cabin." When Weynton jumped up, he about fell over, realizing the liquor had taken hold. Grabbing the chair, he laughed. "Follow me." Both men stumbled on deck to the captain's quarters, beelining it to the captain's chart table.

"Let's see... due West of Peru... here. This chart--here." Unrolling the scroll, he ran his finger across to a group of islands called the "Marquesas." Pulling out his magnifying glass, he scrutinized and then pointed. "There it is, at the top of the island chain." A small crescent island that said Eiao and a dot indicated Hatutu.

Patron stared into the glass, and then looked up at Weynton. "I've never seen this chart, Captain," commented Patron.

"An Inca princess… a map on a skin… that's not much to go on, Patron," Weynton rubbed his whiskers.

"Captain, there was something about her, as if she was telling the truth, and it pained her to divulge it. It was as if it was the one thing of value she had, and she wanted to share it with me. It's haunted me all these years… her beauty, the memory, and the map, the only thing I have to verify the tale." Patron stared.

"Save the rest of that Pisco, Patron. That's good stuff. And put your map away. We're talking drunken nonsense. We might as well sail to California--gold is lying on the ground in nuggets everywhere. Why sail to some cave hidden on a lost island? But you spin a good yarn, Doctor. I enjoy your company. Let's turn in and sleep this one off."

"Good evening, Captain," Patron said as Weynton rose. Bowing, the doctor retrieved his map and bottle, and Weynton returned to his salon.

Shortly thereafter, Pearl tapped on the door and entered with hot soup and biscuits. Finishing his dinner, he went to bed, telling Pearl to blow out the candle. The voyage was over, and a long sleep was needed.

It rained all night, and the following morning, a foggy gloom and drizzle hung in the harbor. True to his word, Lt. Baylor now approached the Cowlitz with six large Songhee war canoes, pulling hard with oarsman. Weynton had been awake for an hour already, anticipating when the tide would be at most advantage to weigh anchor. The Cowlitz cast off six tow lines, and with the power of sixty oarsmen steadying her, the craft pulled up her anchor, and she slowly crept up to the point of the harbor entrance. It was obvious these natives had done this before. Calling out to one another to paddle harder, they expertly guided the Cowlitz into the harbor.

There it was, Fort Victoria. Carved out of a forest, the stockade and blockhouse were surrounded by a sea of tree stumps. Three whitewashed clapboard houses stood out against the dark forest backdrop. All along the North shore was a huge Songhee village. The beach was covered with hundreds of horizontal poles drying out large, cleaned fish in the air. The split board cedar houses were covered in painted deities, and tall poles carved in animal features protruded in several places, some with wings. Smoke covered the harbor and hung under the cloud cover, a steady rain continuing. A floating dock of logs extended out into the harbor, and very smoothly, the natives brought the Cowlitz alongside, enabling her to tie up at the floating deck of logs and split boards. The shoreline was a mob of Songhee natives blowing whistles, chattering a strange welcome song. From the fort gate came an entourage, beating a drum in cadence before a flag bearer. Behind, a contingent of greeters, with Sir James

Douglas riding a fine white horse, following. Arriving at the shoreline, the Songhee became silent. Weynton and his entire crew now walked down the dock to formally greet, with pomp and military order.

"Welcome to the Queen's colony, Captain Weynton," said James Douglas, saluting Weynton.

Weynton saluted back, answering, "On behalf of the Queen, our services are at your disposal, Sir," and bowed.

"Excellent, Captain. We have arranged a celebration in the fort, you and your crew being the honored guests," said James Douglas. "Your ship is in safe hands. Come, we have much to talk about." Turning his horse, he led the color guard and the crew up the muddy road to the fort gate.

Once inside the gate, the crew marveled at the interior of the fort. Neatly arranged barracks, store houses, a small chapel, and government offices circled the entire parade ground. A flagpole stood in the center, flying the Union Jack. A garrison of twenty Royal Marines manned the post, and several company employees were busy doing their morning tasks. A light could be seen flickering in the blockhouse, letting anyone know on the outside that someone was watching them. Weynton and the crew were directed to the mess hall, and upon entering, seated themselves at two long tables. The smell of eggs and sausages was in the air, with fresh bread and coffee being served by two Chinese servants.

Pearl sat with her Makah friends at the table, and excitedly began conversing with the two in Chinook Jargon. Sir James, who sat at the head of the table, overheard her. Intrigued, he brought his attention to their conversation. When the Chinese servant came to her with a pot of coffee, she began chattering in Mandarin. The Chinaman became big-eyed and smiled and answered in his native tongue.

Sir James watched out of the corner of his eye. He passed the plate of sliced bread to her, asking "Would you care for some fresh bread, young lady?" Now, Pearl answered in perfect English, "Thank you, sir. It smells so good," and took the plate, taking a piece and offering it to the Makah. Sir James was in marvel--his first impression of the girl was that of being a peasant Kanaka, but now realizing she was something more, having just witnessed her speak in three tongues.

Breakfast was served with Sir James Douglas giving a prayer, and the joyous crew now stuffing themselves with sausages and eggs. Upon finishing the breakfast, the crew was given a tour of the fort. One of the buildings contained a manufacturing facility. Two large blanket looms were clicking and clacking away, their native operators looking up briefly and smiling. Large tubs of wool were being dyed into bright colors, and spinning wheels were churning away, spinning wool into yarn, creating product for looms. Sir James explained that the blankets were used in trade, and introduced a red-bearded Scotsman, William Sallas, as the carpenter and genius who had constructed the looms. Pearl was in wonder, as she had never seen the likes of a machine that could make blankets.

Sir James continued his tour, and stepping out of the loom house, he pointed out other features of the fort. All of a sudden, Duto came swooping out of a fir tree, landing on Pearl's shoulder. Duto began his tirade of cursing and Pearl calmed him, answering and talking to him in Visayan, and showing him his medallion. Satisfied, he flew up and landed on the block house roof, calling *Caw Caw Caw*. The crew acted as if this were all normal, but the Marines and HBC employees were taken aback in astonishment. Sir James asked Pearl, "What did you say to that raven?" in total disbelief.

"I told him not to bother me right now--that I'm busy," came Pearl's reply.

"Is this bird a pet?" asked Sir James, still in disbelief of what he just witnessed.

"He's more of a protector. He watches out for my well-being," came Pearl's response.

James Douglas now showed the crew the visitor barracks, and ending his tour, he spoke to Weynton. "Captain, may I have a word with you in my office?"

"Of course, Sir. Lead the way," came Weynton's reply.

The office was well-appointed, with large windows to let in light, and a wall covered in books. "Sit down, Captain. I need to brief you on our situation here," Sir James invited.

"Before I offer you a drink, I need to get right to the point. As you are the captain of the company ship, you realize that my authority on land is as yours at sea. Alexander, the company is in a dire situation at this point. You're fully aware of the 1846 Oregon Treaty, the company relinquishing vast pastures and cropland on the Nisqually Prairie, now belonging to the Americans. The loss of revenue to the company is tremendous. And so, here we are, virtually starting over. I'll remind you of the 1849 charter the company has with the Crown--we having four years left to fulfill our contract of colonization. If we fail the terms, our company is gone in this region, and the King will send military and take government control. And so, Captain Weynton, right when we entered into this agreement with the Crown, a gold strike has taken every resource and man to California. We can't fail here, Captain. You have a ship. I have your port. As of this moment, Captain, I'm going to reveal to you that you have become a rich man, a way for the company to buy your loyalty. In the last six months, I have negotiated and purchased vast areas of "waste" land, shall we say. Presently, we have a sawmill to the north, and after logging several acres... by the way, which is some of your return cargo..." (*pausing, puffing, and then continuing*) "...our log crews are being harassed by a 'Cowichan' tribe. My few scouts say that the tribes to the north may plan an attack on the fort. With twenty marines and ten company employees, I'm afraid of the outcome. There are five hundred Songhees here outside the fort who have taken to whiskey and prostitution from Yankee whalers, and they've begun to become beligerant, as well."

At that point there was a knock at the office door. "Yes, enter," came Sir James's call.

The door opened and the person revealed. Sir James turned to Weynton. "Captain, let me introduce William Sallas."

Sallas held out his hand instead of saluting, and the two exchanged introductions.

"Sit down, William," came Sir James's request, arms held out. "I was explaining our situation here at the fort, William. You've arrived at a good time in my and the captain's conversation. I'll go on. One of our treaties and purchases are two islands just to the north." Standing and producing a rolled map, he spread it out on his desk, and revealed a peninsula to the north of the fort. Pointing out several fishing villages, he identified a bay called "Tsawout." "These people are our allies and ears. They have ceded these two islands to the east. We'll call the small one James. I'll keep that one, and this larger island, we'll call it Sallas." William gasped. "William, the north half of the island is yours, and the southern half becomes yours, Captain."

Weynton tried to interrupt, "Land--I have no need for land--I live at sea," came his reply.

Annoyed, Sir James ordered him to "stop" and continued. "There is a large island that is just to the east. It's called San Juan, as our Spanish friends were here first. There are large, open, natural pastures there. The problem is it's unclear as to who it belongs to--us or the Americans--as the treaty was too vague in this detail. And so some of your sheep will go to this San Juan Island, Captain, with herders, to extend our claim and colonization. We need wool for blankets, gentlemen. And so back to your sheep, Captain. I'm giving you each twenty sheep, a total of forty, and William will take the remainder to San Juan."

Both men were stunned now. Captain Weynton scratched his beard, and calculating, realized that by the end of his four year contract, he could be a rich man. "And who will shepherd this flock that you can trust--natives will eat them the first month!" exclaimed Weynton.

Sir James looked Weynton right in the eye. "The girl," Sir James replied.

"What! What girl?" Weynton was mystified.

"The girl with the raven--the one that talks to the bird," came Sir James's answer.

"She's just a child! I promised to return her to her homeland," protested Weynton.

"Captain, I need an informant--someone who can translate--keep me informed of the situation to the north with the Cowichan. The Chief of Tsawout and his son are my friends. They will assist the girl on your island with shepherding, and keep me informed with weekly intelligence. The girl speaks Chinook Jargon, I witnessed it, and perfect English, and God knows what else. She can be a huge asset to this endeavor--maybe even save all our lives here. And so this should be taken as an order by my authority," he explained, looking at Weynton. "Now, let me pour some scotch and celebrate our success in the perpetuation of our colony."

Weynton was speechless.

Sallas was joyous, realizing he was being handed the golden fleece--to own half an island and his own private flock of sheep! He excitedly chatted with Sir James, as Weynton stared in silence.

"Captain, we have your return cargo prepared and manifested: salted, boxed salmon and lumber. You should be underway and returning by week's end. I have three Christianized Songhee that can assist you on your return, as I was made aware of your crew shortages in our conversation at breakfast. I can spare no other manpower, I'm sorry, Captain!" said Sir James.

Weynton continued to stare, saying nothing.

"William, would you be so kind to assist the captain to officer quarters? There is a room prepared for him. If you'll excuse me," and invited the two to leave.

Sallas pointed at the building outside. The captain was already aware of it from his previous tour. Escorting him and holding the door open, they entered, finding a Kanaka house servant, who showed the captain his room. The captain now stared out a window. He spied Pearl, chatting away to a Chinaman hanging clothing on a line. A tear swelled in his eye--how could he leave this child in this wilderness, even worse as a shepherd on a lonely island!? He cursed himself. How foolish of him to let the girl come ashore--or any of them for that matter, the threat of desertion for the gold fields so real. How was he going to tell her--after he had promised her safe return?

At the stockade gate, a detail of armed Marines stood watch, as the offloading of the sheep had begun. Company Kanaka herders and two dogs guided the flock up the muddy road and into a corral at the blacksmith shop. Fresh water and hay were given, and a bleating of contentment was observed by the herders, the flock sensing the ordeal was over. The Singapore salt was now being offloaded as well, the barrels rolled down the floating dock on makeshift rails, and stored in a covered shed on the beach above the high water mark.

Weynton got himself cleaned up with a hot bath and neck shave. It was the afternoon, and he stepped out into the parade ground, lighting his pipe and inspected the sheep corral from a distance. Finishing his smoke, he now smelled food, and followed the fragrance to the mess kitchen. The two Chinamen were busy at their large cast iron stove. Pots simmered, bubbled and steamed, while the cooks added this and that, as they stirred and tasted. Pearl sat at a large chopping block, cutting up a large pile of potatoes. "Captain!" Her eyes got big when she saw him. "Sir, doesn't it smell wonderful in here?" she smiled.

Weynton laughed. "Yes. It is a delight to the nose." He nodded his head. "I see you're making yourself useful. So, tell me.... you understand what the Chinese are saying?" he cocked his head and smiled.

"Yes, sir! Back home, my granny Chinese--she teach me to cook--the language of food in Chinese is easy for me!" she explained.

"You're a remarkable young girl, Juana Pearl. You surprise me on a daily basis," the captain said, shaking his head. "Alright, I won't interrupt your work. After dinner, walk with me to the ship." He looked fondly at the girl.

"Yes, sir. I'd like that. Some of my things need to be washed before we return. The Chinese say I can wash them here," she gleamed.

"Yes, yes. Carry on, Pearl." Weynton turned and left the kitchen.

James Douglas observed Weynton strolling around, puffing his pipe, and left his office to approach him. "Well, Captain, the sun feels good today. I see you've found the luxury of our bath house," smiling and nodding at the captain.

"James, I want the utmost protection of this girl. She's like a daughter to me," blurted out Weynton.

"Of course, Captain. She will not be put in harm's way, you have my word. What is the girl's name, Captain?" asked James.

"It's Pearl. And when I come back, if she has been harmed or worse, you will deal with me, Sir Douglas--but as a man true to my word, as I have taken an oath to the company, I will honor that oath, and recognize you as my superior. Therefore, I will hold you to your word on her safety, and I hope you are successful," Weynton now looked directly into Sir Douglas's eyes.

"I was informed that Pearl is on kitchen duty, talking freely with the Chinese. Captain, I will assign William Sallas as her guardian. She will be in safe hands," Sir Douglas assured Weynton. "Have you told her of her new task, Captain?" asked Sir Douglas.

"Not yet--been trying to find the words. It's not easy. I'll speak with her after dinner," Weynton replied.

"Very well, Captain. Some of yours and my decisions are difficult. We must look ahead, and invest our energy to the future. Thank you, Captain." Sir Douglas walked on.

Dinner was a large feast that evening--venison, salmon steaks, oysters, fresh breads, and potato soup and steamed vegetables. Again, Sir James Douglas observed and overheard Pearl signing and speaking Chinook Jargon to her Makah friends. They were too overwhelmed with the feast before them to notice Sir James eavesdropping. The feasting went on into the June night, the stars sparkling through light cloud patches. After dinner, Weynton found the girl sitting on a bench outside the mess, laughing and talking with Pinto. They were feeding Duto scraps of salmon, laughing at his dancing and obscene language.

"Pearl, come walk with me. Good evening, Pinto." came the captain's greeting. The bird could see more hidden scraps of salmon, so he paid no attention to Pearl walking away with Weynton. Lighting his pipe, he puffed and walked the path to the Cowlitz, both of them avoiding and stepping around mud puddles of rainwater. The guard had given them a lantern at the gate, and Weynton had to hold it high so they could see the path. Seeing a campfire ahead, they found guards with a beach fire going. The dock and boat could be seen in the bonfire light, and another lantern was lit at the end of the dock.

At the catwalk up to the Cowlitz, a lantern hung on a pole, and an armed Marine stood guard. "Good evening, Captain. Your ship is in good order, sir," he said, saluting Captain Weynton.

"Very well, Corporal. Carry on," he replied, saluting back and climbing the plank to the deck portal, quickly unlocking his cabin door.

"I can't sleep in that bed, Pearl, at the officer's quarters. Somehow it's too confining." Weynton now uncorking his favorite whiskey in his cabin, pouring a shot and pounding it, and falling on his feather bed, he put his arms behind his head, staring at the ceiling. Pearl was now inventorying her few things, deciding which ones to take ashore.

"Yes, Captain. I feel safe in your quarters. I always sleep well in my hammock," answered Pearl.

"Juana, sit down, please." The captain continued to gaze at the ceiling. "How would you like it if your parents could live the remainder of their lives in comfort, having enough money to do so?" Weynton asked her without looking at her.

"That is my dream, Captain Weynton. How can you know what I dream?" She was now paying attention to him.

"Pearl--I'll make your dream come true, if you help me once more," he now turned and looked at her.

"I don't understand, sir. I'm confu--"

"Listen to me, Pearl. All of us in life follow the path that has been chosen by the Almighty. Your path is changing. James Douglas has given me title to half an island, and a flock of sheep to prosper it with. I'm asking you to shepherd this flock for one year, and having done so, will return you in one year a wealthy young woman. In the meantime, I will return your brother, Pinto, to your family, along with money to carry them until your return. Mr. Sallas has been assigned as your guardian. Your ability to speak English and Chinook has been recognized by the Chief Factor. I..." he now looked at her. She was sobbing quietly, tears flowing freely, covering her face with her hands.

"I'm sorry, Pearl. I know you want to go home, but if you can wait one more year, your reward will mean a good life for your parents," tenderly hushing her.

"I'm frightened, Captain. I don't feel safe unless I'm around you," she sobbed.

"James Douglas has sworn that you will be safely watched over. The island and sheep are a huge opportunity for you, Pearl. Sometimes in life, those opportunities are rare and extremely rewarding, depending on our taking action." He was now standing behind her and patting her on the shoulder. "Besides, you've got that crazy raven watching over you. You...." She turned and hugged him around the waist, and sobbed into his belly.

"There, there. Come now. Remember all I taught you. Keep your dignity and never show your fear. I'll be back. It's my job, and I've made a bargain with you. I shall fulfill your dream, and in one year take you back to the Philippines a rich girl."

"When will you leave?" she sputtered.

"Three days. Your brother will be returned to the Philippines. You have my word. He will be paid well," promised Weynton. "We'll talk about it some more tomorrow. Let's get some sleep. Dream your dream, only this time, it will come true."

She climbed back into her hammock, and he to his feather bed, and blowing out the candle said, "Good night."

The morning came for Pearl with a loud thumping, echoing through the hull of the Cowlitz. Weynton had been up early. Sleds of raw lumber were now arriving at the dock, being drawn by three mule teams. The consistently shaped and sized timbers had all weighed close to the same--an estimate of loaded weight was made, staying well under the maximum tonnage allowed. Heinz kept a close eye on the cargo being loaded. Kanaka and native Songhee were shouldering the large planks down the dock, a long procession of them. Delivering them to the deck, they loaded the beams into the hold, with a loud "pop," as they were neatly stacked. She arose, bundled all of her things into a pillowcase, and marched onto the deck. Duto immediately spotted her and flew down to the opposite shoulder the bag was slung over. She was angry now. She didn't know why, and gave Weynton a pouting mad look, as she left the ship. She took her kit up the trail, and now at the gate, was not even questioned, already a celebrity as the "Magic Bird Girl." The Chinese welcomed her back into the kitchen, and she occupied herself with the needed chores. She created a small nest and bed for herself in a back room, feeling secure with the Chinese.

Pearl had tied a blue cotton yarn to Duto's leg, identifying him among the dozens of other ravens at the fort. He wasted no time taking authority over all of them, the females all excitedly flashing for his attention. He still maintained his hideout in the Cowlitz stern mast, and now rivals were agitating him, knowing his hideout, and wanting to steal his treasure when he was preoccupied. And so he would make his rounds around the fort, and periodically, fly to the blockhouse roof, where he could observe the Cowlitz, and the safety of his booty.

The rain continued through the day as Weynton and Heinz supervised the loading. That evening, Patron returned to the ship from the officers' quarters, disliking his lumpy bed. The captain was grateful for his company, as the absence of Pearl was duly noted. Asking him her whereabouts, Weynton told the story of her present fate, shaking his head and saying he'd never forgive himself if she perished.

Patron became melancholy as well, the girl and the bird having become a joy in his mundane life. Both men drank heavily to drown their sorrow, with both falling forward onto the table, passing out, and the evening was over.

The morning came, gray, cold, and wet with misty rain. The boxes of salted salmon were to be loaded that day, along with stocks of fresh water and foodstuffs. At the mess table for breakfast, Pearl noticed her Makah friends were gone, and asked Yancy of their whereabouts. She was told they had slipped away in the night, having bartered a skinning knife and some fish hooks for a canoe. Being twenty-five miles from their village, they would not be seen again.

This was her last day with Pinto, and they spent the day quietly chatting in their dialect, at one point going to the small chapel and praying for salvation. She had several messages--tell Mother this, tell Father that--Pinto sensing her anguish of being left behind, and trying to reassure her.

That evening, at dinner, Weynton was informed of the Makah disappearance. "I expected so. They have no contract with the company. They served the Cowlitz well. I wish them luck." He then muttered, "God help us with these Songhee. They will have to sleep on deck. The men will mutiny if they are quartered below, the smell so overpowering. That fish oil they cover themselves with--it's toxic to a civilized man's senses. Mr. Heinz, pass the gravy. Pearl, how was your day?" Weynton asked, trying to be cheerful.

"Good, sir. I translated for the Chinese today with Lt. Baylor. They have not been able to understand the list of foods they requested, and so all are pleased that the list has been made and now understood."

"Excellent. And have you settled in?" asked Weynton.

"Yes, I have a room behind the kitchen. Mr. Sallas has given me a poncho of oil skin, a raincoat," she beamed.

After dinner, the smoking and storytelling began. Weynton requested Pearl to show him her room, and leading him to a back storeroom, found her pallet the Chinese had made for her. A wash basin and small mirror hung on the wall.

"Here, hide this somewhere safe--a small bag of silver shillings. Use it for an emergency," and Weynton passed her a small, weighted leather pouch. "It's not much, but it's all I have at this point, being awarded an island instead of money. You'll be safe here. One last hug," he requested, and then pushed her back. "I'll say goodbye in the morning. We leave on the morning tide." He patted her on the shoulders, turned, and departed.

The remainder of the evening, she wrote a letter to her mother and father in spanish. Pinto quietly watched, assuring her he would not lose it, and promising delivery to their parents. She could think of nothing else to tell them, only to be patient, and that she would return.

The following morning came all too soon, the Cowlitz bustling with activity at first light. Duto seemed confused, after finding Pearl and landing in the kitchen window. *Caw Caw Caw*! She knew he was upset, as he sensed the ship was leaving. Realizing that his nest was leaving port, he paced in the windowsill, cussing loudly. Now understanding his worry, she dressed and walked the trail to the ship. The Songhee were now dragging their longboats down into the water, the departure minutes away. The Cowlitz was still tied to the dock. She came aboard, and the bird landed in his lair on the stern mast. All of the crew were aware of Duto's treasure hideout, and now realized someone had to fetch it, and bring it to Pearl. Confiding in Yancy, she took the bird with her to the captain's quarters, preoccupying Duto, and Yancy retrieved the hodge podge of shells, glass, shiny rocks, and baubles, placing them in a bundled rag, and tying it shut.

Patron and Weynton were going over charts when Pearl was told to enter, after knocking. The doctor gave her a large hug and handed her a parcel, telling her to open it after they had departed. Weynton was stoic, and fearful he might lose his composure. Patting the girl on the head, he assured her that he would return. He then said, "Be gone. Long goodbyes are not in order. Twelve months will pass quickly. Good luck, my dear," and pushed her toward the door.

As she came on deck, Heinz was shouting, "Stand by to cast off!"

She no sooner stepped off the gangplank on the dock, when it was swung aboard. The ship now released its grip from the dock. The Songhee pulled hard on their oars, turning the Cowlitz bow towards the sea.

Frantically, Duto flew back to his stern mast hideout, and realizing it had been pillaged, went into a cursing rage. The girl shone her medallion at him, and landing back on her shoulder, she revealed the contents of the rag bundle, quickly calming him.

Weynton, Patron, and Pinto waved at her from the stern, and soon they were around the point, and had disappeared.

William Sallas was waiting for her at the end of the dock. Pointing towards the fort, he said, "Come. We have much to do."

Sallas Island

William Sallas and Pearl walked back up the trail to the fort. Duto flitted from tree to tree, calling down to her--she ignoring him. "Pearl, you and I have been invited to dinner tonight with James Douglas. You need to bathe and put on your best clothing. I was told for both of us to be there at 6 o'clock," he informed Pearl as they walked.

"Mr. Sallas, I have no shoes and only a sailor's shirt, but I will wash my shirt and comb my hair. It's the best I can do," came Pearl's reply. Walking through the gate and arriving at the mess kitchen, Sallas bid her a good day, promising to return that evening.

The Chinamen were kind hearted, knowing she was depressed about being left behind, and busied her day with friendly chatter and chores in the kitchen. She washed her ragged shirt and hung it out to dry in the kitchen, close to the stove. At the bathhouse, a Kanaka boiled water for her and gave her a bar of lye soap to use. The bath invigorated her. Returning to the kitchen, a Chinaman combed her hair, pinning a small violet on the side. As he promised, Mr. Sallas arrived, wearing his Sunday best shirt and black polished boots.

To be invited to the "Big House" for dinner was a prestigious honor. James Douglas had his own Kanaka cook and house servants, as he, his wife, and children never dined in the mess hall of the fort. They walked across the compound to the Chief Factor's house, and arriving at the front door, Sallas knocked lightly.

A Kanaka servant opened the door, greeted them warmly, and led them down a hall to a closed door. Hearing several voices behind the door, Pearl became extremely nervous and pulled on Sallas's sleeve. "You go--I'll go back to the kitchen," she pleaded.

"Nonsense. Just say nothing. I will do the talking," Sallas scolded her.

The Kanaka tapped on the door, and now another servant opened it from within and gestured for them to come in. James Douglas sat at the head of the table, and upon seeing them, he stood and warmly greeted them. "Come in, come in. Please come and sit over here," he said, pointing at two chairs, the table filled with people all staring at them. "Of course, you all know William Sallas, our loom caretaker, and with him tonight is a new member of our colony, Miss Pearl. Pearl, this is my wife, Amelia, and sitting next to you is my daughter, Cecilia." Now remembering the manners Weynton had taught her, she bowed her head at both. "And this is our second in command, Gov. Richard Blanshard. Of course, you know Lt. John Baylor." Again, she bowed at both men. "And sitting across from you, my two Tsa-wout friends, Joseph Bird Tree and his son Tomas Broken Shell. Please, both of you sit down."

The table was set with silver servers, the room well-lit with oil lamps and candles. A kitchen door was asked to be closed, and James Douglas made a quick and reverent prayer, asking for benevolence. The kitchen door was again opened, and two servers brought pitchers of spring water and red wine. Pearl sat quietly as Sallas directed the Kanaka to pour only water for her.

Cecilia, sitting next to her, was of native blood, her mother being a Cree. She wore a fine silk dress and had ribbons woven into her braids. She took a glass of wine, winking at Pearl.

The pouring complete, James Douglas raised his glass and proposed a toast to the Queen's Colony, and again, "Here, here! God save the Queen!" was exclaimed, and glasses were clanked. The silver servers were now uncovered by the Kanaka, exposing a feast of roast chicken, vegetables, potatoes, and breads.

The banquet was now well underway, with people laughing and joking. Cecilia was now very friendly with Pearl, asking her how old she was. "I'm thirteen. How old are you?" asked Pearl.

"I'm fifteen. So nice to have a new friend. Where are you from?" asked Cecilia.

"I"m from Leyte, an island in the Philippines," she explained.

"Excuse me, ladies." James Douglas was now directing his attention to Cecilia and Pearl. "If I may interrupt," looking Pearl in the eye, speaking perfect Chinook Jargon, "Is the food good?" he asked her in the trade tongue.

Pearl was a bit surprised, as her conversation with James Douglas had always been in English. He had spoken fluent Chinook for years, working at several trading posts and forts in western Canada. He married a Cree princess from the Great Lakes area, and becoming a model company man, had risen through the ranks to become the Chief Factor--the highest rank of the HBC.

Now, without hesitating, she responded to Douglas, "*Muka-muk klose* (food is good)."

"*Ya-kwak-tin pahtl* (belly full)?" he asked her, at which point the two Tsa-wouts began to laugh and Pearl answering.

"*La san-jel kwutl* (belt very tight)," which brought out a roar of laughter from James Douglas and the Tsa-Wouts. Joseph Bird Tree now asked Pearl, "*Klootshman pil-pil chinee* (are you a Chinese woman)?"

Pearl replied, "*Klootshman pil-pil Filipina*," and now a lively conversation began between the four in Chinook, oblivious to the others around them.

110

Amelia excused herself and graciously allowed Pearl her chair so she could sit next to her husband and the two natives and converse.

James Douglas now explained in Chinook to Pearl that Joseph Bird Tree and Tomas Broken Shell would assist her in shepherding on Sallas Island. Daily, they would canoe to and from their village to check on her and give information gathered from the area about the Cowichan intentions. A monthly company boat would supply the sheep station, and the information would be reported by this means. If reports came in of immediate danger, Sallas and Pearl were to canoe back to the safety of the fort.

Now she was beginning to understand why James Douglas had put his focus on her. Anyone not knowing her would perceive her as a common native shepherd girl, not knowing of her remarkable gift of communication, making her a perfect mole or spy.

"Very well, William. All seems understood here. You and Pearl will be escorted with the sheep by a marine detail. The Songhee will be paid to deliver you safely. You'll leave day after tomorrow. Joseph and Tomas will arrive next week. The marines and Songhee will be there long enough to build you a base camp. Three days, I'm guessing. Any questions?" asked James Douglas.

"I've prepared at the company stores our kit, Sir James, as discussed in our previous briefing," he replied, "but there is one problem. Pearl has inadequate clothing, and provision was not made for this in your list of supplies, sir."

"I've got clothing for her," blurted out Cecilia. Both James Douglas and Sallas looked at her, realizing "problem solved."

"Excellent idea, my fair daughter. I admire your generosity, as your father," explained James Douglas. "Please excuse yourselves and take care of this clothing issue," replied James Douglas.

Pearl had never been in such a fine house in her life. Tapestry rugs covered the floors and gilded portraits of English heroes lined the walls. Cecilia led her up a set of wide stairs to a long hallway with several doors. Pushing one open, she invited Pearl in. Cecilia was one of several children of the Douglas family, but she was spoiled more than the others. Large walnut bureaus held silk socks, trousers, and undergarments. A long brass rack held silk and calico dresses, jackets, and blouses. A dozen pair of various shoes and boots were stored in boxes. Selecting one, Cecilia offered them to Pearl.

"Try these boots on. They are too small for me, as I have grown out of them," she offered Pearl. Pearl had never owned a pair of shoes, and Cecilia sensed her awkwardness of trying them on, assisting her in lacing them. She clip-clopped around the room, the new sensation making her smile. Soon,

Cecilia had her outfitted with canvas breeches, a warm fleece jacket, and a knitted wool sweater. Pleased with her work, she stood back and admired Pearl in her new clothing, exclaiming, "Now you're ready for Papa's sheep business. The cold and rain won't bother you."

Pearl was overwhelmed with joy. The clothing and boots transforming her into a different person. She couldn't stop saying thank you to Cecilia and hugged her with delight, laughing and running her hands over the tailored and fitted garments. A tap came at the door, and Amelia entered, telling the girls the guests had gone home and that it was bedtime.

William Sallas was waiting for her at the bottom of the stairs, and upon seeing her in her new clothes, he let out a long whistle, exclaiming, "Look at you!" As Sallas walked her back to the kitchen, Duto swooped down from the block house, confused by her new appearance, and landed behind her, hopping along the ground and following her. Sallas informed her to get a good night's sleep as the next day would be busy and long, packing supplies and preparing to canoe to the new sheep station.

The following day, Sallas awoke her early. Using her Chinook language skills, he gave orders through her to the Songhee on loading the canoe with supplies. Six canoes would be used--one for supplies, one for Marines, and the other four for hauling sheep.

That evening, Cecilia found Pearl in the kitchen helping clean up and gifted her with another bag of clothing. The Chinese had made blackberry pies, and the two girls laughed and indulged themselves at the chopping block, eating half of a pie. Wishing her luck, Cecilia hugged her and departed, the long day over, and Pearl worn out with the chores and preparing.

The morning came, and at first light, the Chinese woke her, feeding her in the kitchen. The Marines and Songhee were already at the beach, preparing to launch. Five sheep per canoe had been hobbled and blindfolded to keep them calm. All twenty bleated simultaneously now, assuring each other of the other's presence.

The rain was drizzling, and she wore her oilskin poncho, her new clothing keeping her warm in the cool marine air. Sallas had acquired a native, cone-shaped hat and placed it on Pearl's head, the rain now dripping off its brim, protecting her from the dampness. A guard of four armed Marines accompanied them in their canoes. Satisfied all was in good order, a command was given to push off, pulling a small, empty seventh canoe. The flotilla of canoes was now underway. Duto had perched himself next to her on the canoe rail, confused as to where she was going. Several of his new friends flew overhead, circling and *caw caw caw*ing, disapproving of Duto leaving the fort.

Now, rounding the point of the harbor entrance and heading north, she could see several islands in the distance. A following, southern breeze helped their progress, and by noon, a large island with a rocky beach was approached, with all canoes safely beaching. Using Pearl as a translator, the Songhee were ordered to unload the sheep and supplies on the beach. A Songhee who was familiar with the island and two armed Marines escorted Pearl and Sallas on an exploratory walk, seeking a suitable spot for a shelter and camp.

The island had been the victim of a forest fire several years prior, and open grass meadows and tree stands were checkerboarded across its terrain. The Songhee guide showed them a spring, bubbling from a small hillock, and close by, a large glacial boulder, the height of ten feet. Within four hours, they had explored the entire island, and Sallas chose the large boulder as the site of their camp. The landing beach was covered with large, bleached driftwood logs. Setting up their white tents, the Marines built a large bonfire, and the expedition settled in for the night on the beach.

The following day, Sallas showed the Songhee laborers the large boulder, the site he had chosen. Using Pearl to communicate, he explained what he wanted for a shelter. A large, rectangular pit was to be dug that butted up next to the boulder. An A-Frame was to be constructed over the pit, using the boulder as the back wall--a wind barrier. The Songhee divided forces, some digging out the pit, others sent back to the beach to begin splitting and making boards, from cedar drift logs on the beach. Using axes, mallets, and wedges, the natives worked through the day, stacking a large amount of planks at the pit site. The pit was dug to a depth of a man's knee, and on the second day, planks were laid up in an A shape above the rectangular hole. By the third day, a fine shelter had been constructed, with a small, iron stove installed at the back of the structure, adjacent to the boulder wall.

The sheep had fanned out across the island, realizing that no predators were around. By the sunset of the third evening, the natives and Marines were preparing to leave the following morning.

The A-frame cabin was warm and accommodating, with the stove heating the large face of the rock and kept it warm through the night. Pearl had brought her few belongings, and had saved Dr. Patron's package to open for a special occasion. When Sallas asked what was in the package, she answered, "Let's find out," and cutting the string and unwrapping the paper was delighted to find a "Spanish Bible." Sallas asked her, "May I have a look?" Seeing it was written in Spanish, he questioned her, "Can you speak Spanish also?"

"Yes. The nuns taught me to read Spanish. Our mass was always given in Spanish," she explained.

113

The cabin was furnished with two bunks on either side, and Pearl had been given a small chest to keep her things in. Placing her new treasure into the chest, she climbed into her bunk, blew out the candle, and bid a good night to Sallas.

The next morning, the Marines were up early, anxious to get going. After a quick breakfast of tea and biscuits, they bid Sallas and Pearl farewell, and soon, the six canoes were underway, heading south back to Fort Victoria. They had promised to return in one month with more sheep and supplies, and now the silence of the island replaced the Marines laughter and the Songhee's construction and chattering.

Sallas had been warned by James Douglas to guard the girl's safety and that no improprieties should occur. Sallas was fully aware of Captain Weynton's warning about her safety. The captain's size and demeanor was enough to command fear of his wrath.

The first days were spent making the cabin more comfortable. Sallas had dug out the spring, and a small pond of fresh water was now available for the sheep. Duto had found a large hollow in an ancient fir tree that had been struck by lightning. Pearl had opened his bag of treasure from the fort, and he busily relocated it up to his safe lair in the tree. There were other ravens on the island, and he quickly made his dominance and authority known.

Their fourth day on the island, Sallas wanted to explore more, so he and Pearl took the small canoe and circumvented the island. On the north shore of the island, a huge, long narrow sand spit reached out into the channel. Looking directly across from the sand spit to the mainland, a native village could be seen in the distance, wisps of smoke rising from plank houses on the beach.

Sallas and Pearl beached their canoe on the spit and walked across the sand. Several squirts of water shot in the air as they walked along. Sallas realized they were in a giant clam bed, and finding a large, discarded empty shell, he used it as a shovel to expose the buried clams. Within minutes, he had several dozen and stowed them in the canoe.

On the east side of the island, looking east, a large group of wooded islands could be seen across the channel, and the dome of a large white mountain lay even further in the distance, its base obscured by the islands. Directly to the south, a huge mountain range of snow-capped peaks commanded the vista across the Strait of Juan de Fuca.

That evening, Sallas made a fine clam chowder, using flour and wild herbs for flavoring. He showed Pearl how the clams had to be placed in a bucket of fresh water to make them spit the sand out from their innards. Then, steaming them, their shells opened, and they were ready for the chowder soup pot.

114

The evenings were spent with a small beach fire, Pearl reading her Bible, and Sallas recording the days' events in his journal. Stories were told by Sallas about a Fort Okanogan, far to the east, where blankets could be traded for a fortune in beaver furs, at an annual rendezvous. The sheep had acclimated well to the island, plentiful grass and forest shrubs to nibble on. And so, after one week on the island, routine and mundane chores had become the daily pattern.

As promised, on the morning of the eighth day, John Bird Tree appeared in their camp, stepping out of the forest and stood before them before either one noticed. "*Tyee, kla-how-ya* (Chief, how are you?)" Pearl greeted him in Chinook.

"*O'lo-mam' ook pi-ah pish*! (Hungry, let's cook this fish!)" he answered and handed a nice, fresh salmon to her he was carrying by the gills.

"What did he say?" asked Sallas.

"He wants to cook this fish. He's hungry," replied Pearl.

The beach fire was still smoldering from the night before, and soon, Pearl had it crackling again. John Bird Tree splayed the fish open into two halves and propped it up next to the fire on some green sticks he had cut from the forest. Pearl and John entered into a lively conversation in Chinook, Pearl translating to Sallas, who would acknowledge and ask questions through her. "Has he heard of any reports of trouble from the Cowichan?" asked Sallas. Relaying the question, John shook his head and answered that most of the Cowichan were fishing the summer run of salmon right now, and he had not heard of any trouble coming.

Caw caw caw came the cry from the tree tops, and Duto swooped in and landed on Pearl's shoulder, continuing his cursing. Knowing what he wanted, she pulled the thong necklaces up from under her shirt, showing him the medallion and medicine bags. Instantly gratified and calmed, he flit from her shoulder to a beach log and strut up and down its length, eyeing John Bird Tree. John Bird Tree was wide-eyed and astonished at what he had just witnessed. By now, Sallas accepted it as routine and chuckled at John, laughing at his bewildered look.

"*Kah-kah ta-ma-no-us shikhs*? (That raven is your magic friend?)" asked Bird Tree.

"*Skook-um se-ah-host*. (He is my spirit eyes.)" she replied, pointing two fingers at her eyes.

John and the bird stared at each other for a long moment of silence, and then, uttering a series of clicks and *tit-tit*s in a strange tongue, the bird hopped over and jumped onto his knee, answering with the same sounds of clicking. John let out a roaring laugh, and the bird flew back to his lair, cawing and being his usual obnoxious self.

115

"*Ik-tah wau-wau*? (What did you say to him?)" Pearl asked John Bird Tree.

"*Kah-kah tyee itl'-wil-lie.* (I am Raven King, as a man.)" He now smiled back at Pearl and quickly changed the subject.

He asked her for her attention, as he had something they should know, explaining, "My people once lived on this island, as you are here. It is a good, sacred place to us. But there is a tribe to the north, the Haida. They are pirates and marauders, stealing everything and taking slaves. They come with one hundred war canoes, having sent out scouts, to find unsuspecting villages. There is nowhere to hide on this island if they know you are here. They will find you. For safety, we moved our people to the mainland. There, we have time to flee into the interior. My people have learned to battle them, and we have medicine that they are afraid of, so they leave us alone. They will see your smoke someday and come. They are still fishing in the north. But soon, if they come this year, you must know this. Make your fires inside at night. We have seen your beach fire every night from my village which says, 'We are here!' Show no smoke with your fire in the day. Make smoke at night. Tomas Broken Shell and I will come daily to the northern tip of the island, where you dug your clams, and watch for them. We have time to escape if we see them first."

Fear now began to overtake Pearl as she translated to Sallas what was being said. She had already been the victim of slave piracy on the other side of the ocean, and the horror of that day was still fresh in her mind.

Seeing her trembling, John Bird Tree patted her on the head and explained she and Sallas would be safe, that they would see them first and could outrun them to the mainland shore. Even now, he explained, his son Tomas Broken Shell, was watching the northern approach to the island.

Now with frantic eyes, Sallas quickly kicked sand on the beach fire. The salmon was cooked and ready to eat at the moment he realized the smoke they were putting up was a signal of their presence.

Seeing the fear in their eyes, again John Bird Tree laughed it off. Breaking a bow off of a fir tree, he used it for a plate to hold a large, steaming steak he cut from the rack and began chucking large chunks of fish into his smiling face. He reminded Pearl of Lolung, the Black Ghost in the tree. He had tattooed lines on his face and curled shells in his earlobes. His soothing aura and fatherly ways soon had Pearl and Sallas calmed down and laughing, once again.

The old elder stayed the entire day and gave them a tour of the island from his perspective. He showed them a burial ground and advised them to avoid it. On the west side, he showed them an oyster bed. He showed them

116

edible plants with medicinal uses at different locations. He was bothered that the sheep had been into his gooseberry patch, and he was annoyed about it.

They found Tomas Broken Shell, concealed on a promontory above the beach, lacing together a new pair of moccasins. John Bird Tree pointed out the vast vista of islands and channels that could be seen from the lookout. Now, Sallas and Pearl understood the value of seeing the pirates first and that their escape window was short, upon sighting trouble. John explained that their camp was the best spot for them, as the north half of Sallas Island camouflaged its presence from someone observing from the north, looking south. It was the smoke that both the natives emphasized was the danger.

Now, with two hours of daylight left, John suggested the two should head back to their cabin. He pointed out his village, across the channel, saying one particular dwelling was his house. He bid them farewell, saying he would be there in the morning to stand watch. "*Caw caw caw*," came a call from the tree top. "*CaCawCa*," answered John Bird Tree, and Duto relocated to a hidden spot and observed Pearl's next move.

Back on the trail, she, Sallas, and Duto arrived back at the A-frame as darkness fell. No beach fire tonight was the new law of the land, and they waited until total darkness to light their stove inside their cabin. Clam chowder, pan biscuits, and tea were beginning to be the standard meal.

The following day, Pearl volunteered to check on the sheep and see if John was there, as he had promised. Sallas agreed, as now splitting firewood for the stove was a necessity. They finished their tea and biscuits, having let the fire burn down to smokeless embers.

She found the flock of sheep at the spring pond, and all was in good order. Duto was enjoying himself this morning as a group of his friends landed from tree to tree, tagging along on the trail.

Now, coming into sight at his lookout post, John turned and acknowledged her presence, as the ravens had forewarned him of her arrival. He was carving a beautiful paddle, and every couple of minutes he would look up and scan the horizon briefly. Talking in Chinook, they carried on a lively conversation. The ravens all quietly sat in surrounding trees, watching the pair. Now satisfied with knowing he was there, she said goodbye, as the walk back to camp was arduous in the drizzling rain, and she had promised Sallas to be back by noon.

Arriving at camp, Sallas had split and cut a nice pile of firewood for the camp stove. Pleased she was back, he felt better after she told him of finding John at the lookout.

The days became weeks, and either John or Tomas could be found daily at their lookout post. Sallas kept a calendar in the cabin, hanging on the wall. As planned, on the thirtieth day, a flotilla of canoes could be seen coming from the south. Lt. Baylor arrived with his detachment of armed Marines and the Songhee canoes, along with twenty more sheep. Soon, they were offloading onto the beach, with the sheep un-hobbled and blindfolds removed. Four crates of foodstuffs were carefully stored in the cabin, and Sallas handed his written report to Lt. Baylor, stating no issues with the Cowichan, as the tribe was fishing to the north. He stated that his concern was about a tribe to the far north, the Haida. He further stated that the sheep were all healthy and that the TsaWout were at their daily posts. Staying only an hour, the flotilla was back on its way, returning to Fort Victoria.

It became Pearl's daily chore to make the morning walk, check the sheep, and confirm that John or Tomas was there. She would bring them biscuits and sweet jam, which they devoured in delight. Every day they would meet, a large number of ravens and Duto would watch from above, in the canopy of the forest.

John would give them treasure when he was there, and they waited like children for their rewards. He offered them small shells and shiny stones. *Click*ing and *cluck*ing, he would call a certain one down from the tree, reward the bird, and laugh as the others called out for their turn.

Soon, Pearl was learning the strange *click* and *cluck*ing sounds, and the ravens began to respond to her calls. If it wasn't sounding right, John would correct her and make the proper *click* and *cluck* tones. Weeks went by, and daily, she would meet at the lookout, with either John or Tomas, learning more and more about the ravens and their language.

John had heard the Cowichans were now done fishing, and their want of whiskey was driving their passion to attack the fort. John suggested that James Douglas parlay with them and give them the whiskey, as their numbers could surely overwhelm the fort. The report was given to Lt. Baylor. Wisely, James Douglas was able to buy some time, arranging a parlay in the weeks ahead and promising the liquor.

It was now the first of October, a chill in the night air. Pearl noticed Duto acting sluggish, his feathers in disarray. He was grumpy, and cursed as his feathers began to molt. It was difficult for him to fly, his new feathers not fully plumed.

One morning, he landed on her shoulder as soon as she stepped out of the cabin. He began cursing and calling out in Visayan, "Give me my medicine! Give me my medicine!"

His medicine! She had forgotten all about it. Lolung had told her to give him one pellet, when he molts, and his heart would be made new again.

Duto was pulling on the neck thong now, as if it were extremely urgent. Pearl calmed him down, and stepping back inside the cabin, she opened the pouch around her neck for the first time. A sweet smell of flowers was noticed when she first opened it, and carefully unfolding it, she found around two hundred green pellets packed together in a small clutch. Gingerly, she pulled one from the mass and carefully folded the cache back into its necklace pouch. As soon as she stepped back out, the bird was there on her shoulder, and she fed him the medicine pellet. He gulped it down and went *"klick klick klick klick,"* shook his head, and returned to his lair.

She made her walk to the lookout that morning, checked in with Tomas, and anxiously returned to the cabin. She and Sallas had decided to canoe over to the oyster beds that John had shown them that summer.

The tide was out, and finding a sandy bite to beach the canoe, they found an exposed beach covered with thousands of oysters. Sallas had brought a large burlap bag, and in no time, it was hard to lift.

That night, Sallas steamed several in a pot on the stove. Two imperfect pearls were found, which brought up the conversation of the pearls found in the Sandwich Islands--the ones she had stolen from Kamehameha. She still had them in Weynton's tobacco pouch, and retrieving them from her storage chest, displayed them to Sallas. Sallas was flabbergasted, as he knew their value was large. The two pearls they had found in their dinner oysters were a dull white and not perfectly round. The Sandwich pearls were a creamy white and glowed, being perfectly round. And the black one--it was hard not to stare in wonderment at it. It was her proud possession—her namesake now--and she carefully counted them and put them back into her chest.

Sallas was in a talking mood, the oysters gratifying his soul. He explained to Pearl that the next supply boat was to bring twenty more sheep, which would be taken to the San Juan Island. Before the flotilla arrived to pick him up, he was ordered to have scouted the northern tip of San Juan Island, for a good landing spot for beaching the sheep. He had put it off for several days, for fear of the Haida. He could no longer wait. He would go tomorrow in the canoe, cross the channel, and be back in three days. For her safety, Sallas wanted her to go with John or Tomas back to their village for the two nights and return each day to watch the sheep. Sallas questioned Pearl if that was alright with her, that he now trusted John and Tomas, as they displayed Christian values, and he felt she would be perfectly safe.

"I'd love to go to John and Tomas's house!" cried Pearl. A chance to get off the island appealed to both of them, the monotonous and mundane chores of their time there beginning to wear on them.

"Good. I'll walk with you tomorrow to the lookout. We'll explain the situation to John." Sallas pondered. "When I get back from the island, we'll shear the wool from our sheep," he told Pearl. "Alright, lights out. We'll get an early start in the morning."

They were up early, ate more oysters for breakfast, and divided the remainder, some for Sallas and his scouting trip, the others to be taken with Pearl to the village as a courtesy. Tossing Pearl's bag over his shoulder, they were off on the trail that was well blazed by now. Duto and his friends always remained above and ahead of them, the birds enjoying the daily routine. Finding John at his post, he was busy cracking a fresh, cooked crab he had brought for his breakfast--a large, flat rock being his table.

Pearl explained what Sallas had told her the night before, conferring in Chinook. John smiled and shook his head, and then explained that the Haida danger was passing, as by now, it was too late in the year for them to be this far south of their home islands, and yes, he would be delighted to introduce Pearl to his family.

Pearl showed him the bag of oysters, and he laughed. "*Chet-lo wapato kloshe*! (Oysters and potatoes so good!)" he cried.

Now wishing her well, Sallas was on his way back down the trail. John finished his breakfast and threw the scrap shells out on the ground around him, his ravens swooping in and quarreling over them. John made a harsh cawing and *klick*ing sound, and the birds became quiet immediately.

Pearl asked him how he acquired his gift to talk to the ravens, and he explained to her,

"Among my people, one must go on a fast and search the forests for a guiding spirit in life. Sometimes it takes years to find it, but once you do, the spirit communicates to you, and your heart is then given up to that spirit on a daily basis. For your reverence to the spirit, it watches over you.

"I was a young man, searching for this vision, and had been in the forest alone for several days. I was unfamiliar with the area, and one day, a bad wind and rain storm struck. I stumbled along looking for shelter in the dark, when I stumbled and fell down the side of a steep path. I landed under the base of a huge fir tree. The size of its trunk broke the wind, and I fell asleep in the dry needles at its base, feeling lucky to have found it in the dark.

"The next morning, the sun woke me as it shone on my face. As I lay on my back, I looked up into the tree, and staring back at me were a hundred

120

ravens, all being quiet and watching. When I lifted my head, they were all standing around me, silent. One big fellow jumped on my chest and began to *click* and *cluck*, dancing on my heart. In my mind, I knew what he was saying-- that they were there to protect me, and to follow them, as a large, killer bear was in the area.

"Somehow, I found myself *click*ing and *cluck*ing back to him, saying I would follow. With that, the flock rose into the air, and I followed them back to the shoreline. In gratitude, I dug clams, broke them, and fed them, and they have been with me ever since."

"Where did you get your Christian name, John?" she asked in Chinook.

He explained, "A few years after meeting my raven friends, I went with some traders to a fort, far to the south. We canoed many days, then took a trail to the Nisqually, and from there to Fort Vancouver. There, I met James Douglas, who insisted I be baptised, and we became friends, as he speaks Chinook very well. Because of this, he returned with my trading party. He liked the harbor he found on the south of the island and chose his site for Fort Victoria.

"We've been talking all day. Look, the sun is falling," pointed out John. "We go now to my house." He waved her up.

His canoe was hidden behind some driftwood on the sand spit. In short order, he had the girl and her bag of oysters loaded and pushed them off the beach. Now paddling away from the shore, Duto glided down and landed on her shoulder. Both she and John laughed at him, not wanting to be left behind.

The tide was changing, and the current was strong. John paddled for a point far upland from his village to allow for the drift. The village was appearing larger as they approached, and now, Pearl could make out details of the place. A longhouse lay parallel to the beach, totems and fish drying racks scattered all along the front. To the north of the longhouse were four separate houses which were heavily carved and painted. John pointed out his house--a huge beak of a bird protruding from the face of the house, with a feathered raven's body painted on the wall. The eyes of the painted bird stared out to sea, as if warning its presence. The beak served as a covered porch.

From out of nowhere, John's ravens came swooping in from Sallas Island and landed on the house, using the roof line and protruding beak as a roost. Their canoe was now a hundred feet from the beach, and Duto was up and away to join his friends.

Children were running and playing, and a woman emerged from a door under the protruding beak and met them on the shoreline, as the canoe beached. "Pearl, this is my wife, Sweet Smoke." Immediately, the two women began to chatter in Chinook. John laughed at them and walked away.

121

Sweet Smoke was gray-haired and had three dark lines tattooed on her chin. When Pearl gave her the bag of oysters, she laughed and said, "Yes, yes, come in. Come in, child."

John had disappeared, and so holding her hand, the elder woman led her up to the house. It was enchanting. The porch floor was smooth and polished cedar planks. The protruding beak provided shelter from the rain. On either side of the door, two smaller painted ravens greeted you.

Upon entering, Pearl had to adjust her eyes. Rays of sun lit the interior. Beams of light shone through a smoke hole in the ceiling, glowing through a smoking haze. Whale oil lamps flickered on either side, the smell of fish overwhelming.

Sweet Smoke called out to the inhabitants, scattered about in its dark shadows. Someone made a joke, and there was much laughter, easing the tension of the moment. Soon, cousins and aunts were all around her, enjoying the new company of the girl named Pearl, that they had heard so much about. A large, stone hearth was in the back with several iron pots that were steaming with fish stew. The walls and pillars were carved with beautiful spirits of their guardian world. She caught herself staring at their raw, magnetic beauty, as the spirits were always staring back at her. A long table ran down the center of the home, ending at the hearth. The children got out a shell and stick game and taught her how to play, while the elders set the table for a small feast.

John appeared, and calling everyone to the table, said a prayer to *sagh-a-lie ten-as* (God Child--Jesus) in Chinook, everyone bowing their heads and putting their palms together. Another prayer was said to the raven, and other spirits were mentioned, as well.

The evening was full of games and stories, food, and laughter. For the first time in a long time, she lost herself in the attention and the wonderful culture she had entered. Having eaten so much, everyone retired one by one. Sweet Smoke unrolled a fresh cedar mat for Pearl to sleep on. She was asleep within minutes.

She felt her shoulder shaking. It was John. "Time to get up. Let's go," he whispered in Chinook, "It's raining." Putting on her oil skin and conical hat, she found the front door left ajar, so she could see it. John was on the beach, holding the tail of the canoe, waiting for her. Pushing off and underway, Duto made his morning appearance, demanding to see his medallion. Satisfied, he hopped to the head of the canoe and scouted ahead, acting important, and occasionally muttering, "Dirty bastards! Dirty, dirty bastards!" John recognized the English curse words and scolded Duto with the *klicka klat* talk. He gave John a look and winked his eye.

122

John pointed out some ominous clouds to the north, saying a storm was coming. He paddled hard with Pearl in unison. The wind came up, and white caps began breaking around the canoe. They reached the slack water of the Sallas Island sand spit as the wind and rain began a furious thrashing. Squalls of dark columns of water approached, the wind now howling.

Once off of the beach, the wind and rain weren't as violent in the forest, and both she and the old elder made it to the cabin in a quick fashion. Pearl got the fire going, as the rain would wash away the smoke in short order. Duto rode the storm out in his lair, his friends finding shelter in various places in the forest. John had some dried fish, and so a stew of potatoes was boiled up.

The storm continued all day, making it impossible to return to John's house that night. The next morning, the storm had passed, and John resumed his post at Look Out, while Pearl found her flock of sheep, and all were accounted for. She fretted through the day, and soon rejoined John at his lookout. They were chatting with the birds, and suddenly John jumped up, and pointed to the south of the channel. It was Sallas, on his way back. "Quickly, I must go," she told John.

Returning to her cabin, Sallas was already there, exhausted. She got some embers glowing and made Sallas a stew. He briefly described his ordeal. Crossing the channel on the morning of his quest, the tide had carried him to the northern tip of San Juan Island, at which time the storm had come up. The tide was carrying him out to bad water, and he desperately paddled to a small island, the current ripping and racing on either side. Finally, beaching in a small bite on the little island, he felt fortunate, as the sea was blowing and capping hard. Stranded on the little island for the day, he quickly realized he was in a burial ground. Hiding the canoe and building no fire, he hunkered down for the night. The following day, the storm had passed, and now just a short distance away on a head land, he could see a fine sand beach. He paddled to it, and within five minutes was standing on the sandy beach. Finding a trail up from the beach, he followed it and arrived at a promontory. He could see a great distance, with open patches of meadows sprinkled through the forest. His return by canoe was less eventful, but he was exhausted from all the paddling, fighting with the current and tide. He got in his bunk and was sleeping deeply, instantly. She pulled out her Bible, read some verses, prayed, and blew out the candle.

Sallas was up early the next morning. Today, they would shear the sheep. He had built an ingenious corral around his water pond so that the sheep could come in at night to water. By closing a hidden gate, it was easy to capture the animals and shear them for their wool. Pearl would hold a cloth over their eyes while Sallas hobbled their legs, and with Pearl holding their necks, Sallas would have them shaved in five minutes. The work continued all morning until they had a mountain of wool, and with the last one schorn of his wool, the product was stuffed into two large, canvas sail bags.

That evening, Sallas discussed their options with the wool. It belonged to them, but the only buyer was the HBC, and since there was no competition, a tuppence was paid. The wool at the fort was being spun into yarn and woven into blankets with the looms that he had built for the company. It was as if he was a slave to his own creation. And then that's when he hit on it--he'd build his own, and Pearl could weave it!

Spinning the yarn was easy and boring. Weaving the loom was a skill Sallas would teach Pearl. Building the loom, he had two choices--build a primitive loom, or buy the milled lumber to build it as he had done at the fort. He then explained his lack of funds. Hearing all of this, Pearl volunteered. "I have some money. Weynton left it for me--the captain. I'm sure he would like to see his sheep farm making blankets."

Joyously, Sallas assured her that her investment would be tenfold and that wool blankets were what the natives wanted, and their margin for trade would make them wealthy.

And so it was. Pearl invested Weynton's shillings for a blanket business. Both she and Sallas would capitalize on their situation and resources and would survive on their far away, isolated British colony.

The monthly supply canoes arrived on time with the twenty sheep to be delivered to San Juan Island. Accompanying the entourage was Charles John Griffin, an agent of the HBC, assigned by James Douglas to scout and colonize the San Juan Island. Assisted by two Kanaka sheep herders, they were the company's investment to fulfill their contract with the Crown in England.

The canoe party wasted no time on the beach at Sallas Island, offloading the supplies and quickly delivering them to the sheep camp. Two armed Marines were to stay with Pearl at Sallas Island, camped on the beach in a military tent. Sallas got the party underway, taking advantage of the tide to carry them across the Strait of Haro to his landing spot he had discovered.

Because of Sallas's scouting trip, he safely guided them across. Approaching the northwest tip of the island, he found his sandy beach. Griffin and his Kanaka sheep men were joyous in finding the island's inhabitants were friendly. Lummi fishermen, who lived in a hidden cove in a longhouse, wanted to trade with the company. These were winter camps, with most of the people at other locations, roaming the Salish Sea to harvest its bounty of fish. Griffin and his herders found several old native fish camps that appeared to have been abandoned for some time. Sallas and Lt. Baylor bid them good luck, and they returned to his namesake island.

Lt. Baylor and the supply party camped for the night on the beach at Sallas Island, roasting salmon and eating oysters. Pearl produced her small bag of shillings, as she and Sallas explained to Lt. Baylor that they wanted to requisition the supplies, to build a loom.

Days turned into another month gone by, and the supply flotilla arrived with more sheep to be delivered to San Juan Island. William and Pearl were pleased, as the finely milled lumber and hardware for their loom were neatly bundled in one canoe. Lt. Baylor acknowledged that James Douglas was delighted with their new colonial enterprise.

Sallas worked full time on the project now. He constructed a shed to house the loom and then began the meticulous assembly of the design he kept in his head.

Pearl had her daily routines now, checking on the sheep, digging clams, picking berries, and visiting with either Bird Tree or his son at the lookout station on the north bluff. Pearl and Duto always enjoyed John Bird Tree and his flock of protectors, talking, chattering, and teasing one another.

She was now talking with the birds as John had taught her, using eye movements, *klick*ing and *kluck*ing and *caw*ing in response. She would pick up shiny stones and shells on the beach and use them as rewards, the birds becoming in a frenzy, to be awarded a prize from her.

The birds in the perimeter canopy kept a vigilant watch over the two, taking turns swooping down as they were called out by her. John Bird Tree realized the girl had a gift and was one with his same spirit protection. He realized she had been sent by one of the Raven Spirits. In their long afternoons of standing watch, he divulged much of his learnings to her, fascinated with Duto and his devotion to the girl.

Back at the A-frame cabin, William taught Pearl how to spin the yarn on a spindle, which was now their evening pastime. The loom was finally finished and Sallas demonstrated its workings to Pearl. Coaching her for several hours, she now had it working like a science and could produce a blanket in two days. It took four sheeps' wool to make one blanket. With the forty sheep they had, within a month, they had ten wool blankets, a trade commodity that could sustain them on the island.

Pearl's communication with the Tsa-Wout was now producing bad reports of an uprising from the Cowichan. Two more months went by with the regular supply canoes delivering more sheep for San Juan Island. An invitation was sent to Sallas and Pearl to spend Christmas at the fort with James Douglas.

San Juan Island

James Douglas had arranged for two more Kanaka herdsmen to stay at Sallas Island over the Christmas celebration, giving Sallas and Pearl a chance to celebrate the year. Cecilia was thrilled to see Pearl again, the two having bonded previously. Pearl was anxious to hear of any news about Captain Weynton's return in the Cowlitz to Fort Victoria. All that James Douglas could do was assure her of his scheduled arrival in June, and that he would be pleased with her blanket enterprise, as was he.

The Christmas dinner was a grand affair in the Chief Factor's house. Afterwards, the Chinamen had created fireworks from black powder, and put on a grand display on the parade ground. Small rockets were shot into the sky, and a string of firecrackers were lit, scaring the Indians around the fort. James Douglas had to call for "enough," as the Songhee were now wailing in their village, thinking they were under attack from the fort.

Calm was restored, and the rainy evening came to an end. Staying in her kitchen quarters, the Chinamen laughed and giggled about the evening's surprise fireworks show. Pearl was fascinated with the firecrackers, and without hesitating, the Chinamen gave her a large string of poppers, wrapped in wax paper.

The new year came, 1851, and Pearl and Sallas went back to their endeavors on Sallas Island, tending the flock, weaving blankets, and assisting in the monthly shipment of sheep to San Juan Island. Pearl continued her afternoon meetings at Lookout Point, the Indians and ravens putting on daily entertainment.

Pearl and Sallas used empty supply barrels as vats to dye their wool in, and soon, Pearl's blankets took on a design of her own.

John Bird Tree put out the word among the Saamich tribes of Pearl's blankets being offered for trade, and she was invited back to his Raven House to trade with the local Saamich. Because of her Chinook Jargon skills, she acquired a large amount of otter and beaver fur along with dried foods of berries and fish. It would take two canoes to ferry all the goods back to Sallas Island.

Pearl had been accepted as one of the family in the Raven House, and her visit was extremely enjoyable, she being showered with loving attention.

The morning of her return from the trading venture at Raven House, John and his extended large family were helping to load the goods onto the canoes on the beach. During this activity, Pearl wanted to explore the beach to the south and informed John of her morning walk, and that she would be back in a half hour, walking the mile long beach.

Duto was waiting for her as usual, and hopped from drift log to drift log down the beach, cawing and making his presence known. Reaching the end of the beach at a rocky spit, she returned and could see John's family, still loading the canoes in the distance. She was within thirty yards of the canoes and houses, when out of the forest and onto the beach came two brown bear cubs, cavorting in the sand. Pearl stopped and laughed to herself, as the two rolled and tumbled in play, not seeing her. As she stood and watched, all of a sudden, out of the forest, came a huge brown bear, lumbering down to the water where her cubs cavorted.

Duto landed on Pearl's shoulder and squeezed it, showing fear but no sound. The huge bear now stood on her haunches, having detected danger in the air, and sniffed her nose into it, as she turned and saw Pearl standing on the beach. Instantly, Duto sang out a call of emergency, continuing in a frenzy, calling for backup from the Raven House. And now, the monster dropped to all fours and was charging Pearl at a quick speed. Duto launched from her shoulder and flew directly into the face of the charging giant, and got her to stop. She began to swat at him. By now, a hundred ravens were on the two cubs, pecking and tormenting them, making them squeal in terror. Hearing and seeing this, the mother bear now turned her attention away from the girl and charged back at the flock that was attacking her cubs. The ravens scattered on her arrival, but now the flock got between Pearl and the bears on the beach. The sow had enough, snorting loudly, and then guided her cubs back into the forest.

John Bird Tree and his men came running down the beach with spears and bows, but the incident was over as quickly as it had happened. John Bird Tree praised the ravens, and everyone on the beach now was in awe of Pearl, sensing that she was protected by big medicine.

She returned to Sallas Island with the bounty of trade goods. The story of the bear attack did not please Sallas, as he remembered his commitment to her safety. Sallas rewarded Bird Tree and Broken Shell with a blanket, pleased with the trades that had been made.

Spring came, and the last days of May brought high anticipation of the arrival of the Cowlitz and Captain Weynton. The Cowichan had contracted influenza through the whiskey trades, and an epidemic was sweeping them. The Saamich were nervous, knowing they could be next, hearing wailing cries from distant islands of the Death Song.

This report reached James Douglas through Pearl and Sallas, via the supply canoes, as reports were coming in from all over the region of an epidemic. The supply canoes arrived at Sallas Island a week late in June, explaining the Cowlitz had arrived. Presently, she was being loaded with lumber at the log dock at Fort Victoria.

Pearl was elated! She had survived the year, and after fulfilling her debt to Captain Weynton, was now ready for him to take her home. Sallas hated to see Pearl go, but by now was totally aware of Pearl's background, and understood her desire to return to her parents and culture.

"Did you see him, Lt. Baylor?" asked Pearl. "Did he ask about me?" asked Pearl to Lt. Baylor.

Lt. Baylor scratched his chin and invited Pearl to sit on a beach log. "Pearl, I've been directed by James Douglas to disclose the unfortunate news, that your Captain Weynton was dishonorably discharged from the service of the company. I'm sorry." Lt. Baylor now stared at the girl.

"He's not on the Cowlitz?" Pearl cried in disbelief.

"No, ma'am, far as I can tell, it's a totally different crew--except there's one fellow, a 'Yancy.' I believe I recognize him from the year before," said Baylor.

Sallas, now overhearing all this, said, "Pearl, go back to the fort. I'll take care of the sheep."

Pearl had not been at Fort Victoria for six months, the Christmas visit now a distant memory. As the canoes entered the harbor and the Cowlitz came into sight, she was stunned at how much it had already changed. A dozen houses were now outside the fort, with fenced pastures around the stump land, and small garden plots everywhere to be seen.

The Cowlitz was at the dock, a scene of activity, loading lumber. Duto found his old roost above the block house roof. Pearl first found her Chinese cook friends upon entering the fort. They confirmed what Lt. Baylor had told her, that Weynton and his crew were gone.

Now wanting to know the truth of the matter, Pearl, without hesitation, barged into James Douglas's office and broke into tears. "What happened to Captain?" she wailed in tears.

James calmed her down and told her to sit down. "I'm sorry, Pearl. Our Captain has hit on some bad luck, or he's a scoundrel and deserves his fate. I'd like to think he's a victim of a bad situation, and I do not wish to judge him until I hear his side. I'll tell you what I know. On his return, a whaler in distress signaled him for assistance, and not just any whaler--it was a Queen's whaler. He refused to come about and assist, and abandoned the queen's merchant whaler, and her want of help. The whaler got lucky, recovering her stores from another passing whaler, and returned to England via the Argentina Horn. The whaler reached London ahead of the Cowlitz, who had returned from around the "Cape." When the whaler reported the Cowlitz's conduct to the Admiralty in London, Weynton and his crew were arrested, on arriving in London. They are no longer employed with the company. That is literally all I know, Pearl. I'm so sorry you're so disappointed. Go find Cecilia. She wants to see you," he said.

Bewildered, Pearl walked out to the parade ground. Seeing her, Duto landed on her shoulder, told her he was going to the Cowlitz, flapped his wings, and away he went. Pearl followed, walking out the gate and down the road to the dock. Sitting at the dock smoking a pipe was Yancy, Duto's foul-mouthed friend. Duto landed at his feet, and the sailor gave out a roar of laughter, the two now cursing each other out.

Arriving moments later, Pearl laughed with joy to see the old salt and the bird going at it verbally. "Miss Pearl," greeted Yancy, now rising and taking a bow, "such a pleasure to see you again," he smiled.

"And good to see you, Yancy," she laughed with joy. "Please, tell me of the captain and my brother, Pinto," she pleaded.

"I was hoping to see you," replied Yancy. "I'll tell you what I know. Here, sit down," he offered up his box he was sitting on and re-lit his pipe. "When we left Victoria last year for Owyhee, we hit a terrible storm a week out into the Pacific. It was so ferocious and continuous that it pushed us far to the south, way off course, before it finally subsided. Our fresh water supplies had been tainted and salted with raging seawater. When Captain Weynton could finally plot our location, we had to make for the closest islands to find water. That island turned out to be in the north of the Marquesas, having to sail into the southern hemisphere to find water. Upon finally finding this atoll, a group of islanders took pity on us, and helped us. In a few days, we recovered enough fresh water to carry on. For some reason, the islanders turned from very helpful and peaceful, to very violent and threatening. Feeling our lives were in danger, we quickly got back underway, heading back to Owyhee. Somehow, the islanders had tainted the water with a voodoo herb, and the entire crew began to hallucinate. It was during this period that a whaling ship was passed by--and Weynton, fearing we all had some kind of spreadable disease, kept going, refusing the ship aid, protecting it from doom. We remained in this stupor for some time--days--until the tainted keg of water had all been drunk. After opening a fresh keg of water, that had not been voodooed, we recovered. These incidents were a blank in the ship's log, as days went by until Weynton and our crew recovered. The missing report did not go well when we landed in London. Our story was not believed by the courts, as the whaler reported us to the authorities as scoundrels. For some reason, the company fired the whole crew except for me, saying my conduct in Owyhee was good and that I had performed well under harsh conditions.

"What happened to my brother, Pinto?" she pressed him.

"Ah, yes, Pinto. I almost forgot. Weynton was true to his word and took your brother back to Matalom, hoping to see James Brooke again. Weynton escorted your brother ashore, they said their goodbyes on the beach, and we made sail for the China Sea. Never did see Brooke, though."

"Can I come back on this trip? Tell the captain I can work for my passage home," pleaded Pearl.

"After what happened on the Cowlitz last year, the company has abandoned the Far East Route--too many pirates. We're going round the Horn, Miss Pearl. The Cape days are over."

The reality of her situation was now overwhelming—the year-long anticipation of waiting, and now everything had changed. She was earning wealth now, with her blankets in demand. Her flock had grown threefold, and now Weynton was gone. It all belonged to her now. She couldn't abandon the flock, and Sallas needed her. And she had become part of Bird Tree and Broken Shell's family. She believed Weynton would come back, and so it was her duty to maintain his holdings until he returned. She walked back up the road to the fort, and this time, politely knocked at James Douglas's office door.

"Come in. Ah, yes, Pearl. I'm glad you're back. I've been thinking about your situation. Sit down, let's discuss things," he said, looking up from his desk. James Douglas was fully aware of her feelings and now expected the decision she was giving him, "to stay" and wait for Weynton to return.

It was now agreed that the current situation was prospering on Sallas Island, and the supply canoes and sheep deliveries were to continue to San Juan Island. Bird Tree and Broken Shell were to continue as "scouts"--eyes and ears for the trouble from the North, rewarding them with trade tokens at the fort.

"Pearl, tell Bird Tree that I have reports of Tlingit and Haida raiding in the North. One of our outposts, Fort Selkirk, was burned and looted by war canoes. Tell him to be extra observant--keep a keen eye," James Douglas explained to her. "Also, there are reports of a German measles epidemic coming down the whole Pacific Coast. Do not intermingle with strangers outside the fort. I'll have Lt. Baylor return you to your island tomorrow. Get some rest, Pearl," and Douglas ended the conversation.

Pearl got her otter pelts graded at the commissary and was pleased with her two large boxes of trade goods she received. She visited with Cecilia in the Chinese kitchen, and the day ended quietly.

The next day, her return to Sallas Island was uneventful, and Lt. Baylor departed within ten minutes of putting her on the beach, returning to the fort. William greeted them on the beach, pleased she had filled the shopping list he'd given her. All too soon, she was back at her routine, tending the flock in the morning, checking on the lookout, and returning to weave the loom or spin yarn. She had given Bird Tree the message from James Douglas, and now there seemed to be more of an urgency and nervousness at the lookout post. Bird Tree and Broken Shell no longer played the games with the ravens, but just sat quietly, and stared out into the straits for any movement.

One morning, she found Bird Tree at his usual perch, and beside him was a large seal skin bundle. He arose, and picking the bundle up, held it out to her--a gift from his family to her. Excited, she asked to open it, and untying the leather cord, found a beautiful, carved, black raven mask head with a cape and wings of black feathers. Bird Tree explained that she had become powerful medicine to his family, after the bear incident on the beach. The family had lovingly created the regalia, and if she would wear it and dance at the next Potlatch, she would be protected from all evil. Pearl loved it, and the old man helped her put the raven mask on, her arms draped in the black feather wings, with a mantel of feathers covering her legs.

Duto and his friends went berserk, hopping and dancing around her. Bird Tree explained the dance she must make, and to observe her teachers, who were shaking their tails and doing hop-hops. Cawing and gyrating their wings, they fluttered in the air all about Pearl. She began to copy Duto's movements, and soon, it was telepathic. She knew the next move he would make, and she would make it in unison. Bird Tree laughed heartily as the two were now on the same wavelength, and it was comical to see the two interact, even delighting the other ravens of the performance.

"Enough!" laughed Bird Tree. "Yes, you have the power, Pearl, and you can use it to protect yourself against the Tlingit. You see, the raven is sacred to all tribes on the forest water. We have many different raven societies, stories, beliefs, and customs. Each tribe has their own view of him as a spirit. Long ago, my people lived on the San Juan Island. We prospered there, the shellfish being numerous. We were attacked by Tlingit Haida, and we called our protector ravens upon them, who attacked them on the beach, as they approached our village. There were a thousand ravens, and they swarmed upon them, many having their eyes pecked out. They retreated, but others on the other islands did not have our protection, and they were taken away as slaves to the north. My people now feared the isolation of the island, and they moved to where we now are, being able to flee if a heavy attack occurs. If they come again, I'm hoping our protection can call our raven friends again, and attack them on the beach, as they attacked the bear on the beach that was going to kill you. So put your bundle away. We will potlatch in October, when the ravens molt, and you will be a holy one in our society."

That evening, Sallas was happy to have her company again and asked about her day. She explained the wonderful Raven Dance, and how she and Duto had connected mentally. Sallas had created a large map of San Juan Island, with charted islets, sheep camps, fishing villages, trails, and watering holes. He had named an islet "Pearl," that he had first landed on in the storm, and she was proud to point it out and put her finger on it, even though she had never been there.

The lambing season had been good. The blankets were piling up, and summer days rolled by. One morning, arriving at the lookout, Bird Tree was not there. A low mist of rain fell across the channel, the mainland barely visible. She reported it to Sallas, having a bad feeling, as she knew he or Broken Shell should be there. Sallas shrugged it off, saying, "Let's wait and see."

The following morning, she found the same conditions, no one at the lookout. It was raining hard on the mainland and channel. Sallas was alarmed now. With no scout posted, the island was vulnerable to a surprise attack, with no chance of escaping. He and Pearl would canoe to Victoria tomorrow to report the situation.

That night, a roaring Nor'wester ripped across the inland's seas and islands. Pearl and Sallas were up all night with the whale oil lamp burning, as trees could be heard crashing to the forest floor all around them, from the raging wind. The high wind continued through the next day, and the seas continued as rolling white caps.

The wind finally subsided, and both she and Sallas searched the island for spooked and stray sheep. They both arrived at the lookout on the bluff, with no sign of Bird Tree or Broken Shell. Looking across the channel, and now being able to see the distant village, Sallas was bothered by the fact that he could see no smoke coming from their cooking fires. "Alright, Pearl. Let's get these sheep all bunched at the water pond, and we'll take the canoe to Victoria. Something is wrong," as Sallas stared out at the distant village.

"I'll stay. The flock needs me here. You go, I'll be fine. I've become one with this place. The ravens will protect me. Go. Go quickly. What has happened to Bird Tree?"

"Alright. I'll return with answers and help. I promise to be back tomorrow. God, forgive me for leaving you here, but yes, two hundred sheep need vigilance, and I believe we have sixty blankets produced in stock--a small fortune. Let's get back to camp. I'll leave immediately."

Taking an overnight kit with him, she helped him lift the concealed canoe and carry it to the water. The water was calm, the day was bright. She watched him paddle out into the channel and head south towards the point. She watched him until he was just a speck, and then another speck, and another, and which speck was he? All of a sudden, specks were everywhere, her mind confused as to what she was seeing.

Canoes!--war canoes, a hundred if not more! She could no longer tell which canoe was Sallas, but could see them clustering in one area. She panicked and ran from the beach. By now, Duto was aware of the danger. Her mind raced, the war flotilla approaching from the south. How can it be? At the cabin, she put out the *Caw Caw Caw Caw* call, and Duto flew into the sky, frantically calling for protectors, and disappearing over the canopy.

Duto was now talking to her through mental telepathy, telling her to put the mask on. "The Raven Mask! Bird Tree said if I danced in the regalia, I would be protected from evil," Pearl recalled. Pearl untied the bundle, and without hesitation, she put the Raven Mask on along with the winged cape of feathers, hurrying and trembling with fear. She racked her brain. "What else? What else can I do to scare them away?" she wondered, looking through the cabin stores. The firecrackers! The Chinese Firecrackers--if they attacked the cabin, she could throw the firecrackers out the door and maybe scare them away. She could now hear them in the distance, rowing towards her beach. Staying in the dark of the forest, she dodged from tree to tree, until she was at the beach. There they were, a fearsome sight. At a quarter mile, she could see their tattooed faces, with pikes and spears in the air. A war chant was heard, as they all rowed in unison.

Duto was now telepathing her, telling her to "dance on the beach log, as we had done that day with Bird Tree." "I'm coming, trust me, dance on the log now," he mentally told her. She appeared now onto the beach and began to hop down it, doing the dance that Duto had taught her. A great cry and commotion came from out on the water, the Tlingit seeing the Raven Spirit dancing on the beach. One lone canoe approached, slowly, as Pearl continued to dance and twirl on the beach. She could see their faces, and in utter horror, she realized she could see Sallas's head on a spear, extended from the bow.

They were a hundred feet away now, and she felt she was going to faint from fear. Suddenly, *Caw! Caw! Caw!* It was Duto! He had returned and immediately went in to the synchronized dance with the girl. Duto kept telling her in Visayan, "Keep dancing, damn it! Keep dancing, damn it!"

The war canoe had come to a stop, and all were mesmerized and entranced by the Raven Dance. All of a sudden, from out of the north and across

133

the canopy came a cloud of 1,000 ravens, diving at the lead war canoe, and attacking the eyes of the Tlingit. Screams of fear and pain could be heard across the water, as the birds relentlessly dove and attacked from all directions.

The war canoes were in full retreat now, and regathered a half mile off the beach. The ravens now returned to the canopy of trees on the beach. Pearl slipped back into the forest and retrieved the firecrackers at the cabin, returning to a hiding spot on the beach. Now, Duto gave a command for another attack, and the black cloud of ravens flew at the flotilla again, challenging it to leave the area.

Pearl sparked her steel and flint fire starter, and the Chinese firecrackers exploded across the water, the unrelenting flashes and pops peppering the beach. That was enough for the Tlingit. Before the ravens could be upon them again, they paddled frantically to get out in the eastern channel, and soon, as quickly as they had appeared, they had disappeared.

Pearl hid for a long time in the forest, tracking the flotilla in the shadows from the east side of the island. The ravens now all kept their distance, ranging in the treetops all over the island. They watched her from a distance, as she still wore the regalia, its medicine having been displayed. She stayed hidden on her way back to the cabin. Arriving, she fell inside and latched the door, collapsing and sobbing on the floor.

The horror of Sallas's head on the spear was rampant in her mind. She trembled in fear, and passed out from total exhaustion.

Caw Caw Caw. She awoke, still wearing her mantel of feathers. The mask of the raven was looking at her, as she opened her eyes. *Caw Caw Caw.* The mask stared at her. It was Duto! He was calling her. She arose and stumbled outside. The bird immediately landed on her shoulder, wanting to see his treasure. Flashing it for him, he relaxed and indicated to her she was safe for now.

Duto wanted her to follow him, and he flit from one rock to another, calling her to the beach. She cautiously peered out at the beach and seashore from behind the last tree. Duto beckoned her once more, from a drift log on the beach. Looking at him, she now saw it--a column of smoke in the southern distance. After ten minutes, she could see it was a large vessel. It was now a mile from her, and a cannon shot was fired, skipping a ball into the eastern channel.

She was the Hudson Bay steamer the "Beaver." Two paddle wheels on her broad sides pushed her along at four knots. She pulled up into the anchorage of the bite, now swinging into the wind and dropping anchor. She gave a loud blast three times on her steam whistle, and Pearl waved her arms to answer. Her davits were swung, lowering two longboats, and soon, two platoons of armed Marines were on the beach, directed by Lt. Baylor. Baylor found Pearl still wearing her plumage of feathers. The Marines were transfixed with her appearance. Lt. Baylor soon had her briefing him, his first question being, "Where is Sallas?"

She sobbed and told him the story. Bird Tree having disappeared, the terrible storm, and then Sallas leaving for help, and then the attack occurring. Lt. Baylor then informed her of an attack on a Port Gamble, to the south. The Beaver was now chasing the attackers, and how many canoes were there? Which way did they go? The Marines swept the island, and returning, informed Lt. Baylor that indeed, she was the only one there. The Marines made camp on the beach, and Lt. Baylor wrote his field report to James Douglas. The Beaver did not stay long, and returned to Fort Victoria.

The camp was somber. If Pearl was right about what she said, 1,000 Tlingit warriors, in one hundred canoes, were somewhere to the north. Many of the Marines had known Sallas. The thought of him being murdered and decapitated infuriated them. Lt. Baylor spent the night in the cabin. Pearl feared being alone, and her shock still overwhelmed her.

The Beaver arrived the following morning from Fort Victoria, anchoring at the same spot as yesterday. Soon, a longboat was making for the shore with another group of armed Marines aboard. Lt. Baylor was waiting for them there. Beaching, a corporal stepped out, saluted, and handed the lieutenant a leatherette of dispatched orders. The Lieutenant entered the mess tent to get out of the wind, and soon had the orders unfolded, reading them with eyeglasses. Lt. Baylor looked up at their faces and spoke,

"I'll read you boys the orders… and you too, Pearl. Listen up." He began reading, "Upon receiving your intelligence, and with other news coming in throughout the region, a decision has been made to change Sallas Island to a strategic, military observatory, and the existing sheep farm is to move to Bellevue, of San Juan Island. By my authority, William Sallas's sheep shall become the property of his heirs, and that Juana Pearl will maintain the flock, and is to accompany her flock and loom to Bellevue, transported as soon as possible by the Beaver. Mr. Griffin, camp supervisor at Bellevue, has been ordered to assist her well-being and comfort. Be advised--the TsaWout village has been wiped out with measles and fever. Reports are the whole village perished. I have bad feelings about our friends, John and Tomas. Proceed with this order immediately, and protect the island accordingly, setting up a twenty-four hour watch on all perimeters. Godspeed. Expect provisions and further orders after the Beaver returns to report." Signed, James Douglas.

Pearl fell into the sand and wept. Bird Tree, Broken Shell, and their beautiful family and village were no more, as if extinguished like a candle flame. Her only friends were now all gone. She was being "ordered" to another strange place. Lt. Baylor patted her on the head, and all the Marines assured her she was in safe hands, and that San Juan Island was a much safer place, now being populated with Kanaka and Englishmen.

Pearl composed herself, and Lt. Baylor reminded her of the urgency of the orders. She estimated they had two hundred and fifty sheep, and that it would take two trips, the bulk of the work ferrying the flock in the longboat out to the Beaver, resting at anchor.

Preparations were made, and early the next morning, the Marines had one hundred twenty-five sheep crammed on the deck by 10 AM. Pearl had her belongings bundled and stowed. She would travel both trips, her presence assuring the flock of sheep and calming them.

The loom was dismantled and carefully transported and loaded onto the Beaver. Wasting no time, they were underway at 11 AM, setting a course for southeast. The Beaver crossed the strait in slack water, and cautiously steamed down the west coast of San Juan Island. By 5 o'clock, a settlement could be seen above a fine little harbor--a floating log dock reaching out to deep water. The Beaver had hailed here many times before. Her skipper expertly pulled her bow up to the end of the dock, and had her safely tied up in minutes.

A clapboard house could be seen on the bluff, surrounded by rail fences and shed outbuildings. A large flock of sheep could be seen to the south in a huge, sweeping pasture.

Pearl tenderly helped offload the flock, having names for several and knowing their personalities. By the time the sun was dipping behind the range of mountains to the west, the offloading was a success. The creatures were safe in a corral with feed and water.

Pearl spent the night on the Beaver, given quarters by the captain, knowing she was important to James Douglas. Duto had found a safe roost on the wheel house, and had stayed incognito and out of sight.

They returned early the following morning, arriving at Sallas Island in the afternoon, having to buck a strong tide in the strait. She boxed the few remaining things in the cabin and rolled up the map of San Juan Island that Sallas had created. It was hard for her to go. She had found peace and security on the island, had made good friends, and now it was to be a distant memory. The following morning, by 9 A.M., the last of the flock had been loaded. Without hesitation, the Beaver weighed anchor, her steam whistle sounding their departure. Her paddle wheels began to churn, pushing her out towards the strait.

The beach of Sallas Island was now a cluster of white military tents, and several beach campfires smoldered smoke from the night before. Suddenly, from over the forest canopy came a cloud of ravens. They swarmed and circled above the Beaver in an endless circle, staying above her as she crossed the Haro Strait. Throughout the crossing, several would land on the Beaver, resting a few minutes, then taking flight. Upon crossing the strait, the multitude of ravens landed in the forest of San Juan Island. During this display, Duto remained on the wheel house roof, calling out to his companions and encouraging them on.

As before, the Beaver arrived that afternoon at the Bellevue Cove, and had the flock of sheep unloaded by nightfall. John Griffin, the camp supervisor, provided Pearl with a spare room in the big clapboard house. At dinner, she explained her past two years on Sallas Island. The Kanaka and camp laborers had all been invited by Griffin to meet the new colonist. They all had heard tales and rumors about her, and her reputation and notoriety preceded her. The Natives all recognized her as a walking, Raven Spirit deity. And now, here she was, sitting at their table. Quickly, she was recognized for her knowledge as a sheepherder. The conversation turned to the everyday chores and techniques, and they all traded information and jokes.

John Griffin announced his plan for her flock of sheep. He had determined that the north end of the island needed further development, and that two Kanaka herdsmen and she would relocate to those pastures, to build a new cabin and station. The company had pushed a road north from Bellevue down the center of the island, with several branches breaking off to different springs and pastures. He now unfurled a large rolled map of the island, covered with spring locations, open pasture locations, camps and stations. The road dwindled out to the northern tip of the island on the map, and was marked as a trail to 'Sallas Landing' and 'Pearl Island.'

John Griffin pointed out a small cove on the north end of the island marked 'Lonesome Cove' on his map. "Here is where to build your cabin. A spring is close by," he pointed on the map. "Here, to the west, is a Lummi longhouse, a fishing village, who supply us with salmon for our salt boxes. They are friendly and on good terms. Tomorrow, you can move your flock, and my workers will escort you and help build a cabin," he instructed Pearl.

Still in fear of the Tlingit invasion and murder of Sallas, Pearl asked about the danger. "What if the Tlingit come back, Mr. Griffin? What am I to do?"

"Flee and hide. This is a large island, not like the one you've come from. They won't pursue you much further than the beach, so make a plan. We all live under this threat and have to deal with it. The report I get from James Douglas is that the Crown is going to send an expedition force of military and navy to crush these barbarians. Until then, we must keep our vigil. Jack and Pineapple will be with you, as well as the dogs. You'll prosper here, Pearl. Try and forget about Sallas Island."

The evening ended with a prayer. The Kanaka said a prayer in Owyhee, and the Songhee chanted a strange chorus, their wives making eerie bird-like shrieking chants.

The next morning, Pearl was up early, as the smell of cooked bacon wafted into her room. Outside, the sheep town was already a scene of bustling activity, as the sun rose. Supplies had been loaded on a two wheel cart, hitched to a small donkey. Jack and his wife Weehee, a Lummi native girl, supervised its loading. 'Pineapple', an old Kanaka, was bringing the flock in from the pasture with dogs, moving them up the road.

Pearl followed the smell of bacon to the outdoor kitchen, a stone chimney with a roof and no walls. The cook was a Kanaka--huge, fat, and round. He liked Pearl and handed her a steaming plate of eggs, bread, and bacon. The chatter was a strange combination of Kanaka, Salish, and Chinook, all blending into sentences that everyone understood.

Jack brought up another donkey with a pack saddle, as Pearl finished her breakfast. "C'mon, Pearl. Let's get you loaded up. We'll come back for your loom and blankets next week. They're safe here." Jack soon had her belongings lashed down. Duto flew down from a distant perch and landed on the pack saddle, announcing his arrival. Of course, Pearl flashed the medallion at him. Jack and Weehee laughed with big eyes, as they knew the story of the bird and the girl.

Now leading the two donkeys, the small entourage headed up the road behind the flock of sheep, being pushed along by the dogs and Pineapple. The south of the island was open, rolling meadows, but soon the road was into a forest, which opened into another meadow, then through a forest, and another meadow. A distant herder in a meadow towards the saltwater waved, his flock grazing close by.

It was a 13 mile walk to their destination, an open glen with a spring of water, which they finally reached in the late afternoon. The herders had a tent made of old sail cloth, and quickly had it standing, with a campfire going. Jack guided Pearl a short distance through a tree stand. Here was 'Lonesome Cove' that Griffin had pointed to on his map. The beach was rocky, and she well recognized the distant islands to the north.

That evening, Duto called in his flock of friends, and they surrounded the glen, cawing from the treetops. As the sun went down, they all quieted down and settled in for their nightly roost.

Pineapple got out his flute and played while Weehee chanted along. They enjoyed Pearl's company, and Duto was the best entertainment, dancing in a circle around the fire, cursing in English and Visayan, with no one but Pearl understanding him.

The next morning, Pearl was awoken to voices outside the tent. Listening from inside the tent, she understood the words--a friendly good morning and pleasantries being exchanged. Leaving the tent, she found a group of six Lummi men with axes and saws, talking with Jack and Weehee. Jack was directing them to build a corral around the spring to keep the sheep out, and keep the water clean. He then pointed out the site for a log cabin. Seeing Pearl, one of the Lummis pointed at her and gestured *Caw Caw*, it's the "Raven Woman," pointing her out to the others. Smiles were exchanged and coffee offered to the workers. They passed around a tin bowl of coffee, each taking a gulp and passing it on, until it was quickly gone.

Soon, the trees at the edge of the glen were being cut. Working all day, a nice pile of log poles were stacked up. Within days, the glen became a stump meadow with a fine, little mud-chinked cabin that stood in the center. The spring was now fenced in. Pearl directed the Lummis to build a large, covered porch on the cabin, that would accommodate her loom.

By the end of the week, the Lonesome Cove sheep station was up and operating. As promised, Jack and Weehee returned to Bellevue, and brought back her loom and cache of blankets. The Lummis enjoyed Pearl and the Kanaka's evening suppers, and returned nightly with fish and clams, telling stories and jokes. They were fascinated with Pearl and Duto, staring in silence, as the two talked back and forth.

Pearl unrolled Sallas's map one evening, pointing at 'Pearl's Island,' and asking where it was. The following day, the Lummis guided her to Sallas's Landing, showing her the island, acknowledging it was taboo to go there, being a graveyard.

They invited her to their village via a trail heading south to a hidden harbor. There, a huge cedar longhouse, two hundred feet long, stood on a beach of solid shells. Totems and fish drying racks were up and down the beach, along with a dozen canoes. Sixty people lived in the village, mostly women, children, and elders with a dozen head men. She was well received, as the cabin builders had spoken of her mystical relationship with Duto. She mingled with them freely, fully understanding their Chinook dialect, sampling different foods, and marveling at the carvings and basket work.

Pearl and Weehee worked hard to turn the little cabin into a safe, warm refuge. With the help of Jack, she had reassembled the loom on the front porch, and on rainy days would work diligently, creating her own designs.

Duto had become lethargic, with little energy, his feathers in disarray. One morning, as she stepped out, he was perched on the loom, a dozen black feathers lying on the ground. "*Caw Caw Caw*! Son of a bitch! Gimme my medicine! Gimme my medicine!" he demanded.

Knowing what he wanted, she fetched a pellet from the pouch necklace. Holding it out, he gulped it down with no hesitation, and flew off to the spring for a drink. That night, Pearl and the Kanaka were awoken to a blood curdling bleating of desperation coming from the sheep. The sheep dogs began barking incessantly.

Grabbing their staffs and long knives, Jack and Pineapple rushed into the dark at the sound of the desperate bleating and barking. Pearl and Weehee could now hear Jack and Pineapple cursing loudly, with growling and yelping following.

It was some time before they returned, needing and fetching a lantern. "Wolves," cried Jack. "Wolves have killed some sheep. Give me the lantern. I need to build a big fire. Quickly!" Jack soon had a bright fire burning at the holding pen, exposing five dead sheep, and several hobbling around, lame and wounded. "How many did you see, Pineapple?" as Jack walked back into the light of the fire.

"Three, maybe four, very vicious dogs!"

"Help me with the wounded sheep. Maybe we can save these two," pointed Jack.

Pearl and Weehee helped calm the flock, as the men doctored the bleeding sheep. At early dawn, Jack lit out on a jog run, going for help down the road at Bellevue. By afternoon, Jack was back with three mounted horsemen carrying rifle scabbards. A hunting dog was soon on the scent of the wolves, and off down a forest trail the group went.

Jack and Pearl were distraught. Eight dead sheep, with five wounded. The animals were like pets, and the loss was saddening. Pineapple cheered everyone up when he mentioned they'd be having barbecued ribs tonight, saying it could have been worse. The men stood vigilant that night by the bonfire, the flock safe at hand, with the dogs guarding also.

At sunrise, several rifle shots were heard in the distance, and five minutes later, another volley echoed across the island.

Later, at breakfast, a Lummi runner from the village came. He told them of four wolves being cornered and shot, and maybe one was wounded and had gotten away, and to be on the lookout for a wounded wolf. Just as he finished his announcement, another volley could be heard in the distance. The Lummi smiled and said, "Number four."

The rains had set in, and the gloomy days were made for weaving blankets. One evening, the Lummi visitors were highly troubled and agitated. Reports were coming in of massive death plagues of smallpox and cholera, wiping out the whole native population, up and down both coasts of Vancouver Island. There was fear in the air, and the sense of celebration was gone. It was confirmed a week later, when Jack returned from Bellevue, with supplies and news. Trading at Fort Victoria had come to a stop, as whole economies of tribal existence collapsed, with whole villages now ghost towns. There was no one to do business with now.

Griffin had been a wise supervisor and had all company people inoculated on a recent visit from the steamer Beaver. He was nervous about Pearl, not knowing her status, and that if she needed inoculation, she was to proceed immediately to Bellevue. Jack had assured him that she had been inoculated, having seen the scar on her arm and discussed it one evening with her in conversation.

Finishing his report of the news, Jack pulled a manila envelope of parchment from his shirt and handed it to Pearl. "Griffin said to make sure you get this," handing it to Pearl. It was from Captain Weynton!

"He's coming for me! I knew it!" she cried.

The envelope was stamped with a wax seal, and trembling, she broke it and unfolded the script done in quill. It read:

"My dearest Juana Pearl--how I hope this letter reaches you and that you are safe and well. I've fallen on hard times, my credentials stripped and my money spent on lawyers and legal fees. I returned Pinto safely to your home island, as I promised. I also promised to take you home, and in a roundabout way, I will with this letter. I want you to sell the sheep to the HBC, wholesale, and with the earnings, buy your passage home. I have contacted James Douglas with a letter of my intentions. The balance remaining will help put bread and soup on my table. Best of luck, Your Captain Weynton."

The Cascades

The Fall weather was balmy and sunny at Lonesome Cove Camp in 1852. The pack of wolves had been eradicated, and life was peaceful at the sheep station, becoming routine. Pearl anticipated hearing from James Douglas, but no news arrived. On Christmas Day, the company herders were called in to Bellevue by Griffin for a large feast of roast pork. Rum and wine were served, and soon a raucous of laughter and joking filled the cook house mess, one outdoing the other in storytelling.

Griffin stood up and quieted everyone, proposing an announcement. "We've had a good year--a little problem with wolves, but that is over with. Our success has been duly noted by the company, and so I have received word that James Douglas will arrive next month with 1,000 more sheep and more people to care and handle them. Our task at Bellevue here will now be supported with several new arrivals, so I ask all of you to assist them in becoming comfortable on our island."

Pearl was delighted to hear the news--a chance to speak with Douglas and discuss Captain Weynton's wishes, and an answer to how was she going to get home. She, Jack, and Weehee returned to Lonesome Cove the following day. Pineapple had graciously volunteered to stay behind and watch the flock.

Sure enough, James Douglas arrived the fifteenth of January, the Beaver pulling a small flat boat loaded with sheep. The Beaver was to spend the week ferrying the 1,000 sheep from Fort Victoria to Bellevue. Griffin sent a runner to Lonesome Cove, requesting Pearl to come as soon as possible. Upon hearing the message, she immediately set out for Bellevue. She'd never walked the 13 miles faster and by early afternoon was at the big clapboard house. Arriving in the rain, she knocked on the front porch door. A familiar Kanaka servant opened the door and welcomed her in. Seeing her, Griffin heartily welcomed her into the parlor.

Sitting there was James Douglas, smoking his pipe. "Pearl, Pearl, so good to see you again. Let me first give my sympathy for what you endured at Sallas Island--terrible tragedy of William. The island is a military outpost now--I hear you've done well here in our new colony, having contributed much in labor and support. I'm grateful. I have received a letter from our Captain Weynton, expressing his wishes to sell your flock to the company. I trust you have received the same information in a recent letter?" he asked her.

"Yes, Mr. Douglas. The Captain says to sell the sheep and buy my passage home," she replied.

"And your feelings, do you want to return?" asked Douglas.

"Yes, I would, if possible," she answered.

"Very well. In six months, a schooner, the Yukon Queen, is scheduled to sail to Owyhee after picking up lumber and salmon in Ft. Victoria. I will make arrangements with the company to further your passage from Owyhee to your Filipina Islands."

"Oh, thank you, Mr. Douglas," cried Pearl, bowing and smiling with a gasp. "Mr. Douglas, I have over one hundred wool blankets that I need to redeem or sell--can you help me?" she now pleaded with him.

"Blankets! My warehouses are full of blankets--there is very little trading at the fort. The pox has destroyed the economy. I can't help you with that one, Pearl, but I must ask one more favor. Will you stay and manage the flock here until your ship comes? I need you to show the newcomers how to survive here," he told her.

"Yes, I'll work the sheep, sir, until my ship comes--what month does it arrive, sir?"

"Scheduled for the middle of June to arrive--so I will have you come to the fort in May, so that you may prepare for the voyage. I'll make sure you have some traveling money. The remainder will be sent as a voucher for Captain Weynton in London. Are we understood?" he asked the girl. She nodded yes.

"Now, run along. Griffin has been appointed Chief Factor of San Juan Colony, and I have much to discuss with him. I'll see you in May. Good luck," and with that, Griffin showed her the front door, and as soon as she was outside, she did three cartwheels and gave a yahoo yell.

Duto was sitting on a barn roof, waiting for her. Sensing her excitement, he swooped down and landed on her shoulder. She slept in the herder's bunk house that night and the following morning was up and gone at first light. The rain drizzled down on the long walk back to Lonesome Cove.

Jack, Weehee, and Pineapple were sad to hear of her leaving them in June and begged her to change her mind. She had to go back--her mother and father needed her. Somehow she must sell the blankets and bring the money back with her to the Filipinas.

The sheep were in good hands, and idle days of watching the flock had begun to concern her, as she felt isolated and not able to trade her blankets. Somehow, she must break even for all her hard work and be redeemed.

Days passed, and one evening, the Lummis made one of their regular visits to the sheep camp. A conversation was struck up among them, sitting around the campfire. A discussion of canoeing to a distant beach, a Spring trading tradition, became the main topic. The Lummis discussed trading their excess dried fish harvest for a cedar canoe. It was agreed upon that they would leave the day after next and to make arrangements. They would be gone for ten days.

Overhearing the conversation, Pearl inquired about other trading at this distant beach, as it sounded like it was a regular trading rendezvous. She was looking for pelts--the mainland still being a rich source of the commodity. The Lummis explained to her that most trappers took their pelts to Fort Nisqually, to the south, the HBC trading post for the interior. The Lummis acknowledged that sometimes they had seen trappers heading south for the fort, passing the trading beach, on their way to the fort. If she took her blankets to this place, she may get lucky and return with the pelts and triple her earnings. Pelts were in high demand now at Fort Victoria, with two thirds of the entire population of Vancouver Island now wiped out from disease, with no one coming in from the woods to trade.

The promise to James Douglas had been to watch the sheep--yet they didn't need her anymore, and so the chance to leave the island on a quick bartering trip seemed to her to be a good chance to take advantage of. Seeing an opportunity, she decided to join the little canoe trading voyage. In exchange for five blankets, Pearl commissioned a canoe and four paddlers to haul her and her bale of blankets, and return her with her acquired pelts. She'd be back in ten days and could begin preparing for the voyage home in June.

The following day, the Lummi loaded her bale of blankets onto a large canoe in Lonesome Cove. That afternoon, three more canoes arrived, loaded with dried fish. The party stayed with the canoes on the beach, spending the evening around a campfire, making prayers and offerings for a safe voyage.

Around three in the morning, Pearl, Duto, and a dozen Lummi fishermen broke camp and left the beach to catch a tide that would take them down the east side of San Juan Island.

This was all new scenery for Pearl, the internal waterway dotted with small enchanting little islands, much like her own Philippine Islands. By late morning, they had reached the southern tip of the island, and a large flock of sheep from Bellevue could be seen grazing on the point, only looking up momentarily to watch them pass, then returning to grazing. Crossing a small channel, they now paralleled the shore of Lopez Island, one she had heard about, but only seen from a great distance.

By late afternoon, they came to a distant point. A cabin was seen in a meadow, smoke coming from its chimney. Sheep grazed up to the tree line across the open meadow. On a beach, at the very southern tip, the canoes made landfall. All day long, a huge flock of ravens had tagged along on the shoreline, and landing in the distant trees, they rang out a chorus of roll call.

144

The leader of the Lummis, Chief Saclamito, invited Pearl to walk with him to the distant cabin. Arriving, she instantly recognized Kohnoho, a Kanaka herdsman, as he greeted them at the door of the cabin. Pearl was disoriented, and he explained to her that she was at a new sheep camp, that had been commissioned by James Douglas. The camp was named "Colville" in honor of the governor of the HBC back in England. The company was trying to duplicate their success on San Juan Island. Kohnoko asked where she was going, and she explained to him the distant trading beach and her desire to trade her blankets. Kohnoho acknowledged that he knew of the place and had heard of it as a "good camping ground" or "Muck-kul-tee-ho." The distant mainland could be seen to the east, a large channel separating them.

The following morning, the Lummi waited for slack water on the tide change, and at ten o'clock, the little flotilla labored across the channel, the wind favoring them, and at their backs. Having crossed the channel, the lead canoe made for a small islet, and having passed it, a narrow passage was revealed, the tide now racing and carrying them through. The current being so strong, the canoe men had to keep dipping their paddles to maintain their heading and not allowing the craft to get sideways in the ripping current and whirlpools. Within fifteen minutes, the current calmed, and they entered into an inland sea.

By afternoon, they came to a thumb of land, with a huge beach and wooded nob on the western shore, protruding into the waterway. The canoes beached, and camp was made. The Lummis were very familiar with where they were at, finding fresh oysters for dinner.

The following day, they proceeded south, passing distant fishing camps on either shoreline, smoke signaling their habitation. By noon, they rounded a point on their western shoreline and could see a distant white beach, with smoke trails rising from it. Chief Saclamito got Pearl's attention and called out as he pointed to the south, saying,

"Muck-kul-tee-ho. Muck-kul-tee-ho."

Off to the left, a small island with an abandoned fishing camp could be seen. The Lummi pointed out to Pearl a group of Orca whales that were hunting in the bay--spread out in a mile-wide circle in groups of two. The bull thrashed and crashed about in the center of the circled pack, scaring the schools of fish in all directions, into the jaws of the surrounding groups of two.

It had rained all morning. As they approached Muk-kul-tee-ho, a patch of blue sky was opening above the beach. Its white sand and bleached driftwood beckoned in the distance. Hauled up above high tide line on the beach, thirty to forty canoes could be seen, their skid tracks in the sand.

The Lummis called out to some clam diggers on the shoreline and were given directions where to beach. Whereupon a group of "cousins" appeared and got the craft safely ashore.

Within the hour, they had all of the dried fish and blankets secured at a beach camp. The canoes were rolled up on logs, used as rollers, to the high ground.

Up past the driftwood on the beach line, sand dunes rolled up to a flat bench of a sand. The flat top of white sand was covered with two dozen cedar houses and mat shacks--some with porches and totems guarding their entrance. This was the village of the Snohomish tribe, its importance as a trading location known to all the tribes for one hundred miles. Dogs and chickens roamed about, and children were in loose groups, playing games and laughing.

The Lummi cousins invited the group into a long, mat house, its interior lit with oil lamps. A smoking pipe was offered, passed around, and then the joking and storytelling followed. A big iron pot of fish stew bubbled in the center on a cooking fire. The soup was served in carved, cedar bowls. Chief Saclamito inquired about trading their fish for a canoe, and the haggling back and forth began. An agreement was reached, which seemed to satisfy the Lummi, and the pipe was passed again, to seal the deal.

Now, Chief Saclamito introduced Pearl, who had been sitting quietly in the background, waiting for her turn. He explained who she was, the "Raven Woman," and upon hearing this, the chatter arose in the mat house, whispering in ears and eyes darting. They had heard about her and her ability to talk with the ravens. Because of this, she was looked upon as a spirit, and they avoided to make eye contact with her. Chief Saclamito explained she had blankets to trade for pelts--and were any available for trade? Upon hearing this, a Snohomish headman spoke up in Chinook Jargon. He indicated for Chief Saclamito and Pearl to follow him.

Leaving the mat house, they followed him through the village to the tree line. A short distance into the forest, they came to a small log cabin. Several horses were in a corral in the clearing. The Snohomish headman called out loudly. The plank door on its leather hinge opened. A woman in a buckskin dress, decorated with shell and elk teeth, invited them in.

A small stone hearth and chimney had a crackling fire going. Another woman sat by the fire, doing quill and beadwork on a pair of moccasins. These women appeared to not be of the Snohomish people, their clothing and hair not familiar to Pearl. An inquiry was made as to the man of the house's whereabouts, being informed he was relieving himself in the forest and to wait, as he would soon return. The women spoke Chinook, and upon hearing who

Pearl was, their eyes got very big, and they remained silent, refusing to speak anymore.

Soon, the door sprung open and a wild looking man in fringed buckskin, braids, moccasins, and a large beaded sash entered, bellowing, "Visitors! Who have we here?"

The Snohomish headman introduced Chief Saclamito and Pearl, saying to them, "This is Swakane Jacque."

Swakane Jacque asked them if they'd like some coffee, and both without hesitation answered, "Yes!" Instructing one of the women to brew some, she answered in a strange dialect, pointing at Pearl. Swakane Jacque scratched and rubbed his bearded chin, saying, "She tells me that you're the 'Raven Woman' spirit--is this true?"

"Yes, I've been called that before," Pearl answered in Chinook.

"These women are afraid of you--assure them you will cast no evil harm towards them," he replied.

And so Pearl explained that she and Duto would not harm them, and standing, she opened the door and called out for Duto. Waiting in the treetops, he swooped down and landed on her outstretched arm, hopping to her shoulder. Cawing and clicking, she flashed the medallion around her neck, and he instantly became silent. The women and Swakane Jacque smiled and grinned in disbelief. The women now lost their fear, and offered Pearl some dried biscuits and honey.

The coffee was now brewed and passed around, and the conversation began flowing. Chief Saclamito explained that Pearl wanted to trade her blankets. Swakane Jacque replied that the natives in this region were all fishermen, and yes, there were trappers who had passed through here, but things had changed. The territory had become part of the United States, and the Hudson Bay Posts had moved to the North. Fort Nisqually was being abandoned by the British. To the south was now an American village called Piner's Point. A man there named Denny was buying any local pelts, what few there are. The trappers had moved off to the east, where colder winters made the pelts thicker and more valuable."

He further explained to her that if she hung around long enough, a trapper would pass through, but no guarantees he would trade for her blankets.

Pearl hung her head, realizing that two years of weaving may have been for nothing. Seeing her dismay, Swakane Jacque offered her his services. He was a trader in deerskins and would soon return east to his permanent home. He volunteered to take her there, where many pelts could be traded for.

Pearl perked up upon hearing this, "How long does it take to get to this place?" she asked.

"Three weeks--a trail over the mountains," he told her.

"How will I get back?" she asked.

"One of my sons will bring you back--three weeks to travel, a week's rest and trade, and then three weeks to return," he answered.

It was mid March, which would place her return the first week of May. It was a huge gamble, but she felt she could make it back to Fort Victoria in time to catch the ship to Owyhee. He explained that the winter pelts would be waiting for her and that she had a good opportunity to trade and multiply her wealth.

"When are you leaving?" she asked.

"In two days. I've been watching the snow melt on a distant mountain, the sign that it is safe to travel. We have wintered here and are anxious to return," he replied.

"What will I pay you with?" she asked him.

"Oh, give my women here each a blanket, that should make them happy," he answered.

"What about returning?" she asked.

"Another two blankets should be payment enough," he replied.

"What about a horse to haul the blankets?" she was now getting down to business.

Jacque smiled, "Two blankets."

"How about food?" she asked.

"Ahh, you are a shrewd one," he smiled. "I shall guide you, feed you, pack your goods, and return you for eight blankets," he stared at her, a serious look on his face.

"Done. And I will let your wives choose. What are their names?"

"This is Morning Sun and her sister Horse Catcher. They are Entiat women--my wives for twenty years now."

The women also spoke Chinook Jargon and now realizing that Pearl would be traveling with them, warmly bonded with her, flooding her with questions. Duto had found a roost on a rafter beam and stared down at the chattering bunch.

It was arranged for Chief Saclamito to return on May fifteenth, to fetch her back to Bellevue on San Juan Island. He was to inform the sheep station at Lonesome Cove of her mission. She would then come for her belongings and Bible then and then say her goodbyes.

The following day, Chief Saclamito and the Lummis were on their way back, with the new canoe they had traded for, pleased with the trade they had made. Pearl and Duto watched them depart the beach at Muk-hul-tee-ho, paddling north on their return to San Juan Island, until they were a speck in the distance.

Morning Sun and Horse Catcher were busy throughout the day, preparing the packs for the string of ten horses belonging to Jacque. The ponies were all hobbled in a corral, and Jacque spent the day grooming their hooves, rubbing them down and feeding them extra hay. The ponies were like his children, and they would clamor for his attention. Each one had bonded with the mountain man and were at ease in his presence. He had traded his cache of deerskins for powder, knives, pots, lead, coffee, and calico cloth. His wives had traded for mother of pearl shell and blue glass beads, to decorate their hair and clothing.

Several Snohomish people came and bid farewell at the cabin that evening, knowing they would return in the Fall with another cache of deerskins to trade, a pattern and routine they had maintained for many previous years.

The morning of departure came, and a misty, foggy rain fell. Two ponies were loaded with hay in bundles, one for Pearl's blankets, and three more with provisions and the trade goods. Pearl had never ridden a horse, so was given instruction by Horse Catcher. Pearl followed Morning Sun and her horse, with Horse Catcher at the rear of the string. Jacque rode out front, his musket draped over the cantel on his saddle.

The tide was out, making an easy, sandy trail along the shoreline, and soon Muck-hul-tee-ho was far behind them, as they headed east. They left the beach at noon, heading into a swampy river delta. They followed a winding trail through a vast forest of ancient cedar trees, some so huge it would take six men holding hands to surround them. Jacque constantly stayed well out in front, scouting the trail for danger. Bear were coming out of hibernation, with a voracious appetite and were unpredictable at this time of year. Leaving the swampy delta, they broke into a forest of giant firs. The trail meandered through the forest, and by late afternoon, they arrived at a small fishing camp on the riverbank. Fish traps were set all along the river, and drying racks of fish were scattered about. Jacque knew this group of people well, and they were received warmly.

The horses were unpacked and hobbled, and all attention in the camp was directed to the arrival of the guests. When Duto landed on Pearl's shoulder, the locals quickly sounded their alarm and fear, realizing who she was. Jacque quickly explained that she was a good spirit and to treat her as an honored guest, to avoid her displeasure. Hearing this, they soon were offering baskets of berries and cooked venison, bowing to her and avoiding eye contact.

149

That evening, Pearl sat with Morning Sun and Horse Catcher around the fire. The women brewed coffee and offered it to their hosts, as Jacque got his long stemmed pipe out, packing it with tobacco and passing it around. The talk was about the trail ahead and what to watch for. Assurances were given that it was now passable, but still muddy and slick in some places.

They were up early the following morning and back on the trail. A steady drizzle of rain fell, which resulted in large drops splashing on them from the overhead canopy of the forest. By late morning, the trail came to a large, sprawling gravel bar on the river. Taking advantage of this crossing, Jacque led the pack string across to the opposite bank of the river. They continued east on the north side of the river, the trail meandering through the forest and following the river. Jacque continued to stay well ahead of the pack train, so as to stumble across any danger, he could deal with it and protect the women and horses.

A shot rang out in the forest, the horses startled and stopped in their tracks. The group stayed stationary for a good fifteen minutes, and finally, Jacque appeared ahead on the trail. "It's our lucky day. I've shot a nice elk. It's ahead on the trail," he beamed with pleasure.

Proceeding ahead, they came to a nice cow elk, conveniently lying adjacent to the trail. Morning Sun and Horse Catcher squealed and laughed with delight. The creature's meat, hide, and teeth were coveted by the women, and they wasted no time skinning and quartering the prize. Within an hour, they had the beast butchered and neatly packed and distributed on the ponies.

Jacque was making for a well known campsite, an opening in the woods from a past forest fire. The grass was abundant there, for the horses to graze and rest. It was twilight when they finally reached the spot, and Jacque quickly sparked a campfire, while Pearl searched for firewood in the dimming light. Soon, Jacque had a roaring fire going, which now provided light to unpack the horses and hobble them. All were anxious to eat the elk roast, and soon the smell of the cooking meat permeated the air. Jacque unrolled a large skin tarp, and with the help of Pearl, they soon had a nice shelter over their heads.

Duto swooped down from the treetops and was given a chunk of a meat scrap. Having his fill, he returned to a treetop roost to settle in for the night. Morning Sun baked some large potatoes on hot rocks next to the fire, and soon they were feasting on the bounty, eating their fill till they could hold no more.

Fully content now, laying on their bed rolls under the tarp, Jacque told a story of killing his first elk when he was a young man. Pearl now asked him, "Jacque, where did you come from? How did you get here?"

"My father was a Frenchman, a voyager and trapper in the far east, an area known as the 'Big Lakes.' My mother was a Cree woman, and one winter, when I was very young, he failed to return in the Spring. No one knew what happened to him. He just disappeared into the wilderness. So I was raised by the Cree and learned to trap and hunt. As years went by, I kept heading west, chasing better trapping areas, and by 1825, I was trapping in the Rockies, close to a trading post called Saleesh House. There, I met a group of Sinkiuse, returning from the buffalo country to their homeland. Traveling with them was Morning Sun, whose temptations I could not resist. She told me of a great land untouched by trappers, rich in beaver and fox. Fort Okanogan was in the region, providing a place to trade, and so I fell in with them. They took a shinin' to me, the tribe, and the fur trappings were as she had said. And so I ended up being a part of the tribe and accepted as one of them. After a few years of trapping--a hard lonely life--I acquired two more wives, Horse Catcher and Talks Too Much."

"Wait, wait," said Pearl. "You have another wife? Three?" she asked.

"Yes, she's at our village in the Swakane," he answered. "Anyway, these three wives and our children are excellent deer hide makers, skinning, curing, and smoking. Several years ago, we discovered that we could trade them at Muck-kul-tee-ho for a much better profit than at Fort Okanogan. So now you know all about me," he sighed. "That's enough. I'll stand first watch. The rest of you get some sleep," and he disappeared into the shadows, calling softly to his ponies. The fire dimmed, and the women traded conversation softly, until Pearl was deep in sleep.

Pearl was awoken by the ponies raising an alarm. The three women sat up and looked fearfully about. *Caw, caw, caw!,* came the alarm of Duto, and he swooped in and landed on Pearl's shoulder. Morning Sun called out for Jacque, who appeared from the shadows and warned her to keep quiet.

"Throw some wood on the fire. There's something out there," he warned.

"What is it, a bear--they smelled the meat?" she asked, fearfully.

"No, I think not. Do you smell that rotten smell in the air?" Jacque's eyes darted in all directions.

The horses were now pawing the ground, nickering wildly and kicking at the shadows. All of a sudden, a rock came from the darkness and struck the campfire, sending up a shower of sparks. And with that, a screeching howl and gut wrenching snort came from the darkness.

Horse Catcher screamed, "It's the man-beast, the Sasquatch!" Another blood curdling howl came from the other side of the camp, the women now in pure terror. From the darkness, the sound of sticks click clacking together could be heard, and then another long, agonizing wail and screech came from the distance. Jacque fired his musket towards the howl, and again, another rock landed in the fire, kicking up sparks. Handing the musket to Morning Sun, he

151

hollered at her to reload it, pulling his pistol and skinning knife from his waist belt. Again, more click clacking of sticks out in the darkness and a foul odor now being unmistakable. Jacque fired his pistol toward the stick clacking noise, and then there was silence. Morning Sun had the musket reloaded and traded Jacque for the pistol, to reload it. Out in the forest, the sound of crashing, breaking brush and snorts receded into the distant night.

Pearl was trembling so hard that she had bit her lip and could taste blood in her mouth. Never in her entire life had she known fear like that. The horses, Jacque, and women were equally as frightened. The howl of the creature was something out of the supernatural world. Duto was upset, as well, cursing and *caw cawing*, not able to understand what had just happened.

The fire was built up to a roaring bonfire, with no one being able to sleep. The rotten smell was gone, and the creatures apparently had disappeared into the night. The ponies were badly stressed and bunched up together, close to the bonfire. Jacque soothed and comforted them, but their ears remained perked and pointed in all directions, listening for danger. Horse Catcher made coffee, and it was passed around and gone instantly. The cold chill still lingered in their bodies.

Jacque and Morning Sun recalled an encounter years before, having spotted three of the hairy beasts below them, crossing the river. The creatures seemed to sense their presence and were vacating the area to avoid contact. Stories had been passed around among the tribes for years, as encounters similar to what they had just endured were familiar in the tales.

The fire was kept roaring all night, and at first light, there was no hesitation of leaving the area. Pearl indicated to Duto to scout from the sky, and he acknowledged, understanding the danger and fear all morning. He would reconnoiter in both directions on the trail and every half hour land on her shoulder and report his findings to her. The bird brought a sense of calm back to the group, for they understood the value of what he could see from the air.

The forest was endless and the trail barely recognizable, as they plodded along. They were climbing into foothills now, the snow-covered peaks and crags loomed before them. Pearl could not imagine how they were going to cross these peaks, their lofty, steep slopes reaching into the clouds. To the North, she could hear water cascading, and as it grew louder, a magnificent waterfall was seen in the distance. The climb was becoming steep and muddy, and periodically, the women would dismount and walk the horses through dangerous areas. The temperature was dropping also, as they continued to climb towards the snow capped sentinels.

On the fifth day of their journey, Jacque took them into a high mountain valley, following a small stream that coursed and zig-zagged, through large granite boulders. That afternoon, they reached an open meadow of grass. Jacque had the pack train stopped, explaining this was the last grass to graze the animals on. "We'll camp here for a full day, rest the horses, and allow them to graze." Pearl was grateful for the rest, her rump and thighs sore from riding.

The mountain air was crisp, cold, and fresh. Elk steaks, potatoes, and coffee revived the group. The horses seemed to know what was ahead on the trail, munching on the alpine grass and hungrily filling their bellies.

The value of Pearl's wool blankets were now appreciated, as Horse Catcher and Morning Sun cloaked themselves from the cold wind coming down the valley. The stop and rest the following day was good judgement on Jacque's part, as an incessant rain lashed at their camp all day. The tarp kept them dry, and the women worked on repairing horse tack, under its protection.

The next morning, the clouds were gone, the eastern sunrise beckoning them to mount up and continue. Far up the valley that morning, they came to a mountain stream that cascaded down from a steep slope. A faint trail could be seen, switchbacking up its side. Jacque dismounted, ordering the women to do so also. "We'll walk the horses up this slope--watch the trail for loose rock," he advised.

Back and forth they zig-zagged, Pearl's legs beginning to burn and ache. By late afternoon, they finally reached the crest of the ridge. The view was a sprawling, sweeping vantage of the forest and valley they had just left. Even Duto had grown tired of flying at this elevation and began roosting on a pack of one of the horses. Breaking over the ridge, the trail entered another hidden valley, and patches of snow could be seen on the opposite flank.

In the basin of the hidden valley, they camped for the night, the cold of the mountains chilling their bones. Morning Sun sensed Pearl's uncomfortable chill. In sympathy, she wrapped her calves in rabbit fur leggings and gave her elk skin moccasins, lined in fur to wear.

There was a sense of urgency and uncertainty in Jacque's manner now, knowing that Spring snow storms were still a possibility. He was up early the next morning, urging them not to delay. A quick cup of coffee and hard pemmican was breakfast. The rain was back, and the warm wool blankets and oil skinned ponchos were their only protection in the biting wind.

Climbing another switchback to a saddle on the next ridge, the hardship of the trail and weather was beginning to take its toll. Cresting the ridge, an ominous sight loomed ahead--another valley filled with snow, the trail vanishing under its mantel. Jacque knew the trail well, having memorized several landmarks over the years. Jacque pulled out a pair of snowshoes from his kit, and leading his horse, he blazed a trail through the snow packed valley.

Pearl was afraid to get off her horse, and sensing this, Morning Sun asked her, "What's wrong--are you frightened?"

"I've never seen snow before--I won't disappear in it?" she asked.

In astonishment, the others laughed. "Step off your horse--it's only a few inches deep, see?" encouraged Morning Sun.

Finally, she stepped down from her mount. Picking up a handful, she held it to her nose to see if it had a smell. "Can I taste it?" she shyly asked.

The others broke out in a huge laugh. "Yes, taste it, you'll like the flavor," Jacque teased her.

"I don't taste anything," she questioned him.

"Alright, enough fun. Let's get moving," he barked.

By dark, they reached a stand of scrub, stunted alpine firs. The lower dead branches were easy picking for firewood, and soon they had a roaring campfire blazing. Some bundles of hay were broken out for the horses and spread around the fire, so the animals could warm their backsides while eating.

The next morning, it was business as usual, the cold pushing them onward with a sense of urgency. The snow was deeper now, and the horses labored and puffed steam through their nostrils. In the distance, two treacherous looking peaks stared at them. Jacque was heading for the low point between them. Stopping the train to catch their breath, he scanned the surrounding peaks. Snow fields loomed in the heavens above them, a sight of sheer beauty. Jacque warned them to all be silent and not to make any loud noises, explaining, "You see that shelf of snow up there," pointing above a cliff. "That could come down on us, an avalanche--we must proceed very quietly and as quickly as possible. No talking, laughing, or coughing. This is a very dangerous part of the trail," he warned.

For a good hour, the pace was quick, horses and humans alike sensing the danger in the air. Finally achieving the passage and out from under the escarpment, Jacque stopped the train amid some large boulders. "We'll stop here for the night. One more day till we get to the summit," he explained to Pearl. Coffee was brewed while the exhausted horses had their packs removed. Jacque rationed out the hay and made a mental note. They had enough hay for two more days in the high country.

Warming her backside by the fire, Pearl marveled at the majestic beauty. Suddenly, out of the corner of her eye, she detected movement on a distant lofty ledge. Terrified for a moment, still thinking about the man-beast encounter days before, she pointed out the creature to Jacque, "Is that one of those man-beasts--up there!" she pointed.

Jacque squinted and spotted the creature. "Ha! That's a mountain goat. Damn, I could hit him from here, but the rifle shot would bring the whole mountain down," he lamented.

"A wild goat?" she asked.

"Yup--I fine skin of white hair too, if we could get him--but it's too risky to shoot--it's his lucky day. I've seen a flock of the damn things on the side of a mile high cliff, the wall being straight up and them cavorting about, defying the law of nature, as if they enjoyed the thought of death. One of God's miracles in these mountains," he mused.

They awoke the following morning to a light snow falling. Urgently, Jacque had them moving again. As the sun broke over the mountains, the snow stopped, and the clouds opened to a royal blue sky. Ahead lay one more snow field, which gradually rose in elevation and funneled into a distinct narrow pass between two jagged mountains. Jacque was elated, telling the women, "Thar she is. Siwash Pass. Keep moving, we don't want to get stuck up here in a blizzard. It can change in the blink of an eye."

By mid afternoon, they had reached the summit. The horses were exhausted and spent. Stopping only for ten minutes, Pearl stared in amazement of the majestic view. For as far as the eye could see in any direction, jagged, ragged peaks were stacked up against each other. The air was thin, and Pearl felt dizzy, gasping in big gulps of air. The sun was beginning to fall in the West, and Jacque figured they had two hours of daylight left. The sky was cloudless, and a full moon appeared in the east.

"You women up for some night riding?---it's a full moon on this white snow. We should take advantage of it," he pressed them. It didn't matter what they thought. He was the boss, and their safety and well-being was in his hands.

After the sunset, the temperature became brutally cold. At this elevation, firewood was extremely scarce, and so the full moon was a good omen to allow them to keep going. In the middle of the night, they finally approached a treeline at the edge of a snow field. The horses were staggering, cold and exhausted. Before a fire could be made, all pitched in to unload the poor creatures. Finally, a fire was coaxed to life, coffee brewed, and everyone fed. Jacque rubbed the animals down and tended their needs, melting snow in a leather bucket with hot stones and watering each one. At this elevation, there were no predators, so no watch needed, and the group instantly fell asleep from exhaustion in the alpine glen.

Pearl awoke early, it still being dark, feeling cold snowflakes melting on her face. The others were still sleeping soundly, the exhaustion from the last three days overwhelming them. She lay there and pondered her situation. Had she made a bad choice in coming over these mountains? Her desire to sell her blankets and bring wealth home to her mother and father had pushed her judgement. She had no idea of the danger of mountain travel--being from the tropics and never experiencing this kind of "coldness." They had already encountered some strange howling beast, she had seen the fear in all of their eyes, even the horses. The trail was laced with danger--falling rocks, precipices, avalanches, severe cold--and she was only halfway across and had to come back. A sense of fear and optimism overwhelmed her, and she softly sobbed, muffling the sound.

Duto had roosted as usual in a nearby tree, and sensing her anguish, landed next to her face. *Caw-caw-caw*, he called and strutted protectively around her, assuring her safety that he was watching.

Horse Catcher stirred and soon was up, waking the others. With snow falling again, there was no time to waste. Bringing the fire back to life, she brewed coffee and handed out pemmican. The horses were restless, sensing the urgency to get down the mountain. They had finished the supply of hay they packed, and the creatures were fully aware of the situation.

The train was underway by dawn, the snow continuing to fall lightly. They were now following a stream, a game trail of deer tracks following its course in the snow. By mid-morning, the stream had become a small river, picking up tributaries, as they descended along its length. In the distance, Pearl could hear water cascading and roaring, and soon, they were on the edge of a large waterfall. The trail broke off into a steep mountainside of forest, the trail deep with snow, switchbacking down its slope. Finally, just as the sun was setting, they arrived in a valley. The same river meandered down its length. Along the river bank, small patches of new grass were beginning to green. The snow still blanketed most of the area, but the patches of thin grass were a welcome sight for the horses.

Pearl was now accustomed to the routine and helped to unpack the horses and set up camp before dark. Again, the coldness of the night fell upon them. The snow had stopped falling, the sky being clear, and the chill was such that the horses breath was seen as large puffs of white vapor in the light from the campfire.

Sitting around the campfire, she explained her closeness with Duto, showing them the medallion and medicine pouches around her neck. The medallion flashed in the firelight, and instantly, Duto swooped down from the tree

156

and landed on her shoulder. Jacque assured her the worst was over--to sleep well, as they would press hard again one more day, to get to adequate forage and grazing for the horses.

They were up and moving again at dawn, the sun breaching over the mountain, and a warm wind was blowing at their backs. Jacque called it a "Chinook Wind," and by afternoon, they were out of the snow, following a distinct trail through a forest of pine trees. Duto had selected one specific pack horse to roost on his pack, as the train ambled along. He would curse in English throughout the day, entertaining the group with his antics and bad language. Finally, by late afternoon, they emerged from the forest into a huge burn area of fallen, blackened trees--with lush, green grass ankle deep. The horses kept stopping to grab a bunch to chew on, and finally, Jacque pulled up at a small stream that entered a river, and camp was made.

"We'll stay here all day tomorrow and let the horses rest, eat, and drink," he announced. The women cooked up the last of the elk steaks, and laughter and contentment returned to the party that evening. Morning Sun cut some willow cane growing along the river, and sitting by the fire, she whittled out a three prong spear on the ends, splaying them open with a small stone.

The following morning, she took Pearl out to a gravel bar in the river. She pointed out schools of dark trout swimming in the shallows and demonstrated how to spear them. Pearl quickly caught on, and within an hour, they had two dozen fish speared. Roasting them on a stick, the party ate fresh fish all day, as the horses overcame their weariness and grazed on the lush grass.

The next day, back on the trail and following the river, they came around a small hill, and before them sat a huge lake. The forest skirted its shore around the entire distance. Flies and mosquitoes began to plague the party. Horse Catcher pulled a leather bag from her pack kit and smeared her arms and face with a foul smelling grease. Jacque and Morning Sun followed her earnestly and offered the salve to Pearl. "What is it?" she turned up her nose.

"It's bear fat mixed with herbs--the mosquitoes will not bite you if you smear it on," explained Jacque.

By late afternoon, they had skirted the north shore of the lake, following a well-defined trail. It was almost dark when they came to the shore of another lake, whereupon camp was made at a distinct and well used site of previous travelers. Pearl stayed close to the campfire through the evening, as the heat and smoke were the only refuge from the swarms of mosquitoes. She had bites on her hands and ears and scratched at them mercilessly.

157

They were on their way again early the following day, leaving the lake area, swarming with the bugs. Heading southeast now, they climbed a ridge and then meandered along its back, gazing down into a valley below. A whitewater river ran through the valley below, heading south, but they continued riding the ridges, heading in a southeast direction.

That night, they camped on the north side of a large bald mountain. The hillsides were covered in early Spring wildflowers, and Duto was excited to encounter a new species of bird he was not familiar with. It was like a small raven, only with bright, white markings and a long tail. They were nested in several bushes at the base of the mountain, and they would gang up on him and run him off as he approached their nests.

Jacque and his wives were in familiar country now and pointed out specific rock formations and streams, having names for them. There was a sense of anticipation and excitement, for they were entering the backcountry of their home, the Swakane Canyon. That afternoon, they came upon several beaver dams and their ponds. It was tricky, getting around the flooded areas of the beaver dams, but Jacque knew the trail well and wound his way through the swampy area. For the first time, the forest was now beginning to thin, and a new terrain, one of which she had never seen, began to become more prominent, filled with low, green, scrubby bushes, or "sagebrush," as Jacque called it. Frogs were croaking in the bottomland of the canyon. Jacque explained that this was the meaning of Swakane--or "canyon of frogs." They made camp early in the day at a beautiful, lush green meadow. The frogs croaked well into the night, and the sky was a carpet of stars, shining down upon them.

Jacque explained to Pearl that they would be at his home by afternoon tomorrow. The women were excited of the prospect, for they had wintered at Muck-hul-tee-ho and were anxious to see relatives, their children, and friends. It was fortunate they were home, as their food stocks were low, and the horses were weary from the trip. The evening was warm and balmy. A small fire was tended for cooking some frog legs that Morning Sun had caught in the creek bottom.

Pearl began to feel lightheaded, and beads of sweat formed on her brow. She turned in early to her bed roll, wondering if the frog legs had made her sick.

The following morning, she awoke and was gravely ill. Fever and sweating had begun to consume her, and she ached all over, her muscles and joints burning with pain. Jacque realized instantly she was gravely ill and constructed a travois. Two poles were drug by a horse, with a stretcher across the back. There was urgency now to get to their home, as the girl was now in and out of consciousness. The horse drug her down the bumpy trail on the pole skids, the jostling making her situation worse. Stopping in the shade of a large pine tree, the women carried water from the creek bottom to bathe her sweltering body and try and cool her down. "C'mon," cried Jacque, "We've got to get her to the cabin!"

An hour later, as they crested a small hill in the canyon bottom, there was their destination. In the valley floor below, sat a fine log cabin, surrounded by six teepees, with horse corrals around the perimeter. A dog was barking, having first realized their presence, and Jacque fired his musket in the air to announce their arrival. All over the camp, children and adults could be seen scurrying about. Two boys quickly jumped on horses and galloped excitedly towards them, whipping their steeds with quirts.

As they came alongside, the women suppressed their excitement, explaining Pearl's situation. The women quickly took the boys mounts, putting them in charge of the travois, and galloped back to the cabin, to prepare it for the sick girl.

By the time the pack train reached the cabin, the celebration had been squashed, as family members were made aware of the situation. Cold spring water was being fetched from the spring, and Jacque gently lifted the girl into his arms and carried her into the cabin.

Laying her down on a pallet of mountain goat pelts, the women stripped her and began fanning and bathing her with the cold spring water. They had seen this same illness in Muck-hul-tee-ho and had watched Hudson Bay trappers perform the same tactics, saving the person's life.

Duto was frantic--*caw-caw*ing and hopping around on the cabin roof. The children began to throw rocks at him to shoo him away, but quickly Jacque stopped them from harming the bird.

They could do nothing now but wait and hope for Pearl's recovery.

Dream of Horses

The cabin was well-built, having squared logs that were dovetailed at the corners and chinked with straw and white mud, with a closing door and window. The entire floor was made up of flat river stones. The hearth and chimney were stones of black basalt, that were mortared together with white mud. Bear and sheep skins covered the floor. Two large sleeping berths lined a side wall, covered with mountain goat fur. Quill and beadwork bags hung from pegs along with weapons, pots, and cooking spoons. Herbs, roots, and dried meat hung from the rafters, giving the cabin a pleasant odor. Through the night, Morning Sun and Horse Catcher labored over the girl, fanning her with reed fans and bathing her in cold spring water. A window above the girl had been opened to let in fresh air. The medallion, medicine bag, and Duto's treasure bag still remained on her naked body. She clutched the thongs, as if not to remove them, delirious in high fever. At one point, Pearl went into convulsions, squirming and thrashing unconsciously, her body overwhelmed with heat. Pacing back and forth on the window ledge, Duto began cursing her, telling her to wake up. The women tried to shoo him away, but he refused to leave.

"Leave the bird alone" Horse Catcher softly whispered to Morning Sun. Horse Catcher held out her arm as she had seen Pearl do, and instantly, Duto fluttered from the window ledge on to her wrist. He let out a *Caw! Caw!* and jumped from her wrist to the girl's left hand that lay at her side. Using his beak, he gently opened her palm and began pecking and swiping softly in her hand. Duto spoke to her in Visayan, confusing the Entiat women. Pearl began to stir, as if acknowledging Duto's communication. He continued the soft pecking and strange Visayan chants. The bird paused and put his ear up to her belly. Raising his head, he repeated the strange chants and lightly pecked at her midsection. Satisfied, he hopped up to her necklaces and began pulling on the medicine pouch, violently. Cursing and struggling, he continued trying to tear the bag open. Finally, in frustration, he stopped and looked at Horse Catcher and cried, "HELP ME, GODDAMNIT!" The astonished women seemed to understand and opened the bag for the bird, using a razor quartz knife to cut the cinch. Two hundred small, green pellets spilled out into Horse Catcher's hand. Duto wasted no time and hopped back to her wrist. Delicately, he selected a pellet from the pile in her hand and jumped back to the girl's bedside. Tapping her cheek with his beak, he laid the green pellet on her pursed lips. The bird now turned back to Horse Catcher and demanded, "GODDAMNIT, HELP ME!" Horse Catcher quickly poured the pellets back into the pouch and then gently opened Pearl's lips, allowing the pellet to fall into her mouth. Satisfied, Duto returned to the windowsill and began his pacing back and forth. Horse Catcher returned the pouch to the girl's neck thong and then continued her fanning. Morning Sun resumed bathing her in cold spring water.

All through the night, no one slept in the little village. Prayers and chants could be heard, coming from the glowing teepees. The air was filled with a sweet sage smoke holding prayers sent to the Creator. It began to rain, sprinkling lightly, and as the morning sun broke on the horizon, a large rainbow appeared in the valley of the Swakane. The rain stopped, and the rainbow disappeared. As if by magic, Pearl's eyes began to flutter, and she regained consciousness. The fever was gone, and Morning Sun began to cry, realizing the crisis was over--the girl would live. "I'm hungry," Pearl weakly whispered to Horse Catcher.

Horse Catcher tried to spoon feed the girl some fish soup, but Pearl had fallen back into a deep sleep and was unresponsive again.

All day, Duto paced back and forth on the window ledge, watching her motionless body, her chest barely indicating breathing. By late afternoon he began cursing and hopped from his perch to the bed. He began again lightly pecking the palm of her hand. All of a sudden, a big smile appeared on Pearl's sleeping face. Within minutes, her eyes fluttered open, and she began speaking in Visayan to the crow. Duto seemed to be relieved, now that the ordeal was over. He flew back to the window ledge and cried, "Son of a bitch, I'm hungry!" went airborne, and he was gone. "I'm hungry too!" cried a laughing Pearl. Within an instant, the gloom over the village turned to joy and laughter. Swakane Jacque had stayed in a teepee all night, praying and chanting into the next day. Informed that Pearl was talking and eating, he came out of his teepee looking totally exhausted. He wasted no time, not even to eat, and hastened to the creek to sweat in a lodge of willow and deer hide. After purifying in the sweat lodge, he jumped into the cold creek and then returned to sleep in his teepee. The following day, drums were beating, and people sang and danced. News had spread of the arrival of the immortal Bird Woman, after witnessing Duto's interaction and the appearance of the rainbow. Horses, excitement, and celebration were everywhere in the village. Several distant cousins had heard the news and had come to pitch their teepees, so as to see this magic girl. Pearl was still too weak to participate, lying in the same place for three days. The women were kind and shouldered her when she felt the urge to relieve herself. Horse Catcher had to close the window shutter, as it had become full of curious, staring faces. The elders and headmen were allowed to see the girl, and she would nod and thank them. Everyone in the camp and village was now made aware of Duto. He was perched in a high tree, watching. Instructions were given to small boys not to harm the spirit talking bird.

The following day, Chief Chilkosahaskt of the Entiat tribe arrived, along with his son, LaHompt. The Chief's village was another fifteen miles up the Big River from a place known as The Water Reeds (Entiat). Their entourage included several travois of tents and food. By nightfall, fifteen teepees were pitched and scattered across the valley floor of the Swakane. News traveled quickly on the river, and Chilkosahaskt had come to see for himself, if the story of the magic bird woman was true. Of course, Jacque had brought back a passel of trade goods, and so the camp was alive now, with gambling and trading.

The Chief and his son asked to see the girl and were escorted into the cabin by Morning Sun and Horse Catcher. The old Chief was surprised to find a young, fifteen-year-old girl, who could be mistaken to be one of his own people. The moment was awkward for the chief and LaHompt, who just stared at Pearl without speaking. She was feeling much better, sitting up in her bed. One of Morning Sun's daughters was combing her hair. Finally, the chief questioned her in Chinook Jargon, "Who are you?" Instantly, she replied in Chinook that she was from a distant island and was here to trade blankets for pelts. Realizing he could communicate with her, he asked about her "spirit bird" and if Duto was good or evil. Pearl assured Chilkosahaskt that Duto was not evil, even though he spoke "bad" words. She convinced the chief that the bird would bring them no harm. Acting greatly relieved, the chief and his son looked at each other and laughed, excused themselves, and stepped back outside to join the celebration.

Swakane Jacque questioned Pearl, "How are you feeling? You know you are pressed for time--are you strong enough to return in ten days?"

The thought had been playing in her mind while she recovered. Time was running out to do her blanket trading and return to catch the ship at Fort Victoria. "I'm feeling better, Jacque. I think I can ride in a few days, but who will trade for my blankets?"

"There's been discussion outside about helping you with your blanket trading. We have a few pelts here, but I explained to them that you don't want to piece the bale out---that you want two bales of pelts for the bale of blankets. Our Wenatchi friends are here, and they speak of an old trapper in the upper river valley who traps beaver. They call him 'Pancake Johnny.' They say he has several bales of beaver pelts, and many wives, and that he would probably trade for blankets to keep them happy. Morning Sun and I will leave in the morning to fetch him here with his furs. You can then do your trading. Just to make sure you get back safely to Mukulteo, I will return you back over the mountain trail myself."

"Oh, thank you Jacque!" she exclaimed and reached out with open arms to hug him. "I'm so grateful!"

"You get some more rest. Morning Sun and I will be gone early in the

162

morning to fetch this Pancake Johnny. We'll be back in three or four days."

The following morning, while the entire camp was still slumbering from a night of storytelling and gambling, Morning Sun and Jacque departed with fresh horses, and three pack ponies. They would make their way down the Big River to the confluence of the Wenatchi River and then head up that river to a place that was called "Where the Water Comes Out." Pearl awoke that morning and was informed that the two had left an hour earlier. By late morning, the camp was up and moving, and as quickly as the celebration had begun, it was over. By sundown, the visitors had departed, and the Swakane was now quiet, except for the bullfrogs croaking in the creek bottom.

That evening, by the hearth fire in the cabin, Pearl described a powerful dream she had to Horse Catcher, when she was delirious with fever. "I was in the middle of a large herd of horses, galloping towards the sunset. There was so much joy in my heart that I didn't want the experience to end."

"That is a good and powerful dream!" Horse Catcher pondered and finally spoke. "You say you experienced 'joy,' so it is a good thought and vision to keep in your heart. You are well now. Jacque will return in two days, hopefully with your pelts. He will take you back, as promised. I will take you root digging tomorrow. We can find you medicine to bring back your strength."

The next morning, the heat of the day began early. Shimmering heat waves appeared on the distant black rocks of the coulee. Horse Catcher had her two young sons catch and saddle two sleek, fat mares. Pearl had not left the cabin in almost a week, and now, stepping out into the warmth of the morning, she marveled at the beauty of the place. Across the whole vista, the village sat in a "hidden bowl" in the coulee. Looking up, she gazed at rolling hills waving in a sea of yellow sunflowers. Sprinkled about were patches of wild Blue Camas flowers. As the wind blew, the whole coulee consumed one's vision, with the endless motion of the waving flowers. The boys helped Pearl into the saddle, and the four of them headed down a distinct trail through the flowers. The ride over the Cascade Mountains had seasoned Pearl to the vigors of trail riding. She felt relaxed and at ease, letting the horse take her at the mare's leisure. At a cleft in the bottom of the coulee, a natural spring of artesian water bubbled from beneath a giant, granite boulder. Below the spring, a stream meandered, lined with chokecherry trees and elderberry bushes. The trail followed the high water mark of the stream. All along, magpie nests crowded the elderberry bushes. The birds sounded their displeasure of being disturbed in their nesting areas. Duto cawed with delight from a distant pine tree, watching the boys dismount and begin collecting eggs from the nests. "We will leave them here. They are having fun. Come, we will ride only a little further," said Horse Catcher. She led Pearl to an opening in the chokecherry grove that opened out onto a flat bench of lush bunchgrass, flowers, and wild herbs. Dismounting, she tethered the horses saying, "You see the blue flowers?" looking at Pearl.

"Yes," acknowledged Pearl.

"Take the sharp stick, and at the base of the flower, dig around the stem," and she demonstrated to Pearl the technique. Loosening the soil around the plant, she gently pulled the stem up, revealing a small bulb the size of her thumb. "We use these to make our pemmican bread cake," Horse Catcher explained. "Here's a digging stick for you. Put the bulbs in the basket."

Pearl soon had the technique down, and within an hour, as the two talked, she was able to fill her woven basket with the little bulbs. "Come this way. I will show you the river," Horse Catcher beckoned to Pearl. As they approached the lower end of the bench, they came over a slight rise that had obstructed the view. Before Pearl was a wondrous sight--the Big River valley. The river was wide with sand bars and sand bluffs on the distant shore. The table land above the sand bluffs was an endless vista of sagebrush, rolling over countless coulees and canyons to the north and south. Within the coulees and dry washes, small herds of horses could be seen grazing, scattered far and wide.

"Are those Jacque's horses?" Pearl asked Horse Catcher.

"Ha! Those are Sinkiuse ponies. They have thousands. They stay on that side of the river." She further explained that the Entiat people had maybe eight hundred horses. "We breed them for quality and stamina. The Sinkiuse are more about quantity." Horse Catcher now pointed to a huge, steep cliff to the south, on their side of the river. "That cliff is where we get our deer. Several people go to the mountain behind the cliff. We drive the deer herds over the edge of the cliff. This gives us meat to last through the winter and hides to trade with. After the hunt, we have a large horse race and celebration with the Wenatchi, who take part in the hunt as well. Tribes from far and wide come to this horse race and event, as the summer salmon are running. It is a happy time of feasting on the deer meat and fish. Much trading and gambling takes place around the horse races. You must come back someday and spend more time here. It is a good place," explained Horse Catcher. "You see that distant trail under the cliff? That is where Jacque and Morning Sun went and will return. Come, we'll go back to the cabin now."

The boys had disappeared from their egg gathering quest and were at the spring waiting for the women. The four gathered and rode back through the cleft in the rock and ascended the prairie across the little valley to where the village sat. Pearl had quickly bonded with the Entiat people. Her facial features and skin tone were remarkably like theirs, and they had already begun to accept her as one of their own. She could understand their dialect--a mixture of Chinook and Salish, and communicating was becoming easier. Horse Catcher made her a fresh herbal tea from plants she had collected that day and instructed Pearl to drink and rest. She would need to build her strength up for the coming trip crossing the mountains. The next morning, Horse Catcher boiled her some of the fresh magpie eggs. She then peeled them and mixed them with wild onion and served Pearl a hearty breakfast with coffee. "Come, we will purify you in the sweat lodge."

The sweat lodge was down by the creek. Horse Catcher built a small fire and began heating stones around the edge. "Your dream--do you remember any more details?" she asked Pearl.

"No, I only remember the total joy and happiness I felt, riding in the middle of the herd of horses towards the sunset," she explained. Horse Catcher responded, "When you were delirious on your deathbed with the fever, your guardian spirit crow pulled your medicine bag from your neck. I opened it, and the bird took a green pellet from my hand and dropped it into your mouth. Within two hours, your fever broke," she explained. Duto was observing the two chatting from a roost in a nearby pine tree. Upon hearing this, Pearl looked up at him, held her arm out, and called him with a strange word. Immediately, he swooped down and landed on the girl's arm. She stroked him and praised him fondly. Cawing in appreciation as she flashed the medallion around her neck, Duto then flew back to his perch in the tree.

The sweat lodge was stifling inside. Just when she thought she would pass out, Horse Catcher raised the flap and helped her out of the steaming hut. Without hesitation, she gripped Pearl's hand and pulled her into the cold creek water. Pearl let out a shriek, the icy water biting into her body. Both laughing, the women dressed and walked back to the cabin.

From the cleft in the rocks in the basin, a rider galloped towards them, waving his arm and shouting. It was "Brave Horse," a boy from the Wenatchi tribe. He reigned his pony in and came to a stop. Tears were streaming down his face. "What is it !? What is wrong?" begged Horse Catcher.

Catching his breath, he sputtered between sobs that Swakane Jacque and Morning Sun had been murdered. Horse Catcher fell to her knees and wept uncontrollably. Soon, others had picked up on the news, and now the whole village was wailing and crying. Pearl at first did not understand, but soon realized what was being said. She also began to weep. At the cabin, several people gathered, crying and holding each other. Brave Horse explained that Jacque and Morning Sun had been returning with Pancake Johnny, and one of his wives. In tow were the two bales of beaver pelts to trade for the blankets. They had been camped on the Wenatchi river on their return, when a group of four Suyapenex (white men) entered their camp on friendly terms. Pancake Johnny's wife was in the bushes picking berries and was unseen. She watched as Jacque offered them coffee, and no sooner said, the men pulled pistols and shot the three dead on the spot. Horrified, she watched the four men throw the bodies into the river and ride off with the horses, furs, and supplies. She had stayed hidden in the berry bushes, too scared to move until dark, and then hurried down the river trail that night to the Wenatchi village. Brave Horse further explained, "I must go now to Chilkosahaskt and bring him this bad news. Chief Tecolekun wants to know how the Entiat will respond, since Jacque and Morning Sun are their people." Hopping back on his horse, he galloped back down the basin and to the river. He would be in the chief's village in two hours and give him the dreadful news.

A slow drumbeat pierced the air of the Swakane. The death song and a wailing, crying chant continued through the day. Horse Catcher and Talks Too Much both cut their braids off at the ears and sat on the ground, wailing and scratching their arms and faces, until they were bloody. The death song continued into the evening, rising in crescendo in waves, then falling off to sobbing and crying. Pearl felt helpless, not knowing the grieving custom, and could only stand to the side and quietly sob. The whole scene was tragic and heartbreaking, as the two departed were key figures in all of their lives.

The wailing went on all night, and by morning, Pearl couldn't stand it any longer and climbed the hillside. She settled on a boulder in the sea of sunflowers. She could still hear the wailing below. She needed to compose herself and gather her thoughts. She realized the predicament she was in. Jacque was her ticket back to Mukilteo. With him gone, she was stuck with her bale of blankets and no way to get back over the mountains. The ship at Fort Victoria would leave without her. She bowed her head and wept. Her gamble had failed miserably. What would happen to her, she pondered. Duto landed on her shoulder, as she cried with her head hung between her legs. He had grown to love the girl, and he had seldom seen her cry. He pecked the back of her neck, soothing her, and patiently waited until she composed herself. She looked at the bird and laughed, "We'll be alright, you and me!" she promised Duto. "I will somehow get us home," she assured the bird. The two sat on the boulder all morning, listening to the grieving below. Her eye caught some movement at the rock cleft. Turning her attention to it, she saw six riders galloping towards the log cabin and the teepees. The riders dismounted at the cabin, and the wailing stopped. A crowd of people gathered at the cabin. Pearl realized something important was happening, as she could hear excited and agitated voices coming from below. She hurried down the slope of flowers and joined the group in front of the cabin. Brave Horse had brought back LaHompt and three warriors. Also with them was a young girl, who looked to be the same age as herself.

Seeing her, LaHompt addressed Pearl, knowing she was confused and frightened. "Bird Woman, you are to go with my sister, Achneen, to my father's village. You will be safe there. It is not good for you to stay in the Swakane. There will be much grieving and starving here in the days ahead. We are going to track these devils down, kill them, and get our horses back." She had no chance to reply, as shouts rang out from several warriors--"I will go with you and avenge my father and mother's death!" Maintaining control over the situation, LaHompt accepted the new warrior volunteers and told the others to remain behind and protect the now shattered village. Within a half hour, the war party was heading back down the basin of the canyon, south to the Wenatchi village.

The girl, Achneen, stayed behind, and after comforting her cousins, she approached Pearl, speaking in Chinook. "We cannot stay here. They will cry and wail into the night until they pass out. Trust me. Come with me. Gather your things, your blankets, and your bird. We will camp on the river tonight," she told Pearl. The hysterical chants and shrieks resumed with the monotonous tom tom drum beating out the rhythm of the song of death. Achneen helped Pearl load a pack horse, realizing no one else was interested in giving assistance. It would only be light another hour, and Achneen wanted to be out of the Swakane by dark. For Pearl, it was a relief to be away from the death song, and she quietly kept her horse to the rear of Achneen's lead horse. It was pitch dark now, but the horses and Achneen seemed to know the trail. At a rushing stream that emptied into the Big River, Achneen stopped. Tying the horses to a driftwood log, she sparked a campfire and got it going. Its light and warmth were a comfort after the stressful day. Achneen fetched a small clay pot from her pack kit. Filling it with water from the stream, she brewed an indian tea for the two to drink. She offered Pearl a pemmican biscuit. Realizing she had not eaten for two days, Pearl hungrily munched on the food. Feeling sympathy for her, Achneen offered another biscuit, and Pearl did not hesitate to accept it, thanking her in Chinook. Both girls were exhausted from the events of the last two days and were soon in their bedrolls, lying by the campfire.

The rising, morning sun in their faces, both girls awoke at the same time. Achneen doused the smoldering campfire and packed the bedrolls. Duto had sat and watched over Pearl diligently through the night in a pine tree close by. Soon the group was back on the trail, heading upriver to Chilkosahaskt and his village. Pearl marveled at the surrounding scenery. The river was wide, twisting through gravel and sandbars. Sometimes two or three or four channels would fan out and then come back together. On the opposite shore, sand bluffs loomed at the riverbank. At their crest, miles and miles of rolling hills covered with sage brush dominated the landscape. Scattered throughout were patches of green bunchgrass and the wild sunflowers. The well worn trail that they were on coursed through large boulders and crossed several springs that emptied into the river. Achneen gave her more pemmican and asked about the crow that had been following them all morning. She knew about Pearl's magic with the bird and wanted her to disclose more about the mysterious bond that the two had.

"Yes, he was given to me by my uncle, a wild man of the jungle forest. He commanded the bird to watch over me and protect me, and he does," she tried to explain.

Pondering this, Achneen responded, "Yes, but it is said that you talk to the bird, and he talks to you---for us to see it, we look at you as a good spirit sent to us. As he protects you, you will also protect us. My father, who is our Chief, says you are good medicine for our people."

They had been on the Big River trail for two hours. Breaking over the crest of a small hill, Achneen pointed out the chief's lodge in the distance. A cluster of teepees could be seen in a cottonwood grove surrounded by several corrals of horses. A fast-moving river lay between them and the village, spilling in to the Big River and creating a large sandbar. Achneen stood on the bank of the rushing river. A boy sat at a holding corral on the far bank. She whistled loudly, signaling him, and moments later, three boys were paddling three canoes towards the girls and their horses. Beaching their canoes, they had expected Achneen's arrival and now plagued her with questions about the war party that had been sent out. Achneen waved her arm, angrily scolding them for being disrespectful to "our guest." She commanded them to unload the packs and the blanket bale, warning not to get them wet in the canoe crossing. "C'mon Pearl, let's go find my father." She coaxed Pearl into the canoe and then pushed them into the fast current. Achneen skillfully pointed the bow upriver, and paddling ferociously, got them across in good order. Duto sat on a boulder, flapping his wings and cawing, disturbed by the danger of the fast running tributary. A huge bed of tule reeds and cattails surrounded the landing on either side, as campfire smoke drifted through the air. Jumping out of the canoe, Pearl followed Achneen into the village. Scattered throughout and on the outskirts, plots of corn and potatoes grew everywhere. The corn stalks were ankle high, and potato leaves sprouted from hundreds of little mounds. Several peach trees were green and awakening. All around were horses in several corrals. A dozen teepees were scattered through the willow and cottonwood, and chickens could be seen pecking at the ground. Smoke was coming from behind a large boulder, and as they walked around it, an earthly, crude cabin appeared. It was half sunk in the ground, its walls above ground being driftwood that had been cut to fit. The whole thing was covered with heaps of tule mats. All around were racks of fish, drying in the air and sun. Another corral, with beautiful horses within, was adjacent to the cabin. Smoke was coming from a hole in the tule mats, and a dog lay on his side in front of the hide door flap. Achneen shooed the dog away, opened the flap, and announced her arrival. She urged Pearl to come inside. "Come in--meet my mother," she offered. A woman stirred a pot on an open stone hearth and was introduced as "Yacosit." She smiled and nodded at Pearl. Two other women were pounding dried corn, taking turns at the pestle. "This is Squenhnmalx, or Soosee, we call her, and this is SpoKoKalx. Where is father?" she asked the group of women.

"He's on the mountain. A rogue stallion is trying to steal the mares. They are trying to catch him," explained SpoKoKalx.

"How is Horse Catcher?" asked Yacosit, the formalities over with.

"She is not good, Mother. She immediately cut her hair, bloodied herself, and will starve for some time now. It is so sad to see," Achneen bowed her head as she spoke.

"I pray our boys will return safely," muttered SkoKoKalx and hit the pestel extra hard in the corn bowl.

Yacosit told the girls to sit down and offered up corn bread and soup in two bowls. The girls ate hungrily and said nothing. Yacosit offered more food to eat and was politely declined. She commanded to Achneen, "Take Pearl outside to rest in the arbor." Leaving the cabin, Duto immediately landed on Pearl's shoulder. Knowing what he wanted, Pearl flashed the medallion, and he was off, landing in a nearby cottonwood tree. The arbor was a shaded roof covered with evergreen bows. It was sweet-smelling. Its floor was a mattress of ferns covered with mountain goat hide. Pearl lay down in its shade, and for the first time since she had crossed the mountains, she felt relaxed and at ease. She fell into a deep sleep.

Down river, LaHompt had gathered more Wenatchi warriors. Pancake Johnny's wife had then led them back to the site of the massacre. The killers had a two-day head start on the war party, but the trail was still fresh, as no rain had fallen. The outlaws had wasted no time putting miles between them and the scene of the crime. They had pushed their mounts hard over the Indian pass called "The Swauk," and then headed south into the land of the Kittitas. By the third day, the bandits had arrived at a log cabin blockhouse. It was situated on an open plain and surrounded with corrals. The stockade had been designed as a refuge of defense, with rifle ports built in to all four of the blockhouse walls. The bandits celebrated their haul--the pelts, horses, and kits of Jacque and Pancake Johnny being worth considerable money. All night they drank and gambled into the next morning and then passed out in a liquored stupor. Tracking the outlaws trail to the blockhouse, LaHompt and his fifteen warriors now stalked the perimeter of the place, known by locals as "Robbers Roost." They could hear the drinking and cursing coming from within, but after weighing their chances of an attack, convinced themselves that to attack the formidable enclosure would be suicide. Instead, they would steal all the horses and as the Suyapenex pursued them on the open trail, they would pick them off and kill them through ambush. An hour before sun up, the warriors made their move. The cabin had grown silent. A posted sentry, a young boy, had fallen asleep. LaHompt and Tekolecum crept into the corral on foot and unlatched the gate. Finding a lead horse, they silently walked the animals out the gate, not waking the sleeping sentry. The warriors regrouped a mile from the blockhouse, as the sun began to rise. Silently, without crying out, they brought the herd to a gallop and steered them to the north. The sentry boy awoke with the bright sun on his face. He was horrified to find the entire corral empty of horses. He sounded the alarm inside the drunken, passed out scene of the blockhouse. Enraged and cursing, the bandits spilled out of the blockhouse and into the morning sun. It took another hour to find four saddle horses and pursue, but now the warriors were miles away. At Swauk Pass, the warriors split the herd into three groups. They left the main trail, and each took old hunting trails, known to them for crossing the mountains. LaHompt and Turtle Eyes found a good spot for an ambush, for as they pushed their group of horses up a mountainside, they spotted their pursuers far below. All four men had chosen to follow LaHompt's trail, and so now was his chance to avenge Swakane Jacque's murder. Taking the high ground and planning a quick escape, the two stealthily waited, knowing the first arrow shots had to be lethal. Now, there they were, a rock's throw away. Both warriors shot their arrows simultaneously. LaHompt hit the thigh of the leg of the lead bandit. Turtle Eyes's arrow sliced open the arm of another. The four carried double barrel shotguns and concentrated their fire on Turtle Eyes, having not seen LaHompt. Turtle Eyes fell dead in a heap. Seeing this, LaHompt retreated to his hidden horses and escaped, driving the three horses he had recovered before him. The four had not seen LaHompt escape and were now too busy tending the nasty arrow wounds. They then stripped Turtle Eyes of his weapons and mocassins, and then scalped his head. They chased his horse for a while, but could not get close to the Indian pony and gave up. Feeling the effects of their hangovers, the four returned to Robbers Roost, as if successful.

They displayed the scalp and bow as trophies, playing down their arrow wounds as just a skin nick.

LaHompt rejoined his group at a chosen, hidden spring on the back side of the mountain. All were exhausted from the vigors of pursuing and retreating. Returning to the Wenatchi village, the people fell into a dark mood, as Turtle Eyes was one of their warriors. His family fell into mourning and sang the death song. Several lamented his slaying, vowing to return and seek revenge on the bandit blockhouse. LaHompt had enough of the war trail. He had found Jacque and Morning Sun's horses. Feeling sorry for Turtle Eyes's family, he gave the rest of the captured horses to them. The white man's guns were just too overpowering. He would think twice next time about attacking, after seeing how the buck shot had cut his friend to pieces.

The following day, as they passed Swakane Canyon on the river trail, LaHompt had the horses returned to Jacque and Morning Sun's family. It had been nine days since the murders, and LaHompt wearily paddled his canoe across the Entiat River, returning home. Chilkosahaskt was sitting and staring at the hearth fire, already aware of LaHompts return, when his son lifted the door flap and entered the cabin. There was a subtle glance between the two of a father/son love, and then came the business of telling the chief what had happened. Chilkosahaskt shook his head and was silent. Swakane Jacque, a French trapper, had come to the Entiat many, many years ago. He had married the chief's cousin, Morning Sun. The Chief was also good friends with Turtle Eyes, and their deaths caused great sorrow for the old chief. "We'll talk again in the morning. I must think about things," he told his son. "Have your mothers feed you and rest. You have acted as an honorable man." A large, fresh salmon steak was put before him with cornbread and dried peaches. He ate his fill and retired to his teepee.

The next morning, LaHompt was back at the cabin going over the raid with the chief. Chilkosahaskt evaluated each detail of each situation, and continued to ask more questions. Finally satisfied with his briefing of the raid, he now explained to LaHompt, "So, you know of this girl, the one they call "Bird Woman?"

LaHompt acknowledged "Yes, Father."

The Chief went on, "I'm glad she is here. I've spent some time with her this week. She speaks Chinook very well and is keenly intelligent about the world outside of ours. She is a walking spirit, protected by her raven. I wish her to stay among us as long as she wishes, as I feel her medicine is good for our village. She's been sleeping in the women's teepee, where Achneen is," explained Chilkosahaskt. "I told her that most of the beaver have been trapped

171

out, except for a few small pockets, by the French Fur Brigades from many years ago. I told her that our people traded only for horses and buckskins, but I would be glad to trade those for some of her blankets. She's stuck on trading for beaver pelts, as some distant Fort Victoria will give her gold for them. She explained that she worked for the Hudson Bay Company and was aware of the old Fort Okanogan to our north. I told her that after you returned from the war path and had rested, you would guide her to the old fort. I think she will be disappointed, as you and I both know that there's very little trading done there now."

Pearl had spent the week during LaHompt's raid in the care of Achneen. The two girls were only a year apart in age, and they bonded with each other quickly. Achneen had given Pearl beaded buckskins to wear and braided her long hair with hawk feathers, which annoyed Duto. She had been schooled about the surrounding valley and its hidden dangers, along with the serene beauty. The Sacred Mountain, where the chief ranged his horses, had an immense, sloping, broad, open pasture across the face. It was covered with green bunchgrass and wild mountain flowers. Hundreds of horses could be seen grazing on its slopes. Scattered across the ridges were lookouts of young herdsmen, who kept the herds from straying away. Wisps of smoke signaled their camp locations.

Achneen and Pearl were picking berries down by the river, when Chilkosahaskt spotted them and approached on horseback. "Pearl, I have spoken with LaHompt, and he has agreed to take you to the old fort--the Okanogan Fort. It is a two day ride on the river trail, so you must prepare for your journey today. Achneen, you will go too, if you wish." With that, he wheeled his horse and galloped up the river trail and disappeared.

Early the following morning, LaHompt, his sister Achneen, and Pearl were on the trail heading north, leading two pack horses with the bale of trade blankets and provisions. They followed the Big River's western shoreline and bank. About two miles above Chilkosahaskt's village, they came to a narrow, treacherous trail that crossed a rocky, steep cliff above the river. Loose stones covered the narrow path, so LaHompt had them walk their mounts and pack horses past the dangerous crossing. Safely past the cliff, they were now back on their horses, following a well-defined trail. The Big River at this point did a sharp bend, tracking easterly. As they progressed up the trail, a cabin by the shoreline came into view. Achneen explained to Pearl that this was her uncle's cabin, Wapato John. "He is Chilkosahaskt's brother," she explained. The cabin was surrounded by corrals, fenced vegetable gardens, and a small orchard of apples and peaches. Barking dogs announced their arrival, and being alerted, Wapato

John now sat on his front porch and watched them approach. Duto had found a perch on one of the pack horses. As they approached, he took off and flew to the cabin roof and began his pacing back and forth. Introductions were made between Pearl and the old elder. Wapato John scratched his whiskers saying, "We have heard of you, Bird Woman. I am honored to meet you. Come in. Have some coffee."

The interior of the cabin was an array of trade goods with ropes, saddles, halters, and dried foods hanging from the rafters. Immediately, Pearl struck up a conversation in Chinook Jargon and asked him, "Why are you called "Wapato John?"

Wapato John chuckled and replied, "When I was young--your age--I traveled and followed the Big River all the way down to the salt ocean. A British trading post is there--a Fort Vancouver. I spent quite a bit of time there observing their habits. They taught me how to grow things. So I returned with potatoes, corn, and fruit trees, which you see growing here. I eat a lot of potatoes, and so my people have named me as such." He now changed the subject, asking, "Where are you taking these girls, LaHompt?"

"Uncle, Pearl has many blankets to trade. She is seeking beaver pelts," he explained. "She wants to go to the old fort and try and trade them," he further explained.

Wapato John chuckled, "I think you're going a long way for nothing," adding, "Perhaps it will be a good experience for you. Are you staying here for the night?" he then asked his nephew.

"I think we'll keep going. We can reach the Chelan by evening," LaHompt replied. "We'll stay a night on our return," LaHompt promised him.

The horses were now watered and rested. Munching on bunchgrass, they were refreshed for the trail ahead. Instead of following the trail that went up the Big River, the trio climbed one that zig-zagged up into a dry coulee, leaving the Big River valley behind. Thickets of wild elderberry and wild plum choked the trail, as it climbed and wound through islands of pine trees and sagebrush. Climbing a switchback trail at the back of the coulee upon a steep grade, they broke over the crest. Pearl gasped at what she was looking at. A turquoise blue lake a mile wide disappeared into the Cascade Mountains to the west. To the east, the lake opened up into a broad basin. At the far end and shoreline, a grove of trees could be seen with the cones of many teepees poking up in numerous places. The beauty of the whole lake valley was stunning.

Achneen and LaHompt were both amused by the big smile on Pearl's face, as she stared in wonderment. It was another two hours before they finally entered the grove of trees at the south end of the lake. Dogs and a throng of children announced their arrival. Dismounting, Achneen explained to Pearl that these people were close cousins and that they would take care of their needs for the night. Seeing a group of women she recognized, she introduced Pearl with much laughter and joking. LaHompt went and found the chief, Innomeseecha, to give him a brief council to answer questions about his recent raid and the deaths that had happened. LaHompt explained the reason for their visit. Hearing this, Innomeseecha wanted to meet Pearl, the Bird Woman, as he had heard about her story. She was summoned to his teepee, and LaHompt introduced her. The old Chief offered her food and coffee. They sat, and while she ate, Innomeseecha peppered her in Chinook with questions about the outside world. Pearl could now hear Duto cawing outside. Standing, she beckoned the chief to come with her. Duto was high up in a cottonwood tree. She saw him, held out her arm, and he instantly swooped down and landed on her wrist. The two exchanged words in Visayan, and Pearl flashed her medallion. Just like that, he was satisfied, and away he flew to another lofty perch. Of course the chief and his people had all witnessed the interaction and were stunned. Achneen and LaHompt chuckled, as they'd seen it all before. That night, the Chelan village was alive with dancing and singing, celebrating Pearl's presence. Salmon, trout, and sturgeon were roasted on fires. Much joy and laughter sounded from the crowd, assembled in a giant circle within the canopy of trees. Pearl and Achneen stayed in a teepee that was exclusively for visitors. The interior was rich in soft furs and bearskin rugs. The trail ride had tired both girls, and they didn't hesitate to lie down and rest. On the other hand, LaHompt was being chased and wooed by several maidens, as his reputation was now in the history book of the tribes. As an eligible bachelor with many horses, the young girls followed him around the village. He disappeared into a secluded teepee surrounded by much laughter.

Pearl was the first to awaken the following morning. She was anxious to get to this Fort Okanogan and wanted to leave as soon as possible. She awoke Achneen and hurried her, telling her to go find her brother. Achneen had a good idea of which teepee he was in. Finding him, she rousted him out and got him moving. Two of the village women had a cooking fire going, making coffee and pan bread. The travelers ate hastily and then retrieved their horses from the corral. There was no fanfare or goodbyes, as they got mounted and left the village heading east. About a mile from the village, the trail descended a dry coulee, which emptied back out onto the shore of the Big River. Reaching the bank, they followed the trail north. Across the river, hundreds of horses could be seen grazing in a panorama of rolling grass hills. By midday, a village loomed ahead, straddling both sides of a river that emptied into the Big River. A cluster of matted, sunken houses and teepees were distinct now, with little activity present. LaHompt called out as they entered the village, and finally, an old woman emerged from one of the sunken mat houses. "Greetings! Where are all the people?" LaHompt inquired.

"Everyone is upriver at the fish traps," she pointed upstream of the tributary. "Who are you? My eyes are weak," explained the old woman.

"I am LaHompt, son of Chilkosahaskt," he answered. "This is my sister, Achneen, and our friend, Pearl," he politely answered to the elder.

"Ah, I know your father. Put your horses over there and come in. You must be hungry," she offered.

Dismounting, LaHompt explained to Pearl that this was the Methow tribe. They lived all along this river that went deep into the mountains, fish being their source of economy and sustenance. Duto found a roost in a tall pine tree and observed the three below enter the mat house. Fish stew and fish cakes were served, with the old woman enjoying their company. LaHompt inquired about staying the night, and the old woman pointed out a lean-to down on the bank of the Big River. They made a comfortable camp there and built a fire before dark. Pearl could see another village across the Big River, in a dry coulee, that came down to the riverbank. Several teepees and horses were noticed, and Pearl asked LaHompt who they were.

"Those are Sinkiuse, not Methows," LaHompt instructed her. "All those horses you've been seeing all day--they belong to them," he pointed out. The Methow village was quiet and silent that night, but across the Big River, the Sinkiuse village was noisy. The games and gambling lasted into the night, their voices and laughter carrying across the river and easily heard at the lean-to.

The next morning, Achneen was first up, brewing Indian tea in her clay pot. A quick breakfast of pemmican cake and tea, and the trio saddled back up. "Let's get started," ordered LaHompt. "We can make it to the old fort by midday, if we leave now." LaHompt swam their horses across the Methow River and waited while Pearl and Achneen made two trips in a canoe, to bring the blanket bale and their supplies across. Repacking the horses, they resumed their journey on the Big River trail, heading easterly. By afternoon, the old Fort Okanogan was in sight. Teepees fringed its outer palisades, with two distinct blockhouses guarding the warehouses and trading post. As they approached the last quarter mile to the old legendary fort, the surroundings began to look bleak. Overgrazing had turned the landscape into sand and dunes. Tumbleweeds could be seen piled up against bleached, rotting old log warehouses. A tattered UnionJack fluttered on a flagpole in the central plaza. Three lone Indians, sitting on blankets, watched as they approached. Pearl's heart sank--this did not look good. She had hoped to see a large enterprise of trappers bringing their pelts to the fort, but this scene was desolate. LaHompt asked the three men sitting where the "captain" was, and they all pointed to the only structure that appeared to be inhabited. Two dogs lay in its shade, uninterested in the trio. Half a dozen white hens scratched and pecked in the dust. Pearl and Achneen stayed with the horses, as LaHompt approached the door and called out in Chinook a friendly greeting. A bearded white man in fringed buckskin stepped out, his rifle barrel pointed at the ground. "Who be ya?" he asked in Chinook.

"I am LaHompt, from the Entiat tribe. These are my sisters," he motioned behind him, not taking his eyes off the man's rifle. "We've come to trade with you," LaHompt explained.

"Trade!? Trade what?" the bearded man questioned.

"My sister has many fine wool blankets she wishes to trade for pelts," LaHompt boldly announced. The man began to laugh and then laughed even harder, until LaHompt and the two girls were smiling also, not understanding what was so funny.

Composing himself, he leaned the rifle against the porch post, satisfied there was no danger. "My name's Francois Duchouquette. I didn't catch your sisters' names," he spoke, pulling a cob pipe from a pocket and sticking it in his bearded mouth.

Pearl answered in rapid Chinook, "My name is Bird Woman and my sister is Achneen, and we did not spend three days on the trail to be laughed at and made fun of," she barked at him. Duto watched from a blockhouse roof and sensed Pearl's anger and let loose with a slurry of profanities, this time in English. Francois stood frozen, his cob pipe falling from his mouth. Duto continued to hurl obscenities at the man in English, and finally, Pearl called up to him and told Duto to stop. Francois turned his stare from Duto to Pearl, still sitting on her horse.

Picking up his pipe, he waved them in saying, "Come in! Come in! I'll make coffee! Good to have folks to talk to! Come in. Come in." The girls dismounted and helped LaHompt tether the horses. Francois had retreated back inside, leaving the door open. The three cautiously entered with Francois calling out to them, "Come in. Here, sit at this table." He lit a candle, and the room brightened up. A fireplace covered with deer antlers on the mantle had a smoldering flame flickering. The old plank floor was wavy and lumpy in places. Behind a long, waist-high counter running down the center of the room, many barren shelves could be seen. Francois bent over the fireplace flame and coaxed a pile of coals together, placing a fresh pot of coffee on them. He positioned himself at the table with his guests and sat down. Looking at Pearl, he questioned her, saying, "Bird Woman, why did you think there were beaver pelts here? Please explain this to me."

Pearl explained the last two years, working on the sheep farms for the HBC. She explained that many, many times at Fort Victoria and in the sheep camps, stories were told of this great "Fort Okanogan," where beaver and pelts were abundant for trade.

Francois acted dumbfounded, saying, "You… you actually know James Douglas?"

"Of course. I've stayed in his house. His daughter and I are good friends," she explained.

Francois shook his head and smiled. "I could tell you was different when ya barked at me from the saddle. Uh, forgive me… let me explain what has happened here. Yes, you heard right. Those stories were true up until five or six years ago. For twenty years, the trappers would rendezvous and trade here, and yes, you heard right, that at one time, you could've traded your blankets for pelts. But nothing lasts forever, and five years ago, suddenly, the whole region was trapped out. The brigades moved north, to a place called Fort Hope, and this place became a ghost of what it once was. The HBC still wished to maintain its territory and holdings, though. My father was the head clerk here, and he left a year ago with 100 pack horses, hauling away anything of value that the company owned. You see, the powers that be on the other side of the world--the Queen--decided to give all of this to the Americans, and now the boundary is some invisible line, somewhere a hundred miles to the north. Soldiers were here last month--American soldiers--a dozen of them on horses, saying that this was a new territory called 'Washington.' So all I am here is a caretaker. The HBC is trying to sell their holdings below this forty-nine line boundary to the American government. So I'm sorry, miss Bird Woman. I will soon lose this worthless job, and I have nothing to trade or offer you. If you keep going to Fort Hope, you may have some luck trading there," he offered.

"How far is that?" asked Pearl. "Better than two hundred miles… take ya a week," he scratched his beard. The coffee boiled, and he poured each a tin cup-full.

LaHompt advised Pearl, saying, "We can't go two hundred miles. We're not provisioned for it," hoping to talk some sense into Pearl.

"I know, I know, we'll go back," Pearl sighed. "At least I had to try. I'd heard stories of many fabulous pelts to be had."

LaHompt urged her, "We might as well go back to the Methow village, there's plenty of daylight left."

"All right, let's return," Pearl reluctantly conceded. They had only been at the desolate fort for one hour and were now back on the trail, retracing their path. By twilight, they approached the Methow village. The village was alive with activity this time, the tribe having returned that day from the fish traps. All three were worn out. Dismounting, they walked their horses into the edge of the village. They were already expected, as the old woman had told of their leaving that morning for the fort. So their return was no surprise.

They were then greeted by a Methow woman. "I am Sindee Green Baskets. I know you, LaHompt. Who are your friends?" she asked him.

"My sister Achneen and our friend, Pearl, the Bird Woman," he volunteered.

Green Baskets wasted no time. She approached Pearl and grabbing both hands, looked her in the eyes, face to face, and pleaded, "My son is very sick. He has fever. I fear he may not live through the night. Many people say that you, the Bird Woman, have special medicine that can cure the fever sickness. It has been witnessed."

Pearl now realized her perplexing situation. How was she to explain that she was not a doctor and that her protector, Duto, had saved her life? "I'm sorry Green Baskets. I'm not a doctor. I don't know how to help your son," she tried to reason with the distraught mother.

Green Baskets' demeanor changed, as if a mother sow bear protecting her cub. "You will come with me under your own will, or you will come with my knife poking you in the back," she hissed.

LaHompt tried to calm the situation down. "Whoa, easy now, woman," and he turned to Pearl, saying, "It can't hurt to try and help the boy." Directing his attention back to Green Baskets, he asked, "Where is he?"

She pointed across the Big River, saying, "My son is in the Sinkiuse camp. His father is Four Eagles. Now hurry, we must go," she insisted. A group of Methow boys stood behind her, and she commanded them to take the horses to the corral. She ordered their gear and bale of blankets to be stored in a nearby teepee. "I'll get the canoes ready. Get your gear stowed and meet me at the river immediately."

As soon as she was gone, Pearl asked, "Who is she? What's happening LaHompt?"

"She is Sindee Green Baskets, a very powerful woman in the Methow tribe. She is married to Four Eagles, a Sinkiuse Chief from across the river. There is his village," he pointed. "We are on Methow land, and Sindee has demanded that you come. She won't hurt you. She's just a desperate mother trying to save her child. Trust me. Achneen and I will go with you," he assured her. Duto landed on her shoulder, sensing something wasn't right. She flashed the medallion, and he calmed down and flew off. At the riverbank, Sindee motioned for LaHompt and Achneen to share a canoe and motioned for Pearl to get in to hers. The Sinkiuse camp was a quarter mile away, downriver on the opposite bank.

Sindee led the way, paddling with strong, determined strokes. Pearl still felt apprehensive. If the child died, would they blame it on her? She asked Sindee a blunt question in Chinook. "Green Baskets, do you know what smallpox is?" not turning around in the bow of the canoe.

She answered, "He does not have the 'pox,' Bird Woman. I know this. Most of my family, my mother and father, were killed by the pox. Many years ago, a man in robes gave the arm medicine, to those of us who were not afraid. Most people ran and hid, but someone grabbed me along with several other children and forced us to take the arm medicine. Soon, almost all my people died but me. The Sinkiuse took pity on me, took me in and raised me as one of their own. No, my son does not have the pox. He is very sick, will not take food or water, and is motionless with a high fever."

Just as the canoe was pulling up on the beach below the village, Duto landed on Pearl's shoulder again. Startled, Sindee began to chant an ancient prayer. Between the beach and the village, a group of people greeted Sindee on the short trail. She urged Pearl to stay close and follow her. A crackling fire silhouetted a large group of Sinkiuse people standing around it. This was a large village, with at least twenty teepees, which were scattered in a large circle on the coulee floor. A large teepee with stars and horses painted on it was approached. Sindee lifted the flap and pulled Pearl inside, with Duto remaining on her shoulder. Relieved to see her, Four Eagles hugged his wife, and both kneeled by the boy. The child, lying motionless, was sweating profusely. Sindee urged Pearl to come and kneel by the boy. Upon doing so, she looked into the pleading eyes of Four Eagles. Pearl asked for water and a cloth. Hanging over the boy from a teepee pole was a large bladder of water. Pearl took the cloth provided, dipping it in water, and bathed the child's face. She wrung the cloth out then took more water and squeezed the rag over his mouth. A trickle of water fell in to his throat. Pearl continued this for some time, but the boy lay unresponsive. Pearl wanted to burst into tears, as she felt the boy was near death. Duto, who had stayed on her shoulder the entire time, now began tugging at the thong holding the medicine bag around her neck. "Give him some," ordered the bird in Visayan. Pearl did not hesitate. She removed the medicine bag and spilled the contents into her palm. Quickly, Duto walked down her arm and selected a green pellet. She then lowered her arm to the boy's pillow. In two hops, Duto was next to the child's face and dropped the green pellet into his open mouth. Duto cocked his head, looked at Pearl, and demanded, "God damnit, help me!" Quickly, Pearl squeezed another rag full of water into the boy's mouth, and the pellet was washed down. Duto returned to Pearl's shoulder, and she continued to bathe the child's body. An hour passed, and the boy still lay motionless. Now, with a loud squawk of impatience and cursing, Duto flew up and hovered at the water bladder. With lightning jabs, he stabbed several holes in the water bag with his beak. The water showered down onto the boy's body. All of a sudden, the boy lifted both arms and began to cry. He sat up and asked for more water to drink. Stunned, Four Eagles ran out and quickly returned with a gourd of fresh drinking water. The boy was fully awake, the fever gone, and he thirstily drank the water from the gourd. Outside, a cry of excitement and exaltation rang out. The boy, whose name was Snorting Bull, was alive and talking. Some had witnessed the magic of the "Bird Woman" and were in awe of her presence. The parents crooned over their son at his bedside.

Pearl slipped outside. The cool night air revived her from the ordeal. There sat LaHompt and Achneen. A cheer went up from the gathered crowd. Achneen jumped to her feet and hugged Pearl. She whispered in her ear, "You are very powerful now! These people will reward you!"

"I'm exhausted. I need to sleep," came her smiling answer.

"This way. I will watch over you," Achneen said as she took Pearl's hand.

Entiat: Place of the Tule Reeds

Awakening from a deep sleep, the sound of children giggling and laughing could be heard. The previous night had been exhausting, mentally and physically, and Pearl mulled over her situation. The warmth of the pallet of robes and rabbit furs was difficult to leave. She slowly sat up on the heap, contemplating her next move. With Swakane Jacque gone, her return to Fort Victoria and catching the schooner back to Owyhee was impossible. Her desperate attempt to trade her blankets for pelts at a rendezvous that no longer existed had failed. Perhaps Chilkosahaskt would take pity on her and trade for a few horses, enough to bargain passage back over the mountains. She could get back to the British fort and wait for the next opportunity to sail to the Sandwich Islands.

Combing her hair, she realized children were peeking at her through the teepee flap. Fully awake now and thirsty, she stepped out of the lodge and was startled at the sight. The entire Sinkiuse band was sitting and staring at her silently. From the crowd, LaHompt arose. He smiled broadly and approached her, saying, "Sister, they are all in awe of you! Some saw you heal Snorting Bull last night."

As he spoke, Duto flew down from a pine tree and landed on her shoulder. A cry rang out. "Look! It is true! She is the spirit Bird Woman!" A tom-tom beat began along with a shaman, chanting and singing with the whole tribe joining and repeating his chants in a loud chorus. She was brought a blanket to sit on and several bowls of various foods and fresh water. Realizing her celebrity status now, she returned smiles and nods to the crowd as they sang to her. The singing continued for half an hour, but now subsided as Chief Four Eagles stepped forward and approached her. He sat cross legged in front of her, asking in Chinook, "The food is good?" Pearl nodded yes and smiled. Returning her smile, the chief then explained his gratitude to her, wanting to give her a gift, as Snorting Bull was alert and recovering. Calling out to a group of boys, they soon led four beautiful white mares and a coal black stallion to stand before her. Four Eagles explained the quality of the horses and to accept them to show his appreciation. Now appeared Sindee Green Baskets, who presented Pearl a beautiful, beaded buckskin shawl with matching beaded leggings. A beautiful Sinkiuse saddle was placed before her as well. Pearl could only smile and shake her head in disbelief at the generosity being shown.

Pearl now arose and addressed the crowd, saying, "Thank you. Your gifts are too generous! I'm glad little Snorting Bull has recovered. I only came up

181

here to trade blankets at the Fort Okanogan. I did not foresee myself receiving gifts. Thank you very much."

Four Eagles was pleased and now questioned her. "You have blankets to trade?"

Pearl nodded, saying, "Yes, but there are no longer pelt traders at the old fort, and so I'm returning to Entiat. Maybe Chilkosahaskt will trade some horses for my blankets."

Laughing, and not to be outdone, Four Eagles boasted, "Chilkosahaskt will only offer a few horses--I have thousands of horses. Where are your blankets?"

Seeing an opportunity, Pearl explained that the bale of blankets was across the river at the Methow village. Upon hearing this, the chief commanded a group of braves to fetch the blanket bale. A large canoe was dispatched, and an hour later, the large bale was dropped before Pearl and Four Eagles. Asking LaHompt to help her, they cut the thongs on the bale and rolled out several beautifully patterned blankets. A squeal of delight went up among the Sinkiuse women. Four Eagles examined the weave and then wrapped one around himself. Getting more serious now, Four Eagles asked, "What is your price?"

Pearl smiled and silently held up one hand with one finger and the other hand with two fingers, indicating two blankets for one horse. But the chief misunderstood, and not wanting to be embarrassed, he whispered to Green Baskets. They bantered back and forth in whispers with each other, saying, "Did she say two blankets for one horse or two horses for one blanket?"

Green Baskets warned, "Be careful Four Eagles, she has much power and saved your son's life--do not insult her! You have more horses than hairs on your head--the blankets are good--maybe magic, too--give her the two hundred horses."

Finally, the chief looked at Pearl and smiled, "Alright, it is done! Two hundred horses for your one hundred blankets! My braves will take you to Corral Creek Canyon. There, you may select the two hundred horses."

Astonished at what had just happened, LaHompt excitedly whispered in her ear, "You are very rich now!"

"Where is this Corral Creek Canyon?" asked Pearl.

"A three-hour ride from here to the south. It is not far," explained Four Eagles.

"What about our horses in the Methow village?" she asked further.

"My braves will take them downriver. There is a secret crossing where you will bring your horse herd across the river. Your saddle horses will be waiting for you on the other side at this place. I will send word to round up a large herd. You and your friends can leave tomorrow. Please be our guests. Enjoy our food and celebration," the chief graciously offered. LaHompt and Achneen looked wide eyed and grinned at Pearl, nodding their heads yes, yes, yes.

Throughout the day, Pearl was showered with attention. Everyone was in awe of her closeness with Duto. He stayed perched on her shoulder, not wanting to be trifled with by curious children. Venison roasts and salmon steaks were cooked on a large, communal fire that evening. Singing and games lasted into the night. Pearl was finally grateful to bed down and relax. All of the attention had exhausted her. Upon awakening the following morning, she found the chief, LaHompt, Achneen, and a group of men already preparing for the ride south. Her beautiful gifted saddle was cinched to one of the gifted white mares, with LaHompt and Achneen riding bareback on two of the other white mares. The black stallion and the fourth white mare were led on horsehair ropes. The entire village assembled, with warm wishes and goodbyes offered. Green Baskets held both of Pearl's hands, thanking her again and again for saving her son's life.

The riders now departed, climbing out of the dry coulee on a well-used horse trail. They headed for a distant ridge, ever climbing out of the breaks of the Big River. Duto circled high overhead, riding a thermal column of hot air, never flapping a wing, and silently watched the string of horses below. Reaching the summit of the ridge, Pearl was astonished at the vista before her. Below, to the south, was the broad, Big River valley. The river coursed and wound its way far into the distance, disappearing towards Entiat. On the western horizon, the whole backbone of the Cascade Mountain range stretched either way for as far as the eye could see. Gazing at it, she had absolutely no idea where she had crossed its wall of glaciers. To the east, a rolling prairie of bunchgrass, wildflowers, and sagebrush stretched into infinity in the distance. They proceeded southward down the ridgeline, with its predominant elevation allowing them to see far into the distance. Below in the breaks, leading down to the banks of the Big River, hundreds of horses in different groups could be seen grazing. Large, black boulders littered the landscape as if they had fallen from the sky. Finally, after riding all morning, the trail emerged from the mysterious black boulders to the top of a vast canyon. Being at such a high elevation, Pearl could see Lake Chelan in the distance. A whiff of smoke could be seen rising above the Chelan village on its shore. Now, the group descended a well-worn trail. Rounding a bluff, a large, flat terrace of a meadow appeared. At its far end, a giant corral of brush and logs encircled a huge herd of horses. Below the corral were three teepees in a grove of cottonwoods along a creek bottom. Their arrival was no surprise, as these were Four Eagles' people, and warm greetings were exchanged. LaHompt estimated there were three hundred horses in the corral. Having been herded into the corral earlier that morning, they were skittish and nervous. Four Eagles wanted to waste no time, saying, "Bird Woman, choose your horses quickly. You have two hours. Then, we will drive them to the river and the crossing."

Sitting on a corral log, LaHompt pointed out "keepers" to Pearl, who made her selections known to the herders. Skillfully, one by one, they were cut out and segregated to one side of the corral, as the rejects were turned loose. Finally, the count of two hundred was completed. The herders kept them bunched and pacified in the corral, waiting for the chief's orders. "Are you satisfied with our trade, Bird Woman?" the chief asked Pearl, smiling.

"Oh, yes! There are so many! They are beautiful, but how will I get them all back to Entiat?" she asked.

"After you cross the Big River, your string of pack horses will be waiting for you on the other side. Those people have been instructed by me to help you take the herd to Entiat."

"Alright, let's go!" called out the chief to his band of herders.

Opening the gate, the herders started to calmly walk the horses down the canyon. The canyon was lush with flowers and green growth. The sun was shining in Pearl's face, and a sense of joy all of a sudden overwhelmed her. *It was the dream,* she thought. It was happening! The same dream she had when she was sick with fever! She had seen all this before--the horses, the sun in her face, the beauty and joy she felt--she was living the dream! As they loped along and descended the canyon, a giant, black boulder appeared on the hillside. It was a monster of a boulder, far larger than any others. It had split in half from the sheer volume of its weight and mass. Without a word being spoken, the whole procession stopped, as if by magic.

Four Eagles rode up to Pearl and spoke to her in quiet Chinook Jargon, saying, "This is a Spirit Rock." "The ancient ones are here. Stay here, and I will give an offering and prayer to allow us to pass safely." Dismounting, he climbed the hill to the massive, split boulder, leaving an offering of tobacco and a respectful prayer. Returning, he quietly remounted, and without a noise, the herd was moving again. Reaching the bottom of the canyon at the banks of the Big River, a giant, crescent sand bar stretched out before them. The sandbar reached far out into the river. At the water's edge, the herd rested and drank. On the other side, their packhorses and three braves could be seen, waiting for them. Riding up alongside Pearl, the chief explained, "This is where I leave you. I will now return to my village," adding, "This canyon is a holy and sacred place

184

to the Sinkiuse. Never return here without my permission. This sandbar is the secret crossing, but you have no use for it, as this place is sacred and the Sinkiuse will not allow intruders in their horse sanctuary. Say hello to Chilkosahaskt for me! Tell him I will see him at the horse races this summer. Thank you again Bird Woman, you are always welcome among the Sinkiuse."

The Chief then barked commands at his herders, who then pushed the herd out onto the sandbar. Where the sandbar disappeared into the middle of the river, the water was only waist deep to a man, all the way to the opposite shore. The current was slow and easy, barely touching the bellies of the horses. LaHompt, Pearl, and Achneen watched as the last horse climbed the bank of the opposite shore. Saying their goodbyes, the three followed the hoof trail out on to the bar. LaHompt led the way, with Achneen following and Pearl trailing behind her. The late day sun was hot, and Pearl's head drooped from the long, tiring ride.

Something caught her eye. Achneen's horse was walking the waterline of the sandbar, and swirls of golden sparkles glittered in the sun of the watery hoofprints. The sight transfixed her, mesmerizing her attention. Looking behind her, the hoofprints in the sand and water of the white mare she was on also sparkled in the sun. Finally, they reached the opposite shoreline and the awaiting horse herd. Seeing them safely across, Four Eagles waved, turned his horse, and headed back up the canyon with his people. LaHompt took charge now, as this was "his" side of the river. The three herders were young Sinkiuse boys who said very little, knowing what their task was.

LaHompt pondered the situation. There was still one hour of sun left in the day. "We'll stay here tonight. Tomorrow, early, we'll push the ponies through Chelan and make Wapato John's by sundown."

The night went by without incident. The group posted a steady watch, with the only sound being the quiet flow of the river. LaHompt had his herdsmen up early at first light, eating pemmican in the saddle, and now he pushed the horses up from the bottom land. Bringing the herd up the narrow trail to Chelan was tricky. The area was infested with rattlesnakes, and the wranglers struggled to keep them moving without panicking. By late morning, they had reached the Chelan village by the lake, stopping only briefly. LaHompt was able to gain some help from his cousins. The three cousins, combined with the three Sinkiuse, gave them a total of nine. Pearl had proven that she was as good as any of them on a horse. The Sinkiuse knew which horses were the leaders and lariated them with horsehair ropes behind their saddles, thus encouraging the entire herd to follow. Down the south shore of Lake Chelan they came, a spectacle of wild horses being manipulated by the herders. Now, leaving the lake basin and up through a dry coulee they proceeded. At the crest of the coulee, they turned and crossed a low ridge, putting them in a different canyon that descended to Wapato John's cabin by the Big River. Arriving at dusk, Wapato John was delighted to see them.

"Uncle! Uncle! The Sinkiuse have made Pearl very rich!" cried Achneen. She then described their trip to the old fort, and coming back, how fate and luck had found Pearl. Wapato John was pleased to hear of her success, saying, "I think that magic bird knows what he is doing," and then winking at Pearl. Up early the following day, the herd was pushed the last eight miles south to the Entiat sacred mountain. Learning of their approach, Chilkosahaskt brought herders to meet them and assist the tired bunch the last two miles of the treacherous part of the narrow trail. The sight of the wild herd was exhilarating. Their lead horses were turned loose, scattering them into "bands" that covered the sweeping face of the sacred mountain.

"Father, there are *no* beaver pelts at Okanogan," cried out LaHompt. "The Sinkiuse now know Pearl. This is their trade for her blankets," he said, sweeping his arm across the scattering herd.

"She even looks 'Sinkiuse' now, sittin' up in that fancy saddle!" laughed Chilkosahaskt. Proudly now, the old chief led the tired trio back to the village. A large gathering of people assembled at the corrals, smiling and quietly nodding at Pearl. Chilkosahaskt explained to Pearl that the people were still mourning over Swakane Jacque and Morning Sun's murders. To further the grief, while they had been gone, Chilkosahaskt's nephew, Steps On A Snake, had fallen from a horse and died. The people wanted to celebrate Pearl's success but instead remained subdued out of respect for their fallen tribal members. Duto was back at his routine, the observer from above. The cottonwood and willow grove of trees in the village gave him a perfect place to roost and watch over the girl. Chilkosahaskt instructed his wives to prepare Pearl with her own teepee and allowed her to rest for a day. Sleeping heavily, she awoke in the late part of the following morning.

LaHompt and Achneen were on the mountain, tagging and wrangling horses. Chilkosahaskt lay in his hammock outside his cabin, waiting for Pearl to appear. Finally seeing her step out, he waved and summoned her over to his presence. "Sit down, Pearl." He then pointed. "Over there, in those bowls, cornbread and fresh salmon. Eat." He directed her from his hanging perch. "Tell me about your journey upriver," he enthusiastically asked in Chinook.

She went over the week's activities. The Chief stopped her at intervals and ask for more details. Pearl then relayed to Chilkosahaskt that the clerk at the old fort had told her this land was now called the Washington Territory, controlled by Americans. Chilkosahaskt now pressed her with more questions she could not answer. The Chief then disclosed to Pearl that while they had been gone upriver, he had seen two strange men with conical hats and long braids across the river. The two appeared to be exploring, traveling with two burros packing their gear. He approached them, and seeing they were not whitemen, he managed to communicate from where they came--a place called "Cathay." Immediately, Pearl realized that Chilkosahaskt had seen Chinese men, which intrigued her. *What were they doing here?* she wondered. "Chilkosahaskt, I must ask your advice. I have no way to return to Mukilteo, as Swakane Jacque's band is in mourning. I'm now stuck here with two hundred and five horses. How do I sell my horses for gold?" she boldly asked.

The Chief thought for a spell before answering, "In mid-summer, a large horse race and gathering is down river, on the Wenatchi Flats. There, you can barter your horses for the yellow dust."

"Can I stay with you and your people until then?" she asked the chief.

He laughed, saying, "You are one of us. You are always welcome here." He now pointed at the distant, sacred mountain and explained, "Near the top, to the left on the bald ridge--do you see the seven benches cut into the mountain?" Squinting and searching, she could make out seven distinct platforms climbing like a staircase to the top. "I will go there tomorrow and be gone nine days to bury Steps On a Snake. LaHompt and Achneen will watch over you," he assured her.

That evening, LaHompt and Achneen returned from the pastures on the mountain. Cutting a hank of horsehair at the mane where it starts at the shoulder, all two hundred and five horses had been tagged with her sign of ownership. Achneen kept the horsehair and now sat beside Pearl, teaching her to weave a lariat rope. LaHompt and his sister had become close friends with Pearl, with days and evenings teaching her the ways of the Entiat people.

In the days ahead, Pearl could see Chilkosahaskt's mourning camp on the sacred mountain. Each day, he would move camp up to the next bench and resume his chanting and praying. He used a different drum and different prayers at each of the stations. Using smoke, he put the prayers on the wind. His wailing chants could be heard far below in the village, coming from the distant peak. On the end of the seventh day, he entered the graveyard and buried Steps On a Snake. Pearl contemplated going back to Swakane Jacque's mourning tribe, but there was no point in it. She'd wait for the horse trading and races in mid-summer and with the gold dust she'd acquire, buy herself a guide and outfit, and pack back over the Cascades.

And so Pearl spent her Spring picking berries, fishing, and being taught the ways of the "horse culture." Several of her mares were having foals now, and by the end of June, she had two hundred and fifty horses.

Her evening chats by the fire with Chilkosahaskt were fascinating. She asked many questions about his people, with each one leading to an incredible story. The Chief explained that he was the "third" Chilkosahaskt and that it meant "Standing Cloud." His band had come here some two hundred years ago from the south. They had seen the same cloud in the distance for three days as they came up the Big River. Arriving at the place of the Standing Cloud, they found the sacred mountain, and at its base was the Entiat river. In his opinion, no other area on the east slope of the Cascades was as ideal for living. The area boasted a bounty of wild game. The river teemed with fish, and the ground was full of camas, onions, berries, and wild herbs. Miles of rolling coulees covered in lush, bunchgrass made it horse heaven. He explained some of the meanings of the different tribes, that Wenatchi meant "Where the Water Comes Out," the Entiat was "The Place of Tule Reeds," the Chelan were the people of the "Deep Water," the Methow known as the people "In Between," and that the Sinkiuse were people "Of the Rock Island." The old Chief was fascinated with Pearl's interaction with Duto. As she had many questions for the chief, so it was that he asked several of her. Her knowledge of the world beyond Entiat kept him captivated. The fireside chats were rewarding to both, and by the end of July, both had bonded with a strong friendship. Achneen and LaHompt continued to teach her the secrets and art of raising horses, managing the mares to run with certain stallions.

One evening, by the fire, Chilkosahaskst told LaHompt to gather some people in the morning and go south to the "deer jump" to help. Normally, Swakane Jacque's band would lead the hunt with the Wenatchi, but their mourning continued, and they could not and would not participate. The "deer jump" was a huge cliff south of the Swakane on the Big River. LaHompt's men and the Wenatchi hunters would start at the Chumstick Mountain. A long line of riders would push the scattered deer herds south, funneling towards the cliff. On either side of the final approach, women arose from hiding places, waving blankets and creating panic. The creatures would end up running off a precipice, falling 1,000 feet to a crushing death below.

The hunt was a success, and LaHompt returned to Entiat, his pack horses loaded with venison and hides. "Father, the Wenatchi have told us that next week at the horse races, Americans with cavalry horses and soldiers will be there. They are coming from the south, from Kamiakin's land, and then going north to all of the forts," he explained.

"Good! I will go to their leader and ask that they capture the men who murdered Jacque and Morning Sun. Pearl will need help. She has one hundred horses to sell. You can drive them to the Wenatchi river bar. We will camp there," explained Chilkosahaskt.

For the next two days, the Entiat people were busy preparing for the horse races with much speculation and anticipation in the air. The morning of the departure, Pearl was amazed at the number of people who came out of the hills and accumulated at the village for the trek south. Over one hundred fifty people of families were mounted and leading pack strings of supplies and tents, with many dragging bundles of teepee poles. Children sat on travois being dragged, with several dogs following the long line of riders. The herders had pushed Pearl's horses and their own ahead of the procession, and slowly, the whole parade headed south following the river. At the entrance to Swakane Canyon, Chilkosahaskt sent a rider with two pack horses of venison and dried salmon to the grieving band. Stopping only to water the horses, the group continued on. Duto had been perched and was riding on Pearl's packhorse when suddenly, he cursed in Visayan, rose, and flew far ahead. Coming over a rise, Pearl spotted in the distance a hundred crows, swirling and flying in a circle, with another hundred on the ground, hopping, cawing, and feeding. On the ground was the butcher site of bones from the deer jump hunt. Duto's brethren were picking the bones clean. Landing on top of a heap of bones, Duto announced his arrival. In doing so, a large opening was created in the flock, who stood back and gave him all the room he wanted. Pearl called out to him and told him to behave, chuckling at his arrogance. The whole tribe pointed and laughed at Duto, now feeling a bond with the bird. As the pack train approached the confluence of the Big River and the Wenatchi river, a wonderful sight was unfolding. Hundreds of teepees covered the valley floor, with vast herds of horses mixed among them. A large campground in some cottonwoods was waiting for them on the north side of the Wenatchi river, their traditional, reserved location for this event and spectacle. The rendezvous had been happening for as long as anyone could remember. The Nez Perce, Cayuse, Walla Walla, Palus, Kittitas, Yakama, Sinkiuse, Spokane, Methow, Chelan, and Wenatchi were all here to trade, gamble, race, dance, and feast. The Entiat people wasted no time raising their teepees, with their large horse herd tended to and grazing close by.

The first night, the camp was full of old friends stopping by and exchanging information and gossip. The word was put out that Pearl wanted to sell her horses for gold. The problem was, there were thousands of horses in the valley, and their owners were there to gamble the horseflesh in wagers, not purchase them. The next day, a brave asked to see Pearl's horses. He was "Stinging Hornet," a Sinkiuse. He knew the story of how Pearl had acquired

189

them. "Bird Woman, you have horses from a good stallion. I know him. I have gold nuggets, but I am here to gamble, not buy. There are races tomorrow. I will wager my horse and rider against your black stallion and rider for this bag of gold nuggets against your one hundred horses. He held it out for Pearl to inspect. The bag was heavy, containing enough nuggets to fill two hands held together. Standing by her side, LaHompt urged her to take the bet. He proposed that *he* would ride her black stallion and win her the bag of gold nuggets. *Why not*, she thought. *I still have one hundred and fifty horses if I lose, and if I win, I'll have the means to get back to Fort Victoria and catch the ship home.* "Agreed!" Pearl acknowledged now to Stinging Hornet and handed the bag of gold back.

That night, the whole valley was in celebration. Feasting, dancing, singing, and wagering took place for the next days races. The races were to be held across the river on a large, table top flat bench. Late the next morning, the races began. Huge piles of booty, blankets, saddles, food, clothing, and horses were counted for each race. The races were a half mile across the flat around a well ribboned pole and then back to the finish line. Each race took about an hour, as most of the hour was spent piling up the wagers and then collecting the winnings after the five-minute race. Pearl watched as Four Eagle's band wagered against a Cayuse band. The Cayuse horse and rider won the race. Four Eagles took it all in stride, laughing off the loss. Seeing Pearl, he approached her, holding out his hands. "Bird Woman, it is good to see you! Where is your raven bird friend?" he joked with her. Smiling, she held out her arm, and from nowhere, Duto landed and announced his arrival, giving them both a big laugh. "I hear your black stallion and LaHompt are racing. Tell him he is up against 'Crazy Whip' and a very fast horse. I favor my old black stallion, but Crazy Whip is a skilled rider, having won many races. LaHompt will have to be at his very best to win!" Four Eagles advised her.

Now it was time for Pearl's big race. LaHompt had spent the morning rubbing the horse down and lightly exercising him. Crazy Whip and LaHompt now led their horses to the starting line. Crazy Whip's horse was a shimmering, buckskin stallion painted with lightning bolts. The crowd went into a frenzy, betting and hollering on the sidelines. Two heaps of booty accumulated as the boys calmed their horses and held them. The starting judge now ordered the boys to mount, and a hush fell over the crowd. Holding his arms over his head, he quickly dropped them and yelled, "Hi EEE!" The race was on as the two bolted away. LaHompt stayed abreast with Crazy Whip all the way to the ribbon roundabout pole. As the horses reached the pole at the same time, Crazy Whip had the inside. Coming around, he had gained just enough to whip his horse on the haunches, the strings striking LaHompt's horse in the eye, causing him to pull up. That was all it took. The remaining ride to the finish saw LaHompt eating Crazy Whips dust. Pearl felt heartsick. She soon realized that no one was feeling bad about losing, but just trying to figure out how they would win it back in the next race. Chilkosahaskt teased her, laughing and saying, "In the Spring, your one hundred-fifty horses will give you that many more in foals back. Maybe next time you will win a bag of gold!"

The races continued through the day with the same exuberance. By evening, the winners were sharing their food with the losers. There would be one more round of races the following day, a final chance to win something, if you were a loser. The socializing went well into the night. The following morning, the sleepy valley was awoken by a messenger scout. A cavalry of soldiers was coming down the Wenatchi river and would be there within an hour. Soon, the column was in view, winding down the river trail. LaHompt counted seventy-five mounted cavalry, several Yakama scouts, and a pack train of over one hundred horses with burdens. The cavalry soldiers sabers glinted in the morning sun, making the line of horses flash and sparkle from a distance. The cavalry was on the Entiat camp side of the river, with their approach ending at Chilkosahaskt's teepee. The old Chief would have preferred to have kept his distance, but now they were all around him. The entire valley of teepees--all of the tribes--were now aware of the military's presence. A stillness and quiet came over the scene. Chilkosahaskt ordered Pearl, Achneen, and his wives to stay out of sight. A soldiers drum began, ra-ta-tat-tatting, as a color guard of flags and six mounted riders approached Chilkosahaskt, standing in front of his teepee. Dismounting, two of the soldiers came forward to the chief.

"I am General George McClellan of the U.S. Army," one of them boldly announced. "Do you speak English?" Chilkosahaskt stood silent.

Now, the other white man broke in, saying in perfect Chinook, "I am George Gibbs, translator for General McClellan. Do you speak Chinook?"

"Ah--yes, yes," announced the chief, now understanding. Graciously, Chilkosahaskt invited them to sit down, saying, "How can I help you?"

And so very formally, through the translator, General McClellan informed the chief of his authority, as adjutant for the U.S. Government. He told the chief that his job was to protect all of the Indians that were camped here and that it was necessary for the tribes to work with the Army. "We are in need of fresh horses. That herd over there--does it belong to you?" the general now asked Chilkosahaskt. The Chief shook his head no, saying, "Those horses belong to Stinging Hornet."

"Bring this man--this Stinging Hornet--to me," the general now commanded the chief.

191

"He is across the river, at the Sinkiuse camp at the race track," Chilkosahaskt answered and pointed. The Chief now ordered two of his braves to fetch Stinging Hornet.

While they waited for him, Chilkosahaskt took the opportunity to report the murders of Jacque, Morning Sun, and Pancake Johnny. The general acted surprised and angry now, answering, "I have heard a story of four miners who claim they were attacked and had arrow wounds to prove it. They claimed that they killed three renegades in self-defence. As none of the miners were killed, I have no reason to pursue that case now. I'll assume justice was bestowed on the three who initiated the attack and were killed."

Chilkosahaskt could see there was no point in arguing and now wanted nothing to do with the arrogant general. Coffee was offered to the group from a uniformed man, and the chief declined, fearing treachery and poisoning. Soon, Stinging Hornet approached the parlay and formalities were exchanged. "I'd like to buy fifty horses," the translator spoke for the general to Stinging Hornet.

"What is your offer, General?" the Sinkiuse asked.

"I will give you fifty Army blankets and five pounds of coffee," came the translated answer.

"I have no need for blankets, and I do not drink coffee," Stinging Hornet did not hesitate his answer. "I will sell you my horses for gold."

"Mr. Gibbs, tell this man that the U.S. government does not give gold to Indians and that, if I choose, I may just take the horses and return them at a later date. So tell Mr. Stinging Hornet that he will take the blankets and coffee under my orders and put his X on the requisition that he approves the exchange." Chilkosahaskt and Stinging Hornet realized the situation was turning bad and that there was no hope in resisting. "Lt. Hodges, break 50 blankets out and five pounds of coffee. Have him sign the order!"

"Now, this race across the river--it is today?" the General asked his translator.

Glumly, Stinging Hornet answered, "Yes."

"Good. We'll camp here tonight," he informed his officers. And with that, he ended the meeting, tipping his hat at Chilkosahaskt. The races that day were less dramatic--more of a show for the blue-coats. The tribes of the valley were aware of the encounter with Chilkosahaskt and Stinging Hornet and how they had been coerced and forced to trade. The old Chief found out from the Yakama scouts that the column would go up the Entiat side of the Big River, as they proceeded north. That meant they would pass through his village, and he was concerned. The Chief did not want the general to force any more trades on him for his corn, peaches, or horse feed for some moldy, old moth-eaten blankets.

192

That night, he summoned LaHompt and a handful of fast riders, saying, "Go back to our village. Get there before the soldiers arrive. Behind the peach orchard is a den of skunks. Capture them, and make them do their business as the soldier column approaches."

LaHompt and his friends quietly disappeared into the night, heading back upriver, knowing the skunk round up would not be pleasant. The soldier column was up early, sounding reveille on the trumpet, waking the entire valley. With a display of pomp and regimentation, they soon were on the river trail heading north, with the Yakama scouts leading the way. Chilkosahaskt was in no hurry to follow them, as he knew his village would smell badly for the next two days. LaHompt and his comrades had managed to snare five of the foul creatures, and in doing so, they had paid the price. The little black and white beasts were tied with their snares at various points around the village in the willows. Jumping into the Entiat river, the boys gasped as they tried to wash the stench off. By late afternoon, the column was approaching the crossing of the Entiat river. Because it was mid-summer, the river was now only waist deep--low enough to wade the horses across. The soldiers assembled on the bank, seeing the tops of the teepees in the cottonwoods on the opposite side. Watching them cross from hideouts in the trees, the boys did their awful, foul task. Each climbed down from the trees, and cutting the tether of the harnessed skunks, they held their breaths and began dragging the furious creatures behind them at a full run. The skunks spewed their foul secretion, and soon the cloud was upon the soldiers as they entered the village. General McClellan cried out "My God Lieutenant, we can't stay here! Double time the column! Keep moving!" Several men were now vomiting, overcome with the rancid air. The horses began panicking, and soon all formation and order was abandoned, as it was every man for himself. The stampede ended up a mile north of the village on a large flat below the sacred mountain. Here, order was restored just as dusk was settling on the valley. In the middle of the night, the wind shifted and began to blow upriver. The smell was again upon the sleeping brigade. Disgruntled and annoyed, they were forced to break camp before dawn, finding it necessary to distance themselves from the Entiat valley. Repacking the train had been done with haste in the dark, as a hurry-up attitude was upon them to escape the odor. At first light, the column found themselves on a narrow, rocky trail on a cliff above the Big River. Bad footing resulted in two pack horses, their loads shifting, plunging to their deaths in the swirling river below. Witnessing the event, the whole column was shaken and nervous. Finally, the last of the pack horses were across and resumed their trek up the well-defined trail. Arriving at Wapato John's in the afternoon, the soldiers took advantage of his trading post supplies and horse feed. They used the excuse that they were there to protect him and that he should be obliged to offer them whatever they wanted.

Three days later, back downriver, Chilkosahaskt decided it was safe to go home and broke camp on the Wenatchi bar, leading his people back to the Entiat village. As the old chief approached his home from the south, and as if by magic, a dark rain cloud unleashed a torrent for fifteen minutes, washing the lingering odor away from the village. LaHompt and his friends welcomed the band home, laughing hysterically in telling about the stampeding soldiers and the "skunk attack." Pearl had taken her loss of the wager in horses all in stride. The Entiats laughed it off as well, saying, "No one can 'own' horses--that humans were only borrowing the horses' souls as they were needed." She was becoming one of them, and they regarded her as a "spirit being."

A month had passed since the soldiers visit. One day, Chilkosahaskt was canoeing on the Big River and was approached from upriver by another canoe. It was Otter Chaser, a Methow, paddling down the river at a rapid pace. "Cousin, what is your hurry? Let the river do the work!" the chief called out to him.

Recognizing him now, Otter Chaser stopped paddling and called out to him, "There is much death upriver! Smallpox! Four Eagles' band has been wiped out! The Methows have gone into the mountains to hide for fear of catching it! I'm going to stay in the canoe and paddle it to the ocean!" he wailed. Keeping his distance, he continued downriver and disappeared.

Realizing the danger, Chilkosahaskt returned to his village and informed his people not to travel north and to stay away from the path of the disease. He sent LaHompt south to warn the Swakane band. Halfway there, LaHompt was met on the river trail by another rider coming in his direction. It was Laughing Wolf, who stopped LaHompt from a distance. "Come no further LaHompt! I was coming to the crossing to warn your father. Many are sick and dying from the pox in the Swakane. Tell your people to stay away! It is not good! I am not feeling well myself." Waving goodbye, he turned his horse on the trail and rode off. Returning to Entiat at a gallop, LaHompt informed Chilkosahaskt of the encounter with Laughing Wolf and the grave warning. Chiilkosahaskt had heard the stories of his younger brother, Wapato John, and of his witnessing the horror of the pox. Wapato John had been all the way down the Big River, employed at Fort Vancouver. He had seen whole villages of Wishram wiped out by the disease, viewed from a canoe as he ventured downriver. Pearl explained she had seen the ravages of the pox also, having witnessed it on Sallas Island and at Fort Victoria.

"LaHompt, post scouts and sentries at the north and south approaches

194

to our village. If someone approaches, we will meet them in force and stop them from a distance," the chief ordered.

Days passed, turning to Fall. It was now October. One morning, Duto landed on Pearl's arm and raised his usual commotion until he was flashed the medallion. He was looking scruffy this morning. His feathers were in disarray, as his molt was beginning. "Feed me! *Caw, caw, caw.* Feed me! God dammit, give me my pellet!" he demanded. Removing the medicine pouch, she carefully pulled a green pellet from the contents, offering it to him in the palm of her hand. Cawing with delight, he gulped it down and flew up to his haunt in the cottonwood trees. Now, a long, cold winter enveloped the Entiat village, as they kept themselves isolated from the outside world.

The early Spring of 1854 brought news from the surrounding areas. Sadly, the Swakane people had been wiped out by the pox as well as the Sinkiuse band of Four Eagles. Sindee Green Baskets and her son, Snorting Bull, had been picking berries in the Methow mountains when the plague had hit their village and so were spared by this twist of fate.

One afternoon, LaHompt came galloping in to the village, filled with excitement. "Where is Chilkosahaskt?" he anxiously asked.

"He's taking a sweat bath, by the creek," came the answer.

Calling for him, the chief appeared, annoyed, asking, "What is it?"

"I was hunting, south, downriver at Two Tree Coulee. Two strange men wearing large cone hats with tight eyes," he said, pulling the corners of his eyes, "approached me, talking in a strange tongue, whining and begging and pleading! I galloped away for fear of the pox!" explained LaHompt.

Chilkosahaskt recalled the two men he had seen the year before with the burros, as they fit the description that LaHompt was giving. "We shall return, as they might follow you here! We must stop them from coming here!" the chief cried with urgency.

Hearing the conversation, Pearl invited herself along. She remembered the story Chilkosahaskt had told about his encounter and her assumption that they were Chinese. She was curious and had nothing to fear, for she had her protector, Duto. LaHompt quickly got a small group of braves together. He led his father and the group back down the trail to where the encounter had occurred. Duto trailed behind, circling from high above. Sure enough, an hour down the trail, the foreigners were spotted. The Entiats stayed out of sight, observing their actions. Pearl was signaled to dismount, approaching the braves and their covered hideout. The two men were stumbling along, wearing only a rag around their waists and conical hats. One of the chief's braves, Kicking Horse, suggested that they could be witches, spreading the pox, and to shoot

195

them down from a distance. Chilkosahaskt pondered this as the men got closer and within arrow range. Pearl could now hear them--they were speaking Mandarin, and she understood their words.

"No, Chilkosahaskt, don't shoot them," she whispered and pulled on the chief's arm. "They are praying and pleading to a God called 'Buddha.' I do not think they are witches. They sound like men in total despair," she continued.

"You understand them?" Chilkosahaskt looked baffled. "Tell them to stop--come no further."

Pearl advised the chief. Stepping out of concealment, the chief shot an arrow, thumping into the ground at their feet. Both men fell to the ground on their knees and began to sob for mercy. Their skin was bloody, torn from thorns and scratched by the buck brush. They continued to wail and bow on their knees, begging for their lives.

"*Ting shai, ting shai, ting shai!* (Stop, stop, stop!)" called out Pearl from her hiding place. This instantly silenced the wailing men, who now raised their heads to see where the voice was coming from. Without showing herself, Pearl asked them in Mandarin, "Who are you and why do you come here?" Startled and astonished by the voice in their language, the men announced their names, "KaPing" and "QueYu," and that they were brothers who were prospecting.

"If you are prospecting, where is your outfit?" she asked in Mandarin. They explained that they had gone up a dry coulee and found nothing. On their return, two mountain lions had stalked and attacked in the night, killing their burros and causing the two to flee for their lives in panic. They had run for miles, afraid the cats were still chasing them. Now they offered a reward in gold if the braves would return and fetch them their kits and belongings.

Pearl translated to Chilkosahaskt what she had just learned. "It could be a trick--to lure us up that box canyon with a trap waiting for us," the old chief was cautiously muttering. "Ask them if they have seen the smallpox."

Chilkosahaskt wanted to hear their reaction to the question. Still hiding, Pearl called out the question in Mandarin. Quickly replying, the Chinese explained that they had been vaccinated in Hong Kong in order to board the British ship. They further explained that they were not sick and had not been with anyone who had the pox. Again, they begged for their lives and offered gold as a reward. Pearl translated this to Chilkosahaskt from her hiding place, as the chief continued to glare and stare them down. He kept another arrow knocked in his bow, ready to shoot them down in a blink of an eye. "Tell them to stay where they are!" the chief barked fiercely, not taking his eyes off them.

Pearl commanded them not to move and then asked, "How much gold are your two lives worth?" in Mandarin.

196

KaPing quickly answered, "We have three ounces of gold, hidden where the lions attacked us. It is yours if you help us retrieve our equipment," he begged.

Pearl wasn't sure how much three ounces of gold was worth, or even what that quantity was. She now tested him, saying, "You want us to go face two mountain lions for three ounces of gold? We have better things to do!"

Still the Chinamen could not see Pearl, only hearing her voice. Still pleading, KaPing offered one more payment, saying, "Alright, I have a golden Buddha medallion. You can have it, as well. It's all we have. I beg you!"

Again, Pearl translated the proposition, and finally, Chilkosahaskt looked over his shoulder, saying to LaHompt, "Take three braves, and with one of the foreigners, have him guide you to the place of the lion attack. The rest of us will stay here and hold the other foreigner until you return." LaHompt and his warriors were quick and surrounded the two, crashing out of their hiding places behind the boulders. Once more, from her hiding spot, Pearl commanded the two men in Mandarin that one would lead to the spot of the lost equipment, and the other would be held under guard until they returned.

Chilkosahaskt waved his arm, saying, "Be quick. We will take these foolish men's gold, and if they are lying, we will cut their tongues out. Go, now!"

Kicking Horse put QueYu on a saddle, swatting the horse's rump, and began heading for Two Tree Coulee. LaHompt and his cousins tied KaPing's feet and hands. Satisfied at the outcome of the encounter, Chilkosahaskt disappeared back into the rocks to talk with Pearl. "Come with me, Pearl," he told her. "We shall return to the village. Tomorrow, we will see if they are who they say they are." Duto had watched the whole event unfold and had grown agitated and nervous when hearing Pearl's voice doing the negotiating. He now flew to her shoulder, demanding a look at his shell medallion. Chilkosahaskt shook his head and laughed, kicking the flanks of his pony. "C'mon. Let's go."

The following afternoon, LaHompt came galloping back into the Entiat village. Finding his father and Pearl, he explained that the Chinamen were telling the truth. Kicking Bird had found the broken camp. One cat had drug a dead burro to a hiding spot and was standing over it when discovered. Ruthlessly, the brave had shot three arrows in quick order, all of which found their mark. As the cat let out a gurgling death scream, the other cat, which was nearby, fled for its life. As it turned out, the Chinamen had a lot of gear---two large chests with a tent, shovels, pans, ropes, and tack. Packing their horses, the group had to walk out of the coulee. They had returned that morning to where LaHompt and the others held KaPing hostage. Realizing they had told the truth, LaHompt cut KaPing free from his bindings. "They have stopped downriver at Little Spring

197

Coulee. They are happy and want to give you the gold that was promised," LaHompt further explained.

"Good. Return to them and tell them I will come to see them tomorrow morning," the chief advised his son.

The following day, Chilkosahaskt and Pearl rode down to the Chinamen's camp. They had pitched their tent on a sandy beach and were panning at the river's edge, as the two approached. Pearl addressed the Chinamen as she pulled up her horse and stopped. Staring KaPing down, she now addressed them in Mandarin, saying, "Good morning. I see that you have recovered your belongings."

KaPing and QueYu could now see the face speaking their language. Staring at her in disbelief, they now watched her raise her arm, still seated in the saddle, as a large raven landed on her wrist. KaPing was now shaking but bravely asked, "How does an Indian girl like you know our language and speak our dialect in this far away place?"

"I am not one of these people. I am Filipina, from the Filipina's Islands," Pearl answered in Mandarin.

Now even more bewildered, KaPing repeated, "How did you come to be in such a far away place?"

"Ha! I rode here on a horse!" was all that Pearl would offer. "The Chief has saved you from perishing--a certain death. He has come to collect the gold that you bargained for," Pearl announced. Without hesitating, KaPing pulled a small bag from his pocket and removed a small gold medallion from his neck, offering them to the chief, sitting on his horse.

Chilkosahaskt now addressed them in Chinook, with Pearl translating in Mandarin. "It is good you are honest men and have kept your word. What are your plans now? You have no burros."

KaPing replied, "This morning, we discovered a small pocket of gold on this beach. We would like to work it, and with the gold we find, buy two horses and some food, and then we'll be on our way."

Chilkosahaskt was not expecting this answer. He thought about it momentarily and then agreed, saying, "Very well, but stay out of my village. Several people think you are witches. They might kill you. I cannot guarantee your safety. You must find your gold and leave as soon as possible. We will check on you in one week." His demands were translated back to the Chinamen.

Returning to Entiat, Chilkosahaskt and Pearl studied the sack of gold dust and the little gold medallion. His curiosity quenched, he told Pearl that she could have both, as she was the one who had negotiated for it and that he had no use for gold. The following week, the chief and Pearl returned as he promised. They were amazed at what they were looking at. KaPing and QueYu had dug a shallow ditch from the spring in the coulee, routing it to the river beach. A large, "cradled" box was being rocked back and forth by QueYu, as KaPing shoveled the sandy gravel into its hopper. The water from the ditch fell into the cradle at a constant rate, allowing the shoveled mix to wash away. Trapped in small grooves carved at the bottom of the cradle, the heavy gold dust settled. KaPing would then scrape out the grooves and pan the mix with more water, separating and removing the pure gold. Curious now, Pearl and the chief asked to watch the process. Duto kept his distance, watching the Chinese, not sure if Pearl was in danger. The conversation was friendly, with periodic laughter, and so he was content that they were no threat to her. Getting down to business, the Chinese now offered a thimble full of gold dust, the equivalent of an ounce, for two horses and some dried fish. Agreeing to the offer, Pearl explained that they would return the next day with the two horses and dried fish.

The next day, the exchange was made, the thimble full of gold for two horses and one of the chief's baskets of dried salmon. KaPing now pleaded his case to Chilkosahaskt, saying, "We are very low on supplies. There is a soldier fort at Walla Walla, many days' ride to the south. We will pay you more gold to guide QueYu there, so that he might return with the goods we need."

Pearl translated this, and Chilkosahaskt pondered over it before giving his answer. "I have a brother, Wapato John, who can take you there if he agrees to your offer. I will tell him of your words. Maybe he will agree, maybe not," came Chilkosahaskt's reply.

Arriving back at Entiat, Chilkosahaskt sent a messenger to his brother. The following day, Wapato John appeared at the Entiat village. "There are two Chinese brothers camped downriver. They have found some gold and offer to pay you with it, if you guide one of them to Walla Walla," the chief explained.

"This is good," replied Wapato John. "When General McClellan and his army appeared and camped at my place, they helped themselves to whatever was on the shelves and pilfered my gardens, saying they would pay me back when they return next year. I have no faith that I will ever see the payment. Because of this, I myself, need to take a pack train to Walla Walla and restock the goods stolen from me. So yes, I will take payment for one of them to ride along," explained Wapato John to his brother. "Tell these Chinese that I will depart in three days and to have LaHompt bring this QueYu to my cabin. If I don't see him in three days, I will leave without him." Wapato John then departed and returned to his cabin upriver.

Chilkosahaskt, with Pearl, rode back downriver to inform the Chinese of his brother's decision. KaPing and QueYu were pleased to hear that Wapato

John would help them. Chilkosahaskt explained that LaHompt would return tomorrow and escort QueYu north to his brother's cabin. The Chief warned QueYu that the round trip would take over a month and to be prepared for a harsh, desert trail. KaPing explained to Chilkosahaskt that he would be no trouble, staying at the camp on the beach and continue to work the small pocket of gold. Bowing several times now, KaPing offered Pearl and the chief tea from a steaming pot that was sitting on the campfire. The tea had a distinct flavor--the same flavor as the tea that the old Chinese granny had given her when she attended school. She was becoming more at ease around the Chinamen, allowing Duto to sit on her shoulder while she enjoyed the tea and Mandarin conversation. Likewise, KaPing and QueYu were in awe of Pearl, astonished at their luck in finding someone that could speak their dialect in this vast wilderness. Chilkosahaskt was fascinated to watch and listen to the dialog he could not understand. Periodically, he would stop Pearl and inject a question. The Chinese had created a comfortable camp. One of the trunks was opened and expanded out to become a giant cabinet on legs, containing dozens of small drawers. An open tent displayed a small shrine to a Buddha statue, with a candle burning in a glass globe before him. A hearth of stones with an iron crossbar held a hanging soup pot, which was ingeniously set up for cooking. Of the two brothers, KaPing appeared to be the dominant one and more outspoken. QueYu was the quiet one who said little, even when spoken to. Dutifully and as promised, LaHompt was at the Chinese camp early the next morning to escort QueYu. The Chinese had already packed their two horses and were eager to see LaHompt.

He urged QueYu to finish his breakfast so they could get started. Soon, they were on the trail, backtracking north through the Entiat village, following the Big River trail to Wapato John's cabin. Reaching his cabin, he was pleased to see them. The next day, he and QueYu departed, leading a long string of pack horses towards the distant Fort Walla Walla.

Days went by, and one morning, Chilkosahaskt found Pearl at the river, washing and bathing. Staying in the water, she said, "Good morning. What's for breakfast?"

"I think you and I should ride downriver and check on the Chinaman. I like that tea that he gave us," the chief answered. "Meet me at the corrals in one hour," he told her.

When Pearl appeared at the corral an hour later, the chief had their horses bridled and ready to go. He enjoyed the rides with the girl and their conversations. And as always, there was Duto, flying from tree to tree and rock to rock, watching over her. Chilkosahaskt called out a greeting as they rode in to

KaPing's camp. The Chinaman was hard at work, rocking the cradle box, and welcomed the chance to stop and visit. He offered up the green tea in tin cups, and the three sat down, exchanging pleasantries. KaPing divulged that the gold pocket was playing out and that he was working harder to get half the gold he was getting a week before. He explained that when QueYu returned, they would move on in search of another pocket of gold-bearing gravel. The Chief asked KaPing "What have you been eating?"

"I finished the dried fish I got from you. I have a little rice, and I catch crayfish in the water reeds," explained KaPing.

"I don't like to see anyone go hungry. We have enough cornmeal to share some. I will have Pearl bring you a sack tomorrow," the chief generously offered.

"Thank you. You are very kind. I must return to my cradle rocking and take advantage of the daylight," KaPing now insisted. Pearl held out her arm, and from a boulder perch close by, Duto landed, walked up her arm, and roosted on her shoulder. Back on the trail, she looked back to see KaPing staring at their departure. He waved at her, and she impulsively waved back.

The next day, she returned alone with a five pound sack of cornmeal. Still laboring over his rocking cradle, he stopped and wiped his brow. Smiling, he greeted her "Welcome, welcome!" in Mandarin. "Sit down! Have some green tea." He gestured with his hands. "Ah, very nice!" he said, nodding his head as he accepted the bag of cornmeal. Now relaxed and drinking the tea, a more personal conversation evolved. He explained that he was from Macau, or Hong Kong as it was also known, and had grown up there. He had several brothers, QueYu being one of them. Their grandfather was a master blacksmith and forged tools and weapons for the wealthy class. Their father was a doctor of medicine and had the means to educate his sons. When news of the gold discovery in California had reached Hong Kong, they had taken advantage of their grandfather's connections with the wealthy class. They had found passage on a British merchant schooner. He and QueYu had sailed to San Francisco. Arriving in California in 1850, they had grubbed and panned for three years, making only daily wages and enough to survive. They had prospected up into the Siskiyou mountains, heading north, and eventually reached the lower Big River. Following the Big River, they ended up at where they were now.

Pearl now opened up, explaining her last four years and her quest to somehow make it back to her family and island. Before long, the two were both experiencing a mutual attraction, their eyes locking and gazing at each other fondly. "I have a little rice. Would you care to have some?" he politely offered.

"Oh yes! I haven't had rice since the Christmas dinner at Fort Victoria!"

she eagerly nodded her head. Boiling some crayfish, he diced them up, spiced them with herbs, and poured the sauce over a large bowl of white rice. He offered the girl chopsticks, but she had already begun spooning the meal into her mouth with her fingers. She laughed, saying, "No," and waved the chopsticks away. The afternoon passed quickly with the two drinking more tea and gazing at each other longingly. "I have to go now. They will wonder why I stayed so long," she told him.

"Will you come back tomorrow?" KaPing asked, hopefully.

"Maybe. I need to check on some horses. If not, I will see you again," she coyly smiled at him.

The following day, she couldn't get KaPing out of her thoughts. The rice had brought back memories of home, and she enjoyed his conversation. Filling a buckskin bag with some dried peaches, she headed back downriver to indulge in another visit. There he was, hard at work laboring over his cradle, and did not notice her approach. Duto landed in his camp and announced her arrival. Pleased to see her, he dropped everything and welcomed her. As she handed him the bag of dried peaches, their eyes locked, and in that moment, they both knew there was a mutual attraction.

"Sit! Sit! Have some tea!" he offered her. He explained that he had been up since first light and that the pocket of gold dust had just about played out. Taking the morning's effort, a pinch of gold dust, he dropped it into a tin cup and added some water. Swirling it with his finger, he offered it to Pearl, saying, "Look. The gold sparkles in the water from the sunlight. Not much for a half day's work," as he shook his head.

Pearl took the cup and continued swirling it with her finger, the tiny flakes flashing in the sunlight. Suddenly, as she stared at the cup, the memory of the sparkling horse hoofprints on the sandbar upriver came back to her. "I have seen a place upriver where the water sparkles like this," she explained. Hearing this and trying to suppress his excitement, he casually asked her to explain. "A year ago, the Sinkiuse gave me horses for blankets that I had--a trade. We crossed the Big River at a sandbar, driving the horses. Out on the sandbar, I looked down and saw sparkles of light in the watery horse hoofprints."

"Do you remember where the place is?" KaPing pressed her. "Yes, but Chief Four Eagles told me not to return to the place, as it was regarded as sacred ground to the Sinkiuse." Pondering more about the subject, she now explained that Four Eagles and his band had all been wiped out by smallpox.

"Since these people no longer occupy the land, perhaps it is alright to at least go to this place and investigate," KaPing coaxed her.

Again, she was nervous about the prospect. She remembered Four

Eagles praying at the massive rock in the coulee and sensing the place was alive with spirits. "I will talk to Chilkosahaskt and LaHompt about this and if it would be safe to return there," she offered to KaPing.

"Very well. If it is a place of much gold, I will share it with you--whatever is found," he promised.

Returning to Entiat that late afternoon, she casually proposed the question to Chilkosahaskt and LaHompt over the dinner meal. "Chilkosahaskt-- with Four Eagles and his band now gone, is it safe to go across the river?" she asked.

"Safe? What do you mean?" the chief looked at her, wondering. Without divulging the secret of the gold, she explained that she wanted to return to the place of Corral Creek and the sandbar crossing.

"Why do you want to go there?" the chief asked curiously.

"I saw many wild horses there across the river--if LaHompt and I could catch some, it would add to our herd," she explained.

"I suppose there is no harm in it. I am of Sinkiuse blood, and they belong to any Sinkiuse that can catch them. Now that Four Eagles is gone, I see no reason why it would be a problem. The only danger is Lolowkin, Chief of the Southern Sinkiuse. If his braves find you on their land, they may not be so friendly, but they are far out on the plateau this time of year, gathering duck eggs at a distant lake. I am good friends with Lolowkin, so I see no danger in it."

"Then you would allow LaHompt and I to go there and scout the possibilities?" she asked.

"Alright. Stay in the breaks and the coulees. Do not venture out onto the plateau," he made her promise.

"The Chinaman says his diggings have played out. He would like to ride along and search for a new place," she cautiously pushed the old chief.

"Ha! Very well. When his brother returns, I suppose they will be moving on anyway," the chief replied, not giving it much thought. Chilkosahaskt now offered more advice to her and LaHompt about where the springs were across the river and where they might find bands of wild horses.

The next day, while LaHompt prepared for the three day scouting trip, Pearl returned to KaPing with a spare horse. "C'mon. Bring what you need. Chilkosahaskt has given us permission to cross the river!" she explained. Wasting no time, he, she, and Duto returned to the corrals at Entiat. LaHompt had two pack horses loaded with food and blankets, and soon, they were on the river trail heading north.

Stopping briefly at Wapato John's cabin to rest and water the horses, they pressed on and made it to the Chelan village on the lake that evening. Chief

Innomeseecha was delighted to have visitors. LaHompt explained to him the purpose of their trip. The Chief shook his head, saying, "Broken Sun's people were across the river two months ago catching wild horses. There are a few horses remaining. You might catch a few if you're lucky," he offered. The Chief was curious about KaPing, asking many questions of Pearl about who he was and where he came from.

The following morning, LaHompt led them to the crossing on the Big River. It was as Pearl remembered it the year before--a large, crescent sandbar on the opposite shore, extending halfway out into the river. LaHompt led the way. The water level lapped at the soles of their feet as they crossed on horseback towards the outer reach of the sandbar. Reaching the other side, Pearl explained in Mandarin to KaPing that this was the place where the horse hoof prints sparkled in the sand. Within five minutes, LaHompt shot a rabbit with his bow. Skinning the creature, he built a fire and prepared some lunch.

"We'll go up the coulee to the corrals and see if any ponies are lingering around the creek," LaHompt told Pearl. "Your friend can stay and search for the yellow dust. We'll be back before dark." Leaving KaPing at the sandbar, the two rode up the canyon, coming to the huge boulder that had split in half. LaHompt and Pearl had observed Four Eagles the previous year approach the monster rock in reverence. Now, he too dismounted, handing the reins to Pearl. Walking up to the monolith on foot, he made a prayer and an offering of cornmeal. Returning to his horse, he commented to Pearl, "Let's go. I don't like this place. The Sinkiuse are afraid of spirits that lurk here." Kicking his horse, he again urged, "C'mon. Let's get out of here!" Climbing the faint horse trail, they now came to the corrals in the meadow below the creek. The teepees were gone, and there was no sign of anyone or wild horses present. "I think Innomeseecha is right--the Sinkiuse have been here and drove Four Eagles' horses south," LaHompt told Pearl. "Let's go back to the river. We are chasing ghosts here," LaHompt suggested. Heading back down the canyon, again LaHompt stopped at the massive, split boulder. He dismounted, approached it, and left an offering of kinnickanick tobacco.

It was sundown when they reached the sandbar. KaPing was wild-eyed with a big grin on his face. Without a word, he handed Pearl a tin cup. She almost dropped it, fooled by its heavy weight. The tin cup was half full of yellow dust, shocking Pearl when she realized what it was. In Mandarin, KaPing explained he had panned gold all afternoon, the results being astonishing. Excitedly, he explained to her that she had led him to a bonanza--a place so thick with gold that both of them would be very rich in no time. "You will return to your island and your family and be a very wealthy woman! There is enough gold here to make us rich beyond our dreams!"

LaHompt could tell they both were very excited. Looking into the cup of gold dust, he could not comprehend what he was looking at. Wealth to him was many fine horses and several wives. A tin cup half full of gold dust meant nothing to him. Little did he realize that what he was looking at was the final chapter of his people and their way of life. KaPing was educated and could better understand what they had discovered. He had learned about what can happen when word of a gold strike got out, the lesson learned in California. Him being a Chinese, he would quickly be rubbed out. He realized that the discovery must be kept secret and to not disclose anything about their find.

"I'll go tether the horses and get us another rabbit. We'll camp here tonight. You two talk too much!" LaHompt laughed at them and disappeared.

"Pearl, come with me!" KaPing pulled her by the hand. Twenty paces out onto the sandbar, at the water's edge, he had excavated a large hole. Reaching into the hole, he pulled out two large scoops of the sandy, quartz gravel. Plopping the mix into his pan, he began to swirl the contents, spilling out the debris and waste. Within two minutes, half of a thimble full of gold lay in the bottom of the pan. Now even Pearl was realizing the magnitude of the find. What had taken KaPing five hours of hard work at his beach site at Entiat, he now produced within three minutes with little effort. Depositing the gold in his poke bag, he now pulled out two more scoops from the hole, repeating the process. Again, in short order, he produced another half thimble of gold. Within ten minutes, he had extracted an ounce of gold from the sandbar. "Pearl, we have to keep this a secret. If word gets out about this place, there will be a thousand miners here within weeks. Say nothing about this place to anyone. When QueYu returns, I will send him downriver to bring a work party back," he explained. KaPing carefully filled the hole back in with sand and washed it with water to make it look natural again. LaHompt returned with a fresh rabbit. That evening, Pearl and KaPing concealed their excitement, changing the conversation to the subject of all the wild horses disappearing. The next day, they broke camp early, crossing the river, climbing out of the valley, and returned to the Chelan village. All along, Duto circled above, watching the trail for the girl.

"You were right--the scattered herds are all gone!" LaHompt informed Chief Innomeseecha. Pushing on, they arrived at Wapato John's cabin at dusk. John had still not returned yet with QueYu from Walla Walla. The three spent the evening chatting with his wives and family. Early the next day, they were on their way.

By late morning, they had arrived back in Entiat. Chilkosahaskt was pleased to see them, saying, "Well, what did you see? I know Lolowkin, and he would have captured most of Four Eagles' horses."

"We saw no horses," LaHompt lamented. "It's as if they were never there," he added.

Pearl then explained to the chief that KaPing had found another site to pan for gold, playing it down as insignificant. Hearing this, LaHompt verified her story, only saying that the Chinamen would move on after the return of QueYu.

Ten days went by, and finally, Wapato John rode into the Entiat village with QueYu. The Chinaman's pack horse was loaded with fresh supplies. He had brought back flour, rice, tea, and many necessities. That evening, KaPing revealed to QueYu that Pearl had led him to the sandbar full of gold. "QueYu, take our two horses and this bag of gold. Go downriver, back to the Siskiyou mountains. Bring back a workforce of men," KaPing advised his brother.

QueYu was gone early the next morning. Around noon, Pearl arrived at KaPing's camp. "I've been thinking, Pearl. You need to come with us--to the sandbar. When QueYu returns, your ability to speak with the Indians and their respect for you is needed. There are many Chinese coming who will work for me and QueYu. To guarantee our success, I need you at the sandbar to help communicate. Once a large workforce is at the sandbar, our safety will be in our numbers there. Until then, we need you there to help guarantee our success in holding the diggings for ourselves. We will reward you with more gold than you've ever dreamed of! One year from now, you will be able to buy your own ship and crew, return to your island, and live like a queen for the rest of your life!"

Sir James Brooke (White Rajah of Sarawak) - Wikipedia

Sir James Douglas (Chief Factor - Fort Victoria) - Wikipedia

Chilkosahaskt (Standing Cloud, Chief of the Entiat)

Wapato John and Chilkosahaskt (Half-Brothers - Entiat Tribe)
University of Washington Libraries, Special Collections, NA 784

Quanah Parker (Chief of the Comanche) - Wikipedia

Peter Wapato (Son of Wapato John) - Chelan Historical Museum

THE CHINA DITCH

BELOW THIS SIGN YOU CAN SEE THE REMNANTS OF THE
CHINA DITCH BUILT BY CHINESE MINERS SOMETIME BETWEEN 1860
AND 1880. THIS DITCH CARRIED WATER FROM A DIVERSION POINT
THREE MILES UP THE METHOW RIVER TO SLUICE GOLD FROM THE
COLUMBIA RIVER SANDBARS A MILE OR TWO DOWNSTREAM. AFTER
THE CHINESE MOVED ON, SETTLERS USED THE DITCH TO IRRI-
GATE ORCHARDS ALONG THE METHOW AND COLUMBIA RIVERS UN-
TIL A 1948 FLOOD DESTROYED TWO MILES OF CANAL AND
FLUME. BY THEN, THE CHINA DITCH HAD PRODUCED A FAR
GREATER VALUE IN APPLES THAN IT EVER HAD IN GOLD.

TED BORG-HISTORIAN

The China Ditch (Pateros)

214

EARTHQUAKE POINT

This site on Ribbon Cliff called Broken Mountain by the Indians experienced a violent earthquake in December, 1872. The shock split the mountain, forming the cliff to the west and causing a huge rock slide which stopped the flow of the Columbia River for several hours. The black ribbons of the cliff are lava-filled fissures. Plateau lavas of the region later covered this rock mass. The white volcanic ash in road excavation is so recent as to have buried undecayed logs. It was blown from Glacier Peak, a volcanic cone, 50 miles to the northwest.

Washington
State
Department
of Transportation

ERECTED BY THE
WASHINGTON STATE DEPARTMENT OF TRANSPORTATION
IN COOPERATION WITH THE WASHINGTON STATE
PARKS AND RECREATION COMMISSION

Earthquake Point (Entiat)

215

Chinese Miner - Pateros Historical Museum

Serpent Rock (Corral Creek Canyon)

216

Matalom Pirate Tower (Leyte)

Matalom Catholic Church (Leyte)

217

Bells of Balangiga (Returned to Samar December 2018)

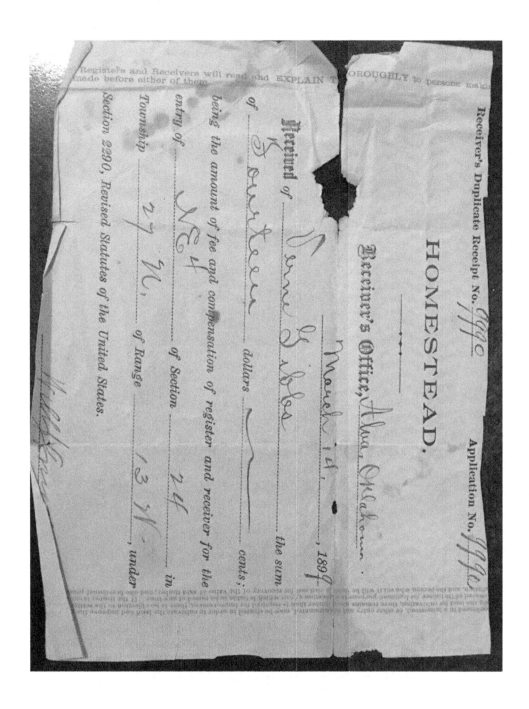

Homestead Receipt (1899) (Verne Gibbs) (Oklahoma)

Brusco, 55 Apache (1971)

Brusco and Zeke, 55 Apache (1971)

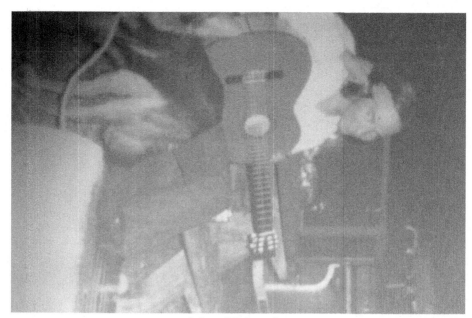

Jake, 55 Apache

Jake, 55 Apache

Wendell George (2019) (Chilkosahaskt's Great Grandson)
(In D. Withrow's Man Cave)

Andy Joseph with Lorna (1996) (At July Grounds, Nespelem)

Brusco and Milton Gibbs (1996) (Pheasant Hunt - Coulee Dam)

Cedar Moon and Douglas Withrow (2019)

The China Bar

That evening, back at Entiat, Chilkosahaskt noticed that Pearl was brooding and had a quiet nature. "What's the matter? You don't seem yourself--you're thinking about something," the chief pressed her.

"Yes, I'm afraid of the future, the seeds I have planted," the girl quietly muttered.

"Go on--tell me. It can't be all that bad," the wise old chief coaxed her. "Let me guess. I notice that you seem to have become very close with your friend KaPing. Tell me--you have deep feelings for him?" he asked.

"Yes, he is a good man--a very smart man. It is easy for us to talk. We seem to know each other's thoughts," she replied.

"Go on," the chief coaxed her again.

"When we went looking for horses, that was a partial truth. I told KaPing of a sandbar where there might be gold. That's why he traveled with LaHompt and I. Sure enough, he found gold at this place. He has sent his brother, QueYu, to go and fetch men to help pan it out. I wasn't thinking this would happen--only that he and his brother would find some gold and be happy. Now, he has asked me to accompany him and his men to this place. He has guaranteed me enough gold to be very rich. I am happy here, yet my desire to return to my island, Leyte, still burns in my heart," Pearl explained and began to cry in her hands.

"I see. Where is this sandbar?" The chief looked at her with apprehension.

"It is at the bottom of the Corral Creek Canyon," she slowly spoke, looking him in the eye.

"That is Sinkiuse land--one of their horse canyons." The chief shook his head.

"Yes, I know this, but Four Eagles and his people are all gone," she reasoned with him.

"That makes no difference. Lolowkin will not allow intruders in that place. You and KaPing would be in danger." Chilkosahaskt scratched his chin in thought. All of a sudden, he changed the subject. "A messenger from the Wenatchi came to me while you were on your horse hunt." He added, "There are soldiers in the Wenatchi valley. They have come to summon all tribes to a great council next year at Walla Walla. They say we must sign a treaty to share the land with the whiteman. I am too old to go, so I will send LaHompt. Tecolekin of the Wenatchi will also go to represent his people. I have bad feelings about this--when soldiers tell us that we will 'share the land.'" He thought some more and then continued, "So if white people are coming to our land and protected by soldiers.... Perhaps this is an opportunity for you to get some gold and return home before the white man finds it and takes it for himself. You are protected by the spirits, Pearl, and they have guided your path to this gold." He went on, saying "I can speak to Lolowkin, as we are good friends. I will ask him not to harm you or attack you--but I can only ask. He has many warriors, and there may be some who do not like his decision. Either way, you must stay on your guard at that place."

"Will you allow KaPing to stay at Little Spring Coulee until his brother returns?" asked Pearl.

Chilkosahaskt nodded, saying, "You say he is a good man. You have been here long enough. You are one of us. The question is, do you trust him?"

"Yes, he has a good heart. He is no threat to the Entiat people," explained Pearl.

"Very well, but when this group of Chinese men show up to work the gold, I want them to keep moving when on our land, not stopping until they are far upriver," he warned her now.

"I will tell KaPing of your words and warnings," said Pearl, as she still hung her head.

In the days ahead, Pearl and Duto visited KaPing daily at his campsite. He continued to pan and work for gold as more of a pastime now and cover. He continued, knowing gold is where you find it, and that he might be five shovel scoops away from a "placer ledge." He was now getting only half a thimble of gold a day, working diligently for ten hours. Pearl enjoyed his tea and conversation, as his education was vast. He could always give an answer that she understood when asking him questions.

He was fascinated with her notoriety and her relationship with the raven. Her travels and experiences would play in to their conversations, and he found himself falling in love with her.

Three months had now passed since QueYu had headed south in search of laborers. KaPing began to worry of foul play, dying on the trail, or that murder would find QueYu and the possibility of him not returning.

One morning, KaPing arose early to the sound of a *thump! thump! thump!* and then a low drumming got his attention. There, under a pine tree on the hillside, a male grouse displayed his plumage. Two of his lady grouse danced before him. KaPing was able to crouch and sly up on them with their preoccupied courtship going on. He then jumped up and whacked two of them dead with his shovel. Pleased with himself, he took his morning bath and cleaned up the camp. His food was almost gone, the bag of cornmeal long since consumed. He had one last cup of dried rice he'd been saving. He put the forest grouse in a cooking pot along with the cup of rice and then proceeded to put on his finest clothes. Pearl arrived at her usual time, in the late morning. She could smell the cooking from a distance and was surprised when she rode into KaPing's camp.

"You're not working today?" she asked.

"Chinese holiday!" He grinned. "Sit! Sit!" he directed her.

"That smells good! What's in the pot?" she laughed.

"Rice and wild chicken! Two in the pot! With special secret spices! Here, have some tea," he offered her. "Pearl, I'm worried about my brother, QueYu. This is wild country--cougars, murderers, rattlesnakes, disease--it's all out there," he lamented. "Maybe he will not return. He should have been back by now."

"That is a possibility, KaPing. This is a wild country, and there are many risks on the trail," she acknowledged.

"Either way, you and I, Pearl, have to find a way of getting that gold without creating a stampede of miners, who would quickly overwhelm us. So, we need each other--we need to be partners, and I find myself now asking you to marry me," he stated bluntly.

Pearl laughed out loud. "And how do you plan on marrying us? You're a Buddhist, and I'm a Catholic!" Again, she laughed out loud.

"We don't need their blessing, Pearl. Where are they in this wilderness? All we need is to answer to our God in our hearts, saying so verbally to each other's face. Let us be cast down as not worthy of our faith, if we go against one another."

Holding out his arms, she fell in to them, crying in fear, "But I have to go home to my island!" she pleaded.

"Let's work hard together, Pearl, to get this gold. After we have it, I promise that I will personally escort you back to your island."

"Do you promise me that?" She looked into his eyes.

"If we become rich, which I'm certain we will, I will take you anywhere in the world you want to go," he whispered in her ear. Looking at him, she sealed it with a long kiss to his mouth.

The next day, Que Yu appeared on the trail downriver. Behind him was a pack train of ten mules, and he was accompanied by a dozen men walking, wearing conical coulee hats. The two brothers were overjoyed to see each other, excitedly exchanging a rapid conversation.

Duto was nervous seeing all the unfamiliar Chinese. He flew from his roost in a tall pine and landed on Pearl's shoulder. *Caw-caw*ing at the strangers, he warned them to keep their distance. The newcomer Chinese all fell to their knees and began to nod at Pearl. QueYu had told them the story of the "Bird

Woman" and how she had led KaPing to the golden sandbar. Now in her presence, they were in awe of her.

"Stop that nonsense!" blurted out Pearl in Mandarin dialect.

Astonished, they all now stood up and continued to mumble and nod. Anxious to get moving after waiting for weeks, and mindful of Chilkosahaskt's warning to not linger, KaPing announced that they would be leaving in the morning. "Do not unpack your kits. We will leave at first light in the morning."

"I'll join you in the morning, when you come through Entiat," Pearl informed KaPing.

Returning to Chilkosahaskt's village, she learned that LaHompt and Achneen had gone into the mountains to gather berries and would not be back for three days. She spent an emotional evening with Chilkosahaskt and his wife, Spokalax, both of whom hated to see her go.

"You can always come back--you belong here!" the chief assured her.

"I will! I will! It's only a days ride," she reminded them. "Chilkosahaskt, I want you to have my horses, as a gift for being so kind to me," she cried, tearfully.

"They will still be yours when you return," the old chief laughed.

The village was awoken early the next morning by barking dogs. KaPing and QueYu, along with their little ragtag army, stood waiting across the Entiat River, hesitant to cross. Pearl came down to the river and waved them across, saying to come ahead. She was ready, having packed her things and food on two pack horses. Her saddle horse was a fine buckskin, which she had bonded with. After the Chinese waded the river with their pack mules, she led them through the village. A few old women were up cooking breakfast and stared at the Orientals walking past them. Their hats, attire, long braids, and manners were totally foreign to the Entiat people. Continuing on, past the rocky cliff trail north of the village, they pushed on to Wapato John's cabin. Reaching his corrals, Pearl reminded KaPing that they were not to linger on Entiat land. Camping here was not an option.

Wapato John and QueYu had become friends on the trail, and so a brief visit was done out of respect for each other. After watering and resting the mules and horses, they continued on the trail, only this time, instead of climbing the coulee to Lake Chelan, they would stay on the Big River trail. It was a harsher trail with steep, vertical grades and many rock hazards. This way, they would avoid the Chelan village and not attract attention.

Duto flew high overhead in a gliding circle, watching Pearl and the Chinese below. That afternoon, they reached the Chelan River, where it emptied into the Big River. Successfully crossing the icy water and continuing north, they reached the horse crossing and could see the sandbar extending out from the other shore. Their presence was discovered by a group of Chelan people who, from a distant ridge, observed the Chinese with curiosity.

Early the next morning, Pearl and KaPing led the group across the Big River and on to the sandbar of gold. Reaching the opposite shore, KaPing told his workers to unpack their kits and goods and pitch their tents. By noon, the shoreline adjacent to the sandbar had become a permanent camp. KaPing and QueYu were in charge of the operation. The gold was to be split four ways, going to KaPing, QueYu, Pearl, and the workers who panned it out. QueYu had brought two rifles back from the Oregon country, and so an armed guard was posted on the hill above the diggings. They watched for anyone who approached from up or down the river.

A systematic system was laid out to retrieve the gold. They began panning the tip of the bar at the center of the river. The plan was to work the sandbar in increments, digging and panning towards the shoreline and the camp. It was apparent that by the end of the day they had found a rich placer. Each panful washed out produced five dollars in gold.

That night, the laborers were overjoyed with their share of the day's work. KaPing had set up a table with a scale on the sandbar, weighing each man's tote bag and dividing it accordingly. There was no need for greed or thievery. Each man knew they were sitting on a bonanza, and with hard work, all would walk away with a fortune. It was beyond their dreams as to what they were sitting on. By week's end, it was apparent that each had to hide his accumulated wealth and secret their hoard in some hidden spot for peace of mind. The laborers began to fan out on the banks surrounding the golden bar, each building a small dugout into the hillside, using driftwood, boulders, and whatever the landscape offered to construct a hovel to live in. Each had a secret location to hide his gold, usually in the dark of night. Pearl, QueYu, and KaPing were in the same predicament as to where to hide their growing treasure. There was no need for the three to pan gold, as their daily take in shares was unbelievable. Pearl found herself helping the camp cook, Charlie Wu. The cook was earning the equivalent of the others, his cut coming out of the daily quarter share of the laborers. The Chinese had brought all the trappings of their culture. Their camp was hung with paper dragon lanterns, which glowed eerily at night. Their meals were various fish caught from the river with rice, along with the abundant rabbits that seemed to be everywhere. Watching old Charlie Wu and conversing in Mandarin, the cook taught Pearl how to prepare delicious, spiced Asian food in the camp kitchen. Today, he was preparing a rabbit stew. He showed her several of his ancient, passed on secrets of how to use herbs and spices, garnishing the rabbit meat with ginger root. He placed a fleck of the ginger root on her tongue, and her eyes lit up.

"Pearl, I have good news!" KaPing called out to her. "I went exploring up the canyon this morning. I found a good place to build a cabin for us!" He beamed.

"How far is it?" Pearl wanted to know.

"It's a half hour walk. C'mon, I will show you," he said, turning his head and nodding at her to follow. She followed him out of camp, and instantly, Duto came down from his roost and landed on her shoulder.

"Why do you not want to stay on the river?" Pearl asked, as she walked behind him.

"There are several reasons. I will explain later," was his only answer.

Pearl instructed Duto to fly ahead. She knew she was in Sinkiuse country now. As they came over a small knoll, they stopped to rest.

"You see that giant split rock up there?" he looked at her and pointed. "That's where our cabin will be, in the crack between those huge boulders," he explained.

Pearl was shocked! He was pointing at the Spirit Rock that Four Eagles and LaHompt had offered tributes and prayers. "I don't think that is a good idea, KaPing. That Spirit Rock is holy to the Sinkiuse." She nervously shook her head "no."

"You tell me that those people of Four Eagles all died of smallpox. They are gone now." We have been here ten days and have seen no one. The split in the boulders--it is the perfect place to build my foundry. The crack is a natural chimney."

"What's a 'foundry?'" Pearl was still frowning "no."

"I will build a 'bellows' at the floor of the crack. There is a natural draft of air rising in the giant crack, like a chimney. There, we will smelt the gold down. We'll be able to get a hot enough bed of coals to melt the dust into solid gold, using a crucible."

Still shaking her head, she pointed at the giant rocks, saying, "You say you will melt the gold there--between the crack in the black rocks?"

"Yes! I want you to keep working in the kitchen. QueYu and I will work up here daily until it is finished. Trust me. It will be good for us. There's two years worth of panning out there on the sandbar. We need a 'headquarters' and a safe place to hide the treasure. C'mon, I'll show you," he said, pulling her hand.

Pearl had only stared at the monolith from a distance. As they came up to it, she shuddered in awe at how immense it was. Standing at the base of the six foot wide crack, she could feel the natural air moving across her face, drawn in to the updraft. The immense crack rose straight up, vertically, fifty feet up to the top of the twin boulders. There was an aura of the place, and Pearl could understand why the people held it in reverence.

Duto landed at the top of the crack. Staring down at her, he cawed his warning to her. Heeding his warning, Pearl urged KaPing that they should leave. Refusing to accept her fear of the place, he laughed and chided her, saying, "Alright, let's go--but when you come back in one month, it will be your new home." He winked at her.

As he had promised, he was gone the following morning with QueYu from the river camp. The two packed in supplies and tools up to the boulder camp and went to work, constructing the smelter and the cabin. The month passed by. Pearl and Duto helped Charlie Wu in the kitchen, and each day, QueYu and KaPing would return from the smelter site, exhausted from their labor. The sandbar operation was continuing its "high yield." No one paid much attention to the two bosses, as they were on the sandbar all day, working feverishly to get their quarter share.

Pearl had learned to weigh the gold each evening at the scale table. Each miner would stand in line, and as they came off the bar, they would have their tote bags weighed, giving up three quarters of the bag. Their share remaining in their bags was usually around a hundred dollars, which was unheard of for daily wages. If they had chosen to work in the whiteman's labor camp, they would have been paid two dollars a day. With a daily bag full of gold, they would head for Charlie Wu's kitchen, pay him his share, and eat large meals. After dinner, they would group up and gamble and smoke until midnight, then each would retire and hide his gold.

One evening, at dinner time, KaPing arrived back from his daily task at the smelter. "It's ready. We will move to the boulder cabin tomorrow," he told her. "We will come to the river camp daily, in the evening, when they come off the bar. We will weigh our daily take and return to hide it. We will be much safer at the boulder cabin."

The following morning, the mules and the horses were rounded up. KaPing broke their camp down and loaded their belongings on the mules. The laborers on the sandbar were aware KaPing and Pearl were relocating. They hardly looked up from their pans, as the two pushed the pack train up the bank and onto the canyon trail. Cresting the familiar knoll, Pearl could now see the black monolith further ahead. It was now encircled with corrals! As they approached, she marvelled at the ingenuity of the two brothers creation.

A chimney arose from the top of the crack--a long, boxy tower of green willows woven together and then covered with a layer of mud. A facade of hewn logs with a door was across the face of the crack. A roof of skins had been covered with sod. A front porch of flat stones had been embedded in the ground, with a hammock swinging in its shade.

Pushing the mules into the confines of the corrals, KaPing and QueYu both beamed at Pearl, proud of their handiwork and the look of wonder on her face. Whatever menacing fears she had felt previously of the place were now gone. The cabin looked very inviting, an oasis in the middle of nowhere. The front door lured her in. The interior was 'window' less. The rock walls rose fifty feet high, up to the skin and sod covering. Lighting a candle, KaPing urged her to follow him. All along the left wall, for forty feet, were sleeping bunks and shelves. The walkway led to the back, where a potbelly stove was arranged next to a hearth. The stove had a tin pipe that routed the smoke into the willow rattan, mud-covered chimney flue over the hearth. The entire floor was embedded with flat, smooth stones. Pearl was amazed at what they had created.

"Now, I'll show you the best part!" KaPing urged her back outside. He led her all the way around to the other side of the crack, stepping a few feet into its interior. There, a large bellows had been constructed of leather and wood, its nozzle pointed into the hearth on the other side of the wall.

"Here, you can work the bellows in the shade, out of the wind and sun! I can smelt the gold on the other side, at the hearth," he explained to her.

Now KaPing looked up and pointed. "That's a roost and a hut for your magic bird," he grinned. Sure enough, a perfect little shelter was straddling the crack, far above.

"It's our home, Pearl! There's a lot of gold down there. We're going to be here for a while." He put his arm around her and kissed her on the forehead.

QueYu was in charge of the company supplies. Realizing the kitchen stores were half gone, especially the rice, he informed KaPing that he should leave immediately for Fort Walla Walla to re-supply.

"Yes, I agree QueYu. We've spent a lot of time on building this smelter. Our workers will rebel if we do not feed them. Yes, take a large amount of gold, and buy a pack train full of commodities. We can sell specialty items to the workers and get some of the gold back--twice what we spend on the goods! Pay your friend Wapato John to guide you. Be generous with him."

Pearl caught the two best saddle horses in the corral, and by noon, he was packed and leaving on the trail, back down to the sandbar and across the river, heading to Wapato John's cabin.

It was the first of October, 1854. The warm summer days were still lingering. Duto was grumpy and looking scruffy. His molt of feathers was coming on. She had been with him long enough to recognize the change and was waiting to hear him demand his little green pill. Duto had found his roost up in the crack the first night that Pearl had stayed in the cabin. He had already begun to stock it with his daily findings--a small mollusk shell, a shiny piece of quartz, and a yellow piece of bone.

One morning, he waited impatiently for her to emerge. He was immediately on her shoulder as she stepped outside. She automatically flashed the medallion at him, but that wasn't what he was after. He began tugging at the pouch string around her neck and cursing her. "Damn you. You're late. Give me my medicine!"

Laughing, she removed the pouch. Carefully, she undid the drawstring, as to not spill the contents, and removed one green pellet. She held it up to him on her shoulder, and he instantly gulped it down. With that, he flew back up to his roost and began a tirade of cursing the foulest English sailor slang that had ever been heard.

KaPing was going to the sandbar daily now and spending most of his time watching and observing. He kept the camp going, finding firewood and catching fish. Each day, as the men came off the sandbar, KaPing was waiting for them at the weighing table. With his constant presence, there was no chance of sneaking the gold off the bar.

Pearl would ride her horse daily to the river camp in the afternoon. She sometimes would give KaPing a break and do the weighing at the table. Occasionally, Pearl would see riders on the opposite shore, on a distant ridge staring down at the scene on the sandbar.

The November winds arrived from the north, bringing an icy chill to the air, even with the sun shining. The rock cabin KaPing had built was protected from the wind. The little potbelly stove heated the rock walls, making the interior very comfortable. KaPing and Pearl had come to being intimate in the dwelling, sleeping with each other nightly.

One morning, stepping outside, he was surprised to see an inch of snow on the ground that had fallen the night before. QueYu had not arrived back from Walla Walla, and KaPing was concerned he could become stranded on the high desert plateau if heavy snow fell. The camp supplies were dwindling down, with maybe one more week's worth of food to feed the brigade of Chinese. That afternoon, his worries were over. Pearl came galloping into the river camp on her horse.

"They're here! They're here!" she excitedly told KaPing. "Wapato John and KaPing are up at the cabin! Go! I'll watch the scales!" she commanded KaPing.

Sure enough, QueYu and Wapato John had returned and crossed the high plateau land. They had chosen a trail that entered Corral Creek Canyon from above. The corrals were full of pack mules and supplies, a very welcome sight. Accompanying the two were five more Chinese laborers who had come to sign on with KaPing's company. KaPing was delighted, offering green tea to the newcomers and asking dozens of questions.

QueYu had kept quiet at the fort about their golden sandbar but had confided in the local Chinese, telling them of the opportunity to work for high wages. He had no problem recruiting the men to come work on a quarter share basis.

The following day, Wapato John was anxious to get home and see his family and was up and gone with his pack string at first light. QueYu had brought back a winter's supply of feed, flour, rice, bacon, dried goods, and a whole list of sundries. They were able to store most of it on the shelves of the rock cabin, but it was evident a warehouse more central to the diggings at the bar was going to be needed.

Utilizing his new labor force, he had the five men construct a very large, stout dugout just downriver from the China Bar, at a running spring water location. The supplies were now transferred to this location, and just like that, QueYu was selling his stock and wares for twice of what he had paid for the goods. Now that QueYu was back, he took up the job at the weighing table, freeing up KaPing.

KaPing had found a stand of rock maple trees in a spring area, farther up the canyon. Spending a few days of gathering the hardwood, he now built a large bonfire in the center of an empty dirt corral. The result was a large heap of hardwood charcoal pieces, which he collected and brought inside to his hearth. One morning, he explained to Pearl, "My grandfather was a metallurgist, creating weapons for the Chinese elite. I would work the bellows for him and learned and watched his techniques. QueYu has brought molding clay from Walla Walla. I will show you the process now, as I need your help. The gold medallion Buddha that I gave you, when I was bartering for my life, was made in this fashion." KaPing then pulled out a small disc from a pocket, a green jade Buddha mounted to a Chinese coin. Flattening out a piece of clay the size of an open book, he pressed the jade medallion into the clay several times, each time creating a perfect mold in the likeness of the Buddha coin. When he was done, he had the mold for two dozen coins. He placed the mold in a large cast iron frying pan, buried it in coals, and baked it for one hour. From one of his trunks of goods, he produced a ceramic crucible and a set of iron tongs. He placed the Buddha coin mold to the side of the hearth but still kept it very warm. Now, he

233

built a pyre with the hardwood charcoal.

"Alright... you Pearl must go around back to the bellows and begin pumping air into the hearth here. Do not stop! Keep a steady pumping until I tell you to stop," he directed her. He filled the crucible with the gold dust and carefully placed it in the pyre of charcoal with the iron tongs. She dutifully took her position behind the wall of the hearth at the bellows and began pumping the bellows handle. The nozzle on the other side now flamed the charcoal and crucible into a white hot blast.

"Don't stop! Keep it up!" she heard KaPing yell at her through the hearth wall.

Within ten minutes, the crucible glowed with a molten, shining soup. With the tongs, wearing leather gloves, he extracted the crucible from the coals and poured each Buddha coin mold in the sheet of baked clay.

"Stop Pearl! No more pumping! Very, very good!"

She walked back around to the front door and to the hearth. She watched as he shattered the mold and then picked each golden orb up with the tongs, dropping them into an iron pot of water. Picking up a warm medallion, he handed it to Pearl to examine. It was as he had said--a perfect copy of the medallion he had given her when he pleaded for his life.

"Each weigh a perfect ounce," he proudly boasted to her. The Buddha was seated on the golden disc, making it a beautiful medallion. She marveled that KaPing had created such a dazzling golden coin. He wiped the coins down with an acidic solution, and now they shone brightly in the cold sun.

"I have something to tell you and show you," KaPing announced. "While you have been at the scales every day, I secretly dug a chamber under this giant rock. Now, it is time to show you the secret. Come with me." He grinned at Pearl.

Taking her back inside the rock cabin, he made his way back to the hearth. Crouching now in front of the hearth, he raised a large flat stone on the floor, revealing a dark hole below. "Follow me," he winked. Lighting a candle, he stepped into the hole and onto a small ladder. He disappeared from Pearl's view, as she peered over the edge. He called to her, "C'mon--step onto the ladder."

At first, she was astonished to see this secret opening in the floor. The entrance captivated her curiosity. Stepping onto the ladder, she climbed down and entered an underground cavern. The ceiling was the massive boulder above them. Her eyes now adjusted to the candlelight, and she gasped at what she saw. A beautiful Buddha sat in a shrine on an altar. Several offerings were placed on the altar as well. A tapestry rug lay on the floor before the altar, allowing one to pray on their knees to the Buddha. KaPing now lit two candles on the shrine and kneeled and prayed to the Buddha. Bowing several times, he now placed the two dozen freshly minted coins on the altar as an offering for safe keeping.

"What is this? How did you do all of this?" she was astonished at what she was looking at.

"I dug this cave under the boulder with a secret entrance. We have to have a safe, secret place to hide all this gold," he explained. "The Buddha deity watches over our treasure, keeping it safe for us," he further explained. She now noticed the candle flames on the altar pulling sideways, towards a shaft of light in the wall.

"What is that light?" she asked KaPing.

"That's daylight. I hollowed out a pine log and use it as an air duct, for ventilation. That way, the incense and candle smoke has a way out." She now felt a draft of air coming down the ladder hole across her face and towards the hollow log.

"Let's go back up," he directed her and blew out the candles on the altar. Both climbed back up the ladder, and he now slid the large stone back into place, sealing the entrance with a loud *thunk*. "You and myself are the only ones who know of this cavern. Not even QueYu knows of its existence. Tell no one of what you have seen, Pearl. If we are to leave here rich, then we must be extremely cautious," he seriously advised her.

The winter snow storms were now upon them. Work had come to a stop on the China Bar. The conditions were far too frigid and hostile. The bar became frozen in ice, making it impossible to pan in the freezing conditions. The Chinese laborers spent their days gambling and spending their hard-earned gold dust at QueYu's dugout store. The camp was sufficiently provisioned, thanks to QueYu's trip to Walla Walla. He was already planning another trip to Walla Walla in the early spring, realizing how lucrative his store was becoming. The Chinese had discovered a large herd of mule deer wintering just upriver. Weekly forays brought back plenty of fresh meat to supplement their rice diet.

Up at the boulder cabin and away from the river camp, KaPing and Pearl worked their forge daily, melting down the bags of gold dust they had collected and placing the fresh coins in the Buddha cavern.

Duto sat up in his roost, high up in the chasm, and watched the daily routine below. He would swoop down onto Pearl's shoulder periodically through the day and make demands of her. The snow was two feet deep, making travel impossible. The horses and mules were beginning to show signs of stress and starvation, with the temperatures remaining below freezing. Finally, in late February, a warm wind began to build, coming up from the south. It blew warm, dry air all day long, melting and evaporating virtually all of the snow. By evening, what had been knee-deep snow the night before was now bare, dry ground--not even muddy. Pearl recalled Swakane Jacque calling it a "Chinook wind." Within hours, the warmth in the mountains melted large snowfields, and the streams became swollen with rushing water. The next day, the Big River swelled to her high water marks on the banks and covered up the golden sandbar with a rush of fast water. The animals were able to graze again, but it would be another month before the China Bar reappeared, allowing the Chinese to resume their enterprise. At the first opportunity, they were back with their shovels, pans, and cradle boxes, systematically sluicing the sandy gravel from dusk to dawn. Almost daily now, new Chinese were showing up in camp, asking to sign on. Word had spread among them on the lower Columbia about the China Bar, and now with the snow gone, groups were arriving. KaPing and QueYu signed on another twelve men but now began receiving protests from the firstcomers, saying it wasn't fair. Chinese were now being turned away with no options as the China Bar was protected by armed guards.

Another makeshift camp sprung up across the river on Chelan land. Within a month, it had grown to fifty men. Fanning out and prospecting, one of them had found a dry wash coulee, whose sand contained the yellow dust. Packing the sand on a long trail to the Big River, there they panned the mix. The newcomers were now making good, daily wages.

Que Yu, not expecting the rush of customers, informed KaPing and Pearl he was leaving immediately for Walla Walla and more supplies. "I'll fetch my friend, Wapato John, to push another pack train for us," he assured KaPing and Pearl.

"I want to visit Chilkosahaskt. I will go with you," stated Pearl. "I will be back in one week," she promised KaPing.

The next day, the two crossed the river at the China Bar and followed the Big River down to Wapato John's cabin. He was expecting them, knowing QueYu was going to need more supplies after the long winter.

"It is good to see you two! Come in!" he greeted them from his rocker on the front porch.

Duto flew off of Pearl's shoulder and landed on the familiar roof of the cabin. Pacing back and forth, he announced his authority to anyone who would listen. Inside, Wapato John fed his guests and exchanged local news. "Many of your friends, the Chinese, have come upriver. They always pay me in gold here at my trading post. I, like you, am running low on supplies. I'm glad you're here. We'll travel again together to Walla Walla, and I'll accept your payment as a guide. I must warn you, Innomeseecha is watching the Chinese closely. The

236

Chelan people are not happy with the situation. I think as long as you stay away from their village on the lake, you will be alright."

"What about the Sinkiuse? We have not seen them at the diggings," Pearl cautiously asked Wapato John.

"They have gone south, to confederate with Chief Kamiakin of the Yakama. He is calling for a war, to run the white man out of this region."

"A war?" asked Pearl in a hushed tone.

"It appears, yes, it's highly possible," answered Wapato John. "Their soldiers and their white chief have called for a grand council at Walla Walla. We will wait and see the outcome. And, yes, we must go and get the supplies before this council happens in the late spring. We will go in the morning."

At sunrise, they were up early and on the river trail to Entiat. Reaching the village, Chilkosahaskt was elated to see Pearl and Duto after the long winter. QueYu and the chief's brother visited for a short time, and then they continued down the trail, pushing their long train of pack mules.

"Tell me--how have you been?" Chilkosahaskt pressed her.

"Very well. I have brought you some of KaPing's green tea and some rice," handing him two small paper packages. Pleased, he handed them to his wife, asking her to brew some of the tea. At that moment, LaHompt and Achneen burst through the teepee flap, overjoyed to see her.

"Sister, you are well! It is good to see you again!" they both greeted her.

"So KaPing is treating you well?" the chief now inquired.

"Yes, he is a kind man. We have plenty to eat and a warm cabin. We are finding much gold!" she enthusiastically offered.

"I see… and are you with child yet?" the chief matter of factly asked.

Blushing and embarrassed, she only would shake her head "no" and quickly changed the subject. She asked about the horses.

"Some were lost in a blizzard, but the Chinook wind came just in time to melt the snow, saving many from starvation. Soon, many foals will be born--we were lucky!" the old chief explained. "LaHompt and Tekolekun will go to Walla Walla next month and listen to the words of the white man's great council. We are not sure what it is they want. The Yakamas are calling for war. We are hoping for a peaceful treaty," he explained to her. "We have seen many of KaPing's Chinese brothers coming up the river. We tell them there is no gold here and to keep moving north. I have seen Lolowkin, and he is not happy with your gold camp and hopes that all of you will soon move on. He and his braves are now far to the south, counseling with the Yakama. When the Sinkiuse return, it could become a bad situation for you and KaPing," he warned her.

Pearl answered, "KaPing's men are armed with guns. I don't think they plan on leaving any time soon."

"Well, for now, Lolowkin has his hands full. We will see what the outcome is at the Walla Walla council."

Pearl and Duto spent several days in the comfort of the chief's village, enjoying the companionship of Achneen and LaHompt. The morning of her departure, LaHompt volunteered to ride with her back up the river trail. Within a mile of the China Bar crossing, he turned back, wishing her well. KaPing was glad to see her back, allowing him a break from the weighing scales at the diggings.

Weeks passed, and by mid May, QueYu and Wapato John appeared one day with their pack train, coming down the canyon trail to the boulder cabin. That night, a grand celebration took place in the river camp. The commodities brought a great relief to the bleak existence of the miners.

With each passing month, more Chinese appeared, working the dry gulch across the river and trading at QueYu's store. Placer gold had been found further up the Big River, below the Methow village. Now, a large camp of Chinese worked it, much like KaPing's sandbar but not near as productive in gold. The Chinese built all sorts of shacks and dugouts to live in along the riverbank, antagonizing the Methow people with their proximity. Just below the Methow village, the miners had begun digging a long ditch of water along the Methow river, routing it down to where the river emptied into the Big River, and onto the sandbar. Using water from the ditch, they set up large rocker cradles, a much quicker way to extract the gold dust from the gravels. The Methow people were upset with the growing influx of Chinese, but peace was maintained as long as the Chinese stayed on the sandbar and did not venture up the Methow's river.

KaPing had acquired a large supply of garden seeds on QueYu's second visit to Walla Walla. Above the boulder cabin, where the Sinkiuse had built a large corral, he and Pearl diverted the creek water into a huge, cultivated garden. Potatoes, beets, corn, beans, and melons were now flourishing in the loam soil. Pearl, with Duto watching, would spend long days working the garden, pulling weeds and nurturing the plants. KaPing dug a deep root cellar into the side of a hill adjacent to the garden and now stockpiled potatoes and dried beans in the cool darkness of its interior. Word quickly spread among the miners of the fresh vegetables that were now available. Daily, she would haul the morning's harvest down to the scales at the China Bar. By days end, all of the vegetables would be gone, traded for gold dust.

QueYu's store was becoming equally as lucrative. Tea, rice, gunpowder, fish hooks, and medicine were in high demand. By mid August, again QueYu needed to re-supply. Informing KaPing and Pearl of his departure, she again rode along with the pack train to Wapato John's cabin. He was expecting QueYu and joined the train with his outfit. As they approached Chilkosahaskt's village, Duto flew ahead and announced their arrival. The old chief and LaHompt knew the raven by sight now, so by the time the pack train entered Entiat, word had spread, and a large crowd gathered to greet their arrival. Chilkosahaskt was pleased to see Pearl, as always.

"Daughter--sit--tell me of your days!" he enthusiastically persuaded her. "I see your bird is as feisty as ever!" he chuckled.

She brought the old chief melons, and cutting one open, she offered the sweet, pink fruit to him and LaHompt. As before, QueYu and Wapato John wasted no time visiting and were gone within the hour with their long string of mules.

Now, the conversation became serious and full of concern. "LaHompt returned two weeks ago from the great council at Walla Walla. He was threatened with his life if he did not put his mark on the treaty. We do not understand what it says--only that the white men are coming and that they want this land," he explained.

"What is an 'Iron Horse?'" he now asked Pearl.

"I do not know, Father," she truthfully replied.

"They say an iron horse will come and and cross the mountains on our land--so we must move and allow it to pass. I do not understand this," he muttered in Chinook.

"I will ask KaPing what an iron horse is--he may know," she volunteered.

Staying only two days, LaHompt again accompanied her back up the river trail, as she worried about tending her garden. Back at the boulder cabin, she told KaPing of the old chief's concern and asked if he knew what an 'iron horse' was.

"I have seen one in California--a large, iron smoking machine on iron rails that pulls wagons behind it," he explained. "They were using it to haul gold ore out of the mountains," he elaborated.

"Why would they bring an iron horse here?" she wondered out loud.

"Maybe they have found gold in the mountains," was the only explanation he could give.

Weeks passed, and late September saw the return of QueYu and his pack train of supplies. This time, he had brought back passengers with him. At the fort, he had convinced three Wishram women to accompany him back to the China Bar. These were no ordinary women. They had been selling their favors at the fort and were now looking for new business. QueYu housed them in a log shack behind the dugout store. News of the soiled doves traveled quickly, bringing even more business to his enterprise. Not only that, QueYu had returned with a large supply of the poppy drug, Opium. Many miners were soon addicted to its power, creating labor problems on the golden sandbar. Several quickly lost their hard earned gold to the pleasures of the whores and slavery of the drug. Fights were breaking out in all hours of the night, and many men were only working half a day, just enough to feed their habit. KaPing realized the situation was getting out of hand and confronted QueYu, demanding he stop selling the drug.

"You have your vegetable business, I have my store--do not tell me what I can and cannot sell!" was his harsh reply to KaPing. Hatred now developed between the two brothers. Neither would speak to the other.

Duto had gone through his molt and received his green tablet, and now, the end of October brought the first snowfall. By mid November, a freak, early blizzard of snow brought freezing conditions and put a halt to work on the sandbar. KaPing and Pearl spent their days at the forge, casting dozens of the Buddha medallions from the season's take of gold dust. The shrine in the underground cavern was becoming laden with the treasure.

Now, with nothing but time and boredom on their hands, the miners became slaves of the wicked drug and the vices of the river camp. There were two murders that winter amongst them, and Spring could not come soon enough. The men were all broke now, having gambled, smoked, and whored the entire winter and spending what was left in QueYu's store.

The thaw came, and work resumed on the China Bar. It was now April of 1856, and Pearl was a woman of eighteen years of age. Her passion with KaPing had not produced a child, and she wondered if it were her or him who lacked the ability.

"KaPing, let's take our gold and leave. We have plenty now. You can sell our interest to QueYu," she tried to reason with him.

"We can't leave… the sandbar is only partially worked, and we are selling our vegetables for a lot of gold! How can we walk away from this kind of income? No, we must stay and wait for the right time to pull out," he insisted with her.

Pearl felt perplexed and discouraged. She was in love with KaPing and could not walk away from him. They had a comfortable life. The gold was buying all the commodities and luxuries they needed. Duto had become quite content also. His roost was full of treasure trinkets he had collected. A huge flock of ravens regarded him as their "Imperial King." Several of his lady birds would banter for his attention, bringing him tidbits of food and bright, shiny objects.

240

Pearl had grown tired of wearing the three necklaces around her neck, finding them annoying as she worked the garden. One evening, with Duto on her shoulder, she entered the underground vault, after KaPing had removed the flat stone. Lighting a candle, the cavern illuminated, and Duto saw its contents for the first time. The altar of the Buddha was covered with the dazzling, gold medallions. Duto quickly grabbed one and held it in his beak.

"No, put that back!" she ordered, grabbing it from his beak. "We'll keep your medicine and your treasure bag down here for safe keeping," she explained, removing two of the necklaces and placing them on the altar. She placed the week's take of gold dust in an enamel cabinet. The season's hoard would be melted down into the medallions in the coming winter. She continued to wear the mother of pearl medallion, the one she had won so long ago on her distant island. As long as she wore it, Duto was bound to her, and she'd grown accustomed to his constant protection. Flashing it at him daily, it was his constant reminder of his purpose.

Days turned into weeks, weeks turned into months, and months turned into years. Pearl and KaPing had become well established at the cabin above the China Bar. Twice a year, they would order supplies via Wapato John's pack train to Walla Walla. The rift between KaPing and QueYu had only deepened, and the two refused to talk or acknowledge the other. The vegetable garden had tripled in size. Chinese from up and down the river would venture weekly to the scales at the China Bar and buy corn, melons, and beans. The sandbar was still producing gold but not nearly in the quantity that it had been in the first years. The "garden" was becoming their gold mine.

QueYu's store had prospered as well, supplying all the vices that the lonely miners could waste their hard earned gold dust upon. The dry gulch across the river had continued to pay wages to the Chinese who worked it. The Chinatown upriver at the the Methow sandbar had grown to an immense size. Over the years, the camp had swollen to almost two hundred Chinese. Working their cradles and pans and utilizing the ditch of water they had dug, they had extracted a huge amount of gold at the site. Over a period of time, the Chinese miners had enticed the local Methow maidens into their camp, offering cooking pans, needles, and calico cloth in exchange for the pleasures they could give. Some had stayed permanently, becoming addicted to the Opium devil drug and pipe. The riverbank had become a decadent little town of shacks and dugouts, housing gambling tables and drug smoking dens. White men were now venturing into the area, but the sheer number of Chinese were enough to keep them moving further upriver. They were searching for hard rock mines or opportunities to farm the land. Pearl continued her visits to Chilkosahaskt. She considered the

241

Entiat people her other family. She had suppressed her longing to return to her island, her dedication and love for KaPing outweighing the desire.

Tekolekun had been murdered by intruding white miners in the Wenatchi valley. Lolowkin, who was now known as Chief Moses among his people, continued to keep his warriors from waging war, knowing the army would quickly retaliate. A trading post at the confluence of the Wenatchi and Big River now supplied newly arriving pioneers. A priest, Father Respari, had built a small log church, attempting to convert the Wenatchi people to his faith.

Far to the east on the Spokane plains, Chief Kamiakin and his confederacy of warriors had been defeated in battle. The calvary, out of Fort Walla Walla, had pursued them and handed them a sound drubbing and defeat. After that, all talk of defying the white man's encroachment subsided.

The government had given up on pursuing a railroad through Chilkosahaskt's valley, and now, for the most part, his existence and village had gone unnoticed. The Chinese were now in great numbers between QueYu's store and the fifteen miles to the Chinatown at the Methow. Their sheer numbers were enough to intimidate anyone from pushing them off the Big River. KaPing's sandbar was almost panned out, yet he and Pearl's vegetable business had grown in such volumes that it had become their gold mine.

By 1872, there were over four hundred Chinese in the region, all of them buying vegetables from KaPing and Pearl. Daily, the produce was hauled to the sandbar, where trading at the scales in gold dust was carried on all afternoon.

It was no secret among the Chinese of the treasure of gold that KaPing and Pearl had acquired. An honorary, time-practiced custom was immediate death for anyone who tried to break KaPing's Tong and attempt to steal from him. Nevertheless, an armed guard was always posted at the corrals of the boulder cabin. Pearl reminded KaPing that Duto would sense danger and sound the alarm if a threat approached. His roost, high in the crack, had become a throne, and he was constantly surrounded by his "queens."

It was mid December, and the heavy snows had still not come. Wapato John had delivered their winter supplies the week before. This time though, he had brought back a surprise. In crates, he had brought back dozens of glass jars, packed meticulously, so as not to break. He had seen pioneers canning fruits and vegetables at the fort. He had watched and learned the process, boiling the glass jars, blanching the vegetables, and then sealing them in the clean jars with a hot, paraffin wax. He demonstrated on an outdoor hearth. Going through the process, he cut up several peaches, blanched the fruit, spooned it into the hot jars, and sealed the top with wax. He had brought back five hundred glass jars. He kept one hundred for himself and his garden. He explained to Pearl that everything in her garden could be put up this way in the glass jars and that the food would keep indefinitely, clear into the next year.

Carefully, she and KaPing stored the glass jars on the shelves inside the boulder cabin. Realizing the potential now to store and save the food for the winter months, they discussed how the following year, they could stockpile shelves of food without it perishing.

"We can grow more carrots and buy Chilkosahaskt's peaches," she advised KaPing.

"Yes, and I would say buy more jars when Wapato John returns to the fort in the Spring," KaPing added.

"We will require the empty jars to be brought back, after the customer has eaten the contents. That way, if they are lost or broken, the customer pays for a new jar if he does not have one to trade in," insisted Pearl.

"It is a good idea, my love! Let's do this canning thing for three more years, build the business up, then sell out the operation to the highest bidder! We'll take our treasure, buy a ship and crew in San Francisco, and sail to your land, as I promised you!" he boldly announced.

Pearl giggled with delight. "I love you, my KaPing!" stomping her feet on the floor in rapid bursts. To celebrate the new business plans, KaPing got out a bottle of rice wine. It was a cold evening but still not freezing. They sat out on their front porch, both in his and hers rocking chairs, gazing at the moon hanging in the distance. Sipping the wine, they reminisced about the years of hardship and work they had endured. Several ponies and mules grazed in the surrounding corrals, quietly in the moonlight, munching on grass.

"I remember when we came here, long ago, being fearful of this place. Now, it seems like home, and I will miss it when we finally depart," she lamented to KaPing.

"I will miss it also, but every time we almost get ready to leave, another business opportunity comes our way and falls in our laps! This time, we will go… in three years, you have my word and promise," he assured her. "Let's go to bed, my queen."

Both had been asleep for two hours when KaPing sat up in bed. Outside, he could hear the horses and mules in the corrals, whinnying and braying and charging about recklessly. Two dogs were barking nonstop. Stepping outside, he summoned the night guard.

"What is it… a cougar?"

"Not sure, Master, they are all acting crazy," he answered. Assembling in a tight herd, as if for protection, the horses now ran around in confusion in the corral, as if wanting to escape. Now, coyotes called out from the surrounding

243

hillsides, their yips and howls adding to the dogs at the cabin, who were still barking. Even Duto was upset now, cawing nonstop from his roost up in the crack. Pearl now emerged, hearing all the commotion.

"What is it, Duto? What is happening?" she called up to him.

"Demons! Demons are coming!" he shrieked at her.

"KaPing, I think the Sinkiuse are going to attack!" she called out to him.

Having no sooner called out her warning to him, a huge *BANG* rocked the floor of the canyon, and the earth began to shake violently. A loud, terrifying groan could be heard as the earth ground against itself, and now the shaking became so violent, that boulders and landslides began crashing down the hillsides. Terrified, KaPing and Pearl looked up the canyon and in the moonlight could see the earth rolling with huge tremors. Again, another loud *BANG,* and the deep grinding and groaning pierced the moonlit night.

In horror, they watched the boulder cabin become unhinged, the two massive rocks shaking so violently that the chimney and roof collapsed into the crack between them. The rolling tremors had now flattened the corral fencing, and the terrified herd ran off into the night.

The shuddering tremors continued. Screams of hysteria could be heard coming from the river camp below. For a full ten minutes, the shaking and tremors were relentless. In absolute horror and fear, KaPing and Pearl embraced each other, anticipating the end of their lives was upon them. The shaking now began to subside. Now, another ominous sound traveled through dark--a large roar in the distance not like anything they had ever heard. Within ten minutes of hearing the strange roar in the distance, a huge cloud of dust now enveloped the entire canyon. Gasping and coughing, trying to breathe, Pearl began to wail and cry in KaPing's arms.

"What's happening?! The world is ending!" she beseeched him in sheer terror.

"It's an earthquake! There's nothing we can do! We'll have to stay out on the open ground until morning!" his voice cracked.

Now, another surge of tremors and the awful groaning and grinding was coming up from the earth below. Their night guard had run off in terror into the darkness. KaPing called out to him but received no answer. The dust was making it hard to breathe. KaPing quickly fashioned some breathing masks, tearing apart his nightshirt and covering their faces. They huddled through the night in the openness of the flattened corrals. Duto had found Pearl's shoulder and refused to leave her. He was confused and did not know what to do.

All that night, aftershocks continued on the hour. By first light, the dust had settled, revealing a shocking scene. The cabin was demolished, caving in on itself. The two massive black boulders had swayed against each other. All around, the landscape was totally unrecognizable from what it had been the day before. Horrified and in shock, KaPing finally composed himself. "C'mon, there are probably casualties and injuries in the river camp. We need to help!" He brought Pearl to her senses.

The trail down to the river camp was unrecognizable, strewn with boulders and debris. Reaching the river camp, the calamity was appalling. Weeping Chinese covered in white dust stumbled about, incoherent. The Big River had turned into a lake. The sandbar was totally submerged. The large body of water was growing and creeping up the bank, past the high water marks. The camp and the miners' shacks had been flattened. To compound the situation, aftershocks and tremors continued. A gut wrenching death wail and crying was heard all along the shoreline, as the surviving miners were still in hysterics and frozen with fear. Several had been cut and were bloodied with broken bones from the panic of the previous night.

"Pearl, we need to go back to what's left of the cabin! We need bandages and medicine. Come with me!" he urged. "These men need help!"

Climbing back up the riverbank and picking their way through a broken trail, they could now hear another roar off in the distance. It came from downriver, to the south. Circling high overhead, Duto sounded his warning--his danger caw. They stopped and focused their attention at the lake of water below. Suddenly, it was moving--faster and faster, until it was a wall of whitewater, crashing down the river, destroying everything in its path. The whole east bank of the Big River was now scoured out, and in one raging moment, the China Bar was washed into oblivion and history. In seconds, the roaring volume of water consumed the entire camp, along with its refugees. Rushing back to the scene, the two were shocked at how close they had been to death. The monstrous river wave had wiped the existence of the rivercamp and sandbar off the face of the earth. Standing in disbelief at the scene, KaPing and Pearl both wept, the continuing nightmare still putting both in a state of shock.

Pearl finally composed herself. "KaPing, we must go and check on your brother, QueYu. They may need our help."

"It's Buddha's wrath that has brought this calamity down! His gambling tables, whores, and Opium dens were surely intended to be wiped off the earth! Why should we help him? We have our own problems to worry about!" KaPing uttered in anger at the thought of helping him.

"For GOD's sake, they're human beings. We at least need to see if we can help," Pearl cried.

Reluctantly, KaPing followed Pearl down the trail to the hillcrest where QueYu's store and establishment could still be seen. QueYu had built his little sin city on a flat above a sand bluff along the river. A spring was located there, and the bench could be seen from both directions. The monstrous wave had passed by, but the higher elevation of QueYu's hamlet had escaped the destructive wrath. People and confusion could be seen in the distance, as the earthquake had done damage. QueYu was lucky, though. His dugout store had, by a miracle, survived.

"Those people don't need our help! C'mon, we need to get back to our cabin, or what's left of it!" Pulling her hand, he demanded, "C'mon, let's go back!"

They retraced their steps back to the obliterated China Bar and found the river running hard and swift. The crossing had vanished. Across the river to the south, they now witnessed another strange appearance. A geyser, shooting water two hundred feet into the air could be seen. The whole landscape had transformed into something it had not been the day before.

Duto had been circling all morning, observing Pearl from above. Confused and unsure, he maintained his vigilance over her for any approaching danger. Finally, he spiraled back down, landed on her shoulder, and demanded to see his medallion.

Arriving back at the demolished cabin, the scene was heartbreaking. Tremors still continued, and the two were afraid to enter the crack in the boulders to try and salvage items from the debris.

"We need to catch some horses. We'll go upriver, to CheSaw's camp and get help!" KaPing shook his head as he tried to find answers for their situation.

The horses and mules had scattered and fled in terror, running up the breaks at the top of Corral Creek Canyon. After hiking up past the vegetable gardens, Pearl could see a group of them hiding in a grove of birch trees. Spotting her prized saddle horse, she called to him, soothingly, and without hesitation, he came to her, as if seeking the security of her voice after the terrifying night before. With her horsehair bridle, she quickly had him under control and was able to coax five more horses from their hiding places in the grove. She wrangled the bunch back to the broken corral, giving them hay and calming them down. She and KaPing then got a makeshift corral stood back up. It was dark before they finally had the fencing repaired. The two were exhausted, having not eaten all day. Building a large bonfire to stay warm, the two slept on the open ground, as the earth continued to periodically shudder through the night. The morning was cold. Awakening to the bad dream, they got their horses saddled.

"We've got to get help before the snow flies. We'll go north, along the Breaks. We can't cross the river here now. C'mon, Pearl, we've got to hurry, before it snows!"

Reaching the top of Corral Creek Canyon, they turned north and followed the ridgeline. Staring down into the valley of the Big River, they could now see the aftermath of destruction from the big quake.

Landslides of debris had choked the river. Its course was now vastly modified and changed from what it had been for centuries. By afternoon, they reached Four Eagles' former home, the coulee across from Chinatown at the Methow river. Reaching the river bank, a hundred Chinese could be seen, panning Sinkiuse land. Across the channel, for a mile running down the bar and bank, four hundred Chinese worked their sluice boxes. They worked in teams, hauling pay dirt in sacks on their shoulders, dumping them into the hoppers of the Long Toms that were all along the shore, fed by a long wooden flue of water on stilts. KaPing spoke with several Chinese that were panning and learned the earthquake had done damage but that the river had not backed up this far, as it had at the China Bar. The frantic digging continued, trying to beat the coming snows. CheSaw's store and town of vices was being repaired. Arranging a ride across the river on a canoe, they swam their horses behind them.

CheSaw was a cousin of KaPing. Having heard of KaPing and QueYu's success, he had financed a company of men to come upriver, establishing themselves at this place. Utilizing QueYu's pack train to Fort Walla Walla, he had established the first trading post in the blossoming Chinatown. Gold was suddenly discovered even further up the Big River, a Chinese digging that had come to be called "Rich Bar." His store served both locations, and he had become wealthy in a few months. The store, a dugout, was faced with vertical whip sawn lumber. Its interior was crammed with supplies.

CheSaw and KaPing had not seen each other for some time, but the greeting was warm and friendly.

"Chee--it is good to see my old cousin. Tell me what you know of the big earthquake. It has destroyed the China Bar and our cabin," KaPing lamented and got right to the point.

"It is bad to the south--a giant mountain fell into the river above Entiat on that bad stretch of rocky trail. The mountain dammed the river and stopped its flow, creating a giant lake behind it. When the water finally broke through, it created a lot of destruction. I was told Wapato John's cabin was flattened by the quake and that he and his family survived and went to the Chelan village for help. Your brother's store, as I have been told, survived, but we were unsure of what had happened to you and your Tong of men."

247

Hearing all this, KaPing replied, "My sandbar and camp are all gone. Every single man that worked for me was swept away, to their deaths in the torrent. Pearl and I need help. Can I hire some of your men to help us rebuild our cabin before it snows?"

"Yes, yes, of course, cousin. I will help you! I have a large boat that we will send downriver with workers to help you. As I can help you, perhaps you can help me. Now that your sandbar is gone, you need a place to market your vegetables. I will give a good price for them and send my boat down weekly to pick the produce up. I can sell the food in my store, and we will both profit. Do we have a deal?" Chesaw had KaPing over the barrel.

"You are shrewd, cousin. I feel I have no choice but to say yes. I will sell you our vegetables if you help us out of our predicament. Yes, I agree to your proposition," agreed KaPing.

"Very well. Tomorrow, I will send four men with you and your wife in the boat back downriver to help you rebuild. Do you wish to sell your horses?" CheSaw now offered.

Hearing this, and before KaPing could answer, Pearl interrupted, saying, "I will take our horses back. I must go and find Wapato John. You go in the boat with the workers. I'm going to Entiat to check on my people. Chilkosahaskt can help us. I need to get his wisdom," Pearl demanded to KaPing.

And so it was agreed upon. Chinatown had become a sprawling squalor. Dugouts lined the riverbank for half a mile and the smell of sewer was in the air. It had become a foul place of rotting deer bones and dog and human feces, and it was swarmed with flies and rats. The rush for gold left no time for a man to clean up after himself.

"I'm going to the Methow village. I will stay there tonight with the horses. I have friends there," she told KaPing. "You go with the boat. I will see you in five days." She cracked her quirt, kicking the horse into a fast gait and leading the other with a horsehair rope. Fifteen minutes later, she rode into the Methow village of teepees, with Duto riding on the rump of the spare horse.

Instantly, a cry rang out. "It is the Bird Woman! The Bird Woman is here!" The excitement got the dogs barking, and now all of the teepee flaps were opening to see what the commotion was.

Walking steadily towards her, an old, grey-haired woman held out her hands and approached. It was Green Baskets! Hopping down, Pearl embraced her, and the old woman wept. Composing herself, the old woman led Pearl to her teepee.

"I am forever grateful to you, for you saved my son's life. I saw you do it, with the bird in the teepee, long ago. My son and I were in the mountains picking huckleberries with the Methows when the 'pox' hit Four Eagles' band. They knew it was bad, and so they did not come across the river. The Methow tribe fled to the mountains. My son and I followed. It was a difficult time for us, but we came back to our village many years later. We found three Chinese men on the river, digging their holes. From that day forward, they just kept coming, sometimes three or four more, everyday. Before we knew it, there were too many to fight, their numbers too great, living all along the banks of the Big River. Soon, many of our foolish women were enticed with gifts they could not resist: cooking pots, knives, combs, cotton shirts. It was irresistible. Soon, many became pregnant and had become sexual slaves. They were drugged and abused. The stories are too terrible to tell." She began to softly weep.

"Snorting Bull is one of Chief Moses' warriors now. He stays at the big camp, on the rock islands. He has told me that he will make war on the Chinese, that Moses has given the nod to let Snorting Bull lead a party of warriors to run all the Chinese out of the territory. Now, the earth has trembled, and they say it is the sign to make war. You are in danger now, Bird Woman, for they know you are with the Chinese," she warned Pearl.

"What do you know about the Entiats? Chilkosahaskt's people--are they alright?" she pressed Green Baskets.

"I was told the Entiats survived, no one dying. The river surge faded before it reached there. Not such good for Wapato John, though. The surge wiped out all his corrals, and the quake flattened his trading post. I have heard that he left and is in the Chelan village."

Pearl was exhausted. The old woman fed her well, and she fell asleep on a rabbit fur robe.

The following morning, she awoke late, the long sleep much needed. Finding herself in a hurry to get going, she quickly had her horse saddled, roped KaPings horse, and was on her way. She said goodbye to the horse wranglers at the corrals and headed south for Chelan. She had hoped to see KaPing and the boatload of workers go by on the river, heading down with the current. She had a late start, and the boat party had more than likely passed hours earlier. The late morning was clear, sunny, and cold. The horses' breaths plumed white as they rode along. High above, Duto, ever circling, was watching below. Her thoughts were of Wapato John and his family and hoping they were safe. She would help him recover financially, if he needed it, she thought to herself.

She was now climbing the basin trail, leaving the Big River valley, zig-zagging up the switchback pack trail. She was another hour from Innomeseecha's village. Curiously, she could now look back up river and see the once China Bar and the massive double rock of a cabin back in the coulee. She

249

checked the shoreline where the bar once was but could not see KaPing's boat beached. Finally cresting the valley, she could just see a glimpse of QueYu's town, smoke rising from their cooking fires.

Duto was now riding on the rump of the trailing horse as they approached the south end of the lake. The bird had been dozing in the sun, and he had let his guard down. Suddenly, from out of nowhere, Pearl and Duto were surrounded by a group of warriors. Their manner was that of menace. They knew who the Bird Woman was and that she had big medicine.

"What do you want? Why do you come here?" their leader barked, adding, "There is no gold in this lake!"

"I'm on my way to see Wapato John to help him," Pearl reasoned with them.

"Wait here!" the leader ordered, turning his horse and galloping back to the village. He left his group of warriors hovering around her. These were young bucks, their arrows nocked on their bows, ready for a fight. They glared at Pearl and Duto with darting, nervous glances. Minutes later, several riders approached from the village at full gallop. It was Chief Innomeseecha and Wapato John! Relieved to see him, Pearl called out, demanding, "Uncle, tell them to put down their bows!" Innomeseecha gave a sharp, barking command, and the gang of warriors disappeared back into the brush.

"Pearl, the chief here is not happy with the Chinese. He says that you are one of them. He says the Chelan may make war on the Chinese. He says he wants you to turn around and go back. He knows you and I are friends and that Chilkosahaskt's word protects you. He will look weak among his people if he accepts you. I will go back with you to the washed out crossing and get you back across safely." Now more sternly, he kicked his horse forward and barked, "Turn your horses. I will go with you!"

Riding a short distance, he ordered her to stop. "There is a spring here to water the horses. We will camp here tonight." With the danger of the hostile Chelans now gone, John built a fire and explained what had happened. His whole outfit had been destroyed by the river rage and the earthquake thrashing. He had sought higher ground, taking his whole family up to the higher lake elevation. The Chelans, out of sympathy, were going to let him settle on a point of land, further up the lake. Chilkosahaskt and his people survived the quake with little damage but took it as a bad sign. Word had spread among the tribes that the earth was angry because the Chinese had dug so many holes on her face. The earth was shaking like a dog with fleas, trying to get rid of the Chinese, and there were more whispers of war.

250

Leaning forward, he quietly dropped his tone, saying, "Not far from here, on the riverbank, is a canoe, hidden in the brush. I will take you across to QueYu's store. From there, you can return to your cabin at Corral Creek. I'm afraid it's the safest place for you to be now." He had barely finished his statement, when the earth began to shake violently again. Lasting only eight seconds, it was over by the time they jumped up to steady the hobbled horses.

The next morning, Wapato John broke off of the main trail, following a faint path in the sagebrush. High above the washed out riverbank, he exposed a canoe, hidden in the sagebrush, perfectly camouflaged.

"I'll hobble the horses and take you across. I'll return and bring your horses back in the Spring, when I pack up for Walla Walla."

Crossing the river, both were transfixed by a geyser in the distance, shooting stinking, sulphuric water into the air. The current was taking them down to the bluff below QueYu's settlement. As they approached and landed, a large group of Chinese stared at them. Beaching the craft, Pearl recognized several of the men. Some of the men were crying, pointing at a form covered with a blanket on the beach.

"What is it? What has happened?" she asked, sensing something bad.

"Boss Man KaPing…. He dead!" came a mournful cry, with several pointing at the blanket.

"WHAT!? No, no, no, no!" Pearl hurried to the blanket heap, lifting the cover. Her dead husband, swollen and grotesque, stared back at her. She fell to her knees, sobbing uncontrollably.

He had been found on the river shore, hours earlier. Pulling her away, Wapato John escorted her up the path to QueYu's store. Bursting through the door of the dugout, QueYu was found sitting at a table, staring down at the river. He was ashen, and it was apparent that he'd been weeping. Upon seeing Pearl, they both embraced and sobbed sadly for several minutes. Finally composing themselves allowed Wapato John to ask QueYu what had happened.

"He was found this morning, a bullet hole in his heart. My Tong is organizing to hunt the killer down." He now asked Wapato John why he was there.

Pearl explained the events of the last three days, and now, she suspected treachery from the men in the boat.

The Massacre

QueYu's grief was quickly overcome with anger, now having heard Pearl's story. He urgently had several armed men mounted, bound for vengeance. Leading them up the river trail, Pearl and Wapato John came to the washed out camp, covered with twisted limbs and mud, and the sandbar that had been flushed away. A large boat was beached on a patch of mud, its bow tied to a muddy log. Footprints led up the bank, through the twisted mess to the boulder cabin trail. Taking the lead, QueYu lead the group up the rocky, broken trail. Arriving at the shattered boulder cabin, four Chinese were found seated around a campfire. QueYu ordered Pearl to remain silent, as he would do the questioning. Silently, Duto circled above.

"Greetings! Is that your boat down on the river?" QueYu asked the four men, who were all now standing.

"Yes, we have come to take vegetables back to Chinatown," came the answer.

"Where is KaPing, the owner of this place?" came QueYu's next question.

"He fell from the boat. He could not swim and drowned," the big one now answered. "We tried to find him, but we finally gave up."

"You are a liar. I am his brother, and he could swim very well!"

"We were in rapids. He fell in. After we capsized, he must have hit his head on a rock," another man pleaded their case.

"And I shall put a bullet in each of your hearts, as you did to him!" snarled QueYu, raising his rifle.

"NO--NO!" a third man begged. "Bing Ho and I are innocent!" he exclaimed, falling to his knees and begging for his life. "Those two--they killed him, trying to make him talk where his gold is hidden---we had nothing to do with it! CheSaw ordered us to come and help restore his cabin…. We are innocent, I swear. It's those two who are the assassins!"

BingHo now chimed in, coming to his defense, saying, "The big one, with the pistol--he and his gun shot Boss KaPing and threw him in the river! KaPing told him all his gold was in the territory bank at Walla Walla. He did not believe him. Those two--they beat him trying to make him talk! ChopSee shot him. They drug his body to the river and threw him in!" The sordid tale of murder was now unfolding. "They told us they would kill us if we told of what happened!" BingHo now wailed for mercy.

ChopSee now tried to pull his pistol out in anger and shoot BingHo. The pistol only made it halfway out of the belt, and QueYu shot him through the head, his body lurching several feet back from the impact. In panic, the other assassin tried to run, and QueYu put him down with a shot to the back of the neck. QueYu's men now wanted to kill the "talkers," but he told them to put their guns down.

"I know CheSaw. He is an honorable man. He would never have conspired for this to happen! You, Bing Ho, go back to Chinatown and tell CheSaw what has happened! Tell him my brother's murder has been avenged and that my 'Tong' will cut the throats of any man who tries to steal from us again. Leave now, and do not come back!" QueYu commanded.

The two Chinese helpers were now escorted down the trail at gunpoint. Reaching the boat, they began pulling the craft upriver along the shoreline in the slack water, disappearing around the first bend. Back at the collapsed cabin, QueYu ordered his men to dig out the collapsed heap. "These men will stay and help you, Pearl. They need to be quick--it could snow any day now."

Confident that Pearl was in safe hands, Wapato John hugged her and said goodbye. "Our horses are still hobbled across the river. I must go now. I promise to return in the spring."

QueYu and Wapato John rode together back to the store. Arriving, QueYu beckoned for John to come in. Making tea, he conversed with his old friend in Chinook Jargon.

"I have heard reports that the Indians are talking of war with the miners who are on the river. What do you know about this?" QueYu asked.

"It is true. You are on Sinkiuse land on this side of the river. The Chelan and the Methow warriors are not happy with the situation either. Their women have fallen for the vices from the hundreds of Chinese on the riverbank. Chief Moses gave his word to Chilkosahaskt that he would not harm the Bird Woman at her cabin at Corral Creek. That, my friend, is truthfully all that I know," answered Wapato John.

"Thank you, old friend, for the information. My men will accompany you next spring on the next pack train to Walla Walla. Have a safe winter, and go now. We will protect Pearl," Que Yu assured him.

Back at Pearl's shattered cabin, QueYu's men began digging out and salvaging what they could. The two boulders had convulsed so violently that the once six foot wide crack was now four feet wide. The glass Mason jars were a total loss, all being shattered. Food stocks along the shelves were a total loss, as well. Some whip sawn boards, the pot belly stove, and KaPing's teapot were pulled out of the tangled mess of sod and dirt. On the backside of the boulders, Pearl found the bellows totally wrecked and shredded.

"Where you want cabin built, missy? No good living inside rock! Earth still shaking!" the workers informed her.

Pearl was uncertain what to do. The treasure lay under the massive boulder, but the flat, stone entrance lay under a heap of debris. She knew that some way, some how, she had to dig it out in secret, without raising suspicion that it existed. Standing by the crushed bellows, she spotted something she recognized, but it meant nothing to anyone else. Barely exposed, the old log air vent that KaPing had so carefully concealed was now peeking out from under a pile of debris. It was full of dirt, giving no indication as to what it was.

"Build the cabin on the backside of the boulder, here, where it's shady in the summer." She pointed at the area where the crushed log vent could be seen.

The workers went into action and within three days had a plank board shack constructed. The little pot belly stove heated the interior as they finished up the whip saw board roof.

KaPing and Pearl had dug several root cellar dugouts on the nearby hillside. All had collapsed on themselves, but the industrious Chinese were able to dig them back out, saving the crop of potatoes and turnips. On December twenty-first, the first day of winter, it began to snow--and it snowed hard for two days, bringing the mining season to a halt up and down the river.

QueYu's men had constructed a lean-to on the face of the old cabin on the opposite side of the boulders of Pearl's shack. The snow was a foot deep now, and they hunkered under its roof, surrounding a warm campfire.

"You men can go back to QueYu's town. I will be alright now," she informed the group one morning.

"QueYu say we stay and protect you," came the answer.

Duto's roost up in the crack had been destroyed during the quake. Realizing her shack was now behind the boulders, he had reconstructed a roost with sticks on the backside of the crack, high above on a rock ledge. He could now stare down upon her little board shack. One morning, she insisted on speaking with QueYu. Escorting her down to the hamlet on a path beaten in the snow, she approached the store and brothel of Opium dens. The camp had swollen to over three hundred miners, waiting for the thaw in the spring. The place was alive with the pungent smell of Opium smoke in the air. Pearl found him in the gambling tent at one of the many tables crowded with loud, raucous Chinese.

"I must talk to you… now!" she hollered in his ear.

Picking up his tokens, he led her back over to the dugout store and into a hidden room within its interior. "My men are treating you well? What can I do for you?" he sat down and lit a candle.

"I don't like your men there all the time, up at my place. They stay up late all night, smoking and gambling. I cannot sleep!" she informed him.

"Very well. I will inform them to keep quiet when you are sleeping," he replied.

"No! I want them gone! There is no danger up there," she insisted.

"I'm sorry, Pearl, but they are under my orders to stay and protect you. Fate has turned you and I into partners now," he looked her in the eye.

"What are you talking about? The vegetable gardens are mine, now that KaPing is dead. I, as he, want nothing to do with your business here," she insisted.

"You are protected by my 'Tong,' and because of this, you are now part of this operation," he dryly informed her.

"I don't need your protection. My bird watches over me and my well being!" she hotly stammered now.

"Let me explain, Pearl--Your gardens now feed hundreds of men, and without food, they cannot work, and without work, there is no gold. My business is about supplying men with what they want, in exchange for their gold. It is known that the Indians do not like us here and that there has been talk of an attack. Wapato John told me that Chief Moses will not attack Corral Creek and its gardens as long as you are there. You have become an insurance--that we will not be attacked as long as you are here. Therefore, my men have been instructed to guard over you. CheSaw and I now have a business deal. He will send his boat once a week when your harvests begin. I will keep your share of the profits here, for safe keeping. When the diggings finally pan out, as they will someday, you will be allowed to leave here very rich."

"So you're telling me that I am your prisoner?" she questioned.

"No, no, no. Just look at it as economics. Things have changed--your vegetable business is now under my protection, and so you must reciprocate with your service of staying here," he smiled at her.

"What about my husband!? What have you done with his body?" she now shouted at him.

"All Chinese wish that their bones be buried in Cathay. His casket will be returned to San Francisco and placed on a schooner to take him back. No worry, I will cover the expenses." He further added, "I don't believe the story that KaPing sent your gold to the territory bank in Walla Walla. I know my brother better than that and his way of thinking. It's enough of a story to fool everyone else but not me." QueYu was staring her down. "I have no interest in any wealth he may have hidden, for my own treasure is countless now. My only concern

255

now is our safety on this side of the river, and you are a key ingredient to that concern.

"DO YOU UNDERSTAND NOW!" he quipped.

She stormed out of the dugout. Her armed escorts were waiting for her. Duto landed on her shoulder, realizing she was upset. Following on her heels, QueYu barked at her guards, "Do not keep this woman awake any longer at night with your gambling and loudness! If she complains again, I will have you all beaten!"

Arriving back at the cabin, the confinement now became extremely boring. Her guards had heeded their boss's warning and now were quiet at night, allowing Pearl to sleep. The faint tip of the protruding ventilation log was just outside the corner of her shack, now covered in snow. She realized that if she started digging, the guards would figure out what she was doing. There was no way to conceal the diggings of dirt in the white snow without raising suspicious interest. No, she would have to wait until spring. There was nothing she could do but play their game. Realizing this, she now befriended all the guards, pretending she enjoyed their company. Duto would spend the nights in her warm shack, waking her every morning, demanding to see his medallion and then to be let outside.

Finally, in late February, the warm winds came, thawing the frozen ground. The miners returned to their diggings in the dry gulch across the river as others headed back upriver to Chinatown and "Rich Bar." One day, QueYu appeared at the shack. "The men say you are in good spirits. I am glad. I want you to supervise these men on the functions and plantings in your gardens. Your friend, Wapato John, has been summoned. He and my pack train will go south. I want you to inform him of your needs, be it seeds, shovels, hoes, whatever, or things you need here at your shack. The expenses will be paid by me," he informed her.

Pearl seethed with anger inside but realized she must suppress it, as if she was happy with the situation. The following week, Wapato John did arrive with his string of pack mules. He had brought back her favorite horse, as he had promised. She had not yet hatched her plan for digging out the treasure and so made no mention to him about her status as a "prisoner."

"So, all of your Mason jars were shattered in the big earth shake?" he questioned her.

"Yes, broken, every single one," she confirmed, pointing at the debris field in the crack between the rocks.

"Mine, as well. The trading post roof collapsed, and the next day, half the place was washed away," he lamented. "I will bring more back. Do you have a list for me of things to bring back?"

"Yes, a long list, as QueYu is paying the bill. Bring back as many glass jars as you can," she informed him.

The green grass shoots were now showing, allowing the pack train to forage in the canyon. The following day, Wapato John was gone at first light along with QueYu's mules and keepers.

The arduous, backbreaking job of preparing the garden beds for planting was now delegated out. With this much manpower, Pearl was able to double the size of the cultivated fields. Corral Creek was now channeled into several irrigation ditches. By April, turnips and potato seeds were in the ground. Corn was then planted, and sentries were posted at night to keep the mule deer and rabbits from eating the new sprouts. By mid April, Wapato John appeared on a warm afternoon, coming down the canyon with seventy-five mules, loaded with packs. Excited to see her old friend, she invited him into the shack for corn cakes and coffee.

"I brought you every glass jar that could be had at Fort Walla Walla. Not sure how many got broke on the way back, but I started out with eight hundred," he laughed. "I will take one hundred, as before, and you can have the remaining seven hundred. Tell me, is everything alright here for you, now that your husband is gone?"

Biting her lip, she answered, "Yes, I'm still grieving for KaPing, but his brother treats me fairly. KaPing wanted to see this vegetable canning business succeed, so I'm trying to fulfill his final wishes," she confided.

"Alright, my family and I are building a new trading post up on the north shore of the lake. If you need me, that's where I'll be. Do you have any messages for my brother, Chilkosahaskt?"

"Tell the chief that I am well and not to worry about me," she advised Wapato John.

"Alright. Stay here in this place. You are safe here," he emphasized.

"Yes, I understand. Come see me this summer!" She gave him a big hug.

Pearl had now devised a plan to dig out the treasure undetected. Wapato John had brought back several packets of herb seeds. She ordered the workers to break ground adjacent to her shack. She would personally attend this patch herself. She had the workers fabricate a willow, mesh fence, which encircled the herb patch, keeping out the rabbits and mule deer. One evening, as the men always congregated at the lean-to on the other side of the boulders,

257

she quietly began digging at the inside corner of the shack, heading for the crushed ventilation log just outside. Putting the spoils and diggings in a burlap sack, she drug it outside, dumping the fresh earth in the herb garden. She blended it in and then went back inside, repeating the process late into the night. Each time she went outside, she pulsed with adrenaline, hoping no one would spot her in the dark. Exhausted finally, she covered the hole with a tule mat in the corner, placing a cabinet over it to further conceal the entrance. On the second night, she was now tunneling under the ventilation log, following its path down at a ten degree angle. She remembered the log's shaft of daylight, shining on the Buddha's face. She was confident that if she followed the log down to its depths, it would lead her to the cavern, which may or may not have collapsed during the earthquake calamity.

Because she was fully in charge and now on good terms with the gardeners and guards, she told them they could gamble and smoke until midnight, and that she would not complain to QueYu about it. The ruse worked, and while the Chinese were preoccupied nightly with their gambling and smoking, she used the distraction to her benefit, tunneling deeper and dumping the soil in the herb garden.

It was now June, early summer, and the gardens were beginning to produce. Beans were in abundance, and Pearl supervised long days of canning the harvest. CheSaw's boat was now coming weekly to a makeshift dock that had been constructed at the mud patch on the river. They collected sacks of potatoes and turnips and were beginning to sell the jars of beans.

Duto had a large flock of queens that followed him around throughout the day. They would all perch on top of the big boulder above the lean-to, watching the daily activities below. Daily, they would pick over the workers' dinner bones from the night before. The workers had grown accustomed to the flock and paid them little attention.

No one had detected her digging activity every night in the shack. She was good for three or four sack loads and then quickly got fatigued dragging the dirt out of the tunnel. Her progress seemed painfully slow. One night, she had pushed twelve feet down the shaft and came to the end of the ventilation log. She expected to break into the chamber at any time, but now realized the Buddha cavern had caved in on itself during the big shake. Disheartened, she emerged and brushed the dirt off. This was going to take a lot more effort and time. She couldn't give up, though, as a fortune in gold lay just a few feet away. Not only that, she realized that Duto's magic pellet bag had been left on the altar, and that somehow, before October, she had to find it before he molted.

258

Undaunted, she continued her nightly excavation. It was getting more difficult, dragging the bag of dirt up the shaft. The candle was burning up the air supply, and she felt lightheaded, coming out often for fresh air. On a final trip into the shaft one night to finish filling the burlap bag, her little spade struck something hard. Clawing and brushing away the dirt, she realized it was the top of the head of the Buddha. Excited and pleased with herself, she drug the bag back up the shaft and once more spilled the contents in the herb garden, undetected. The following day, to her surprise, Wapato John appeared with his pack train on the way to Walla Walla.

"Come with me. I want to show you something!" she proudly boasted. Leading him to the dugouts in the hillside, she raised the hide flap of a door. Inside, along the walls, were shelves of canned beans and cucumbers. Smiling in amazement, Wapato John praised her.

"We have not canned anything yet. We have been busy building our trading post and cutting hay. I have spoken to QueYu. His wranglers are again coming with me. What do you need from Walla Walla?" he asked.

"More glass jars! I've already used half of what you brought in the spring. Bring back as many as you can," she insisted.

"Alright, more glass jars. Chilkosahaskt sends his greetings and misses you. You should go see him. He is getting old," Wapato John advised.

"How is LaHompt?" she asked John.

"He is well and happy. He has taken a wife. Their horse herd is quite large now, thanks to you." He patted her on the shoulder.

She wanted to explain her predicament to her old friend but refrained. She had to get her hands on the treasure before she could leave and so acted as if all was good.

"I'll see you in seven weeks. Take care. I can't stay any longer." Within the hour, he was headed up the canyon.

She anxiously waited for sunset that evening, and when she was sure the Chinese were fully involved in their gambling game, she crawled back down into the tunnel to continue digging. She exposed the smiling Buddha almost to his base, but her sack was full of dirt now. Struggling, she pulled the sack up and out of the hole. She had no sooner emerged from the tunnel, when a knock came at the locked door. Hurriedly, she covered the hole with the tule mat and cabinet. Opening the door a crack, she could see it was QueYu. Without letting him in, she asked, "What are you doing up here so late?"

"May I come in?" he asked.

"Yes. Let me put a shirt on." Quickly, she brushed the dirt out of her hair and wiped her hands and face clean.

259

"Come in. Is there a problem?" she nervously asked. "There--sit there," she directed, keeping the candle between them and shadowing the cabinet in the corner.

"I brought the men some rice wine this evening to reward them. They have been doing a great job in the gardens. I see they are gambling and smoking--they are not disturbing you?" he asked.

"No, we have an understanding--as long as they go to bed by midnight and are quiet, they don't bother me," she offered.

"I want to reassure you that CheSaw is paying his monthly bill for the vegetables. I am holding your share of the gold for safekeeping. I have been told that you have several hundred Mason jars of canned vegetables. We will have plenty to eat this winter. KaPing would be proud of you."

"Yes, proud of me... but not so of you! He despised your wretched Opium and prostitution business!" she fired back at him.

"It's all about supply and demand Pearl. If I did not supply the drugs and women, then someone else would. Business is business. I'm simply the middleman. Miners must have their pleasures at the end of the day. No one, I presume, has approached you for sexual favors?" he now coyly asked.

"No, that has not been an issue," she snapped at him.

"They have been warned. If someone violates you, they will not live to see another sunrise," he assured her. "What's in the burlap bag?" he pointed.

"Uh... oh, that.... It's horse manure from the corral, to fertilize the herb garden," she tried to act bored.

"I see. Very well. I'll be going now--just wanted to check on you. Good night." She could hear him laughing and joking outside, and then there was silence.

Trembling, she realized how close she had come to being caught at her secret venture. Duto was cawing at the front door. He wanted to be let in to see that she was all right. Calming him down, she collapsed on her pallet, the close call draining her. She slept until late morning.

Arising, she went through her morning routines. The day could not go by fast enough, and she pulled weeds to get her mind off of the smiling Buddha. She could think of nothing else. She waited impatiently that evening for the men to eat and begin their gaming. She was hesitant after the close call the night before, but she finally removed the cabinet and mat and slid down the tunnel.

Now she was down to pay dirt, being at the top of the altar table. She had to carefully sift through each scoop, looking for the Buddha coins. Finally!! A gold buddha coin emerged, falling from the scoop of dirt. Then another and another! Something was not right, though. The altar had been stacked and covered with the medallions. By the time her sack was full of dirt, she only had six coins to show for the evening's work. Crawling back up and out and catching her breath, she could still hear the men gaming outside. She closed up the entrance, made some tea, and pondered the situation. She had been in the Buddha chamber dozens of times. The medallions had been neatly stacked in rows on the altar table, completely engulfing it.

The shaking! The tremors! That's it! she thought. They had all fallen to the floor! She would have to keep digging. She worried now. Duto's treasure bag and medicine pouch had been placed right at the base of the Buddha, and they were no longer there. For two more nights, she removed the dirt from the altar table, finding only another dozen medallions. She knew if she dug down three feet, from the edge of the altar, she would find the hoard of medallions.

Weeks passed, and she continued to dig, finding nothing. One afternoon, while supervising in the gardens, she looked up to see Wapato John coming down the canyon. It was none too soon. It was August, and she had used up her supply of canning jars. The gardens were still laden with produce, and more canning could be done. He had brought back another five hundred jars. She had her workers unload the jars off of the pack mules.

"You look tired, Pearl. Have you not been getting enough rest?" he asked.

"I'm alright…. There's just much more work this year--the garden's are so large now," she sighed.

"Well, I'm glad to be home. I'm anxious to get the harvest in at the new trading post and try my luck at this canning. The wife of my son, Peter Wapato, gave birth while I was gone. I'm in a hurry to see the new baby. I'll see you in the spring. Good luck this winter!" Wapato John waved, pushing his mules down the trail.

CheSaw's boat was coming twice a week now. The vegetables were in high demand at Chinatown, selling out quickly. The gardeners were sleeping earlier now, after working all day in the hot sun. It made her digging project somewhat easier, not worrying about being caught at her secret endeavor. Finally, she reached the prayer carpet on the floor of the cave. It was covered with the gold coins, as she had expected. Each scoop held four or five medallions. To her relief, she finally found Duto's treasure bag and his medicine pouch. Climbing out of the tunnel, she closed up the entrance. Catching her breath, she made tea and then dumped the contents of the treasure bag out onto the table. *THE PEARLS!* Years earlier, she had placed them in Duto's treasure pouch of shiny baubles and had forgotten all about them. One was a large black orb, the size of a cat's eye. The others shimmered in the candlelight--

261

a dozen of them, the size of garden peas, some creamy white, some black as ink. She got tears in her eyes as she thought of Pinto and her so innocently collecting the oysters in the Sandwich Islands, not realizing they were property of the King. She put them all back in the pouch and put the necklace back on. Now, she carefully opened Duto's medicine bag and was relieved to see the green tablets had not been damaged in the dry soil. She counted the green tablets out--there were two hundred and thirty-one still in the pouch. She divided them in half, placing some back in the pouch and back around her neck. The other half she placed in a glass Mason jar, screwing its pewter lid back on tight. She would be more careful this time. By dividing the tablets, she felt safer, having two different stashes, in case one was lost. She had recovered two hundred medallions, but she knew there were hundreds more, scattered all over the cavern floor, still to be sifted out of the dirt. Nightly, she continued her scavaging, finding more and more. One evening, in early October, she noticed two black feathers at the shack door as she came in from the gardens. Landing on her shoulder, Duto was scruffy and irritable. Stepping inside, he began his tirade of cursing, wanting his green pill. The Mason jar of tablets was in the cabinet over the tunnel hole. She fetched it, dumped one in her palm, and fed it to him. Swearing and cross, he demanded to go back outside.

Pearl managed to find more medallions that night. Finishing the ritual, she stepped outside with the burlap bag of dirt. *SNOWFLAKES!* It was snowing hard now. She hesitated to dump the bag, as it would stand out on the white ground. Taking it back inside, she added wood to the pot belly stove and fell asleep.

The following morning, to everyone's amazement, six inches of fresh snow had fallen the night before, turning the canyon white. Caught off guard, Pearl and her gardners worked frantically through the day, digging out hundreds of squash that were still on the vine under the snow. Their efforts paid off, for the temperature fell to twenty-five degrees that night, far below freezing. The next day, more snow arrived, and it was evident that the harvest was over. The conditions all but shut down the gold diggings up and down the river.

There was no way she could hide her digging spoils from the nightly excavation in the Buddha chamber. She had hoped to recover all the treasure and steal away with it on some moonlit night. She calculated that still half of the treasure lay buried in the dirt of the cavern. If she could sneak away with even half the treasure, she knew she'd be safe once she got to Chilkosahaskt's village. The early snow had thwarted her plan. She couldn't leave the remaining medallions buried… and an attempted escape would be risky, leaving her tracks and path in the snow. No, she'd wait one more winter and in the spring dig the remaining coins out.

The door on her shack only locked from the inside, and now she fretted about the several jars of medallions she'd recovered, hiding them under her bed pallet. She decided that the safest place to hide them was in the half excavated cavern, placed back on the Buddha altar for safekeeping. She climbed back down the tunnel, taking the jars of gold and Duto's medicine jar of green tablets, placing them back at the base of the smiling Buddha on the altar. Emerging, she closed the tunnel back up for the winter. After it was all said and done, she felt greatly relieved. The staying up late at night and the dusty digging had worn her down. She needed to take a break and get back to sleeping normally.

After washing up, she fell onto the sleeping pallet and was slumbering heavily within five minutes. She began dreaming, seeing her one-armed father on the bank of the river, tossing stones from his shrimp trap. *Click, click, click.* She could hear the stones clicking as he tossed them from his trap. *Tick, tick, tick.... Click, click, click....* He was standing in the river, waving at her. *Click, click, click.... Tick, tick....* Pearl opened her eyes. A chill was in the shack, and she reached over to swing the door open on the pot belly stove. Grabbing a stick of firewood, she poked the coals. *Tick, tick, tick, tick, tick, tick....* The open door of the stove now illuminated the room as a flame sparked brighter. Squinting, she stared across the shack, seeing two red, frowning eyes looking back at her. As her eyes adjusted to the dim light, she suddenly realized in horror that she was looking at a giant, diamondback rattlesnake. He was coiled, head cocked in the striking position, under the table, not more than three feet away. The stick in the stove was now flaming brightly, revealing the size of the devil serpent.

She lay motionless on the pallet, frozen in fear. Her mind raced, wondering what to do. If she bolted for the door, he would surely bite her. The snake, now fully illuminated, dropped his head and began to slowly slither towards the cabinet over the tunnel hole. She felt totally helpless, her body muscles locked in terror. The flaming stick of wood now popped a spark out onto the dirt floor, causing the snake to coil again. Out of the corner of her eye, in the dim light, she now spotted her little spade shovel leaning against the wall. Finally, the serpent dropped his head and began slinking again for the cabinet in the corner. In one swift motion, she threw her blanket over the beast. Grabbing the shovel, she began swinging and chopping violently on the surging, squirming mass under the blanket. Shrieking in terror, she bolted for the door, jumping outside. Instantly, Duto heard her terrifying scream. Flying from his roost, he sailed through the open door of the shack.

263

The snake's back had been broken in several spots, but his head was still swaying back and forth, writhing in pain and unable to strike. Without hesitation, Duto jumped onto his back, clutching the serpent in his talons, and began pecking and stabbing the snake's eyes. By now, the Chinese had awoken, hearing the blood curdling scream of Pearl. Too fearful to enter the shack, they all watched as Duto fearlessly pounded the serpents head with his sharp beak until the snake lay motionless. Finally gaining his courage, one of the Chinamen entered the shack, grabbing the tail and buttons, and drug the bloody carcass out into the snow.

The snake was a full eight feet long--a monster. His girth was as big as Pearl's thigh. Covered with blood and exhausted from his attack, Duto jumped up onto Pearl's shoulder, lovingly swiping his beak back and forth on her arm, relieved she had not been bitten. She soothed him and called him "good boy," stroking his back and assuring him the danger was over. Everyone was pumped with adrenaline. The Chinese built a large bonfire and stayed up all night, including Pearl, who retold the nightmare story several times.

The winter was long and monotonous. Every night, before going to bed, Pearl took a long stick and poked around the shack, checking for any more intruders. CheSaw's boat was coming down the river weekly, returning empty jars and loading fresh jars that held the stored vegetables. A horse was now used to pull the heavy boat back to Chinatown. A well-worn path had been plodded in the snow along the riverbank, pulling the boat through the slack river water.

By early March, the snow had begun to melt, and life returned to the diggings up and down the river. Pearl had her gardeners turning the garden plots' soils, preparing them for the planting. First on the list, she had the herb garden turned and cultivated. She hesitated to open the tunnel now, fearing it full of snakes. She had a phobia of being trapped down there, unable to get out if a serpent blocked the tunnel. One evening, she finally got her nerve up and opened the tunnel entrance. She peered into the black abyss, working up her courage. She threw several small stones down the tunnel, listening for rattles or hissing. Satisfied, she slowly crawled down the tunnel, a stick in one hand, and a lit candle in the other. To her relief, the cavern was just as she'd left it. The tranquil Buddha smiled at her, assuring her everything was alright. She worked off and on for another month. Some evenings, she just couldn't bring herself to continue. The work was exhausting, hauling the dirt out of the long tunnel. She continued to find medallions. The altar now was covered with thirty-seven Mason jars of gold, and the cavern floor was still only halfway dug out. She had to hatch a plan and somehow get all of the heavy jars out and escape to Entiat.

One morning, QueYu appeared with several of his men, as she and her workers were finishing breakfast. "Good morning. What brings you up here so early?" she asked the boss.

"I'm sending a pack train to Walla Walla for more supplies. What items do you need?" QueYu asked.

"Where is Wapato John--he always takes care of that for you?" she looked puzzled.

"I sent for him, but the answer I got is that he cannot come. Chief Innomeseecha forbids him from helping us any longer. My men now know the trail well. We no longer need his services. We do need more pack horses and mules, so my men will take all the livestock you have up here with them."

"You can't take my horse. He's mine!" Pearl protested.

"I can take him, and I will! You have no need for him. We need every animal we have to pack back all the supplies we need."

The morning was spent rounding up the herd, and by noon, a string of fifty horses and mules were plodding up the canyon trail, heading south.

Pearl bided her time, supervising the garden work. CheSaw had returned most of the empty Mason jars, and Pearl neatly arranged them on the shelves in the root cellars, counting out over 1,000. When the pack train returned, she would waste no time and make her getaway. She needed her trusty saddle horse and at least two mules to pack the heavy jars of gold. She figured she could sneak out the back of the canyon and ride south along the Breaks until she was across from Entiat. From there, she could summon help.

To her dismay, when the pack train returned, all the livestock were taken to graze in the coulee above QueYu's store, including her horse. She protested to QueYu about it, wanting her horse returned. He sensed that she might try and flee and refused to return him. Not only that, he doubled the guards at the gardens, including one now who watched over her herb garden nightly.

She toiled through the summer, hoping that if she played the game, they would let their guard down and she could escape, somehow.

By September, the 1,000 Mason jars had been filled with produce, stored in their cellars. The harvest of potatoes and turnips had been good, with dozens of burlap bags filled and cached away. One day, as she watched the workers harvest the last of the squash, a movement caught her eye, high up on the ridge in the back of the canyon. Squinting and shading her eyes, she saw a dozen riders on horseback, gazing down at the canyon below. She looked away to see if anyone else had detected them, but they all had their heads down, engrossed in their work. When she looked back, all she saw was a cloud of dust.

That winter, she fell into a deep depression, beginning to give up hope. *To hell with the gold*, she thought. *I can't stay here much longer. I'm a slave and a pawn. I'll bury the gold, escape, and come back and get it.* She knew that if she fled, they would tear the shack apart and find the secret tunnel and treasure chamber. She'd wait for spring thaw, bury the gold outside somewhere on a moonlit night, then head south on foot. Duto was her only friend now. She would have to have faith in his protection watching over her on the escape across the Breaks. Duto felt her misery and stayed inside with her through the winter, perched all night on the back of a chair.

It was now the spring of 1875--three years since the earthquake and murder of KaPing. As the snow departed, more and more Chinese were arriving at the diggings, all latecomers who had been lured by tales of get-rich-quick. For Pearl, it was back to the same routine and what was expected of her. She would wait till the spring pack train departed, taking all the horses and mules with them. She figured she could outrun any pursuers, as they would be on foot too. QueYu had delayed the trip, wanting a good count on the empty, glass Mason jars and so waited for the last batch to come back from Chinatown. He sent word for Pearl and her workers to meet the arriving boat in the morning and help unload the fragile, empty jars.

She had identified a good place to hide the gold outside. She'd found an abandoned badger den under a black, basalt boulder. The badger had piled the diggings in front of the den, so she could quickly use the soil to cover the hole back up and make it look natural. She'd have to do it in broad daylight, when the guards weren't around.

As ordered, she and six porters marched down the trail to the wobbly dock the next morning. The boat had just landed, and QueYu was there, firing orders at the group. "Hurry! Hurry! The boat needs to come down to the store after you offload the jars!" The jars were in several Methow woven baskets, packed in straw. "Quick! Quick! Make your count, Pearl!" QueYu quipped.

"I count two hundred and twenty-one jars, QueYu," she informed him.

"Quick! Quick! Back to work! Make more vegetables! Chop! Chop!" he commanded. "We go now!" and pushed off with his boatmen. He stood proudly in the center of the boat, as an admiral commanding his crew. When the boat was out of earshot, the whole group of porters made fun of QueYu's performance, chuckling under their breath. Even Pearl had to smile.

Back at the garden camp, a large fire was built, boiling a big iron pot of water to wash the jars clean. It had become just another routine, one they had all done many times. They were soon to learn that the routine was just about over with. April had turned into a beautiful, sunny month on the plateau palouse region. Sunflowers, bunch grass, and camas were bursting from the warm earth. Spring rains coaxed the hills into a lush green.

The Sinkiuse had also been waiting for the thaw. Now, the ponies were fat and strong. A raid on the Chinese would take a full day of well-planned tactics. The warriors would then scatter, giving no chance of retaliation. They could retreat fast and far, with plenty of grass to keep the horses moving. Lolowkin, or Chief Moses, as he was now called, had given the order in council that winter. It was decided that Snorting Bull would lead the strike. All the tribes were upset that the Chinese were destroying the river valley with their thousands of holes. Snorting Bull had seen the Chinatown on the Methow river bar many times. He would visit his mother, Green Baskets, at the Methow village, just up river from Chinatown. He saw the destitution that had befallen his mother's people and heard the stories of the abuse of their women. It was not difficult to convince the chiefs in council to go to war. The issue of the "Bird Woman" in Corral Creek was brought up. Snorting Bull was reminded of Lolowkin's promise to Chilkosahaskt, that the woman should not be harmed. "I know much about this woman. She saved my life as a young boy," he explained as he stood up before the chiefs. "My mother witnessed her magic using the black bird. Her medicine is strong, for the bird talks to her, and she talks to him in a strange language we cannot understand. I will capture her in the raid, myself, and will insure myself that she is not harmed. This way, Lolowkin, you do not break your promise to Chilkosahaskt."

The chiefs all nodded that this was good but then asked, "What will you do with her?"

"I think she is a witch and a sorceress. Yes, I am afraid of her. I do not like being intimidated by a woman in my own country. I want her to go away and not come back. We will retreat after the raid to the buffalo country. We will take her with us--I will sell her to the Cheyenne as a slave!"

Snorting Bull had established himself as a brave man and one to listen to. He was now twenty-seven years of age and had been to the plains to hunt buffalo on three other past occasions. He had stolen several Blackfeet horses and was deadly on horseback with a lance, killing many buffalo. A year earlier, he and his cousins had driven a herd of five hundred horses across the northern plateau to Fort Sheppard, just across the forty-ninth parallel. There, at a Hudson Bay Trading post at the mouth of the Pend Oreille river, he had traded for the herd of horses. Snorting Bull had shrewdly bargained for firearms. Fifty French cap and ball muskets and ten navy cap and ball pistols were traded for the five hundred horses, along with a Henry yellow boy carbine that was displayed on the wall. The result, not counting the firearms the Sinkiuse already had, was a formidable little army.

Now, sitting in the council with prestige, Snorting Bull reminded the chiefs, saying, "How can we talk of war with the whites when we have allowed these Chinese devils to overrun the Big River? Before we can even consider war on the white's, we must eliminate these Chinese, first! Yes, I seek vengeance, it is true. They have overrun the place of my father, where I learned to ride a horse--my country! And they have overwhelmed my mother's tribe with the evil devil smoke and brought disgrace to the Methow women! I know that land well, my chiefs. I have thought many days, long and hard, about how to attack. I will take one hundred fifty warriors up Chief Moses' coulee--to the creek of the waterfalls. From there, we will head north across the plateau, to the field of sacred boulders. There, we will split up. Fifty warriors will drop down in the Breaks and swim their ponies at a chosen spot on the Big River. Reaching the other side, they will sit and wait in ambush. The remaining hundred warriors will go north, to the place the Okanogans call Foster Creek, and follow it down to the Big River, where the Chinese are at a place called 'Rich Bar.' There, the attack will commence, pushing the Chinese downriver to the Chinatown. There, we will rout them and continue to push them south into the waiting ambush. The ambushers will then come back across the river, and from there, we will sweep south, finishing off whoever remain. Myself and the fifty warriors will attack Corral Creek and the Chinese store on the riverbank. The other one hundred warriors will sweep south, flushing the Chinese out at the dry gulch across from the store. Whoever are lucky enough to survive and flee downriver will be met at Rock Island and finished off." It was a brilliant strategy, and the chiefs approved wholeheartedly, putting the plan in motion.

Now, it was that fateful day.

The Sinkiuse warriors, one hundred of them, mounted and armed, had crossed the Big River in the night at the "Rich Bar." They had hidden behind a sand dune, waiting for the Chinese to come down to the sandbar and begin their labors that morning. All of a sudden, a wave of shrieking Sinkiuse warriors bolted from their hiding spot, splashing down the river on horseback. The Chinese were run down and lanced, fighting back pathetically with shovels. The ones who tried to outrun the onslaught were shot down with rifles and pistols. The dugout camp was fully aware of the attack now, and over two hundred Chinese dropped everything and ran for their lives towards Chinatown, eight miles to the west. The Sinkiuse kept up their relentless attack, running down the terrified celestials and lancing them in their tracks. By noon, what was left of the terrified refugees began to spill into Chinatown. Full blown panic resulted with the four hundred

Chinese at the diggings. Half of them decided to flee and run south, straight into the ambush that was waiting for them. The Chinese in Chinatown had a few trade guns that were used for shooting rabbits. CheSaw's Tong had six riflemen, their combined police force. With a few swords and knives, they were no match for the Sinkiuse buffalo slayers that were coming at them, armed to the teeth. The five minutes of unorganized resistance was quickly smothered by the stampede of killing warriors, shooting pistols at close range, and using a withering, arrow attack. A full chaos of retreat was now on, the Chinese running for their lives. Many jumped into the river, trying to hide behind floating logs, but Snorting Bull's riflemen picked them off, like shooting ducks in a barrel.

The raiders now slowed their pursuit, having run their ponies for eight miles. Chinatown was full of loot and booty, and the Sinkiuse helped themselves while they began to torch the place into an inferno.

The fifty Sinkiuse, who had waited in ambush, had picked the spot well. Hiding behind a steep slope of boulders above the river trail, the path choked down to a mere forty feet in width. Spread out over a quarter of a mile, the Sinkiuse waited until the path below was crawling with terrorized Chinese. At a predetermined signal, they let go with a barrage of lead, dropping most of the helpless miners in their tracks. Now, it was up to the ambusher's speed at reloading their guns, allowing a few lucky stragglers to get through. The few lucky ones continued fleeing south, through the dust and pandemonium, to the dry gulch diggings. The Chinese kept coming through the gauntlet and kill zone, being pushed by the marauding horsemen behind them. Finally, the fleeing Chinese dwindled to nothing, and the ambush was over. Only a few Sinkiuse had been wounded, non fatally. Well over two hundred Chinese had been slaughtered between the Rich Bar and Chinatown. Corpses were seen floating down the river. Snorting Bull had observed the ambush high on a ridge across the river. He and a few of his cousins had watched over the carnage below. He had not taken part, as he had given his word to capture the Bird Woman, which was now where he was headed. He now signaled for the fifty riflemen to return. Once they were across, the attack would resume, down both sides of the river. He seethed now with rage, inciting his warriors with their splendid victory to follow him south.

The killing fuse had been lit among the warriors. The deed was only half done. They must finish and wipe out Corral Creek, QueYu's store and settlement, and the dry gulch miners. Snorting Bull's strategy was now evidently brilliant. As the refugees would come running into the dry gulch diggings, he would swoop down Corral Creek Canyon in surprise, creating a pincer movement on both sides of the river, squeezing the survivors into his trap. Now

269

he came charging down the upper reaches of Corral Creek, undetected, a mile from the Chinese gardens and Pearl's shack.

Pearl was busy boiling the glass jars in the iron pot of water when, all of a sudden, rifle shots were heard coming from across the Big River. At the same time, Duto landed on her shoulder, frantically warning her, saying, "Devils are coming! Hide! Hide!"

Now she could hear gunfire coming from the gardens from up above. She could hear screaming and Chinese pleading for their lives. She ran to her shack, taking Duto inside with her. She'd have to protect herself and the bird somehow, not knowing what to do. She could hear a barrage of rifle fire now, just outside the door. She bolted the shack door and pushed the table in front of it. Outside, the killing and carnage was brief, ending as quick as it had started. She could hear Snorting Bull demanding through interrogation as to where the Bird Woman was. Her shack was pointed out, and the Chinamen were shot immediately. Fifty-five warriors, including Snorting Bull, surrounded the shack on horseback in a giant circle around the double boulders. Each held his distance, fearful of the place. Whatever the taboo was, it was common knowledge among them, and each held back at a distance.

Snorting Bull rode up to the door on his war painted horse and called out to her. "Bird Woman, it is I, Snorting Bull, the one you saved so long ago! Come Out! I will save you today! Come out, I say, to save your life. Chilkosahaskt's word protects you!"

Upon hearing this, Pearl realized she had no other options. The boy she had saved so long ago was now guaranteeing her life. She pulled the table away from the door and unlatched the bolt. Duto was on her shoulder as she swung open the door and faced the war chief. He was terrifying to look at. He wore a crown of buffalo horns, plumed with hawk and eagle feathers. A bone breast plate and silver armlets were all that covered his upper body. He was painted totally black, with red dots everywhere. His buckskin leggings were covered with hawk feathers. His bow cover and quiver were slung across his back, fringed in horsehair and silk ribbons. Two butcher knives on either side of the saddle were beaded and protruded within easy reach. A tomahawk hung from his breechclout. He carried a .44 caliber Yellow Boy rifle over the cantel of his saddle, and his horse was a spectacle, covered with feathers and paint. When she looked up at him, she almost fainted at the sight of his satanic look, an incarceration of the devil himself.

"Stop where you are! STOP! Tell your spirit bird we will not harm you! Do not use your magic against us! Do not make us kill you!" he fiercely commanded her.

270

Rifle fire from across the river became intense now, as the sound of screaming and wailing carried across the water. For a long minute, nothing was spoken, as the carnage in the distance continued and could be heard.

"Tell your bird to fly away--I do not trust him," he ordered.

Pearl whispered to Duto, telling him to go to his roost. He cursed bitterly and complained, saying, "You son of a bitch pig bastard!" and flew up to his roost. Startled to hear the bird speak, the Sinkiuse were now extremely nervous about the situation.

Snorting Bull called out for a saddle horse. "Hold your hands out--tie her hands--you will ride with us. Do not try and escape! Laughing Dog, take thirty warriors and attack the Chinese store on the river. Finish them off! Take pack horses with you. Take what you can, then burn it down! I will wait one hour here for your return! HiYee! Be quick! Go now!"

Sporadic gunfire was still heard from across the river. The war party split up, the thirty warriors with Laughing Dog galloping off towards QueYu's store. A full assault was now upon the settlement.

QueYu was lucky. He had heard the gunfire across the river at the dry gulch. He could see the attack happening, fifteen minutes before Laughing Dog was upon them. The two dozen inhabitants of the gambling hall and brothel wasted no time in fleeing, using several canoes and CheSaw's boat to escape in the nick of time. QueYu and his guards grabbed what wealth they could but basically escaped with their lives. When Laughing Dog and his braves reached the settlement, it was totally abandoned. Within a matter of minutes, the place was looted and set ablaze. Across the river, dozens of Sinkiuse on horses had driven the Chinese up against a natural basalt wall and had killed every single one, raining arrows down upon them. The entire Big River valley, for thirty miles, had been wiped clean of Chinese. Many escaped down to the Wenatchi valley and headed south over Colockum Pass, never to return. The raiders, now having laid waste to QueYu's store and brothel, returned to Snorting Bull and his warriors, who now stood guard over Pearl, lashed to a horse.

"I see you have all returned safely. They did not put up a fight?" Snorting Bull questioned as he inspected them.

"They escaped in canoes. No one was in the settlement. It was abandoned and deserted. We loaded six pack horses with goods from the trading post. It is all burning now!" Laughing Dog reported.

Duto had remained at his roost in the boulder crack but was now extremely agitated over the rough treatment Pearl was receiving. Duto now sent out his distress call, and within minutes, his two hundred queens came flying from every direction, landing on top of the massive double boulders. A

271

tumultuous cry of cawing rang out from the giant flock, with a menacing look in their eyes.

A wave of apprehension and fear was now upon the Sinkiuse.

"It is a place of sorcery. Burn the shack down!" cried out Snorting Bull. "We go now!"

The Sinkiuse now threw firebrands and flaming tumbleweeds into Pearl's shack. Within minutes, it was a roaring blaze. Duto and his queens became airborne, flying in a giant circle around the column of smoke, continuing their crescendo of cawing. The sight brought fear to the Sinkiuse, and they kicked and whipped their horses away, sensing a dark and evil spirit. All of a sudden, the flock dove and attacked the fleeing horsemen. They swooped down and pecked the horses' and Sinkiuse's eyes, creating complete panic and a stampede. Duto had singled out Snorting Bull as his own personal target. Snorting Bull was now whipping his horse hard to escape as he led Pearl's horse on a rope. Tied and still lashed, she was helpless. Duto dove in close and raked his talons across Snorting Bull's face, drawing blood and enraging the chief. Regrouping and landing briefly on a pine tree branch, Duto attempted to assess his next move.

That was all the time the chief needed. He quickly nocked an arrow and let it fly from his bow. Seeing the arrow launched, Duto spread his wings to flee, but he was not quick enough. The arrow slammed him hard into the tree trunk, piercing his wing and knocking him senseless. He quivered and shuddered, as the arrow had pinned him to the tree. He now was motionless.

Tied and watching from her horse, Pearl was stunned to see the event unfold. She screamed out, "DUTO! DUTO! Oh, no, no, no, no…. DUTO!" She shrieked and wept.

Other Sinkiuse had used their bows and guns on the bird attack, and now several were dead and flopping around on the ground. The gunfire and carnage scattered the remaining queens. Still in great fear, the Sinkiuse regrouped and fled to the top of the canyon. Being pulled at a gallop, Pearl, with Snorting Bull, reached the crest of the canyon. Stopping and waiting for the others to catch up, she wept and stared at the lower canyon. Two columns of smoke were seen, one from the flaming shack, the other from QueYu's destroyed nest of vices.

"You bastard! You didn't have to kill my bird!" she hissed at the chief.

"Your medicine is broken. The bird is dead! Tie her mouth shut. I will hear no more of her talk!" he commanded. "We will camp at the Lone Butte. We must travel hard and fast--we will disappear like the wind! HiYee!"

Breaking out onto the flat plateau, the war party moved quickly east. By dark, they arrived at the knob protruding from the flat prairie. With lookouts perched on top of the small butte, they watched for any chance of pursuers counter attacking them. The warriors built no fires that night and were up and moving at the crack of dawn. They were headed for a spring at a natural crossing of the Grand Coulee, a place they called "Squaquint." Their families of elders, wives, and children were camped there, waiting to rendezvous with the raiders and flee to the east to buffalo country. The location of the spring was a sanctuary for them, in the heart of their homeland, which very few other people knew about. For hundreds of years, they had camped and hunted at this spot, an oasis in the vast Grand Coulee. The coulee was over fifty miles long and only could be crossed laterally in this location, due to the steep, basalt walls on either side. Below the spring, the Sinkiuse had scooped out a small pond. It had become the watering hole for game in all directions in the vast sea of sagebrush. Pushing their exhausted horses harder, by afternoon the war party had reached the natural cleft in the coulee's basalt cliffs, which secreted a faint path to the coulee floor. In the distance, forty teepees could be seen, pitched in a cottonwood grove around the spring. Two hundred horses grazed around the grove of trees. The camp now came alive, as a scout arrived and announced that the war party was coming down the cliff trail.

Pearl was thirsty, raw, broken, and sore. The site of the camp filled her with apprehension. Without Duto to guide her, she felt alone and vulnerable. As the warriors approached, excited drums began to beat, and women trilled and screeched their battle cries, searching the faces for their husband or brother. The horse culture was now in its finest moment. Returning with horses loaded with booty and pig tail scalps of the Chinamen, the victory of removing the "hole diggers" from their country was now celebrated. Singing and chanting, the women swayed in a long line as the warriors rode past and displayed the collection of war booty. A feast of mule deer followed. The storytelling and eating went late into the night. Pearl had been lashed to a cottonwood tree with two young boys charged to guard and watch over her. The following day was spent with more feasting and dancing. The Sinkiuse's horses were like family to them. Several of the horses were paraded and honored. Their bravery and stories of the attack were told and embellished. Grains and wild plums were given to the chosen ones, and ribbons were tied in their manes, to identify their status. Two horses had come up lame in the retreat. With solemn chanting and tears, they were humanely put down and cut up and roasted. By eating the meat, the creature's brave soul became part of the tribes' spirit.

Sunflower, a young daughter of Snorting Bull, now approached Pearl in pity. Seeing her cowering under the tree, she offered Pearl some of the

273

horsemeat on a skewer. Pearl graciously took the stick of meat and began to devour it hungrily.

"My grandmother, Green Baskets, told me the story about you--how you saved my father from the death fever. She said that you are a good spirit--that you came from far away with your magic bird, bringing gifts of warm blankets."

Pearl smiled at the young girl. "You are brave to feed me and talk to me. What is your name?"

"My name is Sunflower. Some say you are a witch."

"Your father is a great man, but he does not understand me. No, I am not a witch. I am just like you. Do not be afraid of me. I will not hurt you."

"Sunflower! Be gone! Go to your mother!" It was the chief, sternly approaching and waving the young girl away.

"Your daughter has no fear, much like you," Pearl spoke, looking up at the chief.

"If she had seen your black magic that you used in the canyon--the bird attack--she would then fear you," he replied. "I still fear you and do not trust you. Treating you badly, though, could bring bad medicine for my people. I will untie you and let you walk and ride among us, but if you try and escape, my warriors will hunt you down and cut your ears off. We're going to the buffalo country, and I want none of your bad magic put upon us."

"Why have you spared my life, if you fear me so greatly?" she asked.

"Lolowkin gave his word to Chilkosahaskt that you would not be killed. I am enforcing his promise, as my word is my honor. I am taking you far away from my country and warning you never to return. Do I have your promise that you will not try and escape?"

"You have my promise, for I have nowhere to escape to. I am lost in this desert and am at your mercy. Do not fear me, for you have killed my connection to the spirit world, and my power is gone." She hung her head in silence.

With that, he turned and walked to a nearby teepee. Conversing with several women who were seated, he pointed at Pearl. Several nods were exchanged, and he walked off, disappearing into the maze of teepees. Two women now approached Pearl. They cut her rawhide lashings loose and offered her water from a gourd. Placing a blanket around her, she recognized it as one of her own.

"I am 'Wind on the Grass,' and this is my sister, 'Singing Bird.' You will come with us." She was taken inside a teepee, given more food and water, and told to lie down and rest. "We will leave this place tomorrow. You must regain your strength, as the trail is very difficult. Do not worry--we will watch over you. Sleep now."

Not feeling threatened now, Pearl fell into a deep sleep, having not slept for the last three days. She awoke the next morning, a tickling sensation on her face. She opened her eyes, seeing Sunflower smiling and tickling Pearl's face with a turkey feather. "Come, wash yourself in the pond!" the girl urged her. Stepping outside, the camp was being broken down, getting ready to travel. Without hesitation, as they had been waiting for her to awake, her hosts began to dismantle the teepee she had slept in. Pulling Pearl by the hand, Sunflower led her to the small pond, only knee deep. "Wash the trail dust off. Hurry--we are leaving soon!" the girl advised her. The sleep and rest had replenished her, and now the bath invigorated her.

"Sunflower, where is this buffalo country that we are going?" asked Pearl.

"I have never been there. It is to the east, towards the rising sun and beyond many mountains. It will take us many sleeps to arrive there," she explained.

Pearl scooped more handfuls of the cool water, washing her face and hair. *Caw Caw Caw* came a cry from the cottonwood treetops. Looking up anxiously, hoping to see Duto, she made eye contact with the raven, realizing it was not him. The bird quickly took flight, heading back west. She watched the raven disappear and muttered a prayer, "Thank you Duto, for all that you did for me."

"Come--we go now!" It was Singing Bird, urging Pearl to come out of the pond.

The tribe was already moving out... a long line of families, walking and riding abreast, headed straight east towards the morning sun. Dogs were seen loaded with food packs, walking transports that would be eaten later--both food and dog. Wind on the Grass and Singing Bird had a fresh pony, painted and saddled, waiting for Pearl to mount and ride. Sunflower jumped onto a travois, pulled by Singing Bird's saddle horse. Excitement and laughter was in the air, as the highly anticipated journey to the buffalo lands was finally underway. For three days, the dust cloud of people and horses migrated east, stopping at chosen water holes and only resting briefly. They rose every morning before sun up and pushed towards the now visible distant mountains. On the fourth day, they left the flat, desert plateau of sagebrush, winding through low, rolling hills, dotted with pine trees. By evening, they had reached a Spokane village, who were allies and friends of the Sinkiuse. Resting and trading for two days, they now continued east, following the Spokane River. Plodding along the river trail, the people finally arrived at its headwaters, a huge lake and home of the Coeur d'Alene tribe. Several villages were scattered around its shore. Again, these were old friends of the Sinkiuse. Several hunters with their families would accompany them to the buffalo lands, guiding the mass of horses and people through the mountain trails.

By now, no one noticed or paid much attention to Pearl. She quickly picked up the routines of Wind on the Grass and Singing Bird, assisting them in setting up and breaking down the camp daily. Wind on the Grass was one of Snorting Bull's wives and not his favorite. He would walk his camp every evening, checking for problems, giving advice and encouragement. On this evening, he chose to stay in her teepee. Sitting by the cooking fire, he made conversation with the women and Pearl.

"You are good with horses. Chilkosahaskt's people taught you well." He now spoke to Pearl.

"Your father gave me two hundred horses for saving your life. I had no choice but to learn the ways of the horse people," she answered in a deadpan voice.

"So why did you not stay with Chilkosahaskt and his people? Why did you join up with the Chinese?" he now questioned her.

"At the secret crossing, where your father took me to cross the Big River with the horses, I saw gold in the sand. I wanted to return to my homeland, and the gold was the means to pay for it. I showed the Chinese the place, and you know the rest of the story," she answered.

"Yes, I know the story--the Chinese kept coming until they were like ants in the sand. They destroyed my mother's people with their ways. And you--you built your cabin on a Sinkiuse sacred shrine. You were very foolish!"

"Why is the broken boulder a sacred place?" Pearl cautiously now asked.

"That is the place of the serpent king. We do not go near it. We pray and make offerings to it, that the serpent king will let us safely pass and that his children will not bite us with poison," he explained. "You can never return there. We have given you your life, and if you try and go back, we will kill you."

"What will you do with me then?" she asked.

"That is a good question, which I cannot answer." He quickly changed the topic, asking for more venison and dog soup. Singing Bird signaled for her to not agitate him, and ask no more questions.

The travois' and teepee poles now had to be abandoned. They were cached at a spot along the trail to be retrieved the following year when they returned. On the other side of the Rockies, they would cut new teepee poles. All of their belongings were now packed on the horses. The high, mountain trail was steep and rocky. The tribe was now in deep forest, ascending a narrow, rugged trail in single file. The terrain brought back memories to Pearl of when she had

276

crossed the Cascades twenty-two years earlier with Swakane Jacque. The trail was steep and dangerous, a relentless climb upwards. For another three days, they camped on rocky, broken ground in the deep forest. The trail was faint and would disappear, but the Coeur d'Alene guides knew every rock outcrop and every meadow and pushed the people on. The air was thin and cold, and the horses were now becoming weak from lack of forage. Finally reaching a crest and an open lookout, Pearl gasped at the backbone and vista of the Rocky Mountains.

The descent was not much easier, the trail still broken and steep. Finally, after two weeks of leaving the pleasant valley of the Coeur d'Alenes, they arrived in a mountain valley, lush with grass. A stream meandered down its length, with columns of steam rising in different spots. Excitement and joy was with everyone, as camp was quickly established. With the stress of the mountain crossing behind them, dogs were killed for cooking pots, and the horses spread out, grazing after days without grass.

Singing Bird now coaxed Pearl to follow her, saying, "Come, wash yourself in the warm water."

Dozens of people were seated along the wandering stream, soaking in little pools of steaming water.

"What is this place? Why is the water not cold?" asked Pearl.

"It is called 'LoLo,' the place where the water comes out of the mountain hot. Here, sit in this pool," she urged.

"You go first," Pearl was being cautious. Removing her buckskins, Singing Bird immersed herself, giving out a sigh of pleasure. Without hesitation, Pearl now stripped, sitting down in the pool with only her head exposed. She had never experienced in her entire life the feeling of hot water engulfing her body. She smiled and luxuriated in its relaxing feeling, laughing at the pleasure it brought.

"This is wonderful. I never want to leave this place!" Pearl giggled.

They rested for two more days, allowing the horse herd to regain its strength. Breaking camp, they followed the meandering stream down the valley. The surrounding mountains now became round, rolling hills, dotted with patches of forest. Game was plentiful. Several deer and elk could be seen grazing in the distance on green meadows The stream emptied into a broad river valley. The river wound like a snake, far into the distance for as far as they could see, shimmering in the sunlight. Late in the day, they arrived at a large fork in the river. Here, they made camp.The following day, women and young boys spread out across the river prairie, cutting teepee poles from stands of lodgepole pine trees. More hunters were sent out to find elk and deer. A week of resting and drying meat was in order, in preparation for venturing out onto the vast and endless prairie.

Singing Bird explained that this river was known as the "Clark," named after a white man who had ventured down it decades earlier. The other river, at the fork, was the Blackfoot River, which flowed out of their enemies' country.

"We are low on powder because of the Chinese war. Snorting Bull says we will follow the Clark into the buffalo country and avoid contact with our enemy. We do not fear the Blackfeet, and normally we would follow their river, but we will avoid them this time, until we can trade for more powder," she explained.

Pearl was now thirty-seven years of age. Her hair was beginning to slightly grey. Years of living in the desert had etched wrinkles on her face, and she could feel her youthfulness slipping away. As she ventured further east, all hopes of returning to Fort Victoria and catching a ship home were just a blurred, faded dream. She was becoming depressed with anxiety, having no idea of what her fate may be and what was waiting for her in the future. She thought of trying to escape, but the thought of having her ears cut off quickly suppressed the idea. No, she'd make the best of the situation on the hopes that she would meet another kind man who would hear her story and somehow help her find a way back home.

The tribe was moving again, heading southeast and following the wandering Clark River. It was June now, and the days were long and warm. Scouts were sent out now in all directions to thwart an enemy surprise attack. Soon they would be in Crow country, who in the past were inclined to trade and parlay with the Sinkiuse. One afternoon, a scout came galloping fast and hard towards the column, headed by Snorting Bull. Reigning in his mount in a cloud of dust, he pointed to the east, saying, "A large camp of Crow, three hours ride from here!"

Snorting Bull gave the order to make camp. Assembling two dozen well-armed braves, they rode off in the direction of the Crow village. They would approach and decide what the Crow's intentions were… peace or war.

Now as they approached from a distance, they could see the Crow's teepees, a large village of over two hundred lodges. Hundreds and hundreds of horses grazed on the surrounding prairie. Snorting Bull and his braves had been spotted, and now galloping out to meet them were at least a hundred Crow. This was a test of Sinkiuse bravery, and not one man flinched or showed fear, as the Crow confronted them. Suddenly, Snorting Bull began to laugh, as he recognized an old friend.

The Crow

Snorting Bull and Pretty Eagle had met six years earlier. While scouting for buffalo, both had come upon one another in a remote draw on the prairie. Approaching each other with apprehension, they had smoked and assured each other of good intentions. Combining their skills, they had continued scouting together that day, discovering a large herd of buffalo in a hidden valley. Both had then parted ways as good friends, anxious to return to their hunting parties and report the location of the herd. The following day, Snorting Bull's party of Sinkiuse hunters found the herd, and by noon had slain over one hundred of the shaggy beasts but had scattered the remnants from the hidden valley. Arriving after the fact, Pretty Eagle and his Crow hunters were extremely disappointed. Seeing an opportunity for an alliance, the Sinkiuse decided to share the kill with this band of Crow. Now, six years later, Snorting Bull and Pretty Eagle came face to face again.

"My old friend, I have come to hunt the buffalo again, and as before, we will share with you," announced Snorting Bull to Pretty Eagle.

"Yes, I see that! And would you like to tell me where they are hiding, old friend?" laughed Pretty Eagle.

"Let us smoke again, and we will find them together," assured Snorting Bull.

The apprehension and adrenalin now faded as Pretty Eagle invited the Sinkiuse to his village, signaling them to follow. The visitors were welcomed into the village. That night, a celebration of friendship and hospitality was offered. Pretty Eagle had many wives who had many sisters and cousins. They entertained the Sinkiuse braves late into the night. Telling each other of many fights with the Sioux and Blackfeet, their common enemy, both tribes were very much at ease around each other.

"You are very far west from where we met six years ago. Why is that?" asked Snorting Bull.

"The Sioux have infested our hunting grounds. They are vast in numbers, too many for us to fight alone," explained Pretty Eagle. "They make war on the blue coat soldiers and attack anyone they find," he further explained. "We have made a treaty with the blue coats, as they have offered us protection. Now, we have been pushed to this place on the prairie. The buffalo are hard to find now, as the Blackfeet and Sioux keep scattering the herds. We will join forces, old friend, and find where the buffalo are hiding." The pipe was passed again. Both chiefs now had a better sense of confidence and well-being for their people. The alliance would strengthen the security of both tribes.

The following morning, the Sinkiuse were slow in awakening, scattered all over the Crow village. Finally finding and mustering all of his braves, Snorting Bull got them mounted and started back to their camp, three hours away. Pretty Eagle had invited the Sinkiuse to camp alongside his village, as the prairie was vast enough, with good grass for both of their horse herds. Snorting Bull had accepted the invitation and indicated he would return with his people.

After an hour on the trail, as they were returning back, a rider approached from the west, galloping towards them. In a cloud of dust, he reigned his horse in before the group of warriors. It was "Little Weasel," a fourteen year old boy, gasping for his breath.

"The Blackfeet! They came in the night and stole our horse herd!" he finally managed to blurt out.

"The people--are they alright?" Snorting Bull nervously asked.

"Yes, but they are scared! We do not know how many Blackfeet are in the area!" he stammered.

Without hesitation, the group whipped their horses into a full gallop, fearing for their women and children. After pushing the horses to their limits, they could finally see their teepees in the distance. Arriving, the scene was chaotic, with confusion and panic. With only a few remaining horses, the Sinkiuse felt extremely vulnerable. They had set up a perimeter of defense, suspecting a full blown attack now at any time. Calming his people, Snorting Bull assured them of their safety now. He quickly organized a party of warriors to pursue and try and get the stolen horse herd back. Exchanging their exhausted horses for the only fifteen that had not been stolen, he and fourteen braves picked up the trail of the Blackfeet thieves. By afternoon, Snorting Bull and his braves were becoming fatigued, having been up all the previous night, and now had been riding hard all day in pursuit.

They were in unfamiliar country, and the Blackfeet were a cunning foe. All of a sudden, from out of nowhere, a swarm of one hundred Blackfeet emerged from a hidden ravine on their flank. Putting up an unorganized resistance, the Sinkiuse were quickly surrounded and massacred. The Blackfeet were swift with their grisly celebration, scalping and stripping the Sinkiuse of weapons and booty.

Being preoccupied with their victory, one lone Sinkiuse scout managed to escape, heading south back to the raided camp. Arriving after dark, the scout alerted the people of the massacre, and a wail of grief rang out, the eerie death song being chanted by the murdered husband's wives.

Both Singing Bird and Wind on the Grass shrieked and wailed in emotional pain. Feeling helpless, Pearl tried her best to comfort them. Snorting

Bull had been a fearless leader, whom everyone respected. Several of the slain warriors were the core of the tribe's defense, and now panic was once again upon the shattered camp.

Charging Horse, a warrior who had stayed behind at the Crow camp the night before, now took responsibility for making a decision.

"We must break camp at once! We will go to the Crow village and seek their protection! We must hurry. Load what horses we have. We must leave immediately. The Blackfeet will surely attack us tomorrow!" he cried out.

Coming to their senses, the Sinkiuse realized that Charging Horse was right. A rider was sent to the Crow camp asking for warriors to come and guard the rear of the fleeing tribe. The teepees were stripped of their hide covers, leaving the skeletons of poles behind. Within an hour, one hundred of the grief stricken Sinkiuse, along with a few Coeur d'Alenes, were marching in quick order towards the Crow camp.

The messenger to the Crow camp had been successful, and just before dawn, the fleeing people were met on the trail by Pretty Horse and two hundred Crow warriors, assuring them of their safety. The Crow now fanned out in all directions on the flanks and the rear of the distraught refugees. The exhausted Sinkiuse could now slow their pace and calm the panic amongst them. By early morning, they stumbled into the sanctuary of Pretty Eagle's village. Sympathizing with their loss, the Crow warmly accepted and fed them. Enough teepee poles were rounded up for the Sinkiuse to erect eight teepees, giving the women and children a place to lay their blankets.

By afternoon, Pretty Eagle and his warriors returned to the village with ominous news. Scouts had seen signs of Blackfeet war parties in various locations. It looked as if the Blackfeet had been spying on the Crow, waiting for an opportunity. To the misfortune of the Sinkiuse, they had unknowingly fallen into a Blackfeet plan to attack the Crow. The lone Sinkiuse scout who had escaped the massacre had seen over a hundred Blackfeet warriors. However, the various signs and tracks that the Crow scouts had seen indicated a far greater number of enemies lurking out on the prairie. Pretty Eagle held a council that night, and it was decided to break camp and head south to the safety of the soldiers at Fort Ellis.

Pearl spent the night in a crowded teepee with no one getting much sleep. The apprehension of what was going to happen next had all of them in fear. Some of the women and children had lost husbands and fathers in Snorting Bull's massacre, and sobbing and crying continued through the night. The following morning, word spread quickly that they were breaking camp. It took a couple of hours to round up the horse herd, but by late morning, five hundred

Crow and their Sinkiuse allies were plodding across the prairie in a broad column. Pearl, Singing Bird, and Wind on the Grass were given horses to ride. Pearl did her best to try and comfort them, but the two hung their heads and were unresponsive.

Fort Ellis was a three day march to the southeast. The Crow had not been successful in finding buffalo for some time, and now older or lame horses were butchered to feed the people. By the end of the second day of marching, cavalry scouts from the fort intercepted the approaching wave of people and horses. Signaling with a white flag, they waited on a low hill until Pretty Eagle and three warriors rode out to parlay with them.

The corporal signaled in hand signs, "Who are you, and where are you going?"

Pretty Eagle signed back, "We are Crow. We come in peace. The Blackfeet,our enemies, chase us."

The corporal now discussed the situation with his three companions. Realizing they were on friendly terms and under treaty with the Crow, he now signed back, "You are approaching a U.S. military post. What are your intentions?"

Answering in sign language, Pretty Eagle messaged, "We come in peace. We are hungry. We seek the protection of the soldier fort from our enemy, the Blackfeet."

The corporal now hand signed the answer, "Very well. Proceed, but you will be met by many horse soldiers tomorrow."

Pretty Eagle acknowledged that he understood. With that, the calvary now turned their horses and hastily galloped off to the east. The following day, Crow scouts reported seeing a large column of dust on the horizon. Within an hour, seventy-five calvary were flanking the Crow on either side, their saber scabbards glinting in the morning sun. A bugle sounded, and now a group of mounted officers stood in the path of the people. Their pennants and flags fluttered in the morning breeze. As they had yesterday, Pretty Eagle and three braves rode out to meet the waiting officers. With a stern look on their faces, the same corporal from the day before hand signed to the chief, "Tell your braves to sheath their weapons. You will be escorted to the fort. Any display of aggression and you will be shot."

Nodding he understood, Pretty Eagle ordered his companions to holster their rifles. Seeing that they understood and were complying with the order, a Lieutenant shouted out some orders, and the bugle conveyed his command to the surrounding calvary. Turning their mounts, the officers now waved at the Crow to follow, maintaining the straggling column on either flank, as if herding cattle. The Crow horse herd followed the exodus, and by afternoon, the stockaded fort was in sight. A small, meandering stream was nearby, and the soldiers indicated for the Crow to stop and make camp there. By nightfall, the exhausted people had raised their teepees and shared what meager foods they had remaining. The Lieutenant and corporal returned with a detail of armed guards and requested a council with Pretty Eagle. The Chief invited the two officers into his teepee. A pipe was smoked, and the conversation began through sign language again. The corporal explained that his chief, a Major Sweitzer, needed a count and census of the number of people in the Indian camp. They were to muster in the morning, the men on one side of the fort, and the women and children on the other side. The men would leave their weapons in the teepee camp.

Pretty Eagle agreed but pleaded that his people were hungry and needed food. The corporal assured him that food would be given after the headcount was made. Again, Pretty Eagle agreed to the terms and indicated that his people would come to the fort in the morning. Satisfied with the agreement, the lieutenant and corporal returned to the fort and reported to Major Sweitzer.

Word was passed through the Crow camp that the following morning, all were to go to the fort and they would be given food. The warriors did not like the order to leave their weapons behind, but Pretty Eagle insisted, saying he had given his promise to comply. At sunup the next morning, a bugle could be heard blowing "Reveille." Pretty Eagle ordered six young boys to stay behind and watch the horse herd. He now took the lead. His people and the Sinkiuse began walking to the fort, a mile away.

When the mass of people came within a hundred yards of the fort, the gate swung open, and a large troop of cavalry formed across the front of the stockade wall, as if they were going to charge. The Lieutenant and corporal rode out to the approaching chief. Pretty Eagle calmly walked forward, showing that his hands were empty. He signaled, "We have come as you asked. We are not armed. Make your count. The children are hungry."

The corporal now hand signed back, "Tell your women and children to line up on that side of the fort. Tell your braves to line up on the other side." Canvas tarps had been erected on both sides of the fort with tables and chairs under their shade.

Pretty Eagle now turned and addressed his people, explaining what the soldiers wanted and to form a line on either side of the fort. "Give your name and age. Do what they say, and they will give us food," he assured them.

The two lines now formed. The women and children line was three times longer than the men's line. Soldiers with fixed bayonets were now stationed every ten feet along both lines, with a menacing and nervous look on their faces. A clerk sat at either table with a quill and ledger, deciphering each name as best he could on paper. He guessed the age of each, if they could not answer. The process was slow, and the sun began to swelter. Children began to cry, suffering from being made to stand out in the glaring heat. The pickets had no compassion, barking at the women and threatening with their bayonets, demanding for them to make the babies stop crying.

Pearl was about halfway down the line, and after standing and waiting for two hours, it was almost her turn at the clerk's table. Singing Bird was ahead of her, and after she gave her name and age, the clerk stood up and mopped his brow with a handkerchief. A bucket of fresh water sat on a chair behind him, and he ladled out a long drink for himself. Sitting back down, he barked, "Next!" without looking up from his ledger. "Name!" he barked out again.

"Juana Melendres."

He now looked up from his ledger at Pearl. "Say that again?" he asked, looking at her, curiously.

"Juana Melendres, sir!" she repeated.

"You are Mexican?" he inquired.

"No, sir, I am from the islands of the Philippines and once worked for the Hudson Bay Company," she replied in perfect English.

"Why are you with these people?" he now questioned her.

"I was kidnapped in a raid on the other side of the mountains and have accepted my fate with these people."

A papoose began to cry in line. Without hesitation, Pearl stepped around the table, dipping the ladle in the bucket.

"What do you think you're doing?" bellowed the clerk at Pearl.

"I'm giving that child water, whether you like it or not!" hissed Pearl.

Astonished, the clerk dropped his quill and sat back in his chair. Cooling the child with the drink, the baby stopped crying.

"Do you speak Crow? Do you understand these people?" he now asked her as she returned the ladle to the bucket.

"Yes, I understand them. I can communicate with them," she replied.

"Alright then. Sit down here and help me--it will make this go much faster," he ordered her.

"I will help you if you give them water to drink," Pearl demanded.

Pondering it for a moment, he replied, "Fair enough. Jones, walk down the line with the water bucket and give them all a drink! Sit down here, Señora Melendres," he now changed his demeanor and harsh tone.

In that instant, Pearl, whom none of the Crow knew, became a woman of much respect. As each woman and her children stepped forward, Pearl was given a look of wonderment and gratitude. Asking their names and ages, she translated for the clerk. Within an hour, the count and census was over with. Now, Pearl demanded of the clerk, "We were told we would be given food," staring him down.

"That's not for me to decide," he answered. "Come with me. You won't be harmed," he told her.

Guiding her with his hand on her shoulder, he led her around to the gate entrance and the compound inside. Approaching a whitewashed building with a shaded porch, he beckoned to the guard standing at the door.

"I need to see the major at once," he told the guard.

The guard nodded, stepped inside briefly, and reappeared. "Alright, he will see you. Step inside," the guard acknowledged.

Entering, the major and the lieutenant were both seated, smoking cigars. "What is it Cranston? Who is this squaw?" questioned the major.

"Sir, this woman was in the census line. She speaks perfect English and speaks Crow."

"What?! A squaw that speaks English?" the clerk now had the major's full attention.

With that, Pearl blurted out, "I am Filipina! I speak English, Spanish, Chinese, Chinook, and Sinkiuse. I understand the Crow and can communicate with them. And my name is Juana Melendres, and you will refer to me as such, Mr. General!"

The major's cigar fell from his mouth, and he grabbed it, brushing the hot ashes from his uniform tunic. "What in blazes?! Where did you come from?" he asked in bewildered astonishment.

"I came across the ocean on a Hudson Bay Company ship to Fort Victoria. I crossed the mountains to the Big River. In a raid, I was kidnapped by the Sinkiuse, who brought me here to the land of the Crow."

The major and the lieutenant were dumbfounded. "Who are these Sinkiuse you speak of?" the lieutenant now asked.

"They are horse people from across the Rocky Mountains. They have come here to hunt. The Crow are their friends. The Sinkiuse chief was killed by the Blackfeet two days ago. Out of fear, they have come here with the Crow to seek protection."

The Major now asked, "How many Sinkiuse are with the Crow?"

"I'm not sure--maybe around eighty people, as the chief and fourteen warriors were killed by the Blackfeet. There are also a few Coeur d'Alenes--

maybe nine or ten. We are all hungry. You told Pretty Eagle that you would give us food," she now demanded.

"Yes I did, and I will keep my end of the bargain. The problem is that I can't feed five hundred people daily and my own troops too. I will requisition two beeves and a barrel of flour to Pretty Eagle. He will have to send out hunters to find game. Lieutenant, take your men and cut two beeves out of the corral, and give them a barrel of flour. Hungry Indians are dangerous Indians. Go now. Take care of it."

"Yes, sir. Right away, sir!" The Lieutenant was up, saluted, and headed for the door.

"Lieutenant, have the cook bring myself and Miss Melendres some lunch," he beckoned, stopping him in the open door.

"Yes, sir!"

"Miss Melendres, may I call you Juana?" the major politely asked.

"Yes, you may call me by my first name," Pearl replied.

"Juana, I need you to tell Chief Pretty Eagle to tell his people to stay away from the civilian village--the place they now call Bozeman. Tell him not to let his people or horses stray towards the town. It is only a couple miles from here. General Custer's expedition discovered gold in the Black Hills last year, and now every tin cup gold miner from here to the Mississippi has invaded Montana territory. The result is that the Sioux are on the warpath and that the people of Bozeman will shoot first and ask questions later. I don't want to see Pretty Eagle's people needlessly shot down. Do you understand?"

"Yes. Where is this Bozeman?" she asked.

"My men purposely escorted Pretty Eagle's people around and away from the town. It is two miles to the west of the Crow camp," he explained. "Will you please make sure that Pretty Eagle understands this?" he reiterated.

"Yes, I will tell him." Pearl nodded her head.

The Major could now see that Pearl was staring intently at the wall behind him. He spun around in his chair to see what she was transfixed with. "You're staring at the map?" he now asked her.

"Yes. It is a map of your Montana country?" she asked.

Smiling, he now answered, "In a way it is--this is a map of the entire United States." Pointing, he added, "We're right here--Montana territory."

"Where is Fort Victoria?" she asked.

"Well, that would be right here, just above Washington territory." He pointed it out.

"And where is the Big River?" she asked.

"I assume you mean the Columbia River. That would be all along here." Again, he pointed. "The Rocky Mountains, they run from here all the way down to here." He dragged his finger across the map. Pearl now stood up and walked over to the map. "Major, where are the Filipina Islands on this map?"

He chuckled. "Those are not on this map…. they are across the Pacific Ocean, on the other side of the world."

"What is this dotted path across the center of the map?" she now was full of curiosity.

"That's the Transcontinental Railroad. They pounded the last spike six or seven years ago! The Sioux call it the iron horse because it can pull many, many cars and wagons behind it. It's also a big reason that I'm here, the U.S. Army, to defend it."

Pearl's mind raced. She could faintly remember Chilkosahaskt's question of, 'what was an iron horse' and that she did not know. KaPing had seen one in California, as she recalled him saying. Pearl looked at the major in confusion.

"Here--over here on this wall--a calendar and a picture of an 'iron horse….' It's called a 'locomotive.' There…. " He pointed to the train on the tracks in the picture.

There was now a knock at the door. "Enter," commanded the major. It was the cook. The guard held the door open as he carried in a tray of two steaming bowls of soup and a freshly baked loaf of bread.

"Here, place it on the desk, Johnson," he directed the cook.

"Will that be all, sir?" he asked.

"Yes, that will be all," the major nodded.

The cook stared at Pearl in disbelief, saluted the commander, turned, and departed.

"I know you're hungry, so let's eat… and then I have some questions for you. I'm curious about Fort Victoria and the Hudson Bay Company. I'm from Pennsylvania and know very little about either subject. I'd like to hear more of your story."

Pearl was famished and picked the bowl up Chinese-style to drink the soup.

"No, no, no--use the silver spoon, like this," the major mused as he demonstrated. She realized she hadn't seen a table setting in over twenty-five years, since Fort Victoria. She watched him take a couple sips, and then she quickly had her spoon working, the soup being of good quality.

The Major now tore off some of the bread and dipped it in the gruel. She watched and copied his actions. Finishing, the major grabbed one of two rolled linen napkins, flapped it open, and wiped off his beard and moustache. Satisfied, he now pulled a fresh cigar from a box on the table. Biting the end off and spitting it in the corner, he lit the stogie with a stick match. Puffing it, he sat back and put his feet up on the desk.

"Go ahead, finish the bread," he coaxed her. He stared at the ceiling, flicking the ashes of the cigar and stroking his beard. He was thinking about something, pondering a scheme in his mind. Pearl finished mopping up the remainder of the soup with the bread and then duplicated his action with the fresh napkin, popping it open and wiping her face off. The Major mused at her and chuckled while he continued to pull on his chin whiskers in thought.

"Tell me, Juana--what are your plans? Do you plan on staying with the Crow? You seem to be longing for your homeland," he barraged her with questions all of a sudden.

She stared him down now, saying, "I've always wanted to return to my islands, but life and fate always seem to steer me in the opposite direction. Fort Victoria is so far away, I'm not sure I could ever find the trail back," she sighed and stared away.

"I have a proposition for you, Juana. Hear me out. The Crow know the Montana territory better than anyone. Presently, a campaign to subdue the Sioux rebellion is underway. I would like to hire some of Pretty Eagle's braves as U.S. Army scouts to help my troops find the Sioux and subdue them. Fort Laramie, our headquarters to the south, is in need of scouts also. Would you be willing to accompany a group of Crow scouts to Fort Laramie? I'll detach an armed escort to assist and deliver the scouts to that command post. I would like you to act as interpreter when you reach the fort. Along the way, you can help assimilate the Crow scouts to the army's way of life."

Pearl looked at him curiously.

"What I can do for you, in payment and service to the U.S. Army, is write orders permitting you to travel south from Fort Laramie to Cheyenne with a civilian freighter, contracted as a supplier. The railroad is in Cheyenne. There, you can board a train to San Francisco, and I can give you a voucher for that. From there, you can find a ship to take you home."

Pearl could not believe her ears--it was as if God was answering her prayers. "I've never ridden a train, major. I don't know how!" she stammered excitedly.

"Ha! You just walk on and grab a seat and it takes you there. You'll be in San Francisco in five days after you leave Cheyenne," he chuckled. "I need you to go with the Crow scouts to interpret and make it a smooth transition so that there are no issues on the trail going down there. You'd be helping the Crow people get their land back from the Sioux, and the army could feed the scouts'

288

families as payment. I'll have a large supply of food delivered here from Fort Laramie. Juana, help me. It's a win-win-win for all of us. What do you think?" he looked her in the eye.

"Where is this Fort Laramie?" her eyes were sparkling wet.

"Well, it's a ten day trip on horses--about four hundred miles to the south."

"How can I say no? Yes, I'll do it. When can we start?" she smiled, shaking her head yes.

"Well, we need the Crow to agree to the plan. You need to sell the idea to them--to Pretty Eagle. Can you do it?" the major looked hopeful.

"I'm gonna try! It sounds good for the Crow, good for me, and good for you!" she nodded her head yes at him.

"Alright, go back and talk to Pretty Eagle. When you have an answer, I'll be here waiting to hear from you. Good luck!" He now walked her to the door, and stepping out onto the porch, he called out "Sergeant Books! Take a detail and escort Miss Melendres back to the Crow camp. See that she arrives there safely!" He now shook Pearl's hand, and every soldier in the compound took notice. Turning, he now disappeared back into his office. Sergeant Books now approached her and tipped his hat, saying, "Yes, ma'am, my name's Bob, and I understand you speak English?"

"Yes, Bob, I speak English, and you can call me Pearl."

Looking confused, he questioned her, saying, "Ma'am, Cranston says your name is Juana Melendres--just don't wanna be impolite, ma'am."

"Well, Bob, Juana is my baptized name, but my friends call me Pearl. And assuming you're my friend, call me Pearl."

"Yes ma'am, very well, Miss Pearl. Come this way. Follow me." Bob called out to two soldiers sitting on the corral fence. "You two, saddle up four horses, and adjust the stirrups for the lady. The Major wants us to take her back to the Crow camp. Hurry up. Let's go!" Within ten minutes, the mounts were saddled.

"Here, ma'am, take this sweet little mare here. She's gentle," Bob directed her. Bob cupped his hands to allow her to step up and mount. Laughing, she pushed his hands away, and in a flash, she swung up and onto the saddle. The other soldiers laughed at Bob's chivalry. "Shut up you two, or you'll be shoveling horse shit for a month!" he barked at them.

"'Scuse me ma'am--uh, Miss Pearl, let me adjust those stirrup lengths for ya."

The four proceeded out of the gate and headed for the cluster of teepees in the distance.

On approaching, the camp was a sea of activity. The two beeves had been slaughtered, and everyone was preoccupied with getting a share. Once the four riders were noticed, all eyes and attention seemed to turn and focus on Pearl. She dismounted and walked the final three hundred steps to the edge of the village.

Seeing her, Wind on the Grass ran to her, giving her a warm hug. "Everyone is talking about you--the brave Sinkiuse woman who stood up to the soldiers today and gave the children water! They want to know who this Bird Woman is," she explained to Pearl. She proudly walked beside Pearl now, and several women began to trill their tongues and yip and hiyee, singing their praises of her bravery.

A group of Crow warriors now stood before her. "You must come with us. Pretty Eagle is in council. He wants to speak to you," they demanded.

She was then escorted to a large teepee at the center of the camp and taken inside. This was the teepee of the shaman, Yellow Wolf. Several elders, along with Pretty Eagle, were having an intense conversation. The interior was smoky, and it took a moment for her eyes to adjust. Pretty Eagle told Pearl to sit down. "We have been told about your bravery at the soldier fort today. We have talked to your people, the Sinkiuse, and they tell us you are called Bird Woman, with spirit powers, and to fear you. They say that you had a giant flock of ravens attack them. Is this true?" asked Pretty Eagle.

"I no longer have spirit powers. My protector spirit, a raven, was killed by an arrow, shot by the now dead chief, Snorting Bull. The bird was my protector spirit raven, who called for the attack on the Sinkiuse warriors after they burned my cabin down," Pearl explained.

There was a long, low, mumbled discussion among the elders. Pretty Eagle asked another question. "You speak the white man's language. They took you into the fort. What did they say to you?"

"They told me to tell you this--that there is a white man's town close by, a place called Bozeman. Tell your people not to go near it or allow the horse herd to stray that way. They will shoot their guns at us, thinking we are Sioux. They cannot recognize a Sioux from a Crow."

Again, more discussion went on between the Crow elders. Through the smoky, dim interior, Pearl could now see a raven on a roost... in the shadows. He was tethered with a thong on a perch, pacing back and forth. The bird was directly behind Yellow Wolf, who now was mumbling advice to Pretty Eagle.

"Yes, my scouts have seen the white man's town. This is good to know. I will warn the people to stay away from that place," Pretty Eagle told her. "Two cattle is not enough to feed us. Does the white chief know this?" he asked.

"Yes, he knows this. He was not prepared to feed five hundred people who appeared from nowhere. He does not have enough to feed us daily. He says he will protect the women and children and allow hunting parties to go out on the prairie and find food while the families stay here, outside the fort."

"Ah, this is good. We, as warriors, are not afraid of the Sioux and Blackfeet. If he will watch our families while we hunt, that is a good thing for us." Again, more discussion was made between the elders.

Pearl was now making eye contact with the raven as the men talked. She made some subtle communication with the bird that was not noticed by the council.

"He had one more message for you, Pretty Eagle."

"Speak--what is it?" the chief encouraged her.

"His soldiers are at war with the Sioux, as the Crow are at war with the Sioux. He is aware that the Crow know this country in every direction. He has asked for ten of your warriors to scout for his troops and to help them find the renegade Sioux. He would like an additional ten scouts to go south to Fort Laramie and assist those troops there. When the Sioux are defeated, the Crow can have their buffalo country back. In payment for the scout's services, he will bring wagonloads of food back from Fort Laramie to feed the Crow people."

There was silence now, as each pondered what she had just said.

The raven became agitated, sensing Pearl's watchful eye, and began cawing. Yellow Wolf tugged on his tether, telling him to remain quiet. The bird continued the cawing, and now the shaman was becoming annoyed. Pearl uttered a series of subtle *caws* and clicking sounds, and instantly, the bird froze on his perch, clicking back at Pearl. She then made gestures with her head and again clicked out a cadence of language to the bird. The raven clicked right back at her, flapping his wings and marching back and forth on his perch.

Stunned and in awe, Pretty Eagle asked Pearl, "Are you talking to him?"

"Yes. He is upset and angry," replied Pearl.

Chuckling under his breath, the chief asked, "And why is he angry?"

"He does not like being tied to the perch. He says that if Yellow Wolf will give him the silver armlet on his arm, he will be his protector and not fly away," Pearl stated, matter of factly.

"What?!" asked Yellow Wolf, not believing what she was saying.

"Can I show you?" Pearl asked, using caution.

"Show us what?" Pretty Eagle was optimistic.

Pearl walked around the council fire and now stood before Yellow Wolf, who was seated.

"Take the silver band off your arm, and give it to me." She looked the shaman in the eye.

Without hesitating, he slid the shining band down from his bicep and pulled it over his hand, offering it to Pearl. The raven became extremely excited now, dancing and hopping back and forth on his perch, clicking in quick bursts. Again, Pearl made a series of the clicking sounds, and the bird froze on the perch.

"Let me see your knife," she asked Pretty Eagle. Slowly, he unsheathed it and handed it to Pearl.

The bird sat motionless, and Pearl cut his tether free from his leg. Using the tether cord, she now slid the shiny, silver hoop over the cross tie of the perch, and firmly lashed it down at the intersection of the cross. The bird seemed pleased, and bent over and held his eye close to its mirror finish, admiring his new treasure.

"He will not fly away now. He has become your protector," she told Yellow Wolf. "You can place his perch outside. He will only fly away a short distance to find food. He will always return to the perch and guard you and your teepee."

All of the men stared in utter disbelief and astonishment at Pearl. Finally, Pretty Eagle spoke, "You may go now. We will discuss what you have told us. I will talk to you again in the morning," he advised her.

As Pearl stepped out of the teepee, a multitude of women were waiting for her. One approached her and placed a beautiful beaded pouch and belt around her waist. Then another approached and placed a beaded necklace over her head. Now a whole group was around her, tying beaded eagle feathers in her braids. Another handed her a beautiful pair of beaded moccasins, saying they would guide her on a safe journey. Singing Bird waited until the adoration had subsided. "Come with me, you need to rest."

Back inside the shaman's teepee, the discussion went into the night. The scouting for the troops was a good proposition, which would help them regain their hunting grounds. Finally, Yellow Wolf spoke. "These things the Bird Woman says are good for us, but the Sinkiuse warn that she has a dark, mystical power. This may be a trick, as we do not know for sure what she was told inside the fort. She says the medicine raven will be here in the morning on his perch. So, let us place the bird outside, and if he is still here in the morning, we will know she speaks the truth. If the bird is gone, then you will have to decide, Pretty Eagle, what to do next."

All agreed that it was a good test, and so the perch was picked up and placed just outside the teepee door flap. The bird stayed on the stand, admiring his new treasure. The following morning, the rising sun shone and gleamed on the silver armlet. Its reflection glinted in the eye of the raven, who hovered over it, refusing to leave his perch.

"The Bird Woman speaks the truth!" "Come see!" cried Yellow Wolf.

Pretty Eagle awoke, and stepping out of his lodge, he saw that it was as Pearl had said.

The raven was not going anywhere, and anyone who approached was met with his flapping wings in defiance. He hovered over the silver hoop, cawing and warning to stay away.

The chief now went to Wind on the Grass's teepee. She was outside, cooking some of the rationed beef.

"Wake your sister, the Bird Woman," he ordered her. Nodding, she entered the teepee and gently shook Pearl awake. "Wake up… wake up! The chief is here!" she urged her.

Coming to her senses, she grabbed a comb and stepped outside. Combing her long hair, she questioned the chief, "What is your decision? It must be urgent?" she smiled at him.

"Your magic with the raven is good! We will do what the fort chief asks. We will scout for the soldiers if he will protect and feed our families," announced the chief.

"Very well. I will go at once and tell him the news." In the distance, a bugle could be heard, blowing "Reveille."

"Good!" He beckoned at a boy and told him to go fetch a horse.

"Let me braid my hair and eat!" she laughed.

Singing Bird helped her with the braiding, entwining the beaded eagle feathers. Strapping on her new beaded belt and pouch and slipping on the fancy beaded moccasins, she looked regal. A white mare was brought forward. Blue handprints were painted on the horse's withers and rump, a sign of peace. In one motion, Pearl swung up onto the horse's bare back and walked the pony slowly towards the fort. The sentries saw her coming, and she entered the gate, unchallenged.

Major Sweitzer was reviewing the troops, who were standing at attention. As she entered the compound, he dismissed them and waved at her to approach him.

"You're up early, Juana. I trust you have good news for me."

"Pretty Eagle has agreed to your request--his men will scout if you will protect and feed his children," she answered.

"Excellent! Excellent! Sergeant Books, secure her horse! Come in, come in. We'll have coffee and biscuits." They both entered the major's office.

293

"Sit down... Does he understand my present shortage of food?" he was anxious to hear the details.

"Yes, it all makes sense to him. He wants to send hunting parties out at once," she advised.

"Of course, of course. The sooner, the better!" He now pulled a cigar from the box on the desk. He licked both sides of the cigar and placed it in his whiskered mouth, not lighting it. "Well then, we'll have to get a detail moving south, immediately--first thing tomorrow morning. It will be three weeks before the food provisions return.

"Alright, I will write you passage orders, all the way to Cheyenne, and a voucher to ride the train to San Francisco."

There was a knock at the door. "Enter." It was the cook again, with a tray of steaming biscuits and a pot of hot coffee.

"Right here, place it right here--pour us a couple of cups, if you will," he ordered the cook.

"Yes, sir--right away sir."

"Thank you. That will be all." He waved the cook away.

"Help yourself, Juana. I will get these orders written up." Using a feathered quill and ink bottle, he spelled out the direct orders and then stamped them with his personal military seal. He then blew on the stamped blotter seal, drying the ink mark.

"There you are--orders for safe passage and a voucher to ride the train to San Francisco, with meals served to you. Don't lose these papers, or you will be out of luck," he warned and winked as he handed them over to her. She folded them twice and carefully placed them in the beaded pouch on her belt.

"Now, I want you to return to Pretty Eagle and tell him to muster these twenty scouts. Have him bring them to the fort this afternoon, as I want to review them. I want you to interpret my orders and message to them, as they will have to take an oath of honor. They will need to make their marks on an official document, for their agreement and services. Do you understand?" the major now asked.

"Yes, I understand. So we'll be leaving in the morning?" she asked.

"Yes. The sooner, the better. Fort Laramie is expecting reinforcements this month for this campaign against the Sioux. So the sooner the Crow scouts get there, the better. Alright, take the biscuits with you. You need to get back and inform Pretty Eagle of the orders," he urged her.

Walking her to the door, he opened it and called out, "Sergeant Books, bring this woman her horse! Lieutenant, I need to see you in my office at once!" he urgently ordered.

Thoroughly excited, Pearl kicked the white horse into a gallop. All she could think about was, *HOME! HOME! I'm finally going HOME!* Charging into the village, she reigned the pony in, jumped off, and hurried to Yellow Wolf's teepee. There sat Pretty Eagle and the shaman, smoking passively. The raven was still on his perch, and he flapped his wings and cawed as she approached.

"It is done! He wants you to assemble twenty men that you wish to scout and bring them to the fort at once. They must take an oath of honor. Ten scouts will leave in the morning for Fort Laramie. They will be escorted by troopers. I will go along to help communicate for the scouts."

"Well done, Bird Woman! Did he promise to bring us food?" asked the chief.

"Yes, that is why we must leave in the morning. He understands the urgency to get the food back here for the people from Fort Laramie."

"Alright, the twenty braves have already been selected. I will speak to them at once. We will be ready by high noon to go to the fort." Pretty Eagle was on his feet and called out to a brave at another teepee. He then disappeared into the village, calling out names.

Pearl held out her hand and arm to the raven on the perch. He jumped and fluttered onto her arm. Bringing him close, she clicked a message into his ear, and then returned him to the roost. The old shaman smiled and nodded at her. She returned the smile then turned and headed for Wind on the Grass's teepee.

"You look excited and happy--what is it?" the women asked. Suddenly, Pearl realized that this was goodbye. She sat down next to them, explaining that she would be leaving. A tear ran down Singing Bird's face. She had grown to love Pearl and had bonded with her.

"I want to see my family again, and if they are still alive. Please understand." She grabbed both of the women's hands and squeezed them.

"If you see Chilkosahaskt again, please tell him that I love him, and I am forever grateful to him. Someday, I shall return." Pearl now became emotional too, but bit her lip and composed herself.

"Yes, it is good. You have come a long way. This is good, that you have a chance to return to your family. You must follow your heart, as we will keep you in our hearts," sputtered
Singing Bird. Nodding, Pearl now assembled her belongings in the teepee. She was going to bundle them in a deer hide, but Wind on the Grass handed her a beautiful parfleche bag.

"Take this. My grandmother made it. I want you to have it," she offered, holding it out.

Drums could now be heard, pounding outside. The women and braves staying behind began to chant and pray for a safe return of the Crow scouts. Pretty Eagle and his twenty scouts were all assembled now on horseback. The chief called out to Pearl in the teepee, and she emerged. The reigns of the white mare were handed to her. Both Singing Bird and Wind on the Grass said their goodbyes and then she swung up onto the horse's back. The chief rode out with the scouts in single file with Pearl bringing up the rear. A long column of people waited for them on either side of the procession. They touched prayer feathers along their flanks and across the scouts' legs. As she passed the last one, she turned and raised her hand, and a tumultuous shout went up of a last goodbye. It was done. She was leaving the Crow and the Sinkiuse behind.

The Crow scouts were soon at the fort, only this time the gate was wide open. They entered the compound in single file, exquisite and resplendent, wearing their regalia of feathered finery. The troops were assembled on either side of the compound. Standing in between them, the major and his officers, with a full color guard, received Pretty Eagle. Drums were rolling, and the lieutenant called out a command, stopping the drum roll. The lieutenant called out another command, and the soldiers swung their rifles to their sides in perfect unison. Now there was silence.

Major Sweitzer now stepped forward and saluted Pretty Eagle, who was still on his horse. The Chief looked confused, and he turned on his horse, asking the Bird Woman to come forward and interpret. Without hesitation, she rode up to his side, instructing the chief to dismount and shake the major's hand. The major extended his hand, and shook the chief's hand vigorously.

"Juana, tell the scouts to dismount. Sergeant Books, take their horses to the corral--grain and water them," the major commanded.

A table and several chairs were brought forth. Cranston, the clerk, then seated himself. Now, Pearl translated the oath of honor, having the Crow repeat in their language. Raising their right hands, Cranston read the pledge slowly, as Pearl translated it. After swearing their pledge of honor to the U.S. Army, each man stepped forward, giving his name, as Cranston duly recorded it. He handed the quill then to each man, having them place an X next to their written names. Now, the major directed Pearl to have the scouts all line up, shoulder to shoulder. The major then walked down the line, shaking each man's hand and looking him in the eye. Behind him, pushing a two wheeled cart, two privates issued each scout an army tunic with brass buttons and a new service revolver, with a belt and holster. The scouts were astonished at being given the uniforms and revolvers. Joy and happiness were seen on their faces. Pretty Eagle was pleased and also given a revolver in gratitude to take back with him.

"Lieutenant, pitch some field tents outside the fort for our new recruits," ordered the major. "Juana, tell Pretty Eagle to pick two leaders among the scouts. Each will be in charge and responsible for the conduct of the other nine. Sergeant Books, take two scouts at a time to the gully behind the fort and train them how to use the pistols. Let them practice and get a feel for the weapons. I don't want anyone accidently shot. Have them remove the feathers and paint and put their tunics on! Juana, can you and the chief come into my office?" He pointed at the whitewashed building.

Pearl signaled for the chief to follow. The chief had never been in a framed building and cautiously entered through the door. He glanced around nervously once inside. Pearl sensed his uneasiness and pulled up two chairs for each to sit on. The major offered the chief a cigar, which he accepted. The major lit his own cigar, then cupped the match with his hands, lighting Pretty Eagles stogie. The chief puffed the cigar to life and then coughed, not accustomed to the heavy flavor.

"Juana, tell the chief I am very pleased and proud of him--that he has made a wise decision for his people," the major directed Pearl.

Pretty Eagle acknowledged and said that the uniforms and revolvers were well received by his braves as a sign of good faith. The conversation went on for another two hours, with both men asking questions and given assurances. Finally, the major was satisfied and told the chief that he could go now and to tell his people to be patient and that food was coming. He also told the chief to send out hunting parties at once to find game and fresh meat for their people. The pistol practicing shots now subsided from behind the fort. The scouts were assembled in the shade of the tents that the army had pitched for them. The chief thanked Pearl, realizing he would not see her again. He then wished each scout well and told them not to fight amongst themselves or be dishonest. With that, he mounted his horse and headed back to his village.

Sergeant Books now approached Pearl and informed her, saying, "Miss Pearl, the lieutenant informs me that myself and ten troopers will escort you, Star Cloud, and nine scouts to Fort Laramie. We'll be leaving before sunup, so I suggest that you get some rest. Here, you'll sleep in the company chapel tonight. Let me show you where." He handed her a bed-roll. Walking her to the little board church, they entered.

"The Chaplin is away... not sure when he'll return. You can sleep on his bunk. There's water in the pitcher. Dinner bell is at 6 o'clock sharp, ma'am." He tipped his hat and then closed the door and departed.

Pearl washed the dust from her face. Sitting on the bunk, she looked up to see a portrait of "The Last Supper." She realized that she had not been in a church in twenty-five years--the last time being at Fort Victoria. She stepped out into the small chapel and approached the little altar and Crucifix. She knelt down and prayed for a long time, asking for forgiveness. It made her feel much better to repent. She had carried so much sin with her for so long that it was a joy to remove the burden. She returned to the bunk, rested, and awoke to the sound of the dinner bell.

She knew the scouts would be confused and needed guidance, so she stepped back outside into the parade ground of the compound. Pearl grabbed a spoon and plate from the chow line and then went to the scouts outside the gate. She gave them all a lesson in how to use the spoon and plate. She then led them in single file to the Mess Kitchen, lining up behind the troopers. In a very orderly fashion, each received his bacon, beans, and a biscuit on a plate. She then escorted them back to their tents outside. When they had all finished eating, Pearl directed Star Cloud and Curly to stack the plates and spoons and return them to the kitchen. Satisfied, she then informed Star Cloud to have his scouts ready before sunup, as they should rest and be ready to go. Returning to the chapel bunk, she said one more prayer, and then quickly fell asleep.

A bugle horn awoke her in the dark, and she realized it was time to get up. She got dressed, gathered her belongings, made the sign of the cross, and kissed the portrait of "The Last Supper."

Once outside, she found Sergeant Books. "Go get Star Cloud and his boys--we'll have coffee and a biscuit and then saddle up!"

The Crow scouts were all wide awake. Pearl waved for them to follow her into the fort. Again, Pearl had to give a lesson on how to use the tin cup. "Hold it out, take the pour, then sip it until it cools off," she explained.

They no sooner had learned the technique and made a few sips, when Sergeant Books bellowed out, "Alright, let's get this circus started! Mount up! Each trooper, take a scout and ride in doubles, side by side!" The bugle now blared a command. Without hardly anyone noticing, the column was out the gate, heading south, as stars still twinkled in the dawn.

They followed a faint wagon road, and that evening, they made camp at a lone spring of water in the middle of the prairie. The Crow scouts were fully aware of Pearl's magic with Yellow Wolf's raven and now treated her with the utmost respect, fearing her. The ten days on the trail to Fort Laramie were uneventful, except for halfway through the trip, a herd of buffalo were spotted. It pained the scouts that they were told not to go after them and to ignore them. Finally reaching their destination, the fort could be seen on the distant prairie. It loomed as a bastion of security on the windswept grassland. Sergeant Books had the scouts bivouac their tents outside the gates, in a designated area.

"Miss Pearl, come with me to report to the commander," Sergeant Books ordered her. Fort Laramie was much larger and older than Fort Ellis, having been established during the Red Cloud wars. Sergeant Books had been there many times and knew right where to go without asking. He handed his orders to the sentry at the commander's office. He read them and then looked at Pearl in curiosity.

"It's alright. She's an interpreter... she's with me. She needs to speak with the colonel." he assured the guard.

"Wait here," he replied, taking the orders with him. Moments later, the colonel returned with him, and Sergeant Books gave him a crisp salute.

"I trust your journey was without misfortune, sergeant?" the colonel inquired.

"Yes, sir--no problems on the trail, sir," the sergeant snapped.

"We've had reports of renegades marauding in the area, so I'm glad that you had no issues. Who is this squaw, sergeant?" he now turned his attention to Pearl.

"Sir, she is an interpreter, sent by Major Sweitzer. She claims she's not an Injun--that she's from some faraway island. She speaks perfect English, sir," came the response.

"I see. My name is Colonel Luther Bradley, and what would your name be?" the Colonel asked suspiciously.

"My name is Juana Melendres. I am a Filipina, and I am respectfully at your service, Colonel Bradley." The Colonel was wide eyed now, not expecting this answer from the beaded and buckskinned dusky maiden.

"Come in, both of you. Please brief me on the Crow scouts that you have delivered. Follow me," he ordered. His office was far more refined than the major's at Fort Ellis. Bookshelves, animal trophy heads, and pictures lined the walls. Pearl and the sergeant sat in leather upholstered chairs and admired the surroundings. After an hour of briefing, the Colonel was satisfied with the information.

"Well, I'm pleased with the major's foresight in acquiring the Crow scouts. General Crook and his battalion will be arriving next month, so this is good timing. We will fulfill the major's request to feed the Crow people. You, sergeant, will return with several wagonloads of food provisions. As for you, Miss Melendres, I have a mountain man scout here at the fort who speaks Crow. Therefore, your services are no longer needed. You may proceed to Cheyenne, as the major requested. Tomorrow, a government contractor, a freighter, is leaving for Cheyenne with a load of buffalo hides. You may accompany him on his wagon. Sergeant, report to the quartermaster, and take her with you. You and he return to my office. We'll see what provisions can be requisitioned to Major Sweitzer. Take Miss Melendres with you. They've been loading the buffalo hides all morning."

"Very good, sir." Sergeant Books stood and saluted.

Returning the salute, the Colonel gave a casual, "dismissed," and then wished Pearl "good luck."

The quartermaster's store house was close by. Sergeant Books led Pearl to a smoky, dingy, small office, where a clerk was asleep, snoring in his chair.

"Ten-Hut!" barked Sergeant Books out loud, and the sleeping soldier shook himself awake, caught in the act of dereliction of duty. Sergeant Books laughed at his joke.

"Wake up, Wiley, you got visitors!" he laughed out loud.

"Well I'll be dipped, Bob Books, howya doin?" Wiley replied, going from anger to to a friendly surprise. "Been a long time ol' friend."

"This here is Miss Pearl. She's gonna travel to Cheyenne with one of your freighters. This here is Sergeant Wiley, Miss Pearl," introducing the two.

"I see. I assume she has some written orders, otherwise... you know the rules Bob," Wiley drawled and spit tobacco juice into a brass spittoon.

"Yup, it's all official. She got her stamped papers.... Hey, Wiley, you and I are to report to the colonel at once! We gotta go! He wants to make a list of provisions to take back to Fort Ellis."

Wiley thought about it and stood up, saying, "Well, come this way, Miss Pearl," as he opened a back door on the back wall. Stepping out, Pearl could see two wagons. A huge man stood on top of a stack of buffalo hides in one of the wagons.

Wiley called out, "Red, come over here," waving his arm at the huge, broad shouldered man. The man jumped to the ground and ambled over to Wiley, Pearl, and Sergeant Books. Pearl thought to herself, *This the biggest man I have ever seen in my life!*. He stood six foot and nine inches, with huge, square shoulders and arms like ox legs. Pearl could see he was Indian, wearing buckskin breeches, and leather teamster boots. His bare torso glistened with sweat.

Wiley now turned to Pearl, saying "Let me see your papers, miss."

Pearl pulled the papers out of the beaded pouch that was hanging on her belt. Reading them, he handed them back to her.

"Red, this woman has orders to accompany you to Cheyenne. You will be paid in Cheyenne, upon delivering her there safely. She speaks English. I'll provide extra rations for the trail."

Red just stood there, saying nothing. Now Wiley asked, "How's the hide loading going? Are you almost done?"

Now, Red exploded, "Damn it, Wiley! I've got two too many women already! Have her go with someone else," the huge Indian growled.

"Can't do it, Red," Sergeant Books answered for Wiley. "She got direct orders from the colonel."

"And who are you?" Red snarled.

"I'm a sergeant, and I can easily have your contract torn to pieces. So do your job and deliver this woman safely. Do I make myself clear, Mr.Red?" barked Sergeant Books.

Wiley now backed up Sergeant Books, saying, "Treat this woman kindly, and if I hear of any abuse, I'll have you thrown in the stockade." The big Indian now became indignant and just shook his head.

"Alright, Wiley, I'll see to it she gets there safe, but I'd be grateful for more chewin tobacco, as I'm gonna need it, overseein' three women."

"You'll get extra tobacco. Now show her where to put her bed roll... the bunks in the stable. I've gotta go. The Colonel wants me and Bob in his office."

Sergeant Books and Wiley tipped their hats at Pearl, with Wiley offering, "He won't bite you... but his two wives might!" Laughing, the two sergeants walked away.

"Come!" grunted Red at Pearl, turning and walking towards a log building. Entering, the room was dim and had a foul smell. Flies buzzed in the air. Two fat women were stacking hides on a cart, and Red spoke to them in a tongue that Pearl was not familiar with.

He now spoke in English to Pearl, saying, "These are my wives, Lingo and Wyanokee. They do not speak English."

Pearl asked him, "What tribe of people are they?"

Red answered, "We are Wichita, traders from the Arkansas River. Our people are very few now. The Spanish and the pox took most of our people. Enough talk--help them load the cart." He turned and walked back to the wagons.

The two Wichita women glared at Pearl. Wyanokee pointed at the stack of buffalo hides, indicating for Pearl to get up on the heap and pull them off. Pearl climbed up onto the pile and began tossing the heavy hides down to the cart. The flies continued to swarm as the fresh hides were uncovered. The heat and foul odor in the room was overwhelming. Finally satisfied, the two signaled for Pearl to come down. The three then pushed and pulled the cart out to the wagon for loading. Two hours later, after three more trips to the storage cabin, the two wagons were fully loaded to Red's satisfaction. Wiley returned, just as Red was lashing down the second wagon.

"Here ya go, Red--some extra vittles and some extra tobacco." He handed the big Indian a canvas bag. Wiley now addressed Pearl, saying, "It's an overnight trip to Cheyenne. You'll leave in the morning. It's about sixty miles. They're taking these hides to the railroad shipping dock. They make the trip once a week. It's a bumpy little road. Tomorrow's Sunday, so we get to sleep late here at the fort, so I won't be seeing you again. Good luck." Wiley tipped his hat at Pearl and disappeared.

The three Wichitas and Pearl slept in the stable that night and were up early. Each of the two wagons had a team of four mules. Red and his wives got them hitched up in a matter of a few minutes. Pearl rode with Red in the lead wagon, while the two wives took turns driving the team in the rear. The wagon road had deep ruts and was bumpy, having been traveled a hundred times over the years. In the late afternoon, Red pulled up the team and stopped at a grove of cottonwood trees that hung out over a small creek. "We'll camp here tonight. Tomorrow afternoon we will be in Cheyenne," he explained to Pearl.

Wyanokee and Lingo knew the routine well, as this was their regular overnight stopping place on the road to Cheyenne. The mules were broken out of their traces and single trees and watered at the creek. Each of the mules were then hobbled, allowing them to browse close by, in the shade of the trees. The day had been extremely hot, and both Wyanokee and Lingo had removed their shirts on the trail earlier that day. As they moved around the camp, their fat, large breasts swayed and bounced freely while they built a cooking fire and prepared the evening meal. Red produced a bottle of whiskey, and packing his pipe with tobacco, he sat on a blanket under a cottonwood. He sat back and puffed his pipe while taking gulps of whiskey from the bottle.

Dinner was salt pork and beans with stale sourdough bread from the fort. Having plenty, the four all had second helpings. Their bellies were full, extended and relaxed now. The Wichita wives began to pass the whiskey bottle back and forth with Red. They offered the bottle to Pearl, but she shook her head "no" and waved them off. Soon, Wyanokee and Lingo were making jokes, which Pearl could not understand. In disbelief, she watched as both women pulled off Red's boots and breeches, exposing Red's giant manliness. In sheer delight, they giggled and coaxed the dangling cock, arousing it into a limb, as hard as oak.The big Indian was like a stallion now, and began banging away on Wyanokee, who was on all fours, coaxing him with pleasure. Wanting her turn, Lingo pushed Wyanokee aside and backed into Red, continuing the spectacle. Both women were clearly drunk, enjoying the lusty fornication. Wyanokee

302

pointed at Pearl, waving for her to come join them. Pearl shook her head "no." She now worried that she might be "forced" into joining them. She quietly got up and slid into the shadows of the cottonwood trees. Now away from the campfire, she stood in the dark by the creek. Their laughing and grunting and sounds of pleasure lasted for another hour. Finally, the three lay motionless in a heap, drunk and exhausted. Pearl peeked from behind a cottonwood, seeing all was quiet now. She could return to her bed roll now and get some sleep.

As she stepped around the trunk of the tree in the dark, a hand grabbed her from behind, violently. Another powerful hand came up and covered Pearl's mouth. She saw the flash of a blade held against her throat. In terror, she froze and watched as several shadowy figures emerged from the grove. Silently entering the light of the camp, with its fading fire, several warriors now stood over the naked bodies of the snoring Wichitas. In a quick motion, two warriors hacked away with tomahawks on the neck of Red. Wyanokee and Lingo both screamed in terror as the braves finished off Red's squirming body. Another warrior now dumped the canvas food bag on the ground. Pearl was still being held from behind, and now the canvas bag was pulled over her head and cinched tight. Her hands were tied behind her back, and she was pushed to the ground and kicked. The renegades were now rifling through the wagons and taking inventory of the loot. Gathering the mules, each was packed with a load of buffalo hides. Red was scalped. His boots, knife, and rifle being awarded to the slayers. The two naked women were gagged, tied, and bound to a mule. Satisfied with all the loot they could carry, the warriors set the wagons ablaze. Pearl was still lying motionless on the ground, bound with the canvas bag on her head.

Suddenly, she was stood up and thrown into the saddle of a horse. Her hands were bound with rawhide to the saddle horn. She heard some yips and war cries as a loud *pop* struck the rump of her horse, which was being led. She was now galloping in a herd of pounding hooves. They galloped into the night, until she could feel the morning sun on her arms. Stopping only briefly, she was transferred to another horse, and the galloping and hard riding continued.

303

The Kiowa and the Comanche

The retreating raiders kept up the frenzied pace. By dismounting and running alongside their horses at intervals, they kept their string of horses from fatiguing, enabling them to cross many more miles. Pearl was on the verge of passing out. The suffocating bag was still over her head, stifling her ability to breathe. Just when she thought she could take no more, the horses finally came to a stop. She could hear Lingo crying now and begging, pitifully, "*Agua, por favor. Agua por favor.*"

"*Callate puta! Te cortare la garganta!*" (Shut up whore, or I will cut your throat!) Hearing this and not able to see, Pearl wondered if these were bandito Mexicans.

The horses were still breathing hard, and she could now hear conversations in a tongue that she could not understand. All of a sudden, the bag was pulled abruptly from her head. Shivering in terror, she now came face to face with her abductors.

These were Kiowa warriors, a raiding party from the far south, of eight young men. They were hunting for Pawnee scalps and to steal their horses. They had come up empty handed and so had pushed further north on their raid. They had found the wagon road to Fort Ellis and laid an ambush for the first passing victims, who happened to be Red and his two wagons. These Kiowa reminded Pearl of Snorting Bull--fierce looking and full of hostile arrogance. Pearl could now see Lingo and Wynokee, naked and covered with dust, with streaks of sweat running down their fat bodies. Both women were brutally lashed to their mules and hung their heads and whimpered pitifully. A warrior produced a buffalo bladder of water and signaled Pearl to open her mouth. A long stream of water was poured into her mouth. Giving her only one drink, he now grabbed one of her beaded moccasin feet. He called out to the others, showing it to them and saying something she could not comprehend. He now approached Lingo and Wynokee, grabbing each by the hair and jerking their heads back. He gave each a brief shot of water. The group was standing on a low hill. Pearl watched as they pointed and talked about something in the flat land below. It looked like a trail, running east and west as far as could be seen. After resting the horses for a half hour, the warriors snapped their quirts and had the mules hustling down the hill. Coming up on the mysterious trail, the horses and mules became skittish. Stopping, Pearl could now see two iron rails spiked to logs that were buried in the grass. Suddenly, she realized, *This was the trail of the iron horse! The trail to San Francisco!*

One of the warriors kneeled down and put his ear to the rail, listening for a long minute. Finally, he stood up and shook his head. Now, one by one, the horses and mules were led across the track. Each animal was nervous, bouncing and leaping over the rail. Remounting, they popped their quirts, heading south again.

Being able to breathe fresh air now, Pearl gathered her thoughts and analyzed her situation. The warriors were young, seasoned horsemen with plenty of endurance. They kept up the hurried pace, continuing to drop to the ground and run along their horses. As the sun was setting, they came upon a small pond. The Kiowa reigned in their horses, as if they knew where they were and had reached the destination. The marathon ride finally stopped.

They made no campfire. After watering the horses and mules, they sat down and handed out pemmican to eat. Pearl noticed she was given a cake to eat, but the Wichita women were given nothing. The two were in bad shape. Their rumps were red with welts, as the Kiowa had inflicted the quirt on both the horse and rider. All three women were still tied at the wrist. Finally, two warriors cut Wynokee and Lingo loose. They then pushed them towards the pond, both crawling on hands and knees, naked and bruised. Reaching the water, their heads were pushed in. Now, both warriors whipped them again on the rump, saying, "Enough!" Pulling them both by the hair, they drug them a short distance and released them in a heap.

Pearl was then cut loose, the rawhide cinches having rubbed her wrists raw. The brave pointed at the pond, indicating for her to stand up, walk, and get a drink. He walked behind her and allowed her to drink deeply. She washed her face and arms off. He then gestured for her to go back and sit. The water had snapped her senses back, but she was so exhausted, she hung her head between her legs and fell right asleep. It was a short nap. Sometime after midnight, someone kicked her thigh, awakening her. It was dark, and she could not see well. Two strong braves stood her up and threw her back into the saddle again, lashing her hands to the saddle horn. Riding out into the blackness of night, the same, quick retreating pace was picked back up.

The night air was cooler, making travel easier on the horses. There was only a sliver of a moon showing for light, but the Kiowa seemed to know exactly where they were going. By morning light, they came to a small creek and rested in the shade of some willows. The stop was brief. They moved on again, only this time, they followed the course of the meandering creek. At high noon, they came to the mouth of the creek, where it junctioned with a slow moving river. The river was fifty feet wide, with low sandy banks on either side. The Kiowas waded the horses and mules into the river, letting them drink and cool off. The

305

river was only belly deep to the horses, enabling them to walk down the center of the river for almost two miles. At a large sandstone bluff, they left the river and continued south on a faint trail across the prairie. All day and into the night, the relentless southern retreat continued. Cresting a low hill in the morning light, excitement broke out among them. In the distance, a huge herd of buffalo could be seen, grazing on the prairie. The Kiowa backed off and made a plan. Their horses were exhausted and in no shape to gallop down the beasts. They decided to take two buffalo hides from the stolen loot and drape them over four hunters. If they approached downwind on all fours, the buffalo would not be alarmed. The eyesight of the buffalo was very poor, and they relied on their noses to sense danger. The other four Kiowa remained behind the hill, holding the horses and hostages. They crouched and watched from the hilltop. The hunters had found a small gully and slowly approached the herd, hunkered down, as if grazing. They were now fifty feet from an unsuspecting cow. Using the rifle they had stolen from Red, the bullet found its target, with three arrows shot immediately, hitting home as well. The cow staggered for four or five steps and fell. Seeing the hunters and hearing the rifle shot, the herd quickly scattered and barreled away. The tranquility of the moment was gone, as they stampeded in panic. Running up on the wounded, breathing cow, the hunters dispatched her with an arrow to the heart.

Giving yells of delight and yipping, the group on the hill now brought the horses and mules down to the kill site. The meat came at a good time, as the Kiowa were beginning to wear out, needing food. The three days of pemmican and creek water had worn them down. Camp was made, and a large fire was built. The buffalo roasts and ribs were racked up on the fire. A steady popping and hissing caused the fire to flare up, as the buffalo fat fueled the flame. The women were pulled from the horses and ignored while the braves devoured the tongue, heart, and liver. Smoking tobacco and relaxing, they began gambling amongst themselves.

Now, a Kiowa approached Pearl and demanded she open the beaded bag on her belt. Pulling out the stamped orders from Major Sweitzer, she tried to pretend they were nothing, and put them back in the bag. The brave scowled and ripped them from her hand. He looked at them, having no clue what they were. Turning, he walked over to the fire, wadded them up, and threw them into the flames.

By now, Lingo and Wyanokee looked like two ghosts, still naked and white with dust. Their inner thighs were raw after three days of riding the mules bareback. Their backsides were covered with welts from the abuse of the whip.

The gambling and laughter continued, and now it was apparent what the stakes were. Winners would be first to have their way with the women. The two buffalo robes the hunters had used were now laid out on the ground. Two warriors stood up laughing and now approached the tied women. Grabbing Lingo and Wyanokee by the hair, they pulled them both over and onto the buffalo robes. They were ordered down onto their knees and elbows. The rape continued of the two Wichita, until each man had satisfied himself.

Pearl wept as she watched the inhumane scene, fully expecting that she would be next, but for whatever reason, she was not touched or violated. As the rape continued, one warrior tossed a rib of cooked meat at Pearl, hitting her mocassins. He nodded at her to eat, as if she was going to be spared. Her wrists bound with rawhide, she did as she was told, not wanting to agitate her captor. The meat tasted good, its warmth filling her belly. Not wanting to witness the scene any longer, she rolled over and passed out from exhaustion.

It was dawn when she awoke, shivering and cold. The campfire was smoldering, no more than a wisp of smoke. All around lay the spent, exhausted Kiowa, sleeping soundly. Lingo and Wyanokee lay motionless on the buffalo robes. Pearl detected some movement in the shadows. She squinted to see what it was. Four ravens were pecking and tugging at the bones of the buffalo kill. Silently, she stood and approached the birds clicking and clucking a message of greetings. The birds all stopped what they were doing and stared intently at her. She continued her clicking and messaging and sat down right next to them. They acknowledged her presence but continued their pecking and feeding. She now held her arms and bound wrists out. She beckoned a raven onto her arms, who marched up and roosted on her shoulder. Clicking and messaging the bird, he walked back down her extended arm and began pecking at the rawhide wrist lashings. The knot was very tight, and she coaxed and coached the bird to untie it. She didn't notice the two Kiowa who were standing at a distance and watching. The bird was trying, but the knot wouldn't budge. Now, she looked up and saw the two Kiowa. Fearing she might be beaten for trying to escape, she told the bird to hop back up onto her shoulder. The two Kiowa now approached her, scattering the three ravens on the bone pile. The raven remained on her shoulder, guarding her, flapping his wings and cawing in menace at the two men. Now, the two Kiowa backed away, fearful and astonished at what they had just witnessed. The other braves were awake now. The two witnesses pointed at Pearl and the raven, warning the others of her witchcraft. The raven now hopped from Pearl's shoulder onto the ground and began waddling in circles around her, stopping periodically and flapping his wings in defiance at the astonished warriors.

Wyanokee now awoke from her misery, moaning and begging for water in Spanish. "*Agua, por favor,*" she wept. Breaking his gaze and stare away from Pearl and the raven, a warrior told her to "*Callate!*" (Shut up!)

Now, Pearl seized on the moment and ordered in Spanish for the warrior to give her water. The warrior hesitated, and now she raised her voice in anger, again repeating in Spanish to give her water.

This time he nodded his head, saying, "*Si! Si!*" and produced a bladder of water. He poured a long gulp into Wyanokee's mouth. The raven continued to waddle in a circle around Pearl. Now, in Spanish, Pearl ordered the brave to approach her and give her water. He did so, but when he got to within ten feet, he tossed the bladder bag at Pearl. It landed in her lap as she sat. Pearl now gave a command to the raven, who jumped back up on the buffalo bones. Standing, the water bag fell aside, and she approached him, demanding in Spanish to be cut loose. Without hesitating, he produced a knife and cut her wrists free of the rawhide lashing. Now the Kiowa asked her, point blankly, in Spanish, "You are a medicine woman, a shaman of the Crow?"

Seeing an opportunity, she used his assumption to her advantage, saying, "*Si.* Yes, I am a shaman of the Crow people."

The brave now answered her in Spanish, "We recognized your beadwork as Crow. That is why we did not harm you. The Kiowa are old allies of the Crow, from long ago. It is bad luck for us to abuse you. Who is your chief?"

"My chief is Pretty Eagle, and he will be glad to learn that you have not harmed me. Why are you treating these Wichita women so badly?" Pearl asked.

"They are old enemies. Their women are like dogs to us," came his answer in Spanish.

"What will you do with us?" Pearl pressed him.

"Ha! We will trade the Wichita women for powder or horses. They will be used as slaves. I will give you to my two wives. You will be their slave!" came the answer in Spanish.

"Why won't you release me, if I am an ally?" she asked further.

"You are too valuable as a slave. My women will be very pleased to receive you, as my gift from the raid," he snapped back. "If the Crow want you back, they will find you and pay me."

"Where are you taking us?" she pressed him further.

"Our village is on the Washita river, a ten day ride from here."

"What is your name?" asked Pearl.

"Sun Hawk, and what is yours?"

"My people call me the 'Bird Woman' or '*Mujer Pajaro,*'" Pearl answered.

Sun Hawk now ordered the Kiowa to break camp and move out. A brave pulled Wyanokee to her feet and kicked Lingo in her ribs, telling her to "Get up!" Lingo lay motionless. Rolling her over, it was apparent that she was dead. Seeing this, Wyanokee let out a wail of grief. The brave swatted her on the butt, telling her to shut up. Pulling the buffalo robe out from under the dead Lingo, he tossed it over a mule. Another brave assisted in getting the fat woman up onto the mule. This time, Sun Hawk offered the reins to Pearl, saying, "We will not tie you. If you try and escape, we will find you, and you will regret it." Pearl took the reins and looked away from the lifeless corpse of Lingo.

Pearl led and walked her horse over to the raven that was still pecking on the carcass. She pulled a shiny blue bead from the Crow belt she wore, placing it in his beak. Taking it, he flew away, off to the north. The Kiowa now kicked the horses into a fast gait and headed south.

The prairie was no longer rolling but flat as a pancake as far as one could see. In every direction, a sea of prairie grass waved in the wind, rocking back and forth from the warm gusts. The Kiowa's pace had slowed down, as they sensed they were out of danger of being followed. Being able to see for miles now, no one could approach them from any direction without being seen. Day after day went by. The landscape was unchanging, a mantle of unending prairie grass. Camping each night at a chosen, known spot, they would cook the buffalo meat from the cow kill. They would then gamble to see who would be first with Wyanokee. Several small creeks were crossed, allowing them to water the horses as they continued the exodus south. Sun Hawk indicated they were in Kiowa country now and that in two days, they would reach his village.

The two days of travel passed, and now Pearl could see a village in the distance. Two hundred teepees were pitched along a river the Kiowa called the "Washita." A sandstone bluff shielded the teepees from the wind. All along the riverbank, hundreds of horses were grazing. A great commotion came over the village upon seeing Sun Hawk and his braves' safe return. The stolen buffalo hides were distributed among the people, a prized commodity. Sun Hawk's wives found him in the crowded commotion and joyously welcomed his safe return.

"I have brought you a prize from the north country--a Crow slave woman." He offered up Pearl to them. "Be careful with her. She says she is a shaman and has magic. She says her name is 'Bird Woman.'" The two wives eyed Pearl suspiciously. One woman opened Pearl's mouth, examining her teeth. The other squeezed her arm muscles. Satisfied, they lost interest in her and joined the celebration of the returning raiders. Pearl saw Wynokee being led away and wondered what her fate would be. Being ignored, Pearl wandered down to the river. The water was inviting, and so she undressed and took a bath. The cleansing invigorated her, after the two weeks of endless riding. Dressing, she climbed up from the bank and rested under a cottonwood tree. She would wait to see what would be done with her.

The celebration had quieted down now. Before long, the two wives spotted her and now approached. Scolding her in their language, they urged her to her feet and indicated for her to follow them. They arrived at a large teepee, with Sun Hawk sitting outside, smoking. He nodded at Pearl but said nothing. Expecting harsh treatment, Pearl was surprised when the women took her inside and offered her soup from an iron kettle on the cooking fire. The women seemed friendly, but she could not understand their language, and so all she could give was a nod of appreciation. Frustrated, the wives called Sun Hawk inside, asking questions in Kiowa. He translated the questions in Spanish for Pearl.

"They want to know how old you are?" he translated.

"Tell them I am thirty-eight years old," she answered.

"This wife's name is 'Song Singer,' and the other's name is 'Rabbit Dancer.' Tomorrow, they wish to travel to Fort Sill. They wish to trade one of the mules for whatever they can get. You will go with them," he explained. He then arose and exited the teepee.

Rabbit Dancer could see that Pearl was tired and weary. She pointed out where Pearl could lie down. Without hesitating, Pearl curled up on a wolf skin robe and instantly fell asleep.

In a deep sleep, Pearl was awakened by a gentle shaking. Startled and fearful, she sat up. Song Singer was smiling at her. The stress of the unknown was now subsiding, and Pearl returned the smile. Song Singer urged her to get up and motioned to come outside. Stepping out into the light, she was surprised to see several other women on horseback. The stolen mules were all on leads, tended by young boys. They were all waiting for her, as if she were holding up the departure. Rabbit Dancer held a saddled horse for her and handed her the reins. As soon as Pearl was mounted, the Kiowa women kicked the horses into motion. The young boys on horseback followed, leading the mules to be traded. As the entourage headed out of the village, the morning sun was beginning to heat up. They rode single file on a well-used trail, singing and chatting with one another. In the late afternoon, an encampment appeared in the distance. As they got closer, Pearl could see it was a cluster of wagons, military tents, and a large corral. Several teepees were pitched around the perimeter of the place. The Kiowa women found relatives among the teepees. They dismounted, set up camp, and began to cook dinner. Pearl overheard several conversations in Spanish. Interrupting two women speaking Spanish, she asked what this place was. Surprised, the women answered it was the traders' camp--the Comancheros--and then resumed their conversation.

It was getting dark, and Pearl sat back quietly in the shadows of the campfire. The Kiowa women were chatting excitedly about the prospect of trading for goods the following day. Rabbit Dancer offered Pearl some cooked meat and pemmican. After finishing, the two broke open the packs, spreading out buffalo robes and blankets around the perimeter of the campfire. Lying down and covering herself, Pearl thought about how well she had been treated and not as a slave or a prisoner.

The next morning, excitement was in the air as the Kiowa women waited for the traders to open their tents and wagons. The traders knew the new customers had arrived the previous evening. In fairness to each other, they all opened for business at the same time. The tents were full of tables of trade goods. Calico cloth, buttons, trade beads, needles, knives, mirrors, cooking pots, sugar, tobacco, and a range of other items were all neatly arranged in rows on the tables. Each trader watched over their table with a protective eye.

The Kiowas had the mules and buffalo hides to trade with, and the haggling began. Pearl followed Song Singer and Rabbit Dancer from one tent to the next, eyeing the goods and trying to decide what to trade for. A large wagon now caught the eye of Song Singer. The trader sat behind two large tables, displaying his wares in the open air. Rabbit Dancer admired several of his jars of blue, glass beads, while Song Singer picked up a large iron ladle and examined it. Three beautiful, silver concho belts were displayed. Rabbit Dancer ran her hand across the shining silver discs longingly. They now walked away, and in hushed tones discussed what they wanted to trade for, pointing and shaking their heads. Their mule for trading was tethered nearby. They retrieved him and walked him over to the trader sitting behind the tables at the wagon. The haggling began, but the trader was not going to give much for the mule, its ribs showing from weeks of hard travel. Rabbit Dancer retrieved two buffalo hides and offered them up. Still, the trader was not giving them what they wanted. The communication was difficult, as it was a series of pointing and hand signs. The white man kept shaking his head "no."

Observing all of this, finally Pearl stepped forward and stated in perfect English, "They want a jar of blue beads, the ladle, and that bolt of cloth for the mule and hides."

The trader was stunned and surprised, hearing the buckskin beaded woman address him in English. "My goodness, why didn't you speak up earlier? Do you speak Kiowa as well?" the trader asked her.

311

"No, but I can hand sign to them, and they understand me enough to get by," she explained.

"Tell them I don't want the buffalo hides, but I will trade one jar of blue beads for the mule," he explained to Pearl. She now hand signed to the Kiowa women what the trader was offering. The women shook their heads no, hand signing that they would look at other tables. Pearl explained to the trader that the women would move on in search of a better bargain.

"Tell me--you seem to be from another tribe. Your beadwork is not Kiowa--who are you?" the trader now questioned her.

"Yes, you are right. I was kidnapped in the north by a Kiowa raiding party. I am told that I am a slave, but they have treated me like a sister so far," she explained.

"I see... so you speak English and can hand sign very well. What tribe are you from?" he asked.

"I am not Indian. I am Filipina. I speak Spanish, English, Chinese, and Chinook. My homeland is very far away, across the ocean."

The trader was listening and in disbelief. "You speak Spanish, as well?" he asked her.

"Si, yo hablo Español," Pearl answered.

"How would you like to go to work for me? Your gift of language is very impressive!"

Rabbit Dancer was pulling on Pearl's arm now, wanting to move on. Pearl told her to wait--the trader was changing his mind.

"Tell the Kiowa women that I will trade the bolt of cloth, the ladle, and the jar of beads for the mule... only if they will trade you for two silver concho belts and a butcher knife, with a bag of sugar."

"What makes you think that I want to go with you?" Pearl asked suspiciously.

"I am a Christian man. I trade with all the tribes around Fort Sill. Many speak Spanish, and with your ability to use sign language, you would be a great asset to my business. I will feed you and give you a monthly wage. You have my word that you will be treated well."

Pearl smiled and nodded at the trader. Now, she translated the offer to the Kiowa women, who became very excited upon hearing the proposition. Now, the Kiowa knew they had something the trader wanted. The women countered the offer, saying they wanted all three of the concho belts, three jars of blue beads, and the butcher knife for Pearl. She now explained the counter offer to the trader, and without hesitating, he picked up all three concho belts and handed them over, saying loudly, "Done!"

All four stood there in astonishment. The trader at his luck in acquiring a translator, Pearl at negotiating her freedom in five minutes, and the Kiowa women who now possessed three of the coveted silver concho belts. The belts were a prized sign of wealth for anyone within the Kiowa tribe.

He then directed Pearl to a chair behind the tables, saying, "Watch the table for me while I put this mule in the corral," a signal that he totally trusted her. Seeing his mistake of bad manners, he now took off his hat, saying, "Pardon me ma'am, my name is John Doan. I'm a trader out of Wichita, Kansas. Be pleased to know your name, ma'am?"

"You can call me Pearl." She nervously looked back at him. "Are you with the Wichita tribe?"

"No, no, no. That's the name of the railroad town north of Indian Territory. I get the trade goods there, then freight them by wagon to Cache. I sell to all the tribes… Comanche, Arapahoe, and Kiowa. I'll be right back, Pearl." He smiled and led the mule away.

Song Singer and Rabbit Dancer were preoccupied with putting on their new belts. The extras in the trade made them giddy. Pearl was nothing to them. She had been given to them yesterday, taken care of, and now traded away the next day. Pearl realized she could have been traded away to a far worse situation and felt fortunate now. The two Kiowa bundled up their goods, smiled and waved goodbye to Pearl. They were in a hurry to go show off their newfound wealth.

John returned with the mule, saying, "I've changed my mind. I've been here for five days, trading. I just sold my livestock that I traded for to a buyer from the fort. I think I'll just keep this mule and fatten him up. Let's pack it up, Pearl, and head for Cache. Help me load these goods on the wagon!"

He climbed up into the wagon bed, and Pearl began emptying the tables, passing the goods up to him. He now lashed the tables to either side of the wagon and tethered the mule to the back. "I'll be right back with the team!" he told her and handed her a licorice whip of candy. Minutes later, he returned with a stout, matched pair of mules. Backing them into their traces, he had them hitched up in short order. He told Pearl to hop aboard as he pulled himself up onto the wagon seat. "Let's git rollin!" He snapped the reins, hollered "GeeHaw!" and the wagon began rolling.

The wagon road ran past Fort Sill, a large compound surrounded by corrals, shacks, and teepees. John waved and hollered "howdy" to several people they encountered, as if everyone knew who he was. By afternoon, the heat was stifling as they approached a large village of teepees.

"Are these more Kiowa people?" asked Pearl.

"No, no… these are Comanche. They surrendered peacefully earlier this year," explained Doan.

"Surrendered? They were at war? With the Americans?" Pearl asked.

"Yep… a fierce bunch of people. They could never be caught or tamed. The army sent word to them that they would be hunted down and killed if they didn't come in peacefully. Wisely, they came to the fort to surrender and now occupy this ground. The army has made Cache Creek their reservation. My nephew and I have set up a trading post here. They have large herds of horses, and the trading is good for both us and them. There's home, up ahead" he pointed. Home was a large corral and sod house with a hide door.

A woman was washing clothing in a tub as the tired team pulled up. "Good to see you, John!" came a cheerful greeting. "Corwin is down by the creek, fishing with the children."

"Lidee, this is Pearl. She works for us now. She speaks Spanish and English. She will solve our communication problems," John explained.

"That's wonderful! Finally, another woman that I can talk to! Come in Pearl, I have fresh cornbread and coffee. Tell me all about yourself."

Pearl hopped down from the wagon and followed the beckoning Lidee.

"Sit down--here, in this chair Your beadwork is beautiful. Did you make it?" Lidee asked.

"No, the beadwork is Crow. It was given to me," Pearl explained.

"Ahh, your people are Crow. Aren't they far to the north?" she asked.

At this point, Pearl explained her long background, with Lidee listening intently.

"Well, it's wonderful to have a new friend in this wild place. My husband, Corwin, will be pleased to meet you. There is an extra bunk, over there. I'll put a fresh pillow and blanket out for you. You must be tired. Lay yourself down."

Pearl suddenly realized how long it had been since since she had carried on a conversation with another woman in English. She had bonded instantly with Lidee and now nodded her head in agreement. "Yes, that would be nice Lidee. I would like to rest." Feeling safe and secure, Pearl was asleep in five minutes, and did so for the next twelve hours.

Pearl awoke to the smell of fresh bacon being fried. The sod cabin had a small, iron cook stove and Lidee was merrily humming a tune as she watched over the sizzling pan. "Good morning. I see you slept well. Step outside and meet the children." She smiled at Pearl.

Emerging through the cowhide door, Pearl saw the three children were seated at a table. Corwin, their father, was busy splitting firewood. He stopped swinging his axe. "Good morning, Pearl! My name is Corwin. These are my three kids--Tom, Mary, and Corwin Jr. Lidee and John told me all about you. Welcome to our little family! Here. Sit down with the kids."

At that point, Lidee brought out a tray of hot biscuits, the bacon, and a pitcher of cow milk. Corwin said grace over the breakfast, and then a lively conversation followed. Just as they were finishing the meal, two cowboys appeared on horseback and approached the group at the outdoor table.

"Morning folks. Are you John Doan?" drawled one of the dusty cowboys.

"No, I'm his nephew. The name's Corwin Doan. What can I do for you?"

"Well sir, my names Harlan, and my pardner here is Frank. We got a herd of longhorns across the Red River. We were told that someone here might know a safe place to bring them across. We've scouted for a crossing, but everywhere we look is quicksand. Can you help us, Corwin?"

"Yes, that river is treacherous to get across. How'd you boys do it?" asked Corwin.

"We was lucky. My horse got mired down, but somehow Frank's horse found some dry footing. He was able to lariat my horse and pull us out." Harlan answered.

"Well, I don't have an answer for you, but maybe the Comanche chief, Quanah, might know where to come across."

"Be much obliged if you could show us where this chief is, if it's no trouble," drawled Harlan.

"No problem at all. I'm happy to help. Pearl, come with me. Your translating will be needed." Corwin walked over to the corral and quickly had two horses saddled.

"His teepee is about a mile from here. Follow me." Corwin directed the two cowboys. The four came to a cluster of a dozen teepees. Several barking dogs now stood their ground, forcing the horses to stop. A group of women sat in front of one teepee, and now one of them chucked a rock at the dogs, demanding them to scatter. With the dog menace gone, the group proceeded up to the group of sitting women. Corwin looked at Pearl, saying, "You're gonna have to help me here. They know me, but communication is difficult." Corwin looked at the women now, saying, "Como estás?"

The women only nodded their heads suspiciously, not answering.

"Donde está Quanah?" he now asked them.

One woman pointed at a large teepee, covered with horse paintings and stars. She stood up, went to the teepee, entered, and moments later emerged with the chief.

Corwin now looked at Pearl, saying, "You need to take over. My Spanish is very limited."

315

The Chief was tall, rawboned, and dressed in fringed buckskins. His hair was braided, with both braids wrapped in red felt. He walked up to the four, asking in Spanish to Corwin what he wanted.

Pearl now took over, replying in perfect Spanish, "Good morning. My name is Pearl. Señor Corwin wants me to translate in Spanish. May we get off our horses?"

Quanah now looked at Pearl curiously, eyeing her Crow beadwork. The chief answered in Spanish, "Yes, of course. Come sit in the shade over here." He then whistled at two Comanche boys who'd been watching and ordered them to take the four horses and tie them.

They all sat under a brush arbor on buffalo robes. Corwin then produced a cigar, offering it to the chief, who waved it off, shaking his head "no." The cowboys now asked Pearl to translate their predicament with the cattle herd. Hearing their problem, Quanah smiled and rubbed his chin, saying, "Tell them there is a way across, but after making the crossing, their cattle will be on my land, eating Comanche grass."

Pearl translated to the cowboys, who now realized the chief was a shrewd bargain maker. As they were discussing their next move, Quanah now asked, "How many cattle are in your herd?"

Pearl translated the question, and Harlan replied, "Around eight hundred, the last time we counted. Tell Quanah we will give him five steers if he shows us where to cross and allows the herd to pass over his land."

Pearl translated the offer, and Quanah smirked and laughed. "Tell them it will cost ten steers, and I will pick them out. Otherwise, go back to Texas," came Quanah's counteroffer. The two cowboys tried another counteroffer of seven steers, but Quanah again held up ten fingers, shaking his head.

"Damn, Frank. We got no choice. Give him the ten steers." Harlan conceded and agreed to the offer of ten steers. "Can he show us where the crossing is today?" the question was directed at Pearl.

She asked the chief, who replied, "Yes, but we must leave at once to make it there before darkness."

With that, the meeting was over, and Pearl wished the cowboys luck. As Corwin and Pearl were about to depart, Quanah invited the two to come along, saying, "Corwin, you and Pearl should ride along with us. I want to discuss something with you."

Translating the invitation, Corwin agreed, realizing a window of opportunity to increase his trading and transactions with the Comanche. "Alright, we will come along. Quanah, can you have someone take a message to my wife? Here, let me write it down." He scribbled on a pad of paper in his pocket:

"Will return tomorrow. Urgent business with the chief. Love, Corwin." He handed it to the chief, telling Pearl to translate and have it delivered to his wife. Quanah whistled for the two boys tending the horses and gave them instructions to deliver the piece of paper. Quanah directed two of his wives to pack some provisions, and within the hour, the group was heading south. Pearl rode between Corwin and Quanah, translating the conversation. The two wives and the cowboys trailed in the rear. The conversation was lively, with Quanah expressing the trade goods that the Comanche wanted in exchange for fine horses. Now the conversation changed, each asking about the other's culture. A whole new opportunity had opened for both, as Pearl's translating revealed things that both men were curious about. When Pearl couldn't understand Quanah's question, she used sign language, which impressed the chief with her ability.

It was late afternoon when in the distance, a long belt of cottonwoods and willows could be seen, spanning from east to west. This was the Red River, the natural boundary separating Texas from Indian Territory. Reaching the north side of the river, Quanah led the party west along its bank. They came to a spot where low sand bluffs were on either side.

"Here is the crossing. This place is only known to the Comanche. It is here that we would bring our stolen horses across from Texas and Mexico. We will camp here tonight and return in the morning," the chief stated.

The cowboys had brought a sack of beans for dinner. Quanah's wives had brought venison, and so a hot meal was prepared on a campfire. The following morning, Quanah assured Harlan and Frank that there was no quicksand at this crossing. The group watched as the two cowboys rode their horses across the river, having no problems. Emerging at the sand bluff on the other side, the two turned and waved and disappeared behind the bluff.

"Let's go back. I'll return in two days with some men and collect our ten steers," Quanah explained to Pearl and Corwin. "I will reward you with one steer, Corwin, for making this bargain happen," Quanah offered in gratitude.

That afternoon, the group arrived back at Cache Creek. "Lidee--a very successful trip! I've created a strong bond with Quanah, thanks to Pearl. We should do quite well in this horse trading business in the coming months."

True to his word, Quanah showed up at the Doan's sod trading post three days later, with a steer lassoed and in tow. The following week, the Comanche brought in fifty horses to trade for John and Corwin's goods. Quanah brought several of his wives to the trading post, who were excited to barter for the many wares that were offered. It became very apparent to Corwin that Pearl had a keen sense of judgement for trading horses. The fifty horses were corralled, and Pearl started pointing out problems with some of the animals. "See that one, how his hind leg is lifted--he's going lame. That one over there, the sorrel--his back is curved deeply--probably carried too much weight at a young age. That one over there, hanging his head--see how his belly is bloated? He looks sick."

Corwin had the rejects cut out of the herd, keeping only the ones that Pearl recommended. Quanah was impressed with Pearl's ability to grade the horses, saying, "Corwin, you have a shrewd and smart partner. She knows and understands horses and has outsmarted the Comanche on this trade." He laughed as Pearl translated for him.

The horse trading became lucrative for John and Corwin. Over a period of several months, they made three different trips to Wichita, driving the horses to the rail head. The stock was sold to brokers, who shipped them by rail back east. Tripling their money, they would buy two more wagon loads of trade goods and return to Cache Creek and start the process over again.

By the Fall of 1877, word had been spread across west Texas of the location of Quanah's secret crossing on the Red River. Almost monthly now, a herd of longhorns would show up at the crossing, being driven to Dodge City. Quanah's people now became wealthy with cattle, acquiring them as payment to cross Comanche grassland. Trading had slowed with John and Corwin, as the Comanche were loaded up with trade goods now. Sitting at the dinner table one night, John and Corwin discussed their options.

"You know, John, this land we're sitting on does not belong to us. I've got an idea--if we go down to Quanah's crossing, we can homestead on the Texas side of the river. You and myself can each claim six hundred and forty acres. We could set the trading post up there and trade with the cowboys pushing the herds at the crossing."

"By golly, that's a helluva idea Corwin! You're right. Business is slow now, and we need to find another spot and relocate. I think we should go at once, before someone else figures out your idea!"

"Very well. We'll leave in the morning and stake our claims. There's a Texas ranger post at Eagle Springs where we can file our claims and make it legal. Lidee--you and Pearl watch over the place. We'll be back in a few days. Pearl, I promise to take you to Wichita in the spring after the trail thaws. You've earned your train ticket to San Francisco!"

Ten days later, John and Corwin returned with exciting news. They had found and excellent place to build the trading post, close to the river crossing. They had also been successful at staking two homestead claims and filing them with the authorities. Hastily, they dismantled the Cache Creek trading post and

318

loaded their goods onto the two wagons. Word spread quickly among the Comanche that they were leaving and moving south to Quanah's crossing. On the morning of their departure, Quanah appeared to say goodbye.

"My friends, I will miss you and our talks at the campfire," he told them.

Pearl translated his message, and Corwin replied, "You and your people have been kind and fair with us, and we will remain good friends."

"It is a good place you are going. Those are my old hunting grounds from many years ago. Many buffalo roamed in that area at one time. I will come and visit you when I get a chance," Quanah promised them.

By evening, the two wagons had reached the crossing. Camp was made, and the following morning, the wagons crossed the river with no problems. Traveling only a half mile, they came to a grove of scrub oak and sycamore trees.

"This is it! This is our land!" announced John and Corwin. "We'll build the store and the house over here, Lidee!" Corwin excitedly pointed out. "These sycamore trees indicate that there's water here, not too far down. We'll dig a well right over here," he pointed.

A week later, John and Corwin had dug down twenty feet and found a good supply of fresh water. They had found a clay deposit down by the riverbank and were now making adobe bricks, drying them in the Texas sun. It became a daily chore with Lidee, the children, and Pearl, molding the bricks and stacking the dried ones at the new homesite. It was beginning to get cold at night, with cold air blowing down from the north. It was obvious they would be spending Christmas in the tents and wagons, as the brick making process was slow and backbreaking.

One morning, a cloud of dust could be seen to the south. As they finished breakfast, two point riders appeared at the homesite. "Morning, folks," the two dusty riders called out as they approached. "We got a herd of cattle coming your way." It was Harlan and Frank, whom they now recognized.

"Welcome, boys! Have some coffee and biscuits. Good to see y'all! How have ya been?" Corwin offered a warm welcome.

"Well I'll be dipped--did you folks give up tradin' with the redskins? What brings y'all down below the river?" Harlan asked.

"Well, the trading business kinda petered out with the Kiowa and Comanche. We figured this place was as good as any to build a store. Looks like you and Frank are our first customers!"

Frank laughed, saying, "Well a welcome sight y'all is! We need coffee, flour, and tobacco. Can ya help us out?

"Got all that and more, no problem," assured John.

Now Harlan hopped down from the saddle, shook the Doan's hands, and asked, "Would ya take credit Corwin? Well be back in two months and pay you with gold after we sell the stock in Dodge City.

"Harlan, your word is as good as gold--credit is no problem," answered Corwin.

Frank stayed in the saddle, saying, "I'll bring up the chuck wagon to get the supplies. I'll tell the boys to push the cows over yonder, away from your place here, Corwin."

By that afternoon, 1,500 longhorns had passed. And so it was, Doan's Trading Post on the Great Western Cattle Trail was in business. Pearl and the Doan's survived the winter with no severe blizzards falling upon them. In late February, they had four adobe walls up, which cut the biting wind. As they were putting on a temporary canvas roof, Harlan and Frank, with their wranglers, returned from Dodge City. As Harlan had promised, Corwin and John were paid in twenty dollar gold pieces for the supplies that had been credited.

"You've been busy, Corwin! I'll be back in the fall with an even bigger herd! By then, this will probably be a town!" laughed Harlan.

John and Corwin's hunch and timing on moving the trading post to this location was none too soon. Almost weekly now, another herd and cattle company from Texas arrived at Doan's Crossing. All the cowboys were given credit on their word, that they would pay the debt on the return from Dodge City.

Another speculator had seen the same potential as the Doan's. Jim Haulk, from Eagle Springs, had homesteaded a mile away and had set up a saloon and brothel. By the early spring of 1878, both businesses were experiencing a flood of cowboy customers.

One warm afternoon, Quanah and several of his people appeared at the trading post. Pearl was busy helping Lidee bake bread in an outdoor brick oven when she looked up and saw them coming.

"*Buenos dias,* Quanah!" came Pearl's friendly greeting.

"Señora Pearl, it is good to see you! They told me that all of you have been very busy here."

Pearl nodded her head, saying in Spanish, "Yes, this is a good place. Many cowboys pass here and barter for Corwin's trade goods. Did you come to visit us?" she asked.

Laughing, Quanah replied in Spanish, "How can I not visit you!? Your adobe is in the middle of the trail!" Now he saw Corwin and John. "Tell them, Pearl, that they have picked a good homesite. This was one of my old campgrounds when we hunted buffalo. There are good spirits here!"

Pearl translated, and Corwin told Pearl to tell him to have coffee and biscuits in the shade with them.The sun was hot, and the shade and refreshments were accepted. After an hour of visiting, Quanah was ready to move on, saying, "The Army has allowed us time to go to our old spirit lands and gather medicine herbs. We must return in ten days or they will send soldiers after us. Pearl, why don't you come along? I enjoy your conversation and company."

Pearl translated the chief's statement, and Corwin nodded his head yes. "Why don't you go with them--you need a break from brick making. Go ahead. You'll have a good time," he insisted.

Pearl vigorously shook her head yes. The brick making chore had become boring and monotonous. She bundled a few things and was ready to go in short order. The Comanche had several spare horses with them for packing. They handed her the reins of a painted mare, and she swung herself up, the horse responding to her skills of control. The Comanche and Pearl headed due west and shortly came upon the tent city Jim Haulk. Quanah kept his people at a distance. Music and laughter was coming coming from the tents, and suddenly, it became eerily quiet. The Indians had been spotted, and now three horsemen with rifles were riding towards them. It was Jim Haulk and two cowboys. Stopping about a hundred feet from the Comanche, Jim called out, asking "Who are you?" Pearl looked at Quanah, who did not understand the words, and so Pearl spoke out.

"We are Comanche from Fort Sill. We have permission to go to our medicine grounds."

Jim Haulk answered, "This is private property. You cannot camp here. We want no trouble with you," waving his rifle menacingly. "Why are you off the reservation?"

"We are only passing by. We are not camping here. We have permission from the Army at Fort Sill to come and gather medicine," she replied.

Jim Haulk now recognized Pearl from his infrequent trips to Doan's trading post. "Ain't you the squaw that belongs to Corwin Doan? I seen ya before."

"Yes. I don't belong to him. I work for him," came her curt answer.

"Well, you keep these people movin'. I don't want any trouble from them," he motioned with his rifle.

"We are only passing by. We are no threat to you. Put your rifles away!" demanded Pearl.

Pearl now advised Quanah. "These are not good men. They are whiskey drinkers. We need to move quickly away from here." Quanah kicked his horse

321

into a trot, and his long string of followers did likewise.

They put the tent city and the threat behind them and continued riding west. An hour later, they came to a beautiful meadow full of wild Texas bluebonnet flowers. The place was located in a slight dip in the prairie. A clear, running creek snaked its way across the bottom land, disappearing to the west. The group halted on the bank of the creek, allowing the thirsty horses to drink. "We will camp here," announced Quanah, waving his arm across the beautiful meadow of flowers.

That evening, a distinct quiet and solitude was upon the camp. It was as if the Comanche had returned home, and each individual was reflecting with the meadow on a personal level. Pearl sensed the spirituality of the evening and quietly spread her bedroll, gazing at the stars before falling asleep.

She awoke the next morning to the smell of meat cooking on the campfires. Several boys, who'd been tending the horses the night before, had shot several prairie grouse with their bows. The birds were roasting on spits, popping and hissing as the juice dripped into the flames. Weakeah, a wife of Quanah, was busy frying corn mush in an iron skillet. She offered Pearl a hot cake to eat. Pearl asked her where Quanah was, and she pointed him out, sitting on a buffalo robe by the creek. Pearl approached him and asked if she could sit down. He was watching several boys, the night herders, taking baths in the creek.

"Of course. Sit down. A beautiful morning," he smiled up at her.

"This is a beautiful place. It is very peaceful here," agreed Pearl as she sat down.

"Yes, this is one of my favorite campgrounds. I was born on this creek, not too far from here," he explained.

"So you know this place well?" she was coaxing a conversation out of him.

"Yes, this creek was the homeland of my father's people, the Nokoni--the Wanderers--and now, the white man calls it Wanderers Creek."

"Where is your father?" asked Pearl.

"Nocona--he died several years ago in the Wichita Mountains. He went there to grieve over the loss of my mother. His camp was attacked by a Ute war party, and he died a short time later from a poison arrow wound."

"And what happened to your mother?" she asked in a soft voice.

"Naduah was captured several years ago by the Texas Rangers at a place to the south of us," he pointed. "My brother and I were out hunting that morning and did not witness the attack. By the time we returned, they had disappeared and taken her back to the white settlements. My mother was a white woman, Pearl," he matter of factly revealed.

"What!? Your mother was white?" she asked in disbelief.

"Yes, she was captured as a young girl, far to the east. She was raised as a Comanche and became one of us. She became the wife of Nocona, and I was her firstborn. After she was captured, they took her back to her white relatives, the Parkers. They say she died a short time later from a broken heart, not being allowed to return to Nocona." He was staring now towards the south, as if he could still see her. There was a long period of silence. Wanting to change the subject, she noticed the boys were diving under the creek water and surfacing with loud laughter.

"They seem to be having a good time this morning," Pearl pointed out.

"Yes, they are becoming one with the creek, learning of its secrets," Quanah mused.

"What do you mean?" Pearl was being inquisitive.

Quanah looked at her and smiled. "All things in this world have a spirit. The creek has a soul, the waving grass has a song, and the animals all have their protective spirits. Every animal in the world is born with the divine spirit of the protector. In order to survive, they channel this protection for themselves and their offspring. It is the gift of the Creator. If you can learn to channel the protection of the animals, you will live a long life. Young children have pure and innocent hearts. The animal spirits know this and are not afraid of them, so it is important for Comanche children to be among the wild creatures when they are young. The boys are made horse herders when they are five years old. They stay out all night and become one with the horse spirit. The horses know the boys' hearts are pure, and they bond with them. They stare into the horses eyes, blow their breath into his nostrils, and become one with his spirit. We do not need saddles or bridles. When we jump on a horse, we become one with his spirit. We can guide him with gentle kicks and taps on the neck. We sing, pray, and dance to the buffalo spirit. We ask that he give us some of his brothers and sisters so that we have something to eat. He hears us and protects us by sending his herds our way. As long as we honor his spirit, he always gives back to us in gratitude. Those boys--they are testing the protective spirit of the catfish. The catfish hide in holes along the creek bank, protecting their lairs. A young boy uses his foot to probe and find the hole. The catfish clamps down on the boy's foot and then the boy reaches down and grabs the fish by the gills. I did it for hours along this creek as a young boy. Watch them. They will catch one here, shortly."

Sure enough, a few minutes later, a boy submerged and reappeared with a giant, thrashing catfish. Everyone laughed as the giant fish was too much for the boy. The fish thrashed wildly and finally broke free from the boy's grasp. His friends taunted and laughed at him, but it was all in good fun.

"I had a protector spirit once--a bird," Pearl hesitantly volunteered.

"You!? Ha, that does not surprise me," Quanah chuckled. "What kind of bird?" he wryly looked at her.

"He was a raven, given to me when I was a young girl."

"And where is your raven now?" asked Quanah.

"I had him for many years--a shaman gave him to me. We became close, and he watched over me constantly. I was captured by people far to the north. A cruel chief shot the bird with an arrow, and I was taken away, never to see him again."

Now Quanah asked, "Do you still talk with his spirit?"

"What do you mean? He is dead," Pearl looked at him curiously.

"Hmmm… the ravens are much like the Comanche. They are a tribe of birds. They have leaders, hunters, scouts, and mothers who are very protective of one another. If you try and approach a nest, they will be in your face, defending their young. They are close to the spirit world, and because of this, he may still be watching over you."

"How would I know if he is still watching?" Pearl asked.

"Enough of this talk. I will take you to a place tomorrow. Maybe there we can find an answer to your question." He smiled and stood up. "That grouse meat smells good. Let's go get some breakfast."

As Quanah and Pearl ate the delicious sage hens, the boys in the creek laughed with delight as another catfish had been caught. This time, they were able to pull the fish up onto the bank. A large iron pot was produced. The fish was cleaned and tossed into the pot, making a fish stew for the people's afternoon meal. The rest of the day was spent relaxing, bathing, and eating. It was obvious that the Comanche found comfort and security in this field of blue flowers.

These people were the Kwahadi, or desert people. Quanah had married into their clan by taking Weakeah as his wife. Through his exploits as a hunter and warrior, he had become their leader. The Nokoni, his father's clan, had drifted to the north, several of whom had been killed in battle, including Quanah's father. The remnants of the clan had married into the Kiowa, with a few rejoining Quanah's clan of the Kwahadi.

Now, these remnants led the people that evening in song and dance. They sang the old chants of the elders and called on the spirits for protection. At sunrise, the camp was up and moving. The horses were packed and readied for the day's ride. Pearl wished to stay in the meadow, as it was so tranquil and beautiful. She was anxious to see this "place" that Quanah had told her that she might find Duto's spirit.

The Kwahadi headed straight south from Wanderers Creek. By afternoon, four large, conical hills appeared on the flat prairie. By sundown, they had reached the base of the tallest hill. Pearl could see old fire pits spread across the base of the hill. Small groups began to cluster around each one, as if the spot belonged to specific individuals. As it had been at Wanderers Creek, the evening was quiet and somber. Conversation was made in hushed tones.

The next morning, Pearl was up early, helping Weakeah build the cooking fire. As the sun came over the horizon, all of the Kwahadi faced east and chanted until the sun was above the flat distance. They offered up smudge smoke to carry prayers into the sky. In complete unison, the chanting stopped, and the people went about their morning chores. Weakeah got out her iron frying pan and began frying corn mush cakes as Pearl quietly watched.

The Medicine Mounds were awe inspiring in the golden morning sunlight. Pearl was transfixed, staring at them, watching the morning shadows disappear. "They are mysterious in the morning sun, aren't they?" It was Quanah, who'd come up quietly behind Pearl.

"What is this place, Quanah? It feels mystical and magical." Pearl continued to stare at the majesty of the Mounds.

"This is the holiest of ground for the Comanche people. We come here to gather herbs and medicine. We are closest to the spirit world here. Do not make loud noises--only speak in hushed tones. We are guests in this holy place." Quanah quietly informed her. He then explained, pointing at each individual Medicine Mound, saying, "This Mound, here, where we are camped, is the Buffalo Mound. We offer our prayers up to the buffalo spirit here. The praying lasts for three days. On the fourth day, we climb the Mound. The buffalo always appear on the horizon, for you can see in a circle for fifty miles. The second Mound is the Eagle Mound, where we can send our prayers on his back into the stars. It is there that we may find your raven spirit. Fill your stomach, for it is a long day ahead. You will need strength for this encounter."

Pearl ate two corn cakes, but Quanah insisted she eat more. Filling herself with another two cakes, a boy appeared, leading three horses. "Follow me," the chief ordered Pearl. The boy handed Pearl the reins then jumped on his horse. Quanah was already trotting away. They rode the short distance to the Eagle Mound. Quanah carried a blanket and large bundle. Dismounting, he told the boy to return at sundown with the horses. Without speaking, Quanah signaled for Pearl to follow. They ascended a distinct path. A half an hour later, they were on the flat summit of the Mound. Picking his way across the top, he came to a fire pit. The remnants of charcoal were present. He rolled out the blanket and hand signed for Pearl to sit down and be silent. From the bundle, he removed his fire starter, a small bow, stick, and pivot stone. Placing some fluff and slivers on the pivot stone, he then held the pivot stones with his big toes. Placing the fire stick into the bowl of the pivot stone, he now rocked it back and forth with the bow, and in thirty seconds, a white puff of smoke appeared. He now bent low, slowly blowing on the tiny ember until a yellow flame burst forward. With a small, ceremonial fire going now, he produced a smudge and offered its smoke in the four directions. Now he pulled from the bundle a long stem pipe. He placed it on the blanket in front of them. Reaching into the bundle, he now revealed a small, silver canteen with burn marks on it. He placed the canteen into the coals of the fire and waited patiently until steam was coming out of its open cap. He picked up the hot canteen with a corner of the blanket and set it aside to cool. From his belt, he produced a small pouch. He took several pinches of its content, placing the pinches in the bowl of the pipe. He took a twig, lit it in the coals, and brought the flaming match to the pipe bowl, puffing its contents. He handed the pipe to Pearl, indicating to pull several puffs into her lungs. The smoke was sweet and had a pleasant aroma. She coughed, and Quanah indicated to inhale a little less. Doing so, she then offered the pipe back, and Quanah took two more puffs. He then handed it back to her, signaling to take two more puffs. Quanah then took the pipe, knocking the ashes out in the firepit and then returned it to the bundle. Quanah then tested the canteen with his fingers to see if it had cooled. It was still too hot to touch. He then signaled to Pearl, with split fingers to both of his eyes, to look towards a rock outcropping, far below on the prairie floor. Pearl stared at it for a long time, and then she saw movement. It was a coyote, and it seemed to be staring back at her, as well. No sooner had she spotted the coyote, when a rush of euphoria came over her senses. She felt as if she were floating, the sensation totally relaxing. She looked at Quanah and offered a big smile, and he returned one as well. Silently, he nodded at her. He now picked up the canteen and took two gulps of the tea. He handed the canteen to Pearl, indicating to take two large gulps. She was in such a state of euphoria that she did not hesitate and swallowed two large gulps, as he directed. The tea was bitter, and it tried to come back up in Pearl's mouth. Quanah covered her mouth with his hand and made her re-swallow the elixir. He nodded assuredly now, indicating for her to watch the coyote in the distance.

She was now totally relaxed, in hypnotic bliss, and stared at the coyote far below. All of a sudden, as if by magic, the coyote turned into two coyotes, then three, and now four coyotes were staring at her. Now, all four were running towards her from across the prairie below. Reaching the base of the Eagle Mound, they raced up the hill towards them. Suddenly, they were right in front of her, leaping over her and causing her to fall back on the blanket to avoid a collision. Lying on her back, she stared at the sky, which had become a brilliant hue of purple. Two small clouds were overhead, and she fixed her stare upon them. The clouds now turned to a dark, ebony blue and then transformed into two ravens. They flew in a wide circle above her, gliding around and around. As she watched, they continued to circle but sank lower and lower until they were sailing an arm's length away. Suddenly, both ravens landed on the chest of both Pearl and Quanah. The raven stared into the shell medallion on Pearl's neck. The bird then stared into her eyes and she could see the reflection of the medallion in his pupil. Like magic, he pulled her soul into his body. Suddenly, she WAS the raven! She flapped her wings and called out a *caw caw caw*! Quanah had become the other raven! She spread her wings and jumped into the air, taking flight. Quanah was right behind her, cawing and following. She could now see their bodies below, lying on the blanket. Higher they circled into the sky until she could see distant mountains that she had crossed so long ago. With Quanah flying alongside now, she crossed the mountains and the sagebrush prairie. She could now see Corral Creek Canyon below! And there was Duto, sitting atop the giant split boulder! She called out a *caw*. Duto was dining with his queens and paid no attention to yet another queen flying high overhead. She again let out a *caw-caw*, only to remain ignored, so she flew on. There was Chilkosahaskt and Lahompt below. They were sitting on horses on a Big River bluff, staring at a boat that emitted smoke, with a churning wheel behind it. She called and cawed to them, but they did not look up, transfixed by the sight of the boat. She flew on, crossing more mountains, and there was Muk-il-tee-oh. The Snohomish village was gone, and the forest hiding Swakane Jacque's cabin was a hillside of stumps. She looked further and saw large swaths of forest that had been reduced to stumps, with little log cabins sitting in the stump fields. Now she was over the ocean, over Owyhee, but quickly flew past, wanting to see her homeland. She was tired now, her wings becoming fatigued. Finally, there it was in the distance--Leyte! She flew over the old pirate watchtower in Matalom, but now everything looked different. Something had happened! It had all changed! Her house was gone! The school was gone! The Chinese granny's house was gone! Lolung, the Black Ghost, was gone, along with his treehouse! All of it, gone! The tree was there, but its branches were broken and twisted. Quanah called out for her to follow him and circle higher. Climbing higher and higher, she looked down and could now see the curvature of the earth below. Quanah went

327

into a long, diving glide, and she followed. Suddenly, they both were circling above the Medicine Mounds. She followed his glide until both landed on the blanket next to their bodies. She now hopped up on to her belly, and stared into her own eyes. Suddenly, she was staring again at the reflection of the medallion in the eye of the raven. Lying there, she watched as both ravens jumped back into the air, taking flight, and resumed their circling above. She rolled her head sideways, and Quanah was staring at her, smiling. His gaze was warm and beckoning, and she took him in her arms, pulling him close. She wanted him... and he wanted her.

Passionately, he now was on top of her and inside of her. She convulsed with pleasure. Another wave of pure euphoria swept through her body. She could hear him breathing hard, as she pulled him into her and now felt him shuddering on top of her, groaning with pleasure. She blacked out from the immense wave of pleasure, exhausted from the long flight.

She finally awoke and sat up on the blanket. Quanah was close by, waving his arm at someone below. It was the boy who had returned with the horses. The sun was low on the horizon, and she realized the day had already passed.

"We must go now," he quietly told her. He rolled up the blanket and sprinkled cornmeal on the spot. She followed him down the trail, off of the Mound to the waiting horses. It was dark when they rode into camp, below the Buffalo Mound. Weakeah sensed Pearl was exhausted and offered her food and fresh water.

"What was in that tea that we drank, Quanah?" Pearl asked the chief.

"We call it peyote. It is a gift from the Mother Earth, a sacrament taken to enter the spirit world. The Eagle Mound let you see the animal spirits today. Do not speak of what you saw--it would bring bad luck."

She slept deeply that night. She awoke in the late morning and asked where the chief was. In sign language, Weakeah explained he had arose early and rode south. She signed that he had gone to the place where his mother had been captured. He would be gone three days.

For the next three days, she observed the Comanche and their reverence for the Medicine Mounds. She helped Weakeah collect herbs and roots around the base of the Mounds. Several Comanche made the pilgrimage to the top of the Buffalo Mound, but in the end, no buffalo were spotted in the distance. Quanah finally returned and announced it was time to go back. "We must return. I gave my word to the general that we would be back in ten days."

They returned to the beautiful bluebonnet meadow and camped there the last night on the old trail. The next morning, they took a wide path around

328

Haulk's tent town to avoid it. Arriving back at Doan's Trading Post, the Doan family was excited to see Pearl, gone nine days now.

"Tell us about your adventure--where did you go? We want to hear all about these Medicine Mounds." They began to beseech her with questions.

Quanah had Pearl translate to Corwin, "Come and visit me at Cache Creek--and you, Bird Woman, I will see you again. May the protector spirits watch over you."

The Comanche were soon gone, crossing the Red River and heading north across their grassland reservation. A week later, a huge herd of longhorns appeared at the trading post and crossing. John and Corwin did a large amount of business with this cattle company. It appeared that their hunch and gamble was going to pay off, better than their hopes and expectations. They were assured that thousands of cattle were coming from the south to use the crossing at Doan's Trading Post. They would need to replenish their stores of trade goods, sooner than later.

Weeks had passed since Pearl's visit to the Medicine Mounds. She found herself feeling sickly and she wondered if she had caught river fever or had eaten bad food. One morning at breakfast, Corwin announced to Pearl, "Tomorrow is May first. John and I are taking the wagons to Wichita for supplies. I hate to see you go Pearl, but I'm a man of my word. I promised you a train ticket to San Francisco, and you shall have it. Of course, we welcome you to stay with us, but I know you well enough now and what's in your heart. You want to see your parents, and your hard work and loyalty to me shall now be rewarded. Are you still feeling ill? I can take you to a doctor in Wichita, if you wish."

"I'm feeling better--probably something I ate. Thank you, Corwin. Yes, it is time for me to go--I will miss all of you."

A farewell dinner was cooked up that night, with emotions running high as Pearl had become part of the family. Tears and hugs were given, and small gifts exchanged. The following morning, the two wagons were crossing the Red River at sunup. Reaching Cache Creek that afternoon, Corwin and Pearl were disappointed to learn that Quanah was at Fort Sill, negotiating grazing leases with cattle barons. Quanah had become a prominent figure among the surrounding tribes. His shrewdness in allowing cattle to cross his land had grown into quite a profit for the Comanche people.

John and Corwin didn't have time to stop, as there was plenty of daylight left for traveling. They followed a well-worn wagon road that they had helped to pioneer. They camped at several known watering holes along the road over the next four days. On the fifth day, they crossed a makeshift log bridge over a

329

small,muddy river. A sign on the far side of the bridge read: Chikaskia River--Welcome to Kansas. They were out of Indian Territory now and spent the night in a rowdy little cowtown called Wellington. They were thirty miles south of Wichita. Wellington was a cluster of sod houses and tent saloons. John had a friend who ran a diner in a large tent, and they celebrated with sizzling beef steaks and garden vegetables. Fortified, they made camp on the outskirts of the little cowtown.

"My goodness Pearl... I've never seen you eat so much!" laughed Corwin. "Tomorrow, we'll get a hotel and a hot bath. Wichita is the queen of the prairie--the city of the future!" he gleamed.

The next morning, Pearl awoke and was sick to her stomach again. She felt weak and lightheaded, and the bouncing of the wagon compounded the problem. Corwin could see she wasn't well. "Hang on, Pearl. We'll be in Wichita by noon. I'm taking you to the doctor."

By late morning, she was feeling better. She could see the outline of the town in the distance. She was excited to see it after hearing John and Corwin talk so much about it. They entered the town from the south side--the "rough" part of town. The district was known as 'Delano," the sinful part of town, on the south side of the Arkansas River. This was the end of the Chisholm Trail, where cowboys blew off steam at the dozens of bordellos, saloons, and faro tables. As they rode down Douglas Street, or Main Street as it was more commonly called, Pearl was amazed at the sights and activities. One saloon after another lined boardwalk streets on either side. Banjo and piano music spilled out into the dirt street, a different song coming from each one. Several bawdy houses and brothels were mixed in above or alongside each saloon. Women clad only in stockings and bustiers sat outside on porches, calling out to John and Corwin as they passed. A fistfight tumbled out of a saloon and into the street. Corwin had to stop the wagon to avoid the spectacle. A crowd of spectators pushed the bloody brawl to the opposite side of the street. Corwin snapped the reins and got the wagon around the fistfight, telling Pearl, "Hasn't changed a bit. Don't worry, it's not this way on the other side of the river." The Main Street ended at the Arkansas River. A wooden bridge crossed it, utilizing a small island in the middle of the river. A flimsy gate stopped them at the entrance to the bridge. A whiskered old man now approached Corwin and the wagon. "Two bits to cross," he called out.

"Two bits!? That's robbery. It was ten cents last year!" complained Corwin.

"Well, you can go down to the cattle crossing and take your chances or pay the two bits--don't matter to me," he cackled.

"Alright, here's four bits to cover the wagon behind me," Corwin grudgingly handed over the coins. The old man lifted the gate, and minutes later, they were across, in the respectable part of town. Ladies walked the boarded sidewalks, shaded with parasols and large sun hats, shopping in the glass-fronted stores. There were dozens of stores of dry goods, sundries, barbershops, bakeries, and hardware stores. Signs lined the busy streets, boasting of their wares and proprietors. Pearl gazed down side streets and could see neat, white washed, clapboard houses with picket fences and shade trees. She had never been in a real town and now gazed in wonderment at the sight before her.

Finally, Corwin pulled up at a Livery Stable, jumped down, and asked the owner to park the wagons and tend the mules. He helped Pearl down and urged her, "C'mon, let's check in at the hotel." They walked a short way down the board sidewalk and came to the Southern Hotel. Entering the lobby, Corwin called out, "Jake, good to see you again. John and I need two rooms."

The clerk behind the desk looked up from his work and adjusted his spectacles and returned the greeting. "Mr. Doan, good to see you again, sir." He then turned his gaze towards Pearl. He motioned for Corwin to come closer.

"Mr. Doan, you know we don't allow Injuns in here. This is a respectable hotel. She'll have to wait outside."

Taken aback, Corwin assured the clerk, "She's a good friend, and she's not Injun, Jake."

"What?! Do you take me for a fool? She's wearing beaded buckskins-- she can't be in here!"

"She ain't Injun! She's an islander, from out in the ocean!" Corwin now quipped with irritation. "I've been staying here for years. Stop this nonsense, Jake, and give me a couple of rooms!"

"I can give you two rooms in the back, as long as you use the back door. And that's on one condition, Mr. Doan."

"And just what are your damn conditions, Jake?" Corwin's temper was now flaring.

"You take her across the street and buy her some civilized clothes. You're pushin' your luck, Mr.Doan, bringing a fringed, buckskin squaw across the river into town."

Corwin scratched his jaw, wondering if he should roundhouse the clerk or settle down and listen to what he was saying. He looked Jake in the eye and asked, "Where'd ya say that clothing store is?"

The clerk pointed out the hotel window. "Right over there, across the street. See the sign? Gambles General Store. Take her over there and get her

331

out of the moccasins and beads… then come back, and then I'll book ya two rooms in the back."

"C'mon, Pearl… follow me." Corwin angrily stormed out. Across the street he marched, swung open the door, and held it open for Pearl, indicating to walk in. Two fair haired women, who were looking at clothing, quickly departed.

"Uhh… good afternoon, sir… uh, I'm sorry sir, but she's not allowed in here." Hearing this, Corwin flipped the open sign to closed, pulled the blind, and locked the door. Folding his arms,he stared her down.

"Lady, you're gonna fit and sell this woman two dresses, some undergarments, a sun hat, and a pair of them button down shoes. I've got all day to stand here, until you make it happen. The sooner you take care of her, the sooner we'll be gone."

"I don't take credit here! You'll have to pay in silver dollars!" she stammered, hoping to scare them off.

Corwin pulled out his tote of gold and silver coins and plopped them on the counter. "Like I said, the sooner you git her fit, the sooner we're gone."

"Well, I declare, I guess I have no choice, Lord forgive me. Alright, step over here, out of sight from the shop window," she hissed.

An hour later, Corwin and Pearl stepped out onto the board sidewalk. The calico dress was light and airy, and she liked it. The button down shoes were uncomfortable to her. She'd had a pair given to her at Fort Victoria, but she had quickly outgrown them two decades ago. She awkwardly crossed the street, her ankles rolling and stumbling. Grabbing Corwin's arm, they both chuckled at her first few steps. Upon entering the hotel lobby, Jake the clerk nodded, saying, "Here's two keys, but she has to use the back door."

332

Return to Civilization

Pearl followed Corwin down the hall to the back of the hotel. The two keys were numbered seven and eight, and he found the rooms at the very end. Opening number seven, he stepped in and inspected the chamber. It was clean with an iron bed. An armoire and chair sat against one wall, a window on the exterior wall. A commode with a mirror had a wash bowl and pitcher of water on the marble top. A kerosene lamp sat on a small table, next to the bed. A porcelain crock sat in the corner.

"There's an outhouse out back if you need to relieve yourself. There's a thunder-mug in the corner, so's you don't have to go out at night. We'll only be here three days. We gotta get back. I'll make sure you're on the train before we leave. There's a Chinese wash house out back. I'll go have them heat you up a bath. I'll be right back," Corwin assured her.

Closing the door behind him, Pearl stared at herself in the mirror. She removed the sun bonnet and ran her hands over the bright blue calico dress. It was as if someone else were staring back at her in the mirror.

A slight tap was now heard at the door. "Pearl, it's me. Can I come in?" Corwin politely asked. She opened the door and smiled. "They've already got hot water on the stove. C'mon, follow me." She followed him out the back door of the hallway. Four outhouses were on either side of a board walkway, labeled "HIS" and "HERS." The boardwalk continued through a maze of clotheslines, with all sorts of garments and towels drying in the sun. The walkway ended at the door of a large shack, smoke billowing from a stove pipe. Entering, they were immediately greeted by a Chinese man and woman, who bowed graciously and pointed towards a huge copper tub in the center of the shack.

The Chinese finished their bowing, and now the woman held out her hand, saying "Hot bath, ten cents. Hot bath, ten cents."

Corwin pulled out a dime from his pocket, paying the woman. "I'll be back later. I gotta go find John," and was gone.

The Chinese woman now scolded the Chinese man, telling him in Mandarin to leave and give the woman privacy. He bowed and smiled and went out the shack's door.

In perfect Mandarin, Pearl now laughed and addressed the woman, saying, "He didn't think he was going to watch me take a bath, did he?"

The Chinese woman put her hands to her face and squealed with delight. "You speak our language! My name is Su Wong. What is your name?" she asked in the dialect.

"My name is Pearl. Shall I undress and sit in the tub?"

333

"Yes, yes, yes. Sit in the tub. I have lots of hot water. I make you very clean with soap!"

The wood stove had several pots of steaming water ready for the task. In a large bucket, she mixed cool and hot water to the desired temperature and poured the steaming contents over Pearl, who was now sitting in the tub. The hot water made her gasp and jump. A second bucket was now dumped on her and then a third. Su Wong now picked her feet up, and with a bar of lye soap, massaged and washed between her toes.

A lively conversation was now chattering away between the two women in Chinese, both enjoying themselves and the moment. Su Wong commented about the shell medallion around Pearl's neck, and asked what was in the medicine bags that Pearl had removed before the bucket was dumped on her.

"They're just things I keep from my past--for good luck," she explained. Su Wong now moved behind the tub and washed Pearl's hair. She rubbed and massaged her shoulder to the point that she thought she would go to sleep.

"Stand up, now. Time for rinse," the woman commanded. Fixing another bucket, she stood on a step stool, and poured the bucket over her head, washing the soap from her hair and body. "Here. Clean towel. All done. You smell like pretty lady now."

Putting back on the new clothes, Pearl felt invigorated and reborn. She bowed to Su Wong, thanking her graciously, and returned to her room. Su Wong had lent her a hair brush, and she combed her hair dry, as she stared at herself in the mirror.

An hour passed as she admired herself in the mirror. Another tap-tapping came at the door. "Pearl. It's me, Corwin. Can I come in?" he asked through the door.

She opened the door, smiling. Corwin was taken aback by her radiance. The bath, washed hair, and new dress made her vibrant.

"Goodness! Look at you! I need to get me one of those baths. Makes you feel like a shiny new nickel! Pearl... I've found a doctor down the street and spoke with him. He would like to see you, and ask a few questions. Come with me."

She came out of the room, and they started down the hall. Remembering the condition the clerk had put upon them, he stopped, finding an excuse. "Wait. I need to pee. Let's go out back first," he said, turning her around. They stepped out back, and he relieved himself in one of the latrines. "Much better. Alright, follow me." They side-stepped around the wash house and walked down an alley to the next side street. Now back on main street, they walked a block on the board sidewalk, coming to a saloon. A set of stairs climbed the side of the building to a second floor office. A sign above the door read:

DOC HATCHER
-- TEETH PULLED $2
-- BOILS LANCED $2
-- BROKEN BONES SET $3
-- WITH LAUDEMEN - EXTRA $1

Corwin swung the door open and announced, "Doc., I'm back. Here she is." The walls were covered in shelves of books and medicine jars. A large poster of a skeleton and skull were on the wall, which made Pearl nervous to look at.

"Ah, very good. Why don't you take a walk and let me have some privacy. Go have a drink downstairs and a cigar. I should be done by then," the doctor suggested.

Corwin winked at Pearl, and he was out the door, his steps thumping down the side of the building.

"Alright, Miss. May I call you Pearl?" he politely asked.

"Yes, that is my name, Doctor."

"Alright, don't be frightened. I'm not going to hurt you. I have a few questions to ask, alright?" he assured her. "How old are you?"

"I'm forty years old, Dr. Hatcher."

"Have you ever seen a doctor before--like, had an exam?"

"No."

"Corwin tells me you've been feeling nauseated and lightheaded, feeling weak. Is that correct?"

"Yes."

"How long ago did these ill feelings begin?"

"Several weeks ago. It's only in the morning I feel sick, and by noon it seems to go away."

"I see. Do you drink river water or well water?"

"I always drink well water. The Red River is far too muddy."

"Yes, Corwin says you're from Texas. Open your mouth, and let me peek inside. Are any teeth bothering you?"

"No. My teeth seem alright."

"Hmm, yes. I see no swelling in there. I have here, Pearl, a listening device. It's called a stethoscope. It lets me listen to your heart beating. I'm going to put it on your chest. It will not harm you. Please sit still." He placed the cup between her breasts and listened for a long time, finally nodding his head with an, "uh huh."

"Alright, I'm going to put the cup on your belly. Just breathe normally." Placing the cup above her belly button, he listened for a long time, moving the cup around. Finally, he got a small smile on his face. He took the earpieces off, saying, "I want you to hear something. Here. Put these in your ears and listen." Holding the cup firmly on her belly, he gazed at her, asking, "Do you hear that?"

"Hear what?" Pearl was confused.

"Listen closely. You'll hear a *ba-dump, ba-dump, ba-dump*. Do you hear it now?"

"Yes. I hear it now. What is that?"

"Pearl, that's the sound of a baby's heartbeat. You are with child!"

Pearl's jaw dropped, "You must be mistaken! It can't be!"

"Pearl, do you have a husband, or were you with a man several weeks ago?"

"I can't believe this. No, I have no husband. No, I have not," and then she stopped.

Dr. Hatcher looked at her, shaking his head. "You are with child, Pearl. That's why you haven't felt well in the morning. Did someone force themselves upon you, Pearl?" the doctor now questioned further.

"No, it wasn't like that. We--I had a weak moment and wanted to be with him," she gasped.

"So you know who the father is?" he asked.

"Yes," and Pearl bowed her head.

"Well, it's nothing to be ashamed of. It's the natural outcome when a man and woman connect. This man--can you go to him and have him help raise the child?" The doctor was now being sympathetic.

"Go to him? No. I'm riding the train to San Francisco and taking a ship home."

"Pearl, you can't travel in your condition. It's too risky to be at sea and be carrying a baby. You need to go back to Texas after the child is born and raise him with the father."

Clump, clump, clump. Corwin was coming back up the stairs now, and slowly opened the door ajar. "Can I come in?"

"Yes, come in Corwin, and sit down. Here, grab this chair."

"Well, what is it, Doctor? Nothing a good dose of bitters won't cure?" Corwin asked.

"Do you want to tell him, Pearl? He needs to know," the doctor asked Pearl.

"Needs to know what? What's wrong?" Corwin was now frowning and concerned.

336

Pearl hung her head and began to cry softly.

"What--what! What's wrong!?" Corwin was frantic.

"I'm with a child, Corwin. I'm going to have a baby," she blurted out.

Corwin put his hand to his brow and stared wildly at Doc Hatcher. "Are you sure, Doc?" he asked in disbelief.

"Just as sure as the sun will come up tomorrow. Yes, she's with child."

"How did this happen, Pearl?" he asked her in disbelief. "Who did this to you?" he demanded.

"What does it matter Corwin…. who the father is?" she stammered.

Groping for an answer, he beseeched her, "It's not John, is it?"

"No, no, no. It's not John."

"Don't push her with questions, Corwin. She's in a state of shock. She needs time to think about things," the doctor quietly advised.

Corwin quietly stared at Pearl now, who was too embarrassed to lift her head and look at him. "Well, that's that. She's s'pose to ride the train in a couple days to Frisco. I don't see…." and Corwin was interrupted by the doctor.

"No, Corwin. She needs rest, good food, and a peaceful environment. I highly recommend that she not get on a train."

"Can she travel in the wagon?" came Corwin's next question.

"I would not advise a bumpy ride on a buckboard right now, let alone one all the way across Indian Territory."

"What shall we do, doctor?"

"I can't help you with that question. All I know is a woman can die very easily from losing a baby and hemorrhaging. She needs to stay here in Wichita, and rest until the child is born. That's the best advice I can give you."

Corwin was speechless. "How much do I owe you, doctor?"

"One dollar will do. But please take my advice, Corwin. She's an older woman, and sometimes these things do not turn out well. She needs rest, good food and water, and light exercise."

"Alright, doctor. Let's go, Pearl," helping her up now. As they descended the stairs, Corwin reached back, holding her hand. On reaching the board sidewalk, he put his arm around her in a fatherly fashion, assuring her, "Stop crying. We'll figure this out. I'm not going to abandon you."

They walked down the sidewalk, reaching the Southern Hotel and entered the lobby. The clerk, Jake, on seeing them, spoke up. "Hey! Corwin! I told you that she can't…."

"Shut up, Jake! Or I'll knock your teeth into Texas!" came Corwin's blunt answer.

"But I told you that she can't…."

337

"I said shut up! Or I'll throw your ass through that plate glass window!"

The clerk knew Corwin meant it, and he said no more. The two went down the hall, and Corwin unlocked her door, entering with her. "Here… lie on the bed. Let me pull those shoes off."

"What am I going to do, Corwin? I don't know anyone here. I feel so alone and helpless," Pearl sobbed.

"I have a friend here in Wichita that owes me a favor. He owns the hardware store where John and I buy supplies. I'm going to go talk to him. He's a Christian man, and maybe he can help us. Stop crying. I'll be back in a couple hours."

Corwin closed the door quietly, walked down the hall, and on seeing the clerk, issued another warning, "I meant what I said, Jake. Don't push me!" and stormed out the front door onto the street.

Walking north two blocks towards the train depot, he came to "Lonker's Hardware." Entering, he immediately spotted Bill Lonker, the owner, weighing nails on a scale for a customer. "Corwin Doan! So good to see you! Let me finish up here. Martha will be so pleased to know you are in town. Sit down, I'll be right with you."

Finishing with the customer, he now gave Corwin a bear hug and offered him a cigar. "Tell me about the new trading post. Martha got the letter from Lidee telling about your new home in Texas."

Corwin explained the success of the trading post at the Red River crossing and handed him a long list of supplies he needed to purchase to take back. Bill looked at the list, explaining, "You'll have to give me a day to fill this order. There's a lot of merchandise to weigh and package. You and John must come to dinner tonight. Martha will have a hundred questions to ask you!"

Corwin decided that this was the opportunity to explain that Pearl was with them, and the situation that was now upon them.

Upon hearing Corwin's story, Bill became more serious, saying, "Let me speak to Martha about this. She's quite connected in the church. Perhaps she knows someone that can help Pearl, but please, come to dinner tonight. We'll discuss it further."

Another customer entered the store, and Corwin used it as an opportunity to excuse himself. "What time shall we be there for dinner, Bill?"

"How about seven o'clock? Bring John and Pearl with you."

Returning to the hotel, John was waiting for Corwin in the lobby, reading the paper. On seeing Corwin, he was quick to scold him. "What's all this talk I hear… you threatening Jake--that's not like you, Corwin!"

338

"Come with me. We need to talk, John," Corwin muttered in a solemn tone.

In the privacy of their room, Corwin retold the diagnosis of Doc Hatcher, explaining he was in such a state of shock, he had forgotten about the promise to use the back door for Pearl's entering and leaving.

"I've spoken to Bill Lonker. He's going to speak to Martha about it. We're invited to dinner."

John was stunned and musing over the situation. "Suppose Bill and Martha can't help--what will we do?" John was fretful.

"Let's go take a bath. We can't go over there tonight smelling like mule-skinners," Corwin suggested.

John agreed, and before they exited to the bath house, Corwin tapped on Pearl's door. She had composed herself and opened the door. "Pearl, at 6:30 we'll go to dinner. I'll knock on your door then."

At 6:30 sharp, Corwin knocked on Pearl's door as promised, and the three went out the back door and onto Main Street. John flagged down a buggy, who taxied them to a residential street of modest houses. Pulling up at a clapboard, white washed bungalow, Corwin helped Pearl step down, and they entered the yard, knocking at the front porch door.

A young girl answered the door, "My goodness, Nellie. Look at you. You're as tall as a wagon wheel now!" John joked with her.

Entering, a warm welcome awaited. Martha hugged John and Corwin, and grabbed both of Pearl's hands, smiling and saying, "I'm so pleased to meet you. Please, come in and sit down in the parlor. Let me get you some cool buttermilk."

Bill had four children, one of them a suckling baby who was in a bassinet. He introduced them to Pearl. "This is Nellie, Charles, George, and baby Ernest. Welcome to our home, Pearl. Corwin has told us all about you!"

Martha had prepared a chicken dinner. Bill had brought a bench in from the porch for the children to sit at, giving the three guests the chairs at the big, round dinner table.

As they all were seated around the table, Martha asked Bill to say grace, and make the blessing on the food. As they all had their heads bowed, Bill wrangled on about all the blessings that had been bestowed on the Lonker family, finishing, "and Father, thank you for bringing this new addition to our family, Miss Pearl--please help her feel comfortable in her new home and bring her good health in the coming months, as we watch over her. In Jesus's name, Amen."

As everyone raised their heads, all eyes were on Pearl, who buried her face in her hands and cried tears of joy, "Thank you so much. I don't know what to say."

"Say you'll stay with us. We want you to be a part of our family!"

"Oh, this is wonderful. Yes, of course. I'll try not to be a burden," she meekly accepted.

Both John and Corwin nodded at Bill and Martha, a gleam in their eyes, with a huge sigh of relief.

And so it was. Pearl had found a refuge, a place of comfort and security in Wichita, the summer of 1878. John and Corwin finished purchasing their supplies and were gone, promising to return in the fall to restock and check on Pearl. The Lonkers made her feel right at home, and Pearl busied herself with the baby, Ernest, learning from Martha the skills of being a good mother.

As September was ending, Pearl's womb was now large and protruding, and one night at the dinner table, Martha began a serious discussion with Bill. "I've been thinking, William. All of the children were born in Springfield, at cousin Mildred's. She's the best midwife there is. I think Pearl should ride the train to Springfield. Nellie's been there several times. She's old enough. She can go with her. What do you think?"

"Yes, yes, Mother. I can do it! Let me go, Father," came Nellie's pleas.

"You might be right, Martha. Old Doc Hatcher is in that saloon more than he is in his office. Have you spoken to cousin Mildred about it?"

"No. I wanted your thoughts first. But if you approve, I'll send a telegraph message tomorrow."

"Alright, let me explain this to Pearl. Martha has a cousin in Springfield, Missouri. She is a midwife, and has brought dozens of babies into the world, including all four of our children." "Since this is your first child, it might be best to have an expert assist with the birth. How do you feel about that, Pearl?"

"Well, I have wondered about that. I just assumed I'd have the baby here, but I trust your wisdom, if you think it's the wisest choice," Pearl answered.

"I think Martha's right. Women have a lot more insight on the subject of childbirth, and yes, you and Nellie are close. She can travel with you on the Santa Fe to Springfield." Nellie squealed with delight. "Not so fast. Let's wait and see what cousin Mildred has to say, but yes, send her a wire tomorrow, and see what she says," came Bill's answer.

The following morning, Bill sent the telegram at the Santa Fe depot. That afternoon, a courier knocked on the door at the bungalow, handing Martha the returned answer. It stated, "By all means. *Stop*. Come at once. *Stop*. I will make the arrangements. *Stop*. Love, Mildred."

340

That night at the dinner table, the details and plans for the trip were discussed. Bill stressed the responsibility on his daughter, Nellie, who was only eight years old. She was a mature child, having watched over her siblings, and had done well in school, already reading books and the newspaper. This, of course, was Pearl's first time on a train, and she pressed Bill and Martha with a dozen questions. It was a two day trip with a one night sleep. Martha would pack a basket of food to take, and assured them that cousin Mildred would be waiting for them at the station to pick them up. Nellie had already made the trip four times, and she assured Pearl not to worry.

The next day, Bill sent a telegram to cousin Mildred, stating the girls would be leaving the following morning, and to pick them up upon their arrival in Springfield.

The morning of their departure, Bill had a buggy pick them up at the house, and he accompanied them to the station. He handed Pearl a sealed envelope, with instructions to give it to Mildred, when they arrived. Bill helped Pearl board the pullman car, followed by Nellie carrying the basket of food. "I wanna sit by the window, Daddy," came Nellie's request.

"No, you let Pearl sit by the window… so others don't bump her walking by. Besides, she'll enjoy the scenery. I'll go back and get your bag on the platform." He quickly returned with the carpet bag of belongings, and stowed it for them in the rear of the car. "Alright, here are your tickets, Nellie. Don't lose them."

The steam whistle of the engine now blew, and Bill kissed his daughter on the cheek. He no sooner had stepped back on the station platform, when the train lurched and began to creep away. He waved at Pearl in the window as Nellie pressed her face against the glass, and a moment later, he was looking at the caboose pass by.

Within minutes, the Santa Fe was up to speed, its steel wheels click-clacking a rhythm, and the car swaying gently back and forth. The coach was only half full of passengers, as more would be picked up at later stops.

A white-whiskered Conductor now entered the front of the car. He pulled out a pocket watch on a chain, checked the time, and made a note with a pencil on a tablet he carried. He looked rather official to Pearl, wearing a blue and brass buttoned top coat and a cap with a gold braid around the band. "Tickets! Tickets, please! Tickets! Have your tickets ready," he called out.

Nellie knew the routine, and patiently waited as he walked down the aisle, punching tickets and answering questions of the passengers. "Good morning, ladies. And where are you headed?" as Nellie handed him the two tickets. "Ahh, all the way to Springfield. Welcome aboard. Do you have any questions, miss?" he politely asked Nellie.

"No. No questions, sir," she politely answered.

The Conductor now looked at Pearl and asked Nellie, "Is this your nanny, young lady?"

Nellie hesitated for a moment, but decided it would be easier to just say "Yes," which she did.

"Very well. The Porter will be coming by later if you need anything else. Tickets! Tickets!" he sang out and moved on.

An hour later, a black Porter came down the aisle, offering water or coffee. Pearl had only seen a handful of the African people walking the streets of Wichita, and now for the first time, she was up close and personal.

"Yes'm. Y'all like water or coffee, mum?" he politely asked Pearl. His teeth gleamed white, and Pearl caught herself staring for a moment.

"Uh, no, sir. Thank you for asking," Pearl replied.

The Porter smiled, surprised at being called "sir."

"Yes'm. I's be back to check on y'all later mum," tipping his hat at Pearl.

The rhythm and swaying of the car soon put both girls to sleep, as they had been awake most of the night before, too excited to sleep.

Pearl felt Nellie tugging at her arm, "Wake up, wake up Pearl," she softly coaxed. It was dark outside the window now, and the black Porter stood in the aisle next to them. He handed each girl a pillow and small blanket, smiled and moved down the aisle.

Pearl needed to relieve herself, but wasn't sure how to go about it. She whispered in Nellie's ear, who smiled, stood up, and signaled for Pearl to follow. At the front of the car, a small side door was pulled open by Nellie, who pointed for Pearl to enter. There was only room for one person--a small bench seat with a hinged cover. Nellie lifted the seat, and again indicated for Pearl to enter.

Pearl could see the railroad ties rushing past, standing over the hole and staring down. She quickly realized the procedure, and sat down to relieve herself. Feeling better, she exited the small stall as Nellie waited for her, and walked her back to her seat.

They both slept soundly that night. Nellie was already awake and eating snacks from the basket when Pearl awoke the following day. By noon, the landscape outside had turned from flat prairie to rolling hills, covered with oak trees.

At three o'clock that afternoon, the Conductor appeared and called out, "Springfield, next stop. Springfield, ten minutes!" He then approached Nellie and Pearl, asking, "Do you ladies have baggage?"

Nellie acknowledged, "Yes," and he responded, "Alright, tell the Porter to help you with your bags. Have a good day, ladies," and moved on, calling out, "Springfield, next stop!"

The car came to a stop at the platform in a cloud of steam. There was a rush to disembark, and Nellie waited until the haste and bustle was over. As if by magic, the Porter appeared and asked Nellie where her bag was. She walked to the rear, pointed it out, and walked back to Pearl.

"Follow me, missus," he politely instructed Pearl. He had noticed her womb and was going out of his way to help. She was a person of color, and her responding to him as sir made him want to show her his appreciation. He held her hand as she stepped off the car and onto the platform. Nellie followed with the wicker food basket.

There was a sea of people and activity on the platform, and Nellie could now hear someone calling out her name. It was Mildred, who had spotted her getting out of the car, but was now invisible, as the child could not see in the throng of people. Pearl spotted the woman waving with a white handkerchief, continuing to call Nellie's name out. Pearl took Nellie's hand with the Porter following, and the trio wove its way through the throng of people.

Finally, they were in her presence—a well-dressed woman with a large, silk and feather hat, holding a fringed parasol. She warmly greeted Nellie, "There you are, my dear. Give me a hug."

She then politely nodded at Pearl, and introducing herself, she asked Nellie if the bag the Porter was holding was hers, and she nodded, "Yes." From a small coin purse around a thong on her wrist, she produced some coins, and tipped and thanked the Porter, who was genuinely pleased at his luck, bowing and tipping his cap.

On the edge of the platform, a shiny, black ebony carriage sat. A well-dressed black man was holding the horse, and she signaled him to fetch the bag. A small, ragged black boy sat on the edge of the platform. The driver instructed him to hold the horse, handing him something, and then approached Mildred and the girls.

"Lawd have mercy... look at chu... all grow'd up, Miss Nellie," as he picked up the carpet bag.

"Heb... you gonna carve me another whistle?" came Nellie's reply.

"Ah, yes, Missus. I gonna carve you a special one... a singun whistle... jus fo yous!"

Mildred introduced the man to Pearl, saying, "This is Hebediah Smith. He and his wife work for us."

"Nice to meet you, Mr. Smith," Pearl acknowledged.

343

He grinned, "Most folks call me ol' Heb, Missus," bowing politely. Heb helped the ladies into the carriage, then climbed aboard and got the hack rolling.

This town was like none she had ever seen. The streets were paved with red brick, and iron lamp posts sat at every corner. The houses were large, made of limestone and brick, with huge front porches, covered with porticos and large columns.

The carriage pulled into a circular brick drive, stopping in front of a massive white mansion house with four chimneys protruding from its roof. Heb jumped down and helped the ladies down to the carriage stoop.

A large, black woman came out onto the porch to greet them, exclaiming much like Heb had done on first seeing Nellie. Nellie ran to her and gave her a big hug, wrapping her arms around her apron. The woman was pleased with the affection, and now addressed Mildred, "Y'all want your afternoon tea, Miss Mildred?" she drawled.

"Yes, tea would be nice, Di…. Dinah, this is Pearl…. Pearl, this is Dinah, our cook and housekeeper… Heb's wife."

"You can call me Di, honey. Look at chu, you 'bout ready to be a momma, I see's," she cheerfully joked.

Instantly, Pearl felt at ease, the anxiety of not being accepted quickly had vanished. And the house--it was something a king and queen would live in, she thought. Stepping inside, it was dazzling for her to look around. Tiffany glassed oil lamps, Persian rugs, and richly carved furniture were everywhere she looked. A large banister and stairwell climbed to a balcony of rooms above.

"Di…. show Pearl where her room is. You, Nellie…. you know where your room is," she winked at the child.

"Oh, I almost forgot," and Pearl handed the sealed envelope to Mildred that Bill Lonker had sent.

Pearl followed Dinah and climbed the stairs to the overhead balcony. The room was stately, with a large bay window, an iron pot belly stove, and four-poster bed. A wash basin with a mirror, along with an ornate armoire faced the bed. Dinah showed Pearl where the chamber pot was, and told her of the privy out back, if she needed to use it. "Wash yo' face and come down for tea, honey," and Dinah excused herself.

A short time later, Pearl came down the stairs and found Mildred and Nellie in the dining room, chatting at the table. "Sit down, Pearl. Have some cake and tea. I've read William's letter, telling me all about you. I'm so glad you're having your baby here. Dinah has been delivering babies all her life, and I, as well. We'll make it as easy for you as possible."

344

"Thank you, Mildred. Your house is beautiful. Where is your husband?" Pearl politely asked.

"Oh, Charles is in St. Louis on business, always traveling about, buying and selling land. He'll be back next week. You'll meet him then. Tell me... the letter says that you're from the Filipina Islands. I'm dying to hear your story. How did you end up out on the Kansas prairie?"

Pearl spent about ten minutes quickly telling her life story, ending with, "...and that's how I ended up here."

"Please, come into the library. I have a book. Show me which island you're from."

Pearl followed Mildred down a corridor, which ended at two large doors. Pulling them open, Pearl was astonished at the number of books in the library-- hundreds of them. Stuffed animal trophy heads lined one wall, and a large fireplace with a huge mantel and clock over it occupied another wall.

Mildred selected a book from a specific shelf, opening it on a long reading table. She thumbed through the pages, finally saying, "Here it is... I knew I'd seen it before," pointing at a map entitled "Las Islas Filipinas."

Pearl had never seen a map of her islands, and stared for a long time at it. Embarrassed, she informed Mildred that she had forgotten how to read.

"Well, this island here has the city of Manila on it," she said, pointing it out. "And this island here has the city of Cebu on it," again pointing it out.

Excited, Pearl now informed her, "Cebu is close to my island. The sun sets on Cebu from where my island sits."

"Hmm, well perhaps it would be this one then. It's called Leyte," she pointed out.

"That's it! My island is called Leyte," Pearl excitedly touched the island with her finger.

"Show me! I want to see," Nellie insisted.

"Why don't you make yourself comfortable in here. Nellie can read to you from this book. I've got some errands I need to take care of," she smiled at Pearl, seeing her excitement after being shown the map.

The days that followed were spent almost entirely in the library, with Pearl selecting books and sitting on a couch next to Nellie, who enjoyed reading the contents to her. Pearl had lost her ability to read, having been away from books for over thirty years. One particular book fascinated both girls, titled "Alice's Adventures in Wonderland," filled with colorful surreal pictures. It became Nellie's favorite, and she would read it over and over again almost daily, pointing at the characters in the pictures, as she read the story. Pearl identified with the story, as it made her think about that day on the Medicine Mounds.

345

Weeks now passed, and it was obvious Pearl was due any day now. One morning, she woke up and could barely lumber herself out of bed. She walked over to the basin to wash her face, and at that moment, her water broke. Panicking, she called out to Nellie to come quick. Nellie's room was adjacent, and she heard the cry for help. Bursting into the room, Nellie grabbed her arm. "What is it? Are you alright?" Nellie looked wild-eyed.

"Go get Di and Mildred. Something's wrong! Hurry!"

Nellie was down the stairs in a flash and found both Mildred and Di in the kitchen. "Come quick--Pearl says something's wrong!" Nellie cried out.

The three hurried upstairs to find Pearl holding the basin to keep from falling, standing in a puddle of water.

Pearl burst into tears--a panicked look on her face.

"It's alright, honey chile…. the baby is coming. Let's get choo in da bed!"

Both women helped her back into bed, assuring her everything was alright and to relax and let the labor begin.

Mildred removed her shell medallion and her leather pouches from around her neck, and placed them on the bedside table. She bathed her arms and legs with a warm washcloth, telling her not to be afraid of the contractions that were now beginning to come.

Pearl asked for Nellie's hand, as the pain was coming in waves now. Di stood on the other side of the bed, coaxing and assuring her to push.

Mildred was up on the bed, between Pearl's legs, who now was also assuring Pearl and encouraging her.

"I can see the baby's head! Push hard, one more time Pearl!"

With a scream of agony, a moment later came a small cough, and the cry of a baby child could be heard.

Cutting the umbilical cord, Mildred smiled and passed the wet, crying baby to Pearl, gently laying the baby in the cradle of her exhausted arms.

"Lawd have mercy! Ain't she a pretty girl-chile!" Di laughed with relief.

The birth was a success, and the room was full of joy and laughter, thankful the ordeal was over, and that the baby girl was healthy.

The women spent the morning cleaning up the room and fussing over the baby. Nellie was in a state of wonderment, witnessing the event and now gently caressing the baby's head, as Pearl nursed her to her bosom. "What will you name her?" asked Nellie.

"I'm not sure. I guess I was waiting to see if it was going to be a boy or a girl. What should we call her, Nellie?"

"I like the name Alice…. the girl who went to Wonderland."

"Yes, I like that, too! A good choice. Yes, we'll name her Alice," Pearl laughed at Nellie's beaming face.

Nellie spent the day at Pearl's bedside. At one point, Nellie asked about the pouches and medallion that sat on the table. "Can I open one?" Nellie asked, curiously.

"I suppose so. I haven't opened them in years. Open that one there--the other needs to remain closed," Pearl pointed out. "Take that China dish and spill the pouch onto that," Pearl directed her.

Using her fingernails, it took several minutes to untie the tightly knotted pouch. Finally, she carefully dumped its contents. Several gleaming white and black pearls bounced across the plate, followed by several small green pellets. Shaking it gently, another small medallion fell out, with the face of a green jade Buddha on it.

"What are these pretty marbles?" Nellie asked Pearl.

"I found those in some shells a long time ago, when I was not much older than you," she explained.

"And what is this pretty green statue?" she held it up.

"That's called a Buddha--for good luck. A very nice man gave me that long ago," Pearl smiled.

The baby fussed and cried now. Nellie placed the plate on the table and caressed the baby as Pearl cooed to her. Mildred entered the room with a tray of juice, fruit, and bread. She ordered Nellie to move the plate, so that she could set the tray down next to the bed. "What have you got there, Nellie? What is that?" seeing the contents on the plate.

"They're things from Pearl's magic bag. Aren't they pretty?" She held up the plate as Mildred set the tray down.

"Let me see that, child," taking the plate from Nellie. She held one of the black pearls up, as big as a cat's eye, and stared at it. "Where did you get these?" she looked at Pearl in astonishment, gasping.

"I found them in some shells in Owyhee when I was a young girl," as she tapped her baby's nose.

Composing herself, Mildred asked, "May I take these and show them to Charles?"

"Of course. They're just good luck charms I've carried for years. Why? Is something wrong?" Pearl asked innocently.

"No, no. Everything's fine. You just tend that sweet baby. Nellie, you stay with her and help," and Mildred hurried from the room with the plate. Finding her husband downstairs in the library, who was looking at land acquisitions on the

347

table, she interrupted, "Charles.... do you have a minute? Look at this," she set the plate on the table next to the documents he was reading.

"My, my, my, what have we here?" looking up at Mildred.

"They belong to Pearl. She said she found them in the Sandwich Islands long ago," Mildred explained.

Charles moved his pipe to the other side of his mouth, and held one of the luminous orbs up to the monocle squeezed between his eye. "Are they valuable, Charles?" Mildred asked as he examined a couple more.

"I would think so. I'm no expert, but the widow Johnson has more jewelry than the Queen of Spain. I think she could tell us."

"Are you busy? Could you go and ask her?" Mildred insisted.

"Well, yes. What is this other stuff--these green tablets?" he asked.

"I don't know. I'll ask her," Mildred fretted.

"Here, put them in this empty candy jar. I'll walk over to her house and show them to her," he volunteered.

An hour later, he returned with the widow Johnson, a thin, small lady whose silver hair was in a bun. She wore an Italian Cameo choker around her neck, and her fingers were covered in sparkling rings.

"Clara... so nice to see you. It's been too long since our last tea. How are you?" as Mildred graciously met her in the entryway.

"Nice to see you, Mildred. You need to send Heb over and pick some roses for your vases, my dear," she kindly greeted her. "Mildred... Charles showed me these pearls. I was stunned by their beauty and quality. I have a jeweler in St. Louis, who I'd like to have make a brooch with them. What I'm saying is, I'd like to buy them from your guest, if she's willing to sell. I'll give her a fair market price, as their quality is exceptional and rare."

"Well, I'm sure she'll be pleased to hear this. Let's go ask her." Clara followed Mildred up to the room, walked in, and introduced the old woman. "Pearl, this is Clara Johnson. She has seen your collection of pearls, and would like to know if she could purchase them from you," Mildred volunteered.

"Huh? My good luck charms, the pearls? You mean you want to give me money for them?"

Clara nodded her head, "Yes," and then asked, "What can you tell me about these? How did you get them?"

"My brother and I were diving for shellfish, for food. When we brought them on the ship, the natives became fearful for their lives, as they explained that they belonged to the king and queen, and that we shouldn't have stolen them."

Clara gasped and gulped. "I'm curious. Is this why they call you Pearl?"

348

"Yes. The remainder of that voyage, everyone began to call me Pearl, and the name has stayed with me since then."

"Well, Pearl. You have something very valuable. I'm a collector of jewelry, and I'm willing to pay you $400 in gold, if you'd like to sell them to me."

Pearl was speechless. Stunned, she asked in disbelief, "What!?"

"I'll give you twenty $20 gold coins, right now, today if you'll sell them to me," the old woman offered.

Pearl looked at Mildred, who nodded her head "yes" with a big smile on her face.

"Yes. Yes, of course I'll sell them. I had no idea they were worth anything," Pearl was wide-eyed and stunned.

"I'll have Charles draw up the bill of sale. You can sign it, and he can put the gold coins in his safe for you. Do we have a deal?"

"Yes," Pearl shook her head in wonderment.

A beautiful baby girl and a clutch of gold coins… all on the same day. Alice and her were truly in wonderland, she thought.

"That's a beautiful baby. I'll send some roses over to freshen up the room," the widow offered as she excused herself.

Nellie and Dinah took turns watching over the baby that night, as Pearl fell into a blissful sleep, exhausted from the long, eventful day.

The baby Alice grew strong, and a month passed by since her birth. Nellie was whining now that she wanted to go home almost daily, that she missed her mother and father. Mildred finally gave the nod that Pearl and the baby girl were strong enough to travel and ride the train.

It was February now, 1879, and the cold North wind had stopped. Mildred prepared a wicker basket with a large handle, lining it with goose down feathers and a small fur blanket of rabbit. The baby was tucked in, and both Pearl and Nellie carried the basket between them out to the waiting carriage. Dinah had sewn the gold coins into a waistband that Pearl wore under her blouse for safekeeping. Charles was away again on business, and Dinah waved goodbye as the carriage pulled out of the brick, circular drive and onto the street. The ride to the Santa Fe depot was cold and drafty. Heb pulled the carriage up to the station platform, got down, and tied the horse to an iron hitching post. He helped the women down and followed them into the station with the carpet bag. The station was warm, a huge nickel plated iron wood stove heating the place. Mildred bought the tickets and chatted with Pearl and Nellie, fussing over the baby and giving last minute instructions.

The train finally pulled in, and it was time to go. Mildred and Heb said their goodbyes. She assured them that she'd wire Bill and Martha, letting them know of their arrival tomorrow.

As they boarded the car, the same Porter greeted them that had helped them weeks earlier. "Mercy, that's a pretty chile!" as he peeked in the basket. "I best throw some more wood on dat stove, warm this car up a bit for you ladies," he cheerfully nodded.

As the train pulled out, Pearl could see a tear on Mildred's face, as she and ol' Heb kept waving, until the car had passed the platform.

Soon, the train was up to speed, the pullman car clickety-clacking and swaying gently, rocking the baby and Nellie to sleep. Pearl enjoyed staring out the window at the scenery, passing farm after farm, across the rolling wooded countryside. They had been underway for over two hours, and Pearl was beginning to nod off when suddenly, horsemen appeared alongside the window, galloping past and overtaking the train.

Suddenly, the train lurched to a sudden stop. Pearl grabbed the baby basket before it hit the floor. As she soothed the baby Alice, two men burst in through the front door of the car, wearing flour sacks over their heads with eye holes. Both wore long trench coat dusters, that were splattered with fresh mud. They both waved pistols in the air, and one now called out, "This is a hold up. Everyone stand up and put your arms and hands in the air. Now, God damn it!" Stunned and shocked, a moment of silence and disbelief was upon the passengers.

"I said stand up and get your hands in the air, or I'll blow your head off! Now!"

Everyone was on their feet now, trembling, and three or four whimpers and muffled crying could be heard. "Anyone in here fight for General Lee and the stars and bars, for Dixie and the 'cause?'"

A man in front of Pearl spoke up, "I did!"

"Who were you with?" came the sharp response from the hooded men.

"I rode with Shelby's brigade, third cavalry."

"Who was your cavalry officer?" they further interrogated.

"Lt. Ruffner. He was killed at the battle of the crossroads."

"Alright, put your arms down. Don't do nothin' foolish, brother. Anybody else?" Again came the warning, "Keep your arms in the air and remain standing, or I'll put a bullet in your Yankee brain."

The two began moving down the aisle, as one held pistols on each victim, while the other frisked each one, removing jewelry, watches, wallets, and concealed derringers and dumping them in a burlap bag.

350

Alice began to cry loudly, annoying the two gunmen. "Shut that God damn baby up!" barked the man with the two pistols in each hand. The two robbers were now at Pearl and Nellie's seat. "Pick that baby up and shut it up," again came the angry command.

The two robbers moved on, frisking the people down and removing their valuables. Outside, three consecutive gunshots were now heard… *bang, bang, bang*.

"There's the signal, Bob… time to go! C'mon," the man with the pistols urged the other with the burlap sack of loot.

"Keep your arms in the air," one hollered as they slipped out the back of the car.

Now, a large group of bandits rode past the windows of the car on either side, and moments later, they were gone.

Finally, what seemed to be an eternity, the wild eyed Conductor entered the car, telling everyone to drop their arms. "It's alright now, folks… the bandits are gone. Is everyone okay? Was anyone injured?"

A wail of crying now began among the womenfolk, as the realization and fear subsided of what had just taken place.

The Conductor moved through the car, and assured each person that the danger was gone. The train sat motionless for another ten minutes, and finally started moving again. Now the black Porter appeared, handing out blankets and assurances. "Dat baby alright, missus?" he asked Pearl.

"Yes, she's fine. I wish I could say that about Nellie and myself. Who were those awful men?" Pearl asked the Porter.

"Dat was dem outlaws! The James brothers and da gang of rebel bandits! Ol' Jesse hisself held a gun on the engineer, and forced him to stop the train!" he said, wide-eyed.

Pearl now realized how lucky she had been, with Alice beginning to cry, just as the bandit was about to frisk her for valuables. She reached under her blouse, and checked the waistband of gold coins cinched around her waist.

That night, it was hard for anyone to sleep. The loss of their valuables and the trauma of the event had everyone thoroughly rattled. The next day, it was a long and monotonous ride across the Kansas prairie. As the train pulled into the Wichita depot, the Conductor ordered all to remain seated, as Pinkerton men wanted to take the statement of each individual, and ask questions about the robbery. Pearl explained her account to the detective, who wore a derby, and penciled her answers down to his questions.

Bill Lonker was waiting on the platform for them. Pearl was greatly relieved to see him, as they stepped down from the pullman car. Bill had heard the gossip of the robbery. Hugging Nellie, he looked at Pearl, saying, "Thank God you're okay. Those thieving devils! They didn't hurt you, did they?"

"Everything is okay, Bill. No, they did not harm us, but it was terrifying to have hooded men holding pistols on us!" Pearl told him.

"Let me take a peek at that baby!" he lifted up the fur blanket in the basket.

"Her name is Alice, daddy. Pearl let me name her. Isn't she beautiful?" Nellie proudly announced.

"That she is. Alright, let's get you ladies back to the house. Martha has a big dinner waiting for you. C'mon," he urged the women over to a waiting carriage and driver. He tossed the carpet bag in the back, and handed the baby basket up to Pearl, after she was seated.

Of course, Martha was horrified when she learned of the train robbery. Nellie retold the account over and over again at the dinner table, each time answering more questions about the holdup.

"Those scoundrels are notorious murderers. They shot and killed many people! That will be the last time anyone in this family rides the train to Missouri, until those bandits are captured!" insisted Martha. "Let's not talk about it anymore. Here, let me hold that sweet baby." She quickly changed the subject.

That spring, Corwin and John returned to Wichita, to resupply the trading post at Doan's Crossing. They were delighted to see Pearl and the new baby Alice. Both were doing well, and enjoyed the generosity and comfort of the Lonker's family. Corwin offered to take Pearl and the baby back to Texas, but Martha would have nothing to do with the suggestion, insisting the baby and Pearl were part of the Lonker family now.

By the summer of 1879, Pearl was helping in the hardware store, stocking shelves and doing odd jobs. She indeed had become part of the family, as Alice had become the center of attention for the whole Lonker clan. Nellie especially watched over the baby girl, seldom leaving her, like a second mother.

By December, Alice was weaned from Pearl's breast and was a plump, healthy baby girl. Pearl one night brought up the subject of her and the baby traveling to San Francisco, and voyaging to the Philippines. Martha and Nellie looked at each other, knowing that the subject had to be discussed. Martha volunteered her advice, saying,

"Pearl, we all know of your desire to go back to your homeland and visit with your family, as you should. Alice is still too fragile to endure a trip like that… a voyage across the ocean. She is so happy and safe here, part of the family. You have enough money to go and visit and return after one year. We will take care of Alice. She will be safe and well-cared for here. I truly wish you would consider it, for the sake of Alice."

Pearl had long thought about this dilemma, traveling with an infant baby, knowing it was risky. "I couldn't impose on you like that. You've been so gracious caring for us. It's such a chore to care for her daily, I...."

"Nonsense!" said Martha. "We love that child dearly. It would break our hearts to see her leave. Please, Pearl, let her stay while you go on this long journey."

Nellie now chimed in, her voice breaking, "Please, Auntie Pearl. Let Alice stay. I promise I'll take good care of her!"

"Let me think about this," Pearl smiled. "I'll give you the answer in the morning."

There was silence at the breakfast table the following morning, as the family waited to hear Pearl's decision. Sensing this, Pearl finally spoke up. "Well, I thought long and hard about this last night. I love this baby so much, as I know you do too. I feel if I don't go and see my mother and father soon, I may never get the chance again. So my answer is yes, Alice should stay here with you, if you're sure about this."

There was a squeal of delight from all the siblings, with Nellie and Martha overjoyed to hear Pearl's decision.

"When will you go, Pearl?" Nellie asked.

"Well, the sooner I leave, the sooner I can come back. I think next week, I'll ride the train to San Francisco."

The next few days saw Pearl busily packing and preparing for the return she had dreamed about for the last thirty years. On her last evening dinner with the Lonkers, she was assured of the baby's well-being. Sitting at the table, she removed the beautiful shell medallion from her neck, handing it to Nellie, saying, "This has always been my good luck piece. Wear it and keep it around Alice. She always liked playing with it when she was nursing."

The next morning, tearful goodbyes and assurances were exchanged, as Pearl kissed Alice one last time. Bill had a carriage pick himself and Alice up at the cottage, and he escorted her to the Santa Fe Depot. She had only spent $50 of her gold the previous year, and had $300 of the gold coins secreted to her waist in another money belt. The train ticket had been $40, and she kept $10 in a small purse for meals.

The pullman car was much more accomodating and luxurious compared to the one she had ridden to Missouri in. She found her seat and waved to Bill Lonker, as it pulled out of the Wichita depot. A Methodist preacher and his wife and child sat with Pearl in the adjoining seats. Very quickly, she engaged in friendly conversation, a relief for the long, six day journey ahead. The trip was uneventful, with no bandit holdups, as she had previously experienced. She enjoyed the mountain scenery, gazing out the window daily at the passing landscape. By the time they pulled into the San Francisco Depot, she had become good friends with the preacher and his wife, and they insisted that she come and stay with them at a relative's home, until her departure. This was fortunate for Pearl, as the city was a bustling maze of streets, where one could easily get lost, or be a victim of "foul play."

The preacher helped her secure passage on the "City of Peking," a Hong Kong bound steamship. Within four days of arriving in San Francisco, she was aboard the steamer, purchasing a small private cabin, and passage for $110. The ship made good time, utilizing both sail and her steam powered propeller. Pearl realized her decision to leave Alice with the Lonkers was a good one, as the food on board was not very good, and she found herself seasick for a number of days, staying in the cabin.

Once, a powerful storm seized the ship for almost three days, her decks awashed with waves, a terrifying experience for her, being all alone. The voyage took its toll on her, but after a little over a month at sea, the ship finally pulled into Hong Kong harbor. She had lost weight and was exhausted from the stress of the voyage. Her ability to speak Chinese quickly became a valuable asset. Through connections and advice of the steamship company, she found safe and reliable passage on a copra trading schooner, bound for Cebu in the Philippines. To her joy the crew were Filipinos, who relished in her stories about America, and her travels throughout.

She had struggled at first, having forgotten her dialect, but by the time the schooner reached the Luzon coast a week later, the words and language had all come back to her. The schooner entered the Visayan Sea, and four days later, they were finally anchoring in Cebu harbor. The sailors found her a safe fishing boat to cross the final hundred miles of the Canigao Strait, and finally, almost two months since she left Kansas and started her journey, there it was-- Matalom!

The fishing boat pulled up onto the beach at the old pirate watchtower, but nothing else looked familiar to Pearl. The seashore looked completely foreign and strange to her memory. She recognized the small island of Canigao offshore, where she and Pinto had been captured by the pirates, but the town itself had transformed into something totally unrecognizable. She spotted an old man on the beach, loading fresh fish into a basket hanging on the side of a donkey. She now approached him and offered a few pesos, if he would take her bags to the church.

"Yes, of course. Put your bags on the burro. I will take you to the church," he readily agreed. "You are not from around here? You come from where?" he asked her.

"My family lives here. The Melendres. Do you know them?" she questioned him.

"That name sounds familiar, but I don't know of anyone around here called that," as he shook his head and scratched his whiskers.

"There used to be houses over there, on that hill. What happened to them?" she now asked.

"I came here twenty years ago, after the big typhoon. There's never been any houses there that I can remember," he shook his head.

As they walked through the town, she searched the faces and landmarks for something recognizable, but was totally at a loss to strike anything out of her memory. Finally, there was the old Spanish church, a beautiful stone edifice that she recognized instantly. The old man dropped her two bags on the steps, and she gratefully paid him three pesos.

Entering the sanctuary, the musty smell and stained glass windows grasped her memory. She knelt, made the sign of the cross, and approached the altar. The sanctuary was silent, and she again knelt and prayed for a long time. Finally, a priest entered from a side vestibule, making his rounds. Seeing her, he cheerfully nodded and said, "Good afternoon."

"Good afternoon, Father. May I speak with you?" she asked meekly.

"Of course. You're an unfamiliar face. I'm Father Sanchez."

"Yes, Father. My name is Juana Melendres. I've traveled very far to come here. You see, I was a young girl who once lived here… thirty years ago. I was kidnapped by pirates. It's a long story, but I have not been able to return until now. I'm seeking my mother and father--Dionisio and Maxima Melendres, who live upriver. They both take communion here in this church."

The priest looked at Pearl, mystified by her statement. "You say you have been gone thirty years?" he now asked in amazement.

"Yes, and nothing looks familiar. Everything has changed, yet this church is the only thing I recognize," she looked bewildered.

"Please, let's go out in the courtyard and talk. Sit by the fountain. It's much cooler and shady there," he urged her. "Follow me."

The courtyard within the stone walls was pleasant, filled with shade trees. They both sat on a stone bench. "I have something to tell you, and it's not a pleasant story. Twenty years ago, a massive typhoon struck this island, killing thousands of people. It was total devastation. This whole barangay was wiped out. The only thing left standing was the church, and even part of its roof was

355

destroyed. The priest also was lost and died in the raging wind and rain. Everyone who lived along the river was swept away by the flood. The wind stripped the jungle of all vegetation. Only bare sticks of coconut trees were left standing. When it was over, there were very few survivors. The church in Cebu sent me here then, to help rebuild and guide the few survivors. That is why you do not recognize anything. What you remember was all destroyed, except the church and the old Spanish watchtower. I can tell you that I know of no one named Melendres in the flock of the church, but I do know of someone by that name. After the storm, several people decided to build a new, stronger church to the north… a place called "Bato," or "the place of stones." There are many rocks there, and so a fine, strong church of stone was built to withstand any more of those types of typhoons. I have given Mass at this church many times, and given communion and taken confessions there. There is a poor woman there, a beggar, whose name is Dely Melendres, who I have taken confession from. Do you know her?"

Pearl gasped, "That is my sister, Father."

"Let me warn you about her. She is crippled, a beggar, who begs in the fish market. She is there daily. I do not know where she lives. It's too late in the day to go. Bato is five miles to the north. You can stay tonight at the nun's convent. There is a Kalesa that can take you to the fish market in the morning. Come, I will introduce you to the Mother Superior."

The nun was very kind and gracious, offering Pearl soup and bread. A small room was shown to her after the meal, and she fell asleep instantly on the primitive bamboo bed. The following morning, the nun gently awoke her from a deep sleep, saying, "The Kalesa is out front, waiting to take you to Bato."

The nun gave her tea and bread, then helped her with her bags out to the waiting two-wheeled horse cart. Pearl thanked the Sister, giving her pesos for her hospitality.

It had rained the night before, so the road was muddy, making it harder for the horse to pull the cart. Finally, the driver got off, and walked the horse, easing the burden for the animal.

Bato was a thriving fishing village--a crossroads and center of activity. The fish market was a long, thatched nipa roofed building adjacent to the beach. Several fishing bancas were on the beach, and anchored just offshore. Each fisherman's family had a stall in the market. The sounds and smells mingled with a sea of human activity. People called out the day's catch and haggled over prices.

Pearl was perplexed as what to do next. The Kalesa driver sensed her confusion, not knowing what to do with her bags. Across the road from the fish market, several vegetable vendors were set up, sitting under thatch umbrellas. "I have a friend who sells vegetables... there," he pointed. "They will watch your bags, while you search for your sister."

"Thank you. Yes, I need to walk around and ask some questions," she was relieved that he had solved her dilemma.

Carrying her two bags over to one of the umbrellas, he introduced Pearl to two teenage girls. "Maria... Luna... this is Pearl. Can you watch her bags while she is in the fish market?" Both girls nodded yes and smiled. The driver now turned, holding his hand out to Pearl for payment. He asked for five pesos, and she gave him seven, pleasing him greatly. He bowed and returned to his cart, guiding it over to a shade tree to wait for another customer.

The girls were selling bananas and mangoes, so Pearl picked out two nice bananas, paying Maria. The market was crowded with people coming and going. Part of the problem was that Pearl had no idea what Dely looked like. She was a nine-year-old girl when she last saw her, and she could barely remember her facial features. Pearl ate a banana, searching the faces of the sea of activity. "Do you girls come here every day?" Pearl asked the two shy teenage girls.

"We come Tuesday, Thursday, and Saturday to sell vegetables," Maria replied. "Where are you from?" she now asked.

"I'm from America. I've come to try and find my sister," Pearl explained.

"You are from America?" Maria asked in astonishment.

"Yes, although long ago, I lived in Matalom," Pearl explained.

"You must come and meet Pastor Thurman and his wife. They are from America," Maria now explained excitedly.

"Oh, there are Americans here?" Pearl was surprised.

"Yes, they are Baptist Missionaries who run our orphanage! Our orphanage grows vegetables and we sell them here," she explained.

"Well, yes, I would like to meet them. Where is your orphanage?"

"It's two miles up the road, toward Hilongos. We can take you there," Luna now offered.

"Perhaps you girls can help me. I'm looking for a beggar woman, named Dely. They say she is crippled, she comes.... "

Both girls raised their arms and pointed at the same time in the same direction. Maria spoke, "There... see her sitting with her head down, the straw hat and bucket?" Pearl was astonished by her luck. If this was her lost sister, a prayer had been answered, given up in the Matalom church, asking God to help her find her family.

She crossed the road and kneeled down in front of the pathetic sight. The woman was dressed in rags, her head down, with one hand held out, palm up. She wore a ragged, straw sombrero hat, covering her face. The rusty bucket held a couple dozen clams. Her feet were black with dirt and calloused. "Dely--Dely, is that you?" Pearl called to her softly.

The woman slowly raised her head, holding out her palm, saying, "One peso for twelve clams," then slowly bowed her head again, as if she had little strength.

Pearl took her hand and softly spoke, "Dely--Dely, it's me, Juana. It's me, Juana."

The woman slowly raised her head, and the two locked into a gaze into each other's eyes. It was her sister! She could see it, staring at her face. At the same moment, Dely realized who she was looking at, and began to tremble and cry softly. Pearl kissed her softly on the forehead and began to cry as well. She tried to hug her but then realized her left arm was hanging limply. She took her hand and held it to her face, as both women sobbed. "C'mon, Dely. Stand up. Let's get you some good food," Pearl sobbed as she realized how emaciated Dely was. She helped her stand, and Dely attempted to grab the rusty old bucket.

"Leave that here. You aren't going to need that anymore. Here, let me help you," Pearl put her arm around her waist. She now realized how badly she was crippled, her left arm hanging at her side, as she hobbled with a distinct limp with the left leg.

Slowly, they made it back across the road to the girls' vegetable stand. Pearl sat her in the shade, next to her bags, and bought bread from a passing cart, and Luna offered the pathetic woman fresh water from a gourd.

"Tell me, Maria... would this Pastor Thurman rent me a room for two or three nights, until I can nurse my sister back to life?"

"Yes, of course. We have a school there with two dormatories. I'm sure Pastor Thurman would help you. He is a man who teaches Jesus's ways."

Pearl looked back across the road. The Kalesa and driver were still there, sitting in the shade. Without hesitating, she hurried across the road. "I'm glad you're still here. Tell me--could I hire you to take me up the road to the Baptist Orphanage?" she pleaded.

"Of course. Did you find your sister?" he asked.

"Yes, she's sitting there, at your friends' vegetable stand," pointing her out.

"The beggar woman, that is your sister?" he recognized her.

"Yes. Bring your Kalesa. We will go now," waving him to follow.

Marching back to the girls' stand, Pearl announced, "Maria, Luna, I'm buying all of your bananas and mangoes. I will give them to the children at the orphanage. Can you take me there?" By then, the Kalesa was in front of them. "Put the bananas and mangoes on the cart. Help me with my sister," as Pearl took charge.

Sitting next to Dely on the cart, as the driver walked the horse along, Pearl finally took the opportunity to ask about the family. She dreaded the answer, knowing that Dely couldn't have become destitute if they were still around. "What happened to mama and papa, Dely. Tell me, I must know."

"They have been gone a long time, Juana... so long ago. We were happy. Pinto had returned, and mama and papa were overjoyed that you were still alive. We all thought you had been lost and drowned at sea. Pinto had a little money, and bought a fishing boat with a sail. He met a woman from Samar whom he fell in love with. He took her back to her family in Samar, and we never saw him again. A couple years after he left, a giant typhoon struck the island. The river was flooded so badly, it washed away the house. Mama and Papa put us all up in a tugas tree," then Dely began to sob. "The wind was so awful, screaming, it knocked down another large tree, which fell on the one we were all up in. It knocked everyone into the river. They were all swept away. I was pinned under a branch, both my arm and leg were squashed, but it kept me from being blown away. I was found two days later by some mountain people, who got me out of the tree. They kept me alive, but realized I was useless, a cripple, another mouth to feed. They brought me to the beach and deserted me. Since then, I have lived off clams and lizards and handouts. I came here when they built the church. They would give me rice to help gather stones to build it."

Tears were on Pearl's face, the story so unbearable to hear. "Where do you stay--where do you sleep?" Pearl was in shock.

"It's nothing... a nest of banana leaves. I only have one good hand. I cannot make a nipa roof. I dig clams in the morning with one hand, enough to buy a cup of rice."

"What happened to Black Ghost, our uncle, the *wak wak* in the tree?" Pearl pressed her.

"The mountain people went to get him, to tell him they had found me. They said there was nothing left... the treehouse blown away, no macaque monkeys, or his black birds. All gone, including him. The tree was nothing more than a trunk with shattered, broken branches. The wind blew it all away!"

Maria and Luna were walking up ahead, and now stopped, pointing at some huts in the jungle. A small sign on the road read "Baptist School and Orphanage." Maria and Luna called out, announcing their arrival, and fifty or sixty children of all ages clamored out of a large open air thatched building, abandoning a white haired white man at a chalkboard. The children all gathered around the cart, welcoming a break in their daily routine.

Now, the white haired Pastor Thurman came out, and quieted the excited group. "Maria… you have brought us visitors. Help them down, children. Show some manners," he commanded them.

Pearl stepped forward, introducing herself, "Father, my name is Juana Melendres, I have traveled very far, from America, and I have nowhere to stay. Maria and Luna said you might be able to help myself and my sister."

"Of course, Juana. The Lord's house is always open to those who seek him." He now was looking at Dely, who he recognized from town. "And this poor soul is your sister?" he asked Pearl.

"Yes, this is my sister. She was one of the sole survivors of the typhoon many years ago. By the grace of God, I have found her and can now care for her."

"Bless you, Juana. I have seen this woman many times… in fact, dropped pesos in her hand. She is lucky you have come along. Her condition has deteriorated over the years." He now saw all of the bananas and mangoes on the cart. "A slow day in the market, Maria?"

Pearl answered for her, "I purchased all of them, to give to your children here. Tell me how much to pay you."

"Bless you, Juana. You have a good heart. We'll worry about money later. Children, unload the cart and have a snack. School is dismissed the remainder of the day!"

Pearl overpaid the cart driver again, and as before, he was pleased and on his way. Hearing all the commotion, Pastor Thurman's wife appeared from a diamond mat nipa hut. "Juana, this is my wife, Elizabeth, the heart and soul of our school and refuge here."

She graciously shook Pearl's hand, and then saw Dely, the wretch standing behind her. "This is my sister, Dely. I need to bathe her. Do you have some soap I can use?"

"Yes, of course. Come this way, the pump is over there, I'll get a fresh cake of soap," Elizabeth offered without hesitation. "I have a clean blouse and skirt she can wear. Poor thing… Maria, bring their bags into the house."

The bath and clean clothes revitalized Dely, bringing a smile back to her face. "Come into the house. I've got dinner on the table," Elizabeth now insisted.

Sitting at the table, the Pastor said a prayer over the food, then entered into a long dialog of the history of the school. "We came here five years ago, from Boston, as missionaries for our Baptist Church. Our original plan was to house, feed, and educate around thirty orphans, but there are so many here, we quickly exceeded that number. We are on a limited budget that the church sends once a year, so our gardens of fruits and vegetables help feed and pay for our school. It is difficult, but by the grace of God, we manage. Please, tell us your story, Juana."

Pearl spent the next half hour telling the tale of her last thirty years. Pearl spoke in English, so Dely of course could not understand what she was saying. Dely was preoccupied with the dinner, gorging herself with bread, fruit, and chicken soup.

"And so you traveled all the way from Kansas, only to find this last survivor of your family... I am sorry for you Juana. What are your plans? What will you do now?" Pastor Thurman questioned.

"Well, I had planned to stay and visit with my mother and father for several months and then return to Kansas, but obviously, circumstances require a change in plan. As soon as Dely is strong and feeling better, I guess I'll take her with me back to Hong Kong, and return to San Francisco."

"Juana, do you have a husband in America... and a marriage certificate with you?" the Pastor now raised his eyebrows.

"No, I'm not married, Pastor." She had mentioned her child Alice in telling her story.

"Juana, are you aware of the 'Page Act,' the new immigration law in America?" he now looked concerned.

"Why, no. The Page Act... what is that?" Pearl could see his concern.

"Three years ago, I wrote a letter to our church in Boston, asking the congregation to adopt Maria and Luna. The following year, I received a formal reply, stating that the U.S. Congress had passed a law--the Page Act--that states ALL Asian women will no longer be allowed to enter the Continental United States. I contacted the American Consul in Hong Kong upon hearing this, and they confirmed it, saying no Asian women could be sold passage tickets on the steamer from Hong Kong to San Francisco. No one told you about this?"

Pearl was speechless and stared at the Pastor in disbelief. "What do you mean? Why? I don't understand!" she stammered.

"There has been a huge influx of Chinese into California over the years... so many that they almost outnumber the white people. A congressman figured that if Asian women were not allowed into the country, the Chinese men would leave, and return to China."

"But I'm not Chinese!" Pearl wailed.

"That's a general term they use--anyone from Asia is considered to be Chinese. They will not sell you and your sister passage in Hong Kong... I'm sorry," the Pastor was soft spoken.

361

"Then we'll go to Manila. We can catch a schooner going to San Francisco," Pearl was shaking her head. "I know people in Owyhee, the Sandwich Islands, who work for the Hudson Bay Co. They can help us."

"The Hudson Bay Co. is no longer in Owyhee. They left years ago and moved their trading post to the gold fields of the Fraser River. If you go to Owyhee, you will end up as a slave in the sugar cane fields. If you try and pay a smuggler to take you to San Francisco, they will take your money, rape you all the way across the ocean, then throw you in the bay before they enter San Francisco. It is a heavy fine and prison if you are caught in human smuggling," the Pastor now advised her.

Pearl was speechless and at a total loss for words. She hung her head and tears fell into her bowl of soup. "I don't know what I'm going to do, Pastor Thurman. I have nowhere to go," she sobbed.

Pastor Thurman looked at his wife. Both were in sympathy and groped for something to say. Finally, the Pastor spoke up, "Juana… You tell me you can speak Spanish, English, Chinese, and Visayan. You could stay here with us as a teacher to the children. We cannot offer you money. Food and a roof over your head is all we can provide. But I think that under the circumstances, God has guided you to us. You're welcome to stay--you and your sister. Take some time and think about it."

Elizabeth now spoke up "Yes, he's right, Juana. You're welcome to stay here and teach the children. I'd welcome some extra help around here. That's enough for one day. You look exhausted. Let me show you to the spare room in the house. Both of you need to rest. Come with me," she directed.

The room was a welcome refuge for both sisters. Pearl helped Dely to bed, then laid on her back and stared at the ceiling in disbelief.

Both sisters awoke late the next morning, hearing the sound of giggling children outside. They emerged from their room and found the dining table with fresh fruit, bread, rice, and juice of the pineapple. Elizabeth heard them talking from the kitchen and entered, insisting they sit down and eat breakfast. She summoned Maria and Luna, saying, "Take Juana and Dely down to the beach. Show them around after they finish breakfast."

The beach was a beautiful spot. White sands with leaning coconut trees lined a turquoise shoreline. Maria and Luna swam in the sea while Pearl and Dely relaxed and talked about early childhood memories.

Pearl mulled over their situation. There was no sense in denying the fact. Pastor Thurman had said that it was the law now, and Hong Kong would not let her return through their port and that she would not be allowed back into the U.S. She'd been in these situations her whole life. She'd have to make the best of things. *These dramas seem to follow me around in life,* she thought. *Somehow, things will work out for the best,* she convinced herself. None of it really mattered now because her sister, Dely, needed her badly. Perhaps the Pastor was right. God had guided her to her crippled sister, and now she had provided food and shelter.

She still had nine twenty dollar gold pieces secreted away in her bag. It wasn't enough to buy passage back for the two of them anyway. Pondering no more, she decided to take the Pastor's offer and teach at the school.

That night, at the dinner table she conceded and accepted the teaching job.

"I've never been a teacher. I'm not sure how to go about it, Pastor Thurman," she confessed. "I can't read or write anymore… I only remember the words and what they mean."

"That's alright, you can teach as a translator. Give them a word in Visayan, then translate it to English for them. You can sound out simple sentences in the dialect, then repeat them in English. They are good learners. We'll start tomorrow. I'll give the morning lesson and show them how to spell the words you translate. We'll be a team!" the Pastor was getting excited.

In the days ahead, Pearl quickly got over her doubts as a teacher, and was now enjoying the role, seeing the children's faces light up as she drilled the words into them. Dely was happy and smiling now. The daily bath and fresh, good food had brought new life back to her.

Weeks passed, and now Pearl had settled into the routine, and had become a part of the school. She and her students both enjoyed the classroom time. The children made her long for Alice, but the baby girl was as far away as the stars now. She would tell a short story each day about her experience in America, then retell it in English. It became a much anticipated part of her class, with the students silent and straining to listen. Her stories of buffalo, bears, Indians and wild horses fascinated them.

Each Saturday, Pearl would go with Maria and Luna to the market in Bato and sell vegetables. It was Pearl's chore to take some of the money from the vegetable sales and buy some fresh fish in the market to bring back. Sunday was a day of worship at the orphanage, followed by a fish fry for dinner.

It was on one of these Saturdays that Pearl sat with the girls under the thatch umbrella of their vegetable display. Maria spotted three sails coming from the north towards Bato.

"Those are fishermen from Samar! They come twice a year and sell fresh shark. Here, take the pesos, meet them on the beach, and buy some! Hurry, they will sell out very quickly!" Maria urged her. Pearl's mind raced as she remembered what Dely had said…. *Pinto had gone to Samar with his fishing boat!*

She hurried down to the beach and watched with anticipation as the three bancas approached. They dropped their sails, and slid to a sandy stop on the beach. A crowd had already gathered with the same intentions as her-- wanting to buy some before it was all gone. There was a total of six fishermen, and she frantically searched their faces for Pinto. Not seeing him, she waited her turn, as the sharks were being cut up and sold.

"How many, Doña?" the fisherman asked Pearl.

"Those two there." She pointed.

"Ten pesos," he held his hand out. She dropped the coins into his hand, and he handed the two sharks to her, both the length of her arm.

"What is your name?" Pearl asked. He looked at her, perplexed.

"Rico."

"Rico, do you know a man named Pinto Melendres--a fisherman?" asked Pearl. He looked at her with a wry smile.

"Yes, I know Pinto…. He is married to my cousin. They live in Barangay Lawaan. They have many children." he nodded.

Pearl was astonished at her luck. "His name is Pinto Melendres… you're sure?!" she pressed him.

"Yes, he is from Matalom, on this island. He met my cousin long ago. They have a large family. I always see him at fiesta… how do you know him?" Rico was grinning now.

"He's my brother, Rico!"

In utter disbelief, Pearl dropped both sharks on the beach and grabbed both wrists of Rico. "You must take me to him!" she pleaded.

Rico shook his head, confused. "What is your name? You are his sister?"

"My name is Juana…. Juana Melendres. Please take me to him-- please!"

"We are traveling south. It will be weeks before we return to Samar. I am very poor and must catch many sharks before we return to our village. I must…."

Pearl stopped him mid-sentence. "I will pay you an American twenty dollar gold piece if you take me to him!" she blurted out without hesitation. Astonished, Rico stared at her in disbelief. It would take him months of fishing to earn the equivalent of twenty dollars in gold. He questioned her, still not believing what he was hearing.

"You will give me twenty dollars in gold to take you to Lawaan?"

"Yes, yes. You have my word! I will pay you when we arrive at my brother's house!"

"And when do you wish to depart?" Rico scratched his head and stared at her.

"Tomorrow morning... and I'm bringing a sister with me. How many days is the voyage to this place?" Pearl excitedly asked.

"Six to seven days, depending on the wind. You will need to bring your own food, as I cannot feed you," Rico replied. Now, he turned and addressed his companions on the beach. "I'm returning to Samar… this woman is paying me to take her to Lawaan. Good luck, my friends. I will see you at fiesta, when you return."

Big-eyed, Pearl asked him, "So we have a deal?"

"You just heard me tell my friends! I will camp here tonight on the beach. Be here at first light in the morning so that we can catch the outgoing tide."

Pearl joyously hugged Rico. "*Salamat, salamat, salamat!* I will be here, I promise!" She turned and ran with excitement to tell Maria and Luna.

Rico hollered at her, and she spun around. "Aren't you forgetting something?" He pointed at the two sharks laying on the beach. Laughing and smiling, she returned and scooped them up.

"Thank you Rico--*salamat*… I will see you in the morning!" she beamed.

"Make sure you bring food for seven days," he reminded her. Smiling, she nodded vigorously.

By the time she reached Maria and Luna at the vegetable stand, she was weeping with joy. "What is it? What?" asked Maria. Pearl explained her unbelievable luck and what had just transpired during the shark purchase.

"God is watching over you, Juana. We are happy for you but sad to see you go," both Maria and Luna lamented.

Pearl insisted that they return to the orphanage at once. Upon arriving, Pastor Thurman greeted them, wondering why they had returned so early in the day. Hearing the story, the Pastor patted her on the shoulder, saying, "We have grown fond of you and your sister. We will all miss you. The Lord works in mysterious ways, and obviously, he has heard your prayers."

Upon hearing of Pearl's plans for departure, Elizabeth began to weep but quickly composed herself, saying, "Come, now... we need to get your things packed. We'll bake extra bread for you to take with you."

When Pearl told Dely about the fortunate encounter on the beach, Dely smiled with a big gleam in her eye and gave her sister a one-armed hug. Her memories of Pinto were distant. It was obvious of the aura of excitement that was now upon Pearl, and Dely could feel her sister's joy. On the contrary, it was a subdued and solemn afternoon at the orphanage, for the children had come to adore Pearl. Her teaching and stories would be sorely missed. The sharks were cut into small steaks, enough for everyone to have a piece, and a farewell dinner was enjoyed that evening. The pastor gave a long prayer and blessing, asking for a safe voyage for Juana and Dely.

Early the next morning, Maria and Luna helped Pearl and Dely load a small burro with their meager belongings and foodstuffs. Pastor Thurman and Elizabeth made their teary eyed goodbyes, and the women departed, heading for the beach at Bato. Arriving, they discovered Rico's companions had already departed a half hour earlier. Their sails could be seen in the distance, heading south in the morning sun.

"C'mon... no time to waste. We have a long way to go today," Rico urged the women. "Here, let's tie your food sack up on the mast to keep it dry." He pushed the banca into knee deep water, then helped the two climb aboard. Paddling to deeper water, he now found the current and raised the tattered mat sail. Maria and Luna sadly waved goodbye from the beach. Pearl and Dely returned the wave until the two were far out in the channel. Catching a following breeze and riding the outgoing tide, the little banca was now cutting a course to the north. Within a half hour, they were passing the church bell tower of Hilongos, poking above the waving coconut trees on the distant shoreline. A dark rain squall now appeared to the north, and Rico hesitated, realizing they should put to shore and let it pass. Normally, he would have surged ahead, but the safety of the women was a concern, and he wanted his gold coin. He decided to play it safe. He saw a beach up ahead, and pointed the banca towards its safety.

Just as he beached, the rain began to fall heavily. Grabbing the food sack, Pearl and Dely scrambled across the beach to the shelter of the coconut groves. They found a crude fisherman's shelter to stay dry under, as the rain was coming down in torrents now. Rico finished tying up the banca and then joined them. Twenty minutes later, the squall had passed, and the rain began to diminish.

"Alright, it's safe now. We can continue. Let's go." Rico checked the sky. Just then, a crow landed on top of the shelter and began to *caw-caw*. Pearl stepped out from under the shelter and looked up at him. He cocked his head, and continued cawing. Pearl answered with a series of caws and then began to *click-click* at him, maintaining eye contact. To the amazement of Rico and Dely, the bird now jumped from the roof to Pearl's shoulder. He gently nibbled at her ear, and Pearl laughed at his tickling.

"My God!" said Rico "It's as if you're talking to him!"

"I am talking to him. He wants us to follow him," Pearl flatly stated. "C'mon, let's see what he wants to show us." The bird flew from her shoulder and landed on the ground fifty feet away. He cawed and beckoned them to follow. All of a sudden, several crows now landed in the coconut trees around them. They continued to follow the one on the ground, who hopped along and continued to urge them to follow. Coming into a clearing, they came to a nipa hut. A man was tending a cooking fire and looked up when the crow announced their arrival. The bird now flew back and landed on Pearl's shoulder. The man stood up from his cooking fire and waved for them to approach.

"I see my friend Matoo has taken a liking to you," the man chuckled.

"Yes, he's quite the talker," Pearl acknowledged.

"Who are you? What brings you here?" The man now wanted to know.

"My name is Juana. This is my sister, Dely, and our friend, Rico. He is taking us to Samar. The rain squall forced us to beach and wait for it to pass."

"I see. Would you like some fish stew?" he offered.

"Thank you--*salamat*--but we are pressed for time. We must be on our way," Rico answered for Pearl.

"I've never seen Matoo on a stranger's shoulder. He seems to like you. What is your secret?" the man asked.

"What is your name?" Pearl asked.

"They call me Milo. This beach is my home--the beach of crows. They call it Owak," he explained.

"So the crows belong to you?" Rico asked.

"This flock belongs to Matoo, who is my protector," Milo answered. Milo looked at Pearl and now chattered a series of clicks, and the bird flew from her shoulder to his.

"How did you acquire a crow as a protector?" Pearl now looked Milo in the eye.

"It's a long story, but Matoo has been with me for over ten years," Milo offered.

"Please tell me the story," Pearl insisted.

"We need to go, Juana," Rico insisted. Pearl held her hand up to Rico, dismissing him.

"Please, Milo, I want to know how you acquired this bird," she pleaded.

"Alright… I'll tell you the story. I think it was eleven or twelve years ago. I was hunting a wild pig with my cousin, away to the south of here. The pig was very elusive, and we tracked him for a couple of days, deep into the jungle. His trail kept climbing higher and higher into the mountains. We would catch a glimpse of him as he climbed further up. We came into a clearing, high up on the mountain, and stopped to catch our breath. All of a sudden, a huge flock of crows surrounded us in the canopy of the trees around a clearing. They were all cawing, making quite a noise. Irritated, I shot an arrow at one and thankfully missed, as I later learned. Suddenly, two dozen macaque monkeys appeared and surrounded us, snarling and showing their fangs. We were terrified, and we stood back to back in the clearing to defend ourselves. That's when we heard a voice, commanding us to put our bows and arrows on the ground. We did so, not knowing where the voice was coming from. Suddenly, Satan himself stepped out into the clearing. He wore a mask and was painted black and feathered up. He commanded the crows to be silent and ordered the macaques to stand down.

"'Who are you?' he demanded.

"'We are hunters, chasing a wild pig,' we answered fearfully.

"'Why are you shooting arrows at my birds!?' he demanded.

"'We were frightened,' came my answer.

"'Well, you are lucky! If you would have hit one, they would have swooped down and pecked your eyes out, and the macaques would've finished you off and chewed you to pieces!' he sternly warned.

"Satan then approached us, removed his mask, and began laughing at us. 'You're a sorry ass couple of hunters…. when did you last eat?'

"We could now see he was a mortal man. 'We've been eating fruit off the trail,' I meekly told him.

"'Follow me. I will feed you. Then I want you to leave my mountain," he commanded. We obeyed and followed him and after about ten minutes came to a huge banyan tree that stood before a large cave in the mountain. The flock of crows landed in the banyan tree as he beckoned us to follow him into the cave. The interior of the cave was furnished in comfort, and he told us to sit on some bamboo chairs. He offered us some cooked *lechon* to eat, which we hungrily devoured. Finally losing our fear, I asked him who he was… and what was this place.

"He explained, 'My name is Lolung… some people call me the Black Ghost. Many, many years ago, a strong typhoon descended upon my old home in the valley below. My birds--my protectors--warned me of its oncoming onslaught. We all fled to this mountain cave to ride the storm out. The typhoon destroyed my home in the valley, and so it is here that I have remained to this day. People never come up here… in fact, you two are the first people I have seen in many years. I live here in peace with my birds and macaques, but it is nice to talk to a human being again, I will admit.'

"We now felt at ease in his company, and a lively conversation continued through the day. We decided it was time to go that afternoon, but he now insisted that we stay the night, as it was getting towards sundown. That night, the conversation continued, and he lamented that he was getting old and would soon pass. He was worried about who would care for his birds and we questioned him about that.

"He explained that he had a secret potion that he gave a chosen few birds--his favorites. It was given once a year, when they molted, rejuvenating the heart, and that the bird would live much longer than a normal crow. He then looked at us, saying, 'Indeed, I might die tomorrow, and the secret formula would be lost. I'm going to tell you both the magic formula and recipe. In doing so, I will give you both a protector, who will follow you to your dying day.' He then divulged the recipe, and how to create this little green pellet. The next morning, he climbed into the banyan tree, creating a huge raucous, and retrieved several objects from two nests. Tying them into bundles, he made each of us a necklace to wear. From that day on, Matoo has always followed me wherever I go and watches over me. We departed from old Lolung and the cave that day, and I have never returned. I doubt that he is still alive. Do you believe me Juana?" Milo asked as he finished the tale.

Pearl smiled and nodded, "Yes, I believe you. I have heard the story and legend of the Black Ghost before." She divulged no more of her secret.

"C'mon!" insisted Rico. "Enough of these stories of witchcraft!" Pearl thanked Milo for his hospitality, said their goodbyes, and were soon back on the beach. Rico launched the banca, got underway, and they watched as Owak disappeared behind them. At sundown, they camped on a deserted beach and continued the next day with favoring winds. On the third day, they rounded a point and began heading east, following the Leyte shoreline. To the north of the channel, a beautiful island could be seen. Its interior climbed up the cone of a giant, dormant volcano, shrouded in cloud mists.

"What is that beautiful island called?" Pearl asked Rico.

"It's called Biliran. The old Spaniards of long ago built galleons up on one of its rivers, floating them down to the sea. But that was long ago." he explained.

On the fifth day, Rico pointed to the east, saying, "On the horizon, you can now see the island of Samar."

They were blessed with fair weather, and on the morning of the seventh day, after leaving their overnight beach, Rico pointed to a small group of boats in the distance. "Those fishermen are from Lawaan. We'll be there in two hours."

"Is my brother among them?" Pearl asked excitedly, as they approached the fishing boats.

"I don't see his banca." Rico scanned the cluster of boats. "There's a friend of mine. I'll ask him." He steered their banca away from their nets.

"Dong, it's me... Rico! How's the catch this morning?" he greeted the man across the water, who was pulling in his net.

"Rico! What are you doing here? I thought you went shark fishing!" he asked, surprised.

"Where is Pinto? I don't see his boat out here," Rico asked.

"He ripped his net on a coral head two days ago. He's in the village repairing it," came the answer. "Who are your lady friends?"

"They say they are Pinto's sisters. They found me by luck and asked me to bring them to him." Rico's outrigger was clipping along, and now Dong waved him off and went back to pulling in his net. Rico kept the banca on a steady tack towards smoke that could be seen on the shoreline in the distance. The clear blue saltwater became murky now as they entered the Lawaan river. Up ahead, a long line of nipa huts on stilts lined the riverbank. As they approached, Pearl could now see the community buzzing with activity. Children were playing, women doing wash on the riverbank, and fishermen were tending their fish drying racks.

"See that house? Where the dog is? I think that's Pinto there, working on that net," Rico pointed out to Pearl. The man had his back to the sea, and when Rico was close enough, he called out to him.

"Hey brother, you can't catch fish when you're sitting on the dock!"

370

The man turned and grinned, saying, "You can't catch shark either when you have a boat full of women!"

Pearl recognized him and his voice instantly and burst into tears. Rico skillfully pulled up to the hut on stilts and threw Pinto a mooring line.

"What brings you here? Your cousin is picking mangoes this morning." Pinto was not paying any attention to the two women, as he joked with his wife's cousin.

"I brought you some visitors--do you know them?" Rico asked.

Pinto and Pearl locked eyes. He could see the tears streaming down her face and her lip quivering. In disbelief, he called out to her, "Juana?"

She held her arms out to him, and he jumped from the dock onto the boat, embracing her, crying out in shock. He took her face and held it in his hands, weeping with joy. Dely could only smile and enjoy the moment. She had been a young adolescent in the family and did not have the close bond that Juana and Pinto had. Finally, after five minutes of weeping with joy, they both composed themselves.

"Pinto, this is Dely, our young sister. I found her in Bato. She is the only survivor from the big typhoon." Pinto helped his two sisters up onto the dock, and the three hugged each other for a long time. Rico sat in his banca, smiling and enjoying the touching moment.

"How did you find them, Rico?" asked Pinto, who was still dumbfounded.

"I was selling shark on the beach at Bato… she came to me and asked if I knew who you were."

Now a large group of children had assembled on the dock, curious with all the emotion and happiness displayed. "These are some of my children, Juana. This is your Aunt Juana and your Aunt Dely," he introduced them. Each child shyly approached and took their Aunts' hands to their foreheads, blessing them in their tradition.

Pearl now hugged Rico, thanking him graciously, and handed him the solid gold coin, as she had promised. His smile was wide, exposing his three front teeth. "I will go now… I have many cousins here to visit." He bowed and walked the plank bridge to the shore.

In the days that followed, Pearl and Pinto talked for hours and hours, relaying what had happened in their lives in the last twenty-five years. Pinto was astounded, listening to Pearl and her travels across the American West. He could see the pain in her eyes when she told him about Alice, her baby, and how a law called the Page Act would not allow her to return.

"We are your family now, Juana… you must stay here! My children and wife will take care of you and Dely. Nothing will separate us again!" he promised.

Weeks passed. Juana did not want to be a burden on Pinto and his family. She took her remaining gold coins and built a stilt house adjoining the others on the river of Lawaan. She bought a fishing boat and put two of Pinto's sons to work, catching fish. She learned the art of repairing fishing nets, a similar skill she had retained from earlier days of weaving blankets on a loom. The fishermen kept her busy, and she, in time, became a respected and favorite member of the community. Children would gather daily on her dock porch above the water, listening to her stories as she repaired nets. It wasn't long before a regular group of crows would visit daily. Her interaction with them and chattering with them delighted the onlookers.

Dely's health had always been poor and fragile. One morning, she awoke sickly, with beads of sweat on her forehead. She fell into a high fever, and three days later, died in the night, delirious with Dengue fever. For a long time, Pearl and Pinto grieved over her passing, mourning and not participating in fiesta or celebrations.

Months and years went by. Pearl's hair had turned grey, and she walked with a stoop now, from constantly sitting and bending over as she repaired fishing nets. She had watched Pinto's children grow and had become their other mother. She was a celebrity in Lawaan, loved by everyone who knew her. Her wisdom and worldliness had promoted her as the village elder. In cases of dispute or conflict, the issue was brought before her. Her judgement and decision was accepted by all, as she commanded great respect. Anyone who threatened her or spoke badly of her was immediately confronted by a host of adhoring fishermen.

It was now the year 1896. There were whispers and hushed rumours of revolution in the air. After three hundred and thirty years of Spanish rule, the people were ready to revolt and govern themselves. The Spanish had subjugated the Filipinos into forced labor, taxation, corruption, and deceit for over three centuries. They had watched, helplessly, as the wealth of their country was shipped out monthly on galleons bound for Spain.

Twenty-five miles to the east of Lawaan was the town of Balangiga. There, a garrison of Spanish soldiers and a magistrate governed the region of southern Samar. The Franciscan friars had built a church there from very early times, the chapel of San Lorenzo. Once a month, a priest, with an escort of soldiers, came to Lawaan to perform Mass, confessions, weddings and funerals. It had been this way for as long as the people of Lawaan could remember. Having no money, they paid tribute to the priest and soldiers with what they had--fish and *tuba* wine.

It was a peaceful co-existence, as the priest and soldiers knew the fishermen were poor and could offer little in return. In the more populated areas of the Philippines, this peaceful co-existence between Spain's rule and the peasants was not as harmonious. The church and magistrate had become greedier, demanding more tribute and forced labor than the local populations could bear. A secret organization with a revolutionary mandate, called the *"katipunan"* was now organizing behind closed doors. They called for the peasant folk to rise up and join a guerrilla movement, based on harassment, and hit and run tactics of vulnerable Spanish aristocrats. They stayed hidden in the mountains and jungles of the provinces, making them very difficult for authorities to confront or eliminate.

One evening, after sundown, a frightened group of fishermen came to Pearl's hut and warned her, saying, " Koncha Kuba is coming! He's going to make trouble for us! What should we do?"

Within the hour, the rebel warrior appeared with his armed escorts and demanded to be taken to Juana Melendres. He was taken to her hut. Since Pearl had been warned, she was ready for the confrontation and now faced him, showing no fear.

"Why do you come here? You know you're putting my village in danger with the authorities. What is it that you want?" Pearl stared him down.

Koncha Kuba was fierce looking. He had a barrel chest, long hair with a feathered top knot, and a long, wicked scar across his nose and cheek. He stood before her, expressionless.

He wore a pistol on his gun belt that held up his loincloth, and his eyes looked right through Pearl with a deadpan stare.

"You know who I am. My men and I have a stronghold deep in the jungle. We need help from your people. You must give us fish and feed us so that we may continue to fight for your liberation. We've come to collect all of the dried fish you can spare."

Pearl replied "We have very little to spare. The fishing has been poor this week because of the full moon."

"I'll be the judge of that. We will take what we need," the rebel leader scowled.

"We don't want trouble with you and your men. We are sympathetic to your cause. Take what you want, but there is very little. We struggle here to feed our own families, so please leave us in peace," Pearl tried to negotiate.

With that, Koncha Kuba ordered his men to go from house to house and take whatever food they could find. Within an hour, the village had been pilfered.

Upon leaving, he warned Pearl not to report the ransacking, as the consequences would be severe for the village.

"We will be back when the moon is dark and collect more of your fish. If you betray us to the Spanish, I will personally cut your tongue out," he warned her.

As promised, the rebels returned two weeks later. Pearl had warned the village to hide at least half of the dried fish, for she knew they would take all that they could find. This monthly visit went on throughout the year. The village was helpless to the armed bandits, and in order to keep the peace, the tribute was given each time. The bandit rebels were maurrading to the east, pouncing on Spaniards who wandered too far from the safety of the garrison at Balangiga. Each time they would strike, they would disappear back into the jungle, before the Spanish soldiers could muster and retaliate.

One day, word came that Koncha Kuba had been killed. The warrior chief had attacked an outlying hacienda and raped the owner's wife. After looting and pillaging the estate, they had retreated back to their jungle hideout. Enraged that his beautiful wife had been violated, the aristocrat paid spies to tell him where the secret hideout was. From a sniper's position on the outskirts of the camp, the vengeful husband shot the warrior king through the neck, killing him instantly. Successfully slipping away, the man returned to Balangiga and reported the location of the stronghold to the authorities. Two days later, the Spanish garrison unleashed a surprise attack on the rebel camp, killing many and scattering the rest.

By 1897, the insurgents had suffered several defeats at the hands of the Spanish. The rebel leaders sued for peace, made a truce, and went into exile in Hong Kong. This temporary peace in the countryside was short-lived, for at the beginning of 1898, the United States declared war on Spain. The United States approached the rebel leaders in exile in Hong Kong, promising Filipino Independence if the rebel army would join the Yankee cause and fight the Spanish. The rebel leaders agreed wholeheartedly to the alliance and sent word for the insurgents to rise up and join the Americans in the fight.

The war was short and swift. The Spanish were defeated in Cuba, and Admiral Dewey of the U.S. Navy sailed into Manila Bay and blew the Spanish Navy out of the water. The U.S. quickly established martial law in Manila with its military forces. Shortly thereafter, Spain signed the Treaty of Paris, relinquishing Cuba, Guam, and the Philippines to the U.S.

The U.S. authorities now brought the exile rebel leaders back from Hong Kong to Manila, and set up a puppet regime controlled by the U.S. Army. Soon the rebel leaders realized they had been tricked, as the U.S. and its military had no intentions of giving the Filipinos their independence. Enraged by the trickery, the rebel leaders went back into hiding, calling for all insurgents to take up arms against the Yankee intruders. Skirmishes were sporadic throughout the Philippines for the next three years. The rebels were no match for the superiority of the American Army, yet the cause was gaining momentum among the peasant population.

Surprisingly, it was relatively quiet and peaceful during this period in Lawaan. The Spanish garrison of soldiers had abandoned their post at Balangiga by the end of 1898 and returned to Spain. For the most part, the rule of the church filled the void. The rebels now sent a new leader into Samar to muster support for the revolutionary cause. His name was General Vinceto Lukban, and his forces were much more regimented and regulars, compared to the bandito rebels of Koncha Kuba. By 1901, his control over Samar was thoroughly established. His forces scoured the countryside, demanding food and support from every village. Lawaan was no exception. Once again, Pearl and her village were subject to monthly visits by the insurgent forces, demanding whatever surplus they had.

The summer of 1901 saw General Robert Hughes in charge of the U.S. Army in the Philippines. He was aware of the threat of General Lukban on Samar. To counter and make the U.S. presence known, he sent a Company of Army Infantry to occupy the old Spanish barracks that had been abandoned at the port of Balangiga. At first, the townspeople were amicable and catered to the needs of the Americans. At the same time, the town folk were sympathetic to General Lukban and his cause. They maintained a delicate balance between the Americans and the rebels, who were hiding in the jungle in close proximity to Balangiga.

After about a month after their arrival, the American soldiers started to become bold and belligerent. They impressed their authority over the town people, subjecting them to harsh demands. All of the young men of the town were rounded up and forced under armed guards to perform work details. Basically, they had become prisoner slaves, and were not allowed to return to their families on a daily basis. This left their wives and daughters vulnerable. The soldiers sensed this and took advantage of the situation. Rape and debauchery began happening nightly. The townspeople now began to hate the Americans and secretly conspired with the rebels to stage an attack on the soldiers.

Again, on a moonless night, the rebels entered Lawaan and demanded food. This time, they also demanded recruits to assist in the planned attack. Their leader bartered for a full hour with Pearl, saying it was her people's duty to join the cause and rise up to fight the Americans. Pearl listened intently to his

375

reasoning and let him plead his case and then answered, "You have no idea of the capability of the Ameicans. Yes, you see seventy-five soldiers at the barracks in Balangiga, but I assure you that it is suicide to attack them. You might have a brief victory, but they will retaliate and kill a hundred rebels for each of their soldiers you kill. They are armed to the teeth, with cannons, guns, and sabers, and an endless supply of ammunition. I cannot allow my village people to partake in this crime. They are poor, innocent fishermen who want nothing to do with your self-proclaimed war. Take whatever food you want, but if you take our young men, who will then catch the fish to feed your little army?"

The rebel leader looked at Pearl with coal black eyes and accepted her reasoning. Yes, leave the fishermen alone--they were more valuable to the rebels as food suppliers.

On Saturday, September twenty-seventh of 1901, the townspeople of Balangiga staged a mock funeral at the church. Several caskets were brought into the chapel of San Lorenzo. A sergeant stopped the procession, suspicious of the activity. Prying the lead coffin open with a bayonet, the soldiers were startled to see a dead child staring back at them. Decomposition had set in, and the smell was putrid. The people explained that several children had died of cholera, and that a service was to be held for them the following day in the church. Satisfied with the explanation, the sergeant let the procession proceed and did not open the other four caskets. Unbeknown to him, the other four caskets were full of weapons--bolos, knives, and spears. The weapons were to be hidden in the church, which was immediately adjacent to the soldiers' barracks. The deception was not detected by the American soldiers. That evening, an abundance of *tuba* wine was handed out to the unsuspecting American soldiers. Dancing, gambling, whoring, and drinking were encouraged by the townspeople. Late into the night, the soldiers drank themselves into a stupor, with many passing out. On Sunday morning, most of the soldiers were still passed out in their bunks. A handful were up shaving and washing, and a few more were in the mess tent having coffee and nursing hangovers.

All of a sudden, the three church bells began to clang away--the signal of the attack. Within moments, four hundred Filipino rebels were upon the groggy soldiers, hacking them to pieces and cutting their throats. It was a complete surprise. Five minutes into the attack, more than half of the soldiers were dead. The hand to hand combat continued, and by the time the soldiers could get off a few shots, the massacre was over. The rebels began to take casualties, and the conch horn of retreat was blown.

Forty-four U.S. soldiers were killed in the attack, including all the officers. Several others were badly wounded, barely surviving. The survivors bivouacked in the church, locking the doors. They defended themselves from the church's bell towers, shooting at the looters and scavengers. The village people and rebels fled the scene, abandoning the town totally. For two days, the survivors remained in the church, fearful to come out and tend their dead and wounded.

On the third day after the attack, a supply sloop entered the Balangiga harbor. Sensing something wrong, the crew came ashore armed, only to discover the carnage at the barracks and around the church. Wasting no time, the survivors and wounded were hastily brought back to the ship. Within an hour, the sloop was on its way back to Tacloban, where another garrison of U.S. soldiers was stationed.

The news of the massacre spread quickly. Captain Edwin Bookmiller in Tacloban mustered a retaliation expedition. Commandeering a coastal merchant steamship, he hastily departed for Balangiga with a Company of U.S. Infantry. They were accompanied by a U.S. Navy gunboat, the Connecticut. Arriving at Balangiga, his troops were shocked at the sight of slaughter. The dead soldiers had been stripped of their clothing, shoes, and guns. The corpses lay rotting in the tropical sun. Captain Bookmiller buried the dead, then ordered the town to be burned to the ground, including the church. He ordered the three church bells to be brought aboard the steamer, after hearing how they had been used to signal the attack. He then ordered the steamer to return to Tacloban and bring back as many reinforcements as possible. In the meantime, he and his company, along with the gunboat, would hold this position and wait for further orders and backup troops.

It took a full month to get a reply via Morse Code and the telegraph. Theodore Roosevelt, the President of the U.S., was shocked to hear the news. The American newspapers printed the story, having not experienced such a defeat since Custer had been killed at the Little Big Horn. The American people wanted swift retaliation in response to the terrible deed.

In true political fashion, Roosevelt wired his Generals, to "pacify Samar," and teach them a lesson of the long arm and capability of the American military might. Upon receiving his telegram, General Adna Chaffee, the military governor of the Philippines, appointed General Jacob Smith, to the task of the "pacification" order from the Commander in Chief.

General Smith ordered and instructed Major Littleton Waller, commanding officer of a battalion of U.S. Marines, with these very words: "I want no prisoners! I wish you to kill and burn… the more you kill and burn, the better it pleases me. I want Samar turned into a 'howling wilderness.' I want every male, ten years of age or older, SHOT ON SIGHT!"

Within a week, Major Waller and his Marines steamed into the Balangiga harbor. Captain Bookmiller and his Company had waited patiently for the reinforcements. Having heard the orders of the President and General Smith, he was now ready for vengeance. In the previous weeks, he had sent out recon patrols and brought in several suspects for questioning. He briefed Major Waller on his gathered intelligence, then asked what his plan was, as they looked at a map of southern Samar.

"Well, Captain, you say there is a large fishing village to the west. Our orders are to seek out and destroy every source of food the rebels have. I mean kill every chicken, every pig, and every carabao that we see. Burn every rice paddy and every village to the ground. What armaments are aboard the gunboat Connecticut?" the major asked.

"She's got a Gatling Gun on her bow and a Hotchkiss cannon on her stern, including munitions of grapeshot canister," the captain advised.

"Very well. I'll take my Marines into the interior, and we'll hunt the little brown niggers down and shoot them like jackrabbits. Take your men overland to the fishing village. In coordination with the Connecticut, flatten the place with canister and Gatling rounds. If any try to escape inland, you are to meet them and finish them off. Then head back east, following the coast, and in the same manner and tactic, in coordination with the gunboat, flatten every fishing village you encounter. I estimate this operation will be over with in a month. Meet me back here in Balangiga in thirty days." Captain Bookmiller crisply saluted the major, saying, "Good luck and good hunting."

Weeks earlier, on the afternoon after the attack at Balangiga, rebels fleeing the area passed through Lawaan, boasting of their treacherous deed. Anyone associated with the attack was now a wanted man. Each knew he must disappear into the jungle, for fear of being pointed out as one of the conspirators. There was no doubt the U.S. Army would come and hunt down the murderers. Pearl was shocked to hear of the treachery and massacre. Her advice had been wise to her village people, "Do not take up arms against the American soldiers."

She knew they would come and seek out the culprits. She was confident that the Army would only want justice and that those who were innocent of the murders had nothing to worry about. There was an uneasiness in Lawaan in the weeks that followed, knowing now that soldiers had returned and burned Balangiga to the ground.

Pearl assured her village people, "When they come, I'll inform them of our innocence, as I speak their language. I will reason with them and tell them the truth. We have nothing to worry about--we weren't involved in the conspiracy. As long as we cooperate with them, I don't think they'll harm us.

Don't be frightened, the Americans are fair and good people." Her words took the worry from their minds, and they assumed their daily tasks of catching and drying fish.

It was a beautiful Sunday morning. The fishermen were enjoying their day of rest. Many attended their small chapel with their families, offering prayers and burning candles. Their fishing bancas were all tied up in front of each man's stilted house. Pearl sat on her waterfront porch, peeling taro root, listening to her nieces sing a song about Jesus.

Suddenly, both girls stopped singing. Looking up from her basket of taro, Pearl now saw what they were staring at--a steamboat with black smoke rising from its stack was coming up into the estuary. The Stars and Stripes flag fluttered from her signal mast. Alarmed, Pearl calmly told the girls to go inside until she could determine what they wanted. The steamer came to a halt fifty yards offshore and dropped its anchor. She expected to see a tender boat lowered over the side and come ashore to discuss their intentions.

Suddenly, she saw flashes of light from the boats bow, and a moment later, the sound of *pop, pop, pop, pop, pop, pop, pop* steady fire from a deck gun. She could now hear screams of terror coming from the houses and see lead bullets ripping their way towards her. Total panic now engulfed the village, as terrified children were cut down in the wave of hot lead. A cannon now boomed from the boat's stern. A shell came whistling in and exploded between her house and her neighbors. The grapeshot tore through the air, shattering her right arm and knocking her down. The concussion of the shell stupefied her. She tried to stand back up but was now caught in the wave of Gatling bullets. Her body was torn to pieces, and she fell back down, watching with dying eyes, as the village was flattened with grapeshot canister. The shell bursts now had set the houses ablaze. Another grapeshot round zeroed in on her, and her body was shredded by the explosion, sending her limbs flying in every direction. The gunboat continued to fire mercilessly for another fifteen minutes, flattening the village and destroying the fishing bancas. When the guns finally stopped, there was nothing but silence and a heap of flaming debris floating on the water. The few that were able to flee the onslaught were met at the treeline with a hail of bullets from Captain Bookmillers hidden soldiers. There were no survivors, as the order had been given to take no prisoners.

The genocide raged for another year. Estimates of a hundred thousand Filipinos were killed or starved to death in the campaign. In 1902, General Lukban was captured by Major Waller's forces in his mountain stronghold, thus ending the Filipino/American War.

Halfway around the world, in previous years, when Alice was two years old, it was becoming apparent to the Lonkers that Pearl was not going to return. They had received no mail from Pearl but understandably so, as she could not write. They had always thought of Pearl as a "Native American" but now were aware of the Page Act. They concluded that she probably could not return because of her Asian ancestry or that she had somehow died. Nellie, the Lonker's oldest daughter, had become a mother to the child. She now called her Pearl, rather than Alice. It wasn't long before everyone in the family was calling the adolescent girl by the name of her mother, Pearl. She had no idea that she was "adopted" and was raised as one of the family. The Lonker's hardware store provided the family with a comfortable lifestyle, as Wichita was becoming a boom town in the cattle shipping industry.

Alice "Pearl" attended the public schools and was mentored by her siblings, resulting in becoming a well-educated teenager. She would work after school in the hardware store. She would assist at the counter, being able to calculate costs and manage the inventory books. At eighteen, she had become a raven-haired beauty, attracting young men into the store with an excuse to buy anything.

One day, a tall, lanky cowboy entered. She caught his eye immediately.

"Ma'am, I need some axle grease for my buckboard wagon... and a gallon of lamp oil. Can you help me?" he politely asked.

"Yes, of course. Over here is a can of axle grease, and on that shelf is the lamp oil," she directed him. "What else can I help you with?"

They locked eyes for a long moment, and then the cowboy stammered, "My... my name is Verne Gibbs. I'm from Medicine Lodge, and I'm just passin through." He then removed his dusty hat and hesitated. "I was wondering... uh... uh... where's a good hotel to spend the night?"

"There's a hotel down the street--The Southern--they should be able to help you.... Anything else you need here?" she slyly asked.

"Much obliged, ma'am. It was a pleasure meeting you." He nervously nodded his head.

Teasing him, she replied, "Oh? ...we've met?"

"Excuse me ma'am, I'd be honored to know your name," he sheepishly asked.

"They call me Pearl.... Pearl Lonker," she smiled.

"A pleasure to meet you, Miss Pearl. Where is a good place to buy dinner?" he was now getting his courage up.

"The Wrangler's Roost has a good steak, across the street from The Southern," she offered.

He thanked her, bowed and nodded his head, and departed. He stopped briefly in the store window, and gazed at her once more. She acknowledged and returned a smile, the gesture that he had hoped for. The next morning, he returned to the hardware store. Pearl was in the back room taking inventory and could not be seen. Seeing the stranger's searching eyes, Bill Lonker addressed him, "What can I help you with pardner?" The man looked bewildered, searched the shelves for an item, and then pointed.

"I need a can of that linseed oil to dress my harness leather… how much is it?"

"The linseed oil? It's two bits a can." Bill pulled it off of the shelf and placed it on the counter. "What else can I get ya?"

"I was in here yesterday…. a lady named Pearl helped me. Is she here today?" he nervously asked.

"My daughter? Yeah, she's here, in the back." Then he bellowed, "Pearl! There's another cowboy up here that needs your help," winking at the embarrassed man.

Hearing her father, she now came up to the front of the store. Seeing the cowboy, she put him at ease, saying, "Good morning, Verne… did you find the hotel?"

"Yes I did… and the steak was the best I ever ate. Miss Pearl, I was wondering if I could buy you lunch for helping me out yesterday?" pulling his hat off.

Pearl turned and looked at Bill Lonker, wanting his approval. He rolled his eyes and stated, "I need to sweep the boardwalk off out front," and disappeared out the front door with a broom.

"I can't leave the store until we close at 5 o'clock," she told him.

"Well, does that mean I could buy you dinner then?"

"Gosh, I'd need to wash and put on some clean clothes. I thought you were just passing through?" she asked.

"Miss Pearl, if I could take you to dinner, I'll put all my other plans on hold," Verne answered.

"I live at number seven, Baker Street. You can call on me at 6:30. Where do you want to eat dinner?" she smiled.

Astonished at his luck, he answered, "Wherever a fine lady like you cares to dine! You choose the diner!" he beamed.

Verne hung around Wichita another week and courted her daily until he ran out of money. By then, the spark had turned to fire, and they both knew they were meant for each other. Verne worked in the stock yards of Medicine Lodge, as a "cowpoke." His job was to prod cattle onto the railcars using a sharp stick, hence the term "cowpoke." At two dollars a day, he was by no means "well off." He lived in a tattered, old military tent. After meeting Pearl and returning from Wichita, he saved and scrimped for two more months, cow poking and breaking mustangs in the evening for a dollar a head. Saving one hundred and twenty dollars, he returned to Wichita and asked Bill Lonker if he could marry his daughter. The father was hesitant but sensed the love between the two, and so permission was granted. The two were married in 1898, a simple ceremony at the Baptist church. The couple then returned to Medicine Lodge, where Verne rented a small, clapboard shack for himself and his new bride.

It wasn't long before she was heavy with a child. Verne was struggling to make ends meet, not accustomed to the demands and costs of a wife. One day, while talking with friends in the stock yards, he learned of an opportunity across the border in Oklahoma. Five years earlier, in 1893, the Cherokee Strip Land Run had taken place. Congress had opened up Cherokee land for homesteading, resulting in a huge wave of pioneers and speculators, pouring into the region. The Homestead Act required the pioneer to "prove up" on the claim, meaning building a home and making improvements. After five years of proving up, the government would then award the homesteader with title to the land. It was now five years later, and many homesteaders had not proven up, abandoning their claim and moving on. Now there were hundreds of one hundred and sixty acre parcels available to the public again. Hearing of some parcels around Alva, Oklahoma, Verne saddled his horse and headed out to investigate in the spring of 1899.

Ten days later, he was back at Medicine Lodge, full of excitement. "Pearl, I've found a beautiful spot--one hundred and sixty acres with a fresh spring. I filed on it... it's ours! We'll leave right after the baby is born!"

Two weeks later, Clara was born, and within a month of her birth, the trio were headed south to Alva on Verne's old buckboard. Pitching his old military tent, he and Pearl began to work the land. A garden was planted, but locusts devoured much of it. The spring that Verne was so excited about dried up in the summer months. After a year of starving and struggling, they both decided to abandon the endeavor and return to Kansas. Pearl was now pregnant again and gave birth to Irene shortly after they had arrived back in Medicine Lodge.

A local rancher took pity on Verne, seeing him struggling to survive. He gave him a job as a ranch foreman. It gave the family a small house to live in and food for the table but little else. By 1902, another child was born--a boy named Lloyd. Verne had worked himself into debt, borrowing and taking future

382

credit on his ranch wages. With three children now, it was a full time job for Pearl to care for the brood. The struggle would continue.

In 1904, a fourth child was born--a boy named Arnold. The ranch was now prospering under Verne's authority and hard work. In appreciation, the ranch owner had forgiven Verne's debt and given him a raise in wages.

By 1910, the age of the automobile and the airplane were on the horizon. The Gibbs family was prospering on the ranch. The children were attending the local school house, and there was joy at the dinner table every night, with enough food to make them happy. Then, tragedy and calamity struck. Arnold was only five years old, still not big enough for school. Clara, Irene, and Lloyd would walk daily the two miles to the school house and return in the late afternoon. The school house had a shallow, hand dug well for water. It was this water well that the disaster was traced to. In the period of a month, Typhoid Fever had claimed all the lives of the children at the school except for two lucky ones. Clara, Irene, and Lloyd fell victim to the disease, all dying within a week of each other.

Verne and Pearl were devastated. Verne took to drinking heavily to kill the pain. Pearl fell into a chronic depression and would stare out the window for hours. Soon, Verne was derelict of his duties at the ranch, brought on by all of the alcohol, and was told by the rancher to pack their things and leave. Things never were the same again for Pearl and Verne. He got a job for the railroad, shoveling manure out of cattle cars, and Pearl found a job in a Medicine Lodge mercantile store. Arnold was raised in the despondent household. His parents were never able to overcome their depression and the loss of the three children.

By the time Arnold was seventeen, he wanted out of the situation and to leave Medicine Lodge. He packed a carpet bag with a few clothes one day and announced to his mother that he was leaving.

"Please wait until your father comes home!" she pleaded with him.

"No, he won't let me go, mother…. you know that," Arnold reasoned with her.

Pearl had saved around five dollars. She dug it out of her dresser drawer and handed it to Arnold.

"Here, take this five dollars…. it's all that I have. And take this seashell medallion. It was given to me when I was your age. I was told that it would bring me luck. Where will you go?" she cried.

"I'll go to Wichita. Maybe grandpa Lonker can give me a job," he assured her.

"Alright, but please write me a letter, and let me know where you end up," Pearl pleaded.

Upon arriving in Wichita, Arnold learned that old man Lonker had sold the hardware store and retired. The old man's memory was failing, and he had no idea who Arnold was. Down to his last dollar and desperate for work, Arnold found a job at a livery stable delivering coal to the houses in Wichita. The work was dirty and arduous, shoveling the coal into burlap sacks. They then had to be loaded and delivered to wherever the customer wanted them dropped. After about a month, he quit and found a job as a dishwasher in the train depot Harvey House restaurant. He struggled but survived, becoming a kitchen worker celebrity among the employees at the station. In doing so, he found job security, and after two years was helping the cook more than he was dishwashing. Soon, he found himself as the night shift cook. The kitchen became his domain, and as he hit his stride, he became a master at preparing the foods on the menu.

In 1925, a pretty, night shift waitress was hired at the depot restaurant. Thelma Louia, a descendent of a French Cherokee family, had grown up in Wichita and now was a vibrant nineteen-year-old. She could drive a Model T and had learned all the new "Roaring Twenty" dances. Wearing lipstick and eyeshadow, she smoked Lucky Strikes, which exemplified her rebellious attitude. Arnold quickly fell for her, and she for him. They were married a month later, at the county courthouse.

All went smoothly, until Thelma got pregnant. She waited tables at the restaurant until she was eight months pregnant, then retired to the couple's rented bungalow to await the birth. A girl was born, Arlene. Not being able to go back to work, Thelma and Arlene became a financial burden for Arnold. The good old days of having two incomes and shacking up in the bungalow were gone. He began working long hours at the depot restaurant, supposedly. The rumour was that he was having an affair with the new waitress that had replaced Thelma. The marriage and relationship between Arnold and Thelma continued to go downhill. It turned for the worst when she told him she was pregnant again, and he refused to believe the child was his.

A boy was born. Arnold had not been seen for three days, and so Thelma named him Milton Verne, knowing Arnold's father's name was Verne. She had been true to him, and it was his son. Arnold would now disappear for days. Prohibition had been in place the entire decade, and now bootlegging had become a regular business. Through his contacts at the depot restaurant, he had become part of the underworld organization who smuggled and sold the booze. He would come home in the middle of the day after being gone a week, hungover, mean, and violent. He'd leave a few dollars on the table after sleeping all day on the couch, then disappear that night and not be seen for another week. The sorry relationship continued until the baby boy Milton was a year old.

On his weekly visits, he and Thelma would fight like cats and dogs, ending with a few dollars on the table and him disappearing again.

It had been days since Thelma had last seen Arnold. It was a Tuesday afternoon, on October twenty-ninth of 1929, when Thelma turned on the radio and could hear the panic coming over the broadcast. Wall Street had collapsed, and with it came the end of the "Roaring Twenties."

Thelma never saw Arnold again. She had barely survived on his weekly handouts of money. With two children to feed, her situation was grim. She had little family to turn to for help. She had never met Verne or Pearl and had no idea how to contact them to help feed their grandchildren. The reality of the grandparents was that they were no better off than her, reduced to beggars as well.

Thelma's father, Pop Louia, had a small pension from the Spanish-American War, and her mother, Mom Irene, had a large vegetable garden and canned the surplus. Thelma took Milton and Arlene to her parents' tiny house, having no other options. The three moved into the storm cellar behind the little brick house on the edge of Wichita. Thelma found odd jobs, doing laundry, ironing, and house cleaning, just barely scraping by on a daily basis. With Thelma gone all day, the chore of caring for the two siblings fell upon the old Cherokee granny. Mom Irene, or Momarene, as she was called by her grandchildren, took pity on the two and nurtured them in the absence of Thelma.

By 1931, it was obvious that Arnold was dead or had no intention of coming back. Thelma filed for divorce, after posting her intent in the Wichita newspaper. The divorce was granted by the judge, which enabled Thelma to find another husband. No one was interested in marrying a woman with two mouths to feed during the Depression, and so their poverty continued into the 1930's. Milton became like an orphan on the streets of Wichita, a loner and a ragged waif. He'd wander the alleys, looking for handouts and tasks that a young boy could handle. He was in and out of school, mocked for his raggedness and poverty. At ten years of age, he found a friend, Lester Brusco, who was in the same situation as him. Lester's father had also abandoned him at the beginning of the Depression. Lester was fourteen, four years older than Milton, and had developed a sense of street savvy, learning how to survive. Lester had a single shot twenty-two rifle. He and Milton would hunt rabbits in the fields around Wichita and use the rabbit meat for trade. They were able to bring some potatoes and baked bread home on lucky days of hunting.

One day at the dinner table, Pop Louia asked Milton, "Why aren't you boys shooting ringneck pheasants?"

"We tried, Pop, but they don't hold still like a rabbit and much harder to hit. The bullets are two cents each, and we can't afford to miss."

"I see... you're right. Knocking a flying chink out of the air with a bullet is next to impossible," replied the old man. After dinner, the old man lit his pipe and beckoned for Milton.

"Come here, boy... follow me." In his bedroom, old Pop had a footlocker, which was always locked up, and Milton had never seen its contents. Producing a hidden key, the old man opened its lid, revealing a uniform and military cap. Digging to the bottom, he pulled out an old, Ithaca double barrel shotgun. Handing it to the boy, he proclaimed, "This will knock those roosters out of the sky. Do you think you can handle it?"

Nothing like it of value had ever been given to the boy. He trembled with excitement.

"Can I have it, Pop? It's mine?" Milton asked.

"Yep, but I got no shells. You'll have to figure that one out. Be careful, it's a twelve gauge, and you'll blow your foot off if you're not careful!"

Shotgun shells were five cents each, and it took Lester and Milton a week of working odd jobs and scrounging to come up with sixty cents. Buying a dozen shells, and after missing a couple of times, the two became deadly with the shotgun. Coming in from the fields in the afternoon, they'd clean the birds they'd shot and sell them for ten cents each.

The bad years of the thirties continued, with Franklin Roosevelt on the radio weekly, encouraging people to hang on and that better times were just around the next bend. By 1941, Milton was thirteen years old, and his pal Lester was seventeen. Both boys were known around town as expert marksmen. There hunting skills had become finely honed.

On December seventh, 1941, the Japs attacked Pearl Harbor, plunging America into WW2. The local Army recruiter knew about Lester Brusco and his reputation with a gun. By the end of January 1942, Lester had signed up and was shipped out to boot camp. Milton had tried to lie about his age to the recruiter and go as well. The recruiter could clearly see that Milton had no whiskers and was barely a teenager.

In early 1943, Milton got a letter from Lester. He had ended up as a sharpshooter for the Army in the Seventh Corp. Lester had mailed the letter right before he boarded the troop transport ship in New York, bound for Africa.

Young Milton had replaced his hunting brother with a bicycle and continued to hunt the wheat fields for pheasants alone. The war was creating food shortages in America. Old friends and customers, who had bought his pheasant over the years, now looked for him in these hard times. The country's citizens were expected to grow gardens, raise livestock and horses, and ration what they could for the war effort. Milton discovered that what once had been a method of survival now had become a skill, and it helped him provide for his mother and sister. Once a week, he'd pedal the bike to the hardware store and buy two boxes of shotgun shells. He'd visit with the locals, sitting by the pot belly stove, and listen to the news and gossip about the war effort.

On one such occasion, the clerk told him the bad news. Lester Brusco had been killed in Sicily, attacking a German machine gun on a ridge. The clerk showed Milton the casualty list in the weekly paper. It was no mistake--Lester Brusco, marksman Seventh Corp, killed in action.

Milton was broken. Lester had been his salvation--had found him when he was at rock bottom. He'd taught Milton how to survive and had become like a real brother. It was like a piece of Milton's soul had been torn out, leaving him so lonely and empty. He disappeared into the Kansas prairie and wheat, being gone for days on his bicycle down dusty backroads.

Over time, Milton overcame his grief. He wanted to avenge Lester's death and kill Germans. He was still only fifteen but had talked about joining with a recruiter. The war was grinding on, and if it was still going when he turned seventeen, they would enlist him. He'd have to wait until October of 1945. He continued his solitude in the wheat fields. By September of 1945, the Allied forces had overwhelmed the Axis powers, and WW2 officially ended.

The Army stopped all enlistments, and after finally turning seventeen, young Milton would not get his chance to avenge his best friend's death. No one was buying pheasant meat any longer, looking at it as survival food. The markets once again had lots of Kansas beef for sale. One day, Milton was bicycling back into town when a blue Ford sedan pulled up alongside of him. "Hey kid... you that feller that used to hunt with Lester Brusco?"

Milton kept pedaling as the driver in the Ford matched his speed.

"Yeah, I knew him.... Who are you?" Milton continued to pedal.

"The name's Fred Burton, and Lester was my Army buddy." The man looked at Milton, then back at the road. At that moment, Milton stopped pedaling.The Ford stopped alongside.

"You were in the Army with Lester?" Milton now pressed Fred.

"Yeah, we were both in the Seventh Corp... in Sicily. We were in separate Companies. I met Lester on the troop ship, crossing the Atlantic. He spoke of you and asked me to look you up in case he didn't come home. My job was to supply aircraft parts in the Mediterranean theatre after we reached the war zone. I never saw him again, but I'm a man of my word, and so I can say I fulfilled my promise to him. I used my connections to get a job here at Boeing, in Wichita, after the war."

"How did Lester die? Do you know about his battle in Sicily? Did he assault a machine gun nest?" Milton had tossed his bicycle to the ground and was now standing at Fred's open Ford window.

"His company assaulted a heavily fortified German hilltop, full of concrete bunkers. Almost half of the company died in the assault, attacking the hill with bazooka squads. He was one of the ones that died that day. That's all there is to tell. He's buried in Sicily, Milton. Hey, listen… I can get you a job, I think. There's a bicycle courier job open at the plant. You lookin' for a job kid?"

"A job! A real job with a paycheck?!" Milton couldn't believe his ears.

"Yeah, throw that bike in the trunk. There's a rope back there… lash it down." Fred winked at him.

"You're serious?!" Milton was stunned.

"Yeah… yeah… get in… I gotta punch a time clock. I'm in a hurry, c'mon," Fred urged.

A half hour later, they were pulling up to the guard gate at the aircraft hangar and office building. Fred flashed a badge through his open window, then explained the situation.

"It's ok… he's with me and applying for a job. He needs a visitor's pass," Fred explained.

"Alright, here's your escort pass. You know the rules," the guard advised and opened the gate.

Milton was no stranger to aircraft. During the war, when he was out hunting, they dotted the skies as they rolled out of Boeing's assembly hangars and were test flown. One no longer looked up when you heard one pass over, they had become so common.

And just like that, he was hired on Fred's recommendation, who as it turned out, was a supervisor and authority within the plant. His mother, Thelma, was extremely pleased and happy for him. Luck had rarely fallen on her son. Within a month of starting the new job, a profound change had come over him, as if he were emerging from a long, lonely darkness. She eagerly listened to him every night at the dinner table, telling about his tasks that day.

"So you just ride that bicycle around, back and forth, all day, and they pay you for it!?" she teased him.

"Yes, Ma. I deliver rolls of drawings and production orders from the engineer's office building to the assembly plant, all day long, back and forth. There's several of us," Milton explained. "Ma, the Foreman told me I gotta wear a white shirt and tie when I'm in the office building…. So I went to J.C. Penny's today and bought two short sleeve white shirts and a black tie." Thelma stopped him.

"Wait, wait... stop.... They want you to wear a tie and ride a bicycle?" she asked in disbelief.

"Yes Ma, it's like a uniform. It's what you wear. It's like if you're in the assembly plant, you're blue collar... and in the engineering building, you wear a white collar, with the tie. It's a culture, Ma--an airplane culture." Milton tried to explain.

"Well let me see you try it on... see my young man all grown up!" Thelma insisted.

Milton had also bought two pairs of surplus Army khaki slacks. Suiting up in the new shirt and pants, he had trouble tying the necktie.

"Well just look at you, Milton Gibbs.... Land o' Goshen! Here, let me fix that tie." She fussed, grabbing the tails and undoing his attempt. "There, look at you!" She stood back and admired. They both looked at him in the commode mirror.

"You're missing something, and I have one." Thelma ducked away and returned a minute later. She held a cigar box out which had been hidden behind a row of books.

"This stuff belonged to Arnold.... he left it behind. I have no want for it. There is a tie clasp in here." She opened the box. "Here it is." She reached over and clipped his tie to his shirt.

"What else is in that box, Ma?" Milton was now wondering, reaching for it.

"Not much--some baseball cards, a watch, that tie clip, a jack-knife, and that shell medallion. I remember him saying that his mother gave him the shell medallion, as I recall."

"Does the watch run, Ma?" Milton asked.

"I don't know, frankly. I haven't opened that box in fifteen years, son." Thelma shook her head.

Milton discovered that the watch still worked. With the watch strapped to his wrist, and the white shirt and tie with clasp, he was transformed in the mirror... into the look of a modern day professional.

The world was changing. Boeing had now retooled from making war time propeller bombers to the age of the jet airplane. A new airline passenger jet was needed, and Boeing was on the cusp of the developing industry. The facility in Wichita now boomed. Milton's bicycling days had now passed. Now he shuttled engineers to and from the plant to the office buildings. A surplus Harley Davidson motorcycle with a sidecar fulfilled the task, and Milton was the driver.

He succeeded in saving some money from his twice a month paycheck. A friend at work had an old 1926 Dodge, and for a bottle of whiskey and sixty dollars, Milton bought the jalopy.

It dollared him to death to keep it running, but he didn't care. It was a newfound freedom to have a car, and the option to go wherever and whenever he desired.

One day, a co-worker at the plant told Milton about a dance that was happening that Saturday at a local town.

"Milton, we should go. Your Dodge will make it. It's down at Wellington at the Eagles. My cousin lives there. She says there will be lots of girls going."

"Wellington, huh? I used to hunt pheasants down that way. It's a railroad town…. The old Santa Fe roundhouse is there," mused Milton.

"C'mon, Milton. The Frankie Horner Swing Band from St. Louis is playing. C'mon, Milton, you ain't doing nothing else."

"Ok, Bob… I'll drive the Dodge if you buy the gas."

Saturday found the two lads rolling south on the paved road to Wellington. The old Dodge couldn't go much faster than twenty-five miles per hour. Nevertheless, they came into town around seven p.m., just as the doors were opening at the old Eagles hall on Main Street. Over fifty cars were parked along the brick street, with a large crowd waiting on the sidewalk for the dance to start. The war had taken its toll on the ratio of young men to women, as there were several more girls in the crowd than boys. The two paid their twenty-five cent entrance fee at the door and entered the musty, old hall with the worn, wooden floor.

The swing band started a lively tune, and Bob easily found a willing girl to dance with. He snapped his fingers and spun the girl to the beat. Milton watched the two as they continued to dance through a couple more songs. Across the floor, a large group of girls were eyeing him and would laugh and look away when he glanced their way. One girl held her gaze on him and continued to stare at him, beckoning for a chance to dance. Shyly, Milton looked away, but every time he looked back her way, the pretty brunette was still staring at him. He finally locked eyes with her and walked over to meet her.

"I'm not much of a dancer miss…. Could I buy you a Coke?" he offered.

"Sure, I'd like a Coke. It's hot in here. C'mon, my sister is working the refreshment table." He followed her over to the table. A punch bowl with paper cups was being served, and a large tub of iced down Cokes were available. Three pretty girls were behind the table, serving the drinks and collecting the nickels.

"This is my sister, Jean," the pretty brunette introduced Milton. "My name is Jimmie, and you are?" She smiled at Milton.

"Uh… Milton…. Milt Gibbs…. Nice to meet you, Jean. Yeah, give me and your sister two Cokes," he replied, handing her a dime.

Now, face to face with Jimmie, he was struck by her innocent beauty. Her black hair was curled. She wore red lipstick and chewed gum. Her pleated skirt and saddle shoes were the fashion of the day, and her youthfulness made her glow.

"Don't stay out too late," Jean teased her as she handed over the Cokes and gave a wink.

Another song was now playing, and the dance floor had become crowded with exuberant dancers. Jimmie grabbed Milton's hand and pulled him to the corner of the auditorium, away from the crowd. "Where are you from, Milt? I've never seen you around Wellington." She broke the ice with a question.

"I'm from Wichita. My buddy told me about this dance, so we drove down to check it out," he explained.

"Oh… you own a car?" she asked.

"Yeah, nothing fancy, just an old Dodge that barely runs," he joked.

"Do you work in Wichita?" she asked, keeping the conversation going.

"At the Boeing plant." He gazed into her dark eyes.

"Wow! You build airplanes?!" she was impressed.

"Sort of. I work with the engineers and the assembly line."

The band now began playing a slow waltz, and looking at him, Jimmie raised her painted eyebrows and cocked her head towards the dance floor.

"Sure… I'm not much of a dancer… you'll have to be patient with me." He took the empty Coke bottles, returned them to the table, and the two slid out onto the dance floor. She made it easy for him, and the two fell into the swaying motion of the crowd. Just as he was getting his rhythm and confidence, the band broke into a hot, swing dance. Jimmie grabbed his hand and skipped around him to the beat. It was wonderful! He hadn't felt so uplifted in his entire life. She laughed and teased him, coaxing him to get his feet moving to the rhythm of the song. From then on, the two were on the dance floor the remainder of the evening. The last dance was a slow one, and she didn't resist when he pulled her in close to his chest. The song ended too quickly, and the auditorium lights came on.

"Could I give you a ride home?" he offered.

"Yes, that would be nice. I only live two blocks away, at 323 West Harvey Street."

Milton searched the crowd and finally found Bob's face. Waving him over, he introduced him to Jimmie.

"Wow! Look at you! Taking the prettiest one home! All I got was a phone number," he joked.

She guided the car to her residence, a modest older home with two iron hitching posts for horses out front. The porch light was on, and Milton walked her to the door. Using his manners, he thanked her for the nice evening and asked if he could see her again.

"Yes, I'd like that--wait a second," she slipped quietly inside and came back with a pencil. On the back of a Juicy Fruit gum wrapper, she wrote her phone number.

"Don't lose it," she teased him.

He called her the next day. She picked the phone up, halfway through the first ring.

"Hey, there's a juke joint up here in Wichita... I can pick you up Saturday. Let's go dancing again," he offered.

"Uh... my Dad would never let me go up to Wichita on a date. He's a brakeman for the Santa Fe. He'd beat the tar outta you if he thought you were getting fresh with me. There's a cinema house here in Wellington, the Regent. There's a good movie playing, 'The Big Steal,' with Robert Mitchum and Jane Greer. I think Daddy would let me go to the movie house with you. You'll have to meet him though, and ask for permission.... Is that okay?"

"Sure.... I'll be at your house at seven on Saturday!" he promised.

Nervous as hell, he tried to calm himself as he pulled up to Jimmie's house on Saturday. On the front porch swing sat Jim Kincaid and his daughter. She waved him up to the front porch. The railroad man flicked his camel cigarette into the grass as Milton walked up and held out his hand.

"Dad, this is Milt Gibbs. Milt, this is Jim." The two shook hands. The lean, rawboned railroad man wore bib overalls, with a gold pocket watch chain draped across the chest. He was tough as a Texas boot, growing up in Odell, (Haulk) Texas in the cotton fields, and his handshake was a firm grip to prove it.

"Nice to meet you, son.... Jimmie tells me you work for Boeing." His voice was friendly.

"Uh... yes sir, that I do. Uh, Mr. Kincaid, I'd like to take Jimmie to the Regent, sir, here in town... with your permission."

"Hmmm... I reckon you would. You got enough money for three tickets?" he looked seriously at the lad.

"Well, yes sir, I do. Who else is going? Her sister Jean?" Milton politely asked.

"Jean? Hell no. I'll be going with you," he barked.

"Oh stop it, Daddy. He's just teasing you, Milt," as she nudged her father hard.

Jim let out a hearty laugh. "C'mon boy, her mother wants to meet you." He held the door open for Milton to enter.

"Ellie, this is Milt Gibbs, the one your daughter has been babbling about all week. This here is Jean, Raymond, and Micah." He nodded towards her brothers and sister.

"We've met," offered Jean. "Welcome to the Kincaid house, Milt," she giggled. "Can we call you Milt?"

Now at ease, he answered, "Sure... Milt, Milton, Mel... take your pick."

"Alright, you kids have fun. You bring her home by eleven, or I'll come lookin for ya, Milt," the railroad man was serious, as he stared Milton in the eye.

The courting and dating went on for the next year. There was no doubt in anyone's mind that the two were meant for each other. So it was no surprise that in the summer of 1950, they were married at the Presbyterian church in Wichita. It was a modest ceremony, with Milton's only family, Pop, Mom Irene, Thelma, and Arlene attending. The Kincaids and some of Jimmie's schoolmates were present, as well. By then, Milton had gotten rid of the old Dodge and bought a sleek Pontiac Chieftain sedan, making monthly payments.

They had little money for a honeymoon--just enough to drive to Tulsa, rent a cheap motel, and buy a hamburger. They had both spent their savings on the first month's rent for a small, brick cottage on Plaza Lane in Wichita. Barely with enough gas to make it back from Tulsa, they set up housekeeping in their sparsely furnished abode. Jimmie found a job, clerking at a Woolworth store downtown. Together, they both saved their money and planned for a future family.

Polio had been a scourge and much-feared disease in the country for several decades. It had overwhelmed Franklin Roosevelt and stricken countless other families, choosing its victims indiscriminately. So when it was announced that Jonas Salk had discovered a vaccine for its prevention, a wave of euphoria could be felt among the general population. The dark cloud of fear and worry was over, and it initiated the "baby boom." The country had been worn down by war and the Depression, and suddenly, the future looked bright and hopeful. Couples could now build families without fear of food shortages and disease.

Jimmie was pregnant with her first child, and Milton had been promoted at Boeing. He now worked as an engineer's assistant in the big office building. At eight months into her pregnancy, the two began to seriously discuss what to name the child. If it was a boy, Milton insisted that he be named Lester, in honor

393

of his best friend killed in the war. Jimmie despised the name, but in order to keep the peace, she said nothing, hoping for a girl.

One night, at the dinner table, she drew a line in the sand. "Milt, if this child is a boy, I refuse to name him Lester. It just won't work for me," she demanded.

"Ah, c'mon Jimmie. You know how I feel about that. Lester's a good, strong name," he insisted.

"I'll compromise with you, Milt. I know Lester Brusco was like your brother, and it's admirable that you want to honor him, but...."

Milton interrupted, "So what's your compromise, Jimmie?"

"When I was in elementary school, I had a crush on a boy in my class, named 'Cole.' I'd like to name our son, if we have a son, Bruce Cole, and if you want to call him Brusco, that's fine by me." She took his hand and pleaded, "Please Milt--not Lester."

"Actually, I like it, Jimmie! Bruce Cole Gibbs.... If you say it fast enough, it comes out 'Brusco.' Yes, that's it--a good name! And what if it's a girl?"

Jimmie laughed, relieved that Milton had relinquished his hard-headed demand. "I think its a boy, Milt. He's been pounding and kicking me like crazy. If it's a girl, I like the name Rebecca."

The following month, at Wesley Hospital on the banks of the Arkansas River, Bruce Cole Gibbs entered the world.

The Wichita Kid

In 1953, an armistice and truce was signed to stop the aggression in Korea. The war had been fought over ideology and the invasion of the communist regime. Our troops came home, frustrated with the outcome but glad it was over.

In 1954, the Polio Vaccine was being distributed in the United States. Within months, the reported cases of contraction shrank dramatically, indicating the disease had been eradicated.

By 1955, America's next generation of youth had awoken. Bill Haley and the Comets, Chuck Berry, and Elvis Presley appeared on the radio, taking the country by storm. Years of war, depression, and disease were over. America wanted to party. The new sound was rock and roll, and it washed away the memory of three decades of misery and dreariness.

The new automobiles of the 50's were stylish and personalized, making a statement about whoever was behind the wheel. Jobs were plentiful, and the banks made credit easy, fueling the economy and the future.

The television was the new "must have." Milton couldn't resist. He brought a new black and white T.V. set home that he'd bought on sale in downtown Wichita. Brusco by now was three years old. It didn't take long for him to become mesmerized, sitting in front of the T.V. and watching its daily shows. The Mickey Mouse Club, Howdy Doody, and Roy Rodgers kept his eyes glued to the T.V. screen. Milton liked to watch "Gunsmoke," and Brusco would plant himself in his father's lap, watching Matt, Miss Kitty, and Chester.

A baby girl, Brusco's sister, had now been born. Jimmie named her Lilly. The two children had become a full time job, requiring Jimmie to become a full time housewife to care for them.

By 1956, Elvis had become a household word. The rock and roller had attained super stardom. That year, he appeared on eleven different variety television shows. His smash hit "Hound Dog" was being played on every radio station. The howling beat could be heard coming out of every open automobile window on the road, with the driver "turning it up."

Milton had again been promoted at Boeing, to a production team that was working on the 707. The new jet airliner was to be built in Seattle. At the dinner table one evening, Milton announced, "Jimmie, I was informed today that the company is transferring us to Seattle... on the west coast."

"You can't be serious... You're joking, aren't you?" Jimmie was in disbelief.

"I'm not kidding. In fact, the company is flying our whole team to Seattle next week. I'll be gone for three weeks. The company expects all of us to find a home to rent. By this time next month, you and the kids will be heading for Washington."

The following week, Milton departed for Seattle and returned at the end of the month. He was full of excitement and anxious to move to Seattle.

"Jimmie, everything is so green there! There's mountains with snow, fresh lakes and rivers, and the saltwater ocean! The air is so cool and crisp…. It's the exact opposite of what Kansas is. I rented us a house by a lake in the city. There's a big cherry tree in the backyard. You're gonna love it!" Milton was very convincing.

"But what about our furniture, the beds, and the T.V.? How will we move them?" Jimmie was bewildered.

"Day after tomorrow, the company is paying a mover to come and load our things on a truck. The truck will take the stuff to the house in Seattle at no charge to us."

"Plus, the company is buying train tickets for you and the kids. I'll fly back the day after you guys leave on the train. It's a three day trip on the train, so I'll be waiting at the train station, when you arrive in Seattle, to pick you up."

As scheduled, the moving company was there, two days later. By 2:00 p.m., all that remained in the place was their suitcases. The Gibbs family watched as the big box truck disappeared down the street, to a destination 2,000 miles away.

"Well, let's go… we'll stay at the Broadview Hotel tonight, down by the river. I'll drive you guys to the depot in the morning," Milton assured them.

Milton had them all up early the next day. They had a big breakfast at the hotel, and Milton got them to the depot platform just as the train was pulling in. The train was on a tight schedule and did not linger at the station. Milton got Jimmie, Brusco, and Lilly boarded, finding their seats and stowing their suitcases. A quick kiss and a hug, and the Conductor was already calling out, "All Aboard!" Milton hopped off of the pullman car, and the porter reached down, grabbed the boarding step, and stepped onto the iron steps. The engine sounded a long horn blast, and they began rolling out of the Santa Fe station in Wichita, heading west.

This was an eye opener for the young Brusco. His whole life had been the city park or a trip to his grandparents' house in Wellington. Now, outside the window, before his eyes, a whole new world was racing past. A world that was rapidly changing in this space of time. Rural America was disappearing. Outside, ranches and farms, fencing, cultivated fields, livestock, and little towns went by in the blink of an eye, past the moving train. On board were the seeds and young minds that would usher in the new "Jet Age."

At one point during the trip, while crossing the Rocky Mountains, a kindly porter escorted Brusco forward, walking through two pullman cars to reach the "Vista Dome." The entire ceiling was a clear, plexiglass window, allowing the passengers to stare up at the majestic beauty of the Rockies. The porter pointed out a large waterfall to Brusco as the train rolled past. This was First Class, and Brusco only got a five minute taste of the luxury. The kindly porter returned him to his seat with Jimmie.

Jimmie had brought food and snacks to feed them for three days. She was pleased and relieved when she realized that all Brusco wanted to do was stare out the window... and he didn't like being distracted from the view. That made her job of caring for the two-year-old Lilly a lot easier. By the third day, Lilly was getting cranky. Jimmie and Brusco were both weary and relieved when the Northern Pacific pulled into the platform of Union Station, downtown Seattle.

There was Milton, as he'd promised. He searched the windows for their faces as the train pulled up. He saw them and waved back. He had sold the car in Wichita and flown to Seattle in a company plane. The next day, he had purchased another Pontiac Chieftain and was now waiting for them to step off the train. Milton was excited to see his little family. He got their luggage into the Pontiac and headed north on Highway 99.

"Do you know where you're going Milton?" Jimmie was marveling at all the sights of Seattle.

"It's called Green Lake. We'll be there in fifteen minutes."

They drove north over a large hill called Queen Ann and across a large bridge. They entered a district of fine, old Victorian homes that prominated around a lake.

The homes had been built around the turn of the century, when the Klondike gold rush brought wealth and prosperity to Seattle. Circling the lake, Milton came to a street called Latona and took a right. He climbed a short hill and went around a curve, and there was the house. It was a grand, large house that was already some sixty years old. It was weathered and needed paint, but the family took an immediate liking to its spacious, musty old interior.

Brusco spent the summer of 1957 climbing the huge cherry tree in the backyard and riding his bicycle down to the lake. A park surrounded the lake, which focused on a well-groomed path that circled the shoreline. Brusco would ride the three mile path around the lake with his bicycle, enjoying the park with its sights. Hydroplane boats raced on the lake on Saturdays, with spectators, lovers, picnickers, and families watching the event. A favorite pastime was to buy fish and chips at a place called Spuds, walk across the street to the park on the lake, and enjoy the grass lawn, sitting on a quilt. On the north side of the lake was a pancake house called the Twin Teepees. One Sunday morning, while the Gibbs were having breakfast there, Jimmie informed Brusco and Lilly that another baby was on the way.

"What will you name the baby if it's a boy?" asked Brusco.

Jimmie looked at Milton and smiled. "Well, how about James... named after your grandpa.... What do you think?" she asked Brusco.

"Well, I'm gonna call him Jim, not James!" Brusco seriously frowned. "And if it's a girl, what will you name her, Ma?"

Jimmie looked at Milton with that "help me" look on her face.

"Well Brusco, my grandma told a story about a Cherokee nymph girl that had wings like a hummingbird. She lived behind a waterfall and would only come out when the sun shone through the waterfall mist, creating a rainbow. If you were lucky enough to see her, you could make a wish, and it would come true. The Cherokee call her 'Nebanae,' the spirit who hides behind the rainbow. So if it's a girl, we'll call her Nebanae."

A baby girl was born that Fall. Brusco attended the local elementary school, Fairview. The old brick school had been built at the turn of the century. The lofty ceilings and hallways made it difficult to heat, with an ever-present draftiness. Just past the school, blocks and blocks of neighborhood houses had been condemned. Bought out by the federal government, they were being demolished to make way for the new interstate freeway, I-5.

Just as Brusco was getting settled into living on Latona street, Milton came home one day and announced that the family was moving to Lake City, further north, and closer for him to drive to work. It was a newer house for less money, and it cut his commute time in half. So Brusco attended second grade at Olympic Elementary school. The house was two blocks from the school, an easy walk or bike ride. Two blocks in the other direction was a grocery store and Ben Franklin ten cent store. It became a regular, everyday trip on his bicycle to the ten cent store to buy penny candy. For a dime, he could fill a small bag with an assortment of candy.

On a June day in 1960, a weekend, Milton hurried the family at breakfast. A friend at Boeing had told him about a new house, two years old, that was for sale at a bargain price. Milton and Jimmie realized they were throwing money away by renting and felt it was time to buy a house.

Milton didn't have much money for a down payment, so he tried to let Jimmie know to not get her hopes up and be disappointed. If nothing else, it would be a nice family outing in the Pontiac. Up old highway 99, heading north, they came to an intersection called Seattle Heights and took a left on 212th street. An old honky tonk, Barney's, sat on the corner. The sign identifying the place was a giant neon rabbit, his ears waving back and forth. Milton drove a couple blocks and turned again. Here was a street of modest, new homes, one block in length, adjacent to a field of grass. All around the street and field was a forest of evergreen trees. Halfway down the block, Milton found the address of the house for sale. A small sign was tacked to the garage door with "For Sale" written and a phone number. The house was vacant. The owner, a Boeing employee, had been relocated to another state. Peering through the window, Jimmie got excited at what she was seeing and began to beg Milton. "Oh, we must buy this… some way…. I want this house… it's my dream house!" she tugged on his arm.

"Well, I like it too… but don't get your hopes up. We have little money for a down payment."

As it turned out, the Boeing Credit Union held the mortgage to the house. On further investigation, Milton discovered that the Credit Union would make it easy for him to buy it, since he was a well-established employee of the company.

So by the fall of 1960, the house had been purchased, and the Gibbs family moved in. Just to the south was a hamlet called Esperance, where the local school was located. Brusco enrolled in the third grade. He rode a rusty, old yellow school bus that would pick him up daily and deliver him to the Esperance school house. The neighborhood was full of young children, as the "baby boom" was in full swing. Brusco met a kid across the street, his same age. Gordon James and Brusco became inseparable, attending school together and roaming Seattle Heights on their bicycles.

Gordon had an older brother, known as a "greaser" because of his hair style. He played the guitar and was a well-known figure on the local scene. He had all the latest 45 records of rock and roll. Brusco would spend rainy days at Gordon's house, playing his older brother's music on an old phonograph. They memorized the rebellious lyrics and would sing along to the beat.

Gordon loved baseball. He would listen to the Seattle Rainiers on the radio, knowing all the players' names and their positions on the diamond. It wasn't long before it rubbed off on Brusco, who caught baseball fever as well. Milton gave him a leather mitt for his birthday. One of Brusco's favorite pastimes was now playing catch. He and Gordon would lob the hardball back and forth for hours. It soon became apparent that Brusco had a "good arm." Gordon would squat in the catcher's position, and Brusco would wind up and burn a consistent pitch over the plate.

By the 5th grade, Gordon and Brusco were ten years old and eligible to join the local baseball little league, the Mid-City Indians. The coach, Mr. Olsen, immediately recognized Brusco's pitching ability. Within days of trying out, Brusco was made the team's pitcher. Gordon earned the position of third base. Both had given up riding the school bus to Esperance, choosing their trusty bicycles for the task. Staying after school, they'd meet up with the coach and team on one of the three diamonds surrounding the school. They'd practice until dinnertime, then ride home for supper and do homework.

The following year, the team had become a contender, winning many games. Gordon had become a good hitter. The coach had put a long, lanky kid, Jacob Thomason, on first base, who could stretch out and catch the wild throws. Brusco had found his curveball and was striking out batters consistently. The team was on a winning streak and attracting local attention. They were fun to watch, as their confidence was apparent.

The school varsity coach took the time one day to watch Brusco pitch in a game. He had a stellar day at the mound, and his performance was noted by the coach. The Indians won the game handily. After the game, the varsity coach was talking to coach Olsen.

"That kid has a damn good delivery. What's his name?"

"His name is Brusco Gibbs. He's fun to watch on the mound--got a good curveball," coach Olsen bragged.

"Where's he from? I don't recall a Gibbs family from around here," the varsity coach asked.

"His family is from Kansas… from Wichita, he says."

"Hmmm…. Well I'll be keeping my eye on him, an upcoming prospect. So the kid's from Wichita. That wind up on the mound is sinister. The way he loads the ball into his mitt… like a gunslinger…. Ha, he's the 'Wichita Kid!'"

"That's a good nickname for him--the 'Wichita Kid.' I like it!"

A month later, the local newspaper interviewed the coach on his team's winning success. The coach had joked that with the "Wichita Kid" on the mound, their chances were excellent to win the pennant. When the story was printed on the sports page, Brusco from that point on was teased and referred to as the "Wichita Kid." The team went on to win the pennant that Fall, and the nickname became permanent.

At twelve years of age, Brusco had made a name for himself in the small community. Milton was naturally proud of his son and would come to games to root him on. Brusco, Gordon, and Jacob, who preferred to be called Jake, were now like brothers. Gordon had started a baseball card collection, and now Jake and Brusco picked up on the hobby, buying and trading the cards. Across the street from the baseball diamond was a mom and pop little grocery store that sold penny candy. The boys would load up daily on penny candy before practice. A nickel would buy a packet of baseball cards that held a stick of bubble gum. Other boys joined in the trading, and soon Brusco had a collection of over five hundred cards.

Clamoring up to the dinner table one evening, the boy was still chewing a big wad of the pink bubble gum. It irritated Jimmie, and she let him know it. "You quit buying those bubble gum baseball cards! You're gonna ruin your teeth!" she scolded.

"She's right, Brusco…. Every time I see you, you're chewing gum. Spit that wad out and go wash up!" Milton demanded.

Returning to the table after the scolding, Brusco had a glum look on his face. Baseball season was almost over, and the rainy days of autumn had arrived. Sensing his son's moodiness, Milton spoke up. "Hey, I got a surprise for ya. I'm going pheasant hunting next week in Eastern Washington…. You wanna go with me?"

"Really, Dad? Do I get to shoot the gun?" he excitedly asked.

"You'll just be chasing down birds we shoot and learning. Next year, you can go to gun school, get your permit, and then be given a shotgun. This year, you're the bird dog!" Milton laughed.

"Where is this place?" Brusco begged for more info.

"Well, I met an ol' boy out at the plant. He'd been a school teacher in a little town called Almira out in the wheatland. He told me there were hundreds of pheasants roaming around the wheat fields of this town. He knows all the farmers in the area who will let us hunt on their property. His name is Bill Grusom. I'll drive our station wagon, and the three of us will stay at a motel there called the Surprise."

Then, Milton went into a long conversation explaining the craftiness and habits of the ring neck pheasant. They were an intelligent bird and sly at remaining undetected. His years of hunting them as a boy during WW2 had given him fond memories, and he wanted to pass them along to his son. He finally finished his monologue by adding, "And I want you to quit buying that bubble gum! I can't afford to have you in the dentist's office every other month!" He added on a friendlier tone, "You know son, I've got some old baseball cards in a box…. I'll dig them out after supper and you can add them to your collection."

Dinner was finished, and Jimmie was now serving Jell-o to her three children for dessert. Milton disappeared from the table and returned with an old shoebox. He handed it to Brusco. "Those old baseball cards are in there…. An old jackknife is in there, too. Don't cut yourself," he warned. "Finish your Jell-o, then open it up in your room."

Finishing the Jello, he took the box to his room to see what was inside. He found a dozen baseball cards from the 1920's, but none of the players were ones he recognized. The jackknife was old and hard to open the blade. Some old Indian pennies and buffalo nickels lay in the bottom. A shiny, mother of pearl medallion caught his eye. It was the size of a silver dollar. He marveled at the way it caught the light and reflected colors. He tossed it back in the shoe box and grabbed the baseball cards, placing the box back up in his closet.

The hunting trip proved to be a success and an eye opener for Brusco. The wheatland around Almira was immense and flat, much like Kansas. The fields and back roads were crawling with ring neck pheasants. It had taken no time for Bill and Milton to shoot their daily three apiece limits. Milton showed Brusco how to track the downed birds, marking their fallen spot, then rushing there to retrieve them. Upon returning to Seattle Heights, Brusco was filled with anticipation and excitement to go to gun school and be allowed to shoot as well.

One day in November, Brusco returned home from school and found his mother distraught and sobbing in front of the television. "Ma, what's wrong? What is it?" seeing her distraught and crying.

"The President has been shot.... I think he's been killed!" she wailed. From that day forward, a somber mood was upon the land, at school and in public. The assassination had shaken the country to its core. A mood of grief and sadness persisted for weeks, into the winter and new year.

The gloominess of winter passed into spring. It was time for the Esperance school carnival. A contest was held for who could draw the best poster to advertise the event. Brusco worked hard on his poster, a clown juggling balls with each event written on them.

It was a masterpiece, he decided, and was sure to win the contest. An assembly in the auditorium was held to announce the winner. Holding up the winning poster, the principal announced his congratulations to Ruth Baker. She had traced the album cover of a new group called the "Beatles" and made her poster in the likeness of their four heads. Disgusted, Brusco wondered who these Beatles were that had shot down his clown poster masterpiece.

That spring, Brusco and Gordon, along with Jake, practiced daily at the baseball diamond. They were anxious for the summer tournament games to begin. Brusco had worked on his curveball, and Gordon had become a dependable batter. Jake had grown another three inches and could lean and stretch far off of first base. The first game had been won easily, and the second game had been won with Brusco's pitching.

402

It was evident that he was a star pitcher in the making. It was the evening before the third game that changed everything though. A group of neighborhood kids were gathered at a basketball hoop. One of the boys had a new skateboard and was demonstrating his ability to ride it. He made it look easy, enticing Brusco to give it a try. Stepping onto the board with one foot, Brusco pushed with his other foot, bringing it up to ride. Like a bullet, the skateboard shot out from under him, bringing him down hard on the concrete, his forearms taking the brunt of his weight. The result was a compound fracture to his right arm. Hobbling home and wailing in pain, Milton and Jimmie saw the broken arm and rushed him to the emergency room at the hospital. The arm was put up in a full-length plaster cast. Brusco's baseball pitching days were over. The arm mended by September, allowing Brusco just in time to take the gun school course. Successfully completing the course, he could now buy a hunting license.

Now hunting the wheat fields with Milton, Brusco was growing whiskers and learning life's lessons. He was taught the habits of the pheasant, where the watering holes were, and where they liked to "dust" themselves. They were experts at camouflage, hiding in brushy draws and coulees. They loved to eat wheat and would appear from hiding at dusk or dawn to fill their craws. Using stealth and choke points, the hunters could "push" the birds to a point man, forcing them out of hiding, and to flush into the air. Returning to Seattle Heights after the hunt, Brusco was already talking about next year's hunt with eager anticipation. Milton was pleased with his son's enthusiasm, which had formed a new bond between the two.

Brusco had been baptised into Seattle's rock and roll sound, listening to Gordon's 45 records and the stations on his transistor radio. The British invasion was in full force now, exploding on America. The Beatles, Rolling Stones, Kinks, and Herman's Hermits were the talk at school. The new beat and culture consumed Brusco's generation.

Brusco had been blessed with a handsome face, and now, all of a sudden, girls his age were flirting with him. At school, kids were wearing "mod" clothing, a style imported from England. Girls wore white go-go boots, and the boys paisley shirts. Pants of wide wale corduroy of bright colors with a large belt and buckle were the fad. Brusco found himself caught up in the new style. It seemed to attract the pretty girls, which had become his focus.

In 1967, the counterculture was born on the corner of Haight and Ashbury in San Francisco. The rebellious new youth were known as hippies, embracing love and peace. The Vietnam war was raging, and the hippies' motto was to make love, not war. The music was changing also, becoming protest songs against the old school of conservative thought.

A new movement across America was taking her youth by storm, and old principles and values were going out the window. It was also the year that Brusco got his driver's license. The newfound freedom of the automobile brought a sudden change to the boy and his demeanor. He grew his hair out shaggy and long. Wearing Mexican huarache sandals and love beads, his appearance became despised by his parents. The harder they argued about his hippie ways and attire, the more he rebelled and distanced himself from them.

He began staying out late at night, drinking beer at beach parties and coming home in the wee hours of the morning. He had taken up smoking cigarettes, as well, causing his clothing to reek of nicotine and smoke. Jimmie became enraged at the person he'd become. The bickering and arguing with his parents had become constant. They refused to accept this new form of youthful rebellion in their son.

At seventeen, he had found a good job cleaning buildings as a janitor after school. The work would start at 5 p.m., when the businesses closed, and he would work until midnight. His grades in school rapidly went downhill, and by his senior year, he was barely passing his classes. The job was bringing him good money, enough to fuel all of his bad vices. Girls and sex, cigarettes and pot, beer and fast muscle cars had all become his passion. His best friend was now Jake, who was also caught up in the counterculture, just as much as Brusco was. Jake's parents had gotten divorced recently, and it had left him searching for answers. He had moved to his uncle's small farm in Meadowdale. There was a small trailer at the back of the farm, away from his uncle's farm house, out behind the barn, where Jake took up residence.

Both Jake and Brusco were now eighteen. Jake had a Triumph motorcycle, which he'd ride to school. Brusco had a '56 Chevy, with a souped up engine he drove to school daily. On the day of their eighteenth birthdays, the Esperance principal called them out of class and into his office. Each was required to sign up for the military draft. The draft had become a lottery, whereas their birthdates had been thrown into a hat of three hundred and sixty-five numbers. As the numbers were drawn, that became their number on the list of eligible draftees. Brusco's number had come up as one hundred thirty-seven, and Jake's number was one hundred sixty-five. It looked for sure that Brusco would be drafted and sent to Vietnam. Depression came over both boys, as neither wanted to pick up a rifle and kill people in a conflict that had never been declared as an official war.

404

Brusco's drinking and late night escapades became worse as he tried to cope with his fate. Through the course of the sixties, the war had grown larger and loomed in his future. Now, it was his turn to go and fight.

Coming home from a Saturday all-nighter on a Sunday morning, Brusco found both parents waiting for him.

"This is the last straw Brusco.... You're becoming a bad influence on Lilly and Nebanae. We don't want you here any longer. Pack your things and go live with your hippie friends. You don't belong here--we want you to leave," came the ultimatum from both parents.

It was what "The Kid" wanted, both parents pointing him to the door. An hour later, he was driving down the street with all of his belongings in the trunk of the Chevy. He headed straight for Meadowdale and Jake's trailer behind the barn. He already almost lived there anyway, so it was no surprise when Brusco told him of his situation.

Jake had a job pumping gas at a Texaco station after school and made half as much money as Brusco. Between them, they managed to survive the remaining school year, graduating with high school diplomas in 1970. Both boys watched anxiously as the summer months passed. The draft call was getting closer to Brusco. Every Sunday in the Seattle Times newspaper, the government would post how many more numbers were being called up. The country's protest of the war that year was profound and immense, heavily influencing the political climate. The administration had to figure out how to back out of the war with dignity. By Thanksgiving, the Army had drafted to number one hundred fifteen. If the war escalated with another Tet offensive, he'd get called for sure. Jake was feeling relieved, but the month of December passed painfully slow for Brusco, with each week buying a Sunday paper to see the number. Finally, the final call for 1970 was in, the last Sunday after Christmas. The final number was one hundred twenty-five, a little over one third of America's eighteen-year-old boys had and would be sent to kill the yellow man.

On December thirtieth, a new lottery was drawn for the draftees of the next year, 1971. For the first time in many years, the yoke of anxiety was lifted from both boys' shoulders. They, in all probability, would not be drafted. They could pursue life now without that door in front of them, the cloud of uncertainty now gone.

In the winter of 1971, Brusco came back to the trailer from work one day to find Jake tripping on mescaline acid and listening to the Byrds on the turntable. He was laughing and feeling good about life. Plucking away on his guitar, he joked with Brusco, "Hey, take a hit of this brown barrel mescaline. It'll get ya grinnin,'" he laughed and pointed. A sandwich bag held about a dozen hits of the brown pellets of LSD.

"Good stuff, huh?" Brusco examined the contents.

"Yeah, try one, bro.... I'm flying and feeling good. So groovy," he insisted.

Brusco cracked a beer open and popped a pellet into his mouth. Gulping down some beer, he sat back in an easy chair and listened to Jake play his guitar.

The song titled "Ballad of Easy Rider" began to play. Jake knew the chords, strummed, and sang along. Brusco was now rushing on the mescaline.

The next song began to play... "Wasn't Born to Follow."

"Hey, Jake, play that again. You sound good, man!" Jake re-dropped the needle on the record and again played the guitar and sang along. He was harmonizing the lyrics, in synch with the Byrds. The song ended and Brusco insisted, "Stop! Stop! Man, that song got me thinking. We're free, Jake. Absolutely free. Let's hit the road! We'll travel cross country, camp, fish, explore.... We'll find some peyote... trip, and drive on... all summer! Let's save our money and go in the spring. There's nothing holding us here anymore!" Brusco was adamant and tripping.

Jake cocked his stoned head and said, "You're crazy, man.... Where would we go? We can't just sleep out under the stars every night. My motorcycle won't go a hundred miles before it breaks down. That Chevy of yours is a gas hog. We'd be broke by the time we got to Boise!"

Brusco was relentless, saying, "Jakee, listen up.... We get us a pickup, put a canopy on the back, and get a couple of hammocks. We load it up with some canned goods, a good bag of weed, and our fishing poles. We can go to Kansas and Texas. I got close relatives there. We'll fish and camp in the Rockies and chase Colorado hippie chicks. We'll be gone all summer dude!"

Jake was grinning and thinking about it now. "I like it Brusco, but where are you gonna get this pickup?"

"I'll sell the '56 Chevy! I'll take the money and buy us a pickup," Brusco blurted out.

"It's a deal, Brusco. You buy a pickup, and we'll hit the road. We're gonna have to save some money, dude!" Jake was getting serious now.

"Agreed, but if we start saving now, we should have enough money by the end of May. We need a thousand dollars--five hundred to go on, and five hundred to come back. Both of us should be able to save the money in the next four months," Brusco was calculating.

To prove he was serious, the next day after the mescaline trip, Brusco quipped to Jake, "Hey, hop in the Chev with me. I'm gonna go down to the newspaper and run an ad in the classified section to sell the car."

About halfway to the newspaper building, both boys spotted the same thing as they drove by. A Chevy pickup with a "For Sale" sign sat parked on the curb.

"Did you see that? Hey, I'm turning around. Let's go check it out." Brusco spun the steering wheel. Pulling up and parking, they both jumped out. Calling out from a front porch, a voice rang out, "Can I help you boys?"

Brusco turned and politely called out, "Yes, ma'am.... Is this truck for sale?"

The woman turned and called into the house, "Joe, some lads your age are looking at your truck."

Joe came out, talking friendly, and immediately went into a spiel to sell the truck. "Well, it's a 235 three on the tree, half ton with a wrap around glass cab."

Brusco interrupted. "She's a '55... right? Apache?"

"Yup.... My grandpa put that steel bumper on the back. He died and left me the truck. I wanna sell it, and with the money buy a muscle car, like yours," Joe explained.

"How much do you want for the Apache?" Brusco was trying to hide his enthusiasm.

"I'd take $350," Joe offered.

Brusco now played his hole card. "Tell ya what... you give me two hundred bucks and your truck, and I'll give you my '56 two-door Chevy."

Joe got excited, "Really!? Yeah, sure, but I only have $140," he honestly countered now.

"DONE!" Brusco held out his hand. Joe shook it in disbelief.

"You got the title?" he asked.

"Yup, let's trade right here and now!" Brusco nodded.

The deed was done. Brusco and Jake drove the '55 Apache back to the trailer. It was a good trade. The truck was strong running and solid. The cab had a 360 degree view, as the back window was glass to the door post. In the days ahead, both boys spent all their extra time building a plywood top for the bed of the pickup. The cover was only six inches above the bed, giving it a low profile look. Brusco had an old Navajo blanket that he cut into eight inch widths and were used as curtains, or flaps between the gaps. A chuck wagon box was built on the rear steel bumper. Its doors swung open to reveal a camp kitchen. Two

407

hammocks were found to string from the corner of the steel bumper to a nearby tree.

The Apache had "step sides," which enabled Brusco to strap five-gallon jerry cans of gas on both sides--a good precaution to have and not run out of gas. By May, they had accomplished their goal and then some. Eleven hundred dollars had been saved between the two of them.

Jake had heard about a rock festival that was to happen in Marlin, Washington in mid June. The plan was to leave the first of June on their overland adventure, starting off with the rock festival, called "Sunrise 71."

"Ya know, I've been thinking Jakee, maybe we should have a dog. Camping in the Rockies, snakes in the desert… it might be good to have a dog."

"I've been thinking the same thing Brusco. We could go up to the Everett Pound and spring one from death row," Jake suggested.

"Ok… let's go up there and have a look. We're not lookin' for just any old dog though. We might hold off and find a stray on the road," Brusco pondered.

The Everett Pound was out by the dump, an unsavory part of town. Pulling up to the building, a howl of barking could be heard, coming from its interior walls. The boys entered the office and expressed their desire to adopt a dog. Hearing this, the caretaker allowed them to enter the corridor between the barking cages.

"Each cage has a number. Bring me the number, and I'll open the cage," he directed.

An old, grey black lab had caught their attention. His sad eyes were begging for them to let him out. From the corner of Brusco's eye, a shadowy figure caught his eye, pacing back and forth without stopping. He now had Brusco's attention. His eyes were yellow and wild. His markings were collie, but he looked like a coyote.

"Check this one out, Jake," Brusco waved for his attention.

"Yeah… look at him, pacing back and forth. He's the one!" agreed Jake.

The boys returned to the office and announced they wanted the dog in cage seventeen. The caretaker thumbed through his clipboard, "Well boys, this dog has to remain one more week to allow the owner to claim him. Come back in one week."

Disappointed, Brusco said they'd be back next week. That weekend, three days later, Brusco was in the area and decided to stop in and see if someone had claimed the dog. It was Saturday, and this time a different keeper was at the desk.

"Yeah, I was in here a few days ago. We saw a dog in cage seventeen we wanted. I know it hasn't been a week, but I thought I'd check and see if someone had claimed him."

The keeper searched the clipboard. "Hmm... I'd say that number seventeen is a lucky dog. He's scheduled to be put down today."

"Really? The other guy said come back in one week!" Brusco looked surprised.

"Nope, he told you wrong. I was here when they brought that dog in two weeks ago. He's from a ranch in Eastern Washington. They brought him to the city, and he's just too wild. Says here his name is Zeke," the keeper revealed.

"So I can have him?" asked Brusco.

"Yeah... he's a lucky one. Stay here and I'll go get him."

The keeper came back with a homemade leash of rope around the dog. The dog sensed his freedom was at hand and trembled with excitement. The keeper was pleased the dog had been spared and wished both Zeke and Brusco luck.

Returning to the trailer, Jake was delighted to see that Brusco had the dog with him. Jake had traded a bag of weed for an eight-track stereo player and was anxious to install it in the Apache.

"Looks like we're all set to go--tunes, a dog... the truck is running great. Where are we gonna hide the acid?" Brusco questioned Jake.

"I put the LSD in a cigarette tin case. We'll unbolt the battery bracket and slide it under the battery--a perfect place to hide it." Jake winked.

"Wow, that's a great idea!" Brusco admired his ingenuity.

"Well, when are we leaving, Brusco?" Jake asked.

"Well, if you quit your job next week, and my last day is Friday, let's leave Saturday morning! We can find a good campground somewhere around Marlin and wait for the rock festival," Brusco suggested.

"Sounds good to me." He twisted up the last speaker wire. "Hand me that 'Sticky Fingers' tape. Let's see if this thing works." The song "Wild Horses" came booming out of the speaker behind the bench seat.

"Whoa! That sounds great!" Brusco complimented his handiwork.

The week went by quickly, and Saturday morning, the two nineteen-year-olds, Zeke, and the Apache departed on their saga. It was the middle of June and very hot by the time they reached the wheat fields of Eastern Washington. They arrived in the desolate town of Odessa and were quickly pulled over by a sheriff. They were told that there was no loitering or camping in town and to keep moving. On the edge of town, they picked up a hippie hitchhiker who told them that he was going to Wilson Creek, a town next to Marlin, and wait for the festival

409

to start. At Wilson Creek, they found a hundred hippies camped at the grain silos on the edge of town. After three days of hanging out, it was obvious the rock festival wasn't going to happen. The promoters had failed to acquire adequate permits from the county. Five sheriff squad cars rolled in and scattered the campers at the silos. It was time to go.

The boys headed south, down to the southeast part of the state and picked up Highway 12 to cross the Rockies. Just as they were crossing the Idaho line, the sun was going down. The Clearwater River ran alongside the highway. They found a campground by the river, but now it was total darkness, and a hoard of mosquitoes descended upon them. So bad were the mosquitoes that the boys cancelled building a fire and burrowed themselves into their sleeping bags, covering their faces from the buzzing swarms. At first light, both were anxious to leave and wasted no time getting the Apache back on the road. Highway 12 climbs LoLo Pass over the Rockies, and within an hour, the Apache was laboring hard up the grade. By the time they reached the summit of the pass, the truck had overheated. They sat for half an hour and let the engine cool down. The ride down the eastern pass was scary as the truck was heavy with gear, and the brakes began to overheat. Brusco put the truck in second gear, and finally, they reached rolling foothills.

"Let's make camp before dark and get a fire going so we don't have that mosquito problem again," Jake suggested.

Brusco was looking at the road map. "There's a town just up ahead called Drummond. Let's stop there and camp," agreed Brusco.

Pulling into town, Jake saw a small sign in the yard of an old house. It read, "Justice of the Peace," and under that, "Nightcrawlers for Sale." Jake pulled over and shut the key off.

"I'm gonna buy some worms, ask about fishin', and maybe a place to camp. C'mon, Brusco."

The two walked up to the front porch and knocked on the door. A short, bald, whiskered old fellow in bib overalls answered the door. He took a step back and looked at the boys, wide-eyed.

"Afternoon, sir. We'd like to buy some fishin worms," Jake flatly announced.

The man stared without saying anything and finally turned and hollered into the house, "Helen, come here and look at this!"

An old woman appeared behind him and put her hand to her mouth. "Are they Blackfeet?" she whispered.

"No, I reckon they're real, live hippies!

"Where you boys from?" he finally addressed them.

"Washington State--from Seattle, sir," Brusco answered and grinned.

"Well, I'll be damned…. I seen pictures of you hippies on Walter Cronkite but never seen one in this town. I read about you long hairs and problems that you're causing."

"We don't want to be anybody's problem. We just want to know where we can camp outside of town and fish," Jake assured the old gent.

It suddenly dawned on the boys that they were far from home, deep in Montana's redneck belt. Their hair was down to their shoulders. Both wore moccasins, tie-dye T-shirts, and faded, ragged blue jeans. Again, Jake asked, "Can we buy some nightcrawlers sir? And where is a place to fish?"

"Sure, sure… follow me." He took the boys around to the back of the house. On a back porch, he opened an ancient refrigerator. Inside, empty soup cans of dirt held the fishing bait. He handed a can to Jake, who held out two bits.

"On the edge of town, take a right at the cafe. Go a ways and you'll come to a bridge that crosses the Clark. On the other side of the bridge, you can camp and fish. You boys stay outta trouble. I wouldn't hang around here too long. There's a lotta folks here who don't like 'draft dodgers.'"

"We're not draft dodgers, and we're just passin' through." The cocky old fart was pissing Brusco off.

"Just warnin' ya. I wouldn't hang around Drummond if I was you."

The boys followed the instructions and found the bridge next to the river. A picnic table and fire pit were on the riverbank. Brusco got a fire going while Jake tried his luck at fishing. The fish weren't biting, and after an hour, he gave up. Brusco had some stew and pan biscuits cooked up for dinner. Zeke was given a can of dog food, and they discussed where they were bound for the following day. The next morning, Jake was trying his luck at fishing again and not getting any bites. He finally gave up, smelling the coffee that Brusco was brewing.

"All the big talk I've heard all my life about the great fishing in Montana… there ain't no fish in this river!" Jake scoffed.

"Well, let's head for Yellowstone Park. I've heard there's good fishing in the Yellowstone River," Brusco suggested.

As they sipped coffee, a pickup came across the bridge, turned, and pulled up next to the Apache. For a moment, Brusco and Jake feared trouble but then heard a friendly voice.

"You ain't gonna catch any fish here."

Jake walked over to the truck. "Yeah, I figured that out." He laughed.

Three teenage boys wearing cowboy hats sat in the front seat. "Yeah, the Clark's running too fast here. You might catch something here in the late

411

summer," the driver volunteered. Before Jake could answer, the driver now asked where they were from.

"We're from Seattle... Puget sound... on the West Coast," Jake volunteered.

"We never seen hippies! We heard in town you was camped here. We had to come see... kinda boring in this little town," the driver continued. "Does that dog bite?"

"Naw.... Zeke dog--he's friendly," Jake replied.

The three cowboys then got out of the truck and introduced themselves. Brusco walked over and shook hands then offered some coffee in paper cups. A friendly, curious conversation developed. Finally, Jake asked the question, "So you guys being local... you must have your secret fishing holes. We're just passin' through... how bout it--can you tell us where to go?"

The driver chuckled. "Yeah, we know where to fish. Hey, you guys got any of that stuff called 'pot?'"

The moment of trust had arrived. These weren't narcs, and Jake caught on to what he was asking. "Yeah, I'll tell you what... I'll give you two joints if you show us where to fish."

The cowboys got excited now. "Ok, yeah.... We'll take you to 'Seldom Seen.' There's a stream there full of fish for two of those pot cigarettes. What didja call it... joints?"

"How far is it from here?" Jake asked.

"Ten miles. It's up in the Garnet Range. C'mon, let's go! We'll show you where. We can be there in fifteen minutes."

Brusco and Jake instantly broke camp, packing up the Apache. Within minutes, they were following the cowboys up a winding, canyon road. The canyon was covered with meadows bordering a running stream, lined with willows. The cowboys finally pulled off the road and down into an open meadow. Crossing the meadow, their truck came to stop at a large group of willows surrounding a pond. A beaver had built a dam on the stream, with the result being a large pond. They jumped out, eager to explore the magical place.

One of the cowboys explained, "This is an old Blackfoot hunting ground. There's lotsa trout in the pond. Go ahead, throw a line in.

"Hey, we wanna smoke some of that pot. We've never tried it."

"Brusco, twist up a couple of Camels and get these guys stoned... I'm going fishing!"

By the time Brusco had rolled two joints, Jake had caught a nice brook trout. The cowboys laughed at Jake's excitement. Brusco lit the first joint, took a hit, held it, then passed it to the cowboys. They each took a long drag. When it got back to Brusco, he passed and let them finish it. By now, Jake had caught another fish, a big rainbow trout. Having no net, he yanked it out of the water and onto the bank. The fish flopped and fought so hard he tore the hook loose. He made it to the water's edge and was about to swim away, but Jake jumped and lunged, grabbing the fish bare handed. Off balance, he fell on his side into the shallows. The cowboys began to laugh uncontrollably at the spectacle. To see a city boy jump in after a fish was totally comical to them. It was a fun day. Jake got tired of catching fish, landing them one after another. He gave the pole to Brusco and rolled some more pot. A fire was made, and the chuck wagon doors were opened up. Before long, the trout were sizzling in the frying pan. This was what the two had been searching for--solitude in the wilderness and catching and eating wild trout. The cowboys were given a couple more joints that afternoon when they departed back for Drummond.

"We gotta go back to work tomorrow…. Maybe we'll see you guys when you return." They wished each other luck.

Brusco, Jake, and Zeke spent two more days at "Seldom Seen." On the second day, comfortable with the surroundings, they each took a hit of mescaline and tripped all day on the beauty of mother nature. After a late breakfast on the third day, the Apache was packed up, and they headed south down the highway. At Bozeman, they took the Yellowstone cut-off and reached the park gate by afternoon. Jake grumbled about the six dollar fee to enter the park. Brusco had seen the park earlier in his youth and knew about the geysers and bears. Jake had never been this far east in his life. He marveled at the buffalo that roamed the park and walked freely down the roads. They found a campground, with tourist families camped in a condensed cluster all around them. They were clearly out of place and stared at as if they were a park attraction.

"This place is way too commercial, Brusco…. How can you pretend to enjoy this after camping at Seldom Seen?" Jake asked as he looked around.

Zeke was tied to a picnic table, not enjoying his situation. They both looked at him in sympathy.

"You know what…. Let's boogie! We'll drive all night. The cool air of the night is like an air conditioner in the cab of the truck. We'll see where we end up in Wyoming tomorrow…. There's gotta be something better than this parking lot camping." Jake insisted.

"I agree…. We're outta here. Let's go!" Brusco was already untying Zeke. "If we drive through the park tonight, you'll miss all the scenery and attractions…. You realize that, don't you Jake?"

413

"Too many tourists here to even enjoy the attractions. Hell, we seem to be an attraction. I've already caught people taking our picture more than once. Nope, let's drive all night."

Jake was ready to go. By 2 a.m., they were driving into Jackson Hole, in the heart of the Teton Mountains. The bars were just closing, and they found a grassy area in town to park. They threw their sleeping bags on the ground, next to a giant arch of deer antlers cobbled together to make a tourist attraction. At 6 a.m., a sheriff kicked Brusco's shoulder, waking him up. He informed them sternly that this wasn't a camping area, that they were vagrant, and to move on.

They kept heading south on Highway 191, coming to a town called Pinedale. The town was alive with people. A banner flying over Main Street declared that today was the big rodeo. The town was so small that it wasn't hard to find the rodeo grounds. The arena was lined with pickup trucks and stock trailers.

"Hey, let's go get a hot dog," Brusco suggested. They found the food booth. Taking the hot dogs to the condiment counter, they loaded them up with everything offered. Turning around, four big cowboys confronted them.

"Well, look at these ugly little girls, eating weenies. I bet they eat each other's weenie, what do you think, Bill?" the big one taunted them.

One cowboy had a rope and now threw the lasso at Brusco's moccasins.

"Maybe we should string this one up and watch his girlfriend suck his dick," he threatened.

Jake looked at Brusco. "Let's go bro... now. Let's get outta here!" Zeke had been left in the cab. They pulled out of the parking area, the four cowboys pointing and laughing at them.

They continued down 191, checking the rear view mirror for an hour to see if they were being followed.

"Damn it, I think these deerskin headbands are attracting the wrong attention! Everyone thinks we're some kind of rolling freak show!" Jake angrily pulled his headband off.

At the next small town, Brusco spotted a homemade sign that said "Estate Sale."

"Let's stop and check it out, take a breather... let Zeke pee." Brusco pointed at the sign as they passed.

The sale was the estate of a local rancher who'd passed away. Almost two dozen cowboy hats of straw, felt, and beaver sat on a table. "How much?" Jake asked.

"A dollar a piece, take your pick," came the answer.

Both boys found a straw hat they liked, paid the two dollars, and jumped back in the Apache, wearing them. It seemed that Jake was right. The cowboy hats helped to blend them into the local towns they drove through. They camped at Rock Springs that night, got up early, and drove across Utah. That afternoon, they arrived at Green River. The desert crossing had been hot, and they searched for a place to cool off and swim in the river. On a corner at an intersection, Brusco spotted a kid on a bicycle and leaned out to ask, "Hey man, where's a good spot to go swimming in the river?"

The kid pointed back from where the Apache had come. "Go down to Bunker Road, take a left, and it'll take you to the swimming hole."

Following the kid's instructions, they turned around and found a secluded, quiet spot to camp by the river. A cottonwood tree hung out over the Green River with a rope swing dangling over the water. The temperature was 103 degrees, and both boys cannonballed off the rope swing into the river. This was a good place to rest a few days, as no one was around.

It was here that Brusco discovered a major problem. On checking the oil of the dipstick, he found that the Apache was over three quarts low on oil. They carried two quarts in the truck, and after adding them, they found that there was still no oil on the dipstick. They drove to town, bought two more quarts, and added one. Finally, they could see oil on the stick.

After three days of rest, they were anxious to go to Colorado. The drinking age there was eighteen, and they'd heard stories of wild bars in Denver full of young girls. Now leaving Green River and back on the highway, they noticed a plume of exhaust smoke behind them as they headed for Grand Junction. As they crossed the Colorado line, Brusco pulled over and checked the oil again.

"Shit! There's no oil on the stick.... We've probably burned the piston rings out! We've only gone fifty miles!" Brusco lamented.

Adding the one quart they had, they pulled into the next Conoco station. Bulk oil was sold for ten cents a quart in a can. They bought a case of twenty-four cans, for two dollars and forty cents. Thereafter, watching the odometer at thirty mile increments, they would stop and add two quarts of oil to the 235. So to go a hundred miles, it took six quarts of oil.

They pulled into Denver late in the day, having no idea where to stay. Driving around in an older part of town, on West Colfax, they found an abandoned house that was hidden behind tall, overgrown shrubs and trees. Entering the alley, they found a hidden place to park. Under a giant overgrown lilac tree, they lay their sleeping bags.

The next morning, they walked to a nearby cafe and had breakfast. The waitress was young and friendly and asked where they were from.

"Where's a good bar to drink beer and dance?" Brusco asked her.

Without hesitating, she replied, "Go to Stout Street Electric Company…. It's on Stout Street. You'll have a good time," she laughed.

They lingered all day behind the abandoned house. An irrigation spigot still had water pressure, and so both boys cleaned up with soap and water. That evening, they found the bar on Stout Street. Leaving the windows cracked open for Zeke, they parked the Apache a block away. The music was booming out into the street. Upon entering the dark atmosphere, an electronic, pulsating plexiglass dance floor was throbbing. Young teenagers were seen, jamming the dance floor and gyrating. Draft beer was served in pitchers, the tables laden with beer pitchers and glasses. It wasn't long before Brusco asked a cute, long haired girl to dance. She bumped and grinded on him, and they stayed on the floor for several songs.

Jake was playing the field and danced with several girls. At closing time, Brusco's girl invited to have him take her home to her apartment. Her name was Cheri Toronto, and once outside, she was kissing and necking with Brusco. Cheri's roommate--and not and having Cheri's beauty--was up watching television when they entered her apartment. Jake was disappointed, as he couldn't bring himself to make advances towards the homely girl. He plopped down on the couch while Cheri and Brusco retired to her bedroom. The next morning, both girls had to work. Up early and making coffee, they ushered their overnight guests out the door. Still hungover, they drove back to the abandoned house and napped all day in the shade.

"Damn it! It's hot here… must be over a hundred degrees," Jake complained.

"Let's hit the road at sunset. We'll drive all night and head for the Kansas line," Brusco suggested.

They got on the road at dusk, heading south out of Denver, stopping every thirty miles and adding two quarts of oil. Reaching Pueblo at midnight, they took the cutoff onto Highway 50 and headed east to Kansas. After another oil stop, Brusco took the wheel, and Jake fell asleep. Another thirty miles, and Brusco pulled over again, adding two more quarts without waking his pardner.

It was now 2 a.m., and Brusco was having a hard time keeping his eyes awake. Jake was snoring, and Brusco caught his head bobbing twice. He finally spotted a roadside cafe in La Junta that still had its lights on. Brusco pulled into the gravel parking lot and woke up Jake.

416

"Where are we man...? Kansas?" He rubbed his eyes and stared around.

"No, we're still in Colorado. This place is called La Junta. I gotta get some coffee, Jake." Brusco opened the Apache and stepped out. Entering the greasy diner, an ugly, red-haired waitress sat at the cash register and was painting her fingernails.

"The grill's closed. We only got coffee and pie." She looked up at the boys. Not a soul was in the place. They slid into a booth and ordered two coffees. Bringing the mugs, she went back to her chair and continued on her nail polishing. They asked for refills, and the ugly waitress acted disgusted to be troubled again. This time, she left the pot on their table.

"How far is the Kansas line?" Jake was beginning to wake up.

"Maybe twenty-five miles... guessing," Brusco informed him.

Just then, two gorgeous, bombshell Latina girls entered the cafe. They walked over and sat in the booth directly across from the boys. Again, the waitress acted annoyed, having to do her job. The girls were speaking in Spanish and were casting flirting eyes at the boys' direction. Jake cut right to the chase and invited the girls to sit with them. The girls moved to their booth, and a lively conversation began between them. At one point, the girls asked the boys if they liked to get "high."

"Of course!" came the answer.

Now the one girl suggested, "Let's go for a ride. We have some good stuff!"

Paying for the coffees, the four stepped out into the heat of the night desert. The girls were driving a shiny 442 and told the boys to hop into the back seat. The driver went through the gears, pinning the lads to the back seat, jerking their heads as the girl power shifted the clutch. They drove for ten minutes, out into the desert, then stopped the car in the middle of the road and turned out the lights.

"You guys ever had Number One?" the passenger turned around and asked.

"Nope. What's Number One?" Jake asked curiously.

"It's pure THC," she answered. She put a little chunk in a glass tube, lit it with her lighter, and passed it to Jake. "One hit is all it takes," she advised.

Jake and Brusco took two deep, long pulls on the pipe. Jake lit it a third time, and suddenly, his hand just fell away. The rush of the two hits slammed him, and he could not function and strike the lighter again.

"Holy shit! This stuff is powerful!" The rush hit Brusco as well.

"Told ya…. Ya only need one toke. You guys are gonna be really fucked up now," she snickered.

The girls laughed and started up the muscle car and headed back to the cafe. Brusco and Jake had hoped for some fast sex with the beauties, but upon arriving at the Apache, the girls announced they were going home. The lads slowly stumbled out of the back seat. Both girls laughed at the two stoned out hippies and spun out of the parking lot, burning rubber on the highway.

"Sheeez, I'm fucked up," Jake stuttered. "Can you drive, Brusco?"

"We gotta drive, Jakee…. We're sitting ducks here if a cop drives by. The cops probably drink coffee here too." Zeke was whining, not liking being left in the cab. "I'll drive, but you gotta stay awake, Jakee," Brusco demanded. Back on the highway, they became the only headlights in the desert night. On the Colorado/Kansas line, they stopped in a wheat field and oiled up the 235.

The sun was coming up, and the drug was finally wearing off. The two laughed about the previous night. Brusco pulled out a bottle of Southern Comfort, toasted the rising sun that was blinding him, and took a long pull. Jake took the bottle and swigged a gulp as well. "Let's go see Kansas!" he laughed.

By nine that morning, they reached Cimarron, just west of Dodge City. They pulled down a side road that ran along some train tracks, coming to some boxcars on a siding that had been there for some time. Grass was growing around the iron wheels, with no sign of fresh tire tracks in the dust. Using the shade of the boxcars, they camped for the afternoon. The Kansas heat was oppressive, and after the long drive out of Colorado, the two were weary, needing sleep. The place was empty and quiet, and they slept through the afternoon. The consensus now was to travel at night, as the truck was smoking a plume out the tailpipe. Under the cover of darkness and the cooler night air, they continued that evening, traveling straight east through the endless wheat fields.

All night they drove, taking turns at the wheel, stopping every thirty miles and re-oiling. As the morning sun came up, they rolled into Wellington. Brusco was now on familiar ground and drove straight to his grandparents' house--Jim and Ellie Kincaid. The old man was sitting on the front porch swing, having a cigarette and coffee when the Apache pulled up on West Harvey Street.

Jimmie had called the old man and told him Brusco was coming, so it was no surprise. Even so, Jim shook his head and grinned at what he was looking at. The two long-haired hippie cowboys, along with the coyote, jumped out of the bodacious Apache and walked up the brick sidewalk to the front porch.

"Mornin' Grandpa!" came Brusco's greeting. "This here is my buddy Jake and our dog Zeke. Jake, this here is Jim Kincaid."

Ellie came out on the front porch, excited, and gave Brusco a hug. After the introduction, she brought the boys into the kitchen and fed them breakfast. Hearing they had driven all night, she demanded that they take a bath and rest, providing two army cots for their sleeping bags.

After resting for a couple days, the two began to explore the town. They cruised up and down Main Street a few times, garnishing looks as they drove by. It was the third of July, and firecrackers were popping all over town. They bought a string of Black Cat firecrackers and went back to the Kincaid house. The house sat adjacent to an old city park--Stewarts Park. Zeke hated the firecrackers and refused to get out of the Apache, cowering on the cab floor. The boys sat in the park, drinking cold beer and lighting Black Cats with their cigarettes, tossing them in the air.

"Hey…. Y'all got any more beer?" came a voice from behind them. Both boys turned around and were staring at two cute teenage girls.

"Uh… yeah, in the cooler… help yourself!" Brusco open the lid and fished out two cold bottles.

"My name's Brusco… Brusco Gibbs. This is Jake, and who might you be?"

"My name's Gina Bertolucci, and this is Karen Modette. Where are you guys from? We saw you in town." They both accepted the cold bottles. Both girls were lean and pretty, sporting summer tans, with both wearing shorts and low cut tops. Both were barefoot and had southern drawls when they spoke. Instantly, the four were attracted to each other. Within five minutes, it was obvious that Gina liked Brusco and Karen liked Jake. By the second beer, Karen already had her hand on Jake's thigh. The girls asked for a ride in the "hippie truck," saying, "Let's go get some more beer and go out to the lake!"

The lake was a couple miles outside of town, a secluded place. The group found a shady spot and opened some more beers. Brusco took Gina to the cab of the Apache, smoked a joint with her, and commenced to make heated love on the front seat. Hearing them, Jake and Karen got up on the top of the cover over the truck bed and were quickly naked and locked in passion. This went on late into the evening until all four passed out from the passion and alcohol. The next morning, the boys took the girls back to town. They had all agreed that Brusco and Jake would go back to the lake, set up camp, and that the girls would return in Karen's Ford Falcon. The love affair continued for another three days at the lake campground. Karen adored Jake, who would play his guitar and sing to her. Brusco and Gina skinny-dipped all three days in the lake to escape the July heat. Between swims, they lay in the shade, under the tarp, locked at the hips.

419

"What's our plan, Brusco? I could stay out at this lake and do this all summer. This is heaven," Jake smiled in stoned pleasure.

"Well, we're almost out of pot, and we've only got two hundred bucks left. Let's go to Dallas. I've got a wealthy uncle there that owns a large business. Maybe he can give us a couple of weeks' of work. We'll score some pot, then we'll come back here and spend the rest of the summer with Karen and Gina."

The girls protested, "No, don't go yet!" They were having just as much fun as the boys, having never experienced west coast LSD before.

Jake was in agreement though. He convinced Karen, "We'll be back in two weeks, baby! I'll come back, I promise, with a pocket full of money, and we'll party!"

And so once again, the Apache was on the road, heading south to Dallas. At one point, after a thirty mile stop and oiling, they got careless and didn't latch the hood of the Apache properly. The old truck got up to fifty mph, and all of a sudden, the hood flew up, banging against the windshield. Pulling over, they tried to pull the hood down, but it had totally sprung from its hinges. Using a rope, they lashed it to the grill as best they could. They drove until breakfast, stopping in the town of Davis, Oklahoma at a small diner. A sign in the window on Main Street read "Breakfast 99 cents." They pulled to the curb and parked. Walking through the front door, a small bell tinkled as they went in.

Seated throughout the diner were farmers in bib overalls, smoking, eating, and drinking coffee. A hush went over the room as they entered, as all eyes were upon them. The boys both took a swivel seat at the serving counter and looked at each other. All of a sudden, one by one, each farmer stood and walked out, saying nothing. Brusco and Jake looked around, and realized no one was in the diner now, including the waitress.

"I don't like this…. Let's get outta here," Brusco nudged Jake, who nodded his head.

They left town in a hurry, putting ten more miles behind them as they watched the rear-view mirror. Brusco saw a sign that pointed to a public fishing hole in the Arbuckle Mountains. Down a dirt road, they found the spot and camped and fished that day. Jake caught a catfish, so they decided to fry it up, camp for the night, and drive into Dallas the next day. Early the next morning, they drove the last one hundred and fifty miles into Dallas.

Brusco's uncle, Raymond Kincaid, had a fine, upscale house in North Dallas. He owned a plumbing wholesale business, and had become very successful. He liked Brusco, who reminded him of his little brother. Arriving at the house, Brusco's aunt Dolly, Raymond's wife, greeted them warmly. She wasn't too pleased with Zeke though, and she demanded he stay outside.

Raymond was at the office, but he came home for lunch when he heard that Brusco had arrived. He gave the lads a warm Texas welcome, offering the hospitality of his house.

"Well, what's your plan? You're a long way from Seattle," Raymond wanted to know.

"Well Ray, we was hoping that you could give us some work... odd jobs... so we could earn some hamburger and gas money," Brusco answered. "We'll wash your delivery trucks, paint your office... anything."

"Actually, this is good timing. I do have some work. I want landscape curbings poured in concrete all around the house and the flower beds. Can you guys do it?" Raymond asked.

"Sure, you mean mix up concrete in a wheelbarrow and pour it?" Jake asked.

"Yes, exactly. I'll call the lumber yard and have them deliver the concrete sacks and timbers today. You can start tomorrow." Raymond walked the boys around the house, and showed them what he wanted. He returned to the office, and the boys spent the rest of the day digging out the footings for the curbings. After three days, the project was going smoothly, and Raymond was pleased with their progress. By 11 a.m. every morning, the Texas sun was blistering, and by 2 p.m., it was just too hot to work and mix concrete. On the fourth day, it was sweltering by noon.

"Let's go down to the Dairy Queen and get some milk shakes," Jake suggested.

The Dairy Queen was only a mile away. They'd chance driving the Apache for that distance, as the smoke had become alarmingly bad coming out the tailpipe.

The boys sat in the air conditioned seating area inside the DQ, sipping their shakes, and cooling off. Another long hair entered and bought an iced Coke. He sat down in the booth behind them, then casually turned around and said, "Is that y'all's truck?" pointing at the Apache.

"Yup, that's our truck," Jake acknowledged.

"Hey, ya'll wanna buy a lid?" he asked.

Brusco and Jake hesitated. One joint of marijuana in Texas was a felony--twenty years of hard labor at the Seagoville State Prison Farm.

"How much?" Jake asked.

"Ten bucks... it's good sensimilla," he assured them

"You got it here?" Jake asked.

"Out in the car, that blue Plymouth." He pointed.

"Ok, we'll take a lid…. Do you want us to meet you somewhere?" Jake asked nervously.

"We'll do it right here.. Put the ten bucks in my Coke cup. I'll go get it" he directed. Nonchalantly, he walked out to the car with his Coke cup and returned, setting the cup with the straw and plastic lid onto the booth table before Jake.

"I'll see you at the ball game!" he smiled, and walked out. Jake cracked the plastic cup lid open and could see the baggy of marijuana. The blue Plymouth now backed up and departed.

"Let's go…. This makes me super paranoid," Brusco nervously looked around.

The boys walked out to the truck, and Jake pretended to sip on his straw. Jumping in the cab, Jake slid the cup up under the front seat, and fired up the Apache. They got back on the boulevard and headed back for the house. They had only gone two blocks when they passed a Dallas police car at an intersection, and he now turned and got behind them.

"Holy shit, Brusco, that cop is right on our ass. Don't turn around!" Jake warned.

"Damn it! We've been set up. That fucker was a narc!" Brusco muttered as he stared straight forward. "Damn it…. Is he pulling us over?" Brusco clinched his teeth.

"No, not yet…. He hasn't lit us up yet. Stay calm, Brusco!" Jake choked the words out.

The cop continued to tail them now for several blocks.

"What should I do--go to your uncle's house?" Jake was sweating now.

"No, I don't wanna get busted in front of my uncle's house--he'd hate me. Signal and turn, up ahead!" Brusco was lost for answers.

Jake signaled and turned, and the cop did likewise.

"He's still back there, staying with us," Jake muttered.

"Turn again, go left here… SIGNAL," Brusco commanded.

The cop turned, as well, staying right behind the Apache.

"He's still there…. Damn. Why doesn't he pull us over?" Jake was fraught.

"Fuck it. Go to Raymond's house--it's one block away."

Jake now signaled again and turned into Raymond's cul-de-sac.

"He's still back there…. I'm gonna pull into Raymond's driveway," Jake winced.

The driveway was long with a slight incline. The squad car pulled into the driveway as well, behind the smoking Apache. All of a sudden, Jake slammed the three on the tree into reverse, dumped the clutch, and rammed the police car right behind them. The steel bumper and chuckwagon box caved in the cruiser's grill, smashed both headlights, and folded up the hood, wrinkling both fenders as well. Both cops hit their faces on the windshield from the force of the impact.

In horror, Brusco screamed, "What the fuck did you do!?"

"I didn't know he pulled in behind us!" wailed Jake.

The boys now got out and stood helpless at the back of the truck, horrified of the damage to the cruiser.

"Don't resist.... Just let them cuff us and take us away, Jake," Brusco advised.

The two officers got out, rubbing their noses and necks.

Jake was frantic, asking, "Officer, what did we do wrong? Why were you following us?" trying to turn the disaster around. Raymond had come home for lunch and now was standing in the driveway in utter disbelief at what he was looking at.

"How bad is it, Fred?" the one cop asked the other.

"Not good.... This one's gonna be tough to explain to the chief." He ran his hand across the folded hood. Steam hissed from the cruiser's radiator. The grill had impregnated it.

They still weren't handcuffed, and now Brusco tried Jake's approach, "Officers, why were you following us?"

Disgusted, the cop explained, "We were running a license check on your Washington plates and it took a long time. There are no warrants or violations on your truck. They radioed us when we turned into the cul-de-sac. My partner's a rookie. He should not have pulled into Mr. Kincaid's driveway.... Because it happened on private property, we can't prosecute and charge you for the collision. We'll just have to write it off as a rookie error. Let me see your driver's licenses." Brusco and Jake produced valid licenses, and both checked out with no warrants. He gave them back, saying, "I'd advise you fellers to get out of town, and if I see this heap on the road again, I'll have it impounded!"

Slamming their doors and red faced, the cops backed out of the driveway. As they drove down the street, a metallic squeaking could be heard, and a trail of coolant was leaking on the asphalt. A plume of steam shot out from under the rumpled hood.

"What the hell happened here?" Raymond was still in disbelief.

"I saw your car in the driveway when we pulled in.... I decided to back out and not block you! I just didn't see the cop. He wasn't in my door mirror!" Jake was still shaking.

"Wow, you boys are lucky. I still don't believe that they just drove off!" Raymond shook his head.

"When will you guys be done with the landscaping?" he now asked.

"We should be done tomorrow," Brusco replied.

"Well, I think that cop meant business when he insinuated revenge. You guys might want to sneak outta Dallas as soon as possible," suggested Raymond.

The following day, the curbing concrete project was completed. Raymond paid them three hundred dollars cash when he got home. "Well, what's the plan boys?" he asked.

"We talked it over. We were gonna go back to Kansas, but that means driving through North Dallas. The cops are sure to see us. We're gonna sneak out the back streets and go south tonight, after it gets dark," Brusco told him. "Jake wants to see the Gulf and Galveston" Brusco added.

Aunt Dolly fed the boys one more time at supper, and at 9 p.m. that evening, right after sundown, the smoky old Apache limped out of the cul-de-sac. They managed to get out of town undetected and headed south for Waco. There, at Waco, they bought another case of bulk motor oil. By morning, they had reached the Gulf and drove out onto the beach at Galveston. Jake and Zeke both jumped out and waded into the surf. Brusco stayed in the cab and studied the road atlas. They were a long way from Seattle. Brusco took a pencil and did some math. Seattle to Houston was 2,500 miles--divided by thirty equaled eighty-three oil stops. Times two equaled one hundred and sixty-six quarts of oil. *Holy cow!* Brusco thought. One hundred and sixty-six quarts of oil to go home. It looked "not good" for the Apache. It was doubtful the old 235 would go another five hundred miles in the desert heat. Brusco showed the figures to Jake when he got back to the truck.

"I know.... I've been thinking the same thing. Let's do this--we'll head straight west for San Antonio. Maybe we'll find some peyote like we talked about. If we can make it to Albuquerque, we'll sell the truck to a junkyard. We'd then have to hitchhike home, which won't be easy with the dog. To hell with it, Brusco--we just drive the truck till it blows. What other choice do we have?" Jake shrugged.

The Apache left the Gulf that night and headed straight west. In the desert, Jake played Hendrix's "Night Bird" over and over again, smoking joints and singing the lyrics. At four in the morning, after a dozen oil stops, they watched in the headlights several Burma Shave signs pop up. One sign said "Cactus," the next "'Cold Pop," the next "Cigs," the next "Cactus," then the next said "Cold Beer." They were in the middle of Texas desolation, and Jake slowed down, seeing the roadside building ahead. An abandoned gas station, long since closed up, and a cobbled together greenhouse stood in a wide spot in the road.

424

"Let's rest here and wait for this place to open up." Brusco pulled in and shut off the key. The boys kicked back and fell asleep in the cab. Around 8 a.m., a tapping was heard at the window.

A crusty old desert man, whiskered and in sweat-stained clothes stared at them. "Can I help you boys? You broke down?" the man spoke loudly, waking them up.

"Morning, sir.... Yeah, we saw your signs and decided to stop and wait for you to open." Brusco rolled down the window.

"What kinda cactus do you sell?" Jake asked.

"C'mon, follow me," he motioned.

The boys hopped out and followed him to the makeshift greenhouse.Stepping inside,the heat was already stifling from the morning sun. Before them sat table after table of hundreds of varieties of cactus, all growing in little to large, red clay pots.

"Wow, this is amazing!" Both boys were astounded at what they were seeing.

Brusco got to the point and just flat out asked, "Do you have any peyote for sale?"

"What kind do you want? There's six different varieties," the old man gleamed. "I know what you want.... It's called 'star' peyote. I get you hippies in here all the time. Over here, there's a whole table of them." The green, live buttons were the size of a silver dollar, each in its own little clay pot.

"Wow! How much are they?" Brusco was excited.

"A dollar a piece," the old man chuckled.

Brusco quickly counted sixty little pots and said "We'll take the whole table!" The boys rearranged things under the plywood canopy and managed to squeeze all the clay pots in, just behind the cab.

"Can we stay here today? ....park over there in the shade of those trees? We travel at night," asked Brusco.

"I reckon so... since you're paying customers," he generously agreed.

The boys pitched their hammocks in the shade, pleased with their luck.

"Damn, I hope this truck makes it home...we can sell those peyote buttons for five bucks a piece in Seattle," Jake was calculating.

"Yeah, but we just spent our gas and oil money. Let's head for Albuquerque and sell the last of the mescaline. I think there's forty hits left," Brusco advised.

That night, they continued west, camping at Fort Stockton as the sun began to come up. They rested all day and that night, making it to the Pecos River by morning. Miraculously, the Apache continued to drink oil and run. They were now low on pot and asked a group of Mexicans swimming in the river where they could get some. There was none available, but they told of a city park in Albuquerque where you could buy any drug you wanted. The next night, they drove into the city and found the park. To their amazement, the park was crawling with hippies, selling and buying drugs. Within an hour, Brusco had sold the forty hits for eighty dollars, and Jake had found a quality bag of pot. The whole place was surreal, and both boys became paranoid, sensing they were being watched. They parked in a shopping center parking lot that day, rested, then headed west on Route 66 that night. They camped that day in the Navajo desert. They found a roadside picnic table with a shade tree and tied the hammocks between the table and the bumper. Brusco fired up the Coleman stove, and they ate canned chili. At sundown, they headed for Flagstaff. At four in the morning, they pulled into the sleeping town. Jake spotted a sign that said "State University" with a pointing arrow. Jake got creative again, saying, "Let's find the gymnasium. We'll walk right in like we're students and take a shower in the locker room. Nobody will say a word."

As if by magic, the football field appeared on their right and then a parking lot next to the gymnasium. They parked, waited until 7 a.m., then walked right into the locker room. They took hot showers, and no one paid them any attention. Revived, they walked back to the Apache in the parking lot. A campus security car was waiting for them.

"This truck has no parking permit," the campus cop advised the boys. "You'll have to move it off campus or I will have it towed."

Jake started up the truck, the smoke billowing out the back. They drove only a few blocks. The cloud coming out the back made them look like a crop duster airplane, releasing its plume. Jake saw a Safeway grocery store, and he pulled into the back of the parking lot and shut the key off. The truck was dying a slow death.

They got the road atlas out again. If they went straight north, they'd be in the remote desert of eastern Utah. "Let's try and make it to our old camp ground on the Green River," Brusco pointed on the map. They managed to sit all day, incognito, in the parking lot. Again, at dusk, they stealthily slipped out of Flagstaff. The darkness and desolate desert cloaked the smoking beast from the eyes of the law. The thirty-mile oil stops continued. Brusco wondered how the spark plugs could still keep firing. The gallant old 235 Apache lumbered on. At sunrise, they pulled into their rope swing campground on the Green River, much to their relief. They could rest a few days, clean the spark plugs, and maybe, just maybe, they might make it back to Seattle.

After camping on the Green River for two days, they looked at what money they had left. There was just enough for gas and oil, and not a dime more. No food budget. They'd have to go for it nonstop until they got to the trailer in Meadowdale, another thousand miles away. That evening, they realized the adventure was over…. It was time to return to reality. They drove all night and reached Ogden. They found a roadside rest stop and parked there for the day. Pushing on that night, they reached LaGrande, Oregon by morning. They found a riverside city park and camped on the Grande Ronde River. They hung their hammocks for the last time. The last can of soup was heated and served ceremoniously. That evening, they filled up the gas tank and bought twelve quarts of oil at the truckstop. They had five dollars left, with two jerry cans of gasoline. Amazingly, the truck continued to run through the night, reaching Wenatchee that morning. At a Wenatchee Shell station, they spent the five dollars on gas and two hamburgers. They had seven quarts of oil left. They were just barely going to make it. The last obstacle was Stevens Pass, and the Cascade Mountains. It was a dark, rainy morning. They decided to go for it and not wait for darkness. Reaching the summit of the pass, the truck was down to ten miles an hour. The truck was smoking like a chimney, and Brusco guessed the six cylinder engine was running on four cylinders, barely. He free wheeled the Apache down the western side of the pass, cooling the shot engine down. Rolling in neutral, he feathered the struggling engine back to life. He knew if the truck was shut off now, it would never start again. Rolling through Sultan and Monroe, he continued to feather the engine, barely keeping it going. Finally, the last little hill was climbed, and the broken Apache coughed and sputtered into the dirt driveway of the Meadowdale trailer. In the days ahead, Jake got his old job back, pumping gas at the Texaco. He fell right back into his old routine, having his motorcycle waiting for him in the barn. Brusco sold most of the peyote buttons, giving them a little grocery money. Brusco bought some spark plugs, and got the Apache running, just well enough to sell it as a basket case. Searching for a job and having no luck, he called his uncle Raymond and asked for a job in his freight warehouse. Graciously, his uncle gave him a job on the condition that Brusco not reappear with the Apache pickup. Brusco had just enough money to buy a one way ticket to Dallas. Arriving a month later in Dallas after the return to Washington, Raymond gave Brusco an advance for an apartment and allowed him to drive a company truck--one that didn't burn oil.

427

Chase Goes Home

Back in 1875, up Corral Creek Canyon, Duto came back to his senses. An hour earlier, Snorting Bull had put an arrow into his wing, the velocity knocking him out and pinning him to the pine tree trunk. He shook his head, the pain in his wing piercing through his body. His queens were roosted in branches all around him, guarding his situation. On the ground, all around the surrounding terrain, a dozen queens lay dead, their crumpled bodies lying motionless. Snorting Bull and his band of warriors were long gone now, having disappeared with Pearl as their hostage.

The queens began to *caw caw,* realizing Duto had come back to life. Pulling and tugging in excruciating pain, Duto could not free himself. The arrowhead had buried itself in the tree. Its shaft had pierced the skin of his wing but hadn't struck the bone. The more he struggled, the greater pain he felt. He stayed stuck on the tree branch for two days. On the third day, he was dying of thirst. "Son of a bitch!" he cursed over and over again.

Finally, the wise, old Duto had an idea. He called for his queens to roost on the arrow shaft. One by one, they obeyed. As the fourth queen hopped onto the shaft, the combined weight snapped the arrow in half. Duto pulled hard, and finally, his impaled wing slid off of the broken arrow stub. Free from the predicament, he sat on the pine tree branch and assessed his dilemma. He could not extend the damaged, swollen wing. He knew he couldn't fly. Below him, several branches protruded from the trunk, all the way to the ground. Slowly, he hopped down, from branch to branch, his thirst driving him on. Safely reaching the ground, he hopped across the meadow towards Corral Creek. His queens escorted him, hopping ahead and guarding his walk towards the water. Reaching the little stream, he gulped water and rested in the shade of a willow.

His harem began feeding him, bringing him seeds, berries, bugs, and small frogs. Now revitalized, he resumed his quest, hopping towards the lower canyon and the burned-out shack. It took him two days of hopping. Finally, he reached the burned-out mass of smoldering cinders that once had been his and Pearl's home. His roost had not been burned, being twenty feet above the shack and just out of reach from the flames. He could now spread his wing, but the pain was too great to try and flap and become airborne.

Finding another pine tree close by, he hopped up its branches, to an elevation higher than his roost. Spreading his wings, he jumped from the high branch and went airborne in a steady glide. Painfully, he flared his wing to a stop, and safely landed on his roost, high up in the boulder crack. He was safe now. His queens could feed him, and he slowly regained strength in his damaged wing. Every two days, he would glide to the ground, get his drink of water, climb the tree, and then glide back to his roost.

After a month of his recovery, a tremendous wind and rain storm struck the canyon. Sheets of rain and wind blasted Duto up in his roost. The old bird had cleverly situated his roost adjacent to a large fracture that had split off the crack, undetectable from the ground. Duto had discovered the fracture remained dry in rainstorms and so used it as shelter in bad weather. Over the years, he had also used the spot to hide his treasures of shiny keepsakes. Here, he hunkered down and rode out the terrible wind and rainstorm that was upon him.

The following morning, the weather subsided, and Duto emerged to his roost. Preening himself, he looked down to see that the storm had totally flattened the remains of the burned out shack. He now hopped back and forth on the roost, cocking his head, as something had caught his eye below. The morning sun was producing a bright gleam and reflection from the pile of charred wood below. The bright reflection shone up at him, beckoning him with curiosity. He went into his glide and landed on the ground. He hopped over to the charred mass, jumping up onto a blackened board. Waddling down its length, he found where the glint of light was coming from. He cocked his head, studying it with one eye. Under another charred board, right below him, was an opening in the ground. The sun was penetrating the hole, and now he could see far into the darkness of the tunnel. A mason jar glass was catching the rays of the sun. Hopping down to the hole, he realized it was Pearl's secret tunnel. The shining of the gold in the glass jar was too tempting for him, and he had to have it. He stepped into the hole and waddled down the tunnel in the ray of sunlight. Reaching the cavern, there was just enough light for Duto to see the altar and the smiling Buddha. Across the altar sat the thirty-seven glass jars of gold medallions. He was just able to hop up onto the low altar. Walking around between the jars, he spotted one that got his interest. He recognized that it contained his green pellets. Now his focus was on the green pellets, for he knew their value for his survival. He pushed on the jar, trying to slide it to the edge of the altar. Two jars of gold medallions were in the way, and close to the edge. He pushed on them with all his might, sending them over the edge. The jars broke below on the floor, scattering the contents. With the two jars of gold out of the way, he now pushed the glass jar of green pellets over the edge, and the jar likewise shattered on the heap of medallions below. The sun was now rising outside, and the light grew dim in the cavern. Hopping to the floor, he found a green pellet with his beak, then gulped it down. Quickly, he waddled back up the tunnel and hopped out of the hole, back onto the burned up pile of boards. Finding a mud puddle of water from the rainstorm, he took a long drink.

On his walk back to the pine tree, he had a burst and rush of energy. Stretching his wings, he flapped them vigorously, took two hops, and became airborne. Finding a thermal column of rising air, he circled in its pattern, and rose to a tremendous height in the sky. He celebrated his escape from earth, diving and soaring, *caw caw*ing in happiness. Scanning the horizon, he saw no sign of Pearl and her abductors. His best option was to stay at the roost and hope that she would return.

Landing back at his boulder roost, Duto's cocky and bold ways all came back to him, the green pellet flushing new life into the raven. He continued cursing in English sailor slurs and enjoyed bossing his queens around.

Thereafter, on every morning, the bird would make two or three trips into the cavern. He wanted the remaining green pellets, which were now scattered in broken glass, and the gold medallions. Some days he'd vary his chore, alternating between bringing out medallions or bringing out the green pellets. He liked the shiny medallions, but he had to fetch the pellets. Each time he would emerge from the hole out of the tunnel, he'd fly up to his roost and deposit either hoard inside the secret fracture. It became a game with him and routine, like a morning chore. After two months of this activity, he had collected all the pellets and medallions from the glass pile. He had quite a collection in his secret roost now.

One morning, he came out from his secret fracture and out onto his roost. He was thinking about going into the cavern and trying to push one of the heavy jars over the edge. As he preened himself and bitched at his queens, a movement below caught his eye.

It was Mr. Badger, a big one, and he had found the hole. Duto watched as the badger disappeared down the hole. After that, Duto lost all interest of going back into Pearl's secret tunnel.

Over the years, the canyon became a place for the Sinkiuse to avoid. Stories were told of the "Bird Witch Woman" and her flock of attacking ravens. The chance of having your eyes pecked out was enough reason to stay away from the canyon.

Duto remained at his roost diligently for years and years, waiting for Pearl to return. He had learned over the years to always take his green pellet at his molt, the herb renewing his heart. He was outliving his queens now, but he had several to take their place. His reputation in the canyon was "His Excellency," among all of his flocks.

At one point in the 1880's, a supercell thunderstorm washed the canyon in such a torrent that ravines opened up with flash floods. Pearl's giant cracked boulders were at the base of one of these ravines. A wave of water, mud, sticks, and debris crashed into the site of the burned-down shack. The mud and water found the hole and tunnel, filling the cavern with sand and muck. Only a pile of washed-out rocks and small boulders could now be seen, covering all traces of what had once been there.

In the 1890's, White soldiers on horses came, building a fort at the base of Lake Chelan, overlooking the Big River. A road had been constructed using Wapato John's pack trail out of the canyon to Fort Walla Walla. The military graded parts of the trail, and so it was called "The Military Road." The fort at the lake used the road as their lifeline, packing all of their needs by wagons now. The road came down Corral Creek Canyon to a landing on the river, where a flat top ferry, pulled by a mule from either side, got the wagon across.

Duto watched the wagon and horse traffic from his roost. It didn't bother him much, as the road was on the south side of the canyon. No one paid any attention to him. He was just another raven among hundreds.

As the century closed out, the military departed, leaving for a campaign in the Philippines. Orchards began to appear along the Big River. The fruit growers utilized long ago abandoned Chinese ditches dug to sluice gold. Ranchers soon recognized the Corral Creek Canyon as natural grazing land. They discovered what the Sinkiuse and their horses had known long before. The canyon could handle herds of grazing cattle and had year-round water. Soon, the ranchers were fencing and dividing the canyon up into large parcels of acreage.

Shorthorn cattle now grazed around Duto and his roost. The Sinkiuse had all been sent to the reservation in Colville, and the whiteman now had laid siege to the canyon.

Duto continued his vigil of waiting, but Pearl never returned. Each year he took his pellet at molt, rejuvenating, and watched the world go by below him. From his roost, he watched as steamboats began to ply the Big River. Steamboats gave way to a railroad, and he could see and hear the train now, passing below along the river. Its whistle signaled in a new age. The automobile was catching on now, replacing the horse. Duto would watch the horseless wagons pop and smoke, going up the hill on the old Military Road. The road was rough with ruts and in need of improvement for modern travel. The improvement came in the 1950's. Duto watched as heavy equipment came to the canyon. Using graders, bulldozers, and trucks, they turned the canyon road into a vital access point for the whole plateau. Power poles appeared along the paved road with new homes that followed.

It was now 1994, and Duto was down to his last two green pellets. He was now one hundred and seventy-one years old. He knew Pearl was gone and realized his days were numbered.

In 1973, the Vietnam War was in its ninth year. The United States had spent her treasure and her treasured youths' lives for almost a decade. The undeclared war had raged on and on. The American people demanded that it stop, yet the bombing and killing continued.

Brusco Gibbs had come back from Texas. The job in Texas had been a good one, driving a company truck all over the state. "The Kid" was a young, twenty-one-year-old. The lure of Texas had faded, as he constantly thought about the mountains and rivers of home. He'd saved a little money and had bought a '54 Ford pickup, which ran like a top. The call of the Cascades was too great, and he resigned from his job to his understanding uncle. The irony was, as he returned west and was crossing the Idaho/Washington line, he realized he had no plan of where he was going. He was following the same road, Route 2, that he and Jake had followed in the Apache, two years earlier.

He drove through Wenatchee on Highway 2, heading for Stevens Pass. Passing through the town of Cashmere, he saw a sign saying "Peach Pickers Wanted." Following the directions, he came to an orchard, where a farmer was loading bins of peaches with a tractor. The farmer spotted the Texas plates on the pickup, shut his tractor off, and tipped his hat back.

"Y'all lookin for work, huh?"

Brusco nodded his head. "Yeah, I can pick peaches."

"I pay seven dollars and fifty cents for a full bin of peaches picked." The farmer stepped down from the tractor. He handed Brusco a pickers bag with shoulder straps. "Y'all need a three legged ladder, over yonder." He pointed at a walnut tree, used for leaning ladders. "Grab the ladder and start on that row of trees… right there." He again pointed.

The day was sunny and hot. Brusco began to perspire, realizing the work was brutal in order to fill a bin. On the ladder, while reaching to pick, the weight of the bag was grinding on the lower back, the up and down, exhausting on the legs. The peach fuzz was now in his open pores and eyes, causing unbearable itching. After six hours of torture, he got his bin and his seven fifty, and that ended his fruit picking career. It was too late to travel. He went to the local hamburger stand on the highway, Rusty's, and bought a cheeseburger. While waiting for the burger, he stood outside, next to the takeout window and read a local cork bulletin board.

432

"Lost Dog," "DeSoto for Sale," "Pickers Wanted," and then "Trailer for rent on 38 acres, mountain pastures, solitude. $200 a month. Nahahum Canyon, call this number...."

"Your burger is ready, sir!" the girl called.

Handing her a dollar, Brusco asked, "Hey, uh... miss, where is Nahahum Canyon?"

"Across the highway, down that road, and take a right." She pointed.

Finishing his burger, a convenient phone booth was close by. Dropping a dime into the phone, it jingled to life, and Brusco dialed the number. A friendly voice gave him directions to come and look at the rental trailer. Crossing the highway, he followed the girl's instructions and found the mouth of the canyon. He began a long, five mile climb up its winding road. The canyon was beautiful, wide and huge, covered with a blanket of wildflowers and meadows of grass. Hay was cut in the bottom land, and cattle grazed the hills on both sides. The pavement ended at five miles, with another mile to go on a winding gravel road to reach the trailer. The trailer was on the back side of a cattle ranch. It bordered the wilderness. The beauty, solitude, and seclusion of the place sold Brusco instantly. Shaking the rancher's hand, he paid the two hundred dollars. Within a week, after a few trips to town, he was settled into the tranquility of the place. Hanging out in town, he soon befriended the local hippie population. A young, redheaded girl of nineteen was introduced to him one day. Her name was Chris Bitton, and she quickly took a shine to Brusco. He equally fell under her spell. It wasn't long before she was staying at the trailer, full time. Chris had several hippie friends who would come and visit. Soon it became a favorite hangout to smoke pot and drink cheap wine away from the town sheriff. After three months of enjoying himself, Brusco's Texas money was almost gone.

An old sawmill in town, Schmitten Lumber, employed around thirty people. An inside tip told Brusco to apply. The company office signed him up as a "Tail Sawyer," the most dangerous job in the mill. The foreman looked him in the eye and said, "You gonna be able to handle it?"

The job was extremely dangerous. Standing next to a three story band saw, Brusco grabbed the "cants" with an iron hook as they fell from the log and the whirling saw blade. The saw made a high, screaming decibel sound as it sliced the log, spewing a cloud of sawdust into the air. The mill was powered by an old steam boiler from a WW1 battleship. The "Sawyer" controlled a carriage on rails that rolled back and forth, powered by a steam piston called "the shotgun." The carriage had "dog teeth" on it that closed on the log and held it in place. The Sawyer then released steam into the shotgun that pushed the carriage down the rail and the log through the bandsaw. Standing on the other side of the giant saw was Brusco, who would grab the slab as it fell from the cut log and swing it onto a rolling case of rollers, which carried the piece to smaller saws. After a year of the brutal job, he barely escaped with his life during one shift of work. The Sawyer accidently pushed the dog teeth into the whirling band saw, causing it to come off its huge wheels. The blade spilled out onto the mill floor, a twisted mass of razor ribbon surrounding Brusco. By the grace of God, he walked away unscathed, a miracle. If he had been standing a half a step further in any direction, he would have been cut in half. It happened in the blink of an eye, with no time to react. After that, the foreman decided that Brusco had earned a promotion and sent him outside to the green chain where the raw lumber was stacked. In 1975, the year the war ended, Brusco decided to marry Chris. The ceremony was performed on July fifth. The temperature was one hundred and thirteen degrees in the shade that day. Still the cowboy, they honeymooned at the Calgary Stampede, driving her father's new chevy to the event.

After three years of working in the sawmill, Brusco had saved enough to buy five acres of land in Olalla Canyon. Buying the lumber wholesale at the mill, he built a small frame house for Chris. The country now fell into a deep recession, and the sawmill closed down, leaving Brusco and Chris broke. Somehow, he was able to sell the property and new house for a nice profit. With no job prospects in the Wenatchee valley, they decided to move to Everett and seek employment. Answering an ad in the city newspaper, they found a new duplex apartment to rent. The landlord owned an electrical contracting business, and upon hearing Brusco was seeking employment, offered him a job as an apprentice wiring new houses. The job demanded long hours, leaving Chris alone in the duplex. She missed her family and friends from Cashmere, and after six months in Everett, she returned to the river valley. Both lived estranged from each other for another three months, and Brusco ended up filing for divorce, ending the marriage.

He excelled in the electrical trade, learning the craft and began bringing home a sizeable paycheck. He bought a large, liveaboard sailboat, mooring it in the Everett marina. The boat had all the comforts of home. At the dock, he had shore power and a telephone, making it the perfect bachelor pad.

At age twenty-eight, he was accepted into the IBEW apprenticeship program, an accredited four-year school, through Local 191. Completing the four-year course, he took the state exam, passing and receiving his Journeyman's license. Working large, industrial construction jobs, he suddenly was flush with money. He began hanging out in honky tonks and bars, spending the money on loose and fast women. He bought a Harley Davidson chopper, pushing his lifestyle to the extreme. Picking up women in bars for one night stands became a game with him, challenging himself to see how many he could bring back to his bed. This went on for several years, and he began to feel degraded and empty. The alcohol, drugs, and sleepless nights began to take a toll on him.

Cigarettes, pot, and tequila were consumed daily in large amounts. Beer was the chaser, and he found himself consumed and lost in addiction. The party scene had become a game of russian roulette. The deadly disease of AIDS had appeared on the party scene. Almost overnight, the promiscuity of loose women in the bars ended.

In some ways, it was a blessing for Brusco. He was burned out from the lifestyle of chasing shallow women. He missed the old days of living in Eastern Washington, out on the land and close to nature. The city was consuming his soul and spirit, and he felt an intense urge to leave it behind. He still hunted pheasants with his father, Milton. Yearly, in mid October, they continued their father/son pilgrimage to the wheat town of Almira to hunt. The birds had become heavily hunted over the years, pushing their numbers almost to extinction. New farming methods and pesticides had taken its toll on the birds, decreasing their populations drastically. The rendezvous in 1992 spelled an end to the ritual they had practiced for three decades. Not one ringneck pheasant was found in the wheat fields that year. They had disappeared.

On the drive home, Brusco drove through the town of Chelan. Cruising down main street, he spotted an old, dilapidated house on a corner. The house was hidden in a mass of overgrown shrubs and trees from years of neglect. A small sign on a weathered picket fence read "For Sale, By Owner." He pulled to the curb and stared at it, realizing it represented a huge amount of work. He drove on, crossing Stevens Pass, and returned to Everett.

The old house in Chelan stayed stuck in his mind though. He'd always liked the small town atmosphere of Chelan, with the lake being the added bonus. By the end of the work week, he'd talked himself into driving back and inquiring about the old house. If he didn't get out of the big city soon, it was going to kill or consume him, he thought.

Saturday arrived, and he drove back over the Cascade mountains. Arriving in Chelan, he pulled up to the old house and sat and stared at it for some time. He had an impulsive nature, and knew if he pulled the trigger and bought the house that it would change his life drastically. On the sign, a faded phone number was written. Down the street, Brusco found a phone booth at the Shell station.

"Yeah, I'm calling about your house on Woodin Avenue that's for sale."

A nice man answered yes, that Brusco could look at it, and that the owner lived only a couple of blocks away and would meet him there. As it turned out, the owner was the son of an old woman who had lived in the house for seventy years and had passed away. He explained that the house was one of the oldest in town, a leftover from the pioneer days. After walking through the interior, Brusco tried to contain his excitement. He wanted the old house! The man accepted Brusco's down payment, agreeing to give him time to withdraw his pension money from the IBEW to pay the asking price. They shook hands, and two weeks later, Brusco moved to Chelan.

He quickly learned that wages in the electrical trade were not nearly as abundant as in the city. Long periods of waiting on the "dispatch" list for work drained his savings. He concocted up an idea to turn the old house into a mini hotel. After securing the necessary building permits, he spent the next two years remodeling the old historic house into a small hotel, with all the modern conveniences. He succeeded in getting it up and running, renting rooms to tourists. As he had hoped, it supplemented his sporadic electrical wages.

As the tourist season closed in 1995, he found himself deep on the out of work list in the Local Union Hall, with no work in sight. One morning, at the Apple Cup Cafe, he sat reading the classified ads and drinking coffee. An ad with the Colville tribe in Nespelem read "Opening for Journeyman Electrician, who is willing to travel." Calling the number, a voice came back, "Colville Tribe, Public Works."

"Yeah, my names Brusco Gibbs. You got an ad in the paper for an electrician… is the job still open?"

"Yeah, this is Joe Lazard. Have you got a state journeyman's license?"

"Yup, I've been licensed with the state for twenty-two years."

"Oh… okay. Come up to the tribe's conference center tomorrow for an interview, say around 10 o'clock."

"Okay.… Uh, where's the tribe's conference room, Joe?"

"It's behind the July Grounds, the pow wow area, across from the highway from the trading post.… You'll see it."

Brusco was there the following morning, a one hundred and two mile drive from Chelan to Nespelem. It was a two-hour drive across the plateau of sagebrush and wheat fields. Finding Joe in the conference room, the two shook hands.

"Good morning. My name's Joe Lazard." He handed Brusco a business card. "I'm the electrical foreman for the tribe." Joe was well-dressed and clean-shaven. He explained that he was from the "Lake" tribe to the north. It was obvious to Brusco that he was well-educated with the electrical industry, asking questions that only a journeyman could answer.

Satisfied with the interview, now Joe asked, "When can you start?"

"What time do you start in the morning, Joe?"

"Starting time is 8 A.M."

"See ya in the morning Joe."

Thus began a lifelong friendship between Joe and Brusco. Joe had been educated back east, orphaned when his Colville mother had passed away when he was young. He'd been sent to a church school in Maine. The school hadn't broken his native spirit, and after finishing high school, he returned to the Colville Reservation. The tribe had assisted in his electrical education, and he had passed the state journeyman's exam. He now was the only member in his tribe who had a bonafide state license. Joe had a large collection of guns, and his pastime was hunting deer on the rez.

The Colville Reservation is vast--over seven million acres. The tribe's Public Works was charged with maintaining the facilities and infrastructure of an area the size of the state of Connecticut. Brusco was given a service van, and daily was sent to remote areas to assist elders who had electrical problems. He'd been there three months, when one day, he was asked to wire some newly constructed houses at Rebecca Lake. One morning, Joe informed Brusco, saying, "Hey, I hired this tribal member to help you wire those houses. Take him under your wing and show him what to do."

The next day, Brusco was introduced to "Bub" Moon, a big, raw-boned, strong kid who wanted to learn the trade. His hair was halfway down his back, and he carried himself in a quiet, dignified manner. Brusco gave him a baptism by fire on wiring houses, and the kid rapidly caught on. He made several mistakes but learned from them, and after a month, Bub was up to speed and carrying his weight. He took a shine to Brusco, after hearing all his tales of partying and chasing women in the big city. Bub had a wild streak as well, and at age twenty-two had been in and out of trouble with the tribal police. The state had taken his driver's license, but the tribe allowed him to drive a tribal vehicle, as long as he stayed on the reservation. Daily, he would bring electrical supplies from the warehouse at the Tribal Agency to Rebecca Lake. They'd work through the day, with Brusco returning the hundred miles to Chelan and Bub to the agency.

One day, while working, they took a cigarette break. Brusco listened as Bub explained a Nez Perce event that was to happen that weekend on the rez. Curious, Brusco asked him, "So Bub, you're a member of the Nez Perce tribe…. They had a great chief named Joseph. Are any of his relatives still around?"

Bub chuckled and looked surprised, saying, "Yeah... his relatives are still alive. You're looking at one of them. I'm his great great grandson," replying nonchalantly.

Caught off guard with this answer, Brusco looked Bub square in the eye and realized he was looking at a clone of the famous chief. "Holy cow! I can see the old chief in your face.... Wow, I'm honored to know you, Bub!"

The job at Rebecca Lake ended, just as Brusco was notified from the Union Hall that he was at the top of the list and was to be dispatched the following week. Brusco liked the Nez Perce kid and regretted having to leave his yearlong friend behind. Employment on the reservation was bleak, with the opportunity of steady, good wages unavailable. He convinced Bub to come to the Union Hall in Wenatchee and sign up as an apprentice. The only issue was that Bub still did not have his driver's license reissued from the state.

"You can come stay at the hotel in Chelan... no charge. You can ride the public bus. It'll pick you up on Main Street and take you to Wenatchee, to the Union Hall."

And so it was. Bub came off the rez, moved into Brusco's hotel, and joined the Union. The Union Hall dispatched Brusco to a sewage treatment plant in Twisp that needed major modifications. Brusco was made the foreman and given a new company truck to commute to and from Chelan. Taking advantage of his authority, Brusco called the Hall and had them dispatch Bub to his first job, the sewer plant. Bub was now able to commute with Brusco in the company truck, solving his lack of a driver's license dilemma.

On Saturdays, Bub's parents, Roy and Jeannie Moon, would drive the hundred miles to Chelan and bring him fresh laundry and snacks. Jeannie loved to make wild, huckleberry pies, and would always bring two, one for her son, and one for Brusco. One hot Saturday morning, they arrived early. Bub was still sleeping in his unit, but Brusco was up and having coffee. He invited the old Nez Perce elders into his air-conditioned townhouse above the hotel. Jeannie and Roy were pleased with their son's new found path and career and thanked Brusco for helping him. Over fresh coffee and huckleberry pie, they chatted about their drive that morning across the plateau.

"Jeannie, that's a beautiful necklace you're wearing. Is that mother-of-pearl?" Brusco asked.

"Yes... yes it is.... I made this several years ago," she acknowledged.

"Holy Cow! You made that!? That's very cool.... Hey, I've got a mother-of-pearl medallion, similar to yours. It's in an old cigar box.... Let me show it to you." Digging around in a storage closet, he found the old box. Popping the lid open on the kitchen table, he fished through some old coins and agates and finally pulled it out. He rubbed it off and handed it to Jeannie. A hole had been bored on the edge, indicating that it had been on a necklace at one time.

Jeannie held it for awhile, and studied it. "This has some long-time wear on it. See how smooth the edge is? Someone wore this for a long time. Where did you get this?" Jeannie asked.

"It belonged to my Dad…. It was with some old baseball cards in this box. He gave it to me when I was a young boy."

Jeannie now stood up and moved to a wall where a straw stetson cowboy hat hung. She lifted the hat from the hook and held the medallion up to the face of the crown.

"This would make a nice hat band piece." She displayed it for Brusco to see. "Let me take this hat and your medallion, and I'll make you a nice gift," she graciously insisted. "I'll work on it in my spare time…. You can come up to the rez and pick it up in the Fall." Her eyes shone.

"Wow…. Very cool! Yeah, I'd like that! I'll come by your house in October when I go grouse hunting with Joe."

A short time later that month, Bub was reissued his driver's license, so Roy and Jeannie stopped their weekend visits. It was good timing, as the job in Twisp ended. Bub and Brusco went back to the out of work list in the Union Hall, and Bub moved to Wenatchee after being dispatched for work in town.

Sitting on the back porch of his hotel one Sunday, Brusco watched a low flying ultralight, a motorized, powered parachute, fly right over the top of him. The pilot looked down and grinned at him. Brusco jumped up, went down to the sidewalk, and watched the craft fly to the east, towards the little airport. Fascinated, he jumped into his pickup, and arrived at the airport, just as the powered parachute was landing. The pilot taxied onto the grass, and the chute collapsed behind the three-wheeled, motorized frame. The pilot was friendly, and they introduced and shook hands. Mike Huffer explained to Brusco that he was a certified instructor, and asked if Brusco wanted to go up for a ride. Jumping on the opportunity, Brusco hopped aboard the two seater, and moments later they were airborne. So exhilarating was the flight that Brusco arranged for flying lessons. Successfully soloing, Brusco purchased his own flying machine. He spent the remaining summer flying around the Chelan valley almost daily with his new friend Mike.

That Fall, Brusco got a phone call from Joe Lazard, up on the rez. "Hey, c'mon up Saturday. We'll go grouse hunting."

That Saturday, the two spent the day road hunting in the forests of the reservation, shooting several ruffled grouse. Brusco was still using his old, double barrel Ithaca that Milton had given him in his youth.

Driving back to the agency, Brusco suddenly remembered the hat band that Jeannie was making for him. "Hey, pull into Roy and Jeannie Moon's house up ahead.... I wanna say hello," he directed Joe. Knocking on the door, Jeannie opened it and warmly invited them in. She offered them pie and coffee, which they didn't hesitate to accept.

"I'm glad you stopped by, Brusco.... I have something for you." Jeannie smiled.

Producing the straw stetson, Brusco marveled at the beauty of the beaded hat band she had created. The beaded band held the mother-of-pearl medallion, centered on the forehead crown of the hat. Brusco could tell she was proud of it. He tried it on in the mirror and was more than pleased with the piece of craftsmanship she had created. The Nez Perce elder had made something special and given it as a "thank you" to Brusco. He could not thank her enough, and she was pleased with his genuine admiration.

Driving back to Chelan, he kept checking the rear view mirror, admiring his new hat. Crossing the sagebrush of the Columbia plateau, he now descended the road down Corral Creek Canyon to cross the Columbia River at BeeBee bridge. The afternoon sun was in his eyes, and he dropped the visor to shade the glaring sunlight. Suddenly, almost two thirds of the way down the canyon, a ringneck pheasant flew across the road, right in front of the rolling pickup. He slowed down and watched the rooster glide down into a dry wash and land in some brush. Thinking *what the heck,* Brusco pulled over at a wide spot and stepped out with his shotgun. He grabbed two shells, loaded the gun, and began walking down the brush slope to where the rooster had landed. The bird was staying hunkered down, silent and hiding.

Distracting his attention, a raven began cawing, perched on a large, split boulder a hundred feet away. The afternoon sun was bright and caught the reflection in the medallion on the hat band. He now was annoyed with the raven's continuous cawing, distracting him from his prey, as if trying to warn the pheasant of danger. Brusco arrived at the clump of brush, and the raven continued his obnoxious cawing. Brusco was almost ready to turn the gun on the annoying raven, when the rooster flushed into the air to make his escape. Swinging the shotgun up to shoot, the ringneck had flown directly into the sun, blinding Brusco. He hesitated, and then shot both barrels, cleanly missing the bird. In disgust, he watched as the pheasant sailed down the canyon, unscathed. Cursing himself, Brusco now turned his attention to the raven, who was still cawing away. Brusco hurled some obscene curse words at the raven, who continued to mock him. He'd only brought two shells, and looked at the raven, telling him to shut up.

"You're a lucky crow…. I've got no more shells!" he barked at the bird on the massive boulder.

He turned to hike back up the hill, and after a few steps, the raven flew right over his shoulder, landing just ten feet in front of him. Startled, Brusco stopped in his tracks.

He pulled the stetson from his head, and wiped his forehead with his sleeve. Waving his hat, he tried to shoo the raven away. The bird jumped up and flew at his hat, trying to grab the hatband. Now Brusco was pissed and had enough of this arrogant pest.

"Get outta here, you son-of-a-bitch!" Brusco cursed at the bird. The bird did not flinch, and now began walking broad circles around Brusco.

"You son-of-a-bitch! You-son-of-a bitch!" But this time, it was not Brusco cursing! Brusco looked around to see who was making fun of him, hiding in the brush somewhere. The raven now stopped, looked up at Brusco, and opened his beak, "You-son-of-a-bitch!" The raven stared him down and now repeated, "You-son-of-a-bitch!"

Aghast and dumbfounded, Brusco stared in disbelief at the raven, out in the wild, who was calling him an SOB. He looked around, bewildered and confused, wondering if his ears were playing tricks on him. The raven continued his cursing. Brusco was unnerved and began double timing up the hill to get away from the surreal situation. The bird continued to harass him, and he picked up a rock to scare him away. He stopped himself though, as he realized that this was a unique situation. Maybe the raven was someone's pet, and he shouldn't harm him. The bird stayed out ahead of him, hopping and flitting along as he made his way up the hill. By the time he reached the pickup, Brusco was amused and laughing at the cursing bird. The climb back up the hill had been both annoying and fascinating, as the bird would not go away. Winded, he opened the tailgate of the pickup and sat down to catch his breath. The bird now walked in a circle on the road shoulder, twenty feet away, still calling Brusco a Son-of-a-Bitch.

Brusco took his hat off and sat it on the tailgate next to him. The bird stood motionless, staring at the hat. Brusco had the idea to feed the bird and remembered a bag of half-eaten potato chips on the front seat. He jumped off the tailgate and walked around to the driver's door to get the chips. Just then, the raven leapt up onto the tailgate and grabbed the hat by the medallion and tried to tear it loose with his beak. The bird attempted to fly with the hat, but it was too bulky for him to take flight. Brusco forgot about the chips and rushed to save his hat. The bird saw him coming, dropped it on the tailgate, then flew back to the shoulder, at a safe distance.

441

"Hey, hey, hey, you son-of-a-bitch! Brusco barked at the bird, who returned the same language. The bird was upset now, cawing, cursing, and flinging small pebbles with his beak. A truck was now coming down the road, and the driver slowed down, pulled up and rolled down his window. The raven now flew to the top of a power pole, and stared down.

"You need any help? You broke down?" The man was a familiar face from town.

Brusco waved, saying, "Nope, just stopped to take a leak.... Thanks for asking though."

The driver smiled and nodded and continued down the road. Now, another car was approaching. Brusco looked up at the raven on the power pole as he jumped into the cab, and thought, *No one would ever believe me if I told them of this encounter.*

He fired up the pickup and continued down the canyon. The sun had dropped below the distant butte, and it was starting to get dark by the time he got back to the hotel in Chelan. Baking a frozen pizza, he ate two pieces, turned out the lights, and went to bed.

He opened his eyes at sunup. The continuous cawing from a raven outside the window woke him up. He looked out, and below, on the second story deck, a raven was pacing back and forth on the railing. Brusco smiled to himself and thought, *That son-of-a-bitch chased me all the way home from the canyon!*

Brusco raised the window and called down to him, "Good Morning, Chase!"

The bird was silent now, staring back at him. They each eyed each other as Brusco was waiting for the SOB retort from the bird. All of a sudden, the raven blurted out, "*Angkas Matalom!*"

Brusco stared silently, having no clue what the raven was saying. Now the bird repeated himself, saying, "*Angkas Matalom*, you-son-of-a-bitch!" Flabbergasted, Brusco pulled on his overalls, put on his Nez Perce straw hat, and stepped out onto the back porch to confront the bird. As a sign of friendship, he held out a slice of white bread. The bird took it in his beak and moved away on the rail to eat it.

The phone rang inside. On the third ring, Brusco picked it up. It was Mike Huffer.

"Hey, you wanna go flying this morning?"

"Yeah, but come over here, Mike. I wanna show you something," Brusco told him.

Arriving at the hotel, Brusco greeted him at the front desk. "C'mon man, you gotta see and hear this. Follow me."

442

Stepping out onto the second story deck, Chase the raven was still pacing back and forth on the rail. Brusco handed him another slice of white bread.

Mike scoffed, "Yeah, a crow eating and shitting on your deck.... So what's the big deal?"

Instantly, Chase blurted out, "You-son-of-a-bitch!"

In astonishment, Mike blurted out, "I'll be a son of a whore.... He talks! Son of a whore, Brusco, where'd you find him?"

Now Chase mimicked Mike, saying, "Son-of-a-whore! Son-of-a whore!"

"I'll be damned. Brusco, you gotta catch him. Don't let him fly away! You'll be on the Johnny Carson show!" Mike was now excited.

"I don't think I need to catch him.... He doesn't seem to want to leave! I'll put a bowl of water out for him and some scraps. We'll see if he sticks around," Brusco mused.

Chase now repeated his mantra, "*Angkas Matalom! Angkas Matalom!*"

"You hear that, Mike? What's he saying? It sounds strange and foreign!"

"Don't know, dude. It sounds like Hindu or Cambodian maybe. Go to the library and research it." Mike was now just as intrigued as Brusco. He took Mike's advice and went to the library that day but could find nothing to divulge what the words meant. Maybe he could coax another word out of the bird to unravel what he was saying, he thought and pondered.

Chase continued to stay on Brusco's back deck. The two were now gaining each other's confidence and trust. The bird would now alight on Brusco's shoulder and attempt to pull the medallion off his straw hat. It was no use, though, as Jeannie had carefully stitched the medallion and beadwork to the hat. It was becoming apparent that the bird desperately wanted the shiny, mother-of-pearl ornament on his hat. It was his hold on the raven, he realized. Whenever Brusco would leave the hotel, he'd hang the hat in the window, and the raven would march back and forth on the sill, staring at it. When Brusco returned, the bird was still there, staring through the glass window at his desire.

The bird continued his mantra, "*Angkas Matalom,* you son-of-a-bitch!" Brusco could only laugh, wondering what he was talking about.

One morning, Brusco awoke and was surprised to find Chase not on the deck rail. Stepping out on the back deck, he heard him now up in a walnut tree across the alley. He came swooping in, landed on the rail, and dropped a thick, golden coin at Brusco's feet. He now uttered, "*Igawad Juana Oro! Igawad Juana Oro!*"

Big-eyed, Brusco picked up the gold coin. An image of a Buddha was cast into its surface. It looked like pure gold and was heavy in his hand.

"Son of a whore, Chase! Where did you get this?" Brusco stammered.

"*Igawad Juana Oro,*" was the reply of the raven.

Brusco hung his hat in the window, and the bird began to pace on the sill. He jumped into his pickup, drove to town, and showed the coin to a dealer in a coin shop. "What country is it from? And is it gold?" Brusco asked.

The dealer weighed and examined the coin, studying it under a magnifying glass. "Well, it's nothing I've ever seen or run across, but I can tell you this, it's one point one ounces of pure gold, twenty-four carat. Where did you get it?" the dealer asked.

"Uh, my father was in WW2, and he brought it back. He said it was some kind of Japanese loot," the quick-thinking Brusco quipped.

"Do you want to sell it?" the dealer was interested.

"How much will you give me for it?" Brusco asked.

"Well, spot price of gold today is two hundred and eighty-eight dollars an ounce. Since it's a little over an ounce and unique, I'll give you three hundred and twenty-five dollars for it," he offered.

"Ok…. Let me think about it. Thanks for the info." Brusco returned to the hotel and found Chase pacing back and forth on the windowsill. Now Chase was becoming very belligerent with his mantra.

"*Igawad Juana Oro Angkas Matalom!*" he repeated over and over.

Brusco was excited about the gold coin but decided to keep it to himself, telling no one about it. He needed a haircut and decided to reward himself with a trip to the local barber. He left his hat on the hook in the window, and the bird faithfully jumped onto the sill to ogle at it. He drove into town to the barber shop, entered, and took a waiting seat. There was one barber, cutting a man's hair in the chair, and two others were waiting their turn. The shop was air-conditioned, and a T.V. on the wall blared out a commentator calling a major league baseball game. A pile of magazines sat on a table for reading, and Brusco picked up a Playboy, admiring the fold out.

He spotted another magazine, Battles of WW2, picked it up, and began thumbing through it, looking at old photographs. The pictures were from all over the Pacific theatre of war. The black and white photos showed Marines in combat with Jap soldiers on various islands.

He came to a photo titled "Marines Capture Jap Troops, Matalom, Leyte, Philippines." Standing before an ancient Spanish church, the Marines held the Jap soldiers at bayonet point in the old photo. All of a sudden, there it was! Staring back at him! Matalom! He poured over the photograph, but nothing else was revealed.

"Hey buddy, you're next," called out the barber, as he flapped his covering cloth free of hair. When the haircut was done, Brusco asked, "What's the charge today?"

"Still five bucks, as usual," the barber replied.

"Well, here's ten bucks, if I can have that old magazine there." He pointed at the one he wanted.

"Sure, sure, take a couple. I got a ton of magazines, help yourself," the barber chuckled.

Brusco left the shop and went straight to the library again. He found a volume, "Islands of the Philippines" and flipped through it. A whole chapter described the island of Leyte, and turning a page, there it was! A color photo of the old catholic church of Matalom! He checked out the book and returned to the hotel. Chase was on the window sill, marching back and forth. Again, the bird made his demand, "*Igawad Juana Oro Angkas Matalom.*"

Brusco opened the book and showed him the color photo of the Matalom church. The raven went into a frenzy, pecking at the photo and cawing, "*Lagi, lagi, lagi!* (Yes, yes, yes!) Studying the book from the library, Brusco identified the dialect from Leyte as being "Visayan." He knew a filipina that worked in the grocery store deli in Chelan. Jotting the phrase down on a piece of paper, he drove to the store and found her behind the counter.

"Gina, how are you today? Give me a ham sandwich and some potato salad."

She bagged up the food and handed it over the counter, saying, "Anything else?"

"Uh… yeah… Gina, I know you're Filipina. What dialect do you speak?" asked Brusco.

She looked at him curiously. "I speak Tagalog and Cebuano," she offered.

"Have you ever heard of the dialect called 'Visayan?'" he asked.

Of course, Cebuano and Visayan are the same. There are several dialects in my country. Why do you ask?" she asked.

He handed the version of Chase's mantra to her, spelled as closely as it sounded. "Does this mean anything to you?" he asked.

"Well, yes," she said, after looking at it for a long moment. "I think it says I will give you someone's gold if you take me to Matalom."

"Wow, you're sure?" Brusco was stunned.

"Well, yeah…. *Igawad* is 'I will give.' Not sure about Juana, maybe a woman's name… and *oro* is gold. *Angkas* is 'take me with you' and Matalom is an old Spanish town in Leyte, as I recall."

"Gina, how do you say 'I understand' in Visayan?"

"That would be '*Maolagi*,'" she answered.

Excited with his discovery and revelation, he returned to the hotel. The bird was on the back deck, in his usual spot. Brusco flipped open the book again, to the picture of the church in Matalom and pointed to Chase, saying, "*Maolagi! Maolagi!*"

The bird began to dance in a circle, cawing and saying, "*Maolagi! Maolagi*, you son-of-a-bitch!"

Now Chase launched himself and took to the air, flying east. Brusco watched him disappear over the treetops. Brusco cracked open a cold beer and continued to study the book. An hour later, he heard Chase cawing again on the back deck. Stepping outside, to his amazement, Chase had another gold buddha coin in his beak. He dropped it at Brusco's feet and cawed proudly.

Picking it up, he could see it was just like the other one the raven had given him. "Good Boy Chase!"

The bird pecked at the book Brusco was holding. Realizing his desire, Brusco opened the book to the picture of the church, and the bird went berserk again. "*Caw Caw Caw! Matalom!*" the bird acknowledged. Again, the bird took to flight, flying east again.

Like clockwork, he returned an hour later with another gold buddha coin in his beak. Astonished and excited, Brusco now realized he had over a thousand dollars in gold. Where was the bird going... when he flew east? Were there more coins somewhere in a secret stash? Thinking about it, he went back in thought to the first encounter... when he'd shot at the pheasant and missed. Chase had been perched on top of a giant, erratic boulder. Maybe that was where he was going to get the solid gold coins.

The next morning, Brusco put on the straw stetson with the medallion. "C'mon Chase, were going up to Corral Creek Canyon." Jumping into his pickup, Brusco crossed the Columbia River and headed for the canyon. Driving two miles up the canyon, he stopped where the pheasant had crossed the road. Across the coulee, he could see the giant boulder that Chase had been perched on. Parking on the shoulder, Brusco chuckled as he stepped out. Here came Chase, flying up the canyon, and landed on the hood of the Ford.

"C'mon buddy, let's go check your rock out." As Brusco hiked down the slope, the bird flew across the coulee, and landed high up in a crack between the two massive boulders. Reaching the bottom of the incline, Brusco began hiking up the other side of the canyon. All the while, Chase was cawing and beckoning him on. Finally reaching the split boulder, Brusco was out of breath from the climb. Thirty feet above him, Chase was cawing nonstop. Looking at the

446

massive rocks, he now realized it was almost impossible to scale and climb them. He could see the birds roost now, high in the crack, a virtual little fortress of impregnability.

Brusco walked around the edifice, trying to find a place to climb, but it was useless. A large gully ran down the mountain, culminating at the big rocks. He realized he was going to need a climbing rope with a grapple hook if there was going to be any chance of climbing up and seeing what was in Chase's roost. He started back towards the pickup, arriving a half hour later, tuckered out.

Sitting on the tailgate resting, Chase now landed and dropped another gold coin at his feet.

"Wow! What are you hiding up there, fella?" Brusco picked up the coin and petted the bird. He stared at the distant rock, searching for its vulnerability. All of a sudden, it came to him! "I'll fly over! That's it! I can fly right over the top of that baby!" Throwing up the tailgate, he drove back to town, loaded up his flying machine, and headed out to the airport.

Chase had never flown next to Brusco's powered parachute and was curious and watched as he preflight checked the Buckeye tricycle on the grass. He realized the raven would follow him with the cowboy hat on. He pulled on his aviator goggles and tied the straw hat to his chin with stampede strings. Starting the motor and prop, he filled the parachute with air and taxied onto the runway. Throttling up, he was airborne in thirty feet. Chase couldn't believe what he was seeing! Brusco was flying! The raven took to the air and came alongside Brusco, cawing out, "You son-of-a-bitch!"

The pair flew across the Columbia River and headed for Corral Creek Canyon. Brusco spiraled up to gain altitude. At three thousand feet, he peeled off and reduced the throttle, allowing the craft to dive into a long glide towards the mega boulders. The canyon was full of several warm, thermal updrafts. As he encountered them, the energy was transposed to the tricycle, causing it to jerk and buck, creating an unnerving ride. Brusco grit his teeth, and continued the glide. Chase realized where Brusco was going and now flew ahead and landed on his boulder roost.

Calculating his approach, Brusco flew the carriage ten feet over the top of the erratic. He got a quick glimpse into Chase's stronghold but saw nothing. He circled, came back around, and tried a different angle. As Brusco approached, he watched Chase disappear from his roost. As he flew over, he saw the bird's tail feathers protruding from a fracture in the rock, adjacent to the roost. On his fourth pass over, Brusco saw Chase emerge with a gold coin in his beak and hopped up onto his roost. Realizing what he had just observed, Brusco steered the craft back to the river and the airport. Chase came up alongside, holding the gold coin in his beak. As Brusco landed at the airport, he watched the raven land on the hood of the Ford and drop the coin with a metallic thud. Retrieving the golden buddha coin, Brusco loaded the Buckeye flying machine onto the pickup.

That evening, Brusco thought about his options and measured the possibilities. If he could climb the rock, it was still futile, as the gold was hidden in a narrow fracture that appeared to be narrower than his hand. It was obvious the bird had something cached away in the impossible location. The raven seemed to respond to pictures in the book. Maybe he could play a game with him--force him to retrieve the gold coins for a chance to look at the pictures in the book. It was worth a try--make the bird bring the coins to him. The next morning, Brusco hung the hat in the window, and Chase immediately flew to the sill. He drove the pickup to Wenatchee, to the big regional library. He was able to check out four books with pictures relating to the island of Leyte.

Returning home, he teased Chase with the books, opening one to a full page photo of the church at Hilongos. The bird became transfixed with the picture, pecking at it, as if to recognize it. Instantly, Brusco closed the book and held up a gold coin. The bird pecked at the book, and Brusco gave him another flashing glimpse of the photo. Closing it rapidly again, he held the coin in front of the bird and then pointed east. Chase understood and took to the air. One hour later, he returned with a coin and dropped it on the book. Brusco was waiting for him and now opened the book, showing him a couple more pictures. Slamming the book shut, Brusco held up the coin, and again pointed east. The bird again took flight, and like clockwork he returned an hour later with another coin. The game was on! After three more trips, Brusco sensed the bird was tired, and praised him, giving him food and water.

The next day, the book and picture game resumed. Flying back and forth, each time Chase returned with a coin and then was shown more pictures of his homeland. On the seventh day, he started bringing back shiny stones and odd objects. For another week, Brusco continued the picture game, but each time, and old bone or piece of white quartz was brought back. It was clear that the bird had emptied his golden stash.

Brusco was becoming attached to the bird, realizing how special he was. The bird had given up his golden hoard but still repeated his mantra, telling Brusco to take him to Matalom. He sat in deep thought one day, thinking about how he could get the bird back to Leyte. A ship would take far too long, but maybe he could take Chase on an airplane. After all, the bird had rewarded him with enough gold to easily pay for the trip and then some. Inquiring on the phone if it was possible, he was told yes. The bird would need medical papers and to be sedated and caged during the flight. Upon arriving in Cebu, the bird would be quarantined for a week. If he showed no signs of afflictions, he would be released, on the pretense that he was a pet and would return to the States along with Brusco. The trip was going to be expensive, with hotel and airplane tickets for both he and the bird. He returned to the coin dealer in Wenatchee and emptied the bag of thirty-four gold buddha coins on the counter.

"This is the Japanese loot from WW2 that I was talking about. What is it all worth?"

The coin dealer was delighted to buy the pure gold coins. He opened his safe and gave Brusco $11,900 for the pile of gold.

Flush now with cash, Brusco went to the courthouse and applied for a passport. He then bought roundtrip airfares for he and the bird, not exposing his intent to release him. He planned a ten day trip. He'd sit and wait at a hotel in Cebu for the one week mandatory quarantine, then hop a ferry to Bato. Once there, he'd take a taxi to Matalom and the old church to set Chase free.

As required, he took Chase to a veterinarian and had him checked out and certified as being healthy, with the proper travel document. The doctor gave Brusco a sedative to put in Chase's drinking water, along with a cage to transport him on the plane.

The day of departure arrived. Mike Huffer drove Brusco and Chase over the mountains to SeaTac International Airport. The cage was covered with a pillowcase to calm the raven. In the parking lot at the airport, Brusco spiked his drinking water dispenser in the cage with the sedative. Within minutes, the drug took effect, and Chase sat motionless and quiet inside his enclosure. At the check in desk at the airline gate, Brusco handed over the cage to an airline employee and was given a claim number. He was told to report in one week to a certain address in Cebu.

The flight was long and boring. Finally arriving in Cebu, Brusco had his suitcase cleared at customs and then hailed a cab outside the terminal.

"Do you speak English?" Brusco asked the cabbie.

"Yes, of course. Where are you going, sir?" he politely asked.

"I need a good, clean, safe hotel close to the airport.... Can you recommend one?"

"Yes, yes, the Bella Vista... only five minutes away. You will like it. Are you a cowboy?"

"Ha! Yeah, the cowboy hat.... Yeah, you could say that I'm a cowboy. Ok, lets go to the Bella Vista," agreed Brusco.

The hotel was a high rise and very modern, close to the Mactan Bridge. As it turned out, it was perfect for Brusco. Breakfast was served as a compliment, and several restaurants and shopping opportunities were close by. He slept for a whole day, as the jet lag and time zone change had exhausted him. On his second morning, he woke up hungry. He pulled on his denim overalls, brushed his teeth, and put his cowboy hat on. He then went down to the hotel restaurant to have breakfast. Several people were enjoying the buffet, all of them Asian and Filipino. He caught people staring at him numerous times. He was a curiosity, an American in overalls wearing a straw stetson cowboy hat. He got his coffee, bacon, and eggs and found a table to sit at.

"Good morning, Joe!" a friendly young man offered from the table next to him. Brusco responded and tipped his stetson, replying, "Mornin'."

Halfway through his breakfast, a beautiful, young filipina woman entered the restaurant. She briefly glanced at Brusco and smiled, then made her way to the breakfast buffet. Pouring some tea and selecting some *pandesal* bread, she turned and looked for a place to sit. Brusco was watching her, and he realized every table was taken. Seeing her dilemma, he raised his arm and pointed at his table. She smiled and nodded and now approached. Brusco jumped up, took off his hat, and helped her with her chair. She shyly sat down and thanked him in English for being so polite.

"Howdy.... My name's Brusco Gibbs. I'm from America," he introduced himself.

"Hello, my name is Lorna Salizon. Nice to meet you, Brusco," she blushed shyly.

Her beauty was striking, and now up close, Brusco caught himself staring at her, starstruck.

"Do you ride horses and work on a ranch?" she asked.

"Uh... no, I'm not a rodeo cowboy. It's just kinda what I wear at home to keep the sun off my head."

"Are you here on business, or are you a tourist?" she now politely asked in perfect English.

"Well... neither. I'm here to help a friend," he explained, not being sure if he should bring the subject up about the bird.

"Ah... you have a Filipino friend?" she asked.

"Uh... no, actually, I know no one here. I'm here to release a bird into the wild. I look upon him as a friend."

"I see, and where will you release your friend?" she giggled.

"I have to ride a ferry to Leyte. There, I will release him at a place called Matalom."

"That's interesting, Brusco. I'm from Leyte, a place called Tagaytay, which is not very far from Matalom."

"Wow, it's a small world…. So you're here in Cebu visiting friends?" he asked.

"No, I left Leyte years ago. I work as a nanny for a wealthy family in Vancouver, British Columbia… Canada. I'm here to visit my mother and father. I have two weeks off, and I haven't seen them in two years. I arrived last night at the airport. Tomorrow, I will ride the ferry to Leyte," she explained.

Brusco then divulged the story of Chase, hoping the beautiful woman wouldn't think he was crazy. "I have to wait in the hotel five more days until they release him from quarantine."

"I see… and you know no one on Leyte? You're traveling alone?" she questioned him.

'Yes, that's my plan," he grinned.

"You are very brave, or very foolish, Brusco. An American traveling alone in Leyte can have a bad ending."

She had his attention. "Why is that, Lorna?"

"There are bad people, in particular, the NPA communists. You would be a prize for kidnapping and ransoming. Allow me and my family to meet you at the dock at Bato. We will guarantee your safety and safe return," she insisted.

"That would be wonderful! I arrive next Tuesday at 5 p.m. I was nervous about where I would stay after I got off the ferry," he confided with her.

"You will stay at my parents house in Tagaytay. I'll make the arrangements to transport you and your 'friend' to Matalom," she assured him.

The two ended up spending the day together, eating lunch and dinner and having long conversations. He was fascinated with her, and she had never met anyone like him. His stories of growing up in America had her undivided attention. The following morning, she was up early to catch a cab to the ferry terminal. He had coffee with her in the hotel restaurant and helped her with her bags at the curb. They both vowed to meet each other in four days. A compelling feeling came over him. He hugged her and kissed her on the forehead, wishing her a safe journey. Caught off guard, she smiled in embarrassment.

"I'll see you soon. I'll be waiting for you," she promised. Jumping in the cab, she blew a kiss at him, and was gone.

Finally, after a week in the hotel, the quarantine and waiting was over. Grabbing a cab, Brusco handed the address to the cabbie. A short ride took him to a government building, close to the airport. Entering, he produced his claim ticket at the front desk, explaining he was there to pick up his pet raven.

"So you're the owner! We'll be glad to see that bird go! He curses in horrible vocabulary and is terribly offensive. Did you teach him all those bad words?" the clerk spoke in an annoyed tone.

"Uh… yes, I apologize for his bad language. I got him from someone else, a comedian, who used him in a stage act and taught him to curse. My sincere apologies, ma'am," Brusco winced.

"Let's see your passport," she curtly demanded. "Alright, sign the documents here," she ordered. She then got on the phone, talking to an employee. Five minutes later, a man appeared from a side door, holding the birdcage.

"You son-of-a-bitch! You piece of shit son-of-a-bitch!" came the expletives from the hooded cage. "You son of a whore!"

"Get that foul bird out of here!" demanded the clerk.

Grabbing another cab, Brusco went straight to the ferry terminal. Boarding the vessel, he found a seat in the open air, on the upper deck. He was getting a lot of attention on the crowded boat. Chase would curse in low tones, totally pissed off. The words could be heard all around, coming from under the shroud of the cage. Several children were curious, but the slurry of foul cursing made modest adults push the youngsters away.

"Joe, is that a mynah bird?" someone finally asked.

"Yes, yes, he's a large mynah bird, and he's not happy today." Brusco gritted. "My apologies, ladies, try to just ignore it."

"You-son-of-a-bitch!" the rascal cawed.

Several women were red-faced, and scurried away. Finally, a ferry crew member, a uniformed "Captain's Steward," approached Brusco and his cage.

"Sir, can you come with me, please… and bring your baggage," he demanded. Brusco was escorted to a small, empty cabin. The steward held the door open. "Right this way, sir."

Closing the door behind him, he explained, "The Captain has received several complaints about an American cowboy with a cursing mynah bird. There are 'Sisters of the Order' who were offended by the bird's language."

A loud interruption came. "You son of a bitch!" cawed the hooded cage.

The steward smiled and continued, "We are God-fearing Catholics in the Philippines, and we do not condone that bad language in public. The Captain, as a courtesy, would like you to stay in this cabin for the remainder of the voyage, which will be two more hours." He looked at Brusco's ticket and then added, "Those are the captain's orders." He then opened the door and departed.

There was a porthole window in the cabin. Opening it, Brusco stared at the approaching island of Leyte. Ragged, cloud shrouded mountains ran down its interior. The shoreline, for as far as you could see in either direction, was covered with thousands and thousands of coconut trees. The ferry blasted a long whistle, announcing its arrival at the Port of Bato.

A porter came to the cabin and took Brusco's suitcase. He led him to the gangway and rail and down to the dock. Several motorcycles with sidecars and people were there to greet and transport the offloading passengers. He spotted Lorna coming at him, waving her arm and hand. Behind her were two men and a woman.

"Good to see you, Lorna! Thank you so much for being here. I didn't realize the provinces were so rural!" Brusco praised her.

"These are my brothers and sister… Neon and Victor… and Verge, my sister."

The two men tried to grab the suitcase and cage. Chase seemed to have stopped his temper tantrum after leaving the boat. He became quiet now, for he could hear the old familiar dialect.

"Uh… I'll just hold his cage. It's not a problem." Brusco insisted. The group escorted Brusco to a motorcycle with an attached sidecar. Piling aboard, Verge kick started the Honda, and away they went.

Fifteen minutes later, the sidecar pulled into the barangay of Tagaytay. Lorna's family house was old, made of tugas wood that was weathered grey from old times. The open air windows were covered in large shutters, which were open to let fresh air in.

A large group of people had assembled to see the American with the talking mynah bird. A large table of food was put out. Lorna had a lechon pig roasted for the occasion. Bowls of different pancit and pandesal foods, with fresh cut jungle fruit, were full and abundant. The air was abuzz with chattering, laughter, and eating. Brusco was introduced to Lorna's *nanay* and *tatay*. He took both their hands and blessed them to his forehead, a sign of respect. The effect was very pleasing to all who observed the American honoring their customs. The party continued into the evening. Brusco and his bird turned in and went to bed early. The arrangements had been made to take the bird to Matalom in the morning.

He was awoken to sounds in the kitchen, breakfast being prepared. He'd removed the cover from the cage the night before and now was looking at Chase staring at him quietly. Breakfast was finished, and the same group hopped back onto the sidecar, giving Brusco and the cage the front bench seat. A half hour later, they were entering Matalom. The ancient church was close to four hundred years old, and now, standing before it, the time had come to set Chase free. The grounds around the church were empty of people. Chase began to curse and

453

caw, realizing where he was. Hearing his cries, two ravens flew in from nowhere, and landed in the bell tower of the church. They answered his calling caws.

Brusco had prepared for the moment. He had cut the hatband and medallion from the cowboy hat. Opening the cage door with one hand, he held the coveted medallion in the other. The bird hopped out of the cage and onto Brusco's wrist. He stared at Brusco for a long moment then uttered, "You son of a bitch," whereupon he grabbed the medallion in his beak and took flight. He flew up to his waiting companions in the bell tower. He seemed to be showing off his new prize with the two queens.

The deed was done. It was time to go. Brusco was pleased with himself and how it ended, the bird finding instant girlfriends. The payback had been made, and in the process, he'd met a beautiful, intelligent woman. Brusco stared at the jungle and rice fields as they returned to Tagaytay. Lorna took his hand, for she could tell the bird had meant a lot to him. As they motored down the road, Lorna's brothers pointed out that the three ravens were following them. Finally arriving back at the house, Brusco was astonished to see the three ravens land in a giant mahogany tree across the road. The hat band and medallion still hung from Chase's beak. Brusco watched them for ten more minutes, then suddenly, they all took flight and headed north over the coconut canopy.

The next morning, it was time to go. Brusco's quick encounter with the island had left him spellbound. Its beauty was calling him, and he promised himself that he would come back.

"Tell me Lorna, what does Matalom mean?"

"It's Spanish for 'beautiful place.' Do you like my island?" she smiled.

"Yes, I hope to come back someday and spend more time. Can I see you again? Vancouver is a four hour drive from where I live. I could come visit you," he offered.

"Yes of course, I'd love for you to come visit me in Canada." Her eyes sparkled. "I'll be flying home next week... here's my phone number. Please call me," she invited.

The sidecar brought him to the ferry terminal as the boat was loading. They stood on the ferry dock staring at each other. He took off his hat, thanked her for her help, then pulled her close and put a big lip kiss on her. She responded, kissing him deeply on the mouth.

"I'll be home in two days.... I'll call you in ten days, after you get home... I promise!" Brusco searched her eyes. The porter grabbed his bag--he had to go.

She and her brothers and sister watched and waved as the ferry left the dock. He watched from the fantail, as the boat was quick getting into the channel. Arriving in Cebu, he rested at the hotel and flew back to Seattle the following day. Arriving safely back in Chelan, he waited for the days to pass so that he could call the phone number. Finally, on the tenth day, he nervously placed the long distance call to Canada.

A young boy answered the phone. "Can I speak to Lorna?" Brusco politely asked.

A moment later, she was on the phone. "Hi!" she merrily cried out to Brusco. "I can only talk briefly, we were just going out the door. I'm taking the boys to the park. I have next weekend off, two days. I've never been to America. Can you come get me? I'd like to see your hotel in Chelan!" she spoke rapidly.

"Yes--YES! I'll come get you. What's your address?" he was exuberant.

"You can't come here... my employer would not approve. I'll meet you at my girlfriend's house. Here's the address."

Jotting it down and reading it back, they arranged to meet at a certain time.

"And I have something important to tell you!" she added.

"What... what is it? Don't keep me waiting!" he pleaded.

"I'll tell you when I see you next Friday night," she promised. "I gotta go. See you soon!"

The following days went by painfully slow, and finally, Friday arrived. Donning his cowboy hat, Brusco gassed up the old Ford pickup and drove the four hours to the Peace Arch at the border. He'd done his homework and had acquired a city map of Vancouver. He had no phone number, only this address to go to. He was able to drive straight to the address, a long street of well-maintained houses. There she was, sitting on the porch with another Filipina! Both girls jumped up, and Lorna ran to him as he got out of the cab of the truck. Embracing passionately, they both kissed deeply for a long moment in time.

"This is my friend, Mary Lou." She introduced the pretty girl, who had just witnessed their passion.

Brusco politely shook her hand, but now insisted, "Lorna, it's a long drive back. We need to get on the road."

She retrieved her little suitcase and assured Mary Lou that she would call and that she'd be back Sunday night. Climbing into the cab of the pickup, she buckled up her seat belt.

"Brusco, I'm so excited to go to America... I've never been.... It's my lifelong dream!" she excitedly laughed in delight. An hour later, they were going through customs at the Peace Arch. Entering Washington State, Brusco began to point out things of interest along the highway.

455

"You said you had something important to tell me…. What is it?" he had waited for the right moment.

"Yes I do… I think it will please you. Three days after you left Tagaytay, I was at the well pump pitching water for my mother. All of a sudden, your raven landed on the pump handle. In his beak was a beautiful black pearl. He dropped it at my feet and began cursing. I picked up the pearl, and he calmed down and began to speak my dialect, to my amazement! He said to tell you this…. That his name is not Chase… that his name is Duto…. Tell Brusco that I have found my old raven friends, who have led me to a bird shaman in Owak. There, that shaman has the medicine I need. The shaman has given my treasure away again, and I must follow its path and go south to protect a chosen one--a leader of the people, who was born south of Matalom. It is Duto's task now to guard and protect a certain 'Rodrigo Digong' who lives in Davao, Mindanao. Tell Brusco thank you for bringing me home.' And just like that, he flapped his wings and flew south."

Opening her purse, she now took out the shimmering black pearl for Brusco to see.

"Well, I'll be damned…. So he belonged to a Wak Wak… a shaman. No wonder he was so magical and mysterious. I wonder who this Rodrigo Digong is? He's gonna learn some bad language from ol' Chase--I mean Duto. God help him!"

It was ten at night when they finally pulled up at the hotel in Chelan. Both were tired from the excitement of the long day. He showed her the layout of the little townhouse, and she realized there was only one queen bed.

"Let's get something straight, cowboy. I suppose you want me to hop into bed and have sex with you. Well, it's not gonna happen! My virginity is all I have, and you can't have it unless you marry me!"

Brusco smiled and chuckled, "I was already expecting this…. You are a classy lady, and I totally respect you. Tell you what. Let's go get married tomorrow."

Shocked, she couldn't believe her ears. "Are you kidding me…. Look, if you marry me, you're stuck with me for life. There's no such thing as divorce in my culture. It would bring great shame to me and my family…. So you can't walk away if it doesn't work."

"I'm not joking one bit! The moment I first saw you in the restaurant in Cebu, I wanted you. Please Lorna, will you marry me?"

She laughed, "How can we get married? Tomorrow's Saturday. There aren't any government offices open."

"We'll go to Idaho, a place called Coeur d'Alene. There's a little chapel across the street from the courthouse. It's called the 'Hitching Post.'"

"Really--you're really sure about this!?" she stared into his eyes.

"Yup, I don't want to lose you. You're everything I've ever dreamed of-- the whole package."

The next day, they drove to Idaho and were married at the Hitching Post. The fee was twenty-five dollars. On the drive back to Chelan, Lorna could not believe how easily it had happened.

"Are you sure we're really married, Brusco?" she shook her head in disbelief. It was her first time in America, and within twenty-four hours, she had married an American.

Brusco returned her to Vancouver on Sunday night. Seven months later, she had finished her work contract. By then, Brusco had processed her immigration papers and acquired her green card and brought her home to Chelan.

Nine months after the trip to Coeur d'Alene, a shimmering pearl was born--a baby girl in the town of Chelan... the real Treasure of the China Bar.

Treasure of the China Bar (Serpent Rock in the Distance)

References:

Fort Okanogan: Wikipedia

1872 North Cascades Earthquake: Wikipedia

Spanish/Moro Conflict: Wikipedia

Chelan City Thumbnail History: History Link.org.essay

"Raja of Sarawak/Sir James Brooke" (book): Gertrude Jacob, author

James Brooke: Wikipedia

"Eyewitness to Indian Wars" (book): Peter Cozzens, author

Iranun People (pirates): Wikipedia

Caracoa (warship): Wikipedia

Swivel Gun: Wikipedia

Piracy in the Sulu Sea: Wikipedia

FORT VICTORIA JOURNAL/Capt. Weynton - COWLITZ:
fortvictoriajournal.ca/bio-weynton.php

Ships passenger list COWLITZ - sites.rootweb.com/bcvancou/ships/cow.htm

Smallpox Victoria 1862: web.uvic.ca

Smallpox: The key to Confederation: vancouver.mediacoop.ca

Hawaii-Honolulu-Ho'okuleana: totakeresponsibiliy.blogspot.com

Chinook Jargon - George Gibbs: washington.edu

"Four Years in B.C./Vancouver Island/Sallas Island" (book): Sir James
Douglas, author

Bellevue Sheep Farm, San Juan Island: nps.gov

Griffin Journal - 1854 - Belle Vue Sheep Farm Journal - nps.gov

Lopez Island, thumbnail history: historylink.org

THE CHINESE MASSACRE RECONSIDERED: cinarc.org/violence

"Half Sun of the Columbia" (book): Chief Moses, Sinkiuse - books.google.com
Yakima (Yakama) War: Wikipedia

Sinkiuse Indians: books.google.com

WallaWalla Treaty Council: books.google.com

"Last Chief Standing: A Tale of Two Cultures" (LaHompt) (book): Wendell
George, author

Chinook Jargon: chinookjargon.com

Raven Man Totem: pbase.com

The First Ones on San Juan Island: nps.org

English Camp/San Juan Island: nps.org

Snohomish Native People: Wikipedia

Roche Harbor: Wikipedia

Seattle 1841/Piner Point: geologywriter.com

500 Generations of the Methow Valley: methowvalleynews.com

"Pre 1900s Chinese Placer Mining in Washington State" (manuscript):
Lindsey Evenson, author - dc.ewu.edu

Indian Slave Trade/Kappa Indians: book.google.com

History of Chelan County: cityofchelan.us

Pretty Eagle/Crow: Wikipedia

Wichita/Delano Map: wichita.gov

Ren Tap, Pirate King: Wikipedia

History of Wapato Point: wapatopoint.com/history

Entiat People: Wikipedia

Tribal Chiefs: colvilletribes.com

Fort Ellis: Wikipedia

Quanah Parker: Wikipedia

Doan's Crossing: texasescapes.com/towns

Haulk, Texas (Odell): Handbook of Texas Online - tshaonline.org

Medicine Mounds, Texas: Wikipedia

Fort Sill: Wikipedia

Balangiga Bells: Wikipedia

Page Act of 1875: Wikipedia

Matalom: Wikipedia

Jungle Crow: Wikipedia

Great Western Cattle Trail (Doan's Store): Wikipedia

Swakane Canyon: wta.org

Pearl Island (Washington): Wikipedia

Comancheros: Wikipedia

Mason Jars, 1858: Wikipedia

"Alice's Adventures in Wonderland," 1865: Wikipedia

Curly Crow Scout: Wikipedia

Entiat Historical Society

PH Coll 358 B.C. Collier Photographs Photographer: Collier, B. C. Description: Wenatchi (Wenatchee) man named Silico Sasket, Washington, ca.1907 Negative no: NA 644

PH Coll 564 General Indian Collection Photographer: Description: Chelan man known as Wapato John poses with Wenatchi man named Silico Sasket, Washington, ca. 1900 Negative no: NA 784

Balangiga Massacre: Wikipedia

Thank you for taking the time to read Lost Treasure of the China Bar. *It really means a lot to me, and I would love to share this story with others. If you enjoyed the book, the author and editor would appreciate your review on Amazon.*

Made in the USA
Monee, IL
18 July 2021